Place
Terra House
er Hall
Mars Laboratory
King's Hollow
The Howling Meadow
The Wailing Wood
The Orb
Earth Observatory
Venus Library
ercury
ambers
Aer House
Fire Arena
Ai
Cov

ZODIAC ACADEMY

FATED THRONE

CAROLINE PECKHAM

SUSANNE VALENTI

This book is dedicated to the stars. Thanks for sending us mixed messages dudes, you're a real bunch of sparkly assholes.

In light of that we asked Gabriel Nox to write you a prophesy about this book...

"Paiiiiiiin, immense, unimaginable paiiiiin lies in your future if you continue reading this book.
However, there is also some good which awaits, slivers of joy, laughter which will lighten your soul only to ensure it is crushed more thoroughly in the fist of fate subsequently.
Both incredible happiness and intense suffering are coming to you...but if you spill enough tears, you may find the authors of destiny show mercy. It is an unlikely fate, but a possible one.
So spill those tears dear one, capture them in jars and look to the sky to ask the stars to be kind. Because every once in a while, they listen."

P.S. we are the stars - sorry, not sorry.
Gabriel also has foreseen you joining us in our reader group on Facebook so follow your fate and we'll see you there!

WELCOME TO ZODIAC ACADEMY

Note to all students: Vampire bites, loss of limbs or getting lost in The Wailing Wood will not count as a valid excuse for being late to class.

DARIUS

CHAPTER ONE

Agony ripped through my side as a Nymph got close enough to drive its probed fingers into my flesh and I roared a challenge as I swung towards it. The axe Darcy had forged for me in Phoenix fire blazed with blue flames as it carved a path through the air and the Nymph's neck in turn.

The foul creature didn't even have time to shriek in pain before it died and it crumbled to dust which swirled around me on the storm Darcy and Seth had summoned to hide our advance.

Not that that plan had worked. The fucking Nymphs had realised we were here the moment we stepped foot outside the clearing where the clubhouse was concealed. I didn't know if we'd set off a magical alarm when we arrived via stardust or if we'd just been unlucky enough to be spotted, but it didn't matter now. We were right in the thick of the shit storm with Nymphs closing in on all sides.

I pressed a hand to my side, healing the worst of the wounds with a curse as I was forced to pause my advance.

Caleb appeared as nothing more than a blur of red and blue flames as he shot all around the forest with his Vampire speed, the twin daggers Darcy had crafted him tearing through the Nymphs before they even realised he was close.

My skin prickled with the urge to shift and a Dragon's roar left my lips as smoke coated my tongue, but there was no room for me to shift here between the trees. Besides, I liked the way it felt when my new axe carved through my enemies too much to abandon it.

When Darcy had presented us with these weapons, my heart had ached for her. For the pain she was in with her sister and Lance gone and the weight of the world pressing down on her. I shared the torture of their loss with her so I understood the burden of it more than well enough. But instead of crumbling beneath the agony of their loss, she'd risen to the challenge and spent the summer helping us to try and track down the Imperial Star. Roxy had made the sacrifice Gabriel had predicted, stopping Father from finding it for now and we refused to allow her sacrifice to be for nothing. And now that Darcy had armed the four of us with weapons that could withstand the Nymphs and cut through them as easily as if they were made of paper, there was nothing that could stop us from finding it.

Max bellowed a challenge from his position on Seth's back in his huge white Wolf form as they charged through the clearing and he fired an arrow flaming with Phoenix fire right over my head. A Nymph exploded into dust as the arrow punched a hole in its chest and Max guided it back to him on a gust of wind in a move he'd been practicing tirelessly since Darcy had forged his gift. He instantly placed the arrow in the bow and aimed again as I raced forward behind them. Seth's front paws were clad in gleaming metal, the claws able to ignite with Phoenix fire and tear through the barky flesh of the Nymphs like a hot knife through butter.

I swung my axe with savage abandon, black blood splattering my face and arms as I killed again and again but no matter how many enemies I destroyed, it felt like the tide was never ending.

My heart was pounding to a frantic rhythm as I searched the darkness between the trees for Darcy. She'd run ahead using a concealment spell despite my command for us to stick together, and panic was warring beneath my skin for every moment that passed without a sign of her. I'd given Roxy my word that I'd protect her sister before she'd fallen into the shadows and been taken by my father and it was the only thing I could do for her at the moment.

Besides, I'd formed a bond with Darcy of my own in the last six weeks. We'd been meeting up as often as I could get away from the manor in secret so that she could try and burn the shadows out of me. If I could just get free of them then Clara couldn't control me anymore and I'd be able to strike at her and Father. But it wasn't fucking working. I was pushing and pushing for Darcy to use ever stronger flames, but they were coming closer to roasting me alive from the inside out than they were to destroying the shadows. She'd refused to attempt it at all this past week since I'd passed out from the agony of them and Max had struggled to heal me in time to save my life. But I didn't want to stop trying. I needed to break free so that I could stand against my father and rescue the girl I loved.

The pain of my separation from Roxy cut me open and made me bleed with every day that passed.

Father held her life in his hands and he'd threatened her to stop me from trying to track her down. Not that that had stopped me. I knew he held her somewhere in the manor and I'd been spending every waking hour searching for her, but I'd never even found a clue to her whereabouts. But sometimes, in the dead of night, I woke suddenly, sure I'd heard her screaming, alone in the dark.

I hoped that I was just having nightmares. But I was almost certain I wasn't.

A huge blast of Phoenix fire came from the clubhouse at the centre of the clearing and Nymphs screamed as they died beneath Darcy's wrath.

I raced forward, cutting through the Nymphs who were trying to escape her flames until I finally made it to the stone house where she was waiting for us.

For a moment the light from her fire cast her in shadows, making her blue hair appear black as she smiled savagely in victory, looking so like her sister that my heart dropped right down into the pit of my stomach. Guilt rose up in me like an all too familiar curse and I forced my mind off of it so that I could focus on this fight.

"Did we get them all?" Darcy called as her flames guttered out and the illusion was lost to me.

"What the fuck was that?" I demanded as I came to stand before her, my muscles burning with fatigue from hefting my axe which now hung loose in my right hand. "The plan was to stick together."

"Calm down, Darius," she replied, flicking a lock of blue hair back over her shoulder. "I was just rounding up the stragglers."

"You could have gotten yourself killed," I snarled as Seth padded up beside me in his Wolf form and Max slid from his back.

"Well, I didn't. So you don't have to worry about breaking your precious promise," she muttered bitterly.

"It's the only thing I can do for her at the moment," I growled in reply, my heart twisting with the truth of those words. We'd vowed to do everything we could to get Roxy back, but it turned out that there was nothing we *could* do. Not so far anyway. Even Gabriel hadn't been able to *see* anything to help us. The whole situation was fucked.

Darcy's gaze softened at that and she nodded. "I know. But I'm not some fragile thing that needs protecting."

"Well you *are* a princess," Seth teased as he shifted back into Fae form.

Darcy rolled her eyes as she turned away from him flashing his junk and Max tossed him a pair of sweatpants from his bag.

Caleb shot towards us as we waited for him to pull them on, a wild look in his eyes as he extinguished the Phoenix flames which coated his daggers.

"There are more coming," he panted as he pointed away through the woods. "Too many. We need to search this place and get the fuck out of here."

I cursed as I looked up at the huge stone building which had once been home to the Zodiac Guild. Darcy had discovered this place mentioned in an old tome which had been kept at The Palace of Souls and we'd come here as soon as we could, but the damn Nymphs had still been faster. Just like they had at the last four places we'd searched.

I didn't know how they were managing to do it, whether the stars really were against us or if they were spying on us somehow, but it was like we couldn't catch a fucking break.

"Let's make this quick then," Darcy snarled as she turned towards the building and made a move towards the door.

I caught her shoulder, my gaze flickering to Dragon slits as she huffed at me and I moved her aside so that I could go in first. She might not want me to protect her, but I'd promised Roxy and I wasn't going to back down on that.

The door was heavy and stuck as I tried to open it, magic locking it in place. I quickly placed my axe in the holster on my back so that I could concentrate on opening it.

I closed my eyes as I focused on the lock, working my own magic into it and cursing as I struggled to break it.

"Hurry up, man," Seth hissed behind me and I grunted in frustration as the lock continued to hold me back before finally breaking through it with a surge of power.

The door swung open with a groan and I threw a handful of Faelights into the dark space to illuminate it ahead of us as we stepped inside.

The clubhouse was immaculate, dominated by a huge open area filled with leather armchairs and dark wooden furniture. A few doors led off of the central room and we glanced around as we moved further into the space. It must have been spelled to stop the dust from settling here, because though the room looked untouched, the taste of magic on the air was long since faded. No one had been here in a long time.

"We've got five minutes, tops," Caleb warned. "Then we need to get the fuck out of here. I'll check the back rooms." He shot away without waiting for us to reply and the rest of us fanned out to search for anything that could relate to the Imperial Star.

We hunted with a feverish desire that was bordering on aggressive as we tore through the room, using detection spells to locate anything that might be hidden.

I cursed as we failed to find anything, tossing books, ornaments and anything else I came across in a heap on the floor and my pulse pounded as the minutes ticked down.

"Shit," Darcy gasped and I whirled around, finding her in the middle of the room with a tarot card in her hand.

She'd explained about the messages Astrum had been sending the twins from beyond the grave a few weeks ago and the look in her eyes said she'd just found one more.

"What does it say?" I demanded.

The last person who we suspected to have been in possession of the Imperial Star was Astrum and I could only hope that this breadcrumb trail he'd been leaving the twins was designed to lead them to it.

"Seek the fallen hunter." Darcy looked up at me as she held out the card for me to see.

The World tarot card looked back at me, a naked woman dancing above the earth holding a staff in each hand while she was watched by various creatures. That at least was positive – the card symbolised things falling into place, even if the message that went with it seemed like nothing more than a riddle.

"I can't find anything," Max called from across the wide space.

"Me either," Caleb announced as he shot back into the room, his blonde curls dishevelled.

"I don't think it's here," Darcy said bitterly. "We wouldn't have found a card if it was."

A terrifying shriek sounded from somewhere out in the woods and we all looked around in alarm as the Nymph army drew closer.

"Then I say it's time to go," Seth said, moving to join us as he opened an old bottle of whiskey, drinking the few inches in the bottom of it before tossing it aside.

"Yeah, let's get the fuck out of here," I agreed, pulling a pouch of stardust from my pocket.

"One moment," Caleb said, shooting away before I could object.

The howls and shrieks of the Nymphs outside were so close that my muscles tensed and magic raced to my fingertips.

Caleb reappeared with a jerrycan beneath his arm which he must have found outside and as he twisted the cap off, his eyes lit with excitement.

"Faesine," he announced, upending the can in a whirl of motion as he shot around us so that every surface in the building was coated with the incredibly flammable substance.

Seth howled with excitement and I tossed the pouch of stardust to Max as we all moved closer together.

The Nymphs were so near that I could hear their rattles now, the cold feel of their presence dampening our magic as Max took a pinch of stardust out of the bag and grinned around at us.

Darcy caught my eye just as the first window shattered and the Nymphs shrieked with excitement as they spotted us.

Darcy sucked in a sharp breath and my heart leapt as they fought their way inside and the horrifying sight of their gnarled bodies and soulless red eyes made my pulse race.

Max tossed the stardust and I flicked my fingers, flames leaping from my palm and hitting the Faesine. The tremendous whoosh of the fire met with a blaze of heat that washed over us and the screams of the Nymphs filled the air as they burned half a second before the world spun around us and the stars whipped us up into their embrace.

Our feet hit solid ground and Seth howled excitedly as we found ourselves in the dark woodland beyond my family's estate.

I could just make out the colourful lights which had been strung up in honour of my birthday in the grounds. I fought back a snarl as I realised I was going to have to sit through an evening of bullshit as Father put on a show of family love and respect for the press and his fake ass friends. I couldn't even attempt to pull out of it. He'd made it clear that any public show of dissent would cause him to hurt Roxy and I couldn't risk that. He had me by the balls and he knew it.

He'd effectively leashed and muzzled me and there wasn't a fucking thing I could do about it. And the way he looked at me since the start of the summer made my insides boil with hatred. His eyes glinted like he knew something I didn't. Like he held this great secret he was just bursting to spill and every time I thought of him doing it, I was filled with a mixture of dread and a desperation to know what it was.

There was one small sliver of hope which I clung to all the time he continued to taunt me and hold Roxy captive at his mercy. Ever since the night I'd almost killed him, he hadn't once come near me without Clara at his side. In fact, she never seemed to leave his side at all anymore. And I was filled with this deep hope that the reason for that was fear. He knew just how close I'd come to besting him that night. To ending him. And only Clara and her control over me via the shadows kept him safe from my wrath.

So if I could just get him alone, figure out a way to take her out of the picture, then I was sure I could finish him for good. But he was proving to be an un-Fae asshole as well as a treacherous bastard, putting his Guardian between us rather than face me like he should.

"Will you be alright alone in the palace tonight?" Seth asked Darcy, a soft whimper escaping him as I handed her the stardust so she could head home. Obviously a Vega wasn't welcome at a party filled with people who backed our claim for the throne so she couldn't come in. If the press caught wind of how much time we all spent together these days they'd have a fucking field day. It certainly didn't seem like we were on opposing sides of a war to me.

"I'm always alone now," she said in flat tone which made my heart twist with guilt. I was starting to seriously worry about how she was coping. First Lance had been taken from her and now Roxy; I knew Geraldine had been staying with her a lot, but it wasn't the same.

Before any of us could offer up anything in response, she tossed the stardust over her head and disappeared.

We'd snuck out here an hour ago to meet her, the moment she'd figured out our latest search destination but now that guests were starting to arrive for my birthday party, it would be a lot harder to sneak back in. Especially with Father's extra guards patrolling the grounds. He'd supposedly hired them to guard against Nymphs, but they were either just a front to keep up appearances, or they were to make sure no one got close to the house without him knowing in case anyone figured out what he was doing here.

I slipped the axe and holster from my back, pulled my ripped shirt off and glanced at my brothers. There was a simple way to get them back into the building, but doing it meant breaking the code my father had always insisted I stick to.

Why do I even give a shit about his codes?

"You're going to need to construct a decent cloaking spell," I said to them as I tossed my shirt and axe to Max.

"Why?" Cal asked, eyeing me like he couldn't figure out what I was up to even though I had to guess it was clear I was going to shift. Strip shows really weren't my thing.

"Because I'm going to fly us all back in."

"No fucking way," Seth breathed, bouncing up and down on the balls of his feet as Max grinned excitedly.

"You mean it?" Cal asked, his eyes widening.

"Yeah, I mean it. I'm sick of you assholes always being stuck on the ground. It's time you realised how much better it is to be a Dragon than any of your shitty Orders."

Max snorted a laugh and Seth began to howl half a second before Cal slapped a hand over his mouth to silence him.

"Very subtle, asshole," Caleb chastised.

Seth peeled his hand back off of his mouth then leapt forward and ran the pad of his tongue right up the side of my cheek. "Holy shit, I'm so fucking excited I could pee myself. This is as good as the time when I was on the moon and I jumped clean over that crater when everyone said I wouldn't be able to."

"If you piss on me, I'll toss you into the lake," I warned, dropping my sweatpants and handing them and my sneakers to Max to put in his bag too before turning away from them so I had room to shift.

My body split apart and reformed and I fought to contain a roar as fire washed beneath my scales and I flexed my claws so that they dug into the sun-baked dirt beneath me.

I'd only ever let Lance and Roxy ride me before now and I'd been breaking the rules to do it, but that suddenly seemed so pointless. Father was obsessed with the idea of Dragon supremacy, but who gave a shit if I wanted to let some of my friends ride me through the clouds? It didn't make me a fucking pack mule. It just showcased what my Order could do.

I turned my head to look at the other Heirs as they hesitated. I mean, yeah, it was a pretty fucking huge deal, but I needed them to move their asses before Father came looking for me. If he realised we'd left the manor, he might figure out that we'd had something to do with the deaths of a bunch of his Nymphs.

Seth stepped forward first but Caleb shot into action a moment later, leaping up onto my back and settling himself between the spines on my shoulder blades with a breath of excited laughter.

Max and Seth climbed up right behind him and I walked forward several steps as I adjusted to the feeling of them all riding me at once before risking my wings.

"Are you sure about this, Darius?" Max asked, but the edge of laughter to his tone said he absolutely didn't want me to change my mind.

I twisted my head to look at them, blowing a puff of smoke into their faces in answer before snapping my golden wings out either side of me and launching myself into the clouds at speed.

Seth whooped in excitement a heartbeat before a silencing bubble washed over my scales to contain the noise alongside a concealment spell to make sure no one spotted them and then they were all yelling and cheering as I beat my wings hard and shot into the sky.

I flew as hard and as fast as I could, my heart pounding as I broke through the clouds and soared beneath the stars, showing them the world the way I loved it the most for a few endless moments before diving back to earth again at breakneck speed.

The other Heirs all yelled and whooped as we plummeted through the clouds and I twisted through the air to give them a real ride. I could feel them clinging to my spines with all their strength as they almost fell and I released a burst of Dragon fire from my mouth which whipped around us as I dove through it.

I snapped my wings out and swooped over the roof of the manor at the last second before coming to land on the flat roof of the tower which held my rooms.

The Heirs slid from my back, laughing excitedly before I shifted back into my Fae form and I offered them half a smile. It was good to see them enjoying themselves, but I hadn't been able to take real joy in anything since Roxy had been taken from us. My heart felt like it was locked in a cage of ice and if we didn't manage to find her soon then I wasn't sure what would become of me.

I looked towards the other Heirs just as Max disbanded the concealment spell around them and my eyes managed to focus on their smiling faces instead of only seeing darkness where they'd been.

We headed down into my rooms and I used water magic to clean the dirt from my flesh as Seth took to my bathroom and set the shower running.

I changed into the charcoal suit Mom had left out for me and styled my hair like a diligent little Heir as I prepared to face the charade which was my birthday party. I didn't know many twenty-year-olds who chose to celebrate with a sit-down banquet and a formal dance, but I didn't give enough of a shit to complain about it. If I had my way, we wouldn't be celebrating at all. Hell, if I had my way, I'd have spent the day alone with Roxy doing literally anything and it would have been perfect.

Seth lingered in the shower until Caleb cursed him and shot in there to toss him out. Max had cleaned himself off with water magic too and he chuckled as he tightened his tie, a little knowing smile on his face as he glanced towards the bathroom where the sound of them arguing spilled from the doorway.

Seth fell out of the room a moment later, soaking wet and butt naked with his ass leaving a print on my carpet as he cursed Cal out.

Caleb's laughter came from the bathroom and Seth stomped away, drying himself with air magic before dressing in his grey suit. Before he'd even managed to pull his jacket on, Cal shot back into the room and dressed himself in a flash of Vampire speed before coming to a rest leaning against the door and inspecting his fingernails as if he'd been waiting for us for ages.

A knock sounded at the door and I called out for Jenkins to enter a moment before the wizened old butler stepped into the room.

"Your guests are waiting for you, Master Darius," he simpered, bowing low like he wasn't a conniving asshole and I dismissed him with a flick of my hand.

I looked around to make sure the others were ready and Seth used air magic to style his long hair into perfect waves as he hurried to catch up with us.

The closer we got to the banquet hall, the heavier the weight in my chest felt. I didn't want to put on this show. I didn't want to play this part. I ached to make a public challenge against my father and expose his lies and treason to everyone in the kingdom. And instead I was being trotted out like a fucking show pony. It made me sick to my stomach to think of sitting through his bullshit all night, but we had a plan which might just make it worth it.

Tonight, the other Heirs were going to stay with me in my rooms and we were going to use our combined magic to try and locate where the fuck he was keeping Roxy. I knew the power of the Guardian bond would continue to bind her to him even if we got her away from him, but I just had to get her out of his clutches.

If we could just get her back to her sister, I was sure we could find a way to pull her out of the shadows and then the Guardian bond could be dealt with in its own way. Even if the only way to sever it was to kill my father, that was alright because I planned on doing that anyway. His tie to her only gave me more motive.

The sound of a string quartet reached me as I approached the banquet hall and Seth brushed his hand down my back in a comforting gesture as if he could sense how much I was dreading this farce. Max pushed calming emotions over me and I allowed them to slip beneath my skin, needing all the help I could get to hold it together tonight.

Jenkins hurried ahead, announcing our arrival as the huge double doors were swept open and the guests all turned to applaud me as I entered the room.

I smiled politely and let myself be passed from hand to hand as I was greeted with enthusiastic handshakes and praised over everything from the breadth of my shoulders to the cut of my suit to the noble sacrifice I'd made when I'd chosen to become Star Crossed. It was a fucking sham and I hated every moment of it but I smiled and nodded, complimented fugly dresses and praised the beauty of women older than my mother as they pressed their fake tits against me and offered up flirtatious suggestions.

Father was nowhere in sight yet thankfully, but Mildred sped through the crowd with a squeal of *snookums!* before planting a wet kiss right on my mouth and painting aubergine lipstick all over my jaw.

My smile was tight, my posture rigid, but no one noticed. No one cared. They wanted to buy into the pretty lie of my perfect life and get as close to the most powerful Fae in the room as they could manage.

17

Eventually there was a call for us to take our seats for dinner and Mom appeared out of the crowd. She offered me a pat on the cheek and her eyes burned with understanding before she whisked Mildred away, directing her to a seat further down the table from mine so that I at least didn't have to endure her pawing me throughout my meal.

I sat to the right of the chair at the head of the table with Xavier on my left and mother opposite him.

Father's newest groupie slunk into the room while everyone was distracted by finding their places and my gaze snagged on him as he moved to claim a seat at the table. Vard was a Seer who had turned up at the start of the summer claiming to want to help my father rise to greatness, and of course the vain bastard had accepted instantly. I didn't like the Cyclops one bit. There was something seriously disconcerting about him and as he swept his long, black hair away from his face my attention caught on his mismatched eyes. There was a scar running through one of them which had left it swirling with darkness that seemed all too clearly linked to the shadows for my liking.

There were around a hundred guests in attendance and the other Heirs took seats further down the table with their parents where they shot me sympathetic looks as I forced myself to engage in polite conversation and we waited for my father to show up.

Lance's mother, Stella, strode along the table, shaking her ass as she walked and looking like she thought every man here was hers to choose from. But it was more than obvious to me that the only one of them she wanted was my father. Unfortunately for her, despite her continued loyalty and devotion, Father seemed more than happy with the trade he'd made to her daughter so she could shake her ass all she wanted but it didn't seem to be luring him back.

"Happy birthday, Darius," she purred as she dropped down into the chair opposite mine, to the right of where my father was due to sit. "I do hope you've had an exhilarating day."

I hesitated a beat before responding as I tried to figure out if she knew something or if she was just being her usual odd self. The bulk of Father's Nymph army were currently camped out in the grounds of her estate and I'd been hungering to strike at them there since we figured that out. Especially since Darcy hoped to get hold of the soul hat Diego had left for her somewhere in the woods. But there were far too many of them there for us to be able to risk it.

On the raids we'd completed up until now, we'd been diligent in making sure not a single Nymph survived us. Just one witness would have our cover blown and if Father found out we'd been working against him with Darcy, everything could go to shit fast. But as Stella gave me that plastic smile of hers, I felt certain her question hadn't been relating to the fight we'd just had so I just gave her a bullshit smile in return.

"Who doesn't love birthdays?" I deadpanned, making it clear I wasn't much of a fan. At least not this year. But of course she just grinned like I'd told her it had been the best day of my life and took a moment to adjust her short, black hair as she greeted my mother like they were old friends. Mom acted like she was interested in what Stella had to say and of course there was no mention of the fact that they clearly hated each other.

"Lord Acrux and his Guardians, Clara Orion and Roxanya Vega!" Jenkins announced as the double doors swung open and my heart fell right through the pit of my stomach as all heads turned towards them.

I pushed out of my chair, almost knocking the thing to the floor in my haste as my mouth fell open and Father swept into the room with Clara on one arm and Roxy on the other.

She was heart stoppingly beautiful, wearing a full-length black gown which clung to her figure like a spill of ink. Her mahogany hair had been curled and hung down her spine and her makeup was like a work of art, dark and sultry around her eyes which only highlighted the ring of black the stars had given her and her lips were painted a deep, blood red which made me ache to taste her kisses again.

Father moved into the room, strutting like a peacock with an ass full of new feathers, but I only had eyes for her.

The guests had all broken into murmured conversations and gasps of surprise and the other Councillors moved to join my father as he began to spin some bullshit story about how Roxy had seen the light and decided to throw her support in with them.

Roxy didn't add to the conversation, but she offered up her left arm, showing them the Aries brand on her flesh as proof while smiling lightly.

She didn't look my way. She didn't even seem to care where she was. She just stood there as my heart splintered right down the centre and I was frozen, not knowing what to do. I wanted to stride over there, rip her out of his arms and take her as far away from him as physically possible, but instead I was rooted to the spot. I didn't know how to handle this. She wasn't kicking or screaming or trying to escape, she was just standing there like she was made of stone and nothing in the world could touch her. I'd look insane if I tried to prise her away from him by force but was I seriously just going to stand here and stare at her?

My gaze raked over every inch of her body as I hunted for signs of mistreatment, but of course there wasn't a physical mark on her because that would be all too easy to heal. Any trauma she bore was on the inside where no one could see, but she did look slimmer, paler...

I'm going to rip his fucking heart out!

A hand landed on my arm and Max's power pushed against my barriers as he tried to soothe my rage. I couldn't tear my eyes from her, but I could feel my muscles bunching, my hands curling into fists and some tiny, rational part of me knew that if I let myself give in to the desire to attack my father in front of all of these people then it wouldn't help anything. Roxy and Clara would throw themselves between us and as much as I was willing to destroy Clara, I couldn't lift a hand against Roxy. I'd sooner burn my own heart from my chest than put her in harm's way.

With a grunt of effort, I let Max calm me, just enough to take the edge off. To let me think rationally, try and come up with a plan, some way to separate her from my father and keep her away from him.

The Councillors broke apart and Father turned toward me with a cruel smile lighting his face. To anyone else he was just a father wishing his son a happy birthday. But I knew this was a test, a challenge, a game. And I had to figure out how to win it.

"Ah, Darius, I'm so sorry we're late. The girls were a little excitable while we were getting dressed," Father purred as he approached us.

"Excitable?" I asked, forcing my tone to remain neutral as my gaze stayed fixed on Roxy.

She wasn't looking at me, her eyes were on my father as he spoke, her gaze focused on his face.

"It's hard to concentrate when Daddy takes his clothes off," Clara giggled, stroking his arm and running a hand down his chest. Stella stared at them venomously, but said nothing.

Roxy's upper lip pulled back the smallest amount as she narrowed her eyes on Clara and for a moment it seemed like she was angry or bitter or…I refused to even consider the word *jealous*.

"Clara, be a dear and take your seat next to Xavier," Father said, shaking her off dismissively and she pouted as she stomped around the table and dropped down beside my brother. "Roxanya, say happy birthday to my son."

My heart stilled as Roxy turned to look my way, her gaze sweeping over me slowly, like she hardly even recognised me. She was so deep in the shadows that the girl I knew barely even seemed to be there anymore.

She released my father's arm and he gave her a little nudge towards me so that she moved to stand so close that I could have reached out and touched her.

Max released my arm and backed up, tossing a silencing bubble over us to give us some sense of privacy as I could feel the eyes of the whole room on us.

"Happy birthday, Darius," Roxy said, her voice rough and dark like it was swimming in sin.

She stepped closer to me and leaned in, brushing her lips against mine in a cruel mockery of all the kisses we'd shared before. Her lips were cold and her gaze empty. A shiver raced through me as I tasted the darkness on her. There was nothing in that kiss, not a single piece of the girl I loved and it felt like every part of me was breaking apart as I looked down at her in horror, wondering what the hell had happened to her to leave her so empty. How the shadows could have stolen so much and what else my father had been doing to her in the time that she'd been missing.

She pulled back but I caught her wrist, wanting to beg her to come back to me, hunt for some piece of the girl I knew in her eyes. But the moment my skin touched hers, a jolt of pain and darkness speared through me as the shadows in her invaded my body and wound their grip tightly around my heart.

My eyes widened and I struggled to draw breath as spears of agony slammed into me and cut me apart piece by piece. A smile curled up the corners of her lips as she watched me suffer and I was paralysed by the strength of her power.

"Let him go, sweetness," Father murmured, holding a hand out to her with a serene smile on his face. "It is his birthday after all."

Roxy tilted her head as she watched me suffer for an extra moment before suddenly drawing the shadows back out of me. She took my fingers in her grip and gently peeled them off of her arm and I watched her with my heart pounding and shattering and falling to pieces as I hunted for anything familiar in her eyes.

"Don't you know me?" I breathed, unable to hide the raw edge to my voice as I studied the black rings in her green eyes and begged the stars to let her see me.

"You're Darius," she replied, that rough edge still coating her voice. "The man who promised he'd never hurt me, even though he always enjoyed it when he did."

I shook my head, wanting to argue against those words but Father held a hand out to her and she took it with a smile which seemed painted on, but the adoring look in her eyes as she gazed at him was all too real.

"Sit down, Darius. Everyone is waiting for the birthday boy before they can eat." Father pointed me to my chair and I fell into it, not knowing what else to do.

Max gripped my shoulder for a moment, pressing more calming energy beneath my skin before dropping his silencing bubble and returning to his chair along the table.

Father took his seat at the head of the table and heat invaded every cell in my body as he tugged Roxy down into his lap.

A growl ripped from my throat and I half lurched out of my seat, but Clara caught hold of the shadows in me and forced me back down again before anyone noticed. I sat rigidly in my chair, pain and terror shredding me apart as Roxy arranged herself more comfortably on Father's knee.

She didn't resist as he pulled her close but she didn't just sit on his dick either, perching on his knee instead with her spine straight as her gaze trailed over all of the people at the table who were staring at her, before she looked away again dismissively.

Xavier's hand gripped my knee beneath the table and I could feel his own horror at this, but I couldn't spare an inch of my attention for it.

The first course was served and I could only watch her as Father made conversation with people around the table and Clara kept me trapped within my own body.

Stella laughed loudly at everything he said, tossing her short hair and leaning forward so that her tits threatened to spill from her dress and Father hardly even seemed to notice.

He reached around Roxy's back and toyed with the dark curls of her hair where they spilled down her spine and she just sat there, not reacting in any way. No horror or disgust, no pleasure or excitement either. She was like an empty vessel filled with shadow and everything from the coldness of her gaze to the emptiness of her expression made me seethe with rage and fear.

"I can see what had you so captivated, Darius," Father murmured as the next course was served and everyone was distracted. "She really is a beautiful girl. And so...*tenacious*. I have to say I really enjoyed breaking her in and beating that wildness out of her."

"If you've laid a fucking finger on her, I'll cut you into a thousand pieces and burn you alive in Dragon fire," I snarled, but Clara's hold on my shadows stopped me from doing any more than tightening my grip on my goddamn spoon. If I could get close to him, I'd gladly find a way to make a spoon lethal though.

Father didn't bother to respond, only offering a knowing smile as he rested his fucking hand on her hip. Rage unlike anything I'd ever felt before consumed me as I was locked in my fucking chair, forced to endure the show he was putting on for me, taunting me with the girl I loved like she was just some plaything.

I didn't eat a bite of my food as the courses came and went. I had no appetite even when Clara allowed me to move enough to eat. I pushed the odd thing around my plate, but my gaze never wavered from Roxy. And I never stopped trying to fight Clara's hold on me so that I could rip her right out of my father's lap.

As the dessert was served, Father leaned close and whispered something in her ear. She nodded once and got to her feet, turning and sweeping from the room without a word.

Clara released me just as Roxy got to the doors and I shoved to my feet instantly, practically running out into the hallway after her and not giving a shit who saw or what they thought.

By the time I made it out into the hall, Roxy was already at the far end of it and I called out to her as I broke into a sprint to catch up.

She made it onto the stairwell in the centre of the house before I caught up to her and she turned back to look at me with an eyebrow raised like she had no idea what I might want.

"What did he do to you?" I choked, my heart racing as I reached for her, but she shifted so that I couldn't catch her hand and I could have sworn fear flickered in her eyes for a moment before she hid it again. "Tell me and I'll rip him apart for it. Tell me what I have to do to break you out of this."

"Out of what?" she asked in a cold tone.

"The shadows, Roxy, you need to break free of them, you need-"

"Why would I do that?" she asked dismissively. "The shadows bring me more pleasure than you can even imagine. They feed my soul and steal my pain. Maybe you should consider joining me in them."

"Joining you?" I sneered. "The girl I love would never-"

She stepped forward suddenly, her hand pressing to my chest right above my heart as we stood eye to eye with her on the steps.

"That pain you feel doesn't have to rule you," she said, moving so close that her lips almost brushed mine but the look in her eyes was hollow, bottomless, void. "You could join me in the dark. We could have it all."

"What about love?" I murmured, my hands slipping around her waist as I drew her closer to me, wanting to hold on to her until I forced her to come back for good.

"I only love my king," she breathed.

"No," I snarled fiercely, denying her words with every fibre of my being. "You don't love him. You'd *never* love him."

A dark laugh escaped her as my grip on her tightened and a swell of power burst from her hand where it was pressed to my chest, the shadows slamming into me and knocking me back against the heavy doors at the front of the house and pinning me in place.

"Let me know if you change your mind," Roxy said dismissively, turning away and continuing up the stairs towards my father's quarters without a backwards glance.

The shadows held me against the door long after she'd walked away and by the time she released me, she was long gone.

I hunted the entire house for her, but she'd disappeared once more. And I felt her loss all over again, just as sharply as the night she'd been taken. Or maybe even more so. Because until now I'd had hope that I could save her if I could only find her. And now I had to fear if I would ever get her back again.

XAVIER

CHAPTER TWO

"Boy," Father's voice was firm and cutting, carrying from his office and making dread carve a hole through my chest.

I placed my suitcase down, straightened my shirt and took a breath as I approached the door. I could get through anything now. I was about to leave for Zodiac Academy and my magic would be Awakened. I literally couldn't freaking wait. I'd gotten a sum total of three hours' sleep last night and had had to wait all damn day for this moment. But it was night time now. The stars were awake, and soon my magic would be too.

I pushed the door open, lifting my chin as I faced the man who sent fear prickling along my limbs. After everything he'd done, there wasn't a scrap of love in my heart for him. It was hard to remember a time there ever had been really. Admiration maybe, awe, respect – before I realised he didn't deserve any of those things. But any dislike I'd had for him had turned into a potent hate after everything he'd done, the lives he'd destroyed, and the ones he still planned on destroying.

He was dressed in a fine tailored suit, his broad shoulders emphasised by the fitted blazer and his blonde hair pushed back and styled perfectly. He stood from his chair behind the desk, rising to his imposing height.

"Close the door." he commanded and a razor blade lodged in my throat as I pushed it shut with a sharp click that echoed on through my skull.

Father moved around the desk, gazing down his nose at me with undisguised disgust. "You understand the way the wind is blowing, don't you boy?" he asked in a dangerous growl, but he went on before I could figure out what he meant. "The throne is mine for the taking, I will be Solaria's King. And that will make you of great interest to the students of Zodiac Academy.

My arm has been twisted into allowing you to attend, but do not underestimate my influence upon you even when you are no longer under this roof."

I clenched my jaw, keeping my tongue from spilling out a single stupid word. I wasn't going to test him tonight. Not when freedom was so close that I could hear it screaming my damn name.

Father went on, "You will keep your head down and the press will barely know you exist. You will not take interviews unless I tell you to, you will not cause a stir, let alone a scandal. And you will return home whenever I demand it, is that clear?"

"Yes, Father." I bowed my head, playing the good little pawn. I just wanted out. The only problem was Mom. She'd come to me last night, making me swear I'd build a life for myself at school, that I wouldn't worry about her. But how could I do that? Leaving her here was unbearable. I just didn't have a choice.

"Good," he said dismissively. "Go downstairs, Portia will be conducting a brief interview for The Celestial Times before we leave. I will announce your Elements and House to the press after your Awakening is done, then there shall be no more focus on my worthless, spare son."

I nodded stiffly, turning away with that bittersweet slap to the face still stinging my cheek and heading out the door, his heavy presence following me. I grabbed my suitcase and carried it downstairs where a porter was waiting to take it from me. Darius had already gone back to Zodiac a few days ago, insisting he needed a head start on his work and Father had let him go because he always wanted his special Heir to be ahead of the game. I knew better though. Darius had told me himself he was going out Nymph hunting with the other Heirs and Darcy Vega. He'd been telling me about their hunts all summer so I could live vicariously through his stories. I longed to join them, it sounded like something from one of my Xbox games. A real life adventure. And now I was getting my magic Awakened, maybe it wouldn't be too long before I really could help. Though I guessed I knew in my heart that I had a lot to learn before I'd be of any use. Still…

Voices carried from out on the porch, the front door half open and my father's hand suddenly landed on my shoulder as he steered me outside. When I looked up at him, I found him wearing one of his false smiles, his teeth on show and a decent attempt at pride glowing in his eyes. I slapped on my own smile which was equally fake and we stepped outside where the press had set up some lights facing the porch and Mom was there chatting with Portia in a flowing green gown.

"Ah, here's the man of the hour!" Portia exclaimed, her blonde hair bouncing as she hurried up the steps toward me. "You look dashing, Xavier. Let's get a few pictures with your parents." She positioned me between them and they both moved in close as the photographer started shooting. I looked up at Mom with a grin and she shot me a wink that warmed my heart.

When the shoot was done, Portia questioned me about my feelings over being Awakened and starting school, and I was able to let out the bursting emotions inside me over it all. Because I was fucking excited. Star damned crazy happy about it. And by the time I was done telling her about it, my jaw was aching from how hard I'd been smiling.

"It's not fair!" Clara shrieked from somewhere in the house and Father's face turned to thunder.

"Excuse me," he said curtly and Portia waved him off, but shared a brief look with the photographer that said she was curious as shit.

"Go grab your coat, Xavier," Mom encouraged, her eyes anxious. "We'd better head off soon."

"Yes, of course, I won't keep you any longer," Portia said apologetically, starting to pack up her things.

I slipped back inside the house while Mom started making small talk with her slightly louder than was necessary and I shut the door behind me. Clara was on the stairs with a cloak of shadows spinning around her, her hands planted on her hips. Tory stood beside my father in a red satin dress, gazing at him with a doe-eyed look that made my skin crawl. I couldn't even express how angry I was about what my father had done to Tory. I hadn't seen her since Darius's birthday and had no idea where he was keeping her. Now, he brought her out like a dog on a leash. It was fucking sick.

"I was your Guardian first, Daddy, how come *she* gets to go with you?" Clara pouted, her eyes a swirling storm of darkness. I probably should have been used to her calling him *Daddy* by now, but fuck no I wasn't. It still made me wanna vom. Every. Damn. Time.

"Now, Clara, I explained this to you," Father said in a purr that made me equally sick. "Roxanya needs to be seen as allied to me out in public. And you still don't have full control of your power, you cannot pass as Fae yet."

I drifted across the hall to the coat closet, grabbing a smart black one and pulling it on, never taking my eyes off of the circus of horrors playing out before me.

Clara's face twisted in fury and the storm cloud of darkness around her built in size, the strength of her power tugging on the shadows living in me.

"I can control myself!" she bellowed and Father snarled, lunging at her and grasping her throat.

"Silence," he hissed. "Or I'll have you banished from my quarters for a week. Is that what you want?"

"No," Clara whimpered and the shadows died around her while my nose wrinkled.

I tried to catch Tory's eye, but she just gazed at Father with the same intensity Clara was giving him. It was sickening to watch.

"Good girl," Lionel growled. "Now go back upstairs and when I get home, I'll reward you for behaving."

She leaned in for a kiss, but he moved away before she could claim it, placing a possessive hand on Tory's back and guiding her toward the door. He jerked his chin at me in a command and I fell in to step behind them as they exited the house again.

Portia was still there chatting with my mom, but her eyes practically leapt out of her head as she spotted Tory at my father's side. It wasn't like it was fresh news that Tory was aligned with Lionel now, but the press still couldn't lap it up quick enough.

"Oh, good evening, Miss Vega, I wasn't expecting to see you tonight," Portia said in surprise as Father took his hand from Tory's spine.

"Yes, well here I am," Tory said blandly, smiling at Father again before giving Portia a flat look.

"Could I get a few words while I'm here?" Portia asked hopefully, glancing at my father then back to Tory.

"Of course, but make it quick, we need to leave," Father said politely and Portia nodded, hurrying up the steps to Tory with her dictaphone in hand so she could record her.

"Have you spoken with your sister lately? She has been running quite an extensive campaign with The Daily Solaria insisting that you are still planning to claim the throne together. Care to comment?" Portia asked hopefully and I wished I could scream at her and tell her the truth, that my father was a monster, that he was using the shadows to control Tory, that he used dark magic daily, that he was allied with the Nymphs, that he planned on taking over the kingdom and destroying anyone who stood in his way. But I just stood there, my features schooled, my heart pounding out of rhythm.

"Oh, I'm not running for the throne anymore," Tory said simply and my heart scrunched up in my chest. She reached out to run her hand up and down Father's arm. "I've found my true place now."

Portia blinked furiously and Mom carefully kept her serene expression in place, but there was a dark horror behind her eyes.

"By the stars, so you are officially renouncing your claim to the throne of Solaria?" Portia asked, dollar signs flashing in her eyes at being the first to get the scoop on this. *Hell no. Don't do this, Tory.*

"Absolutely," Tory said with a weirdly empty smile.

"That's all for tonight, I'm afraid we don't want to be late," Father stepped in as Portia looked fit to burst with questions. "Jenkins will see you out. Good evening, Portia."

He steered Tory past her and me and Mom hurried to follow, sharing a worried look. She took my hand, squeezing quickly before releasing it and my heart swelled a little knowing I had her secretly on my side, even if she couldn't say it. I just wished I could take her with me tonight and keep her away from Father forever.

The porter was waiting at the end of the drive with my bag and as we crossed out of the gates together through the wards, Father tossed stardust into the air and the world spun in a haze of stars.

My feet hit solid ground and I found myself gazing up at the immense gates of Zodiac Academy; the zodiac circle was engraved at the centre of it, featuring all of the star sign symbols around it. Nerves and excitement warred inside me as Father huffed out a breath.

"They couldn't even lift the wards for one night? This school is forgetting who funds it," he muttered.

"Well at least our Xavier will be safe here," Mom said in a flat tone, but I knew her words were for me.

I'd be safe here from Father. Once I was inside these gates, he couldn't easily get to me. Sure, he could summon the living hell out of me, but that was nowhere near as bad as being hauled out of my bedroom by the scruff of my neck whenever he was in a bad mood. No, here I would have more freedom than I'd ever known in my lifetime. I felt a whinny building in my throat and fought the urge to shift, take off into the sky, circle my new home and let glitter tumble from my flesh. *Later, dude. Me and the sky can get real intimate.*

A few students were already gathered by the gates, most arriving by cars. They were hugging their families, saying goodbye and I realised a little bitterly that my father wasn't going to go anywhere until the stars awoke my Elements.

"Good evening, Lionel," a deep voice called and I turned as Tiberius Rigel strode toward us with his wife on his arm and their daughter following at their heels.

Ellis's hair was dark and thick, framing her strong features which had a hint of her brother Max in them. I'd spent more than a few dinner parties with her, but we never got to spend much time together outside of our parents' watchful eyes. Unlike the way the Councillors had encouraged the four Heirs to spend time together and bond, they'd never bothered to encourage a similar relationship between the younger children in the families. Even if there was technically a chance that any one of us could challenge our older siblings for their positions one day.

No, despite how the system was meant to be fair and we were all supposed to have an equal shot at claiming the role of Councillor one day, it was more than clear to all of us that the eldest siblings were never going to be unseated. They'd been Awakened young and given advanced training in every kind of skill and magic years before even coming to Zodiac Academy. So even if our power levels were a match to theirs, there was no way any of us spares would be able to pose a real threat and everyone knew it. Not that I had the slightest desire to take Darius's place from him, but the injustice of the system still annoyed me.

Ellis smiled vaguely at me and I smiled back, wondering if she'd ever considered the challenge of vying for Max's position worth her time or if she was happy enough in her position too.

"Tiberius." Lionel nodded to him.

Tiberius's gaze fell to Tory beside him, a look of concern twisting through his eyes before he quickly schooled it.

Father tugged her closer without shame as Tory gave him that dreamy eyed look again. I had no idea what the other Councillors thought of my father's new pet, but from the few looks they'd exchanged at Darius's birthday party, I had to think they thought it was weird as shit. The whole kingdom surely thought that too. And anyone who knew Tory would be able to see it the second they got close. But that was the problem, Father didn't let anyone near her. And if he did, he was clearly going to be right there beside her like an overbearing husband. *Ergh. Should not have gone there.*

Tiberius's wife Linda looked around, her nose wrinkled like there was a bad smell under it. She pulled Ellis close, arranging her hair over her shoulders and her daughter indulged it, smiling serenely at her mother's affection.

"Melinda and Antonia will be arriving together momentarily," Tiberius said. "Exciting, isn't it?"

"Quite," Lionel said coolly.

The air shimmered beyond us and Melinda Altair appeared with her golden hair tumbling around her shoulders in soft curls and Antonia Capella materialised beside her, her coppery brown locks pulled up into a chignon bun. They were both wearing fine dresses and I wouldn't have been surprised if they'd come from an interview with the press. Behind Melinda was Caleb's younger brother Hadley with his sharp jaw and blue eyes as piercing as the rest of his family's. His hair was dark though, honey brown and shaved in at the sides. If he was a Vampire, his Order would emerge the moment his magic did, and I imagined they were expecting that, just as Father had expected me to be a Dragon. I wondered if he'd receive the same kind of treatment I'd endured if he turned out to be a Pegasus or something else, or if his family actually loved him and would accept him no matter what.

Beyond Antonia were two of Seth's younger siblings. The twins had grown into their looks this past year; Grayson was tall, his features angular and his eyes dark, his sister Athena was the female mirror image of him, though she had dark purple streaks running through her wavy hair whereas Grayson's was a floppy, brown mess on top of his head. They tickled and shoved each other as they laughed and played, looking like the Wolves they were. I grinned at them and they grinned back, running over to snare me in a two sided hug.

"Xavier! You'd better take me flying soon," Athena begged and Grayson grabbed my face to pull me around to look at him.

"Me first, dude," he insisted and I laughed, shoving them off and throwing a glance at Father whose right eye was twitching. Dragons didn't let anyone ride them, but there was no such law for Pegasuses. Would he expect me to refuse like a Dragon or would he just accept that my Order lived by different rules? Not that I was going to ask for his opinion. No doubt he'd make it perfectly clear if he wanted to.

Hadley was carefully positioning his hair as he walked over to join us, but Ellis held back with her family while her mother whispered something in her ear.

"We've been placing bets on our second Elements, you want in Xavier?" Hadley asked with a dark smirk, his eyes drifting to Athena and lingering on her cleavage peeking out of her fitted blue dress before he looked back at me.

"My bet's on Hadley being a single Elemental," Athena taunted him and Hadley scowled.

"You're just jealous that I'm going to get the best Elements, Athena. Earth and fire." He pushed his fingers into his hair in a way designed to draw attention to his bicep, but Athena's gaze didn't falter from his face.

"Well unlike you, I don't want to have the same second Element as my older brother, because I'm not a little Heir clone. I'm going to have air and water then I'll make a tornado that sweeps you into a lake of my own design so I can drown your vain ass in it."

Grayson barked a laugh, bouncing on his heels. "Maybe I'll get air and fire and firenado your ass too, Hadley."

Hadley rolled his eyes as Grayson shoved his arm. "You wish, Gray."

"What do you think you'll get, Xavier?" Athena turned to me with a bright smile.

I shifted on the tarmac, shrugging. "Honestly, I just can't wait to have one Element, let alone-"

"Nonsense," Father boomed, laughing loudly in that fake way he did at his pretentious parties. He dropped an arm around my shoulders, steering me away from the others and planting me next to Tory. "Xavier will make us proud as a double Elemental." His grip on my shoulders grew painful, like he was warning me to produce two Elements or I'd be gutted. But what did he expect me to do? I couldn't pluck extra Elements out of my ass if I didn't have them. It was up to the stars what I was gifted tonight.

"What do you think you'll get, Ellis?" Grayson bounded over to her like a dog who'd just been let off its leash, apparently having no awareness of her standoffish stance as he slung an arm around her and nuzzled into her hair.

She growled, shoving him off. "I don't know, Grayson."

"She'll have water and air, just like Max," her mother said firmly, elbowing Tiberius who quickly chimed in to agree.

"Yes, yes, most likely," he agreed, smiling proudly.

"Are you gonna pick Aer House then, because your big brother doesn't like you stepping on his toes, does he?" Grayson taunted and she rolled her eyes at him as he tried to paw at her again.

"I'll go wherever I fancy," she said with a cool smile and Grayson barked another laugh.

The gates suddenly opened and my heart beat powerfully in my chest as a tall woman appeared with her dark hair pulled into a bun. I'd seen enough pictures of her to know this was Principal Nova. She'd been especially helpful to my Father lately. Mom had told me she'd sent a letter promising to keep an eye on me while I was here. I mean, it wasn't exactly a surprise to me that Father had the staff under his control considering he pumped Zodiac full of gold whenever the school board asked, but I still didn't like the idea of being watched. This was a big school though and there was no way she'd be able to keep an eye on me twenty-four seven. And just the idea of being able to go about my day without a Dragon Lord breathing down my neck was like fifty million times better than my previous circumstances, so I was calling it a win.

Beside Nova was a woman with flowing raven hair and pale skin; she was dressed in long black robes, looking like some sort of medieval witch. She gazed at my father and the other Councillors with respect, but something in her eyes told me she wasn't exactly thrilled they were here. Her gaze fell on Tory and a squeak of horror left her as she took an abrupt step toward her. "My dear, are you quite well?"

"Quite well," Tory echoed and the professor pulled at her own hair, glancing at Father and quickly schooling her expression again.

"Good evening High Councillors," Nova said brightly, ushering an entourage forward to take all of our bags from us – or our porters anyway. "We are absolutely thrilled to welcome your children to Zodiac Academy."

There were like two hundred other kids waiting behind us but whatever.

"Professor Zenith will be conducting their Awakening as usual," Nova went on. "And we thought it might be apt for the five of them to be gifted by the stars before the rest of the students."

"Oh, that's really not necessary," Antonia said cheerily and Melinda nodded.

"I think it would be appropriate," Father said firmly, directing Nova and Zenith to start walking ahead of us, taking charge.

We followed them through campus and Tory drifted along at my side, seeming disinterested in anything but occasionally gazing wistfully at my father. I frowned at her, wishing I could do something to help her, but as she met my gaze, I could see she was hardly even there. Was Father going to allow her to come back to the academy this year?

The thought of her having been stuck alone in the manor with him all summer was awful. But it wasn't like I'd been able to get near her, and Darius certainly hadn't. Shit, what could anyone even do at this point?

We wound along through the beautiful campus under the light of the stars and the mutters coming from the crowd of freshman behind us said we were the talk of the night. Grayson kept throwing flirtatious looks at the group of fangirls at his and Hadley's heels. Come to think of it, there were a bunch of girls pointing at me and whispering too. Heat blazed along my neck and I turned back to face the way we were going before I tripped over my own feet or some shit.

We reached a sweeping meadow full of tall grass and Nova directed the rest of the freshman to wait by the trees before leading me, Tory, the Councillors and their kids down to the centre of the field.

My heart lifted at the sight of the Heirs waiting for us there. Darius, Max, Seth and Caleb were dressed in smart suits, watching us closely as we approached. I could see their lips moving and Caleb's hand curling around Darius's arm as my brother stared at Tory. The tension in his posture made my chest ache, and he gave Caleb a firm nod even though the action seemed to cause him pain. They were clearly talking within a silencing bubble, but the second we got close enough, they disbanded it and all moved forward to greet their families.

Darius pulled me into a hug, speaking in a low voice in my ear. "This is your night, Xavier. Enjoy it."

I smiled at him as he released me, but my smile started to die as his gaze moved to Tory again and she acted like he was invisible. It hurt me to see the two of them like this. Wasn't being Star Crossed enough? Now my father had to do this to them too? It wasn't right. Sometimes I didn't have any faith in the stars. It was hard to accept they were ever on our side when all I saw from fate these days was bullshit.

"Let's begin," Zenith said brightly.

My heart thrashed against my ribcage as she directed the five of us to stand in a circle and our parents and Tory stood back behind us. It was easier to concentrate when my father was no longer in sight and I smiled at Hadley across from me who smirked like a cocky asshole.

Zenith stepped between us as Nova moved away to watch and Athena and Grayson grabbed my hands on either side of me.

"That's it, hold hands all of you," Zenith said, her eyes sweeping over us with an assessing gaze.

Ellis and Hadley clasped hands then took hold of the twins' hands too so we were all linked in a circle.

"It is my greatest pleasure to Awaken your Elements tonight," Zenith announced. "Now please tilt your heads towards the sky as it is time for the stars to bring forth your inner power."

I dropped my head back, a shit eating grin pulling at my mouth because holy fuck, I was about to get my magic at long last. I wouldn't be totally indefensible anymore. I'd be able to learn and get strong and maybe help my brother and his friends against the asshole of a Dragon who called himself my father.

The stars above were endlessly bright and glittered like a million eyes watching the world unfold below them. I could feel their power thrumming in the air, injecting my veins with a rush of exhilaration. They might have been dicks, but they were going to do at least one good thing for me tonight.

"Virtus aquae invocabo!" Zenith cried up to them.

The air fell still and I stopped breathing as I waited, tension gripping the atmosphere as silence fell around me. Then water droplets dotted my cheeks and I laughed as the swell of my water Element crashed into my limbs, running through my body like an overflowing lake.

Ellis laughed and a sound of excited clapping came from behind me.

"That's my girl!" Ellis's mom cried and Tiberius cheered.

"Wonderful, you two have the Element of water," Zenith announced.

"Guess you won't be drowning me then, Athena," Hadley taunted her and she pouted.

I drew in a breath as the magic in me swirled like a whirlpool. I was a double Elemental. No doubt about it. My star sign was linked to fire so I would have the same Elements as my brother after all. I couldn't wait.

"Everyone focus on the sky. Rogo vim aeris!" Zenith called to the heavens.

Grayson and Athena's hair gusted in a wind I couldn't feel and they whooped excitedly.

"Wonderful, your air Element has Awakened in you both," Zenith told the twins and I grinned as they both squeezed my hands. "Invoco virtutem ignis!"

Heat flared at my feet and I grinned as I looked down at the fire tearing around me in a circle.

"Fuck yes!" Hadley whooped as fire blazed around him too. I grinned as I spotted the fangs in his mouth and the look of bloodlust peering from his eyes as his Order Emerged.

The Heirs all started cheering behind me and a grin stretched across my face that felt permanent. I was free, I'd soon be learning how to wield my power at the academy I'd dreamed of attending my entire life. This day was starting to rival my first flight as a Pegasus.

"Wonderful, Xavier," Mom's voice reached me.

My chest swelled as the Elemental heat spread through my body, warming every inch of me and a sense of real power thrummed in my chest.

"Oh shit." Hadley's eyes turned dark and he gasped, lunging at Zenith who promptly offered her arm to him like she'd seen this happen a thousand times. His fangs sank into her flesh and he drank deeply from her to sate his bloodlust. He finally tugged his fangs free, grinning satisfactorily as he stepped back to re-join the circle.

"You have the gift of fire, Xavier Acrux and Hadley Altair," Zenith announced and I felt everyone else's eyes on me as no one else had yet received a second Element. But earth was last so Hadley would definitely have it as he was a Virgo and the others would surely have it too. I looked back at the sky once more as Zenith cried out her final command to the stars. "Rogo vim terrae!"

I looked down, watching as grass grew up around Hadley's legs, curling hungrily along his body. The same was happening to the twins and they laughed excitedly as they whooped. I glanced at Ellis, seeking the same, but there was nothing there and it took me a second to realise she was staring back at me with utter horror in her eyes. Something tickled my hand and I dropped my gaze to it, my heart lurching in complete disbelief as I found the grass coiling up around my body too.

"Holy shit," I breathed.

"He has three Elements!" Mom gasped and I turned my head to look at my family. Father's eyes were wide, a look of pride filling them that I'd never seen aimed at me in my damn life.

"My son has three Elements!" he laughed, clapping his hands twice in quick succession and heat crawled into my cheeks. I still hated the asshole, but maybe I was a sucker because now he was looking at me the way I'd always wanted him too and it felt really fucking good.

Darius was smiling his head off and the other Heirs looked awestruck. It felt so strange being the centre of attention after so long being locked up, hidden away and ignored. But I quite liked it too.

Tiberius started consoling his wife who'd broken down in tears and my heart hurt for Ellis as a noise of fury left her. She only had one Element, and it had to suck seeing us all gain more power than her. Max snorted, barely concealing a laugh and the other Heirs dove on him, the four of them suddenly tussling and cheering. But it was hard to focus on anything except the look in my father's eyes. The way he saw me as someone of value for the first time in my life. My gut suddenly lurched and my happiness over that fact ebbed away as I realised what it meant.

I cursed the stars for this and their continued fuckery, because as much as I'd wanted my power, all I'd really wanted was a life without my father paying me any attention. But now he would watch me closer than ever, keep me under his heel, ensure this was splashed through every newspaper in Solaria. And I realised with a horrible, confining certainty, that I was never truly going to be free.

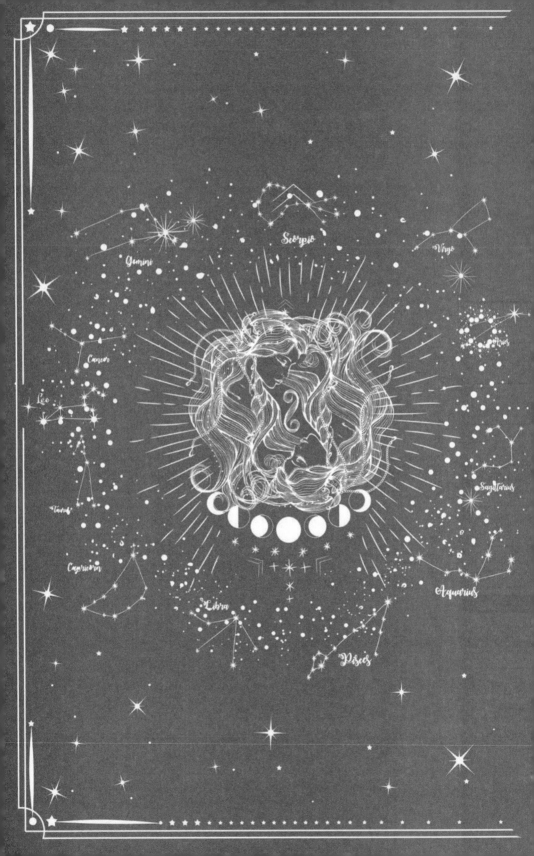

DARCY

CHAPTER THREE

I woke up with a groan, my Atlas alarm telling me it was time to move. But no matter how much of a morning person I was, nothing could make me want to get up today. I'd only gotten three hours sleep since we'd been out hunting Nymphs half the night.

A weight shifted on my bed and my hands slipped into soft fur as I rolled towards the comforting heat of the body beside me. Seth's Wolf form was damn huge, but he still managed to somehow fit in my single bed and leave me with enough room to breathe. I hadn't asked him to stay with me, but I also hadn't asked him to keep me company at the palace all summer and he often had. All the Heirs had.

Another groan in the room told me we weren't alone and I cracked my eyes open, peering through a swathe of white fur to where Max was passed out by the window in a nest of blankets. I snorted at him as he pushed himself up onto his elbows.

"Why didn't you go back to your room when Darius and Caleb left?" I asked through a yawn as I sat up.

"I was gonna, but then I touched this blanket and it was *so* soft. What's it made of, fucking clouds?" Max brushed his fingers up and down it. "Anyway, I made this nest like some sort of Tiberian Rat and camped here. So…this blanket is mine now, yes?"

I blew out a breath of amusement. "Sure, take it."

Seth was still dead to the world, laying upside down with his furry head crammed between the mattress and the wall and his tongue lolling out. *Ridiculous mutt.*

We'd stayed here talking last night after the Nymph hunt, trying to come up with new ways to save Tory, new ways to destroy Lionel, but what had been on all of our minds was Xavier. He had three freaking Elements. And from what the Heirs had said, Lionel was happy as hell about it. But as pleased as I was for Xavier, anything that made Lionel happy was just another kick in the teeth.

I'd been heartbroken to find out that Tory had been at his Awakening too. Right on campus. And now she was gone again and I didn't know how to reach her. Going on the Nymph hunt had been what all of us had needed to keep our minds off of things. The problem was, no distraction ever lasted. It had been bad enough waiting for the Heirs to finish hazing all the freshmen before we left; it had served to remind me of my first night at Zodiac, and made me miss Tory something fierce.

I picked up our latest Tarot card from Astrum which was sitting on my nightstand, twisting it between my fingers. The words *seek the fallen hunter* gazed up at me in shimmering silver letters. As Orion's name was the constellation of The Hunter, Darius had spoken to him about the card. They'd guessed it might have something to do with Orion's dad and the diary he'd been gifted from him. Not that Orion had made any progress with decoding it as far as I'd heard. I never spoke with him directly, but Darius kept me updated. And I guessed that was the new normal. Living as though he was wholly separate to me, like he'd never owned my heart, like I'd never pledged to love him no matter what.

My chest ached at the thought of term starting today without Tory. The summer had been long and painful and I'd had to find ways to harden my heart against all of that. The loss of Orion, then losing Tory after had nearly broken me. But the one thing I'd found to hold onto amongst it all in the end was a purpose. I would do whatever was in my power to destroy Lionel and ensure he never sat his hateful ass on the throne. And I'd rip my sister out of his control and burn the shadows out of her too. Just as soon as I figured out how.

I'd been practising on Darius for months, but no matter what I did, I couldn't seem to work out how I'd rid myself of the shadows. Seth had been dying, Clara had been about to kill us all. It was hard to replicate those circumstances, but Darius had been willing to try anything. It just hadn't worked yet. But it would. And as soon as I could do it to him, I could do it to Tory and Xavier and…Orion.

My heart yanked and pulled in several directions and I pushed out of bed, not willing to stay there and drown in the misery lurking in my soul for a single second longer.

"Geraldine's arriving this morning," I told Max and his brows arched, his excitement clear before he shrugged and ran a hand over his hair, playing it cool, like he didn't bring her up at every given opportunity. He'd grown out the mohawk recently, his hair short all over and giving him a more mature look.

"So?" he asked, getting to his feet and stretching his muscular arms above his head. He'd stripped down to his boxers which had schools of fish swimming across the navy material and I smirked.

"She'll like those," I teased then slipped into the bathroom and shut the door.

I stripped out of my pyjamas, showering and washing my dark blue hair, wondering for the millionth time if I should just dye it red or green or strip it all out and go dark again. But whenever I bought new dye, I couldn't make myself go through with it. It wasn't about Orion. *Screw Orion.* But there was still something holding me back. Maybe I didn't want to let go of the girl I'd been before the two people I loved most in the world had been ripped away from me. But perhaps it was time I accepted that girl was dead and buried, this new version of me fitted with a heart that lived in a fortress and who hungered to take the throne to ensure Lionel never got his hands on it.

The Heirs had been helping to train me up in combat, but nothing could beat the education I was gaining at Zodiac to really become powerful. Some things took time. And I needed to be here so I could continue fighting for my sister. *I'll find a way to free you from the shadows, Tor, just hold on.*

"See you at breakfast, little Vega!" Max called through the bathroom door as he left.

"See you," I called back, tearing my gaze away from the mirror at last. I liked my hair dammit, so why should I change it? The new me could give it a new meaning. It didn't have to be anything to do with *him* anymore. Like he said, blue meant royal in Solaria. *"And to me, blue means you."*

Get out of my head.

I wrapped a towel around myself, pushing the door open and cursed as I found Seth lying just where he had been before only now he'd shifted, so his naked ass was planted on my bed and his junk was in full view.

"Seth!" I snapped, snatching a pillow from the nest Max had been sleeping in and slapping it down on his dick to hide it.

He bolted upright with a doggish yelp, snatching my wrist before I could draw away.

"*Balls*," he wheezed. "How dare you?"

"If you don't like covering up your dick then maybe you should sleep in your own bed sometime." I arched a brow at him and he cocked his head, giving me the puppy dog eyes.

"But you need me," he said.

"I don't need you, Seth," I laughed but he gave me a serious look.

"You talk in your sleep these days, you know? You're all 'help me Sethy, come hug my cute ass. Oh ravish me, Sethy, ravish me!'"

"Yeah, right." I moved to my closet, taking out my uniform and sighing as I ran my fingers over the crest on the blazer. My throat closed up as I thought of Tory. *She should be here. I don't want to do this without her.*

The ache in me over her loss was like a knife twisting in my gut. I never felt whole anymore. Without her, I was half a girl. We were meant to be together. It was how it had always been and always should be.

"See," Seth said darkly. "Whenever your mind drifts it's onto her, or him. That's who you really talk about in your sleep."

"We don't talk about *him*," I muttered.

"I know, but…that doesn't mean you're okay."

"I'm fine," I growled. "It's done, I'm over it."

"Pfft," he scoffed and I rounded on him as fire prickled along my veins.

"Oooh you're getting the flamey eyes." He chuckled, getting out of bed and casually dropping the pillow before tugging his boxers on. "You must be really thinking about him today."

"Stop it," I snarled, but he was right. I'd dreamed of him again, holding me, kissing me, not betraying me. You know, all the good stuff. Shame he had to ruin it.

"Darcy," he said gently. "You know you can talk to me about him, you don't have to bottle it up."

I shook my head, the wound over Orion begging to split open in me again, but fuck that.

"How about I tell you a secret in exchange for one of yours?" he offered enticingly and I frowned, gesturing for him to turn around so I could get dressed. He did so and I figured what the hell, that offer was too intriguing to ignore.

"Go on then, tell me," I said.

"Swear you'll tell me yours after," he said firmly.

"Fine," I agreed. "Now go on."

"You can't tell anyone," he said in a growl and I became even more intrigued.

"I swear it on the stars and all that jazz."

"I might have to actually make you swear it on them in a minute," he said in a low tone.

"Sure." I pulled on my underwear before running a hand through my damp hair to dry it with air magic.

"Okay so…I have this crush. It's a really secret crush."

"God you're gonna start talking about the moon again aren't you?" I said in exasperation. Ever since he'd visited the damn moon over the summer, he wouldn't shut up about it. Like he was some sort of moon wizard now. I mean yeah, it had been cool to hear about it when he'd first gotten back, but four weeks on and the shine had kind of worn off of his moon stories.

He chuckled. "No, but that reminds me of when I was on the moon and I stuck my dick in a moon hole. I have *literally* fucked the moon."

"I know," I said exaggeratedly, laughing as I tugged on my skirt. "And you have *literally* told me every detail."

"Right yeah, well anyways, it's not about my moon crush. It's another crush."

"Okay…" I waited as I pulled on my shirt, but he didn't go on. "Seth?"

"It's kind of a big deal."

"Every crush you have is a big deal, you had a crush on a cookie the other day and didn't eat it for like eight hours."

"The chocolate chips were arranged into the shape of a dick!" he defended himself and I snorted. "Anyway, this isn't like that."

"What is it like?" I pressed, pulling on my blazer before grabbing some knee high socks and sitting on the edge of the bed to roll them on. Seth glanced over his shoulder at me then turned around fully when he realised I was dressed.

"It's like…a crush on my friend," he said coyly and I swear if he'd been a Wolf right then his ears would be flattened to his head all cute like.

"Oh yeah?" I frowned.

"Yeah… Caleb to be exact," he said shyly and my lips popped open.

"No way," I gasped.

"Way," he said with a lopsided smile. "I mean, I always thought he was hot but lately, I dunno…" he ran a hand through his unruly long hair and I jumped up and hugged him.

"That's so perfect. Have you told him?"

"Perfect?" he scoffed. "It's very imperfect actually on account of the fact that he's straight. So obviously I haven't told him. And if you breathe a word in his direction, babe, I will spank your ass red."

I laughed. "I won't." I offered him my pinky and hooked it around his. "Promise. But you should tell him despite all that shit."

"Nah." He waved me off, but I gave him an intent look.

"Seth Capella, life is not guaranteed and with the shit we do most nights, you will regret it if anything happens to him and you don't get the chance to tell him the truth."

"We won't die," he said with a shrug. "We're the Heirs and the Savage Princess. Darcy and the dudebros. Wolfman, Bitey C, Fish Fury, Dragzilla, and the Phoen Dream."

"Okay firstly, never call us those things again, and secondly, we're not immortal, Seth. Just…don't take this time for granted, okay?" I implored. "You never know when the world could just be pulled out from under your feet." My heart knotted up in my throat and I took a shaky breath.

Seth stepped forward, brushing a lock of hair behind my ear with a whine. "We're gonna be okay."

"I don't know that anymore," I admitted. "I used to think everything would just work out one way or another, but now…" I dropped his gaze, trying to ignore the void living inside me, but it was a hungry thing. Sometimes it felt like it was going to consume everything inside me and leave me hollow. If it wasn't for the will to save my sister and my desire to see Lionel brought to his knees, I was sure it would have done so already.

Seth gripped my chin, tilting my head up to look him in the eyes. His irises were deep and earthy brown, full of a hope and positivity I hadn't felt in a long time. Looking at him pulled on some instinctual piece of my soul these days. I'd always felt a connection to Seth, but I'd never really understood why that was when he'd been treating me cruelly. Now, my enemy had somehow become someone I deeply cared about. And though there was still an echo of hurt that lived between us, my hate was now saved for someone much more worthy of it in Solaria.

"You owe me the truth, babe. And you're not walking out of this room until you give it to me."

"I could just put you on your ass, Capella," I warned and he smirked.

"Just try me." He gnashed his teeth together and I blew out a breath, knocking his hand away from my face. "So what's your truth? What are you really feeling after all this time away from Professor Dipshit?"

I didn't walk away like I wanted to. I had made a promise after all. So I swallowed thickly, holding his gaze. "The truth is, I'll probably dream about Lance for the rest of my life. I'll miss him and long for him, but when I wake up, I'll continue as if he was never here. Because that's what he asked for when he betrayed me. And now he's gone, he'll never get back in. No one will. I just can't trust anyone anymore."

"You don't trust me?" Seth whimpered.

"No. There's only one person I trust in this world and she's currently being held by a monster. But as soon as I have her back, I'll keep her close and that'll be enough."

Seth reached for me but I knocked his hand away again, hating the look of pain in his eyes or the way I felt that pain scrape up the centre of my being.

"It won't be enough," he breathed sadly and I set my jaw, ignoring the agonising hole in my chest that agreed with him.

"It will," I growled, stepping past him, grabbing my bag and hooking my Atlas off the nightstand before pushing out the door.

Seth followed me out into the hall in his underwear, abandoning the rest of his clothes in my room. I swear if he started trying to keep stuff in my drawers again like he had at the palace he was going to get a dick punch instead of a pillow slap next time.

My gaze shifted to Diego's old room across the corridor and my stomach clenched, a burning sense of grief driving through me before I forced myself to look away again. I didn't know what had happened to his stuff, but his room had been emptied out and there was no trace of him left behind. Some freshman had probably moved in there last night and it would soon be like he'd never existed. Fae died all the time in Solaria, so it wasn't like there would even be a lot of questions about him. I'd told Sofia and Geraldine over the summer. They knew everything now. I didn't see the point in keeping it from them, and frankly, with Lionel on the rise I'd rather they were prepared to face whatever might come their way.

Geraldine had been distraught and had announced that she would note him down as the first official A.S.S. casualty to die in the War of the Reborn. When I'd asked her what the hell that was, she'd said it was going to be the official name for the fight for the throne which would be remembered by historians for all of time. She also said we'd only just begun to tell the tale of our rise to power. It seemed insane to me, but she was keeping official records 'for posterity' whether I liked it or not and I knew better than to try and change Geraldine's mind when she'd decided on something.

We made it to the stairs where we paused to say goodbye, but as Seth leaned in to hug me, a noise of anguish met my ears. I frowned, glancing up the stairway, spotting Kylie there in her uniform, her lips parted in shock and her eyes full of betrayal as she gazed between us. I remembered her on the stand in court, spitting vicious lies about me and Orion and venom seeped through my blood.

"So you're officially together now?" she demanded, her lower lip quivering.

"Did you hear something?" Seth mused and I turned away from Kylie with a shrug.

"Nope, must have been the wind," I said. "See you later."

"Bye babe," he purred in a voice designed to taunt Kylie and I heard her pleading with him to stop shunning her as he walked upstairs.

My Atlas buzzed in my pocket and I found that my name had been mentioned in a news article entitled *Roxanya Vega Renounces Her Claim on the Throne.*

My heart stopped working, my lungs decompressed. As I stepped out of the door at the bottom of Aer Tower, several lost-looking freshmen bumped into me while I just gaped at the screen, a voice screaming *No!* in my head.

I clicked on the article, knowing I was going to regret it, but I had to know. *Oh my god, what has she done?*

Roxanya (Tory) Vega has spoken last night in an exclusive interview with The Celestial Times renouncing her claim to the throne of Solaria and aligning herself fully with High Lord Lionel Acrux. The Vega princess openly distanced herself from her sister Gwendalina (Darcy) earlier this year after it emerged that a feud between the two of them had sent them spiralling down different paths.

After rumours of Gwendalina setting fire to Stella Orion's house surfaced in July, her growing instability became apparent. Was this a vicious attack on Lance Orion's mother in retaliation for Stella's interview which stated that her son was better off in prison than with a Vega? Perhaps we'll never know. (See page 23 for more information on the Orion/Vega scandal and an interview from Honey Highspell who claims Lance Orion is a victim of a dark Vega plot).

All in all, it seems Roxanya had no choice but to break away from her own flesh and blood stating that Gwendalina was both 'volatile', 'temperamental', and 'aggressive' towards her in the following months.

Witnesses who attend Zodiac Academy with Gwendalina

have confirmed that she has been hoping to make a bid for the throne independently for quite some time, savagely cutting herself off from her sister in the process. Roxanya bravely took a stance to distance herself from Gwendalina and is now keeping company with the Acruxes. Some are naming this move as both honourable and respectful to the Councillors who have ruled Solaria peacefully since the times of the Savage King.

It is unlikely that Gwendalina will ever fulfil her dreams of taking over the kingdom, but it cannot be ruled out. We must simply pray that she wouldn't follow in the violent footsteps of her ruthless father if she ever-

I stopped reading, my blood pumping hot and fast through my veins as I stuffed my Atlas away and released an honest to shit growl. I stalked my way to The Orb, fuming at what Lionel had made Tory do. He was twisting everything, making out that she wanted him, that she'd chosen him over me. It was sick. I wanted to tear his goddamn head off for it.

Fire flared hotter under my skin as my Phoenix reared its head, desperate to be unleashed. A flash of movement in my periphery made me flinch and fire burst to life in my palms as Caleb slowed to a halt beside me.

"Woah, chill sweetheart. I guess you saw the article?" he asked and I put out the flames.

"Yeah," I snarled. "How dare that asshole do that to her, he had no right."

He frowned sadly. "We'll fix it. We'll get her back."

"We've been saying that for months," I said, my breaths coming heavily and I cast a quick silencing bubble around us. "Even if I could burn the shadows out of her, how are we supposed to get near her?"

Caleb pushed his fingers into his curly blonde hair with a sigh. "Darius can get us inside his house."

"So what? She's locked somewhere we can't reach her. And even if we knew where she was being kept, I doubt we could get near her without setting off a ward or – or-" I shook my head in dismay.

We'd been over it all before anyway. We weren't getting near her unless Lionel chose it. And that truth was unbearable.

Caleb knocked his arm against mine and I looked up at him with a sad smile.

"We won't give up on her," I breathed and he nodded seriously.

"Never."

"Maybe Gabriel will *see* more?" Caleb said, his voice heavy. Gabriel had come to me over the summer after inviting all of the Heirs and Geraldine to the palace, announcing it was time to tell them the truth. They'd proved their friendship to the Vegas, and we'd entrusted them with our secret. That Gabriel was mine and Tory's brother. And he was the son of the greatest Seer of the century.

"I hope so," I sighed and he gave me an encouraging smile, though there was a darkness in his eyes that spoke of his doubts too. With Clara and the Nymphs keeping Lionel's movements hidden, it was impossible for Gabriel to see anything tangible that might help us save Tory. Especially with her so far away, lost to the shadows. Darius said we couldn't use the shadows to spy on Lionel anymore either because Clara could sense it. It was infuriating.

I disbanded my silencing bubble as we walked up to The Orb and Caleb opened the door, letting me head inside first. The place was packed and freshmen were clustering together in groups, looking wide-eyed and unprepared - which I imagined was exactly how I'd looked when I'd started here too. Plenty of them glanced our way, nudging each other and whispering. My gaze snagged on the group of the Heirs' siblings holding court at a table beyond the Heirs' red couch. Xavier wasn't among them though and I frowned as I hunted for him before my view was blocked by Geraldine climbing onto the A.S.S. table with two bagels clutched in her hands.

"My lady!" She strode over the table, sending bagels flying everywhere as she used Justin Masters' head to help her climb down on this side then ran towards me like a runaway train.

I laughed as she collided with me, hugging her tight, the scent of butter and fresh coffee hanging around her.

"See you later, Darcy." Caleb shot off to get some coffee as I was crushed into Geraldine's large breasts, wheezing as she squeezed the air out of me.

"It's good to see you too, Geraldine," I rasped.

She pressed me back, looking me over then burst into tears, covering her eyes and turning away from me with a wail. "Oh mangos on a merry-go-round you're so broken, I can't bear it. Your homologous half, your synonymous sibling, your tantamount twin – gone! There has never been such woe as this. To see you here alone, walking through the door of destiny which leads you down a separate path to hers. It is a travesty!"

"Shh." I patted her back, feeling eyes on us from all around. "We'll work it out."

Geraldine wailed, spinning on her heels to look at me again, her eyes red and her face blotchy. "That diabolical, dastard of a Dragoon! I would give him what for alright. I'd pluck his eyes out and fry them up in a funnel cake!"

I steered her back toward our table where the A.S.S. all looked concerned. Justin rose from his seat, wrapping her in a hug and she sobbed loudly against his shoulder.

"It's alright, Grussy," he cooed.

I looked to Sofia and Tyler across the table, their brows pinched in worry as I mouthed a *hey* to them.

"The fuck?" Max appeared, shoving Justin away from Geraldine and gripping her cheeks in a punishing hold. "Why are you crying?"

"Get off of me, you heinous halibut," she demanded, pushing him away and sniffling as she pulled herself together. "Now go back to your salmon pond and leave me be." She shooed him away then walked off around the table with her chin held high before dropping back into her seat.

Justin dusted off his shoulders like Max had left a mark on his clothes, pushing his fingers into his blonde hair and puffing his chest up as he tried to appear as big as the Heir he was foolishly facing off with. "Don't you tell Grussy what to do," he said firmly, planting his hands on his hips. "I won't stand for it."

"Oh yeah?" Max snarled, squaring up to him. "And what are you gonna do about it?" He lifted his chin, emphasising his several inches of height on Justin and to his credit, Justin didn't flinch.

"Perhaps I'll write a strongly worded letter to your father," Justin said haughtily.

"Oh do sit down you valiant woodlouse!" Geraldine cried to Justin. "I appreciate the sentiment, but I am quite capable of sending strong words directly to this cantankerous cuttlefish myself."

Justin dropped into his seat with a pout, but Geraldine patted his hand and his expression softened a little.

Max grumbled something under his breath and walked away to the Heirs' couch. I slipped into my seat as chatter broke out around the room again. Plenty of silencing bubbles went up and it wasn't hard to guess what they were all talking about.

"Did you see the article?" I asked Sofia and she nodded sadly while Tyler looked pissed as hell. He'd put on about twenty pounds of muscle over the summer and his hair was now dirty blonde all over, floppy and glinting with silver glitter.

"My mom will run something in The Daily Solaria to counter it," Tyler promised. "We can do another interview."

I nodded as I picked at a bagel. I'd been putting out as many interviews as I could to try and counter the damage Lionel was doing with Tory, but the plain fact was, all signs pointed to his version of the truth. If we could only expose him for using dark magic and harbouring the shadows then maybe my efforts would be worthwhile, but doing that could possibly mean dragging Darius, Tory and Orion down with them, which I was never going to risk.

I pushed a piece of the bagel into my mouth as I sighed. I was on strict orders to eat three meals a day from Darius after he'd figured out I'd been using healing magic to skip meals back in August. Food just didn't taste of anything these days, but I also knew there was no sense in depriving myself either. I needed to be strong enough to keep fighting the Nymphs, to go after my enemies.

I'd put back on the weight I'd lost when Orion went to prison, but I was all defined abs and muscle tone now considering half my time was spent either training for combat or *in* combat.

There was nothing quite like destroying members of Lionel's Nymph army to ease some of the tension living in me. It was kind of frightening how easy killing them came to me these days. After Diego's death, I knew they weren't all soulless monsters. But the ones we faced were wholly team Lionel. And I didn't feel guilty about burning them up in my Phoenix flames or watching as the Heirs destroyed them with the weapons I'd gifted them. Combining Dragon and Phoenix fire caused one helluva pretty bonfire too.

There were stories being told about the Nymph hunters in the news. The FIB were looking for information on them i.e. us. Some people whispered excitedly about the vigilantes out to save the world, others claimed they were a secret division of the FIB and others claimed we were a bunch of foolish idiots who would end up dead on the end of a Nymph probe one of these days and would only end up making the Nymphs more powerful when they stole our magic. It was illegal as shit what we were doing. But I didn't care. None of us did. We had to kill as many of them as we could to try and land a hit on Lionel that really mattered before it was too late. The FIB weren't doing nearly enough to strike back against the Nymphs whenever they attacked and we all suspected they were being fed false information by Lionel and Stella as they secretly aided them. We'd even put in several anonymous tips to the FIB suggesting Nymphs had been sighted near Stella's house and it hadn't once been raided. *Fucking Lionel.*

So we took our job to go up against them seriously and took out whatever small groups of them that we could find. Barely a night had slipped by over the summer that we hadn't gone after them, but now we were back at school I didn't think it was going to be as easy. I had to concentrate on my studies, advance my magic. It was crucial.

Tyler suddenly tensed up and released an aggressive, horse-like snort and I frowned at him in surprise.

"You okay, Ty?" I asked and he lifted an arm, dropping it around Sofia's shoulders and yanking her closer.

"*Hey,*" Sofia snapped as she lost her grip on a bagel and it went bouncing back onto her plate, but Tyler didn't look at her.

I followed his gaze to the door. Xavier Acrux had just walked in, his dark hair messy and his expression saying he was out of his depth. A group of girls dove from their seats nearby, crowding around him asking for autographs and his eyes widened before he nodded and started signing anything they thrust under his nose.

"He got three Elements, did you hear?" Angelica said as she dropped down beside Geraldine with a cup of coffee.

"Yeah and he chose Ignis House," Sofia said, her cheeks turning rosy.

"He's in *your* house?" Tyler balked and she shrugged, making him snort angrily again.

"Um, Tyler, what's going on with the snorting?" I asked before pushing another piece of bagel into my mouth.

He tore his eyes off of Xavier and looked to me with a pout. "I hoofed down Davros and Brutus yesterday. They arrived on campus early and I beat their asses in Pegasus form. I'm officially the Dom of our herd now." He lifted his chin, holding Sofia tighter.

"Which means I'm his now," she explained, looking at him with a proud smile that said she didn't mind that so much, but then her eyes flitted back across the room to Xavier and I suspected there was something else going on here. "But Xavier Acrux is like...serious Dom material."

"He's gonna fucking challenge me, I just know it. And I only just became Dom. I got one day and now mini-Acrux is gonna try and take it from me." Tyler stamped his foot under the table and I bit my lip to hold a laugh back. I swear I was never going to get used to the ways of all the Orders.

I glanced back over my shoulder just as Xavier broke free of his fan club and his eyes met mine. I waved and his expression brightened as he started heading toward us.

"Oh my stars, he's looking at Sofia," Angelica squeaked.

"Quiet Angelica, we mustn't interfere with the ways of their magnificent kind," Geraldine whispered loud enough for everyone to hear, holding her breath as she gazed from Xavier to Sofia then Tyler.

Xavier reached our table and no one said anything which was super awkward so I smiled at him encouragingly. "Congratulations on your Elements, Xavier. How's it going so far?"

"It's pretty fucking sweet," he said, his eyes flicking from Sofia to Tyler and the tension in the air almost made my ears pop.

"Hey Sofia," he said, smiling awkwardly then nodding to Tyler. "Hey man, I'm Xavier."

"Tyler," he replied, assessing him. "You'll be looking for a herd, I suppose?"

"Yeah, I guess." Xavier shrugged, scratching the back of his head. "Anyways um...see you around?" He was looking directly at Sofia again and I couldn't help but smile as she turned scarlet.

"Yeah, we'll catch up soon," she promised.

"Great." He nodded to me and headed away to join the other Heirs' siblings.

Max and Caleb were sitting on the back of their couch as they spoke to them and I suddenly realised how absent the place was of key H.O.R.E.S like Mildred and Marguerite. It was pretty damn nice actually.

"Do you know him or something?" Tyler asked Sofia with a frown and Sofia cast a silencing bubble before the two of them started having a tense discussion.

I shared a look with Geraldine who cleared her throat loudly, waving her hand and casting a fog of water that surrounded them too, cutting them off from sight. Subtle.

My gaze drifted to where Diego used to sit, his spot now filled by some new A.S.S. member. My heart rose into my throat and I quietly cursed the stars over his death. I didn't have his hat which he'd told me to take; it was almost certainly somewhere in the woods at Stella Orion's house, but getting in there would be all but impossible now with the Nymphs guarding it. And whatever secrets lay with it were lost unless we could figure out how to reach it.

It had been hard to focus on anything else but Tory over the summer and how Orion was rotting in a jail cell. It was like the stars had cast all of our fates to ruin in one fell swoop and laughed as they watched the shattered pieces fall. Now all the Heirs and I could do was try to pick up the pieces and find a way to fix what had been broken. But sometimes that seemed like an insurmountable task. And it weighed on my heart like a tonne of lead.

As always, when my mind drifted, I started spiralling into the pit of despair that lived inside me. So I cut myself off from it once more and forced the pain away. If there was one thing this whole shit storm had taught me, it was that tears saved nobody and dwelling on regrets was as useful as cutting my own hands off. Darius was the only one who understood fully, and together we'd found a way to keep moving, because giving up wasn't an option and talking over and over our woes did nothing but bring us down. One small mercy I'd been gifted was that I'd found a bond with him I'd never expected to have. And though trust was something I doubted I'd ever feel again for anyone besides family, Darius Acrux came surprisingly close. And so did the other Heirs sometimes.

Geraldine suddenly dropped a bagel that was halfway to her mouth, her eyes stretched wide. She released a noise like a strangled peacock then flew out of her seat. Another bagel shot out of her grip as she brought a hand to her forehead and it smacked Justin in the face, the cream cheese making it stick. "Grapefruits in a snowstorm, it cannot be!"

I twisted around, my gaze falling on the girl who'd just walked in the door, my heart lurching, my breath catching, a ringing filling my ears. Her face was pale and everything about her seemed endlessly dark, but it was her. Tory was here.

I sprang out of my seat, rushing toward her as my heart pounded right up into my skull. I couldn't think or breathe, no rational thought entered my head as I collided with her, crushing her against me in a fierce hug while she just stood there.

I half noticed Mildred and Marguerite trailing behind her among more of the H.O.R.E.S and grimaced as I dragged her away from them.

I leaned back to look at her, tears burning the backs of my eyes as I tried to form a question, absorbing the fact that she was really in my arms.

The door opened again behind her and Darius appeared, halting dead in his tracks, his lips parting and suddenly he was upon us, wrenching Tory from my arms and twisting her around to face him.

"You're back," he rasped.

"How did you escape?" I managed to get out, pushing one of Darius's hands off her so I could get close again. I realised The Orb was utterly silent and one look to my left told me Max, Caleb and Geraldine were closing in on us and the rest of the students in The Orb were watching intently.

"Come on, let's go somewhere private." Darius tugged Tory's arm but she yanked her hand free, straightening her sleeve where he'd ruffled it with a pinched look of disgust.

"No thanks," she said, brushing past us and leaving us there in her wake.

I ran after her, pulling her around to face me again, holding onto her when she tried to continue walking. "Tory, it's me, it's Darcy. Look at me," I demanded, desperation clawing at my insides.

Muttering broke out but I didn't care, my heart was trying to climb out of my chest. I'd never expected this. Why would Lionel let her come back?

Tory's cool gaze moved to my face, her expression bored. "I'm sorry, do I know you?"

Marguerite shrieked a laugh and Mildred sniggered somewhere behind me, making my hackles rise dangerously.

"Tory," I growled, shaking her, drawing my Phoenix flames under my skin, trying to urge them into her to burn out the shadows keeping my sister prisoner. "Hold still." The flames reached the very edges of my flesh and a deep, burning creature in me called for the Phoenix that lived in her, but no answer came in return. I gasped, realising what that meant, my grip on her firming.

"Let go of me." Tory tugged her arm away, a swirl of darkness in her eyes making determination storm through me. *I will set you free.*

I reached for her again and Tory raised her hands as if she was about to fight me. But I didn't care. I'd fight through every force in this world to save her.

"Darcy," Caleb shot to my side, pulling me back. "Not here."

Tory looked between us with her nose wrinkling then walked away, heading off to a table full of H.O.R.E.S with Mildred dropping down at her side, smirking darkly back at me. Xavier had risen from his seat, staring from Tory to Darius with a look of horrified surprise written into his features.

"No," I snarled as Caleb gripped my arm tighter.

Darius marched past me after Tory, but Max intercepted him, pushing him back.

"Not. Here," Caleb hissed and I met his gaze, my heart splintering up the middle. But through the fog of emotion clouding my mind, I could see he was right.

I nodded, straightening my spine and fighting not to shake with anger at seeing my sister like that.

Max spoke into Darius's ear and he finally gave in with a growl of frustration, turning back and the two of them headed toward the door.

Caleb moved at my side as we followed and Geraldine raced after us with tears still streaming down her cheeks.

"Oh, my Queen, what will we do?" she begged of me.

I didn't have an answer, but I was going to damn well find one. "I don't know yet, but we'll figure it out."

She nodded several times, tears still flowing freely down her cheeks.

We bumped into Seth outside and he howled to the sky as Caleb explained what was going on. Then we all started moving across campus in a tight group, heading to King's Hollow. The Heirs had increased the amount of protection spells on their hideout tenfold last night, keeping it a haven away from other students or teachers.

When we arrived at the huge tree that gave access to it, we headed up inside the hidden stairway while Geraldine muttered under her breath about barbequing Lionel Acrux and serving him up to a pack of hungry dogs.

My heart blazed with the flames of my Order as I was torn between being distraught by Tory turning me away and relieved that she was here. Because now we had a real chance to get close to her. And that was what we'd been hoping for for months.

We headed into the large lounge at the heart of the treehouse and I looked to Darius, seeing my own pain mirrored in his eyes.

"There's something we can do to help her," I announced and everyone turned to me hopefully. Darius took a step toward me like I was the answer to everything he'd dreamed of all summer.

"Her Order is being suppressed. I couldn't sense her Phoenix, that must be what it is," I said firmly, needing it to be true. Because I knew there was a way to fix that.

"Holy tartlets," Geraldine gasped and Seth howled again.

"Shit, Lionel must be giving her Order Suppressant shots. They can last a few days," Max said and the others nodded.

"But there's an antidote right?" I asked anxiously. Gabriel had told me about it in a bunch of his stories from when he'd attended Aurora Academy.

"Yeah," Darius confirmed, his eyes lighting with hope and I felt it too, brightening up the dark void living inside me.

"Hm, where can we get some of that? It's not exactly something we can buy," Seth said thoughtfully.

"I know exactly who can get it for us," I said confidently.

"Who?" Darius asked with a frown.

I smiled, feeling like we finally had something that could really save Tory at long last. "My brother."

TORY

CHAPTER FOUR

I woke early in a soft bed that felt familiar and strange all at once. There was an ache in my chest and the memory of a dream haunting me as the shadows curled and writhed beneath my skin.

I fought to push them aside as I tried to remember the dream. I'd been standing in the rain on a cliffside and someone else had been with me. Someone who had made my heart beat a lot faster than the slow and steady rhythm it was maintaining now. My lips tingled with the memory of a touch I couldn't place, the taste of something so much sweeter than I deserved...

The shadows writhed impatiently beneath my skin and I rubbed a thumb over the Aries brand on my left forearm as it itched.

I sat up and turned to take my Atlas from the nightstand beside me, my fingers seeking out Lionel's number as the urge to see him grew in me until it was almost unbearable. I'd only been away from him for two nights, but I could hardly think of anything aside from returning to him. How was I supposed to make it through the rest of the week before seeing him again?

I pressed dial and held the Atlas to my ear as it began to ring, my muscles tensing with each moment that passed and the need to be closer to him growing in me as I held my breath and waited for him to answer.

"What is it, Roxanya?" Lionel growled, his voice rough with sleep like I'd woken him and as my gaze strayed to the dim light of the rising sun beyond the window, I realised I must have.

"I missed you," I breathed, the words seeming to form of their own accord on my tongue and my gut twisting uncomfortably for a moment before the power of the shadows within me swept through my limbs, causing pleasure to tumble down my spine instead.

"Who is that, Daddy?" Clara's voice came in the background as Lionel grunted irritably.

"My other love," he explained in a flat tone with a sigh of frustration that made me bite into my lip nervously. "You'll have to learn to cope with the cravings, Roxanya. I don't have time to mollycoddle you every time you ache for me."

"*I* ache for you, Daddy," Clara moaned. "I ache to please you."

"So do I," I said a little petulantly as the sound of Clara moving around on the bed filled the speaker for a moment.

"Good. Then come and see me tonight," he said, making my hopes lift a fraction as Clara started murmuring praises in a husky tone that made my skin prickle. "I have a meeting I want you to attend by my side. And then we are going to need to talk to the press."

"Okay," I agreed instantly.

"Oh, Daddy, let me lick you like an ice cream," Clara begged and I gritted my teeth as I tried to ignore her.

"Come straight from classes. I'll send you the details," Lionel said to me, making some of the tension in my limbs relax.

"I will," I promised.

Clara started moaning loudly in the background and my thumb landed on the screen to end the call as my lip peeled back in anger. I threw my Atlas across the room where it slammed into the wall before thumping down onto the carpet and shadows poured from my skin to embrace me.

My furious outburst turned into a groan of pleasure as the darkness writhed within me. Its caress eased my mind and soothed away whatever had been getting me so worked up. But it was hungry too. The shadows liked to gift me pleasure, but only so long as I fed them in pain. And as a shiver of darkness raced down my spine, my fingers flexed with the desire to do just that.

I let the shadows rise up in me until they were coating every inch of my flesh and I could hardly even see through them while I mechanically pulled on the uniform that was hung in my closet. My hands followed patterns that were ingrained in my memory without me really paying much attention as I brushed my long, dark hair and painted makeup onto my face. Before long, I was ready to go hunting for what the shadows craved.

I paused beside the door, moaning beneath my breath as the shadows stroked my body before forcing my will over them and taking them into my control the way Clara had taught me.

They withdrew reluctantly and I watched in the mirror as they slid back beneath my skin until the only visual clue that they were there at all was hidden in the black ring that surrounded my irises.

My gaze stayed locked on that ring for a long moment as the echo of something important tugged at my memory. I shivered as I almost felt the kiss of snow on my arms, tasted tears on my lips, felt a stab of pain directly into my heart. But as I sucked in a sharp breath at the almost memory, the shadows fluttered in my chest and soothed it away for me.

The hint of a smile touched my crimson painted lips and I pulled my door open as I headed outside.

The corridors of Ignis House were quiet due to the early hour and I walked on silent feet in my stiletto heels down the stairs to the empty common room before heading down the next set of stairs to the exit.

I pushed the door open and stepped out into the cool morning, almost calling on my fire magic to warm me through before the shadows licked beneath my skin and drew my attention away from the cold.

I took a few steps, but a prickling sense of awareness drew my attention to more shadows at my back and I clenched my fist as I reached out with my own hold on the dark magic to claim control of the threat.

There was a grunt of discomfort from the source of the shadows, but the owner of them made no attempt to pull them back under their own control and I slowly turned to look at him.

I flinched as my gaze fell on Darius, standing there in a pair of grey sweatpants and a white tank. His muscular, tattooed arms flexed with tension and his gaze tightened as his eyes moved over me.

"Roxy," he murmured and I fought to stay impassive as the echo of pain and fear washed through me at the sound of that name in his mouth.

But this wasn't the indistinct pain of memories I couldn't quite grasp. It was the smack of electricity slamming into my flesh and burning me from the inside out. It was the taste of charred flesh on my lips and the sound of my screams filling the air. He was responsible for that. And even the idea of lingering in his company had me fearing it happening again. But I couldn't show him that. My king had been very clear about that.

"Why are you standing out here?" I asked him, forcing myself to take a step closer even as I remembered the scent of burning flesh in the air and had to fight the desire to bolt. "You didn't seriously think you could sneak up on me, did you?"

"I was waiting for you," he replied, his brow pinching like he thought I should have expected that.

I released my hold on his shadows a touch as I tried to understand why he'd expect me to be out here this early. But as I tried to figure it out, a different memory rose in me of him forcing me beneath the surface of a swimming pool and bringing my nightmares to life. And the darkness in me ached to make him pay for it.

"Why?" I ground out, my jaw tightening as the shadows whispered dark thoughts in my ears, urging me to claim vengeance for the things he'd done and all the pain he was responsible for. I tightened my grip on them, using them to hurt him.

My lips curled up as a curse escaped his lips and I watched as the shadows dug their claws into him and fed on his pain, filling me with a sense of euphoria that was utterly addictive.

Darius clenched his jaw and I felt a sharp tug on my hold over his shadows as he took back control of them. I expected him to lash out at me and drew on my own darkness even more in preparation to fight him off, but instead he just stepped into my personal space and caught my cheek in his rough palm.

"Because I'm not giving up on you, Roxy. I don't care what I have to do or what it costs to pull you back out of the shadows. I won't stop until you're yourself again," he swore roughly.

For a moment I just stood there, my gaze raking over his face as the shadows rippled through my flesh and I smirked at him.

"You think I'd choose to relinquish my hold on the shadows?" I asked him. "For you?"

"Not for me. For you. For your sister. For-"

The ground beneath our feet began to tremble and I knocked his hand off of my cheek, but took a step closer to him as I raised my chin.

"I think you're under the impression that I'm some kind of damsel in distress, Darius Acrux," I said in a low voice as shadows flickered before my eyes and shimmered over my skin. Even the mention of his name sent the memory of agony pulsing through my chest, but I held the shadows closer to fight off the sensation. He didn't step back as I moved right into his personal space, but he swallowed thickly and my gaze tracked the movement of his Adam's apple as it bobbed before I looked up into his dark eyes again. "But I have everything I could ever want and more with my king. I have power and love and freedom. What else could I possibly desire?"

"You don't have love," he growled, his eyes flashing with reptilian slits as the Dragon beneath his skin peered out at me too. "You don't love that monster. You love Darcy. You love..." His brow creased and he shook his head. "*I* love you. And you promised me forever once. So if I have to-"

"Forever?" I asked, a memory pushing into my mind but fleeing again before I had a chance to look at it.

My heart slammed against my ribs at his words and the memory of my flesh burning and charring while I screamed in agony made bile rise in my throat and a ringing start up in my ears.

I flinched away from him as my king's voice filled my head. *Who do you love?*

"I love my king," I hissed, stepping back and sneering at the man in front of me as he tried to follow.

The shadows rose up in me to soothe the ache of the lightning that had crippled me time and time again. All of that pain, all of that suffering was his fault. Every time I'd been burned by the power of the storm, ripped apart and set alight in the heart of it had been because of him. My king had healed me of that agony and I wasn't going to let him poison me with his lies. The deeper I fell into the shadows, the less I remembered that pain and the more I craved the dark.

Darius took a step closer to me as the expression fell from my face and I tightened my fist, yanking on the shadows inside him as I invaded them with my own.

56

"Stay away from me," I warned him as his muscles tensed against the pain I was driving into his flesh.

"What if I won't?" he gritted out.

"You will," I insisted, pushing more shadows into him and making him swear as he fought to stay on his feet through the pain of them.

"I promised you forever too, Roxy," he growled. "And I intend to keep my word."

My gaze skipped between the black rings that surrounded his irises just like mine and I almost drew the shadows back for a moment before a stab of pain resounded in my chest like a bolt of lightning.

With a hiss of anger, I threw the shadows at him hard enough to knock him back against the glass wall of Ignis House then turned and strode away from him without another word.

I constructed an air shield around myself that was utterly impenetrable as I walked up the path, focusing on the feeling of the shadows as they snaked beneath my skin and soothed the aches in my flesh.

They weren't hungry anymore, sated by the pain they'd caused Darius, and yet somehow I still felt unsettled by the interaction.

I reached into my pocket, my fingers curling around the edge of my Atlas as I considered calling my king again, then sighed as I forced myself to release my hold on it. I'd be seeing him tonight. I could last that long without him. But the ache in my body was only going to grow more urgent until then.

I moved inside The Orb and took a seat at a table to the rear of the room with a single chair at it and a fireplace right beside it, wanting to replenish my magic while I focused on my task. There was only one reason for me to be in this place after all and I wanted to make sure I didn't disappoint my king, so I was going to spend every moment I had studying and perfecting my hold on my magic just like he wanted. The stronger I was, the better I could protect him and that was the one, single thing I knew I needed to do with my life.

I pulled my Atlas from my pocket, my gaze skimming over the horoscope that had appeared on it as I took in the words.

Good Morning, Gemini.
The stars have spoken about your day!
Though it may seem that you are lost in the dark at times, just remember
what is dear to your heart and you will always find a way back to yourself.
Fortune favours those who follow their own path, but beware - pitfalls await
you if you allow yourself to be tempted off of the route your heart desires.

Well, that seemed clear enough. I needed to follow my heart which meant I needed to please my king. And there was nothing that would make me stray from that path in this world or the next.

I took a moment to look at the screensaver Clara had saved on the device for me as I pressed my fingers to the Aries mark hidden on my forearm beneath my shirt and sighed. The picture was a posed shoot of Lionel, standing tall and proud with his shirt off to reveal his muscular physique while he held a sun steel sword in his hand with the tip thrust into the ground. Behind him, an image of him in his emerald green Dragon form was roaring, releasing a burst of flames into the air which highlighted the golden colour of his hair. I closed my eyes to drink in the image, but somehow, behind the confines of my closed eyelids, I found myself imagining a golden Dragon instead.

I frowned as I tried to figure that out and suddenly my moment of peace was interrupted by the pounding of a fist against my air shield.

My eyes snapped open and I looked up to find Geraldine Grus knocking her fist against my shield like it was a door while holding a plate stacked high with bagels in her other hand. She smiled broadly as my gaze met with her deep blue eyes and she waved before pointing at the plate of bagels then at me.

My stomach growled, reminding me that I needed sustenance and I released the magic securing my shield.

"Oh, thank golly for small miracles, I thought you might have been napping like a narwhal in November and you'd have missed out on my buttery bagels while they were still fresh from the bun oven," she gasped while I just regarded her in silence. "How are you, my lady Tory? It has been a long and mournful summer without the pleasure of your happy face and joyful presence to enhance it. I have missed you something chronic. I do hope that loathsome lizard didn't subject you to too many mishaps while we were hunting for you? I swear I don't think I've slept a full wink since I realised you were taken by that rotten reptile and I have been begging the stars to return you every moment of every day. I have been wracking my brain all night, wondering what might help you return to your senses and I wondered if a buttery bagel in the morn might spark something helpful." She placed the tray of bagels down on my table so that she could swipe tears from her eyes before peering at me hopefully like she'd only just realised that she hadn't heard me speak yet.

"You can fuck off now," I said flatly, realising she wasn't going to actually leave unless I told her to.

"I can...I can...you want me to..." She gaped at me like somehow I hadn't been clear while the tears in her eyes built up and up as she clutched her chest like she'd been mortally wounded.

I sighed, flicking my fingers at her and knocking her back several steps with a blast of air magic.

"My lady!" she gasped in horror as I lifted my Atlas again and gave my attention to studying. My king wanted me at this academy to learn so that was what I was going to do. I was going to become the strongest Guardian he could ever wish for then maybe I'd be his favourite instead of Clara.

Geraldine continued to splutter hysterically, making me seriously consider using a stronger show of magic to make her back off before a dark voice interrupted her ramblings. I looked up to find Darius standing there, perspiration now coating his flesh where it was on show and his breathing heavier than usual like he'd been running. I stayed silent as I took him in, the faintest niggle of recognition stirring in me again like his morning routines were supposed to interest me for some reason.

"Now isn't the time, Geraldine," Darius said in a tone that didn't allow for arguments and I cocked my head at him as I tried to figure out what he wanted.

His gaze darkened as he looked back at me and for a moment, I swear I could taste the pain on him as the shadows rose up in me, hungering for more of it.

He placed a mug of coffee down in front of me and I eyed it like it was a bomb set to detonate, though it just sat there innocently.

"I know you're still in there, Roxy," he said in a low voice that made the hairs along the back of my neck stand on end. "And sooner or later, I'll figure out how to save you from this."

Darius turned away without me responding, taking hold of Geraldine's arm as her sobbing turned hysterical and he directed her across the room.

I watched them go with the faintest urge to follow them rising in me before the shadows smothered it out and let me relax back into my chair again.

But as I took a sip of the coffee Darius had left for me, the strangest stirring twisted my gut and for the first time in months, even the shadows weren't enough to quiet the whispers in my mind. But I still couldn't hear what they were trying to say.

DARIUS

CHAPTER FIVE

I flew through the sky with Dragon fire pouring from my mouth time and again as I worked to exorcise some of the ever-present rage in my heart as my wings beat madly in the cool air.

Father had summoned me and the rest of the Heirs to join him at the Palace of Souls tonight and I knew he'd invited the other Councillors too, but I just couldn't decide if this was what we'd all been dreading or if it was just some new power play.

I'd checked with Darcy after we'd been given the summons and she hadn't had a clue about us turning up at the palace which was her home tonight. It wasn't exactly unusual for Father to invite himself wherever the hell he wanted to go and do whatever the fuck he wanted to do, but the location of this had me on edge.

Darcy had gone to speak to Gabriel about it and I was left circling the clouds to try and calm myself enough to endure an evening in his company. I hated pretending to have been thoroughly put back into my place by the things he'd done to Roxy and how he'd left Lance to rot in prison.

I blew out a final breath of fire accompanied by a roar loud enough to rattle the windows in all of the nearby buildings before cutting through the sky towards Ignis House. I hurtled towards the open floor length window on the top floor where my room was, tucked my wings and shifted back into my Fae form at the last moment. I ran several paces across the carpet to counter my momentum and strode towards my closet to dress for the meeting.

Whatever the fuck we were doing, it was official business which meant I needed to be suited and booted, looking my damn best or he'd happily punish me the moment we were behind closed doors.

Over the summer he'd summoned me to his office more than once and commanded me to take a beating from him under threat of Roxy's life, and I'd had to take it like a good little bitch because I knew the evil bastard was capable of anything. Not that I was certain he wasn't hurting her anyway. But aside from my birthday, I hadn't seen her once over the summer. Even though I knew she was being kept somewhere in the manor and I'd searched every fucking brick in the place, used every spell possible to try and reveal the concealment. But there was nothing. The only clues I had gotten at all were the times I'd woken in the night, certain I'd heard her screaming, calling for me, begging me to find her. But once I was awake, there was never anything but silence again.

I didn't know if it was just my imagination being cruel to me or if the stars were gifting me glimpses of what was happening to her, but I got the horrible feeling it might be the latter. Thanks to the fucking shadows clouding Gabriel's Sight, he was having no luck in seeking her out and I'd been starting to consider riskier and riskier moves that could be made to try and find her.

I dressed in a charcoal grey suit with a black dress shirt, pausing for a moment as I pulled the jacket over my shoulders and found it tight around my arms. That thing had been custom made only a few months ago and yet I'd managed to grow out of it already.

I glanced in the mirror at the fabric straining over my biceps and the inch of ankle showing above my shoes before cursing and pulling the suit off. Not that I was really complaining. Last I'd checked, I was on eye level with the piece of shit I called my father but seeing as I'd been making a good effort not to look at him when I was stuck in his company, I hadn't particularly noticed that I was having a growth spurt again. It wasn't all that surprising that my muscles were growing with the amount of training I'd been doing with the other Heirs, wrestling and learning to wield the axe Darcy had gifted me to the best of my ability. But if I was getting bigger in my Fae form then that would be even more noticeable in my Dragon form. And I seriously hoped I was about to become the biggest Dragon in Solaria, even if it was just so that I could watch Father's head explode when he realised his own son had knocked him off of the top spot.

A knock at my door interrupted me as I changed into a black suit instead and I called out for Xavier to come in, knowing he'd been summoned to come to the palace tonight too.

But as the door swung wide and I glanced at it in the mirror, my breath caught.

"Roxy?" I asked, turning towards her sharply and letting the tie I'd been about to put on fall from my hand.

She was wearing a black gown which accentuated the dark rings in her eyes and she regarded me impassively as she stood on the threshold. She was stunningly beautiful as always, but there was hardly anything of the girl I'd fallen for showing in the mannequin model version of her standing before me. There was no scorn in her eyes, no wit on her tongue, even her posture was just so fucking rigid, it didn't seem natural. She was like a painting of herself, all done in perfect proportions but with no life inside her, nothing to say she was anything more than a beautiful decoration designed to be admired and little else. I missed her quick tongue and insults, I wanted her calling me out on having a gold plated bed and a fucking jacuzzi tub. Hell, I'd take her hating me over this...*nothing* creature that stood in her place.

"Your father said I should arrive with you," she said simply, glancing around my room like she didn't even recognise it.

"You're coming too?" I asked, hesitating where I was despite the desperate desire to go to her.

This helpless void of emotion in her cut me open and bled me out, but until I could get my hands on the antidote to the Order Suppressant my father was dosing her with, I didn't know how to try and bring her back to us. We had to be careful who we trusted to get it for us and it took longer to brew than any of us wanted to wait so Gabriel was in the process of getting hold of some faster from his dodgy Alestrian contacts. I didn't really give a shit where we got it from, I just needed my girl back to herself or it was going to kill me.

"My king wants me there," she said, her eyes shining at the mention of her so-called *king*, and I had to grit my teeth against the rage that built in me.

"Do you remember when you first came to this academy?" I asked her, taking a step forward but falling still as she flinched.

It was only the smallest jerk of motion and she raised her chin to cover it a moment later, but I caught the movement and it sent ice running down my spine. Why the fuck was she afraid of me?

"Not particularly," she replied coldly and a distant rumble of thunder reminded me that we weren't supposed to be alone. Fucking stars. I hated them almost as much as I hated the man who had sired me.

"Why did you just flinch when I moved closer to you?" I asked and her brow creased the smallest amount in a way that made me think she hadn't been aware of it. Or maybe she had but she hadn't wanted me to see.

"You hurt me," she replied simply, her green-brown eyes meeting mine. "Always have, always will."

Fuck.

Why did those words cut into me worse than any blade ever could? Maybe because I knew there was truth to them. Maybe because that was the one thing I feared more than anything and I hated that it might be so. I regretted everything I'd done to her more than I could ever put into words, but I couldn't even deny that I was still hurting her. My father should have died at my hands the night he took her. I had been so fucking close to saving her and everyone else from him and I'd failed. And everything that had happened to her in the months since was my fault because of it.

"I'm sorry, Roxy," I breathed but she didn't even seem to register my words, looking back over her shoulder as more footsteps approached. What I wouldn't give for her to call me out on getting her fucking name wrong or to call me a lizard bastard or an arrogant prick or any number of insults. I'd take them all and thank her for them if I could just prise them from her lips.

"Oh, err, hey - am I interrupting?" Xavier's voice came from behind her, which was probably a good thing as the thunder which was crashing through the sky was only getting more insistent and I knew I couldn't linger alone in her company.

"No," Roxy replied simply, like she had no reason at all to want to prolong our conversation. I tried not to let that hurt but it fucking did.

Xavier glanced at me with a question in his eyes and I just shook my head. There was nothing we could do right now with Father waiting for us, but I was sure as hell going to do something soon.

The three of us headed out of Ignis House and started walking for the gates while Xavier asked Roxy question after question as he tried to draw her out of herself. But he got little more than single word answers if she replied at all.

I tried to walk close beside her, but she kept shifting away when I moved near, and I knocked against a solid air shield the third time I attempted it. She didn't even look my way as I tried not to let the rejection bite at me, but this was so fucked up that I didn't even know how to begin fixing it. I just had to hope that Darcy was right about her Phoenix being the key to it, because if we didn't figure this out soon then I was going to lose my damn mind.

We made it beyond the gates where we met the other Heirs and travelled via stardust to the sprawling courtyard outside the Palace of Souls where Father was already waiting.

I exchanged loaded looks with my friends but kept my face neutral as I took in the gathered crowd, waiting to hear whatever the hell he had to say.

Roxy strode away from us the moment we arrived, her eyes lighting up for the first time since she'd appeared at my door as she headed straight for my father who stood with Mom, Stella, Vard and Clara before the gates to the palace.

"Take it easy, remember we've got a plan," Max murmured, placing a hand on my arm as he pushed his Siren gifts at me, offering me a measure of calm as I watched the girl who should have been my mate wrap her arms around my father's neck and embrace him in front of everyone here.

His eyes met mine over her shoulder and the corner of his lips hooked up cruelly like he could feel my fucking heart tearing open as his arms closed around her for a moment.

Fortunately for him, he released her before I lost my fucking mind and launched myself at him. I wanted his death more keenly than anything I'd ever desired and the way he was watching me said he was well aware of the fact. But it didn't matter because he'd placed the only woman I'd ever loved between us and he knew my hatred for him would never outweigh my love for her. She was a shield unlike any other he could have constructed against me and I was tamed by his control over her just as surely as she was by the shadows that had corrupted her.

Silence slowly fell throughout the courtyard as Father stepped away from Roxy and moved to stand in the centre of the space, facing the crowd.

"No doubt you are all wondering why I summoned you here this evening at such short notice," he called out and the other Councillors all exchanged looks, standing a little way behind him and clearly having no fucking idea what this was about.

I met my mother's eyes across the wide courtyard, but she was obviously just as in the dark as the rest of us, so I turned my gaze back to the man running the show to see what the hell he had to say for himself.

"Last night, I awoke with the words of the stars whispering in my ears," Father called loudly to the deathly silent crowd. "They summoned me from my bed and led me to the lake at the edge of my land and there, I saw a vision in the reflection on the surface of the water."

I frowned as I tried to figure out what the fuck he was going on about, but the crowd of onlookers were all watching him with rapt attention so I could only wait to find out where he was going with it. I seriously doubted he'd been gifted a fucking vision though. There was no trace of The Sight in our heritage and he'd never had one before to my knowledge.

I glanced over at Vard, my father's creepy new Seer, wondering if he was going to claim to have something to do with this apparent vision, but he just stood watching, his mismatched eyes fixed on the show, the blood red one seeming to pulse with magic on and off.

"I *saw* destruction, devastation, death and the end of the world as we know it. I *saw* us losing this war against the Nymphs." Screams of fright went up amongst the crowd and the Councillors exchanged shocked glances, confirming that they were as in the dark as all of us, though they seemed to be more interested in hearing him out than interrupting his speech. "Then the stars offered me a deal. One which I felt duty bound to accept as it was presented by the guiding force of the heavens themselves. The true and divine beings who have given us all we have in this world. They gave me and those most loyal to the stars a gift – the Fifth Element."

The silence in the crowd erupted into whispers of shock and suspicion but Father was more than ready for that as he raised his voice to quiet them again.

"They offered me this and all the power that goes with it for the sake of our kingdom. But they also pointed out that our kingdom isn't truly a kingdom at all because it is not ruled by a single monarch the way that they intended for it to be."

He raised his hands and my gut lurched with bile as I felt the dark power of the shadows rising up around us before they even became visible to the naked eye. Father lifted his arms slowly and shadows crept down his hands, coating his fingers and pooling in his palms.

My heart raced in my chest as I looked between the other Heirs in horror, realising that this was it, his play for power. He was going to claim the throne. Which meant he was about to formally challenge their parents. And if he proved his power over them in front of this entire audience and all of the cameras that were trained on him, there would be no denying that he was the most powerful

Fae in all of Solaria. He would claim his position at the top of the pecking order and there was nothing that any of us could do to stop him. Fae took their power and fought for their place and if he was the most powerful Fae of all then there was one clear position for him to assume.

But instead of doing that, of following the guidelines laid out in place for a formal challenge, Father just raised his hands higher, the shadows thickening around him as more people screamed and some of the weakest Fae in the audience bolted like they feared for their lives. And they should have. Nothing good came from the darkness of the shadows. Nothing lived in them but pain and misery and a hunger that could never be sated.

I made a move to step forward, to make my own challenge, to try to force him to face me without putting Roxy between us or do anything at all to stop this horror show from playing out.

But as I tried to move, I found my body locked in position, the shadows within me rooting me to the spot and binding my tongue just as firmly as my limbs. My gaze caught on Clara across the courtyard where she stood in her trailing black gown, shadows twisting between her legs and beneath her skirts in an unnatural wind as she smirked at me with black painted lips. She looked like a witch from an old fairy tale, not the sibling of the man I loved like a brother.

"I am a willing pawn of the stars and I will gladly let fate guide my hand in protecting our kingdom and ruling over all of my subjects!" Father cried, either totally oblivious of the countless horrified, terrified faces before him or fucking relishing every second of their fear. "And I am here to claim my crown."

With a swift strike of his hands towards the ground, shadows burst from him like a blanket of pure darkness, snaking out in every direction and seeking each and every member of the crowd surrounding us.

As they coiled around each person, they tangled them in their grip and forced them to their knees one after another and I watched in horror as the Councillors were all made to bow too.

My knees hit the cobblestones with a heavy thump that echoed right through every bone in my body as I stared at the only man left standing in the entire courtyard while a victorious grin slid across his face.

Roxy was on her knees before him, her eyes glazed as she looked up at him in devotion, one of the rightful queens of our kingdom forced to bow before a monster and quelling any doubts that might have been left about whether or not the Vegas might try and stand against him. It didn't matter that Darcy wasn't here. That wasn't even going to make the news. All that anyone would see was one of the princesses and all of the Councillors kneeling at his feet like adoring subjects.

"This is dark magic!" Tiberius boomed and my gaze slid to Max's father as he struggled against the shadows which had engulfed his entire body aside from his face.

"Let us fight," Melinda demanded, her fangs snapping out as she snarled in a fierce refusal of what was happening.

"You *are* fighting," Father said casually. "And yet you can't break free. So I think that proves I've already won."

Tiberius started cursing and Father flicked his fingers, tossing a silencing bubble over him and the other Councillors as he turned his attention back to the crowd and the cameras broadcasting this fucking farce to the entire kingdom.

"I know that this is new and that you may be feeling concerned. But I can prove to you that the stars know what they're doing in this matter," he called, raising his arms again as he beckoned, looking towards the trees that surrounded the palace grounds like he expected something to emerge from them.

Clara allowed me to turn my head and I caught Caleb's gaze as his eyes widened in horror.

"Nymphs," he breathed, hearing more than I could with his gifts and making my skin crawl as I tried to turn further towards the approaching monsters.

When they burst from the trees led by Drusilla, Miguel and Alejandro in their Fae-like forms, more than one Fae in the crowd screamed in horror but none of them fled and I could only imagine it was the hold of the shadows which kept them in place.

"Don't be afraid!" Father shouted, commanding quiet as the Nymphs moved into the courtyard at an unhurried pace and formed lines behind him. Their grotesque bodies were twisted and rough with skin like the bark of a tree and their red eyes glared out at the crowd of gathered Fae, promising long and agonising deaths to each and every one of them. Drusilla and Alejandro exchanged a smug look and Miguel gazed at them blandly, his eyes unfocused like he had no opinion on the wild events ensuing around him.

"The shadows have gifted me the power to control their kind!" Father cried. "The war is over. With the gift of the stars, I have won it for us in a single night!"

A long and agonising beat of silence followed his proclamation, then all of a sudden some members of the crowd erupted into cheers as Father's smile grew and a chant of *'Long live the King! Long live the King! Long live the King!'* broke out amongst them.

Roxy and Clara slowly stood before him, the only ones of us allowed to return to our feet as Clara pulled an iron crown inlaid with emerald Dragon scales from within her skirts and handed it to the girl who was born to be a queen.

Roxy didn't even hesitate as she lifted it up and placed it on his head, leaning forward to press a kiss to his cheek which came close enough to his mouth to make the Dragon in me snarl with fury and beg to be set loose to rip him limb from limb.

Roxy and Clara stepped to his side then Mom, Xavier and I all found ourselves on our feet, moving to join them.

I ended up right beside my father as cameras flashed and people yelled praise to the new King Acrux. Inside, I was doing everything in my power to fight off the grip of the shadows so that I could tear his fucking head from his shoulders, but externally I stood at his side, the loyal son, helping create the picture of the perfect family he painted us out to be in his lies.

Once the crowd began to quiet, Father strode away from us to stand over the three Councillors he'd forced to their knees.

"Will you serve in my Council the way we all once did for the Savage King?" he asked in a booming voice which carried across the crowd and silence fell once again.

He removed the silencing bubble that had stopped their protests earlier and the three Councillors looked resigned as they exchanged glances.

"I swear my loyalty to the crown," Melinda agreed, the reluctance in her voice clear as Father took her hand and forced her to make that oath before the stars, binding her to her word.

"I swear my loyalty to the crown," Antonia ground out and Seth's shoulders dropped an inch as he watched his mother be forced to bow like that.

Tiberius held out the longest and as my father waited on his oath, I could see the way his eyes tightened against the pain of the shadows which were no doubt being driven into him with more power to force an answer from his lips.

"I swear my loyalty to the crown," he gritted out eventually and with the clap of magic that sealed the oath, it was done.

Solaria was no longer ruled by a Council. We had a monarch. A king who would no doubt be so much worse than the Savage King had ever been.

Father turned and strode towards the gates to the Palace of Souls, the Nymphs parting for him like a tide as he took ownership of this royal place, the people, the kingdom, everything. And all of our nightmares came true at once.

In short, Solaria was well and truly fucked.

ORION

CHAPTER SIX

I sat in the Mess Hall at breakfast, gazing at the slop they called oatmeal in my bowl and trying to convince myself to eat it. Wasting away in here was non optional if you wanted to survive. Fights broke out daily and without magic I had to be physically strong to defend myself whenever I was dragged into it. Which was pretty often thanks to the stars being assholes to me lately.

The small amount of free time I had, I either spent in the gym or in the library. Working out until I nearly busted a lung was the only thing that ever made my misery more bearable. And the rest of the time I spent pouring through every book in this place as I hunted for clues about the Imperial Star or how to break into an old fucking diary locked by a magical password I couldn't guess. Not that there were many passages on either of those things in the tomes kept in the piss-poor Darkmore Penitentiary library. But there was an old section on the royals which mentioned the Imperial Star once or twice. Nothing useful so far though, nothing that could give Darius and Darcy an edge to find it before Lionel did.

Someone slid into the seat beside me and I turned my head, a growl grating against my throat in warning. I found Roary Night perching there, his muscles flexing, his long hair falling around his face.

"I've been watching you," he said casually, like we'd spoken a thousand times.

I grunted, turning away again. "You? Or your little band of followers?" He wasn't one to show off about it, but everyone knew he ran one of the biggest gangs in Darkmore. Unlike the other gangs, the Shades didn't need to go around shouting about how big their balls were to prove their power though. They were the shadow in the dark, the threat you didn't see coming. It was hard to even know for sure who exactly was one of them, but they saw everything that went on in this place. Each and every one of them reporting back to the man in charge. And for a while now, I'd gained his attention.

He chuckled darkly, twisting around in his seat and resting his forearms on the table. "Both."

"Good for you, I hope you enjoyed the show." I stuffed a spoonful of oatmeal into my mouth and he yawned broadly, slinging an arm over my shoulders. I swallowed the tasteless sludge on my tongue, cocking a brow at him.

"I've been speaking to my brother. And he's been speaking to Gabriel Nox..." His brother Leon was a good enough friend to me that I didn't distrust Roary, but I was also planning on collecting friends in here about as much as I planned on starting an acapella band. But now he had my attention. I'd met Leon after he and some of his classmates had been sent to Zodiac Academy for a student exchange back when I'd been a student myself. He'd licked my face which had made me dislike him intensely, but I guessed the over-friendly Lion Shifter had grown on me eventually. His brother was a little more sinister though.

I fell still, surveying Roary curiously. "And?"

"And, I know the truth now."

I dropped my spoon into my bowl and shrugged his arm off of my shoulders. "And what's the truth?" I asked hollowly.

"You're no pervert," he said with a smirk, rubbing his knuckles against my cheek. I batted his hand away with a growl of warning and he laughed lightly. "So we can be friends now."

The table banged as Ethan Shadowbrook, the leader of the Lunar Brotherhood gang in here, slammed himself down on the seat opposite us, his fists hitting the table. "Hands off, Lion. I already called dibs."

"Didn't realise I was building a harem," I said dryly, returning to my breakfast.

The resident nutjob, Sin Wilder, suddenly launched himself to sit on the table cross legged, gazing between all of us with a psychotic look on his face. "What do you call a harem with four swords and no scabbard?"

"What?" Ethan narrowed his eyes at him.

"Boring." Sin jumped off the table and laughed manically as he headed away. The guy was a certified lunatic, but at least he left me the fuck alone most of the time.

"So, remember that offer I made you about those pills that will, you know..." Ethan leaned closer, pushing his fingers into his styled blonde hair. "Suppress the Guardian Bond."

I itched the mark on my arm where the sleeve of my orange jumpsuit was rolled up, the skin prickling as it urged me toward Darius as always. Fuck I missed him.

"I said no," I growled. I wasn't gonna owe this guy anything. I'd fought to keep myself a loner in here and that was the way it was staying. I'd align myself with one of the gangs the same day I'd strip down and bend over for the local pervert Plunger. Last week a guy had made a crack about him drinking tea instead of coffee and Plunger had face slammed him into a wall, then proceeded to drop his pants and dunk his balls in and out of his slack-jawed mouth while shouting *'who likes tea bags now?'*. So, yeah.

"That's the thing. Yesterday I gave those pills to a guy who was suffering from Faemorrhoids," Ethan said, scratching the back of his neck. "They're like a fix-all, numbing thing you see?"

"Right," I muttered and Roary frowned at him.

Ethan leaned even closer, lowering his voice. "And basically, I can definitely get more of them if you want, but the guy got a rash on his balls that was so bad he had to have them chopped off."

"Wow," I deadpanned. "Please send them my way."

"He felt pretty numb while it all happened if that helps. And people call him Eunuch Jim now. He always wanted a nickname," Ethan snorted and Roary shoved out of his seat, giving me a look that said to come and talk to him when the Werewolf was finished offering me ball rash pills. The choices I had in here really were sublime.

A bell rang which sounded the end of breakfast and I pushed out of my seat with plans to head straight to the gym, but I knocked into some asshole behind me and turned around to find Gustard there, his juice spilling all down his chest. *Great.*

The guy had tattoos on his face and was the last motherfucker anyone wanted to cross in Darkmore. But since the stars had cursed me with bad luck for breaking the star vow I'd made with Darcy, I seemed to bump into him ten times a day and piss him the fuck off. I swear I'd been sent to medical five times more often than any other Fae in here, mainly because of this asshole.

"You again," he hissed between his teeth and I clenched my jaw. It wasn't that he on his own was a force of nature, but his entire gang flouted the way of the Fae and ganged up on their opponents ten on one. "Get me another," he growled, trying to dominate me, but for all the stars in the world, I had too much pride to bow to anyone like a little bitch.

"Get it yourself," I snarled, brushing past him toward the doors.

I'd have to pay for that in blood later, but I'd rather that than lose my dignity in this place. It was pretty much all I had left and if I was being honest, it wasn't really intact when everyone in the world believed I'd Dark Coerced a Vega princess into fucking me. I was just some depraved pervert in most people's eyes. But at least I'd done it for the best reason on earth. *Her.*

I headed down to the library, the guards' watchful eyes following me on the stairs. When I pushed through the frosted glass doors, I headed to my favourite spot at the very back of the stacks, one of the few places where I could find solitude in the prison.

As usual, the old guy everyone called Poltergeist was there. He was ancient with his grey beard and sallow skin and he never said much. He drifted to the end of the aisle, throwing me cautious glances before disappearing around one of the stacks. He always haunted this part of the library, but he never bothered me, and I didn't bother him either. And that made him my new best friend.

I grabbed out the tome I'd been reading yesterday, flicking to page five hundred and dropping down at a desk before working through it. I had one saving grace today. A visitation with Darius. It was kind of pathetic how much I'd come to depend on my contact with him. He visited me whenever he could, but now he'd started back at Zodiac, I doubted he'd be able to come as often. I supposed if I had one constant companion in here, it was loneliness. And once upon a time, that wouldn't have bothered me so much. Being a Vampire meant I had an inclination towards alone time. But fuck if I didn't ache for company these days. A very specific kind of company of course.

The Guardian bond tethering me to Darius was always begging me to be with him, and I'd once thought the pain of being parted from him would be unequalled by anything else. But since meeting Darcy and now being parted from her, it paled by comparison. There wasn't a moment that went by that she wasn't on my mind, my memories of her playing on repeat in my head. At least there were distractions in the day, but at night it took everything I had to fight off the shadows beneath my flesh, offering me the sweet bliss of a high that could help me escape from the brutality of heartache. It was a wound that lived on the inside and consumed all the colour in the world until everything seemed grey. She was gone. I'd made her go. And there was nothing I could ever do to fix it.

I spent a couple of hours reading, not finding anything of use and eventually giving up as I realised it must be almost time for visitation hours. I *needed* to see Darius. And I was always desperate for any scrap of news he brought from the outside. After everything that had happened with Lionel during the summer, I lived on Darius's updates like a drug. News reached this prison slowly, the newspapers I got were always a week old, so I was often left not knowing what was going on. I'd been struggling with the fear that my sacrifice had been for nothing after Lionel had bound Tory to him and all the power had shifted in his favour. But now I'd made my bed, I had to lie in it. It was too late for regrets.

Appealing my sentence would only prove I'd lied and ensure Darcy's name was dragged through the mud. Her place at Zodiac Academy would be in jeopardy and she had to keep getting stronger so she might be in with a chance to claim the throne. At least one good thing had come of it all. Blue - *fuck no, don't call her that* - had broken free of the shadows and she was no longer plagued by them. She was so fucking strong. So fucking everything. By the stars, I couldn't believe I'd ever tried to claim her for myself. She was so far out of my league it was unreal.

Despite knowing that, it was still keeping me awake at night not being able to comfort her after everything. She'd lost her sister to Lionel. And I knew the fucking feeling. But now I was stuck in here, useless to her and Darius and everyone I cared about. The only solace I could take was that by staying here, Darcy would keep her place at the academy. And that was what

I held onto to keep me sane.

Books were shuffled along the stack at the end of the aisle and Poltergeist's yellowy eyes peered through them. He liked rearranging the books. He also liked watching me. And as creepy as that was, it kind of beat hanging around with most of the other inmates so I just ignored him and let him do his creepy thing.

A creak sounded on a floorboard behind me and Poltergeist gasped a warning just before a huge fist slammed into my head.

I twisted around with a yell as four strong hands gripped my shoulders, shoving me down over the desk. I spat a curse at Gustard's UnFae assholes as more of them crowded closer and Gustard watched from just beyond them.

I kicked one of the guys holding me in the dick and he yelped as he backed away, clutching his junk with both hands. Another one came to take his place, but I fought my way to my feet, throwing solid punches into the faces of anyone who got near. Blood coated my knuckles as I let myself go fully savage. I'd learned fast to fight for your fucking life and ask questions later in here. So I broke jaws and noses and roared like a fucking demon from hell as I beat the shit out of anyone who tried to grab me. My heart thrashed in my chest and I relished the outlet, sinking into the shadows as they reared up in me, lured by the pain I was delivering and whispering their encouragements in my ears.

Gustard laughed coldly, the sound making adrenaline rush through my veins.

"Hold him down," he commanded and I lunged toward him, trying to break through the ranks to get to their leader, determination and anger fuelling my movements.

"Face me like a fucking Fae," I barked as four of his guys grabbed me and forced me to lay down on the desk on my back.

One of them slammed their fist into my nose and blood poured over my face, pain splintering through my skull as bone and cartilage busted from the blow. I'd faced worse, but I doubted it was gonna end there.

A big asshole slapped a hand across my mouth and my arm was yanked out over the edge of the table. My muscles bulged and I bucked against their restraint as I fought to get free, but there were too fucking many of them.

Gustard stepped forward, taking hold of my wrist and I bit down on the hand covering my mouth as the gang leader pushed my arm down forcefully, bending it in the opposite direction it was supposed to go. Stars exploded in front of my eyes as the bone snapped and my pained roar was smothered by the asshole gripping my face.

I blinked away the darkness curtaining my eyes as Gustard breathed in my ear. "Last warning."

They left me there and I groaned as I tasted blood on my tongue and felt the heavy and agonising weight of my right arm hanging off the desk, unable to move it.

Poltergeist appeared with wide eyes, taking my other arm and helping me off the table.

"You need to see the medic," he croaked in an ancient voice, but I shook my head, groaning as another spike of pain cleaved through my arm. *Fuck.*

"Have to go to visitation," I growled, stumbling past him as blood pissed from my nose onto the carpet. I wiped it away with my sleeve then clutched my broken arm against my chest, biting down on my tongue at the blinding pain racing through the limb. At least I'd made a bunch of them bleed first.

I made my way out of the library with the inmates all staring at me then headed upstairs towards visitation.

"What the fuck happened, One-Fifty?" Officer Cain barked as I reached the top of the stairs. He was a big asshole with close cropped hair and a mouth that never smiled.

"Fell," I grunted, trying to step past him toward the hall that led to the visitation rooms. He shot into my way with his Vampire speed and I snarled a threat, wishing I had access to my own fangs so I could put this motherfucker in his place.

"Well Medical is *that* way." He smirked tauntingly, pointing back down the stairs.

"I'm going to visitation," I hissed and he folded his arms.

"Are you now?" he asked. "Well you're gonna shock that little Heir boyfriend of yours when he sees you like that."

I gave him a cool look then stepped forward again to move past him and he let me go this time. I made it to the line of inmates waiting to be called into a visitation room and propped my shoulder against the wall, grinding my teeth as I tried to ignore the pain in my shattered arm. *Fuck Gustard. Fuck that unFae piece of shit.*

"One-Fifty!" Officer Lucius called from down the corridor. "You're in room eight." She directed me forward, her eyes widening as she took in my face, the blood splattering my jumpsuit and my arm clutched against my side.

She grabbed her radio from her hip. "Oh shit, you need-"

"I need to walk through that door right this second, so get out of my way." I jerked my chin at the room behind her then didn't wait for her to agree, ducking past her and pushing through the door. Darius stood up from his seat at the single table in there, his jaw dropping at the state of me.

"Fuck, Lance, what the hell happened?"

I rushed toward him, using my good arm to pull him against me and wincing through the pain, the Guardian bond purring happily inside me as I released a heavy sigh. *Better.*

Darius slid his fingers onto my twisted arm and healing magic swept into my veins. The bone snapped back into place and I hissed between my teeth before the pain finally ebbed away. He fixed my nose next, cleaning the blood off of me with his water magic and I drew him into a fierce hug the moment it was done, needing him close, craving the feel of him against me.

"Tell me what's going on," he commanded in a Dragon's growl worthy of his father, finally pulling away from me.

We sat down opposite each other at the table and I shrugged. I wasn't going to snitch on Gustard and his lackies in front of the cameras, but there was another group of assholes responsible who I could openly blame. "The fucking stars have it out for me."

"You can't continue like this, you'll end up fucking dead," Darius hissed, his face twisted in concern.

"Don't look at me like that," I demanded. "It is what it is."

He shook his head, then subtly swiped a finger and a chill filled the room. He used his water magic to mess with the cameras, casting ice into them to give us a chance to speak properly. "Lance you have to get out of here. My father...he's taken the throne. He-"

"What?" I gasped, my lungs constricting, horror threading itself into my chest. I knew that we'd been running out of time, but I'd thought there was still some left. How could this have happened? How were we going to stop him now?

Darius started recounting how Lionel had made the Councillors bow to him and moved into the Palace of Souls and I just listened in silent dismay, losing hope by the second. And I'd barely had much to start with.

I cursed, the walls seeming to close in on me. I was so fucking useless in here. How the hell was I supposed to do anything to help?

"I'm sorry," I rasped. "I'm sorry I'm no use, I'm sorry for fucking everything up."

He sighed, his brows tugging together. "Just take the appeal."

"That would only make things worse now," I said quietly. "You know that's true."

"There must be some way," he insisted. "I'll speak to Nova, I'll ensure Darcy's place at Zodiac is secure."

"Elaine Nova's in Lionel's pocket. Any excuse to get rid of Darcy and she'll take it," I spat and silence stretched for a moment as Darius tried to come up with another idea.

"*Fuck.*" Darius slammed his hand down on the table. "Well at least break that star vow with Darcy. You're never going to find out what your father's diary says if you can't catch a damn break."

I drew in a long breath, unable to deny it. But that would mean him bringing Darcy here again. Seeing her, getting her to break the last thing that tied us together. For all the bad luck in the world, a twisted part of me wanted the punishment. I'd broken her. I'd given her no choice. Betrayed her in a way I'd sworn never to. She wouldn't ever trust me again. But I'd known all of that when I'd taken the stand in court, because regardless of the consequences, it was still better than the alternative. She would have lost her claim on the throne if she couldn't be trained. As soon as our secret had been exposed, I had been the one thing standing in her way, the one thing that could cost her everything. And now with Lionel sitting on the throne, it was more important than ever that she would be able to fight him.

"We need this. If your father knew something, then we have to find out what it is. Astrum's last Tarot card said to seek the fallen hunter. And that just has to be your dad," Darius insisted.

"Yeah, maybe," I grunted, scratching at my beard. "Or maybe not."

"The diary has got to be important," Darius insisted.

"But what if it's just a diary?" I croaked, knowing that all the efforts I'd made to crack the password could be pointless, that all the hopes we were pinning on it could be in vain.

"Well we have to find out either way. We don't have anything else to go on," Darius said, sounding tired and I realised he looked it too. He was going through his own kind of hell out in the real world and it pained me to see him that way.

"Alright," I gave in, my chest growing tight at the thought of what I had to do, but there was no choice. Darius was right; so long as the stars were cursing me with bad luck, I'd never figure out how to unlock the diary. "Bring her here." *Oh fuck why do I feel like I'm about to bust a lung at the thought of that?*

I wanted to see Darcy again more than anything in the world. And yet I knew it would crush me all over again.

Darius smiled sadly as he nodded.

"She misses you, you know?" he said darkly. "She won't say it, but-"

"Don't," I growled, my heart crumbling to dust in my chest. "I don't wanna hear it. She should be moving on."

"I think she has," he said earnestly and I wasn't prepared for how much that hurt me. I wanted it, I'd pushed for this, I knew it was what needed to happen. But the thought of her forgetting me, finding someone else, fuck, it was intolerable.

"But that doesn't mean she doesn't miss you," Darius said sadly.

I miss her too. I miss her in every moment of every minute of every day. I will always miss her.

"Is she...okay?" I asked in a tight voice. I generally avoided talking about her with him in any depth, but this question was one I asked often. It gave me some peace knowing Darius was looking out for her, that she was still safe. And I guessed that was the most peace I would ever have over her.

"No one's okay right now, but she's coping," he said with a deep frown. "There's some hope for Roxy. I'll let you know if it pays off."

I knew he couldn't tell me more even with the cameras disrupted, just in case, but my heart lifted all the same. "That's good. Just be careful."

"Always," he promised then he fell into telling me everything about Xavier's Awakening and hinting at how him, Darcy and the other Heirs were all working together to figure out a way to take on Lionel. My heart swelled at the thought. I might have been broken, hurt, and ruined by destroying us. But the sacrifice had been worth it. She was becoming the queen she was always meant to be. It was just hard to accept that I was never going to be her king.

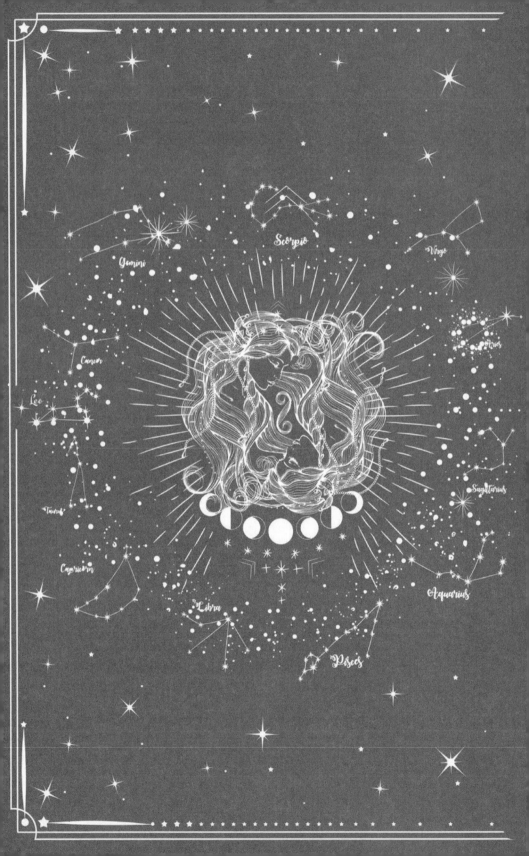

DARCY

CHAPTER SEVEN

All hail the goddamn, asshole of a king. I'd been up half the night again at the Hollow, discussing everything that Lionel's ascension to the throne meant with the Heirs while trying not to lose my mind with fear.

Now, I was lying on the couch after a few broken hours of sleep. My head was pressed to a warm arm and I drew in a breath as the scent of smoke, cedar and coffee reached me. Beyond the window, the dawn was red, the light seeping through the sky like blood. And I couldn't help but feel that the world was wounded.

Everyone knew about the shadows now; it had been broadcasted to the whole world and Lionel had made it clear Tory had the gift of them too. No one would dare challenge him while he held that kind of power, they couldn't. And now everyone in school would fear my sister almost as much as him too.

I sat upright, looking at Darius beside me who had smoke pluming from his nose as he slept, his brow creased with lines as nightmares plagued him.

Geraldine was curled up in an armchair across the room and Max was at her feet on the rug, his arm slung over his eyes. On my other side Seth was curled up like a dog, though he was in his Fae form. My eyes fell on Caleb last in the kitchenette across the room pouring coffee. *Ah coffee. The shit that couldn't solve anything but made everything seem better for five minutes.*

Caleb shot around the room in a blur of motion, planting a cup in my hand with a smirk at the fact that he hadn't spilled a drop. He placed the other down beside everyone else before lowering into an armchair, his ankle balanced on his knee and his hair freshly styled. He was in his uniform and I guessed he'd been up for a while, but you could never tell with a Vampire considering they could do things at ten times the speed of a normal Fae. If they were ever a second late to anything it was absolutely intentional. And a Vampire-who-would-not-be-named was the kind of asshole who used to like intentionally doing shit like that. Damn, why do I miss that?

"What time is it?" I asked as I sipped my coffee, the zing of caffeine helping to rouse me further.

"Half seven," Caleb said. "Nova's called an assembly at eight." He waved his Atlas at me and I searched for mine, finding it wedged under Darius's leg. He jerked awake as I grabbed it, breathing in sharply and looking at me through squinting eyes. "Pinching my ass, Gwen?"

I snorted. "Gross. And don't call me Gwen."

"Why's that gross?" Seth asked as he woke, yawning broadly as he sat up and nuzzled into my neck in his Wolfish way. He did that shit so often these days, I didn't even notice it half the time. "Darius has a lovely peachy ass."

"Because he's in love with my sister which makes him about as appealing to me as a three day old tuna sandwich – no offence," I tossed at Darius and he smirked.

"You're an old tuna sandwich to me too, Gwen," he agreed and I punched him over the name, but couldn't fight a smirk.

"Mmm, tantalising tuna," Geraldine mumbled in her sleep. "Such a large trout you are."

"That's *my* trout she's talking about," Max said cockily, getting to his feet and Geraldine's foot shot out, slamming right into his dick. He crumpled forward with a wheeze and she pushed him aside as he got up, tutting under her breath.

"You are always in my breathing space, Max Rigel, if you don't want your Long Sherman in my way then take your leave."

"How is that my fault?" Max asked indignantly.

"How is it not your fault?" She started doing her morning stretches, bending down to touch her toes and rocking her hips side to side while Max drooled over her and forgot all about their argument.

The first thing I came across as I raised my Atlas was my horoscope and I read it over as I tried to concentrate on waking up and getting my brain into gear for the day.

Good morning, Gemini.

The stars have spoken about your day!

Beware of changes and upheaval throwing you off balance today. It may seem like times are at their toughest, but don't forget that everything can always get worse. So try to remain calm in the face of adversity and play the long game if you wish to succeed.

Great. Even my horoscope knew how fucked everything was right now.

I tapped on FaeBook next to see the world imploding and the first post that came up was one from Tyler.

Tyler Corbin:
Back. The. Fuck. Up.
Does anyone else need a recap right now?
Big L shows up at the palace with some crazy smoke blowing outta his ass, a Vega on his arm and Clara Orion who looks fresh back from the dead (uh, hello? Have you heard of sunlight, dear? 'Cause you got veins coming outta your veins).
Anyways, Big L starts spewing this speech about gifts from the stars and holy Dragons and fuck knows what else, but hold up, was anyone actually paying attention to Clara at this point? The girl LEGIT started floating, no lie (screenshot below).
Now I'm not saying this girl is a zombie dragged outta the depths of hell, shoved in a long (albeit hot) dress with a demon possessing that fine body of hers. But okay, I'm calling it. Because WTF???
King Lionel just took over and the press haven't printed a SINGLE WORD about floaty McGee over here who 'disappeared' years ago and miraculously reappeared like she just popped out of Lionel's buttcrack – and frankly, that would explain the translucence a bit but not enough for me to back the theory a hundred percent. I'm not entirely ruling it out though, because Big L has buns of steel and I wouldn't put it past him to have shrunk her down to the size of Thumbelina and wedged her between them as punishment for drinking his favourite tropical punch Kool-Aid or some shit – but what was she living on up his ass all these years – butt dust???
I digress. Point is, can we all focus on the bigger issue than Lionel taking the throne, that being one scary ass see-through bitch who, rumour has it, calls Big L 'DADDY'.
#nope #Imout #onetickettoanywhereplease #whatdoesbuttdusttastelikethough #crackwhore #oneguywatchedthewholeshowthroughthebackofherhead #ghostestwiththemostest

Eliza Smoot:
Oh my stars! She's a #flyinorion
Cat Vann:
I wouldn't mind getting up in Lionel's #crustycrack
Lacey Ledlow:
I wish I could #tropicalpunch our new king in the face
Gizelle Alea Oyelade:
Do not speak ill of our king or his wonderful Guardian!!
#thetruekinghasrisen
Shabnam Hosseini:
Do you think Big L has a big D? #daddydick
Cynthia Rodriguez:

I'd call him Daddy and let him put me between his buns of steel any day of the week #signmeup #putmeinyourclenchtrench

"*God,* I'm not ready for this day," I said heavily, not even finding it in me to smile at Tyler's post. And that was a damn shame because it was funny as hell. I also figured he could probably know the truth about Clara now as Lionel had outed his shady shit to the whole world anyway so I made a mental note to fill him in.

"Your mortal talk is so weird, is it because they think they're all ruled by Zeus or something?" Seth asked and I realised he was nibbling on a piece of my hair. I batted him away and stood up, draining my coffee.

"Or something," I snorted then headed into the bathroom. Before the door had swung closed, Geraldine strode in behind me, whipping off her top and revealing her large breasts before dropping her pants and walking into the gaudy golden shower which screamed of Darius Acrux.

I brushed my teeth then swapped places with Geraldine in the shower once she was done. By the time we were dressed in our uniforms we found all the guys waiting for us in the lounge, looking casually gorgeous and prepared to take on anything. I just hoped they really were prepared because I had a feeling we weren't going to like the world that was waiting for us outside of this place. I sure as hell wasn't looking forward to facing it, but with all of them around me, everything seemed easier.

We headed down the stairway together and started walking to The Orb where the assembly was being held. Darius tugged on my sleeve beside me, drawing me to the back of the group and casting a silencing bubble around us.

I frowned curiously. "What's up?"

"So, there's something I need to ask you." His Adam's apple rose and fell as he stared at me and I got the feeling I wasn't going to like what he had to say. I swear any news any of us got these days was bad news. I probably should have been used to it by now.

"What is it? You're giving me that doomed Dragon look and I don't like it."

"It's not too bad, it's just…I need you to visit Lance."

"What?" I hissed, my heart rate going from nought to a thousand miles per hour in one second flat. "No," I blurted, my instinct to refuse driving through me. The last time I'd seen him, he'd turned me away, told me to move on, acted like we were *nothing.* He'd ripped my heart out and watched it bleed for him. I wasn't going back there. Besides, he didn't want me to go back there. And I sure as shit wasn't going to be making a visit so he could tell me to fuck off again.

"He's agreed," Darius said quickly as if that made it any better.

"Oh well, if he's *agreed,*" I said sarcastically. "Then I'll fly there right now and skip into his arms like an obedient little homing pigeon. Oh no wait, I'd rather eat Griffin shit."

"Darcy," Darius sighed. "The star vow he broke is putting him in danger. The bad luck he gets means he's coming up against the most vicious assholes in that place over and over again. I had to heal him of a broken arm and a shattered nose yesterday."

I stopped walking, the horror of that news making everything bunch up inside me and hurt like hell.

Darius turned to me with a serious look. "And it's more than that. We need to find out what's in his father's diary. He's never going to get the luck to do that if he remains under this curse."

I drew in a long breath, trying to hear him out through the cloud of rage and betrayal in my head. Slowly, I nodded, giving in. I couldn't just let Orion suffer in there. And though I'd never admit it, knowing that he was being hurt just made me want to tear through the walls of that prison and take him as far away from it as Faely possible. I knew I couldn't do that, but I could do this…

"Okay," I agreed tightly. "But I want to go in and out. Five minutes, that's it."

"Deal," he said, a grim look entering his eyes. "But you *could* talk to him."

"No," I growled. "I gave him a chance to talk and he told me to stay away from him. I'm done, Darius."

He looked like he wanted to say more, but finally nodded and disbanded the silencing bubble. "We'll go tonight."

Shit. Tonight??

"Sure," I forced out like it didn't matter. But it did, hell it really did.

We kept walking, hurrying to catch up with the others while I tried not to panic about the bomb that had just exploded in my face. *It'll be fine. In and out. Five minutes.*

There was a strange mood hanging over the campus as students headed to The Orb, some obviously overjoyed and others sombre. I was definitely in the second party. Lionel taking the throne was the worst thing that could have happened freaking ever. I had no idea how we were going to stop him now. I just knew we had to.

We reached The Orb, heading inside and my heart thumped a little harder at the sight of Nova standing before the faculty at the far end of the room, a wide and disconcerting smile on her face.

I walked toward the A.S.S. table, but Seth caught my hand and tugged me on toward the Heirs' couch. I was extra surprised when Max held onto Geraldine too and she didn't pull away, letting him guide her that way as well. Maybe we all just needed each other a little more today.

I dropped down between Seth and Geraldine, while Max sat on her other side and Darius and Caleb perched on the couch arms. My gaze hooked on Tory who was sitting with Mildred near the front of the room and I hated that I couldn't just go over there, slap that moustached bitch and take my sister back to where she belonged. I mean, I *could*, I just didn't think it was worth the detention or the fight with my sister over it. *Sigh.*

Seth's hand stayed wrapped around mine even when I tried to pull it free but as I opened my mouth to rebuke him, Nova spoke, her voice carrying across the room.

"A new king has risen to the throne, and now we have entered another era. One which will make right the wrongs of old and will see us grow into the Fae we were always meant to become." A few of the staff clapped, plenty did not.

I noticed Gabriel was sitting rigidly in his seat, his hands balled on the table in front of him as he stared coolly at Nova's back. Washer was on his right, shaking his head and muttering under his breath to Gabriel and the way my brother nodded said they were in agreement on something for once.

I shared a look with Seth as my stomach knotted.

Nova went on, "King Acrux has decreed a new law this morning and sent a personal letter to me which outlined the law as it will apply to you all here at Zodiac Academy."

My heart thumped unevenly and I stopped fighting Seth's grip on my hand, squeezing it back.

A ripple of chatter ran through the air which Nova hushed instantly. "As of today, Orders shall no longer fraternise, socialise or cross-breed with one another unless given express permission from the King himself."

The air thickened and it became harder to breathe as shouts of anger broke out around me.

"No way!" Max barked.

"This is an outrage!" Geraldine gasped. "You cannot divide us like colours on an abacus!"

"Sit down!" Nova commanded, raising her hands threateningly and a bunch of the H.O.R.E.S suddenly stood up to join her side. Tory was among them and shadows coiled out from her hands, making a bunch of people scatter from the front rows. "King Acrux has asked me to appoint loyal members of the student body to ensure the law is abided to. Those chosen will have leeway with the law and will be allowed to mix with other Orders so long as it is in the interest of the King. Teachers will also be allowed to spend short periods of time with students who need extra attention, so long as their discussions are focused solely on academic topics. They will be permitted to run classes and detentions as normal providing they abide by the new code of conduct emailed to them by me this morning."

No. Fuck no. We couldn't let this happen.

I got to my feet as Seth and the rest of the Heirs rose too. My hand fell free of Seth's as we braced for a fight and I realised the A.S.S. were all rushing toward me and Geraldine to back us up.

"We won't stand for it," Caleb snarled, his shoulder pressing to mine as a deep growl left Darius beyond him.

"It is the law, Mr Altair," Nova said cuttingly.

A mini tornado twisted in my left hand and flames curled around my right as I bared my teeth at Nova, hatred pouring through me.

"Lionel Acrux will never be my king," I spat.

"You will all sit down or there will be dire consequences," Nova warned and Tory moved forward, raising her hands so smoke blasted out from them.

I gasped, casting an air shield and it combined with Seth and Max's as our magic slid smoothly together. I braced as the shadows impacted with the shield and everyone behind us was protected from the blast as it crashed over the dome like a spill of oil.

The strength of her dark power made me grit my teeth and I forced more of my magic into the shield, losing sight of everything around us as shadows consumed the world beyond it. Screams rang out and adrenaline surged through my veins.

The pressure suddenly eased and my heart stammered as the shadows cleared and I spotted all of the Heirs' siblings on their knees in front of Tory, her eyes swirling with darkness.

"Enough!" Nova yelled. "The King has agreed that any force necessary may be implemented to ensure his new law is upheld. You will all stand down or the punishment will fall on the Fae before us. This is your last warning."

My throat tightened and I looked to the others, seeing the defeat in their eyes.

"Our hearts are made of sun steel and our wills cannot be broken!" Geraldine cried.

"We've got no fucking choice," Darius growled as he gripped her arm, his eyes turned to golden slits as his Dragon form begged to come out.

He locked me in his gaze next and my heart cracked as I felt us being forced into line. He was right. Because what could we do? If we fought this, Lionel could have us arrested. We'd give him the excuse he needed to get rid of us. And we couldn't risk the Heirs' brothers and sisters getting hurt.

I dropped my hands and the others all followed suit. A smile tugged up Nova's lips and anger washed through my chest like a deluge.

"My lady, we will fight if you wish it," Geraldine spoke to me and I looked back at the A.S.S. who were standing behind me like they were ready to go into battle.

I shook my head, refusing to let them all put themselves in the line of fire for this. Lionel was going to ensure this law was upheld, and today was not the day to throw away our lives for a fight we were going to lose.

"Stand down," I told them all firmly and they did so immediately, surprising me with how readily they listened to me.

"Sit!" Nova commanded and we reluctantly dropped back into our seats. She pressed her shoulders back, looking to the few teachers who'd risen from their chairs too, including Gabriel.

He slowly lowered back into his seat beside Washer then his eyes glazed with a vision. My heartbeat stuttered. Could he *see* a way out of this? I had to speak to him. If there was something we could do to stop this, I had to know. If anyone could *see* the way forward now it was him.

"Tory Vega will be leading the King's United Nebular Taskforce here in the academy, and anyone selected will be allowed to mix with other Orders

87

whenever necessary to uphold the new law at Zodiac Academy, reporting directly to me if ever there is a breach." Nova spoke casually as if the fact that she had the Heirs' siblings on their knees before her wasn't totally fucking insane.

"Wait…oh my stars, they're in the *Kunt*," Tyler hissed from somewhere behind me, but even that couldn't make me laugh right now.

Nova hushed everyone once more. "Now please make your way to your classes, ensuring that you divide yourself into your Orders. The teachers of your first classes will all get you acquainted with the new ways of the academy and answer any questions you may have about it. Please pass through the door in single file on your way out. An enchantment is now in place which will mark you with a symbol of your Order. Enjoy this wonderful day."

Mark us?

"Meet at the Hollow at midnight," Darius said under his breath and we all nodded before splitting apart and heading for the door.

"I'll give that crab headed goon of a principal what for," Geraldine hissed as she stalked off ahead of me. "The Almighty Sovereign Society will not stand for this."

I queued toward the exit and caught Sofia's eye as I glanced over my shoulder. She was standing close to Tyler and a look of worry filled their eyes. Just behind them was Xavier and a few other Pegasuses I vaguely recognised. His jaw was pulsing and rage filled his eyes over this. A rage I felt on a soul deep level.

I stepped through the door and the kiss of magic tingled over my skin, the sensation trickling over me and a flare of magic shining beside the Zodiac Academy crest on my blazer. I gazed down at it as the fiery symbol of a Phoenix glittered there. I ran my fingers over the mark with my upper lip peeling back. My sister was the only other Phoenix in existence, so Lionel's little law held a double whammy for me. I was essentially cut off from everyone else in the school. But hell if I was going to abide by his rules anyway.

I headed to Jupiter Hall and queued up outside, finding the floor marked with lines a meter apart which had symbols of each Order next to them. A growl built in my throat as Tyler and Sofia joined me on the Pegasus line and I didn't budge an inch away from them.

"This is bullshit," Tyler spat as the rest of the class started spreading out over the lines and the other Pegasuses moved to stand behind us.

Kylie appeared at the back of the queue, her arms folded and a pout on her lips as she stepped onto the Medusa line. Everyone around her ignored her as usual, but my heart leapt as Tory appeared with shadows in her eyes and strode straight up to her.

"You've been chosen to join the King's United Nebula Taskforce," she said in a flat tone, holding out a rectangular gold pin for her with K.U.N.T. printed on it and I snorted.

A huge smile split across Kylie's face as she snatched it and put it on. "So I can tell everyone what to do?" she asked excitedly.

"You can ensure the law is upheld," Tory corrected then Kylie wheeled toward me, pointing excitedly and a cool anger swept through my blood.

"Darcy Vega is standing with those Pegasuses!" she exclaimed and Tory looked to me, her hair stirring as the shadows writhed up around her. Plenty of the students shrank back against the wall at the sight of them and my heart stammered as she approached me.

"Tory," I breathed, not raising my hands. I would never fight her.

I kept my defences down, gazing into her eyes and I hunted for a piece of my real sister to hold onto. My gut writhed and Sofia caught my hand as if to pull me away, but I stepped toward Tory, seeing if she really would hurt me one on one.

"It's me, Tor," I begged, desperate to get through to her. "Your sister."

"Clara is my only sister now," she said lightly and her words felt like an injection of poison into my blood. *Her fucking sister?? Never.* "Get in line," she warned, but I shook my head as hurt stung my heart.

She raised her hand and shadows exploded toward me. I refused to shield, praying she might stop if she realised what she was doing, but she didn't. They wrapped around my throat and threw me to the floor onto the Phoenix line and I coughed out a breath. The weight of them pushed me down and I gritted my teeth as they tried to force their way under my skin. But my Phoenix flames burned hotter and blocked her out as they flared through me like a wall of fire. It didn't stop her using her power to immobilise me, but the shadows couldn't reach into me anymore. Through all the pain, nothing hurt worse than her being turned against me like this.

She released me at last and I growled as I pushed myself up to my feet, watching as she moved down the queue, checking everyone's marks to make sure no one was standing with anyone they shouldn't be. My heart beat erratically, but I didn't care about the war taking place in my body. We'd soon have the antidote to the Order Suppressant Lionel was giving her anyway, and once her Phoenix was awake, she'd be able to fight the shadows off too. I just knew it.

A sharp clicking of heels told me Professor Highspell had arrived and she swept past me a second later, wearing a fitted red dress, her dark hair tumbling down her spine in soft waves. She nodded to Tory before walking into the classroom and ushering us inside, offering a sugary smile to a few of the boys as they passed her. When I walked by, her green eyes darkened to pitch and I mirrored the same scowl she gave me.

"There is now a new seating plan you must all abide by," Highspell announced before anyone could take their seats and I stood with my arms folded as I took in the newly arranged class. Over half the seats had been pushed to the back of the room in grouped sections and the other half at the front had been exchanged for cushioned chairs with glasses of water on the table and freaking mini muffins beside them.

"The following Orders will take a seat at the back of the class," Highspell called as she moved to her desk – Orion's fucking desk – and took out her Atlas.

My throat tightened as I exchanged a concerned glance with Sofia.

"Heptian Toads, Tiberian Rats, Pegasuses, Minotaurs, Sphinxes, Experian Deer Shifters-" She continued on, each Order heading off to take seats in groups at the back of the class, all muttering under their breath.

When she was finished, she smiled darkly and I wanted to punch that look off of her disgustingly beautiful face. She stroked the glimmering aquamarine necklace at her throat as her eyes scraped across the remaining students waiting to be seated. "The rest of you may take a seat at the front." She gestured to the selection of mostly powerful, predatory Orders at the front of the class and my heart pounded out of rhythm as Harpies, Nemean Lions, Manticores, Vampires, Werewolves, Sirens and the others moved to sit down.

"What is this?" I demanded, my feet rooted to the spot as the rest my classmates swept away toward the comfy seats, some of them seeming far too pleased with themselves as they dropped into them.

Highspell arched a brow at me, seeming shocked that I'd questioned her. "It is the new way," she said lightly. "Classes must now be split by lesser and higher Orders."

"*Lesser?*" I spat. "Who are you to judge that?"

"I am a humble servant of our King," she said icily, her eyes flashing. "And you will not question the ways of our new ruler, Miss Vega."

My pulse hammered in my ears and I refused to take one of those seats at the front of the class.

"This is wrong," I growled and a bunch of people murmured their agreement.

"If you don't like it, Miss Vega, then you may take a seat at the back of the room with the rest of the lessers," Highspell said with a smirk that said she expected me to back down for the sake of a comfier seat. "But as your grades were abysmal last term, I would suggest you take any advantages offered to you in the new world."

"Screw your new world," I spat, turning my back on her and walking to the rear of the class.

"Mr Corbin, be a good boy and please move a seat for Miss Vega so she is placed with the rest of her kind back there," Highspell mocked me, knowing I had no one else but Tory who had emotionlessly taken her seat at the front already.

Tyler casually flipped Highspell the finger, drawing a laugh from a bunch of students around him. I smirked, dropping down beside him with the Pegasuses and gazed calmly back at Highspell, a challenge in my gaze.

Her eyes turned to snake-like slits, showing her Medusa Order peering out of them.

"This will not be tolerated," Highspell hissed.

Tory got to her feet and, like a good little minion, Kylie popped up too.

"Stand up, Miss Vega!" Highspell snapped at me, raising her palms and I quickly cast an air shield around myself.

"No," I said, my breathing coming rapidly.

Mutters broke out behind me as Tory closed in on us and I heard a few mentioning my 'addled mind', making my jaw clench. I'd had enough of this. Enough of the lies, of everyone believing Tory had really changed sides and that I was some lunatic who spoke to ravens in my spare time. And now that Lionel had exposed his use of the shadows, there was no need to protect Darius and the others from people knowing they had the Fifth Element too. Lionel wasn't going to let them be punished for it now that he was in charge and claiming it was some gift from the stars.

I pushed out of my seat and raised my chin. "Lionel Acrux is controlling my sister with the shadows. He forced us to take part in a ritual that-"

"Enough!" Highspell shrieked.

"- brought a meteor down from the sky. Lionel turned it to stardust with his Dragon fire and-"

Highspell waved a hand and a storm of ice slammed against my air shield.

Tory raised her palms, taking Highspell's place against me and I decided to just keep talking until she was able to shut me up, because screw it, what was there to lose now? "It created a portal to the shadow realm!" I cried and I realised a bunch of people were recording me on their Atlases. "He forced me, Tory, Darius and Lance Orion to kneel at the heart of the meteor crater and-"

Shadows blasted toward me and a bunch of students scattered around me with screams, but I was shielding anyone close enough to me. The darkness slammed into my shield and I swore as I had to focus for a moment, straining with the effort of holding them off, but I managed to keep talking for anyone who cared to hear the truth. "We were cast into the Shadow Realm and when we returned, the Fifth Element was gifted to us all, including Lionel Acrux and his followers. It was the same ritual he did years ago to Clara Orion and that's where she came back from. She's been in the Shadow Realm all these years and now-" Power blinded me as the full brunt of Tory's shadows crashed over me and my air shield finally buckled.

I was thrown to the ground and my Phoenix reared up to protect me from their power before they wound around my body and dragged me across the room. I was hauled forward and thrown into a seat.

As the fog of darkness cleared, screams reached me that made my blood curdle.

I twisted around in my seat which had been dragged forward away from any of my other classmates, finding all of the Pegasuses falling prey to the shadows, crying out and whinnying as they paid for what I'd done.

"No!" I yelled, trying to get up, but the shadows were still wrapped around my waist, holding me in place.

Highspell was smiling, delighting in the chaos and when the screams finally stopped, she turned to the board, ready to teach the class while I silently vowed to destroy her.

I flew with Gabriel at my side, releasing all the tension of the day as we twisted through the clouds, flying up above them to watch the sun die. We weren't allowed to do this, but technically Gabriel was teaching me how to fly, so if anyone asked he could cover for us.

"Highspell gave me a week's detention," I said as we hovered side by side, my burning wings flapping behind me as his ebony ones beat in time with mine.

I'd told him what she'd done, not that he could do anything about it, but maybe he'd had a vision that could give us some hope in this situation. I'd held off on asking until now, just wanting to fly and be free and forget all the bad shit that had happened today.

"I despise that woman," he snarled.

"I don't suppose you can *see* a way to get her fired, can you?" I asked, half joking, half serious.

"I'm afraid she's here to stay for now," he sighed.

"And what about Lionel? Is he here to stay?" I asked, my throat constricting as I turned to him.

His grey eyes darkened. "I've been consulting the stars about that all day," he admitted. "There is still hope. But it rests with the Imperial Star."

I nodded and he dove down through the clouds suddenly. I took chase, tucking my wings and swinging away from a herd of Griffins as they sailed beneath us.

Gabriel kept ahead of me as we moved into view of the campus below and I followed at a distance before he flew through his office window. I circled the building once, making sure the coast was clear before doing the same, landing lightly inside. He might have been able to cover us to an extent, but I didn't want anyone looking too closely at how much time we spent together. His connection to me and Tory was still a secret as far as I knew unless Tory had spilled it, but as she barely seemed to know who any of us were, we were hopeful that wasn't the case.

He pushed the window closed and cast a silencing bubble. His office was sparse and I didn't think he spent a whole lot of time here. Gabriel went home most evenings by stardust to see his family and despite him saying I was welcome to go with him anytime, I knew I couldn't leave Zodiac while my sister was here. She needed me, even if she didn't know it. And I had to be around to help her if anything ever happened.

Gabriel moved to his desk, taking a bottle from the top drawer with a few syringes. "Here's the Order Suppressant antidote," he said with a half smile.

My heart lifted and I rushed to take it, but he shook his head. "You're going to be stopped on your way back to Aer Tower, and if they find it, they'll take it then Nova will put you in detention for the evening."

My lips parted on a demand to take it now and find some way to give it to Tory, but I stalled with a sigh. I trusted his gifts. I just had to fight the urge to snatch it, fly to Tory and try and inject her with it right this second.

"If you follow that line of thought, you will still be stopped and searched before you take it – ah, but if you take *that* route, you will be unable to give it to her. No, it's just not going to work tonight." Gabriel shrugged sympathetically.

I sighed and my wings dissolved away behind me. "I hate when you do that," I said, but a smirk tugged at my lips.

He chuckled. "You love it really."

"Yeah, I do," I breathed a laugh but then my amusement fell away as the weight of this day fell over me again. He walked forward and wrapped me in his arms without a word, resting his chin on my head. For a moment the world paused and everything was okay. Just for a second. But what a perfect damn second it was.

"So the Imperial Star…" I started as he released me.

I sat on his desk and crossed my legs underneath me, toying with a lock of my hair. I'd changed into leggings and a crop top for the flight, but now my wings weren't warming me, goosebumps spread across my arms so I urged fire into my veins to keep the cold out.

Gabriel's wings fell away and I examined the artwork of tattoos on his chest, wondering what secrets were hidden within them. Things that had come to pass, things that were yet to. His gift was written into his flesh, future, past and present. There was a ring of star signs over his heart that were joined together in a beautiful circle and he scratched that very spot as he dropped into a chair in front of me.

"I can't *see* where it is," he said with a frown. "But I can *see* that Lance is the key to finding it."

I nodded slowly, biting on my lower lip. "You probably already know this but-"

"You're going to see him tonight?" he finished with a smirk. "He has something very important he needs to do. And you need to help him."

"I'm going to free him from the star vow we made to each other," I said, my chest compressing and I suddenly couldn't meet his gaze. Gabriel could *see* so much, could he see right through me to the hurt I worked so hard to hide these days too? The love that still lived on in me for Lance as fiercely as ever?

"It's more than that," he said carefully, like he couldn't say too much. "Just do whatever you can to help him."

I frowned. "What can you *see*?" I pushed, the secrets lurking in his eyes making my heart beat wildly.

"So many paths," he said with a pained expression that made me worry about how many of them were bad. "Just do your best, follow your heart and all that bullshit."

I laughed softly, but it died away in my throat as I rested my chin in my hand, my elbow propped on my knee. "Is any of it good? Has the future got anything to look forward to, Gabriel?"

A crease formed between his eyes and he scooted his chair closer. "The future is just a roulette wheel, Darcy. Only every outcome is grey."

"That doesn't sound so good," I murmured.

"It is good, and bad. That's life. I guess that's one thing The Sight makes me *see* clearer than anything else. It's all about the choices you make, the actions you take. Cause and effect. If you do nothing, nothing will happen. If you do everything, everything will happen."

"That's…weirdly comforting," I said thoughtfully. "But what about the stars, surely they're deciding all of this? Isn't it all just fate and we're slaves to whatever they desire?"

"The stars will test us. And sometimes they may punish us or gift us for the choices we make, but they don't make our fate. Only we can do that. So go make it, Darcy. You've got to get going if you want to be ready in time."

I slid off the desk with a sigh and he stood up, grabbing a lock of my hair and tugging on it teasingly. "He's going to eat his heart out," he murmured and I rolled my eyes. "I hope he does by the way. I'm still pissed he hurt my little sister. Kick him in the dick for me, okay?"

I chuckled as I headed to the window, pushing it open and feeling him drop the silencing bubble.

"Can you *see* a dick kick in his future?" I asked with a grin.

"Definitely," he said with a smirk.

"Love you, Gabriel," I told him, then dove out of the window, the rush of falling making my stomach spin before my wings burst from my back and I soared along, climbing toward the sky and taking a direct route to Aer Tower in the distance. I got stopped and searched by a bitchy K.U.N.T. of a Harpy when I flew too close to a Manticore, but she let me go with a warning. And I may have not so accidentally started a tiny fire in her hair which wouldn't take root until I was far away and unable to be held responsible.

I made it to my window, landing on the slim ledge before pushing open the tall pane that swung sideways to let me in. I dropped into my room, my flaming wings fizzling away behind me with a lasting crackle.

My covers were suddenly thrown back and Geraldine sat bolt upright from under them.

"My lady!" she cried. "I have been most sneaksome indeed to get in here. That wayward white Wolf let me in and snuck me upstairs under an illusion spell which disguised me as one of his pack. It was quite the thrill ride."

I grinned as I rushed over to her, pulling her into a hug as she stood up and I noticed a bag on the bed.

"What's that?" I asked.

She wheeled around, snatching it up and clutching it against her chest. "It is a gift from your most charming and devilishly handsome brother. He set me on this mission, a task I took as seriously as a cucumber on a bed of flotsam."

"What kind of gift?" I frowned and she handed me the bag with the brightest smile in the world.

I opened it, finding a blue maxi dress inside the same colour as my hair and a velvet box sitting on top of it. I took the box out and flipped it open, gasping almost as dramatically as Geraldine did when I found a silver bracelet inside with a Gemini charm on it.

"I have strict instructions to not allow you to wear anything else but these items, excluding bloomers and shoes of course." She laughed and I did too as she grabbed the bracelet and clasped it onto my wrist. I touched the pendant, turning it between my fingers with a smile pulling at my mouth.

I grabbed my Atlas, but before I could shoot him a text, one came from him.

Gabriel:
You're welcome.

I shook my head with a grin. *Damn sight seeing bastard.*

Geraldine helped me do my makeup and practically forced the dress over my head when I said it was overkill for a trip to freaking prison.

"You will wear it and have that buffoon of a Vampire see how perfectly perfect you are without him. He shall feast on his feelings and his heart shall die a thousand deaths when he sees you dressed up fit for a dinner with the stars."

"I don't want his heart to die a thousand deaths, maybe just like, one death," I reasoned, eyeing myself in the mirror. *This is definitely too much.*

"Nonsense," she chastised.

I turned to face her as she finished arranging my hair over my shoulders. "I'm serious, Geraldine. I'm just going to break off the star vow. In and out. Five minutes."

Her eyes glittered with tears and her lower lip wobbled. "Oh fudge fancies on a Thursday, I promised myself I wouldn't cry." She dabbed at her eyes and waved me off when I tried to comfort her.

"Is it the dress?" I frowned down at it. "It's too much isn't it?"

"No, it's not the dress, it's forbidden love, doomed to never be. Honey pots in a haystack, as angry as I am at that pest of a professor, it still breaks my heart."

"It shouldn't. I'm over it." I pushed down the sharp lump in my throat, moving to my closet and grabbing out a leather coat before shrugging it on. Geraldine shrieked, ripping it from my shoulders before I could do it up.

"No coat. You have your Phoenix to keep you warm!" She pushed me toward the door, twisting the key in the lock and shoving me out of it. "Now go, the dashing Dragon says he will meet you at you know where."

"Great. Thanks for helping me. Just don't cry, okay?" I hugged her goodbye and she nodded several times.

"I won't," she croaked and I headed off down the corridor, hearing her mournful sob following me.

I jogged downstairs and walked outside, a swarm of butterflies in my stomach making me want to throw up. *Five minutes, that's it. I can face anything for five minutes.*

I ignored the yearning in me that wanted so much more than that. But I could never give in to that feeling. His betrayal ran too deep. And when I'd gone to him before and asked him for an explanation, he refused to give me one. It didn't matter that Darius swore that what Orion had done was to protect me, to keep me at Zodiac. Even if that was true, he hadn't had the right to make that choice the way he did. And he hadn't even offered me an answer for that one desperate question I'd needed from him. *Why? Why do this to us, why take everything from me, from himself?*

I'd opened a can of worms now and I couldn't seem to close it as the bastards wriggled out and crawled through my head. I approached the outer fence, checking around to make sure no one was watching. Then I headed off of the path and hurried through the trees to where Darius was waiting. He took in my dress with his eyebrows raising and heat crawled up my neck.

"This was not my choice," I said firmly before he could open his mouth. "Gabriel and Geraldine are entirely to blame."

He laughed. "I'm saying nothing. *Except* that he's going to lose his fucking mind."

I rolled my eyes, stepping back and we walked through the illusion Orion had cast here to hide the gap in the fence. He wouldn't give a shit because he'd moved on just like I was supposed to have moved on. Which I was definitely working on. And most people were convinced of it anyway thanks to my newfound ability to stuff my emotions down so deep that they didn't give me away. So I was calling it a win.

Darius turned me to face him on the other side of the fence with a dark expression. "Since my father has now outlawed Orders socialising, I had to make a last minute change to our plans. I'm not even really supposed to be able to visit Lance because he's a Vampire, but in light of my Guardian bond to him, Father decided to be generous." His sneer gave away what he thought of that. "But obviously I can't disguise you as Max. Oh, and fuck my father by the way."

"Yeah fuck him with a spiky dildo," I agreed. "So what's the new plan?"

"Well it's Gabriel's plan actually. He foresaw this last night and spoke to Dante Oscura. The Storm Dragon's given you permission to use his image to get into Darkmore."

I smiled. "Perfect."

Darius stepped forward and I held still as he carefully disguised me under an illusion spell. It wasn't an awesome idea to risk this right now, but breaking off the star vow was important. And since Darius had told me about Orion showing up to his last visitation bloody and hurt, I couldn't stop thinking about it. I'd kind of compartmentalised it if I was being honest. Thinking about him was dangerous territory as it was, thinking about him suffering was unbearable.

The illusion trickled over my skin and Darius stepped back, smirking at his own work. "Okay, let's go."

He took a pouch of stardust from his pocket and I steeled myself as he threw a pinch of it over us. We were whisked away through a tunnel of stars and my head spun as we were spat out in another part of the world, my feet hitting solid ground. I managed not to stumble too hard, but Darius steadied me anyway as I gazed at the huge complex that housed Darkmore. Damn if I wasn't getting better at those landings.

A car came to take us in and it wasn't long before we were heading underground in the large elevator that led us down into the prison's depths.

My heart rate wouldn't rest and I wrung my fingers together as we descended.

Darius shot me a taut frown. "Are you alright?"

"I'm fine," I said firmly, fiddling with the bracelet on my wrist. "It won't be like last time. In and out Darius."

"Yeah, yeah five minutes right?" He smirked, turning to face the doors again and my heart thrashed harder against my ribcage.

"Why are you smirking?" I narrowed my eyes at him and he shrugged innocently.

"This is just my normal face," he said, trying to flatten his smirk and failing.

"No, your normal face suggests you're deciding whether or not to eat the Fae in front of you," I pointed out. "You only smirk when you've decided you're actually going to do it."

He released a low laugh. "Maybe I'm hungry."

"Well maybe you should have brought a snack."

"Maybe I did." He gnashed his teeth at me and I snorted.

"I'd cook your ass if you tried it."

"Hmm, that's a point. How will I fry you up if you don't burn?" he mused and I laughed.

"Sucks to suck, Darius," I said lightly. "I'm uncookable."

The doors opened and we stepped out into the waiting room. We were only sat down a couple of minutes before we were called, but those minutes felt like an eternity as my nails bit into my palms almost hard enough to break the skin. Darius tried to distract me with a few jokes about how he was going to eat me raw like sushi but I couldn't focus enough to laugh this time.

I followed Darius through the security doors and down the bland corridor, my instincts telling me to turn back, to not walk through that door and see the man waiting beyond it. Because this place was where I'd shattered before, and I couldn't do that again. Not ever.

I stopped in my tracks, frozen in place as doubts gripped me and a voice in the back of my head screamed at me to leave. But in the pit of my stomach, I knew that I couldn't do that. For everyone I loved, I had to walk through that door and face Orion. For us to even stand a chance at finding the Imperial Star, we needed him. And regardless of that, he was suffering in here. Despite everything that had happened between us, I'd never wanted that for him. I couldn't just leave him here to the wrath of the stars. If I didn't help him, he could end up dead the next time some assholes attacked him.

Darius paused by the door, waiting for me with a patient expression. "Are you ready?"

"I don't think I'll ever be ready," I admitted, forcing myself to move and stand at his side. "But let's get it over with."

He pushed through the door and I followed him inside, finding the room empty as I took a steadying breath. I nudged the door shut as Darius flicked his fingers, casting a film of ice over the cameras, covering us from view.

"You've got as long as you want, I've paid off everyone who might cause us an issue today," Darius said, giving me an intent look.

"I told you, I only need five minutes, maybe not even that," I said determinedly.

Darius stepped toward me, dissolving the magic concealing me as Dante Oscura and taking my hand. He squeezed once, giving me an apologetic frown. "Sorry, shrew."

He stepped past me, moving back out of the door and slamming it shut in my face, ice growing over the handle as I lunged at it and tried to open it. I used my fire magic to try and melt it, but the asshole somehow kept it locked.

"Darius!" I snapped, smacking my hand against the wood. *Bastard!*

The door opened behind me and I felt him enter the room before I even turned around. The hairs stood up on the back of my neck and a shiver raced down my spine that made me squeeze my eyes shut. *How can he still affect me this way? After all this time, is it always going to be this hard?*

Fae up, Darcy Vega. Get it over with.

I took a breath, fixed an emotionless mask into place and turned around.

Orion stood there in his orange jumpsuit, the sleeves rolled back to show his thick forearms and a layer of new muscle that seemed to cling to him all over. I dragged my eyes up to his face as my pulse pounded wildly and found a thick beard on his jaw, his mouth flat, his hair getting overly long.

I expected to see a wall in his eyes, forcing me out like the last time I'd seen him, but it wasn't there. He looked…broken. As broken as he'd been back then, only this time all the sharp pieces in his eyes had settled. He'd accepted his fate as I'd accepted mine, and there was a painful knowledge in that which ripped at my insides.

His gaze travelled over me with slow and hungry movements, like he was trying to make an eternity out of seeing me.

"Hello," he said at last, his voice deep and holding an edge of desperation in it that made me ache.

"Hi," I said stiffly, wetting my lips and taking a step closer. "Darius locked me in here, so…"

"Asshole," he muttered.

"Yep." My heart thundered out a wild and yearning tune as it begged me to get nearer to him, to feel the heat of his body meeting mine in the air, to smell his familiar smell and brush my fingers over the lines of his face, seek out the single dimple hiding in his right cheek. But I'd be doing none of those things. Not now, not ever.

When I was close enough, I stopped moving, trying to ignore the way every fibre of my flesh seemed to pulse with energy, driving me toward him. "I don't know how to break the promise, so if you could just show me how," I said, my tone sharp.

He reached out and took my hand, his rough palm meeting mine and gripping it tightly. A small and involuntary gasp escaped me as a light but potent energy rushed through me from his touch. It was addictive, demanding and horribly familiar.

His jaw ticked furiously before he tugged me closer so I was right in his personal space, forced to look up at him and my breath caught in my throat.

"*Lance,*" I warned, unsure what I was even warning him of.

I just needed it to stop. All of it. I couldn't believe after all this time I still felt like this. Like the world began and ended with him and I would never belong to any other man. *But that's not real anymore. He's not mine and I'm not his.*

"Fuck," he growled, clamping his eyes shut for a moment before looking at me again with a tight expression. "How are you?"

I yanked my hand free of his, anger curling up through my body like flames. "How am I?" I scoffed. "That's what you have to say?"

His jaw tightened and he said nothing. Nothing. I wasn't going to demand an explanation from him again though. He'd had his chance the last time I'd come here. But he'd frozen me out and told me to go. That it was over and I needed to move on. So I had.

Every part of me was hot and I snatched his hand again, fire blazing against my palm as I fought not to scold him. "How do I break it?" I demanded.

"Just say the words," he said defeatedly. "Recite the promise and tell the stars you release me from it."

I nodded, keeping my eyes on his as I refused to look away. I thought back on that day we'd made the promise and how, no matter what we'd faced back then, we'd known we'd always have each other. Somehow, I'd fooled myself into believing that. I'd really thought we had a future. I would have fought the stars themselves to keep him. I guessed the sentiment had never been shared.

"I promised to fight for you, whatever it took and you promised it in return," I didn't let my voice shake as I held his gaze and saw a flicker of regret in his eyes. He probably had a helluva lot of regrets when it came to me. "I release you from that bond," I said firmly, keeping my mask locked in place.

I wouldn't break, or cry or let him see a single crack in my façade. I was stronger now. And no man, not even him, would be able to hurt me again.

Magic crackled between us and the feeling of something snapping against our palms rang through my body before I felt the promise lift from my heart. There was something so final about it, our worlds cleaving apart fully like an axe severing the final ties between us. My hand lingered in his for two more seconds before I pulled it free. *Done.*

"Thank you," he sighed and I nodded stiffly. It felt like a thousand words hung between us in the air. But as I backed away, the window of opportunity to say them closed forever. And as I reached the opposite side of the room, it might as well have been a whole universe parting us. His and mine. Planes we could only exist on separately.

I twisted the door handle behind me, but it didn't budge and Orion surveyed me with a tight frown. *Dammit Darius.*

"I'll go," Orion rasped, turning to head through the door that led into the prison. But he paused, glancing back at me, his penetrating gaze drilling a hole in my heart. "You look like a queen, Darcy. I'm looking forward to the coronation." And with that, he left, making the air rush out of me and anger surge up inside me like a tidal wave. I twisted around, casting burning hot air into the lock and finally managed to break it open, stepping out into the corridor where Darius was leaning against the wall with his arms folded.

I strode up to him, slapped him hard then hugged him firmly, because dammit I needed him right now. "You had no right."

He held me close and the feel of him casting the identity illusion tumbled over my flesh. "I know, but you haven't given up on me and Roxy. So I have the same sentiment when it comes to you and my best friend."

I pulled away from him with a sad look. "The difference is, you two actually want each other."

"That's not a difference, shrew."

"Don't call me shrew, Asscrux." I rolled my eyes, but my stomach knotted because inside I knew all I wanted was Orion. But I would never admit it out loud. I'd smother that feeling, push it down until it went away one day. Because if the stars had taught me anything, it was that we didn't belong with one another no matter how much it had felt that way once. *And I'm done breaking for Lance Orion.*

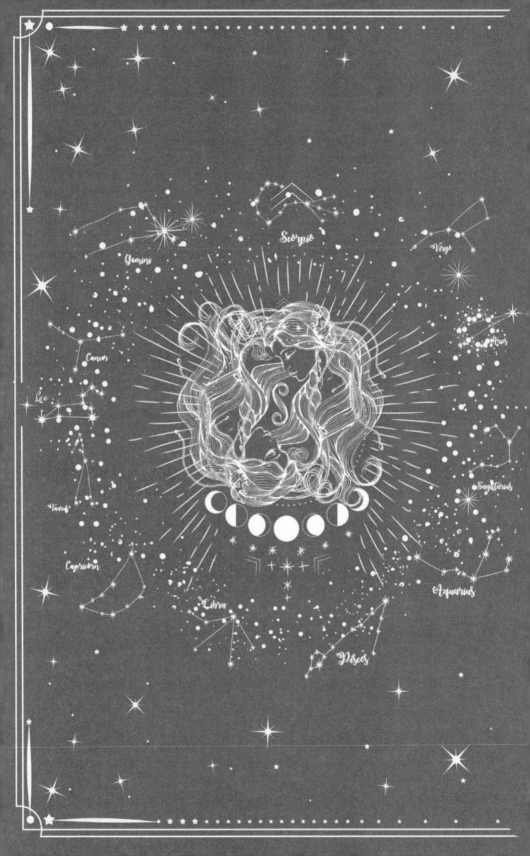

TORY

CHAPTER EIGHT

I sat in Arcane Arts at the end of my table, trying to predict the future with the roll of the dice Gabriel had given me and finding it unclear time and again. Frustration built in me as I continued to struggle with the task and the shadows writhed beneath my skin, feeding on my anger and looking for an outlet for it.

"Tory, I want a word with you at the end of class," Gabriel said as he moved to stand beside me and I looked up to find him standing over me, eyeing my notes with a disapproving frown.

"Why?" I asked, wondering why he seemed to be taking such an interest in me.

"The problem with your predictions is that you need to really connect with your emotions to get a read on your future. And all the time you're letting things get in the way of your true feelings-"

"I don't know what you mean," I replied flatly and he sighed in frustration.

The air shield around me trembled at the touch of his magic against it and I stood abruptly as I tightened my hold on the shield I always kept in place.

"Sorry, I didn't mean to scare you," Gabriel said, stepping back as I narrowed my eyes on him.

The shadows twisted and swirled within me, whispering at me to strike at him for that, but I didn't give in to them. Something in my gut urged me not to hurt him and though I wasn't sure why, as he backed away I found I was glad I didn't have to do any more to defend myself.

"I'm not afraid of you," I replied flatly.

I lowered myself back into my chair and Darcy caught my gaze from the far side of the room. I didn't turn away, holding her eye with an expressionless look that seemed to be making her angry and her brow furrowed as she stared at me, her eyes watering as her fists tightened on the table in front of her.

As the bell rang to mark the end of class, she leapt up and strode from the room, nodding at Gabriel as she went and disappearing before anyone else had even managed to pack their things away.

I bit my lip as I considered whether or not I should call my king, running my fingers back and forth over the Guardian bond mark on my forearm as I considered it. It had been three days since I'd seen him and though I knew he was busy with the changes he had to make in the kingdom, I was certain he had to be missing me too. Or at least I hoped he was. Because without him I didn't have anything.

But he'd also told me to stop calling so frequently and I didn't want to make him angry.

I huffed in frustration and packed my stuff into my bag then turned to leave.

But before I could make it more than a few steps, Gabriel moved to block my path.

"I still need that word," he said seriously, levelling me with a look that said he wasn't going to leave this issue.

I shrugged and moved back towards my chair but he shook his head, pushing his black hair away from his eyes and regarding me with interest.

"Why don't we walk and talk?" he suggested and for some reason I liked the sound of spending more time in his company. There was just something about him that made me feel safe. "I think a bit of fresh air could do us both good."

Technically I shouldn't have been mixing with a Harpy but as there were allowances made for teachers and I was above the rules anyway, I decided not to make an issue of it.

"Fine," I agree, not caring much either way. I just wanted this day over. On Friday I could return to my king and in the meantime, I just needed to study and sleep to make the time disappear. But the more time that passed, the more I ached to return to him and the harder it was to ignore the itch in my bond mark. I'd do it though. For him. Like I promised.

Gabriel led the way out of the building and I trailed along after him, tightening my hold on my air shield as we stepped out into the cool air. Lionel had warned me that Darcy might try and attack me at any moment, especially when I was alone so I had to be on the lookout at all times. Though for some reason I didn't really think she would. But I'd do as my king told me all the same.

"Do you mind if I get my wings out?" Gabriel asked casually, unhooking the buttons on his grey shirt without waiting for my response so I didn't bother giving one. He'd clearly decided he was getting them out either way.

As he removed his shirt, my gaze caught on a tattoo above his right hip of two Phoenixes flying together and my brow furrowed as a memory was tugged to the forefront of my mind before being swept away again on a tide of shadows.

Gabriel rolled his shoulders back and a huge pair of midnight black wings burst from his back as he shifted and I watched a little curiously as he flexed them behind him.

"I haven't seen you shift since you came back to the academy this term," he commented, leading me up the path that led into The Wailing Wood. "Perhaps we could go flying together soon?"

"I don't enjoy flying," I said automatically, unsure where the words had even come from. But as I opened my mouth to counter that comment, I gasped at the ripple of pain which washed through my chest.

I did hate flying. It hurt me. My wings hurt me and I didn't ever want to use them again.

"What's wrong?" Gabriel asked, reaching for my arm but finding my shield still in place which stopped him from laying his hands on me.

I didn't want him touching me. I knew that very clearly and I cut him a glare as I stepped aside, placing more magic into my shield in case he tried again. "Nothing."

"You looked like you were in pain," he pushed.

"You have very little understanding of true pain then," I replied. And I had a lot of understanding of that.

Gabriel chuckled darkly and shrugged. "I know a fair bit. I've been through more than a few battles in my time and I took a bolt of Storm Dragon lightning to the chest once too."

I fell still as he said that, my fists clenching at the memories of being struck by that very thing. A voice in my ear whispering those words. *"This is the full power of a Storm Dragon. Whose fault is it that you have to feel this pain?"*

"Darius," I breathed, almost forgetting Gabriel was there as the memories of being struck with all of that electricity over and over again overwhelmed me for a moment and I was forced to seek solace in the shadows. That had happened to me because of Darius and I needed to keep the hell away from him unless I wanted it to happen again.

I glanced over my shoulder like he might be lurking in the dark, just waiting to pounce and my pulse raced as I drew even more shadows to the surface of my skin, sighing as the fear began to subside and the pleasure of their power took its place.

"What about Darius?" Gabriel asked but I just shook my head. I wasn't supposed to talk to him about that. Not him, not anyone. Only my king and Vard and Clara. I wouldn't be coaxed into saying anything to anyone else.

"He's the worst kind of poison," I breathed. "The kind you don't realise is killing you until you've already taken too much."

"Darius isn't poison, Tory," Gabriel said firmly, coming to a halt at a turn in the path where the trees surrounding us were so thick that I could barely see between them.

"He is to me," I replied. But that was all I was going to say on the subject.

Gabriel opened his mouth to respond, but before he could, a blast of power slammed into the back of my air shield and I gasped as I barely managed to hold it in place.

I whirled around, drawing more air into the shield as Seth burst from the trees, his face set in determination as he cast more air at me and I had to fight to make sure he didn't break through my shield.

I gritted my teeth in determination just as another attack hit the shield at my back and I looked around to find Darius directing water at me, his brow furrowed as he worked to break through my defences.

My heart began to race at the sight of him coming for me, just the way he did in my nightmares, his face set in a cruel mask and his body written with determination.

"Stop," I commanded, raising my hands either side of me as I pushed more power into my air shield and the ground beneath my feet began to tremble as Caleb shot out of the trees and attacked me too.

"Tory!" Darcy called as she stepped onto the path and heat flared along my limbs as I spotted my twin taking part in this ambush as well. They were all against me, just like my king had told me they were. They were going to hurt me and take me away from him and steal everything I cared about in this world if they got the chance. "We aren't trying to hurt you. We just want to help you regain control of your Phoenix. We need you to free yourself from the shadows and-"

"What if I don't want to be free of them?" I snarled, gritting my teeth as the combined pressure of so much magic almost buckled my shield. My king needed me to wield the shadows with him. I wasn't going to let them go against his wishes. I wasn't going to disappoint him like that. It was unthinkable.

"Her shield is about to crack," Gabriel announced as he added his own water magic to the assault and Max and Geraldine emerged from the trees to help too.

"I'm ready!" Caleb called and I spotted a syringe held in his hand which sent fear slicing into me. I couldn't let him get close to me with that thing. I'd die before he did.

My heart was pounding and the shadows were whispering promises of death in my ears as they begged me to use them.

The shadows were always so hungry for blood that they would make me sloppy if I gave them too much freedom. I needed to control them rather than allowing them to control *me*, but I was burning through my power resources and any moment now, they were going to break them down.

"Go carefully," Darius barked. "If any one of you hurts her, I will personally beat the shit out of you for it."

"We are going careful," Seth growled as he increased the pressure of his attack and I felt my shield cracking.

I sucked in a sharp breath and dropped my shield half a beat before it would have broken anyway then yelled out as shadows burst from my body in an explosion of darkness that blotted out the world.

They slammed into the entire group who had surrounded me, hurling them off of their feet and into the trees in every direction and the sound of their screams made me smile savagely as their pain fed my darkness.

I took off running the moment the path was clear, throwing up a huge wall of shadows at my back as I reconstructed my air shield with what little power remained to me and cast a ball of fire to replenish what I'd lost.

Seth was howling in agony in the trees behind me and their shouts and curses chased me away as I kept running and running, not stopping until I made it back to Ignis House and into my room.

I slammed the door closed and pressed my back to it as my chest heaved and the shadows writhed beneath my skin, making me moan with pleasure in payment for the pain I'd fed them.

But as my rampant heartbeat finally calmed, I forced myself to push them back so that I could think a little more clearly. Just enough to remember the orders I'd been given before returning to this place.

I knew what I had to do. What I'd promised I'd do if I was ever foolish enough to let them get close to me. But as I pulled the glass jar from the bag beneath my bed, my hand began to tremble with fear.

I placed it down in front of me before unknotting my tie with shaking fingers and slipping out of my shirt and blazer next.

I sat cross legged on the floor in my bra and school skirt, eyeing the crackling electricity contained in that jar with a sense of dread that even the shadows couldn't keep away.

I blew out a shaky breath and picked up my Atlas, calling my king and placing it on loudspeaker as I set it down on the carpet beside me.

"What is it?' he snarled as he answered and I flinched at the knowledge that I'd upset him, especially knowing I had to deliver this bad news. "I'm in the middle of dealing with an issue with the Nymphs at Stella's manor."

"Can I help?" I asked, hoping he might need me for something and summon me back to him where I belonged.

Lionel sighed irritably before he replied. "Not unless you can come up with a way for them to gain the magic they require without the population noticing that they've been killing again."

"Let's feed them children," Clara's voice came in the background. "Nobody likes children."

"Go and make yourself busy somewhere, Clara," Lionel snapped. "I have no use for your nonsense."

Clara started crying loudly and a cruel smile captured my lips as I heard her running away. *Who's the favourite now, bitch?*

"Between her and her useless mother, I'm at my wits' end," Lionel growled. "I'll figure out the solution to this problem myself. Now tell me why you are calling before I lose my temper."

"I'm sorry, my king. I promised I'd call you if anyone tried to attack me," I said quietly.

"Who attacked you?" Lionel growled, his tone changing to one of interest.

"Darcy. The Heirs. And Gabriel," I said quickly. "I think they were trying to capture me but I managed to use the shadows to escape them."

There was a long pause and I waited for his answer with my heart pounding fear into my veins.

"Gabriel Nox?" he asked curiously. "Why would he involve himself with their foolish attempts?"

An answer came to my lips and I almost spoke the truth of who he was to me, but a moment before I could say the words, the knowledge slipped from my mind again and I couldn't remember what I'd been going to say. I didn't care about Gabriel anyway. Only my king. I only loved my king.

"I don't know," I breathed and he grunted irritably.

"Well, the main thing is that you got away. But you will have to be punished for allowing them to get you into that position in the first place," Lionel growled.

"I know. I'm sorry," I breathed, eyeing the jar of lightning again as fear washed into me.

"Where are you?" he asked.

"In my room," I replied.

"I'll send someone to come heal you in a few hours. Once you've learned your lesson." His voice was eager now and I took some comfort in that, knowing that at least my suffering would please him.

"Thank you," I murmured, reaching out to pick up the jar.

"Give me a moment to get somewhere private. I need to be sure you do everything exactly the way you promised," he commanded and I nodded even though he couldn't see me.

I waited as the sound of his footsteps filled the speaker and closed my eyes as I listened to him breathing, drinking in the sound like it was giving me life.

"Go ahead," Lionel grunted as a door snapped closed wherever he was and I bit my lip as a shiver of fear danced down my spine.

I reached for the jar, picking it up and feeling the power of the runes used to contain the bolt of lightning inside it as I unlocked them the way he'd taught me. This was what I deserved for letting Darcy and the others get close to me like that. For letting them try and take me from my king. I needed this punishment. It was the only way to set things right.

I gritted my teeth as I pushed my magic into the runes, unlocking them as I twisted the lid off of the jar in the same movement.

The bolt of lightning slammed into my chest with a force so powerful that I was helpless to stop the scream of agony that tore from my lips as I was knocked flat on my back while the electricity careered back and forth inside my body.

It lit me up from the inside out, burning and frying and shocking everything it touched before bouncing back around to hit all the same places again twice as hard.

My back arched as I screamed so loud my throat tore and pain unlike anything else I'd ever experienced held me in its grasp and wouldn't let go. It was never ending, this blinding, all consuming agony which sliced through every piece of me until it was destroyed and bleeding for my king.

When it finally stopped, I collapsed in a heap of agony, shaking and crying, the scent of burning filling the air and a ringing in my ears that wouldn't let up.

I could hear Lionel breathing heavily as he listened in to my torture and I latched onto the sound as a groan of pleasure escaped him, the single good thing that I could find in this eternal fire that I was burning in.

"Good girl," he grunted through his panting breaths as I just lay there sobbing and whimpering, unable to move or do anything to relieve the pain in my flesh which went on and on eternally.

The shadows crept closer to me, promising oblivion if I let myself dive into them, but I knew I couldn't do that. Not yet. Not until he said I could.

"Five more minutes to make sure you've really learned your lesson," Lionel said in a rough voice. "And when I next see you, you'll be rewarded for your dedication."

I tried to force a reply past my burned lips, but only a pained moan escaped them as I lay there, almost certain I was dying.

"Remember not to kill the one who comes to heal your wounds," he added gruffly. "I need them alive. Don't let the shadows take them."

Another pained moan escaped my lips as I agreed and he clearly knew I understood as he cut the line, leaving me to lay there and suffer for my failings.

The tears which slid from my eyes only made the burning worse but in five minutes I could escape into the shadows. Five minutes and I wouldn't feel it anymore.

And soon I would see my king again, knowing he was proud of me. That was all that really mattered anyway. So I'd hold onto it with everything I had and be sure to make him proud.

CALEB

CHAPTER NINE

I raced up the pitch with the roar of the crowd in my ears and the Waterball tucked firmly beneath my arm as I headed for the Pit with my jaw locked in determination.

It was the first game of the season and the sixth week of term. Lionel Acrux had taken the throne, we were having fuck all luck finding the star despite the fact Darcy had broken her star vow with Orion, Tory was still well and truly lost in the shadows, Darius and Darcy were so fucking miserable that it actually caused me pain to see them like that and to top it all off I'd been out hunting this morning and had caught an eyeful of Washer's teeny weeny while he was shifting down by the lake. Fucking gross.

But no matter how much everything else sucked, there was one single thing in this world which would always make me smile and bring me and my brothers together. And that was Pitball. I mean yeah, we might have lost our coach and yeah, we had the world's most unenthusiastic cheerleader in Tory and yeah, a win on the pitch wouldn't solve any of the real issues we were facing, but it sure as fuck would feel good. And that was what I wanted. One night to forget about all of it and just pretend the world hadn't gone to shit.

The ground began to buck and quake beneath me as the Aurora Academy Team Captain wielded her magic against me and I hooked a grin her way as I countered her attack with my own hold over the Element. Rosalie smiled like a savage beast as she ran to intercept me, her pretty face splattered with mud and black hair pulled back in a braid.

I was almost at the Pit when she collided with me and I let her take me down as I threw the ball straight for the hole in the centre of the pitch. Darcy took out the Aurora team Keepers with a savage blast of fire magic to make sure I scored the point and the crowd went wild as the ball sailed home.

I hit the ground hard beneath the Wolf girl and she growled as she straddled me in the mud, her thighs gripping tight around my waist and giving my dick some happy ideas.

"Save it for the afterparty, yeah sweetheart?" I teased, giving her a smirk as she lingered with her thighs parted over my hips for a moment.

"Are you going to beg me for a sympathy fuck when we beat you?" she teased, that Faetalian accent of hers only making the idea of that more appealing. She wasn't going to win and we both knew it. The game was a round away from over and Zodiac had the lead even if Aurora was putting up a damn good fight.

"We don't lose," I promised her. "But if you'd like to take a ride on the Zodiac star player..."

"Oh, is Seth offering?" she asked, looking around for him and making me growl as her attention wandered.

"I can make you come better than him," I promised her and she laughed, tossing her braid back over her shoulder as she stood and offered me a hand up.

"Well, there's really only one way to test that theory," she teased, giving me a flirtatious look before flicking her fingers and making the earth buck beneath me hard enough to put me on my ass again.

Seth barked a laugh from his position by the Air Hole and I shook my head with amusement as I got to my feet.

Rosalie was jogging back over to the Earth Hole and I followed her with my gaze straying to her ass more than once. Okay, my eyes were on her ass the whole way, but the girl had a damn nice ass and in my defence, I hadn't gotten laid in like...fuck, I wasn't even sure. Not since Tory anyway. And that was a long fucking time ago.

My gaze flicked over to the cheerleaders where Tory was diligently taking part in her routine even though she hardly seemed to be present mentally at all. She legitimately shot herself twenty meters into the air and sailed back to the ground in a cloud of pink blossom and didn't even crack a smile. It was fucked up.

I sighed as I watched her, my attention moving to Darius who was looking her way too as I'd been sure he would be. It had taken me a little while to get over her, but when I saw the way he looked at her and felt his grief over what was happening to her, it was easy to see that me and Tory had never been in the stars. It had been good while it lasted and I didn't regret any of it, but it had just run its course and I was okay with that now. I'd moved on. Just not physically. But as Rosalie Oscura looked up at me and licked her lips, I found myself thinking that was about to change.

The whistle blew and while I was distracted by Rosalie's mouth, I failed to spot the lump of clay she sent flying at my stomach and I was knocked on my ass by her for a second time. She leapt over me with a howl of triumph, snatching the heavy Earthball that had just shot from our hole and took off with it across the pitch.

"Get your head out of your cockles, Caleb Altair!" Geraldine scolded as she threw her arms out, casting a ripple of earth magic through the ground and managing to knock Rosalie off course so she was forced to turn away from the Pit.

I cursed as I got to my feet, ignoring Max as he yelled at me to buck the fuck up and flipping off Seth as I caught him laughing too. *Yeah, yeah, I let the sexy Wolf distract me, big fucking deal.*

I raced up the pitch, chasing after the Wolf girl as she ran with wild laughter tumbling from her lips before throwing the ball to her team's Fireside.

Darius leapt into his path, an explosion of fire cutting him off and sending the poor guy racing towards Max who flattened him like a steam train. Max tossed the ball to Seth who howled as he ran for the Pit with Rosalie charging behind him with her teeth set in a snarl.

The girl was damn tenacious and she wasn't afraid of throwing a brutal blow either. Stones burst from the ground all around Seth and she shot them at him as he shielded himself with air, making them all ping off in every direction and keeping the rest of us back as the deadly missiles came our way.

The rest of the Aurora team seemed to be in on her play and they charged at us, keeping us back as Rosalie focused on Seth.

He raced on but she threw even more earth up ahead of him, splattering his shield with mud so that he couldn't see out of it and I cursed as he was forced to drop it. The moment he did, Rosalie slammed into him, tackling him and wrenching the ball from his grip.

He grabbed her leg as she tried to run with it, tripping her, but the moment she hit the ground, she sank beneath it, disappearing altogether.

Seth cursed as he stood and we all looked around to see where she'd emerge as the time ticked down on the golden board hanging overhead.

An eruption of earth from the ground sent us all running to the left of the pitch but a moment later I realised that it hadn't been caused by Rosalie and their Earthbacker had created the distraction.

She leapt out of the dirt to the right of the Pit and tossed the ball home with five seconds to spare on the round, ending the game with a scream of cheers from the Aurora Academy students that rivalled the screams the Zodiac crowd made at our win. It had been one of the closest run matches we'd had in a while though and that was a lot to do with the beautiful Team Captain who was currently being swarmed by a crowd of Werewolves who were racing out of the Aurora crowd to congratulate her.

Seth slapped my ass before he jumped on my back and yelled at me to take him for a victory lap. I laughed as I shot into motion, showing off my Vampire speed now that the game was over and doing four circuits of the pitch so fast that everything around us was a blur.

Seth had to hold onto me with a death grip to stop himself from falling off and I smirked as I sped us towards the rest of the team who were all celebrating in a dog pile beside the Pit.

I caught Darcy's gaze as she grinned widely and I smiled back at her, ruffling her muddy blue hair and just feeling glad that she was able to experience this little moment of happiness even if I knew it wouldn't last.

We all clambered to our feet and I slung my arms around Darius's neck, slapping a kiss on his cheek as he gave me that tight smile which I knew was bullshit.

"Afterparty?" Seth asked hopefully, looking between everyone but Max just shrugged.

"We aren't allowed to socialise with anyone outside of our Order, remember? So if we do it'll be a party for six at the Hollow as usual," he said. "I'm surprised we're even allowed to continue Pitball, but if Lionel took that away there'd be a fucking riot."

"Damn that scoundrel and his preposterous laws," Geraldine growled, the Cerberus in her showing as she bared her teeth. "I have a mind to spend the night dallying with a different Order just to defy him!"

"Is that so?" Max asked with a hopeful smile that made me laugh.

He was so fucking into her that it was untrue. No doubt he was going to spend the rest of the night trying his hardest to get into her panties again and she'd make him run circles around her while she tossed fish based insults his way. I'd be able to tell if he'd lucked out in the morning either by the irritating as fuck grin on his face or the petulant strop he'd throw. My guess was it was about a fifty/fifty chance either way.

"Well if it's a Wolves only party then I could bring my pack," Rosalie's voice drew my attention as she wove between the members of our team and came to stand before Seth with a flirtatious smile.

"Are you looking for a pack orgy, babe?" he asked, smirking at her as he pushed a hand through his long hair, but his gaze shifted to me and there seemed to be some reluctance in him that I didn't understand.

"No. Pack orgies don't really get me going," she replied. "I'm an Alpha kind of girl, so unless you have another one of those in your pack?"

"Not likely," Seth barked a laugh before slinging an arm around my shoulders. "But Cal here is all Alpha. So if you don't mind breaking the law..." He left that suggestion hanging in the air between us and though I was fairly certain it was supposed to be a joke, the idea of it was actually pretty appealing.

Rosalie smiled as she looked between the two of us, leaning closer conspiratorially. "I don't know if you know it, but my family are kinda notorious criminals," she whispered, her eyes dancing with amusement as I grinned.

"You're asking if we know that the Oscura Clan are a bunch of thugs and murderers?" I teased, not sure why I found that so funny. But I kinda liked the fact that the squeaky clean Heir the papers loved to think I was really hung around with outlaws sometimes.

They might have held their territory in Alestria which was down in the south of the country, but they were notorious enough for me to know plenty about them even if I hadn't been vaguely related to them too. My mom had told me once that leaving cities like that under gang rule actually made sense for the kingdom. The most powerful Fae held the positions of power and kept the others in check without the Councillors - or I guessed King now - having to travel around the entire kingdom to enforce their power. And a little criminal activity was preferable to having to actually face challenges from those kinds of Fae. At the end of the day, Fae like Rosalie's cousin Dante were content to own their corner of the kingdom and not overstep their territory. So long as they knew when to bend the knee to those who held the ultimate power, there was no point in trying to remove them.

"Well, if you've heard of my Clan, then you already know I'm bad news," she said with a shrug. "So I guess the real question is whether or not you two wanna put your money where your mouths are and break the law with me?"

Principal Nova started talking then, her voice projected over the crowd as she called us all up to stand before her so she could announce the player of the match and present the medals to us for winning. Rosalie headed away from us again to re-join her own team and I walked across the pitch to take my position in the line up.

I ended up standing next to Seth and he leaned in close to me, casting a silencing bubble so that our conversation was kept private.

"Are you gonna kiss me again if we have a three way with her, Cal?" he teased, knocking his shoulder against mine and grinning wolfishly.

"Please. You fucking wish I'd kiss you," I teased him. "You bring that shit up so often that I just know you've been fantasising about it."

Seth glanced away from me, half coughing and half laughing as he shrugged. "Yeah, well, I guess my tits aren't big enough for you, so there goes that plan."

"I'm really more of an ass man," I replied, knocking my elbow against his and smirking as he chuckled.

"Well I've got a damn nice ass," he pointed out. "So maybe my luck is in with you after all. What do you say then? Wanna take my key and shoot up to my room to wait for us? Let's see if the pretty Alpha Wolf really can handle two Heirs."

I shrugged, though my dick was already hardening at the mere thought of it. The last time I'd shared a girl it had been really fucking hot and I seriously needed to get laid soon or my cock was going to fall off from lack of use. Not to mention the fact that Rosalie Oscura was fucking gorgeous and I got the impression that she'd be more than up to the task of scratching that itch in both me and Seth.

"So you're gonna sneak me in there like your dirty little secret?" I teased.

"Yeah. Imagine the shame it would bring on my family if they knew I'd philandered with a dirty Vampire," he said with an exaggerated shudder.

"Well I can't argue against the dirty part," I muttered, glancing at him with a smirk.

"By the stars, don't bullshit me right now, Cal, because the idea of this actually happening is getting me all kinds of hard and if you're just winding me up I don't think I can take it," Seth groaned and I chuckled as my gaze instantly tracked down to his crotch. Sure enough I could see his cock bulging through his pants and my pulse spiked as I let my gaze linger there.

When I looked back up at him, I found his gaze had fallen to the swell in my pants too and I snorted a laugh. "Did we just check each other's dicks out?"

Seth's earthy brown gaze snapped back up to meet mine and he grinned like a predator. "This is fucking on, isn't it?"

At that moment Nova stepped in front of me and placed a medal around my neck and I was forced to disband the silencing bubble as I thanked her and tried to will my hard on away. But the fucker was here to stay and as I looked down the row of players to seek out Rosalie's pretty face, my fangs snapped out too. Yeah, this was fucking on.

The crowd all cheered as Rosalie was awarded player of the match and everyone moved towards the crowd to accept their congratulations.

I caught Seth's arm as he made a move to walk away and leaned close to speak in his ear. "Where's your key then?" I asked, his bicep flexing in my grip as he gave me a heated look.

"Shit, this is going to be even better than that time when I was on the moon and I stuck my dick in that crater," he murmured. "It's in the bottom of my bag. Make sure no one sees your Vampire ass sneaking in or the shame it will bring on me will make me die."

"Please. As if I'd be seen dead sneaking in to fuck a pair of dirty Wolves," I joked, running my tongue over my fangs before forcing myself to release him and shooting away.

Fuck, I was thirsty. The match had made my magic reserves dwindle down to almost nothing and I needed the taste of blood on my tongue, but I was going to give my cock priority tonight. The poor thing had been left on the side lines for fucking months and it was time he got some front row action.

I shot into the changing rooms before anyone else could manage it, grabbed Seth's bag and found his key lurking between some socks at the bottom of it before tossing my own bag over my shoulder and zipping back out of the room again.

I spotted my little brother hanging out at the edge of the stands, waiting to congratulate me and forced myself to stop and talk to him even though I seriously wanted to get the fuck out of here. But it would take Seth and Rosalie a lot longer to walk back to Aer Tower than me anyway, so I guessed I had the time to not be a dick to my kid brother.

"Hey Hadley, did you enjoy the game?" I asked him, tossing a grin at the group of girls who were grouped around him and ignoring the gasps and squeals of excitement that came from them as I gave him my full attention.

He knew as well as I did that these fangirl types were mainly here because of our surname and their dream to suck on some powerful cock. No doubt he was making full use of them while keeping his emotions firmly out of the equation. But fangirl pussy lost its appeal pretty fast in my opinion and I'd found myself wanting something more than that since I'd ended things with Tory. Which was why I hadn't buried my dick in any of these types since it had happened. And no, I didn't imagine I was about to embark on some great romance with Rosalie Oscura, but at least she had something about her and wasn't just begging for my dick while hoping to claim herself a powerful husband.

"Yeah, man, you did good out there. I saw that Wolf chick put you on your ass though," Hadley teased and I grinned at him.

"What can I say? We still won the match, so I'm not too butt hurt over it. You still making sure you feed regularly?" I asked him, knowing I was sounding like Mom but I'd also more than learned my lesson over letting the bloodlust get too much of a hold on me and I didn't want him to end up hurting anyone the way I had. I still got nightmares about that shit from time to time.

"Yeah..." He trailed off, glancing at the gaggle of girls surrounding us and I frowned as I wound an arm around his shoulder and tugged him along with me.

I made sure my grip on him was tight enough then gave him a sharp tug as I forced him into motion at top speed.

Hadley laughed as he started running at my side and we made it out of the stadium, into the dim light of the setting sun and I released him, turning for the path. "I'll race you to Aer Tower," I called, not giving him the chance to refuse as I shot off into the trees.

Hadley's laughter followed me into the woods as he used his gifts to chase me down and I grinned broadly as we ran together. We'd done this more than once since his Order had been unleashed and I had to admit I was loving having someone who could move at my speed to run with.

We shot through The Wailing Wood at top speed and I charged up the cliffside towards Aer Tower with him right on my heels.

I beat him of course and he cursed me as I came to a halt beside the entrance, leaning my back against the wall and tossing a concealment spell up over us as well as a silencing bubble to hide our presence within the shadows.

"Who are we hiding from?" he asked curiously, panting a little as his eyes glittered with the fun of the game.

"I'm here to hang out with a few Wolves, so naturally I have to cover it up," I replied, rolling my eyes at the absurdity of that new rule and he sighed as he nodded in understanding. "Anyway. We didn't come here to discuss that, I wanna know why you don't seem thrilled about drinking blood when it's pretty much the best fucking thing in the world."

"I dunno how to explain it. But it's like, all these girls keep letting me bite them and it seems like I should be loving that, but something about it just leaves me wanting, even when my power reserves are fully topped up." Hadley shrugged and I grinned, knowing exactly what the problem was.

"Yeah, blood whores aren't much fun," I teased. "Especially low powered ones. What you need to do is refine your tastes. You gotta pick the most powerful target you can and then overpower them for their blood. You don't want it offered up willingly and you don't want it unless it's good and potent."

"Got any suggestions for who I should be aiming to drink from then?" he asked, seeming intrigued by that idea.

"A Vega," I joked. "But unfortunately for you, there's no chance of you overpowering one of them now. So I'd have to say one of the other Heirs' siblings. I mean, if you wanna go top shelf that is. Or someone with power as close to matching yours as possible if you can't overpower them - or if they get too pissy about it and you wanna maintain your friendship more than you wanna taste their sweet blood."

"Like Athena?" Hadley suggested, his eyes sparkling as he spoke about Seth's younger sister and I laughed.

"Yeah. Capella blood tastes seriously good. But if she's anything like her brother, you're gonna have a fight on your hands to get your teeth into her. Of course, that's half the fun."

He grinned way too widely at that and I had to wonder if my little brother was crushing on Seth's sister. Probably best not to mention that to Seth though or he might go all protective Alpha over his baby sister and ruin Hadley's chances.

"Alright then. I'll give that a go," he said, smirking at me conspiratorially.

"Sounds like a good plan. Now fuck off and leave me to break the law."

Hadley laughed, giving me a playful shove with his enhanced strength that pulled a growl from my lips before he shot away from me.

I didn't have to wait long for a member of Aer House to open the door to the tower and the moment it swung wide, I ran at full speed in a blur of motion and slipped through it before it could fall shut.

I didn't stop as I raced up the stairs, speeding all the way to Seth's room so fast that no one laid eyes on me before turning the key in the lock and letting myself in.

I glanced around his huge room, smirking at the sight of the bed big enough for ten to sleep in and moving over to the window where I opened the shutters to look out at the full moon hanging low in the sky. If there was one way to turn Wolves on even more than usual then it was by fucking them with the moon watching, and I was more than okay with letting the celestial being watch us. So long as Seth didn't take it as an excuse to start talking about his fucking trip there again.

Seriously, I had half a mind to regret getting him that damn ticket. Aside from the fact that it had put a big fucking smile on his face of course. I couldn't really bring myself to regret that. That said, I was probably going to have to sucker punch him if he brought the moon up one more time this week in my company.

I moved away from the window, grinning like a cocky asshole who knew he was about to get laid as I strode through Seth's room to his en-suite. I tugged off my Pitball uniform as I went and set the shower running so I could wash off the mud and sweat from the game while I waited for him and Rosalie to arrive.

The huge metal showerhead poured down on me like a heated thunderstorm in the open wet room and I stole some of Seth's shower gel to wash with as I stood on the white tiles.

I closed my eyes as I rubbed my hands over my body, inhaling the familiar scent of Seth's wash products as my cock grew hard again while I imagined the things we were going to do as soon as they got here. Which I hoped was going to be really fucking soon because I was already done with waiting.

Before long - and yet still too fucking long as far as I was concerned - the sound of the door opening out in Seth's room reached my ears and Rosalie's throaty laughter filled the air.

"You're not serious?" she purred.

"I swear on all the stars in the sky," Seth replied. "The moon actually spoke to me while I was up there. Like her soul connected with mine."

I groaned internally as I realised he'd just found himself a new poor soul to flood with stories of the fucking moon, though I had to admit that Rosalie didn't sound the least bit bored by the subject.

"I'd give anything in the world to go to the moon," she moaned, her voice all sex which had my hand sliding around the thick length of my cock as I picked up the quickening pace of her heartbeat with my gifted hearing.

"Well, I can't take you to the moon," Seth purred. "But how about me and Cal make you see stars?"

Rosalie laughed again but the sound was cut off a moment later when the two of them appeared in the doorway as Seth pushed her into the bathroom with his mouth against hers.

I watched them hungrily as my heart began to pound and Seth opened his eyes, looking at me over her shoulder as he kissed her and his hands moved down her body.

I stayed under the flow of water as Rosalie broke their kiss and looked at me with a lust filled expression. She was seriously fucking beautiful and I watched hungrily as she pulled her own shirt off before quickly following it with the rest of her clothes, leaving her naked body for me to drool over.

Seth stripped off behind her and the two of them moved into the shower with me, making my pulse race with the anticipation of what we were about to do.

"Come here," I commanded, tugging Rosalie closer and lathering up the sponge again as I began to wash the mud from her body and she moaned with pleasure as my hands explored her flesh.

Seth took the sponge from me, but I didn't stop cleaning her, using the suds on my hands as I palmed her breasts, drawing another moan from her lips that had my cock hardening against her ass in a clear demand. Seth made quick work of cleaning himself then started to help me with her, taking another kiss from her lips as I watched them and I moved my hand between her thighs.

Rosalie moaned as I pushed my fingers inside her, leaning her head back against my shoulder and parting her thighs wider.

"You too, Alpha Wolf," she commanded, taking Seth's wrist and moving his hand down to meet with mine at her core.

I chuckled darkly at the little she-Wolf bossing two of the most powerful Fae in the kingdom around like we were her sex slaves and Seth grinned at me, clearly knowing what I was thinking.

He pushed his fingers inside her alongside mine and there was something so fucking hot about the feeling of his hand against mine while we pleasured her as she moaned and panted for us.

I leaned down to kiss her neck, my fangs brushing along her throat as the scent of her blood called to me and Seth watched us with hooded eyes.

"No biting, Vampiro," Rosalie growled in warning and I groaned as I forced myself to obey.

I had no objections to taking another Fae's blood by force when I wanted it, but the only exception I made to that rule was during sex. If I was fucking someone and they didn't want me biting them then I'd accept it. Even if I ached for blood the way I did right now.

Seth chuckled at my expense then upped the pace of his fingers inside her, urging me to match him as she writhed and panted between us and we worked together to bring her to ruin. Within a few minutes, her pussy clamped down hard around our fingers and she cried out, sagging back against me for a moment while I watched Seth suck on her nipple with a hungry growl.

Rosalie moved out from between us and turned to look at us with mischief glittering in her big brown eyes before pushing the two of us to stand side by side with our backs to the tiles.

"Ora voglio conoscere i tuoi cazzi," she purred and I had no fucking idea what that meant but I was pretty sure the word dicks was in there so I was all for it, especially when she dropped to her knees in front of us.

Her fingers wrapped around the base of my cock and I groaned as she leaned forward to lick the length of my solid shaft before turning and doing the same to Seth's dick beside me.

"Fuuuck," Seth sighed as she said something else in Faetalian which I swear meant she was going to make us both into her bitches, but I had to agree with her when her hot mouth closed around my cock.

I tipped my head back with a groan of pleasure, moving my hand to caress the back of her wet hair as she took me all the way to the back of her throat while pumping Seth's cock in her hand right beside us.

My fangs snapped out and I groaned with the ache to drink blood just as Seth's mouth found my neck and he grazed his teeth across my skin, sending a rush of pleasure coursing down my spine.

I looked at him through hooded eyes as Rosalie slipped my cock from her mouth before taking Seth's instead and using her hand on me.

Seth tipped his head back with a growl of pleasure, exposing his throat to me as he panted under the expert skills of Rosalie's mouth. I couldn't take my eyes off of his pulse as I watched him falling apart for her.

"Stop staring at my carotid and sink your fucking fangs into it already," Seth growled and my heart leapt as I realised he knew exactly what I was aching for and clearly wanted it too.

I didn't need telling twice and I lunged at him, gripping a handful of his dark hair and holding it tight as my fangs sank into his neck. Seth groaned loudly and Rosalie shifted her mouth from his cock to mine again just as the heat of his blood and the deliciously rich power in it flooded through me.

I growled with desire as I tugged Seth closer and his hands slid down my chest as Rosalie continued to switch her mouth between us, our shafts knocking against each other more than once in the transition and the feeling of that somehow only making me harder.

As Rosalie drew Seth's dick to the back of her throat again, his body went rigid and he groaned loudly as he came, the sound of his pleasure making my body tense up with anticipation as I knew it wouldn't take much for me to follow him. But I wasn't ready to end this yet.

I tugged my fangs free of his neck, running my tongue over the puncture wound as I chased the blood that had escaped it and Seth's fingers pushed into my hair as he tugged me closer like he didn't want me to stop.

I pulled away though, reaching down for Rosalie and tugging her to her feet before she could finish me too.

With a shot of motion, I hoisted her off of her feet and ran back into Seth's room before stopping at the foot of his bed and kissing her roughly. The taste of him on her lips had me growling possessively, kissing her deeper and harder, wanting to claim her even more.

Seth followed us into the room, sending a gust of air magic over all of us to dry us off and making Rosalie shiver in my arms as a surprised gasp escaped her lips. I sat back on the bed, turning her so her back was to my chest and both of us were looking at him. Then I pulled her down to sit on my lap as I drove my cock inside her in a purposefully slow move that made her moan loudly.

Seth pushed a hand into his hair, growling in the back of his throat as he watched me fuck her and I couldn't help but get off on the way he was looking at us, my eyes finding his again and again.

He growled louder as we started moving faster and squeezed her breast as my other hand found her clit, the heated look in Seth's eyes as he ran his hand up and down his dick urging me on as she cried out for me, demanding more.

I was thrusting into Rosalie so hard that before long she came all over my cock with a scream that almost had me following her into oblivion and I had to grit my teeth to force myself not to follow. *Not yet.*

She sagged back against me with her chest heaving as she beckoned Seth closer.

"I came here to fuck two Heirs," she teased. "And you're seriously not involved enough for my liking at the moment."

"The girl has a point," I said, my eyes moving to Seth's thick cock which was already hard again from watching us and he shrugged like an asshole.

"Well, if you insist," he said, moving closer. "But to give you the full experience, I really think you're gonna have to take both of us at once. So will you be a good girl and get on all fours for us, little Alpha?"

Rosalie growled in a clear refusal and I laughed darkly before speeding into motion and flipping her on her back on the mattress beside me, holding her wrists above her head so that Seth could move on top of her.

He kissed her and I groaned with longing as I watched her tangle her legs around his waist, wanting to see the moment he drove his cock inside her. There was just something about us both fucking her that I couldn't get enough of and knowing that she had just had me inside her right before taking him was getting me all kinds of turned on. I watched hungrily as Seth pinned her to the mattress, lining himself up to claim her while they kissed filthily.

He thrust in hard and as she cried out, arching her back off of the sheets, I got my wish.

"Fuck her hard, Seth," I growled, my hand finding my cock as I watched the two of them going at it while Seth's powerful body dominated hers and she screamed in pleasure for him.

My gaze hooked on everything about the two of them from the hardness of her nipples to the sweat running down his abs. And best of all the place where their bodies joined as the shaft of his cock drove in and out while I matched the pace of my hand on my own dick to the thrusts of his hips against hers.

Rosalie lunged forward suddenly, rolling them over so that she was on top and she dug her fingernails into Seth's chest to keep him in place beneath her before looking over her shoulder at me expectantly.

"Come on then, Vampiro, let's do this," she challenged and I took my hand from my cock with a filthy grin as I got to my feet and moved behind her.

"Top drawer," Seth growled, pointing to his nightstand.

I shot to it, grabbed the bottle of lube out and was back on the bed straddling Seth's legs on my knees behind Rosalie within less than a second. I slicked my cock and her ass with the strawberry scented lube as she moaned her encouragement and leaned right over Seth to give me the access I was going to need.

Seth slowed the pace of his thrusts inside her as I lined the head of my cock up with her ass and slowly pushed my way in, groaning at the tight fit and closing my eyes to focus on it entirely. I hadn't been lying to Seth earlier - I really was an ass man and the tightness of her body around my dick only made me more sure of the fact.

I leaned forward over her, sandwiching her body between mine and Seth's as I placed my palms flat on the pillows either side of his head and started moving my hips.

Rosalie cried out in pleasure as the two of us quickly found a rhythm together and our thrusts in and out of her fell into sync. I looked down at Seth over her shoulder as I kissed her neck and growled my own pleasure over what we were doing.

It was so fucking hot and exactly what I'd been needing and yet somehow even better than that at the same time.

I could feel the movements of his cock within her and I groaned as she took the two of us with breathy moans of pure pleasure that perfectly mirrored how I was feeling about this.

Rosalie started cursing as her body began to tighten around my cock and I knew I wouldn't be able to hold back from finishing with her again as I started thrusting firmer and deeper, wanting her to come so hard that she saw stars just like Seth had promised.

My gaze met Seth's just as we made her come and I growled a curse as I finished with her, watching pleasure spill through Seth's gaze as he came too and my heart just about leapt out of my chest at how fucking hot that was.

We rode out the wave of ecstasy together then fell in a panting, sweaty heap on the bed while Rosalie muttered something in Faetalian that I couldn't understand but absolutely agreed with. That had been something else.

I didn't even try to move, I just stayed there, letting my eyes fall closed and feeling sleep calling to me as my limbs turned to jelly and I grinned like an idiot.

After what seemed like ages but maybe wasn't really all that long at all, Rosalie got up from her spot between us and I cracked my eyes open to watch her as she moved to stand at the foot of the bed.

"Well, that was fun," she said with a grin, her gaze sliding over me and Seth appreciatively as she casually wandered over to his closet and helped herself to a pair of sweatpants and a shirt.

"Stay," I muttered sleepily, shifting in the bed a little and ending up much closer to Seth. But we'd just fucked a girl together, so I wasn't that worried about being close to him while I was naked, all things considered. "We can do that again in the morning."

"That is a seriously tempting offer, but everyone from Aurora is actually heading back tonight."

"So what? I'll give you some stardust tomorrow," I offered.

"Nah. If I'm lucky my cousin Dante will still be hanging around and he'll fly me back with him," she said with a shrug.

"Dante isn't allowed to fly you about," I said, though I seriously doubted the Storm Dragon gave a shit about the Dragon Guild rules set in place by Lionel.

"Dante is the Dragon born of Wolves, he does whatever the fuck he wants," she growled. "Besides, I'm a Moon Wolf which means I've got all kinds of weird additional gifts."

"I'd love to be a Moon Wolf," Seth sighed. "Me and the moon had such a connection, it seems like I am anyway really. When I was up on the moon-"

"What does being a Moon Wolf have to do with you ducking out on us?" I asked, cutting him off before he could start down that path.

"I see things," she shrugged. "Like connections between Fae. I saw it with Dante and his wife and I've seen it with others too. And as much as I loved being the filling in your dick sandwich - which I seriously did by the way, I'll be getting myself off while thinking about this for years - I also don't wanna be a third wheel."

Rosalie winked at me, gathered up her Pitball uniform, tossed it in an expensive looking bag she stole from Seth's closet then headed for the door.

"See you around, boys," she purred, blowing us a kiss then leaving just like that.

"Do you have a clue what she was talking about?" I asked, turning to look at Seth as he hooked a sheet into his grasp and tugged it up over the two of us.

"Who knows?" he murmured sleepily. "But if you are still horny in the morning, I can suck your dick for you."

A breath of laughter escaped me, but my dick twitched like it didn't hate that idea and I cleared my throat as I looked away for a moment.

"If I stay are you gonna end up spooning me in the night?" I asked, wondering if I should go too, but kinda hating that thought.

"Probably," Seth admitted with an amused snort. "But I want you to stay anyway."

I looked back at him with his recently fucked hair as he gave me the puppy dog eyes and found myself giving in way too easily.

"Alright. I'll stay," I agreed, my pulse picking up as he closed his eyes and shifted closer to me. "But if you end up spooning me then I'm gonna bite you in the morning."

"Sure. What are friends for?" he asked sleepily and I watched him in the moonlight as my gut tightened at his use of that word.

"Yeah," I muttered, frowning to myself as I closed my eyes too. *Friends.*

ORION

CHAPTER TEN

Fuck. My. Life.

I stood in the Magic Compound with my back pressed to the wall that ran down the centre of the huge concrete space. It was fenced in everywhere, all the inmates contained within it as the guards watched from the outside. It was the only place in Darkmore where we were allowed to use our magic, and we only got a couple of hours in here at a time.

I created a sphere of ice in my palm, the relief of using my magic always sullied by the fact that I was stuck in an underground hell for the next twenty five years. *Oh the joy.*

Things weren't all bad I supposed. Now that Darcy had broken the star vow between us, I'd stopped getting into fights twenty four seven. And Gustard was no longer breathing down my neck. I'd also managed to form something of a friendship with Roary Night too. His Shades watched out for me these days and I had to say I liked the guy.

I carved at the ice in my hand, moulding it and shaping it absentmindedly until it was taking the form of a bird. No, not a bird. A Phoenix. *Of course.*

I often dwelled on Darcy, how breath-taking she'd looked when she'd visited, how much I'd wanted to drag her into my arms and beg for her forgiveness. I knew every word of our conversation by heart and regretted at least eighty percent of them. But there was no room for regret in my life anymore. I had to push her away. It had to be like this. Even if I'd tried to apologise, what good would it have done? I didn't want her forgiveness. I didn't deserve it. I never would. So she'd had to come and go. Just like that. A brief encounter which meant more to me than every single day that had passed in this place since. I replayed it, mostly on mute might I add, so I didn't have to listen to the cold detachment of her voice, but the memory of her standing before me in a dress that seemed designed to hook onto my darkest, most fierce desires had me in pieces.

Yeah just keep dwelling on it, asshole, that'll cheer you up.

At least she seemed okay, though I imagined nothing could comfort her over what was going on with her sister. I just wished I could do more.

Roary appeared with a nod before pressing his back to the wall beside me, folding his muscular arms. This was Ethan's turf for the Lunar Brotherhood, while the other side of the wall was ruled mostly by the Oscura Clan. Anyone who wasn't aligned to either gang could move between the two sides relatively ignored though.

"Heads up, Crank's about to blow," Roary warned, nodding to the powerful Vampire who was pretty new to the prison. He'd been losing his shit daily while working on an appeal to get out. But the reason he was here had been splashed through the news. He'd murdered his whole family and buried them with his earth magic fifty feet under in his backyard. *Fucking psycho.*

"He lost his appeal this morning," Roary murmured to me, pressing his back to the wall. "Guy's gonna blow."

Crank was shoving people to the ground and shouting obscenities. The guards were getting antsy beyond the fence and I cursed as Crank cast two wooden blades in his hands, stabbing two Fae in quick succession.

"Hey!" Officer Cain barked from beyond the fence, his taser shooting through the fence at Crank, but the Vampire acted fast, casting a whip of vines to smash it away from him. He dove on a bunch of weaker Fae and started stabbing and stabbing. I stepped forward with a dark growl, raising my hands to try and get the asshole's attention.

"Crank!" I barked.

"Are you crazy?" Roary grabbed my arm, yanking me away but I growled as I shoved him off and I cast a whip of air at Crank's back, sending him smashing to the ground.

Roary swore as Crank leapt to his feet and rounded on us, but I could take this motherfucker on. I damn well wanted to. I had plenty of rage in me I needed an outlet for and the stars were no longer working against me. Why shouldn't I fucking do it?

A spear of wood shot toward me and I twisted my hand to cast my own shield a second too late. Roary tugged me aside and the blade slammed into the wall where my head had been and I sent a barrage of ice shards back at the fucker. He cried out as they sliced into him and a blast of fire tore out around him. Several Fae were set alight, screaming as they tried to run, while others laid charred and burned on the ground. There must have been eight dead already, it was a fucking massacre.

Guards started swarming into the compound and I let Roary drag me away as more Fae fell under Crank's attacks and the guards dove forward to try and immobilise him.

Roary pulled me around to the other side of the wall, shoving me against it with a tut, his dark hair swinging forward over his shoulders.

"What the fuck was that?" he demanded. "You wanna get yourself killed?"

I shoved him off of me, making him stumble back as I snarled. "He was going for the weakest Fae in here."

"How fucking noble of you to want to save them," he laughed. "You wanna stay alive in Darkmore then you need to watch your own back and your allies' backs. That's it."

"I'm not just gonna stand by while people die," I growled.

"It was Fae on Fae," Roary said.

"It was one maniac on a killing spree," I countered. "All I did was turn his attention on me. That's not against Fae law."

"Fae law," he laughed dryly. "The laws don't apply down here. And last I heard, you were convicted for using dark magic against a princess of Solaria. So you've got a moral compass now have you?"

"Shut up." I shoved his shoulders to force him back another step, still hungering for the fight.

"Or did you do it to save her pretty ass and her reputation?" He smirked and I growled at him.

"Shut. Up," I warned.

"Gabriel Nox sent me a letter," he said tauntingly. "It was very enlightening."

"What do you want from me?" I snarled, pushing past him, but he just turned and followed me. "And why the hell is he sending you letters?"

"I dunno, but he had a little note in it which he wanted me to pass on to you." He reached into his pocket and I frowned as my gaze followed it. What the hell was Gabriel playing at?

"Give it here then," I urged.

We turned, pressing our shoulders to the wall as he subtly passed it over, but it slipped between his fingers, fluttering to the ground and I stooped down to pick it up.

"Turdpedo!" someone cried then a heavy splat sounded as something wet hit the wall above me.

Roary yanked me away with a disgusted noise and I stood up with the note in my fist, staring in horror at the honest to the stars *shit* splattered across the wall.

"Oh my, you just missed out on my most spectac-u-lar turd sandwich, boy," Plunger's voice reached me and I turned, finding the grey-haired creep pulling up his pants and I grimaced in disgust. He didn't even wipe. "Must be your lucky day." He turned and walked off and I frowned. Lucky? Maybe he was right. That was two bullets I'd dodged now. And I was pretty sure I would have rather taken the shard of wood to the eye than be hit with Plunger's shit.

"What does the note say?" Roary asked like he hadn't read it and as I skimmed my thumb over it, I felt a magic seal breaking on the surface that meant he was telling the truth.

Most of the guards had run to subdue Crank and help the wounded so no one was watching as I unfolded it and read the message.

You're welcome. My vision showed that turd hitting you right in the mouth,

Orio. Call me your fairy starmother today, because Jupiter is in your chart

and you're about to get real lucky. Follow my list below to the letter. Do

NOT deviate from it.

Love, Noxy.

P.S. You have two seconds before a guard looks your way.

I glanced up, my heart beating wildly as I stuffed the note in my pocket just as Officer Lucius walked into view and gazed over at me and Roary with interest.

"What's it say?" Roary whispered.

"It says you're a nosy fucker," I said with a smirk and he smirked back.

"Alright, keep your secrets, you shady asshole," he laughed, pressing his tongue into his cheek.

The bell chimed, ending the session and I filed out of the compound with everyone else, avoiding the bloody patches on the ground as I went, the bodies already moved and the wounded long gone. I guessed working in Darkmore meant the guards were used to cleaning up a murder scene pretty fast and pretty fucking often too.

My heart beat harder as I made my way out of the yard and we were sent upstairs for dinner. I slipped my hand into my pocket as I kept to the centre of the crowd, reading through the to do list Gabriel had written out for me. Not that any of it made any fucking sense. But I trusted him implicitly, so I was going to make sure I did every damn one of these things, but fuck knew why. Maybe it was so I didn't end up in a body bag at the end of the day. *Comforting.*

I reread the first item on the list.

Let the Wolves include you.

I headed into the Mess Hall and queued up among a group of Lunar Werewolves who were licking and grooming one another while I gave them a deadpan look as they got in my way, hands occasionally stroking me by 'accident' and some going for my star damned dick. *Is this what you want Gabriel? For me to be dragged into a damn Werewolf orgy?*

A hand suddenly groped my ass and I twisted around, finding Ethan Shadowbrook there. He barked a laugh, slinging an arm over my shoulders. I fought my instincts to shove him away and swallowed the growl in my throat as I heeded Gabriel's words.

I swear to the stars, Noxy, if this ends with Ethan Shadowbrook taking me back to his lair and trying to have his way with me, I'll kill you.

"Hey big boy, having fun with my pack?" He flashed his pearly white teeth at me as some of his Wolves brushed past me and started caressing him. He kissed them intermittently, seeming to forget I was there, but keeping an arm locked around my shoulders.

Don't lose your shit.

I hated being tactile with anyone. Anyone except Darcy. Alright, and Darius. Apparently I only liked the D.

Ethan broke a kiss with a tall girl and turned to me again with a crooked smile. "This is fun, wanna make it more fun tonight in the library? Say, eight o'clock?" he offered and I bit my tongue on a fuck no, instead forcing myself to nod.

"Alright," I grunted and Ethan's eyebrows flew up.

"Really?" he asked and his pack started bounding around me, yapping excitedly and motherfucking hugging me. One guy reached for my junk and I caught his wrist at the last second, quickly hitching on a grin to cover my scowl.

"Later," I growled. *This had better be what Gabriel fucking meant.*

Ethan gave me an appraising look, sucking on his lower lip for a second before sweeping past me down the line with his pack, overtaking a bunch of other inmates as they cut to the front of the queue. I blew out a breath, running a hand down the back of my neck before checking the next item on Gabriel's list.

Use the sink at the far end and take what's left.

I frowned, tucking it back into my pocket, figuring that wasn't relevant just yet when I suddenly got the urge to pee. *Fucking Noxy.*

I left the queue, heading out the door and a bunch of guards gave me surly looks as I walked to the bathroom on the next floor down. I slipped through the door, using the urinal before heading to the sink at the far end like Gabriel had said.

Plunger strode in, walking right up to the sink next to mine and proceeded to take his jumpsuit off casual as anything, revealing his hairy grey chest and throwing me a dirty smile.

I wrinkled my nose, ignoring him but saw him drop his underwear in my periphery. *By the fucking sun.*

He propped one leg up on the sink and started trimming away at his pubes with a pair scissors he'd gotten from fuck knew where.

"Yeah, that's the business. Ooh hello my pretty, aren't you a curly silver treasure?" he purred.

Nope I'm out.

I was about to leave when I remembered Gabriel's message and cursed as I forced myself to remain there, taking my time over washing my hands. *This. Is. Hell.*

"Mmm yeah, clippity clip my sweetness. Got to keep you tidy for tonight's activit-ais."

The sound of boots pounding into the room came this way and I looked up as Officer Cain strode in with a furious expression as he spotted Plunger standing there with his cock in hand.

"Twenty-Four!" he bellowed furiously and Plunger knocked the little pair of scissors into my sink, the soapy water hiding them from view. "Get fucking walking. You're going to the hole this time, I've had enough of this shit." He shot forward with his Vampire speed, grabbing his arm and Plunger threw himself against him, rubbing his ass against his crotch.

"Oh my, Officer, do be careful with me!"

"Get your fucking clothes on." Cain shoved him away in disgust and Plunger tugged on his jumpsuit, leaving his dirty underpants on the floor as Cain dragged him away.

I looked down at the water concealing the scissors and cursed the stars. And Gabriel a bit too. *Fucking pube scissors, Noxy??*

I washed them off thoroughly as hell then pocketed them before checking the next item on the list.

Tell the Incubus he looks like shit. You'll know when.

Great, that's gonna go down like a treat.

I walked back upstairs for dinner and grabbed some food, sitting alone while I killed the hour. At five to eight, the Lunar Wolf pack got up and all started howling excitedly as they headed off in the direction of the library, a bunch of them shooting me hungry looks.

I checked the final items on the list for any sign that Gabriel was shitting me about this orgy. *Are you sure you planned for this, Noxy?*

Guess I had to trust his ass though. So I pushed out of my seat and headed to the door, my gaze snagging on Sin who cornered Poltergeist against the wall. "You owe me three tokens for the commissary, ghost man," he growled. "Pay up."

Poltergeist shook his head in a panic. "I – I don't have them. But if I can just have a bit longer I'll-"

"You'll what? Poop them out? I don't have time for your intestines to produce the goods. I've got a need for chocolate that won't quit. And if I don't get chocolate, I get hangry, and you don't want me to get hangry do you, ghost man?"

"N-no. Please, just a little longer," Poltergeist begged and I slowed my pace, taking a breath.

Well this seems like the perfect time to be an asshole.

"You look like shit today, Sin," I called and he swung around like I'd hit him with a baseball bat.

"Come the fuck again, pretty fangs?" he growled.

"You look like shit," I deadpanned, shrugging and he lunged at me with a holler, throwing a fist that I ducked. But he came at me like a savage once more, twisting around behind me and leaping onto my back. His teeth sank into my shoulder and I snarled as I flipped him over so he hit the ground beneath me with a thwack.

"I can bite too, honey pie," he said through bloody teeth, his eyes wild. "I'll bite deep and make you hurt so bad you'll scream for your momma."

"Unlikely." I glanced over my shoulder, spotting Poltergeist high-tailing it out the door. I checked my list as Sin scrambled to his feet.

Take it like a Fae.

I prayed those words didn't have anything to do with the pack orgy Gabriel had set me up for, but then Sin's fist slammed into my face and I stumbled back, tasting blood. He laughed wildly then slapped me on the shoulder as I cursed.

"Have a good evening, bestie." He sauntered off as I rubbed my jaw, stretching it out. *Bestie?*

I headed out the door and made my way down to the library, stepping through the frosted doors. The sound of Ethan's pack howling, groaning and gasping carried from the back of the room and I guessed they'd made a start without me. I read the final item on the list as I turned down an aisle, wondering what the hell Gabriel expected to achieve by all this.

Shoelaces.

I looked up as I tucked the list away, my eyes falling to Gustard who was with some of his gang, all of them crowding around someone further down the aisle. I scowled as I realised they were shoving Poltergeist between them and laughing.

"Does picking on an old man make you feel strong, assholes?" I asked.

Gustard turned his head, sneering then striding toward me as his little gang of shits immediately jumped up at his back.

"Not that it's your business, but something precious has been stolen from me. A blade of fortune grass," Gustard purred, my gaze travelling over the spider tattoo on the side of his face. He smoothed down his immaculate jumpsuit, regarding me as I gave him an icy look.

"I d-don't have it," Poltergeist stammered.

"There you go, he doesn't have it. So I'm sure you fine, upstanding Fae will let him go now," I said dryly then moved to step past Gustard, but a big dude with a large gut pressed a hand to my chest to stop me. His uniform marked him as a Minotaur and his cowish face confirmed it as he snorted angrily.

"Get your hand off of me," I demanded calmly, my skin prickling under his touch.

"Or what?" he laughed, the rest of the group swarming around, closing in on me on all sides while a big girl with buck teeth held onto Poltergeist.

My jaw tightened as I glared at Gustard, ignoring his pets. "I challenge you to fight me like Fae."

Gustard laughed and the rest of his crew did the same. "Do you hear that boys? The big bad Vampire wants to fight me like Fae." He moved forward, smiling at me cruelly. "We're not Fae anymore though. Didn't you get the memo? We're animals. And animals do what they have to to survive."

"What do you want?" I snapped.

"Well some little thief has stolen my fortune grass and come to think of it, you seem just the type of sneak who would do it," Gustard growled.

"I don't have shit," I said dismissively.

The Minotaur pulled my arms behind my back and a Lion Shifter moved forward to pat me down. I huffed out a breath impatiently then my heart lurched as the Lion pulled the pair of pube scissors out of my pocket, waving them victoriously.

"Carrying weapons are we, Vampire?" Gustard sneered, then nodded to the Minotaur who locked me in a choke hold as another two assholes lunged forward to keep me still. "Teach him a lesson, Angus."

My heart leapt as the Lion jumped up and down with the scissors, eyeing my face greedily. My gaze dropped to his feet, his shoelaces hanging open and I guessed Noxy really was saving my ass today. The Lion lunged toward me and I stamped down on his laces, making him fly at me with a yelp of surprise. His aim was thrown off and the Minotaur screamed, releasing me and knocking the others flying as I stumbled away. I darted through a gap in their ranks, glancing back to see the Minotaur falling to his knees, grasping at the scissors sticking out of his throat.

Gustard took his leave, jogging away from the carnage as a guard shouted out and came running over to see what had happened.

I grabbed Poltergeist's arm as he stood stock still staring at the chaos and I dragged him down the next aisle, putting as much distance between us and that bleeding Minotaur as possible.

We rounded into a dark aisle in the far right corner of the library and Poltergeist wheezed as he caught his breath. "Thank you," he said heavily.

"It's nothing," I said, waving him off but he clutched my arm, tugging to make me look down at him.

"I wasn't sure if I could trust you," he whispered in a rush, his yellowy eyes flicking back and forth between mine. "I have so many enemies."

I frowned at the guy, figuring he was paranoid or some shit but then he rolled up his sleeve and showed me the faded mark of the Virgo star sign on the crook of his elbow.

"You're Guardian bonded?" I asked in surprise. "To who?"

"My Ward is dead," he breathed, leaning closer, the small man having to tip toe to speak in my ear. "I once served Kraveen Dire, a friend of your father's. I knew Azriel Orion well."

My throat tightened as shock jarred through me.

"I met you once, when you were just a boy. That was long before I ended up in here for breaking my eternal vow," he went on in a ramble.

"What vow?" I asked in confusion.

"I had to be here, it was my fate. I was a royal guard so I stole from the king, breaking my vow to the royals. My betrayal landed me here." He moved closer, his eyes wild. "I wanted to trust you the first moment you stepped into the prison, but there are so many rumours circling, that you are Guardian bonded to an Acrux. And one must never trust an Acrux."

"Darius is different to his father," I said protectively and Poltergeist's eyes widened. I went on before he could try and question me on that, "What's your real name?"

His eyes flitted left and right. "Jasper Lumien. Listen," he said urgently, his grip tightening on my arm. "Before Kraveen died, your father came to him with a very important message from the Queen to say the wheels of fate were in motion and there was nothing she could do to stop it."

"What?" I blurted and he hushed me, drawing me further down the dark aisle. "Queen Vega?"

He nodded intently. "We were the last, you see?"

"The last of what?" I frowned.

He wet his lips, his voice dropping to nothing but a breath. "The Zodiac Guild."

"You're a member?" I asked in surprise and he nodded again, lifting his thumb to his mouth and biting down until blood was drawn. I frowned as he smeared the drop of blood along the inside of his forearm and my heart stuttered as a sword appeared along the length of it, seeming to shimmer up from beneath his skin, each constellation etched into its surface. I'd seen the symbol before and the breath was crushed out of me as I realised what this meant. My dad had been one of them. The elite society created to serve and protect the royals.

"One of the last tasks set to us by King Vega was to protect the Imperial Star," Jasper whispered.

I grabbed onto him, pulling him closer as desperation filled me. "Where is it? Where is the Imperial Star?" I demanded.

He shook his head fiercely. "I don't know. I wasn't its keeper. Our Guild Master Ling Astrum was given it by the King. The Queen had instructed him to entrust it to our Guild brother, Kraveen Dire, if anything were to happen to them. Kraveen held the Imperial Star for some years, but when he died, it was sent to your father."

"But he's dead now too," I said, shaking my head. "And all I have left of him is his diary. But I can't read it, it's locked by powerful magic and I don't know the word which will open it."

"I think I do," he whispered and my heart thundered against my ribs.

"How?" I growled, my breathing growing frantic. The answer could be so close, if this guy knew how to give me that passcode then the Imperial Star could be in the hands of Darius and Darcy by nightfall. *"Tell me."*

"When Astrum first came to us with the Imperial Star, we bound ourselves," he rasped. "All four of us made a promise. Queen Vega foresaw a terrible fate, that the world would fall under the rule of a fierce and cruel Acrux and there was no other path, no possible way to change it. Solaria would descend into chaos, the Orders would be divided, those of weaker power eradicated in time. Every Fae would be watched and controlled. Our children and our children's children would die if they ever fought back."

"Get to the point, Jasper," I snarled and he nodded quickly.

"We consulted with the stars and the shadows alike," he breathed. "And one answer came to us. The single path, the only hope."

"Which was?" I pushed.

"The Vega Twins. If they could be saved and the Imperial Star could be returned to them, there was a chance that they might succeed against the monster who sought to take their throne," he whispered. "But the price was high," he half choked out. "The King and Queen would fall, and the last of the Zodiac Guild had to give their lives for a new prophesy to arise."

His hand trembled around my arm, but his eyes were full of hope.

"Tell me what I have to do," I begged, certain he held all the answers we'd been looking for for months.

"I'm afraid this is the end of my journey," he whispered, smiling strangely at me. "As one can vow on the stars, one can also vow on the shadows. Kraveen, your father and I did just that. A promise to die."

"What are you talking about? Please, you need to tell me everything you know, you must have some idea where the Imperial Star could be hidden," I demanded, but he shook his head, still smiling that strange smile.

"The stars showed us each our true paths, the last steps they wanted us each to take before their debt must be paid. My task led me here to Darkmore to wait for Azriel's son, to tell him everything so long as he was pure of heart. And now I know that you are, I am left with my final duty to the Guild."

The hairs on the back of my neck stood to attention as an intense energy seemed to surround us. It felt as though the stars themselves were turning their gaze to watch us and my lungs started to labour.

"The stars whispered a single word to me, a word I have held in me all these years, waiting for you. And now I know why," Jasper breathed.

I swallowed what felt like a razor blade in my throat, clinging onto this guy who could change everything.

"What's the word?" I demanded, hunting his eyes as if I could read it from them.

He leaned closer again, whispering it to me in a slow and measured breath. "Ankaa."

My lips parted as I recognised that word. "That's-"

"The brightest star in the Phoenix constellation," he answered for me, smiling even wider. He pressed a hand to my cheek, his eyes brimming with tears. "You look like him, dear boy. It is good to see one last familiar face."

He groaned suddenly and the scent of blood hit my senses though my Vampire was locked down deep inside me. I gasped as he stumbled away, a shank held in his grip as he stabbed at his gut again and again.

"Stop!" I cried, lurching forward to grab him as he started to fall. I caught him before he hit the ground, but he didn't seem to see me, his eyes looking somewhere through me and his lips parting like he was gazing at something beautiful beyond me.

"Wait!" I begged, then turned my head. "Help! I need a guard! Someone help!"

Jasper fell still in my arms and I stared at his peaceful expression in disbelief as the sound of footsteps came from both ends of the aisle.

I was pulled away from him and I fell back on my ass, staring at Jasper as my mind reeled from all he'd told me.

There was one thing that kept ringing in my head like a bell chiming on repeat. I had the password to open the diary, I was certain of it. My father had known this moment would come. And now his secrets were just waiting for me to discover. It didn't matter that Jasper didn't know where the Imperial Star was, because my father surely had.

After a round of Cyclops interrogation, it was confirmed that I had nothing to do with Jasper's death. And thanks to the guards leaving me in isolation all night while they waited for the Cyclops to arrive at the prison for his shift the next morning, I'd had time to train my mind and hide away the secrets I didn't want him to see.

As I was escorted back to my cell, excitement and anticipation laced my veins. The second I was locked up, I hung a sheet over the bars and moved to my bed, grabbing the diary out from where I'd stashed it in a slim hole cut into the mattress.

I sat on my bunk, flipping open the book and taking a deep breath, my heart thudding powerfully in my chest.

"Ankaa," I whispered to the diary and words unfolded before me, spreading across the first page in a hand written note from my father.

> *Dearest Lancelot,*
> *If you are reading this, then the stars have aligned and fate has given the world a chance. I bound this book with a word I saw spoken to you in a vision gifted to me from Merissa Vega. The Queen has seen the path that will lead you to the truth. And it lies within this diary.*

Firstly, I want to apologise to you, my boy. I never wanted to leave you and Clara behind. If there was any other choice in it, I would have taken it. But my death will buy a chance for the world and the kingdom I love so dearly. Merissa gave me a glimpse of the life you have led and I'm sorry for what you have lost, but there is a chance yet for happiness. And that is all I have ever wanted for you and your sister.

When you witnessed my death, I'm afraid it was an illusion meant for your mother to find. When I later discovered that you had seen it, I was heartbroken. But I could not reveal myself to you. For my real death has been planned for years, my boy, and it will have come to pass long before this letter reaches you. My true body will play an important part in your fate, so please forgive me for the pain I caused you.

My heart crushed as I thought of the fire I'd seen him consumed by, believing he was cast to ruin by dark magic. I'd just been a kid and it had seriously fucked me up. How could it not have been real? And what did he mean about his true body being important?

To leave you with your mother troubles me greatly. I've seen what she will become, and it is a sad and unfortunate fact that there is no love lost between us. It pains me to tell you, but our marriage was designed by Lionel Acrux many years ago. Stella was and will always be a close friend of his and I suspect her heart always truly lay with him. But don't pity me, Lance. You and Clara were the true loves of my life, and I regret nothing.

There are many things Merissa was unable to show me of the future, but she offered me these words that she didn't understand herself. 'You are the only one who can save Clara, and you will know how when the time comes.' Whatever fate has befallen her, I know that you will always protect one another and I have faith that you can make it right.

So I entrust my secrets to you and may the stars shine in your favour. The rest of this diary will be unreadable to the disloyal. It is bound by the magic of the Tenebris Lunae and so you may only read it under the light of the full moon. You must destroy this note to keep this secret safe.

I love you, son. And I know you can pass the tests that await you. Wherever I may be, know that I miss you and will be waiting for you beyond the Veil.

A.O.

P.S. Give Lionel Acrux hell for what he has taken from you and what he is yet to take.

I clutched the book harder, my breaths coming unevenly as I flipped through the rest of the pages and cursed as I found them empty. I tore out the note my father had written and read it ten more times before I carried it to the sink, shredded it into tiny pieces and washed it away. The last words of my father. A keen and eternal pain tugged at my chest over his loss. A loss that had never been a magical accident at all. He'd given his life to change fate. He'd offered the Vegas a chance to succeed against Lionel. And I had to make sure I didn't let him down.

But how could I do that when I couldn't even read the diary in my cell? I'd have to sneak it up to the Order Yard once a month, chart the moon cycles... It wasn't going to be easy and I'd have to risk carrying it around with me. And the chances of me being offered time in the yard when the moon was full were low. *Fuck, this is not good.*

"One-Fifty!" Cain shouted beyond my cell and I stood up, folding the diary and stuffing it into my pocket just before he tugged down the sheet covering the bars. He eyed me suspiciously then stepped up to the door and made a radio call to get my cell unlocked.

"Follow me," he growled and I frowned as I stepped out of the cell. It was early as shit; they weren't even taking the count yet.

"What's going on?" I asked.

"Your Dragon friend is here," he said coldly, leading me out of the cell block.

"How is he allowed here outside of visitation?" I balked.

"Special circumstances," he scoffed, glowering at me. Fucking asshole had a serious attitude problem.

"Right, well thanks for making that clear," I said dryly.

He led me up into the visitation corridor but instead of sending me into one of the rooms, he dragged me down to the security door at the end, swiping his keycard against it then scanning his magical signature and taking a retinal scan. My brows lowered as he tugged me through it into a small room where a buzzing, humming magic filled the air. When it stopped, Cain tapped in a code for a thick metal door opposite us and it buzzed loudly as it opened. He guided me outside, nodding to an officer on duty as we passed through the waiting room and over to the elevator where two cameras stared down at us.

"You're taking me up?" I gasped. "What for?"

"Quit talking," he snarled. "Or you can have words with my fucking taser."

He had to make two radio calls and type in another code to get the elevator open. We stepped inside as the doors slid wide and we shot up toward the surface, my heart thumping wildly as I waited to find out what the fuck was going on.

The doors opened again and we stepped out into a large white room, a set of security doors standing just beyond a guard behind a booth.

"Here." Cain shoved me toward the booth and I gazed in at Officer Lyle as he signed a form then pushed it out through a slot for me to sign too.

"It's your lucky day, buddy," he said brightly. "You're getting out of here."

"What?" I gasped, nearly choking on my own damn tongue. "How's that possible?"

How the fuck had Darius pulled it off?

He chuckled, picking up a tray with a ziplock bag of my clothes in it and another with the personal items I'd had on me the day I'd arrived. He pushed them through the slot and jerked his thumb at a door beside his booth. "Head in there to change."

I followed his orders in a daze, stepping through the door and pulling off my prison jumpsuit. There must have been some mistake. How could they just let me go? What had Darius done to buy my freedom?

I started to worry about the consequences of me leaving this place and everything I'd sacrificed to be here. If I left, what would that mean for Darcy? But this surely couldn't be right anyway. People didn't just get released from Darkmore. Not without an appeal at least. *Something is seriously fucking wrong.*

I pulled on the suit I'd worn the day I'd been dragged away from Zodiac and tied on the friendship bracelet Tory had given me. I tucked my wallet into my pocket with my Atlas then hid my dad's diary in the other, my heart drumming out a frantic beat in my chest.

I pushed through the door and lifted my hands up to Cain, showing him the magical cuffs shining on my wrists. "Am I getting these off?"

Cain released a dark laugh, shaking his head at me and dread twisted in my stomach as he tugged me through the security door. He led me outside and fresh air gusted around me, the sun shining down on my face. I tilted my head toward it with a groan of happiness before Cain yanked me around to face a large armoured truck. My heart dropped off a ledge, smashed through three glass roofs and hit the ground with a splat that made it explode.

Lionel Acrux stood there with his arms folded and a dark grin on his face that said I was in a world of fucking trouble. And holy shit did I know it.

My friend Francesca stepped out of the armoured truck in her black FIB jumpsuit, a sharp V forming between her eyes as she looked at me. She moved forward, drawing me away from Cain who headed back inside without another word.

"Lance, you're now under house arrest. It's the King's orders," she breathed, glancing over at Lionel who smirked victoriously.

"I'll ride in the back with him," Lionel announced, opening the door for me and gesturing mockingly for me to get in.

In the pit of my gut, I knew this was worse than staying in Darkmore. My pulse thrashed against my eardrums and I tried to come up with some way to refuse this. But Lionel was the King now, how the fuck was I supposed to get out of this?

Fran gripped my wrist, giving me an intent look that told me to comply before drawing me toward the back of the truck.

I glared at Lionel as I passed him by then climbed inside, dropping into a seat. Lionel followed me in and Fran shut the door for him before moving to drive the vehicle.

"Good morning, Lance," Lionel purred, looking at me like a smug fucking bastard as he cast a silencing bubble around us. "We have a lot to discuss."

"What the fuck do you want?" I spat and he stole the air from my lungs with a wave of his hand.

"I am your King, dare to speak to me that way again and your sister will pay the price for it."

I glowered at him as my lungs began to burn and he continued to hold my life in his grasp, watching me closely as I started to convulse, my eyes rolling back into my head.

He let me breathe again with a casual flick of his wrist and I coughed heavily, choking down a lungful of air as I bit back the curses I wanted to fling at him. I wasn't going to risk him hurting Clara and he knew it. The fucking asshole.

"Now listen to me," Lionel growled, leaning in closer, the scent of expensive cologne and power rolling from him. "You are going to do exactly as I say because I officially own you, Lance Orion. You are *mine*. And if you step a toe out of line you will regret it. You are still a convicted criminal and the entire FIB will come for you if you try to run from me."

I said nothing as my hands balled with rage. All I wanted to do was tear into his throat with my teeth and bleed him dry, but I wouldn't get access to my Order until the suppressant in my veins wore off.

I hated this man, I hated him with the heat of a thousand fucking suns.

"What do you want?" I snarled and he smiled in a way that set me on edge.

"My Seer brought me some interesting information this morning. It seems you are the key to finding the Imperial Star. You have some sort of diary in your possession, yes?"

I gaped at him and I swear I heard the sound of my soul screaming.

"I'll take that as confirmation," he said smugly. "I cannot take it from you as it seems only you can decipher it, but you will work to unveil its secrets and hand them to me. Do you understand?"

Francesca threw a worried look at me over her shoulder even though she couldn't hear what we were saying. But I guessed when the King of Solaria kidnaps you from a maximum security prison, it was unlikely you were heading off on a fun-filled day to the zoo.

"You will agree to this, Lance," he growled, his jade green Dragon peering out of his eyes. "You will swear it on the stars that you will make every effort to find the Imperial Star."

My mouth was too dry, my mind working on overdrive as I tried to figure out a way out of this. He knew about the fucking diary. He was going to lock me up and force me to reveal its secrets to him.

Only...he hadn't explicitly said that. He was asking me to promise to find it. And that was exactly what I intended to do anyway. I might have been a washed up bastard of a professor, but I was still a wily one.

Lionel took a key from his pocket, cocky as anything as he twisted it tauntingly between his fingers. "In return, you will have a house on my property and some semblance of freedom within a shadow ward created by Clara. You will be allowed to see my son regularly and of course, you will have access to your magic and Order twenty-four-seven." He unlocked my cuffs, and magic rushed to my fingertips, the will to fight him nearly overwhelming me. But I couldn't defeat Lionel Acrux, even if it would have been worth it to tear his face off before I went down in a blaze of fire.

Once I got my Order back, I could try and run, but that would only mean the entire FIB would come hunting for me and what were the chances that I could really get out of this truck in one piece anyway? Even if I made it, then what use would I be to anyone? I couldn't be away from Darius for long with the Guardian bond tethering me to him, and Lionel would get his talons into me sooner or later. Besides, it could take a while for the suppressant to wear off and my Order to awaken.

No, the asshole had me cornered.

He offered me his hand, his eyes glittering with victory as I slid my palm into his, my upper lip curling back.

"So we have a deal?" he asked.

"I'll make every effort to find the Imperial Star," I swore and a clap of magic ran between us, binding me to him in this promise. *And I will make every effort to ensure it never falls into your greasy palms, Uncle Lionel.*

DARIUS

CHAPTER ELEVEN

I materialised outside the gates of The Palace of Souls and strode straight forward at a fast pace. The journalists who were camped out there all perked up at the sight of me, scrambling to jump to their feet and intercept me. But I was in no mood to entertain the press tonight and I upped my pace, my chin raised as the guards on the golden gates opened them to admit me.

"Would you like me to call you a carriage, Prince Acrux?" one of them asked and I stumbled a step at that title, wondering what insane parallel universe I'd just fallen into as I shook my head and growled a no at him.

I was already unbuckling my belt and I kicked my shoes off as I prepared to shift. I didn't need to wait around for some damn transport to take me up the ridiculously long drive to the palace itself. I hooked my shirt off single-handedly, and the flash of one of the journalists' cameras went off behind me as they crowded in close to the gates for the strip show.

"If any one of you takes a photograph of my naked ass without my permission then you'll find yourselves out of a job and knee deep in a legal case before you even get home tonight," I snarled, glancing over my shoulder and a flurry of apologies came from them as they all diligently turned away again.

I dropped my jeans into the pile of clothes last and shifted in the blink of an eye.

The moment my enormous feet hit the ground, the cameras all went wild again as they all desperately tried to get a good shot of me in my golden Dragon form. But I wasn't in the mood to pose for them so I let them photograph my scaley ass, grabbed the heap of clothes from the floor into my mouth and took off fast.

I beat my wings hard as I sped towards the palace, the gigantic building dominating the view ahead of me as the countless towers reached up towards the dark clouds above and the moonlight seemed to make the walls gleam.

I didn't know why Father had summoned me back here at such short notice, but I wanted to get it over and done with. We were supposed to be working on our plans to lure Roxy away from the K.U.N.T.s again so that we could dose her with the antidote, and I hated being called away from that. No doubt the others would come up with something without me, but everything that had happened to her was because of my father and I felt responsible for her in a way that pained me.

I dove from the sky outside the huge door which led into the palace, dropping my clothes and shifting back as the guards on the door watched me uneasily. I yanked my jeans back on and kicked my feet back into my boots, but I didn't bother with the shirt, keeping it in my hand as I strode up the steps, my jaw ticking with tension.

Jenkins pulled the door wide before I reached it, bowing as little as he could get away with and murmuring a greeting to me which I ignored. The old fucker didn't even deserve basic pleasantries from me and he wouldn't be getting them.

"Where is he?" I asked, not caring that my boots were tracking mud over the perfectly polished white tiles or that he was eyeing my bare chest with distaste as I strode through the entrance hall.

The palace was familiar to me from the many visits I'd made here over the summer to see Darcy. We'd worked tirelessly to try and burn the shadows from my veins so that I'd be in a position to challenge my father and rescue her sister, but nothing we'd done had worked. Not that that stopped us trying regularly.

"The King is currently occupied in his study," Jenkins replied haughtily. "He asks that you wait for him to-"

I walked away, moving up a flight of stairs and casting slick ice over them to stop the nosey butler from following me as I headed for the study which had once belonged to the Savage King. A bang and a yelp made me grin as I realised Jenkins had tried to follow and fallen.

A door opened before I made it to the study and I smiled as my mom slipped out, her dark hair coiled into some perfect creation as usual and a stunning black evening gown hugging her figure.

"Darius," she cooed, glancing around before moving to embrace me and I smiled as I held her close for a moment. "What are you doing here tonight?"

"I was hoping you might be able to tell me," I replied. "The old motherfucker summoned me. I was just heading to ask him why."

She drew back, her eyes flashing nervously as she glanced down the corridor in the direction of the study.

"He has those *things* in the house," she breathed, her fingers bunching in the skirt of her dress nervously.

"Nymphs?" I asked, my skin prickling at the thought of that.

"Yes. I try to stay out of the way when they're here."

I was filled with the urge to go and find out what he was doing with them, but I hesitated a moment longer, enjoying the small bit of time alone in my mom's company. "How has he been?" I asked her. "Is he leaving you alone?"

"No worse than usual," she replied, painting on a smile which I knew she wore to try and stop me from worrying.

"So, pretty fucking awful then?" I surmised and she just gave me a little shrug.

"He has Clara to occupy him. I'm usually just trotted out for photoshoots and parties. It's a big palace and I can avoid him for the most part."

I sighed heavily, hating that she was living like this, sneaking around and hoping to go unnoticed. It was a lonely, miserable kind of existence and I wished I could just take her away from here so that she could have a life of her own. I guessed making her into a widow would be a good way to achieve that.

"I'd better go and find out why he summoned me," I said, drawing her close again for a moment and she sighed contentedly.

"Is Xavier settling in well?" she murmured as we lingered there for a moment, making up for all the hugs we'd missed out on over the years.

"Yeah," I said, breathing a laugh. "He's got the entire Pegasus herd in a flurry and I don't think he's even noticed. All the mares are trotting about trying to catch his attention while the Dom looks about ready to bust a blood vessel every time he lays his eyes on him. He'll be leading the herd in no time."

A choked sob escaped my mom's lips and I drew back, frowning down at her to find her smiling through her tears.

"Don't mind me," she breathed, waving a hand to dismiss my concerns. "I'm just so relieved that he's finally free to be himself."

"He is," I agreed with a smile, glad to at least have that one thing to be happy for.

Though my heart sank as I considered the girl who had given him that chance. Roxy had forced my father to accept Xavier's Order and had effectively broken the shackles that would no doubt have still been binding him to a life locked up and out of sight if she hadn't. And now she was the one chained to that monster and I couldn't even free her in return.

My mood soured as it always did these days and I placed a kiss on my mom's head before heading towards the study once more.

I cast a silencing bubble as I approached it then felt out ahead of me for the detection spells Father no doubt would have placed along the corridor to sense anyone approaching.

As expected, I found them placed like trip wires across the floor and primed to inform him if anyone walked through them.

With a twist of my fingers, I cast water beneath my feet and raised myself up to float over them, moving along the corridor and stopping outside the door next to his study. He'd have cast a silencing bubble to block the door

147

from the outside, but I knew him well enough to know the best ways around his habits.

I entered the door to the small smoking parlour beside his study and headed inside, crossing the space and moving to the door which connected this room to the one he was in.

I moved to stand beside it, smirking as I slid into the outer edge of his silencing bubble as expected before pressing my ear to the door and casting an amplification spell so that I could hear what was being said inside.

"-go on this way," a woman's harsh voice came. "Our kind have been denied our rightful magic for too long. We swore allegiance to you because you promised that our needs would be met. That we would no longer have to suffer on the edges of society but would have the opportunity to flourish and prosper. And now we are dealing with some rogue Nymph hunters too who are destroying friends of mine whenever they get the opportunity."

"As I have said, Drusilla," my father's crisp tone came next and I could tell his temper was fraying. "What you want is not so easy to give. I have told my kingdom that your kind is under control. If the Nymphs start attacking Fae again then it would undermine my hold over the people. And there have always been hunters of your kind among Fae. You have dealt with them up until now, so I suggest you find a way to deal with them now."

"They're hungry, Daddy," Clara moaned, a pout in her voice. "It hurts me to feel them starve."

"I had assumed you wanted a strong army," a man growled. "Not a bunch of heathens who don't even hold any magic."

Father sighed in frustration and I could picture him pinching the bridge of his nose as he fought a losing battle with his temper. When meetings went badly for him like this, someone usually ended up bloody for it. Maybe that was why he'd summoned me home. He did love to force me to take a kicking after all, using his hold on Roxy to compel my cooperation.

"Perhaps we could come up with something," Stella's voice came next, her tone placating like she was working the peacekeeper angle. "Some outlying town that no one would miss…"

"Ooooh I like that idea!" Clara cried, clapping excitedly.

"Perhaps," Father conceded though I could tell that wasn't an actual agreement. Whatever this was about, he was considering it though. "I'll look into it. But I don't wish to discuss this any further now. See our friends out, Clara."

The man and woman grumbled as they were dismissed, but they went all the same, the sound of the door opening and closing calling to me as Clara began singing happily out in the corridor.

I waited for them to pass the door that led back out there and then eased it open a crack to get a look at them, recognising Drusilla and Alejandro as they muttered irritably and Clara pranced ahead of them like some excitable kid.

The sound of voices drew my attention back to the study as I slipped out into the corridor again and I realised that Father had dropped the silencing bubble.

I moved to stand outside the door, the amplifying spell I'd cast still working so that their words sounded clearly through it.

"I miss you, my beast," Stella purred seductively and I shuddered at the kissing sounds which followed.

"Yes. You make it painfully obvious," Father muttered cruelly, but apparently that rebuke wasn't enough to make her give up.

"Let me have a real taste of you, sire," she breathed. "Let me remind you of how good we were together."

Father sighed as the sound of his fly rolling down came and I scrunched my nose up, taking a step back before he spoke again.

"Have some self-respect, Stella," he growled. "I was fucking your daughter over this desk before you got here and you know it. Desperate doesn't look good on you."

Stella sucked in a shocked breath and the sound of him yanking his fly up again came.

"She can't possibly compare to what we have, Lion," she said, the sound of her crocodile tears starting on the last word. "Besides, you're a king. You can have as many lovers as you please. Why can't we just-"

I decided I wasn't going to overhear anything else that was useful, so I threw the door open and strode inside, pretending I didn't notice my best friend's mother scrambling up off of her knees as I looked into my father's cold eyes.

"You summoned me," I said, my voice dripping with disdain.

"No need for the attitude, boy," he growled. "I only wish to offer you a gift."

"What gift?" I asked sceptically.

"You'll find it in the summerhouse. And don't say I never give you anything."

He flicked a hand dismissively and seeing as I had no desire to linger in his company, I turned and strode from the room, relieved to have been able to keep it so brief.

But as I headed down the long corridors and descended a curving staircase, my heart began to patter with concern over what I was going to find when I made it out to the summerhouse.

When I was growing up, he'd often bought me expensive gifts like cars or motorcycles to reward me for any particularly desirable behaviour. I'd once lost my temper with a bunch of assholes in my school when I was twelve and beaten the crap out of the three of them. The school had called my father to tell him and he'd bought me a million aura speed boat which was currently docked in Skybour Bay. But I hadn't done anything to please him recently that I could think of, so I wasn't sure what I would have waiting for me now.

The summerhouse was to the east of the rear grounds of the palace and my boots thumped heavily down the path which led to the little cottage as I glanced at the white roses which climbed up the walls of it.

When I reached the door, I hesitated for a moment, drawing my magic close in case this was some dumb test then I pushed the door open.

It was dark inside, the open space only lit by a single lamp sitting on a desk in the far corner and I frowned as I stepped inside, not spotting anyone anywhere.

"Hello?" I called, knocking the door closed behind me and feeling like a girl from an old school slasher movie waiting for the psycho to spring from the closet.

I moved further into the dimly lit space, passing a living area with a couple of couches and pausing at the foot of the king-sized bed which was placed against the wall.

A blur of motion caught my attention and I twisted to look towards it a beat before something collided with me and I was sent crashing down onto the bed beneath a hard body, the air driving from my lungs in a whoosh.

The scent of cinnamon filled my nose and I almost swung a punch at the asshole on top of me before his deep laughter had a grin tearing across my face instead and I started laughing too as I wrapped Lance in my arms.

"Holy shit. How?" I demanded, squeezing him tightly as the dull ache in my chest loosened at the feeling of his body against mine. Fuck, I'd missed him.

"The king dick wants me to find the Imperial Star for him. Seems he's got a Seer who knows I'm the key to finding it," he said into my neck and I dragged him further up the bed so that we could lay with our heads on the pillows to talk.

"Vard," I spat. "Father's new pet. Now that he's King, he made that asshole his Royal Seer. He's been using that glass chair in the palace to help him *see* things to strengthen his power."

"Perfect," Orion growled. "Just what we needed – for him to be able to predict us coming for him."

"The stars are against us as always," I agreed on a sigh, but the smile stayed glued to my face as I reached out and brushed my fingers through his dark hair. "Didn't you cut this while you were in there?" I teased and he rolled his eyes.

"I was too caught up pining for you, big boy," he joked in return, his fingers tracing the pattern of the tattoos on my left bicep. It was kinda weird if I gave it too much thought, but the bond demanded we be together as often as possible and after months of surviving on half hour visitation slots, I knew damn well that we'd be glued to each other for a good few days while the magic got its fill.

"Anyway, you didn't let me get to the best bit," Lance went on. "Right before Lionel came and got me out, I managed to figure out how to unlock the diary. My father had left me a note and I really think it's going to lead us to the Imperial Star."

"Seriously?" I asked, my brows going up as hope built in my chest.

"What do we need to do? Is there somewhere we have to go or-"

Lance caught my arm as I made a move to get out of bed and shook his head. "I can't read any more of it until the next full moon," he said, disappointment clear in his voice. "But this is it, Darius. The beginning of the end. I just know it."

"So how are we going to get out of you helping my asshole father?" I asked, scooting forward until my forehead pressed to his and I was surprised when he started laughing. "What?" I demanded, smiling too because it was damn infectious.

"The arrogant motherfucker got me to make an oath to find it," he explained. "But he didn't say a thing about me finding it for *him.*"

I started laughing too and the relief of just feeling something good after so fucking long had my chest swelling with happiness. I knew it wouldn't last, but for right now, we weren't going to talk Vegas or Nymphs or Dragon overlords. I was just going to bathe in his company.

Orion dropped his head back against the pillow, his gaze roaming over my features like he was trying to memorise them and I noticed the movement as he ran his tongue over his teeth.

"Are you thirsty?" I asked and he groaned, nodding slowly.

"But I'm also having trouble keeping my hands off of you right now and I'm concerned that if I bite you we might end up fucking," he joked and I barked another laugh.

"It's probably inevitable after all this time anyway, right?" I carved a hand through my dark hair as he eyed my neck hungrily.

"If only you didn't have that big Dragon dick between your thighs, we could have been perfect," he joked.

"Oh please, we both know you'd be the girl in our relationship," I told him and he rolled his eyes.

"Whatever you say." Lance ran his tongue over his fangs again and I gave him a hard look before tilting my head and offering him my neck.

He held out for all of two seconds before pouncing, grabbing my wrists and slamming them down on the pillows either side of my head as his weight crushed me to the mattress and his fangs slid into my neck.

I growled, caught between my natural desire to assert my dominance and my desire to see him happy.

I mean, we weren't happy. Not really. But I was gonna steal this little bit of joy and hold it tight while I could because him being stuck in that hell had been tearing me apart. And though he clearly wasn't free here, this was a million times better than Darkmore.

Lance finally drew back, smirking down at me with my blood on his lips as he kept me pinned beneath him and I growled as I lunged forward, flipping him off of me and making him into my little spoon as I rolled onto my side.

He struggled a little bit then just gave in because we both knew we needed the contact right now anyway and we were gonna roll with the weirdness like we always did.

"Tell me everything you had to hold back on while I was stuck in that place," he begged, settling in and holding my arm tight around his chest as we ignored the ridiculousness of this and just fucking snuggled.

"Okay. Then you have to tell me about the assholes who hurt you in that place so that I can go in and kill them with my bare hands," I replied.

"Maybe we should focus on your father first?" he suggested with a dark chuckle.

"Fine," I agreed. "But then I'm going down there to kick some ass."

"You're so protective of me, sweetheart," he joked.

"Always, baby," I agreed with a laugh and I held him tighter as I began filling him in on everything I'd had to hold back on when I came to visit him.

Things might still have been pretty fucked up, but now that I had him back again, I had to wonder if the stars might finally be on our side for once.

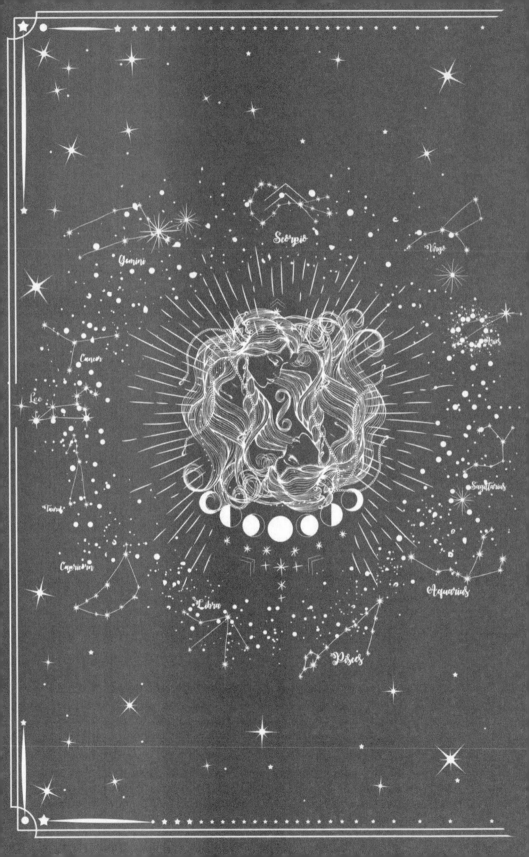

DARCY

CHAPTER TWELVE

I stood in the shower, washing my hair and definitely not thinking about Orion. I wasn't thinking about his dark eyes, or him in that prison jumpsuit and the way his muscles filled it out, the way he'd drank me in like he was a dying animal thirsting for water. Yeah, I definitely wasn't thinking about any of those things as I lathered the soap over my breasts then ran it down my belly, dipping it between my thighs.

A breathy moan escaped me which I tried to swallow because shit, I was not thinking about him and his hard cock sliding in–

"Hey babe!" Seth called, bursting into the bathroom and I screamed in alarm, dropping the soap, stepping on it and sending myself flying as it slid hard under my foot. I caught myself with a gust of air before I bashed my head on the glass and Seth whipped the door open, holding out a towel.

"Get out of here!" I shrieked, snatching the towel, unsure what he'd seen or heard, but none of it was good.

I wrapped the towel around myself as he grinned at me, bouncing up and down like an excitable puppy.

"What the hell, you crazy mutt?" I snapped, raising my hands and casting a storm of air between my fingers.

"I have news," he said excitedly, practically panting as he weaved back and forth in front of me. "I didn't get to talk to you about it before and I've been dying, babe, *dying*."

"So you broke into my room and strolled into my bathroom while the shower was running?" I narrowed my eyes at him and he nodded a little guiltily with a whine.

"Yeah but, it's not like I saw anything. Apart from your ass, and your tits, and that soap you dropped. But I didn't see what you were doing with it."

"I wasn't doing anything with it," I balked, throwing a gust of air at him that forced him to stumble out of the bathroom. I advanced on him, forcing him back again and again as heat rose in my cheeks.

"Sure." He smirked. "On a completely unrelated note, when was the last time you got laid?"

"That's none of your business," I growled, my cheeks growing hot.

"So, Orion?" he guessed with a pitying look.

I snarled, throwing another blast of air at him that launched him onto the bed and he laughed mockingly.

"I can get you laid, just say the word. Do you know how many guys have a crush on you at this academy?" he said, pushing himself upright and making himself comfy against my pillows.

I didn't like how confronting his words suddenly were. I knew there was a reason I hadn't dated anyone else since Orion and I refused to face it. So in favour of not having this conversation, I decided to move it the hell on to something else. *Nope, I am not poking that hornet's nest.*

"What did you come here to tell me?" I asked, moving to the mirror and working to dry my hair with my magic while Seth gave me a grin in the reflection.

"I fucked Caleb," he said and I spun around with a gasp, all of my anger tumbling away.

"What? Seriously?"

"Well, no," he backtracked. "But I did fuck a girl *with* him and there was a lot of eye-fucking between us. Like a *lot*."

It was practically the only good news I'd had in like ever and I was going to lap it up and forget about all the bad crap for a bit. I moved to the bed and knelt on the end of it, smiling at him and soaking in the happiness pouring from him. "Tell me everything."

"So you know that girl Rosalie Oscura from the Aurora Academy team?"

I nodded. "She's cute."

"She's hot. Like fuckable with a capital F. But it was crazy because while she was sucking my cock, I was just looking at Cal, you know?" He bounced on the mattress. "And he bit me, babe. Fucking *bit* me. He was giving me the hungry eyes. It was like Dirty Dancing only instead of Baby in the corner, it was Cal sucking on my neck and fingering my butthole in the corner."

"He did that?" I gasped.

"Well, no," he backtracked again. "But he did do the biting. And then when he was fucking Rosalie and she was screaming like a banshee between us, he looked at me when he came, not her. That has to mean something, right?"

Ohmagod.

"Erm...well did you talk to him about it after?" I asked. "Eye contact isn't exactly a done deal, Seth."

"I know, I know. And no, we didn't talk about it. But he stayed with me in my bed after Rosalie left. And when I woke up in the morning, he didn't even complain about my morning glory digging into his ass or that I licked his face to wake him up. I really considered going down on him to just rip the bandaid off and show him how I feel. Do you think I should have?"

"Um no, that's a bit full on," I said. "You need to speak to him."

"Yeah, I mean I kind of tried to." He hung his head, whining softly. "I mentioned how good it had been seeing his dick driving in and out of Rosalie and I was about to say how much I'd wanted to put his dick in my mouth too, but-"

"You could just try saying, 'hey Caleb, I think you're hot, maybe we could go on a date sometime,'" I said with a laugh. "You don't need to go from nought to blowjob."

"Right...yeah, that makes sense," he said thoughtfully. "I just get so excited."

"It's good you're excited," I said with a grin. "But you kinda need to figure out if he's on the same page as you before you try to suck his dick."

"Okay," he said, nodding seriously.

"So what did you say when you tried to talk to him?" I asked.

"Well, I didn't get far because I started telling him about this time on the moon which I was going to compare to the feeling of my dick against his ass cheeks to when-"

"Was it when you stuck it in that crater?" I pursed my lips and he nodded, giving me an innocent look.

"Yeah, then he punched me in the balls and shot out of the room," he sighed. "It's like he doesn't even like me talking about the moon sometimes."

"Literally no one enjoys that," I said and he laughed like I was joking.

"So anyway, what do I do? Shall I get him a basket full of lube with a message that says 'stick it in me?'"

"No," I said firmly. "Definitely not that."

He jumped up from the bed, starting to pace back and forth, pushing his hand into his hair.

"Is it just about sex or is it more than that?" I asked him and he paused, tipping his head back and howling.

I quickly cast a silencing bubble around us, knowing we weren't supposed to be in here together and not wanting to bring a bunch of K.U.N.Ts down on our heads.

"No, fuck no," he growled. "It's like...when I was on the moon and I could see the earth, I thought about how sad it was that they'd never be together. The moon just watches the earth in all its gorgeous green and blue glory, but it can never, ever touch it. And it made me think of him." He dropped his eyes. "Everything makes me think of him."

My heart tugged and I reached out to catch his hand, making him look at me. "You need to tell him."

He sighed. "It's not that easy." He hung his head. "As Heirs, we're not even really supposed to get with anyone outside of our Orders long term. Plus, like, what would we do about producing Heirs ourselves? I guess we could use a surrogate and then our kids could be brothers and Heirs to both of our seats and that would actually work out just fine, so maybe that's all cool... But regardless of that, if he doesn't feel the same way it could break us. He's my best friend, Darcy. I can't lose him over this."

I frowned, nodding in understanding as I released his hand. "Well, maybe I could try and feel him out for you?"

His eyes lit up and he bobbed on the balls of his feet as he nodded excitedly. "Yes!" He leapt on me, crushing me down onto the bed and I squealed as he licked my face and nuzzled my hair.

"Yes, yes, yes!" he cried, leaning back to grin down at me with his head cocked to one side. "Just keep it subtle."

"I'll be the most subtle, now shut your eyes and get up because I think you just dislodged my towel," I said and he chuckled.

"I've seen it all now, babe. Lucky I've got a new crush. But if he turns me down maybe we can pity fuck each other back to normality?" he suggested like he genuinely meant it.

"In your dreams, Capella." I shoved him back and he jumped up with his eyes shut as I tucked my towel back into place before I got up.

My Atlas buzzed and I swiped it up, hoping to find a message from Darius. He'd gone AWOL all of last night. According to Caleb, Lionel had summoned him home – and by home I meant mine and Tory's goddamn palace – and we hadn't heard from him since. I'd brought a bunch of my stuff back to the academy before Lionel had taken over, but the rest of it was in the Queen's quarters in the palace, and I couldn't see how I'd be getting it back anytime soon.

Seth pressed close behind me as he read the message over my shoulder and I frowned as I realised it was from my brother.

Gabriel:
Meet me beyond the fence. Bring the mutt.
P.S. Delete all correspondence between us from now on.

My heart juddered and I looked to Seth whose brows had arched. Maybe Gabriel was going to give us the antidote for Tory at last. He might have *seen* a chance to inject her with it. He'd been holding the damn thing hostage since our failed attempt, saying he was waiting for the right opportunity, and I was losing my mind with impatience.

"Let's go," I insisted, moving to my closet and taking out some jeans and a sports bra, darting into the bathroom to pull them on. I grabbed a sweater and tied it around my waist before heading to the window.

"Race you there," I said with a smirk.

"Wait," Seth said then stripped out of his clothes, tossing them to me. "Carry these, wench."

"Hey!" I snapped as he howled a laugh, turning and shoving out the door.

I released a laugh as I pushed the window open, leaping out of it and my heart soared before my wings tore from my back in a fiery blaze. Heat rushed through my limbs as I flew across campus, sweeping over The Wailing Wood, the leaves gold and amber on the trees. A white Wolf dove out of the door at the bottom of Aer Tower, knocking a bunch of freshmen on their asses as he bounded along beneath me. He howled to the sky and I echoed the sound, crying it back to him mockingly as I flapped my wings and took the lead, keeping his clothes bundled in my arms. I had half the mind to let them fly to the wind, but I also didn't want to spend the morning with his naked ass.

I landed in a group of trees close to the fence, making sure no one was watching before dissolving my wings and pulling on my sweater as I jogged toward the outer perimeter. I slipped through the secret gap in the fence and Seth's wet nose bumped into the back of my head as he arrived too. He shifted into his Fae form and I tossed his clothes to him, smiling smugly.

"I win," I announced as he pulled them on.

"Try racing me on foot next time," he challenged. "You won't beat me then, little bird."

"I'm good," I said lightly and he shoved me playfully. I shoved him back and the two of us started fighting just as Gabriel popped out of the atmosphere and tossed a handful of stardust into the air. My hand was still locked in Seth's hair when I was dragged into the stars and the air was crushed from my lungs. I gasped at the suddenness of it and took in the whirlpool of endless beauty around me as I was transported across the world.

I landed heavily, losing my grip on Seth's hair and my ass hit the ground, making me huff out a breath.

Seth laughed at me and Gabriel slapped him with his wing as he swept past him and pulled me to my feet.

"How very princessly of you," Seth taunted as I brushed the dirt off my ass.

"I'm the Savage Princess remember?" I lunged at him, but Gabriel looped an arm around my waist and pushed me back with a serious look that made me fall still with worry.

"What is it?" I asked, taking in the group of trees surrounding us, but I didn't recognise this place. "Is it Tory, is she okay? Has something happened?"

"Tory's fine," he said firmly. "Well, if you can call being shadow possessed and Guardian bonded to Lionel Acrux fine, but you know what I mean."

I released a breath of relief. "Can we try to give her the antidote again yet, is it time?"

"No, but soon," he promised and my heart pounded wildly as I clutched his arm. "I've *seen* that we need to trap her to be able to make this work so I'm working on getting us a Nymph cage from some of my friends in Alestria."

"Will that hold her?" I asked.

"Those cages are rare as shit," Seth said. "Who the hell are your friends?"

"Yeah, they're rare, but I can get one. And it'll hold her," Gabriel said, not answering his question. But he'd told me all about the people he knew back home who were gang members and criminals. I was pretty sure he could get his hands on anything if he wanted to.

"So if this isn't about Tory, what is it, Gabriel?" I asked as Seth moved closer with a frown.

"It's Lance," he said and my heart beat even faster, the world seeming to darken around me.

"What's happened?" I demanded, panic flashing through me.

"He's out of prison," he said evenly and my lips parted, no words coming to me as that statement sucker punched me in the gut.

"What do you mean he's out?" I gasped.

"He's not free," he said grimly. "Lionel Acrux has him on house arrest."

I took a steadying breath as I tried to wrap my mind around that. "Why? How? When?"

"Yesterday, and I don't know why yet but I'm sure it isn't good. Darius is with him now. And Lionel has headed into Celestia for a couple of days, so we have some time to go to him. I need to speak with Lance, but I can't do that without your help."

"What do you mean see him? Where?" My mind whirled and Seth whimpered, pressing close against me as he sensed my anxiety over all of this.

"Lance is being held at the palace," Gabriel explained, running a hand through his ebony hair. "I've *seen* a way to get to him, but I need you to come with me. Will you help me?"

I hesitated, still unsure of what this all meant, but I had to help him if he needed me. "Of course. What do I need to do?"

"Follow me," Gabriel said, his wings tumbling away and leaving a single black feather floating down in the breeze behind him. He took his shirt from where it was stuffed in the back of his jeans and pulled it on, covering the artwork of tattoos on his body.

Me and Seth headed after him through the trees, walking down a hill and heading across the gold and orange leaves beneath our feet. Fall was well underway and it wouldn't be long before the lasting kiss of warmth in the air was gone.

The trees grew tighter together until the morning light was blocked out and the shadows between the trunks thickened. We stepped into a hollow where an ancient tree stood at the heart of it, the bark knotted and gnarled, huge roots spreading out beneath it.

There was a symbol etched into the bark of a Hydra and Gabriel took my hand, guiding me toward it. "Place your palm on the mark."

I glanced at him in confusion then reached out and did as he asked, spreading my hand over the rough bark. A tingle of magical energy licked my flesh and the mark suddenly lit up in a white glow.

"There are passages running all beneath the Palace of Souls," Gabriel explained at last. "Only those of royal blood can access them."

"Why can't you open them then?" I asked, stepping back.

"Because your royal blood comes from your father," he said and I nodded, biting my lip as the mark suddenly split apart and the roots rearranged beneath it to form a stairway leading down into the dark.

"Holy shit," Seth breathed. "This is awesome. But why the fuck am I even here?"

I looked to Gabriel for an explanation, but he just smiled like a mysterious bastard and headed down the steps. I'd grown pretty used to Gabriel evading explanations about the things he did, but it was still frustrating sometimes.

I shrugged at Seth and he moved behind me as we followed Gabriel who'd cast a Faelight to see by. As we reached a damp tunnel far below ground, the sound of the roots retreating made me turn back and my heart thudded harder as the ground closed up above us once more, leaving us down here in the dark.

Gabriel directed his floating orb of light toward the wall, pointing out another Hydra symbol there. "You can get out again just as easily."

I nodded, examining the old mark and wondering if my father had once used this passage. Had he stood right here where I was now, with all his plans for the future? Had my mother come here with him? How long had she known they were going to die?

The gifts of a Seer had to be a curse in that way. Surely they'd *see* their death coming long before it ever passed.

We followed Gabriel into the dark, our footsteps the only sound between us as we moved along the narrow passage.

We eventually reached a fork in the path and Gabriel turned right without even hesitating, leading us along until the floor beneath us began to rise.

I tried not to freak out over the fact that at the end of this tunnel was Orion. Which I sort of managed, mostly because I was still processing that shit. I needed to get my game face on because I was wholly unprepared for seeing him again.

"Why would Lionel get him out of prison?" I asked Gabriel.

"You won't like it," he said darkly.

"When do I like anything Lionel does?" I said coldly as worry splintered through my chest.

"Touché," Gabriel said. "Unfortunately, Lionel apparently now has his own Seer. And he's using the Royal Seer's Chamber. Because of him, Lionel now knows about Orion's diary."

"What?" I gasped, horror filling me. "But when you tried to use the chamber during the summer, it wouldn't work for you. How can-"

"Because Vard has been appointed the position by Lionel - who is the King whether we like it or not. And that means the chamber is his to use until you and Tory can dethrone him."

"And this Vard dude is as powerful as you?" I questioned, my gut knotting with anxiety at the thought of that because if that was the case then

I didn't know how we would ever be able to strike at Lionel without him knowing we were coming.

"No fucking way, he's not as powerful as me. But with the use of the chamber, he'll be able to see more than we'd like. Don't worry, I'll make sure that I'm watching everyone carefully though. He won't get around me."

"So has Lionel taken the diary?" Seth asked, his own panic clear. We'd been pinning our hopes on that diary. What were we going to do without it?

"No, it seems it is still in Lance's possession, but I don't know the details. The shadows conceal Lionel's plans to me because he is with Clara so much, but I've *seen* enough to know that we'll be safe to visit Lance and that he may have some answers for us."

"Okay," I said heavily, my gut clenching as this news settled over me. My pulse was thumping so loudly in my ears that it was hard to hear anything else.

We reached a set of stone steps and Gabriel cast a silencing bubble around us as we climbed them. A crack of light appeared around a wooden hatch in the ceiling and as we reached the top of the steps, we had to hunch over beneath the low ceiling. Gabriel and Seth practically had to crouch with how tall they were.

"There, Darcy," Gabriel said, pointing to the Hydra mark engraved on the hatch. I swallowed my nerves, reaching up and pressing my palm to it.

The mark gleamed and a click sounded the hatch unlocking. I pushed it, using my air magic to swing it open. *Well, it's probably best to get this over with sooner rather than later.*

I cast air magic under my feet, propelling myself up into a white kitchenette with blue flowers on the tiles and sunlight streaming in the window. Seth and Gabriel climbed up behind me as I turned toward a large lounge in tones of cream and sandy brown, the whole place gleaming. There were beautiful paintings on the walls of exotic beaches and cliffs and the floor was blue and shimmered like the ocean.

Orion was lying in a huge bed at the far end of the space and Darius was spooning him, the two of them looking freaking serene as they slept. It would have been funny if it wasn't so sad. The damn Guardian bond tying them together had been driving Darius insane these past months. He didn't feel everything the way Orion did as I understood it, but he always pined for him. As I gazed at the two of them, I had the sudden urge to crawl in there and curl up with them. *Yeah, because that would be a totally sane thing to do.*

My gaze tracked over Orion's face and my heart ached with a need it was never going to have fulfilled again. *Lock it down right now.*

Gabriel dissolved the silencing bubble, opening his mouth to wake them, but Seth sprinted across the room, diving on top of them before he could.

Darius roared almost as loud as if he was in his Order form and Orion threw Seth away with the strength of his Order, sending him flying onto the floor with a hard thud. My lips popped open as Seth leapt to his feet again, wheezing as he healed himself then jumping on Darius and starting to lick him.

Orion shot out of bed and his eyes suddenly fell on me, his naked chest heaving. His abs were taut and gleaming and his shoulders were even more built than they'd been before. *Holy shit.*

I forced my eyes up to his face, taking in his beard and unruly hair, not entirely hating the wolverine look, but I did miss his dimple. *Gah.* My heart was fit to bursting as the temperature in the room seemed to rocket up fifty degrees. He darted towards me and Gabriel in a blur and I gasped as he grabbed my hand, tugging me into the arc of his body with his eyes blazing like he was gonna hug me or something crazy. I sent fire magic bursting through my veins and he hissed as I burned his fingers, making him let go of me before I quickly backed up. His brows knitted together and he mumbled something about instincts before he lunged at Gabriel instead, the two of them embracing hard.

"How did you get in here?" Orion demanded.

"The King's passages," Gabriel answered as he released him. "Darcy can open them."

"That's enough," Darius snapped and my eyes flicked over to where he'd pinned Seth to the bed by the throat, Seth's tongue lolling out his mouth as he panted. "No more licks."

He released him and Seth whined in disappointment, but didn't lunge at Darius again as he started wiping the slobber from his face.

Orion folded his arms over his bare chest which I still absolutely wasn't checking out. "So is this some sort of rescue mission because I'm afraid I'm going fucking nowhere." He lifted his wrists and my heart stumbled at the sight of the black rings wrapped around each one like tattoos. "These stop me from going beyond the boundary of shadows Clara has cast around the palace."

I reached out for them on instinct before curling my fingers up and pushing them through my hair instead. *Totally smooth.* He was wearing Tory's friendship bracelet, the leathery vines intertwined together in an intricate design. I wasn't sure how to feel about that. I didn't want to think it was sweet, but dammit I did. Orion's dark eyes lingered on me for a moment, making my heart race as I gave him a cool look in return. *Not that you'll find out how sweet I think it is.*

Gabriel moved to examine the rings on Orion's wrists and I frowned as I realised they were shadows writhing beneath his flesh.

"I knew we couldn't move you from here. But I couldn't *see* why. I can never *see* the damn shadows," Gabriel murmured. "Fuck Lionel."

"Father clearly hasn't thought of everything though," Darius said with a look of determination in his eyes. "You can all get in here."

"What good does that do?" I asked, feeling Orion's gaze on me again which I refused to meet.

I felt like he was trying to examine my very soul, and it was making the hairs on my arms raise. I didn't like him looking at me like that, but a part of me didn't want him to stop either.

"Well I've still got my father's diary. And now I know how to access it," Orion said and I just had to look at him as my heart lifted.

"You do?" I asked.

He nodded. "I can read it under the light of the full moon apparently."

"Which was two days ago so now we've got to wait for another fucking moon cycle," Darius said and Seth punched him in the arm. "What the fuck?"

"Why didn't you text us, asshole. We were worried about you," Seth growled.

"Sorry brother, I left my Atlas back at the academy. And Father let me stay with Orion so I…" He cleared his throat as the two of them shared an awkward look. "We haven't been able to really fulfil the needs of the Guardian bond in a long time."

"Oh, I see. Say no more." Seth winked, strolling casually over to me and slinging his arm around my shoulders. He turned his head, whispering in my ear. "Butt sex."

"*Seth*," I snorted a moment before a freight train collided with us as Orion shoved Seth away from me with a snarl, putting himself between us.

"Woah, what the hell?" I gasped as Orion went full fucking animal, his fangs on show as he glared at Seth in a clear warning to stay away.

Seth gazed back at him with a taunting smirk like he was wholly up to the challenge. But this was not going any further.

I ducked around Orion, shooting him a glare as I moved to stand beside Seth again.

"He's on our side now. Me and him are good," I growled, planting my hands on my hips. "Hasn't Darius explained that to you?"

Orion's pupils were fully dilated, his eyes moving from me to Seth as his jaw worked furiously. "He's explained plenty, but I'm not so quick to forgive," he hissed and my heart galloped faster.

"Trust me, I'm not quick to forgive either," I said icily. "But things have changed with me and Seth. There's a lot that's happened since you've been in prison."

"A *lot*," Seth emphasised.

"I know," Orion snarled, his shoulders tensing and Gabriel moved to stand in front of him and block me and Seth from view.

"Relax, Orio. Sit down. We need to talk about the diary," Gabriel said, gripping his arm tightly and leaning in close to speak in his ear. "Oh and if you ever shove my sister like that again I'll rip one of your arms off." He said it so calmly, but the darkness in his eyes said he'd absolutely do it. *Aw, I love my psycho big brother.*

Orion tsked. "I didn't shove her," he growled then walked over to a drawer beside the bed and took out a leatherbound diary.

"No, you just bowled into me like a stampeding rhino," I said lightly and I swear Orion smirked before he flattened his lips and turned away again.

That small, tiny, infinitesimal sliver of light between us made my stomach flutter and I internally started stamping on every bastard of a butterfly who dared show up for him.

Darius set about casting an illusion spell in front of the windows so it would look like only he and Orion were in here. Lionel may have been away for the weekend, but I wouldn't put it past any of his minions to rat us out if they suspected anything strange going on here.

As I moved through the room, I gazed beyond the floor length windows along the far wall. They looked out onto an L shaped swimming pool and hot tub. I could just make out the palace in the distance and my heart clenched at the thought of Lionel residing in it. It didn't belong to him. It was mine and Tory's and I planned on dragging him out of it as soon as damn possible. Preferably in a body bag.

"Can you go anywhere on the grounds?" I asked Orion.

"Pretty much," he grunted. "Only during the day though. Lionel has guards lock me in here from six pm 'til dawn."

That's gotta be better than Darkmore, right? I moved to sit in a chair, but Seth caught my hand and dragged me down beside him on the couch, nuzzling into my hair. I batted him off absentmindedly, working to focus on the diary and nothing else as my eyes kept skipping over to Orion and the taut muscles of his stomach. I mean seriously, could someone just put a shirt on that man?

You're not distracted by Darius going around all shirtless and shit.

Well he's a tuna sandwich dammit.

Orion started telling us about everything he'd learned from the Guild member he'd met in Darkmore. When he mentioned the password which had revealed a secret message to him in the diary from his father, my mind whirled with all that it meant. Had my mother and his father really foreseen all of this happening? Had they been friends?

"So what does Lionel know exactly?" Gabriel asked, resting his elbows on his knees to the left of me.

"He doesn't know much as far as I can tell," Orion said thoughtfully. "Just that I'm the only one who can read the diary and decipher what's in it."

"How long is he going to keep you here for?" I asked. Was he going to be forced to return to Darkmore once Lionel was done with him? And how were we supposed to stop Lionel getting any information while Orion was stuck here being made to work on the diary? I couldn't help but be relieved that at least he was away from the psychos in Darkmore, but now he was living in a maniac's backyard. It was like being pulled out of a box of acid slugs only to be thrown into a pool of Griffin shit.

"I don't know," he said, levelling me with a hopeless look. My heart clenched. I had the urge to smooth the frown on his brow and tell him we'd find a way to fix this, but it wasn't my place anymore. And he wasn't owed shit from me anyway. "He forced me to make a star vow with him that I'd make every effort to find the Imperial Star. But that's pretty vague so he's left me a lot of wiggle room."

Darius smirked. "My father's so cocky, he'd never even consider the possibility that you might work around his vow."

"Well, that's because he thinks I give a shit about what he'll do to me if he finds out," Orion said dryly and my gut yanked.

"He won't do anything to you," Darius growled, though the silence following his words said we all knew he could make no such promise. And I despised knowing that.

"Have you seen Clara?" Gabriel asked gently and Orion shook his head.

"No," he sighed, then turned to me, his eyes full of sadness. "Is Tory like her?"

"She's not like Clara really, she's just...lost," I said as something inside me shattered.

"I'm sorry," Orion murmured. "Have you made any more progress with figuring out how to rid her of the shadows?"

I shook my head and Darius stood up suddenly.

"Try it now, we missed our session last night," he said, beckoning me up from my seat.

I frowned. I hated hurting him every time I did it wrong, but I knew it was the only way to work it out. "Maybe we should wait until we get back to Zodiac."

"I want to see," Orion said firmly. "Maybe I can help."

"You're not a professor anymore," Seth pointed out super unhelpfully and Orion growled dangerously.

"He knows about dark magic though, idiot." I shoved Seth in the forehead and he grinned at me, looking like he was about to jump up and start a play fight. "Stay," I mocked him like he was a dog, pointing a finger at him and he nipped the end of it with a smirk.

I shook my head at him with a half smile and turned to find Orion standing right behind me, looming over me like a damn tower.

"Come on, show me this shadow shit," he demanded.

"Did you have to come all the way over here to say that?" I muttered, side stepping him and feeling him follow a hair's breadth behind me as I walked over to Darius. Goosebumps rose along the back of my neck and I was glad of my long hair to hide them from the intimidating shadow currently following me. *What was with the stalking??*

I reached for Darius then my eyes snagged on a pile of jewellery, blades, metal objects and coloured stones laying on a table beyond him. "What's all that?"

Orion shared a look with Darius. "Lionel is having his Nymphs bring me all kinds of shit that could be concealing the Imperial Star."

Gabriel started laughing, cracking up and we all turned to him while he tried to pull himself together.

"What's so funny?" Seth asked with a grin.

Gabriel reined it in, shaking his head then his face returned serious. "I can't really say."

"Oh come on," Seth pushed. "You can't do us like that."

Gabriel shook his head. "If I say, it'll change everything."

"So it's good news?" I asked hopefully, but Gabriel said nothing, obviously fighting the urge to laugh again.

"Come on, let's get on with it," Darius said, turning me to face him again and Orion stood beside us, watching closely. *Yep, him just standing there like a big hot Vampire ex-boyfriend is really helping me focus.*

I took a breath, reaching up and resting my hands on Darius's shoulders and letting my eyes fall closed to concentrate. My Phoenix flames burned hotter under my skin as I tried to feel out the shadows living in Darius. He brought them to the edge of his body and they brushed against my flesh like a cold caress. They didn't call to me anymore. There was no way for them to get past my defences. I just wished I could offer the same to those I loved.

My flames rushed out along my arms to meet with the darkness in him, burning it back, but I could only destroy those that coiled outside of his flesh.

"Do it," Darius commanded and I knew he'd cast himself into my flames and be consumed by them if it would help bring Tory back. Because I'd do the very same.

I gritted my teeth and forced myself to do it, pushing my flames into his flesh and urging them to seek out the shadows in him. He hissed between his teeth and my eyes flew open, meeting the deadly gaze of a Dragon as he allowed himself to burn in my power. His skin began to blacken and I groaned as I forced the flames deeper, hating myself for hurting him but knowing I had no other choice.

Orion groaned then suddenly dragged me away from Darius, forcing my arms behind my back and burning himself in my fire as it circled up around me.

"No!" I cried, but he held onto me as he drew me away from Darius and I realised it was his Guardian bond. It wouldn't let him stand by as I hurt his Ward.

Orion clutched me hard against his chest and I quickly extinguished the flames, my heart hammering at the scent of burning flesh. Seth rushed over to Darius, lending him magic to heal fast and I twisted around in Orion's arms, inspecting the damage I'd done to him with frantic hands. My fingers brushed the burns on his chest and arms as I quickly cast healing magic, my breaths coming heavily, matching his. The scent of cinnamon hung around him and I wanted to lean in and drown in it. *Oh god, oh god.*

"Stop," Orion grunted, catching my wrists and I looked up at him, finding his eyes were a sea of pain that I wasn't sure had anything to do with the burns I'd laid on him.

His jaw tightened and he released me, shooting away across the room to stand behind Gabriel on the couch.

I straightened my spine, averting my gaze from him and making sure he didn't see how shaken I was. I was flushed, angry, hurt, turned on, all the emotions that burned. It suddenly struck me that all the times I'd hurt Darius in an attempt to burn the shadows out of him, I'd been hurting Orion too. He felt all of Darius's pain, cursed to feel it and know his Ward was in trouble. But he could never come and help. I couldn't even understand the kind of agony that must have caused him. All this time I'd been torturing him and I hadn't even known. It made me feel sick.

"You can't do it while I'm with you," Orion said with a sigh, but I didn't look at him. I couldn't. If I did right then, he'd see through me to the deep and bloody wound he'd left on my heart that still wasn't healed. "Keep practising at the academy."

"You can record it," Gabriel said to me and Darius, reaching into his pocket for something then tossing Orion an Atlas. "Here, it's got all our numbers in it. No, don't hide it *there*," he said as Orion took one step toward a large blue dresser with little sea animal ornaments on it. "Hide it in the cupboard under the sink."

"Got it," Orion muttered, pocketing it.

I frowned at Darius, silently asking if he was alright and he nodded, but his jaw was tight, clearly frustrated I'd failed once again. As much as I needed to continue trying to destroy the shadows in Darius, I despised the idea of hurting both him and Orion again. But what choice did I have?

I walked over and hugged Darius, thinking of Tory with everything inside me just hurting. It wasn't only him I was letting down, it was her. I just wished I knew what to do.

Seth joined our hug, nuzzling into Darius and whimpering softly. "We'll figure it out," he said, and I wanted to believe that, I really fucking did. I just didn't know what I was doing wrong so I could fix it.

Seth's hand roamed down my back and fell onto my ass, squeezing as he pulled me and Darius closer.

"Er-" I started, but he was suddenly ripped away from me by a whip of air and thrown across the room. He flew over a chair, his foot catching on a vase and sending it crashing into a wall before he hit a window face first.

Gabriel lost his shit as he laughed, this clearly being the exact thing he'd *seen* before.

"What is your problem?" I rounded on Orion with a growl as Seth leapt up and cast two spears of wood in his hands.

"Come on then, asshole," he snarled. "Bring it the fuck on."

"Seth," Darius warned as Orion bared his fangs at the Wolf.

I put myself between them and glared at Orion with my hands raised and shards of ice growing on my palms. "You wanna fight? Then you can have one."

"I'm not fighting you," Orion snarled, trying to side step me so he could aim at Seth, but I moved into his path again.

"If you've got something you want to say, then spit it out," I demanded and Orion's eyes flashed furiously as we just stared at each other.

Silence stretched between us and my breaths came unevenly as I waited for him to spill it. He looked like a predator on the hunt, but I wasn't going to be his prey. Never. Again.

Orion dropped his hands, shaking his head and turning away from me with his shoulders dropping.

Gabriel stood up with a frown, his eyes shooting to the sliding doors that led out toward the pool. "Someone's coming. We have to go."

"Shit," I cursed, running into the kitchenette with Gabriel and Seth.

I glanced back over my shoulder as Darius pressed a hand to Orion's back and they shared a tense look which I didn't understand.

"I'll be back at school on Monday," Darius said, throwing us a taut look.

"I have some ideas on how to remove the shadows, I'll talk them over with Darius," Orion said, like he was speaking to me but he didn't look my way.

"Fine," I said stiffly as Seth took my hand and pulled me down to unlock the hatch. There was a faint marking in the grain of the wood, but it was barely noticeable. It lit up as I touched it then we quickly slipped inside and pulled it shut, my chest tightening as we headed into the dark.

Seth squeezed my hand. "Forget him, babe."

"He's forgotten," I said lightly like I wasn't affected by seeing him again. But I was. And I knew I'd forget about Orion the same day the stars decided to give us all a break and blast Lionel to pieces with a flaming meteor.

Well, a girl can dream.

GERALDINE

CHAPTER THIRTEEN

"**O**h, by the light of the big, blue moon,' a narwhale sang in the great lagoon, 'I am but a fish in need of a kiss, and I tell you this as my dying wish.'"

"What song is that?" Angelica asked as I sang my dilly dally to the stars, offering it up to them in hopes of buying us some good fortune after a long day of classes.

It was dark out here between the trees and there was no one to hear us despite the silencing bubble I'd used to hide our passage.

"It's nothing, dear Angelica," I said. "Merely a ditty to appease the stars on this – the night of the great A.S.S. ramming."

"Are you certain you want to stick with that name?" Angelica asked, that dubious tone to her voice which she kept using when I brought this up.

"Angelica, dear," I began on a sigh. "Are we or are we not about to meet in a clandestine, Order mixing, law flouting, gathering of the biggest A.S.S.es you know?"

"Well, yes, but-"

"And are we, or are we not about to ram our truth down the throats of those vile K.U.N.T.s?" I proceeded.

"Yes. But-"

"So are we A.S.S. ramming or are we ramming the K.U.N.T.s? Because so help me, Angelica, I can't think of a simpler way to phrase our noble work."

She seemed on the cusp of further nonsensical arguments when we rounded a turn in the bend and we came upon the place where it was all to take place. The first official meeting of the A.S.S. since that unworthy reptile had placed his scaley behind upon the throne of my ladies and sullied it with his loathsome presence.

The clearing in The Wailing Wood was the perfect place for a secret meeting of the most devoted royalists I knew, and tonight we would begin upon our journey of support which would see our ladies reclaim their birth rights.

I placed the box of buttery bagels I'd been carrying down upon a convenient tree stump and sighed as the sweet scent of victory called to me on the breeze.

The crescent moon was low in the sky, but Justin had already arrived and was valiantly hanging little balls of fire around the place like a diligent dung beetle, tirelessly working to get the job done.

"Hey, Grussy," he said as I pushed my silencing bubble out to encompass the entire clearing, smiling at me like a happy little caterpillar.

"What fine little balls you have," I praised and he opened and closed his mouth a few times before I pointed to the fire balls he'd created. Sometimes, he really was rather dense.

"Oh…thanks. I actually wished to have a word with you, Grussy," he said, taking a step forward as Angelica busied herself creating little cups out of ice for everyone to drink their champagne from like a good little lamb. It was a celebration after all.

"Well make it fast, floppy worm, I have much to do and little time to do it," I said, awaiting his promised word.

"It's about…our arrangement," he said slowly, glancing over at Angelica who was listening in like a nosey nelly and I gasped as I threw a second silencing bubble over us to make sure my most secret secret was kept on the low down.

"Oh, what a time to bring up such a thing!" I cried. "On this most important of days! At this most important of meetings! During the A.S.S. ramming! Why would you wish to sabotage my A.S.S. ramming?"

"Grussy," Justin pressed, clearly taking no heed of my distress. "I know we agreed to keep it secret until graduation and to…play the field."

"What is this field of which you speak?" I asked in confusion.

"I mean…you know, how we said that we'd spend the time before our marriage having sexual relations with other-"

I clapped a hand over his flapsome jaw and looked around in alarm, noting Angelica's raised brow of judgement even though she could not hear us. But she always did have a way with her intuition and no doubt with that single eyebrow proclamation she was telling me that she'd figured it out. She knew of the way Justin's family and mine had agreed to join. She knew that the two of us were due to be wed after graduation. She knew how we had agreed and how we had also made the choice to water our lawns with a range of hoses in the meantime. 'Play the field' was clearly Justin's utterly confusing way of saying that I was spending time riding the Long Sherman, hopping on the wishing fish, writhing with the slippery sea serpent and bending the

172

salmon. Yes, that eyebrow said she knew it all and now the whole academy would know too.

"What on earth possessed you to bring up our arrangements now, you meddlesome moth?" I asked him incredulously.

"Because I think that we should stop seeing other people and just come out and tell everyone about us," Justin said as if this were the place for such a declaration.

"And you thought now was the best time to try and tame Lady Petunia?" I gasped. "Right when I have her all primed for a ramming?"

"Your vagina is primed for-"

"Good sir! Please do not be so uncouth. I cannot have this discussion right now. And I cannot agree to any such thing at this moment. You do not just announce to the lawn in the midst of summer that she shall only taste rain henceforth! I need my lawn watered in more ways than that. What of the hose? What of the bothersome barracuda?"

"The what?" Justin frowned and I flushed red as thoughts of my dear, sweet, badly bred basking shark swam through my mind and for a moment I couldn't breathe.

I was saved from answering the vexing cricket by the arrival of the rest of the Almighty Sovereign Society as they began to appear between the trees and I made a hasty retreat.

I hurried around the circle, making sure everyone had a bagel from my box, handing them out so that everywhere I looked there was a buttery bagel in hand and a look of most reverent devotion upon their faces.

I was about to begin when Milton Hubert stomped through the trees, seeming to take no care to remain silent.

"Do sit down, Milton," I encouraged, refraining from making a joke about bulls in china shops though the notion did strike me, bringing a chuckle to my lips.

He took a seat beside one of Justin's tiny balls and I gasped as the firelight caught on the glorious ring he had freshly hanging from the base of his nose.

"Dearest Milton!" I cried, my eyes wide as I realised what this meant. "Have you taken on a herd?"

"I'm about to," he said proudly, lifting his chin so that his nose ring caught the light again. "My family were in talks with several other Minotaurs over the summer and at the weekend I beat all the other bulls to the centre of the Gelopian Maze. I got my nose ring for winning and I'll start meeting some cows soon so that I can build my herd."

"Oh joyous day!" I said, throwing my arms around his neck and squeezing him tight. "We must all have a toast before the ramming begins!"

I turned away from him to find my glass, but as I hunted for it, my Atlas began to buzz in my pocket.

I pulled it free and my cheeks flushed as I spotted Maxy boy's name appearing upon the screen.

Justin was casting a curious look my way and I quickly switched the device off before putting it away again and raising my glass for all to see.

"To Milton getting his nose ring!" I called out and Milton stomped his foot happily as everyone raised a glass in a toast.

We took a sip of our drinks and I smiled warmly at everyone as the bubbles tickled my tummy and I was filled with pride at the sight of so many varied and wonderous Orders all joined together in one place.

"It is my great honour to be holding this somewhat clandestine meeting of the A.S.S. despite the ridiculous laws of the scoundrel who has stolen the crown from our fair ladies," I began. "I am as thrilled as a chicken crossing the road to see you all here, flouting the grossly outrageous restrictions he is trying to place upon our kind. And though our queens are not currently here, I know that they would be truly bolstered to see so many fine faces, standing up against this Orderist collywobble!"

Cheers went up amongst the noble A.S.S. and pride beamed through me like sun through the fluffiest white clouds.

"All of us here stand united in our faith in the Vega line. We stand against persecution, inequality and unworthy Dragon scoundrels. This is not just a meeting of the Almighty Sovereign Society as usual, but it is indeed the beginning of the rebellion!"

"Long live the queens!" Sofia cried and more scallywags joined in, bringing a smile of greatest joy to my face.

"Indeed!" I agreed wholeheartedly. "We here are the first to see the light and my father has found even more likeminded souls out amongst the masses. Lionel Acrux may have stolen the crown with dark magic and deceit, but his reign will not be a long one. He will be cast asunder by our ladies before long and we shall live to see the rise of the Vega line once more. Who here will stand with me against the K.U.N.T.s? Who here will fight for what is right?"

Cheers of joy went up and I beamed, feeling the full force of the A.S.S. ramming building up all around me.

I opened my mouth to go on, but before I could, I felt a press of magic against the wards I had cast to keep unwanted nincompoops away from our fine and noble meeting and I gasped as I turned around, hunting the trees for a sign of the intruder.

I raised my hands, pushing back against the magic that tried to break through my own, grunting as the scoundrel coming against us used brute force and took me unawares, breaking through my wards.

"We are under attack!" I called, looking out into the trees and gasping as I spotted a flash of white racing towards us.

I conjured a spear into my hands as I prepared to stand and fight and the rest of the A.S.S. stood at my back, valiant and stalwart in the face of impending doom.

"Gerry?" Maxy boy's voice called to me and though I had no business in trusting an Heir, my stomach did flip flop and my tension did ease.

"What are you doing breaking into a private meeting you cantankerous clam?" I called back, sucking in a gasp as he burst through the trees riding on the back of a fine white Werewolf, looking like some warrior of old, galloping in to save the day.

"The K.U.N.T.s are coming," he called. "We overheard Highspell. She caught wind of your meeting and they're on their way to catch you all. You have to run."

I pressed a hand to my heart as I looked around at the A.S.S. ready to fight if that was what was called for.

"Is there time for us to escape?" I demanded as Seth skidded to a halt before me and Maxy boy looked down at me from his back, shirtless and salacious and making my mind go all of a dither for a moment.

"Yes. If everyone splits up now. I set a river racing across their path to slow them down, but my magic won't hold much longer and Nova will expel all of you if you're caught meeting like this," he grunted and I noted the tension in his muscles, realising he was indeed wielding powerful magic to aid us in our hour of need.

"You heard the man!" I called. "Vamoose! Take to the skies, the land and the sea, get yourselves away from here before that mindless mannequin and her platoon of K.U.N.T.s are upon us!"

The A.S.S. sprung into motion, many of them shifting, grouping together in their Orders and taking off into the night. The flying Orders flew skyward and dear Angelica paused to burn all remaining items of clothing with her Dragon Fire before taking off after them.

"Come on, Grussy," Justin urged, snuffing out his little balls and peeling off his shirt as he prepared to shift into his Cerberus form and I knew in all good sense that I should go with him, but Maxy boy held out a hand to me and in a moment of madness, I wished to take it.

Indecision froze me and Highspell's voice called out through the dark. "I want anyone found out here detained for Cyclops interrogation! If we can prove they were meeting in secret then we can report them to the King!"

"Be gone you braggards," I hissed, smacking Seth on his hairy behind and waving them all away as I turned to the clearing, wielding earth magic to grow new vegetation over the last of the evidence.

Justin whimpered before taking off into the trees as I'd insisted and Seth howled as he raced away too.

I pushed more power from my body as I made greenery grow over every scrap of evidence and Mildred's heinous voice called out as she spotted me.

"I see one of them!" she shrieked, her undercut snout poking through the trees as her beady eyes glared at me.

"For the true queens!" I cried, throwing my hands in the air and creating an enormous crater beneath her feet which she tumbled down into like a turd in a toilet.

I was fully prepared to stand my ground and make her pay for ever choosing the Dragon imposter over my ladies, but I was suddenly whipped off of my feet in a whirlwind of air magic and the world went topsy turvy all about me.

I landed in strong arms and my heart leapt as I found myself held against my Maxy Boy as Seth ran beneath us, the two of them having circled back for me and Seth howling in victory as we tore away through the trees.

"I've got you, Gerry," he purred in my ear.

"Oh you cunning cuttlefish," I cooed, relaxing back into him as we tore away from the K.U.N.T.s in the direction of King's Hollow.

He chuckled behind me as he held me close and despite the fact that he was an Heir and a scoundrel, I found myself smiling. For a man who claimed not to support the true queens, he had just put himself at great risk for the A.S.S. and that meant more to me than he could ever know.

So perhaps there was more to him than met the eye. He had just aligned himself with the supporters of the royal line. And just maybe, that meant there was hope for him yet.

DARIUS

CHAPTER FOURTEEN

The stardust brought us to the courtyard just outside the palace gates after a long week at school and I shared a look with my brother that spoke louder than words. We had our game faces on already, the cold masks the Acrux name required of us. But as the reporters spotted us, I found I wanted my position even less than I ever had. I fucking hated this legacy. I wished I could cut my ancestry from my body like the rot it was. And I wished more than anything that I didn't have so much of my father in me. If I hadn't, if I'd been stronger and more willing to make up my own mind and stick to my convictions then maybe none of the things that had pushed Roxy away from me would have taken place. Maybe she never would have said no to me when we'd had our Divine Moment and I wouldn't have deserved all of the shit the stars were sending my way now.

I couldn't even count the number of times I'd dreamed of that night going differently. And of the man I would have been for her if she'd given me the chance to prove I could be. But there were some things that night had changed in me which I wouldn't want to take back. Because losing her for the man who had donated his genetics to my creation was the final straw to have broken all ties I'd still felt to him. Any loyalty I'd been clinging to or desire to please him and make him proud had withered away with every second that had passed since.

What he was doing to her now only made my hatred burn deeper and my thirst for his death more potent. When his time came it would be bloody and brutal and agonising and it still wouldn't come close to payment for all he'd caused. But I'd relish every fucking minute of it no matter if it happened in the blink of an eye or if I was gifted months to slowly carve him apart.

I strode forward with Xavier at my side, trying to ignore the flash of the cameras as Fae yelled questions at us, hoping to get an answer for the biased rags they reported for.

"Are you settling in well to the palace?"

"How are you finding your father's new regime?"

"Is it true that Lionel is considering Order segregation throughout the kingdom?"

"Do you believe in your father's vision for a new Solaria?"

"Prince Darius, can you tell us how it feels to be next in line for the throne?"

That one pulled me up short and I cut my gaze to Gus Vulpecula, the sneaky little Fox Shifter who always managed to get the story he wanted no matter how loosely his facts were based on the truth.

"What did you just call me?" I snarled, unable to help myself even as Xavier snorted a low warning in his horsey way. I'd let it slide the last time someone had called me a prince, but I didn't want it catching on. I was an Heir just like my brothers and I had no intention of rising above them.

"Prince Darius," Gus replied, a cunning smile on his lips that said he'd gotten me right where he wanted me. "Your father is the King. His Heirs have also been gifted the Fifth Element, so it only stands to reason that you are now more powerful than the other Heirs. Just as your father is more powerful than the Celestial Councillors. So, it's a simple assumption to make that they will go on to form a Council in support of you while you sit upon the throne after your father, is it not?"

A low growl escaped my lips at the thought of me betraying my brothers like that and Xavier took a step forward, plastering on a fake smile as he saved Gus from having his head ripped off by intervening.

"Right now, we are simply adjusting to Father being the King. We certainly aren't thinking about Darius or anyone else taking his place any time soon, so maybe we should just focus on the matter at hand for the time being?"

Xavier nudged me to get my ass walking again and I flicked a glare at Gus while he smirked like he'd won some point here. I mentally promised him a horrible death if he kept pushing at me like that.

The golden gates before The Palace of Souls opened and a fucking horse and carriage pulled up before us to take us to the palace doors. It was a long walk but this shit always seemed unnecessary to me.

Xavier exchanged a look with me, rolling his eyes where no one could see and I hopped up into the damn thing before taking a seat as the cameras continued to flash like mad as we were driven away.

I tossed a silencing bubble over us and sighed loudly. "I don't know how much more of this I can endure," I growled, heat lining my palms as my fire Element moved to the surface of my skin.

"I know. I hate having to come and see him too, but Mom is all alone here with him and I worry about her," Xavier said, reminding me that I was failing yet another person I cared about.

"I feel so fucking useless in all of this. Why can't we catch a damn break?" I asked bitterly. "Everywhere I look, people I love are being hurt by that monster and we can't even stand against him publicly. He has me by the fucking balls and the longer it goes on the more reckless I feel like becoming. Like maybe I should walk right into the palace and shift on his psycho ass and bite him in half before he even realises what happened."

"You know that's not how it would go," Xavier said sadly. "Tory would jump between you and Clara too and then-"

"I know," I snapped, hating that I was now being a dick to him too, but this useless feeling was driving me to be the worst version of myself.

Xavier clapped a hand on my arm and I sighed as I forced myself to get it together.

The carriage pulled up before the palace doors and we got out of it, heading inside as two doormen tugged the doors wide. We followed Father's butler, Jenkins, as he offered up a formal greeting.

By the stars, I hated that old bastard. He'd seen so much of what our father had done to us over the years and I swear he got off on it or something. His expressionless face never so much as twitched to give his feelings away, but more than once when he'd found me bleeding on the floor after one of Father's beatings, there had been this wild kind of light in his eyes that told me he would never be someone I could ask for help. I didn't know what my father had done to earn such unyielding loyalty from him. Maybe it was nothing more than admiration for the sick and sadistic creature who had been responsible for bringing me into this world, but whatever it was, I wished nothing but ill will to him.

We finally arrived in the sprawling throne room and I had to force myself not to react as I found Father sitting on the dark stone throne with its back shaped like fifty Hydra heads for the Savage King's Order.

Roxy was perched on the step sitting by his fucking feet like a dog while wearing a trailing black gown and the Dragon in me shifted angrily at the sight of her. She flinched a little as she saw me and my teeth snapped together as I fought to contain my rage.

Clara was perched on the arm of the throne, stroking Father's hair and kissing his neck as he barely even seemed to notice she was there, his cold eyes fixed on me and Xavier as we approached. Mom stood on his other side in an emerald dress, perfectly made up as always with that plastic doll look on her face that I loathed so much. Lance's mother, Stella was beside her, all in black like a gothic Barbie doll and a cruel smile on her lips as she watched me and Xavier carefully.

"Seriously?" I snarled as Jenkins left the room and the door closed behind him. "Claiming the throne wasn't enough? You have to sit a Vega at your feet too?"

"Well, I could have her sucking my cock if you don't think it's enough," Father replied with a cruel twist to his lips and it took everything in me not to lunge at him as my entire body flooded with rage. "Would you like that, Roxanya?"

Roxy lifted her head to look at him, blinking slowly and shrugging one shoulder. My girl would have punched him in the fucking balls for even thinking about that and I hated to see her so fucking vacant over the suggestion. At the very least I could be glad that she hadn't been too enthusiastic, though my gut clenched at the thought of him making her do that.

Clara hissed like a snake and moved her hand down Father's chest possessively. "Daddy doesn't fuck the whore," she growled and Stella clucked her tongue, narrowing her eyes on her daughter. "I'm the favourite. *I'm* the one who gets to please him like that."

It felt like my lungs fucking decompressed at those words as relief filled me in a wave. I'd been driving myself insane worrying about that, night after night wondering if he was forcing her to give her body to him and hating myself more than words could convey for not being able to rescue her. That had been my worst fear for her in all of the nights she'd spent locked up at his mercy and though I knew she had to have faced so many atrocities from him, the fact that he hadn't been raping her sent relief through me in droves. I swallowed thickly against the surge of emotions in me as I looked at Roxy helplessly, aching to just grab hold of her and take her far away from this place. I'd give up everything to do that. To just pick her up and run and run until Solaria was no more than a distant memory of a nightmare we'd escaped and I could know that she was safe at last.

"For now," Father added dryly. "It has occurred to me that poor Roxanya is in a predicament with the new regime though. With crossbreeding outlawed, and no male Phoenixes currently in existence, she cannot procreate. I have been considering making an exception for near extinct Orders like hers. And of course, a Dragon with our fire gifts and ability to fly, not to mention our immense power would be the closest thing to a match for her. A child inheriting either Order would at least be powerful, even if their blood was mixed."

"You can't seriously be thinking about making her have a baby?" Xavier demanded and I stiffened as Father's hateful gaze slid to him.

"Mind your tongue, runt," he snapped. "I am yet to decide on what to do about anomalies such as you. You have Dragon blood as pure as spring water running through your veins and yet you turn into a fucking horse when you shift."

Clara cackled loudly and Mother's eyes glimmered with barely restrained emotion, but Xavier just held his head high and took the insult like the Fae he was. Anyone could see how fucking powerful he was in every way that counted, and Father's Orderist bullshit couldn't change that.

"I have a few matches in mind for you, but of course I cannot risk wasting a female Dragon with good breeding on you if you may pass on this condition. So, for now, you will just remain as you are."

Neither of us replied to that, probably because we were just relieved he hadn't found a fucking Mildred to chain Xavier to. Yet.

Mother's eyes had tightened as she listened in on our conversation, but she didn't open her mouth and didn't move an inch, making me wonder if Father had placed new Dark Coercion on her. In fact, I didn't need to wonder, I knew the old bastard would have done it without a thought.

"But in answer to your question about Roxanya's fertility options, I am still undecided. Perhaps you would like to put the bastards in her belly, Darius? After all, your blood isn't tainted and I have no particular objection to you fathering bastards so long as you're producing fine Dragon Heirs with Mildred too. I'm sure Roxanya would be accommodating to you if I told her to be. Wouldn't you?"

Roxy turned her dark eyes on me and there was no mistaking the shiver of fear that ran through her at the prospect of that. My heart bunched as I saw it. What had he done to make her fear me like that? Why did she flinch and recoil from me like she was expecting me to attack her at any moment?

"You're forgetting the stars won't allow us near each other," I snapped. "So even if you wanted to force us to do that, the stars would never let it happen."

"You're right," Father sighed, leaning back in the throne and gripping the heads of the stone Hydras that created the arms of the chair. "I suppose if I decide to follow through with that idea, I'll have to put the bastards in her myself."

Clara snarled loudly and shadows rose up around the room as she lunged towards Roxy as if she'd been the one to suggest it, but Father managed to catch her arm to stop her.

"I haven't made any such decision, my love," he said to her firmly. "You are still my favourite. But you won't be if you attack my pet."

"I can give you bastards if you want them, Daddy?" she offered and he laughed coldly before pushing her back to stand to the side of the throne, looking away from her.

"What use would I have for Vampire bastards? Your Order is as common as soot and worth a whole lot less. Besides, you're a void of darkness inside, Clara. I can only imagine you're barren anyway."

Clara's face scrunched up in pain and she burst into tears before jumping up and tearing away from us with shadows billowing around her in a sea of darkness. She ran up the stairs at the side of the huge throne room and her sobs echoed back to us as she raced away.

No one said anything for a long moment and I actually almost felt sorry for Clara. Not that she deserved anything less than an excruciating death for her part in all the evil my father had brought upon Solaria, but sometimes I wondered if there was anything of Orion's sister left in her. Especially as I was so adamant that Roxy was still trapped inside the vacant vessel which currently sat before me. But then my girl hadn't spent years alone in the Shadow Realm, so it was a lot more likely that she was still essentially herself beneath the corruption.

"I'll calm her down for you later, Your Highness," Stella simpered, rounding the throne and moving up the steps to take Clara's place on my father's left. She reached out to run a hand up his arm and the look he gave her had me wondering if he was still screwing her too despite the way he'd shot her down the other day. *Fucking hell.*

"I didn't actually summon you home for the chance to have this thrilling discussion," Father said once Clara's sobs had faded into the distance. "Today I intend to begin cleansing Solaria of all of its issues and the stars have guided me towards the first and most worthy cause which requires my attention."

"You don't need to bother with that star bullshit in front of us," I said in a low voice as I glared at him. "We all know that you're just a psychotic megalomaniac who has such a hard on for power that you'd do anything and everything to claim it."

"You will not disrespect the King like that!" Stella exclaimed but Father silenced her with a shake of his head.

Father's fingers curled into a fist as he glared back at me but rather than strike me himself like I'd expected, he nodded once at Roxy who immediately got to her feet.

Shadows darkened her eyes until all I could see in them was black as the thick fog of the dark power rose up all around her.

"Please don't," Xavier begged at my side, trying to move in front of me but I just flicked my fingers, creating a lasso of water magic to tug him away from me before she could strike.

He may have had three Elements, but he had very little control of them and there was no way for him to fight off my magic.

The shadows struck me right in the chest as Roxy drove them into me and I grunted as I took the hit, refusing to even shield against them as I accepted the pain she was driving into my body. I didn't care what happened to me now anyway. I only cared about doing anything and everything I could to save her from him.

Darkness flooded my vision as the pain of a thousand cuts slicing into me from the inside filled my body and I dropped down to one knee as I fought to stay conscious.

Just as I was certain I was going to black out from the agony, a fist crashed into my jaw and I was knocked onto my back before a heavy boot slammed into my side over and over again, catching me in the face too.

I cursed as I clenched my teeth against my father's assault and rolled onto my side just as Roxy pulled the shadows back out of me.

"Heal him and make sure he's presentable before you join us on the balcony," Father's voice came from far away and I grunted in pain as I moved onto my hands and knees, spitting out a mouthful of blood as a procession of footsteps moved out of the room and Stella muttered something about me learning respect.

A soft hand caught hold of my chin and I looked up at Roxy in surprise as I found her there instead of Mom, tilting her head to one side curiously as healing magic slid from her fingers into my skin.

"Do you truly remember nothing?" I asked her as the taste of my own blood lingered on my lips.

I rocked back onto my knees before her as her touch awoke every aching piece of my heart, but as I looked closer, nothing in her expression said she knew me at all.

"About what?" she asked, her gaze cold, expression void. Other than the flickers of fear she sometimes directed my way I never got anything else from her and that was somehow more gutting than if she'd been sobbing and broken in a more obvious way. This felt like she wasn't even her anymore. Like every stubborn, infuriating, obnoxious, addictive, delicious, beautiful piece of her was gone. Like she might as well have been dead. And I was the one who had killed her. Father clearly had her in the grip of Dark Coercion as well as the shadows and whatever the fuck he'd done to her to make her fear me, and I was lost without a way to combat any of it for her.

"Us," I breathed, catching her hand as she moved to withdraw it and pressing her fingers to my cheek like if I just held her there, I could force her to feel it.

She stiffened as I held onto her but didn't do anything to stop me as she remained crouched in front of me with her gaze hunting mine. I didn't try to hide anything from her, showing her every broken, bloody, hurting piece of my soul because it belonged to her anyway.

"I remember..." For a moment it was like a cloud shifted across the sun and the light shone free within her. But I barely even saw it before shadows swept over her eyes and she drew back with a sharp inhale, wincing a little as she stood again, looking down at me. "I remember all the reasons I have to hate you. And you're just lucky my king doesn't want you dead, or I'd make sure you were."

"You don't hate me, Roxy," I growled as I got to my feet and towered over her, but as I tried to take a step towards her, I found she'd frozen my feet to the ground.

The chandelier above our heads began to make a loud jingling sound as vibrations rocked the foundations of the palace due to us being left alone, but I didn't fucking care. I needed to speak with her and the stars weren't getting a say in it this time.

"No, I don't hate you," she agreed and I swallowed thickly as she moved closer to me, brushing my father's boot marks from my shirt before tucking it in for me. I inhaled deeply as she smoothed the creases over my shoulders then traced her fingers across my chin as she washed away the blood there using her water magic. She ran her dark gaze over me critically, tiptoeing up to push her fingers into my hair and I growled with the ache in my heart as my hands slipped around her waist and I tried to draw her closer to me. "I don't care about you at all."

I froze at the coldness of those words as she spoke them, and she was gone before I could fully comprehend how clearly she'd meant them too. That had been the truth. The honest to stars reality of the person she was now. She didn't care. Not about me or Darcy or any of her friends or anything at all aside from that fucking animal who had stolen her throne.

My blood pumped hot and furiously through my veins as my heart broke for her all over again. But I wasn't given the luxury of having a moment to process the cruel words as she wrapped a rope of air magic around my wrist and tugged me out the door after her.

The chandelier fell still as I followed her, and I had to fight to get my mask back in place as she led me through the palace and down a long corridor towards the west wing.

"Where are we going?" I asked when she offered up no explanation. There were plenty of members of staff scurrying to and fro in the hallways so at least the stars left us alone as we walked.

"The Reception Hall," Roxy replied flatly, not even glancing back at me. "My king has an announcement to make to his subjects."

"What's wrong with any of the halls and ballrooms down this end of the palace?" I muttered, mostly because I was feeling like I'd been sucker punched and I just wanted her to fucking talk to me.

"Since my king took possession of the palace, some of the rooms and wings have locked themselves and as of yet he hasn't had the chance to figure out the spells that unlock them again," she replied without a single inflection in her voice.

"Wait - are you telling me the palace has locked itself to him?" I asked, my mood lifting at the thought of that.

"In part," she replied. "For now."

A smirk lifted my lips at that little nugget of truth and I filed it away as I wondered whether there might be some way for us to make use of that against him. The palace had clearly been spelled to keep it protected from usurpers and as I was certain that Darcy hadn't had any issues like that while living here, I had to hope that there was something at work here specifically targeted against my father.

We reached a heavy wooden door and Roxy glanced my way as she pulled it open before stepping through it and leading me after her.

I followed her, schooling my features as I stepped out onto a balcony where Father stood above a crowd of onlookers as they cheered for him in a huge hall with white pillars running along the length of it.

Roxy's magic tugged me along as we walked to join Mom, Stella and Xavier where they stood watching at the back of the white stone balcony and I found myself standing so close to her that our arms were brushing against each other.

I looked down at the girl the stars had picked for me while her adoring gaze stayed fixed on Father and I breathed out slowly as the ache in me became unbearable. Gabriel was supposed to be getting the Nymph cage to us within a matter of days and I was so hopeful that we would be able to bring her back to us once we could reawaken her Phoenix, but every second that this went on, I felt like my soul was being shredded and the stars were fucking laughing at us.

"I stand before you today to speak of a grave matter that has come to my attention recently," Father called as the crowd quieted to listen to him. "A matter which I know has been concerning Fae all over the country for quite some time. Of course, I am speaking about the lack of midnight amethyst stones in our great kingdom."

I fought the urge to arch a brow as I tore my gaze away from Roxy to look at my father. What the fuck was he talking about? Who gave a shit about midnight amethyst being hard to come by recently? I mean, yeah, there had been a bunch of stories about how the stones which were the luckiest objects in Solaria had been dwindling in numbers over the last ten years or so, but I'd never really paid those stories much attention.

Less powerful Fae relied on things like lucky stones to get them through life, but I preferred to chart my own path. Besides, it seemed fairly obvious to me that if enough people really believed that those rare stones might change their lives then they'd be in high demand. Fae who owned them would be secretive about them and guard them carefully. Plus they were damn rare in the first place.

"It has come to my attention that a conspiracy has been taking place beneath our very noses," Father growled, allowing smoke to slip from his lips to showcase his Dragon for the crowd and cameras watching him. "A group of Fae have been stealing these precious stones and hoarding them away to make sure that their kind are the only ones to benefit from owning them. This group of Fae are all of one specific Order. A prey Order. The kind to seem inconspicuous, innocent, harmless even. And yet many members of their kind - if not *all* members of their kind have been quietly stealing these stones and using them to gain power and influence in their communities while robbing hard working, more powerful Fae of their rightful places above them."

The crowd began to boo and shout for answers and I glanced beyond Roxy to Xavier, wondering if he had any idea what the fuck was happening here because I was getting the horrible feeling that I might just know, and I really didn't want to be right. My brother's eyes widened a fraction and he gave me the hint of a shrug as I turned my gaze back to watching my father as he riled up the crowd.

"These Fae - no, these *Rats*, have been working to gather midnight amethysts for years. Slowly increasing their power and influence despite the fact that their very nature demands they stay at the bottom of the pecking order. And to prove to you that I am correct in this discovery, I have brought their leader here for you to see."

Father waved a hand towards a door at the far side of the balcony and two of the palace guards dragged a terrified looking Fae out to kneel before my father. His hair was ice white and his skin the colour of paper, his features slightly pinched like a rodent's and his grey suit dishevelled. I would have guessed he was a few years older than me, but the cut of his suit looked expensive and despite his clearly terrified expression, something about the way he was put together told me he was important.

"I present to you, Eugene Dipper, High Buck of the Solarian Mischief of Tiberian Rats," Father called. "And the instigator behind this treachery to our nation."

"I'm not!" Eugene squeaked. "I didn't steal anything, I swear. I'm a collector - I paid for all of my stones and I made no attempt to conceal my ownership of-"

"So you admit that we found a hoard of over eight hundred of these rare and valuable stones in your possession?" Father demanded and my gut fell as I saw this for what it was. He was turning everyone against this man and every one of his kind. And surprise, surprise, Eugene Dipper just happened to be the leader of one of the Orders my father hated the most.

"L-like I said, I didn't steal anything," Eugene stammered, casting a terrified look between my father and to my disgust, myself and Xavier too like we were complicit in this.

"Well, we will soon get to the bottom of that," Father replied, his lip curling back in distaste as he flicked his fingers and Eugene was dragged away again.

The crowd booed and catcalled after the Tiberian Rat Shifter, their minds already made up about him despite the fact that he didn't seem to have done anything wrong as far as I could tell. There was no law against buying multiple rare items even if they did hold a sway over luck or good fortune. But my father had made him out to be some kind of thief, stealing those things from other Fae. And the assholes in the crowd were dumb enough to lap it up.

My stomach churned as Eugene screamed while he was dragged out of sight and my arm twitched where it hung beside Roxy's. The back of her hand slid against mine, causing heat to prickle across my skin and for the briefest moment, her little finger hooked around mine, making my heart leap as I looked down at her.

She didn't look back, didn't blink or react in anyway as our hands stayed joined for just a few seconds before she released me again. But it had happened. I just didn't know if that was proof that some part of the girl I loved was in there fighting to get out or if I was just kidding myself because I needed to believe that so desperately.

"I propose we start up an inquisition into the matter of the theft of luck from the Solarian people!" Father bellowed, gaining screams of support from the crowd as he looked down over them. "Every Tiberian Rat in the kingdom is formally requested to come to the new Nebular Inquisition Centre that I have opened up in outer Caronis. It is a holding facility where you will be questioned by a Cyclops who will get to the bottom of these accusations. If you are innocent, then there is no need for you to refuse this request and you will of course be released. But if you are guilty then the people of Solaria will have their answer - and I will demand payment for this theft in blood!"

The crowd roared even louder as my father stood there, lording it over them and smirking in that fucking way I'd always known proceeded violence in him and it fucking terrified me.

That wasn't going to be an inquisition. There would be no Tiberian Rats found innocent. I wasn't a fucking fool. And once he'd proclaimed the lot of them to be guilty of stealing everyone's goddamn luck, he'd come calling for that blood payment.

It would be genocide. And I knew in my soul that the Rats would just be the beginning.

King's Hollow was full with all of us here, Geraldine bustling about like a mother hen while Darcy sat in the armchair opposite mine beside the fire. The others had plenty to say but I just gazed into the flames with my brow furrowed and my heart aching.

"It will work," Darcy insisted and I glanced up to find her looking at me. Or more like glaring at the doubts which were clearly written across my features.

"I know," I agreed. "She won't be able to escape the cage or cast the shadows beyond the confines of it. But..."

"But?" she demanded and I knew she was just worked up on behalf of her sister, and if she needed to use me as I punching bag she could.

"I just know my father. He's not one to do things by halves. Yeah, he got her to give herself up to the shadows and he bonded her to him to make her feel loyalty to him even when the shadows are numbing everything else. But I don't think that would be iron clad enough for him. He would know that the moment she was away from him we'd be trying everything we could to bring her back to us and yet he still sent her here alone. There's more to this that we aren't seeing, and I'm just concerned that releasing her Phoenix isn't going to be enough to bring her back to us."

"You're wrong," Darcy growled angrily, getting to her feet. "I know my sister and I know she is still in there fighting for us. I'm not giving up on her and once her Phoenix is released, I just know it will be enough to pull her back from the shadows. He could have placed a thousand Dark Coercions on her, but it won't matter because they'll all be burned away the moment she can use her Order form again. Once the shadows' grip on her loosens we'll be able to figure the rest of it out."

"There still isn't any way to sever the Guardian bond though," I muttered bitterly, knowing I was only riling her up, but I couldn't help it. All the time that I was parted from Lance while he was in prison, I'd felt the ache to be close to him so desperately that it cut me open. And even though I could visit him more frequently, it still wasn't enough. I'd been going back there almost daily and yet I still yearned for him, worried about him, cared for him. We couldn't do anything to stop Roxy from feeling that way about my father too. And it would be even worse for her because the Guardian felt it all five times over. As the Ward, I got the easy ride, only really feeling that way because he'd been gone for so long.

"Well, there is one way to sever the bond," Darcy growled. "We just have to cut Lionel's head off."

"Assuming that won't kill her too," Seth piped up helpfully. "Because my mom once told me that Guardians can't survive the death of their Ward. She said they'll throw themselves between them and death or follow them into it if they fail, so-"

"Shut the fuck up, Seth, that's bullshit," I snapped.

I got to my feet and glared at him and he stepped up to me instantly, bumping his chest against mine as he growled in response to the challenge I was offering him.

"Back off, man," Max demanded, moving to grab my arm as he tried to force me back and the Dragon in me stirred with rage.

Caleb caught Seth by the shoulder and drew him back too and Seth muttered something about reptiles being fucking crazy as he tore his gaze from mine. I blew out a mouthful of smoke as I strode away to the kitchenette, shaking Max off as he tried to push his gifts over me to help calm me down.

"Stop that," I snapped, grabbing a bottle of whiskey from the cupboard and pouring myself a way too healthy measure before sinking it in one and enjoying the burn of the liquor on the way down.

"She should be leaving The Orb soon," Darcy pointed out, getting to her feet. "Maybe we should get into position."

"Yeah," I agreed, tugging my shirt over my head and rolling my shoulders back as the urge to shift rippled across my skin. We were about to herd the girl I loved into a fucking cage like a sheep being herded by a wolf pack and the thought had me more than a little on edge.

"Oh magical muscles, look at the size of that six pack!" Geraldine gasped as she looked at me. "You truly are one beastly specimen of a man, Darius Acrux. No wonder my lady Tory is so enamoured with your swollen banana. I did sometimes wonder if she'd been drinking at the moose juice when she kept falling under your spell, but getting a close up look at your man-parcel really has me all of a dither-"

"Stop looking at his fucking man-parcel," Max snarled, moving up behind her and slapping a hand over her eyes as I snorted a surprised laugh. That girl was seriously off her fucking bagels but there was something about her that was growing on me. The beastly specimen comment probably helped.

"Do not tell a goose where to gander, you overgrown seahorse!" Geraldine cried, scrambling to get out of Max's arms as he glared at me like this was somehow my fault.

"Put your fucking shirt back on, man," he snapped at me.

"I'm about to shift," I replied, shaking my head as Caleb laughed his ass off and Seth looked like he was a popcorn bucket shy of settling in for a show.

"Unhand me you slippery sea urchin!" Geraldine shouted, throwing a hand into Max's stomach and knocking him off of her with a slap of water magic.

"Well stop staring at Darius's dick then," he growled.

"Excuse you, sir, but I am doing no such thing! For one, the delicious Dragon has not revealed his man ham for the room to peruse at leisure, so I was only appreciating the powerful physique which he uses to please my lady! And for two, I would never lay so much as a chin whisker upon the flesh of the man my lady is destined to love by all the stars in the sky! I am merely expressing my approval for his ability to pleasure her physically, even if his personality has left a lot to be desired-"

"Hey," I growled as Darcy muttered, "She's got a point." But neither Max nor Geraldine were paying any attention to either of us anymore.

"Well if you don't want him, then don't fucking look," Max demanded. "I don't like it."

"And why should I care what a villainous cad such as yourself thinks? You don't even believe I am capable of making decisions about my own life correctly."

"That's because you're prone to making terrible fucking decisions!" he yelled and my brows went up as I realised this fight was clearly about something way bigger than her checking me out, but I had no fucking idea what.

"Guys, let's just take it down a notch, yeah?" Seth suggested with a little whimper to show how much he didn't like this arguing, but Max and Geraldine didn't seem to give a shit about that.

"I am not the one who got my tail in a knot over a little arranged marriage!" Geraldine cried. "You seem to be under the misguided impression that I belong to you just because I tangled with your tentacles once or twice, but you are very much mistaken in that belief! I made myself clear to you when I said that I had made my choice and you are the one who refuses to listen. Now, if you'll excuse me, I have a princess to rescue!"

Geraldine turned and fled the room, disappearing down the stairs and leaving all of us feeling seriously awkward as Max ran his hands down his face and groaned.

"Fuck. My. Life," he said and I glanced between Seth and Cal, wondering if they had any idea what was going on.

"Did she say arranged marriage?" Darcy asked in a soft tone as she stepped forward and tugged Max's hand from his face.

"Yeah," he sighed. "She told me about it a while back, but they've been keeping it secret so that they can fool around with other people for a while. I was hoping to get her to pick me instead. And the other night after I saved her from Highspell, we went back to mine and she kissed me. I guess I stupidly thought that meant she was changing her mind."

He looked so fucking defeated that I didn't even know what to say as Darcy glanced back over her shoulder in the direction Geraldine had taken. "Let me go and make sure she's okay to go ahead with the plan." She took a few steps towards the door then paused, shooting Max a sympathetic smile. "I'm sorry, Max."

The moment she was gone, Seth stepped forward and wrapped his arms around Max, howling for him as he looked so damn hopeless that it cut into me.

"Who is she marrying?" I asked, hating seeing him in pain like that. I swear it seemed like none of us could catch a fucking break at the moment.

"Justin Masters," he spat, his lip curling back in disgust. "He's a great big Royal ass licker and I guess that's all she gives a shit about."

"You want me to accidentally barbecue him the next time I see him in my Dragon form?" I offered and Max laughed.

"I heard he's got a hot sister who graduated before we came here," Caleb added. "I could bang her and make a sex tape. His family wouldn't seem like such amazing Royalists if everyone knew she'd been sucking Heir cock."

"Let's not do anything too hasty," Seth laughed kinda aggressively as he slapped Cal on the shoulder harder than necessary. "No need to go whoring yourself out, Cal, let's just fuck the guy up and threaten his balls until he agrees to break it off. No cock sucking required."

"Sure," Caleb agreed, blowing out a laugh as he glanced at Seth then looked to me quickly. "Not by the Masters chick anyway."

Seth smirked at him and Max groaned loudly. "Stop flirting, you two, you're just making me feel worse about my shit."

"Flirting?" I balked, glancing at Seth as he shrugged innocently.

"I can't help it if all of my friends are stupidly hot and I like to suck the odd dick from time to time," he said innocently. "But if you guys ever wanna ditch the girl drama and build a sausage heavy harem then I wouldn't take a whole lot of convincing," he said, his gaze falling to my bare chest for a moment before he looked at Cal again and winked.

"Right. Well, as much as I like brunettes, I'm currently hooked on one who needs us to chase her into a cage and drug her, so shall we get on with that?" I suggested and they all agreed.

"I'll go check that Darcy and Geraldine are in position," Cal said before shooting away and I nodded to the others as I hoisted myself up and out of the hatch set into the roof.

I stripped out of my shoes and jeans, tossing everything down into the treehouse before taking a running jump off of the roof and shifting into my enormous Dragon form, my golden scales catching the light of the setting sun.

I refused to focus on all the things that could go wrong with this plan and instead set my mind on the small pinprick of hope that it was going to go right. That I might just be about to get my girl back and we were finally going to strike a blow against my father that could really make a difference.

Because if this went to hell, I was out of fucking ideas. And I didn't even want to consider what that might mean for Roxy.

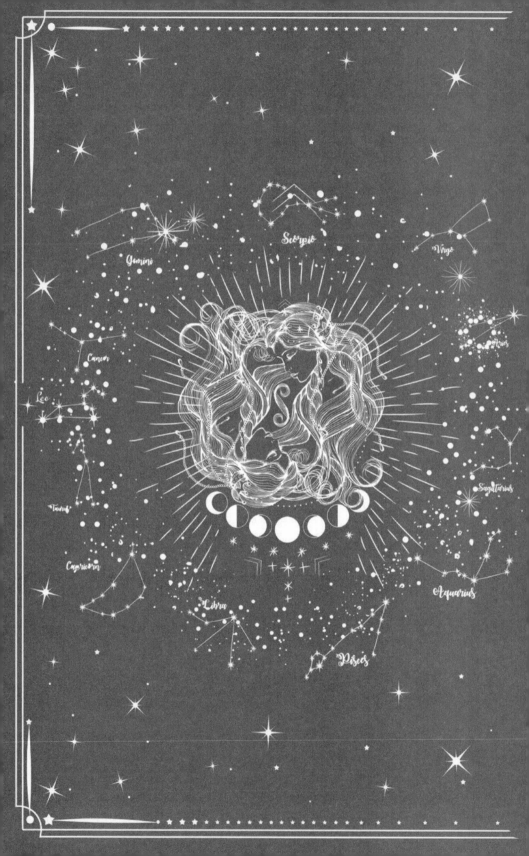

TORY

CHAPTER FIFTEEN

I stepped out of The Orb after dinner with Mildred at my left and Marguerite on my right as the two of them prattled on about wedding dresses and I tried not to feel sorry for myself because it was a Sunday. Five whole days before I could return to my king. I knew it had to be this way, but five days had never felt so damn long.

"I am more concerned about practicality than flamboyance," Mildred scoffed at some comment Marguerite had made. "The main thing that matters is that it comes off easily for our wedding night so that I can produce a fine Dragon Heir for the next generation of Acruxes-"

My fist snapped out so suddenly that I wasn't even certain when I'd decided to strike her, but as my knuckles collided with her bristly jaw, a dark smile pulled at my lips and the shadows in me stirred with hunger.

"What the-" Mildred began, rolling her shoulders back and bunching her muscles as the Dragon behind her eyes glared at me like it wanted to bite my head off.

"Go blather about weddings somewhere else," I growled, shadows slicking down my arms and pooling around my fingertips. "The shadows are hungry. And if you don't fuck off, I'll let them feed on Dragon tonight."

"Catch you guys later," Marguerite gasped before scurrying away, but Mildred wasn't so smart.

"You might be important to the King, but I am going to be an Acrux before long, so you'd do well to remember that I-"

With a flick of my fingers, I sent her sprawling back away from me, driving the shadows into her chest as she squealed like a stuck pig.

"I'll be telling the King about this!" she gasped.

"The King doesn't care about you," I growled, advancing on her with my eyes full of shadows and pleasure tracing patterns down my spine. "You're just a walking womb with Dragon blood in your veins. And guess what? You don't need legs to give birth. So I suggest you listen to me when I tell you to run from me or you'll be finding yourself without the necessary limbs to comply."

Mildred shrieked in pain as I drove the shadows deeper into her but before they could get a true hold on her, she shifted, tearing through her clothes and expanding in size so rapidly that all I could do was watch.

She roared at me in her mud brown Dragon form, swinging her head around to glare down at me with beady eyes set deep in the scales of her head.

The shadows rolled over me as I stood my ground, my heart pumping furiously as I felt fully awake for the first time in a long time and Mildred released a blast of Dragon fire right at me.

The shadows rose up in a cloud to meet her flames and my eyes lit with hunger as I fought to control them, their power almost overwhelming me.

An enormous roar broke through the air, drawing my gaze skyward as a golden Dragon five times the size of Mildred dove from the sky and collided with her.

I sucked in a breath of fright as my gaze fell on Darius and the echoes of a thousand tortures bit into my flesh. Memories of pain and suffering surfaced in me at the sight of him and the fight went out of me as I pulled the shadows close defensively.

As the Dragons tumbled across the path, a torrent of students appeared from The Orb to watch and scream in shock so I took off.

I strode away with the shadows curling through my fingers as I took the path into The Wailing Wood and left Mildred and the other Dragon behind. Though I tossed more than a few glances over my shoulder as my brow furrowed with concern over something I couldn't quite place.

I tugged my Atlas from my pocket so that I could just look at the screensaver of my king for a few moments, but a notification flashed up on it which I'd been tagged in.

Tyler Corbin:

Looks like love's young dream isn't so sweet after all. @DariusAcrux was just seen swooping in to give his fiancé @MildredCanopus a beat down Dragon style in the name of love for his true mate @ToryVega. This young Pegasus saw it all going down and I swear, Mildred still has that moustache in Dragon form as well as that pig snout. Anyone else think she might have some pig grandparents hiding somewhere? For all that the great and honourable King Asscrux has to say about pure bloodlines, you'd think he might have noticed that the Canopus family have been boning farm animals...
#isawtrotters #hewontwannaporkthepork #ibetshehogsthecovers #jurassicpork #porkasaurusrex #piginawig

Stacy Denny:
Someone needs to wrap that pig in a blanket and roll it off a cliff!
Desinie Bass:
She's Mildredful. If Darius Acrux has to marry her then I'll never forgive the stars...
Alexandra Lanoville:
This little piggy went wee wee weeee in her panties when Darius dive bombed her! #sendthatpiggytomarket
Stacey Braum:
Old Macdonald had a farm E-I-E-I-O, and on that farm he had a Mildred E-I-E-I-O – with a moustache here and a big wart there, here a hair, there hair, everywhere a bear hair. #E-I-E-I-Ho
Jessica Glosson: *S*
he so ugly, when her Momma dropped her off at Zodiac she got a fine for littering
Jodie Fleming:
Mildred takes so many Faeroids she'll probably be the one impregnating Darius on their wedding night #peenqueen #dragonatrix

A snort of laughter escaped me and I frowned as I tried to figure out why, but my Atlas started ringing before I could give it too much consideration.

I pursed my lips as I saw Clara's name illuminated on the screen but answered all the same. She was never far from my king so there was always the chance that I might hear his voice in the background of the call, even if he hadn't wanted to speak to me directly.

"Yes?" I asked, keeping my pace up as I moved deeper into the woods.

"Daddy has a message for you," Clara sing-songed. "We're going to stay in the city for the week."

"Why?" I growled, my gut lurching at the idea of him being even further away from me.

"You always have so many questions," she huffed. "Nosey, nosey. I have half a mind to ask Daddy to let me punish you again the next time you're home with us."

My jaw clenched as I remembered the way Clara had made me suffer whenever I failed on her instructions with the shadows, but I didn't back down. It may have been agonising to allow her to force them so deep inside of me, but that was also exactly why my hold over them was so strong. Besides, the punishments always put my king in a good mood, so if I had to suffer to please him then I would.

"I just need to know where he is," I ground out. "You know the way the bond makes me ache when I'm not close."

Clara huffed out a breath, but this was the one thing that we could always see eye to eye on, so she finally gave me what I needed. "He's got some information on a network of Tiberian Rats who have been trying to flee the Nebular Taskforce rather than face the inquisition. We're going hunting." The glee in her voice was unmistakeable and I sighed with relief.

"Okay," I agreed. "But you'll be back at the palace when I return on Friday?"

"Maybe," she taunted and my grip on the Atlas tightened to the point of almost breaking it.

"Clara!" Lionel barked in the background and my heart soared at the sound of his voice even if it was rough with irritation. "We're leaving now. Have you delivered the message?"

"Can I speak with him?" I gasped.

"Sorry, Daddy doesn't want to speak with you right now," she said and I could hear the smile on her poisonous lips. "But don't worry - I'll make sure he enjoys his time away from you so much that I'm sure he won't miss you at all."

"Clara, just let me tell him I-"

The line went dead after she cackled a laugh at my expense and I shrieked in frustration as I hurled the Atlas away from me, letting the shadows blossom all around me in a thick cloud until the force of their power drove deep enough into my skin to take my fury away and left me trembling with the pleasure of their power.

I closed my eyes, moaning softly as I tipped my head back and just bathed in them for a long moment.

"Well shit, babe, if I'd realised what a turn on the shadows clearly are to you, maybe I would have understood why you love them so fucking much," Seth's voice broke through the heady fog of the dark power within me and my lip curled back as I looked to the right of the path where he was standing between the trees butt naked and holding a leaf over his cock which didn't even come close to hiding it. "Made you look," he taunted but before I could reply, a crash of raw power slammed into the shield at my back and I cursed as I was knocked to my knees, barely managing to keep my shield intact.

I twisted to look over my shoulder, finding Darcy hovering a few feet above the path while fiery wings burned brightly at her back and her blue hair billowed around her.

"You should probably run," she warned me, giving me half a second's notice before a blast of air magic slammed into my shield again.

I snarled as I managed to regain my feet, but Seth threw his own air magic at me from the right and I stumbled towards the left side of the path between the combined strength of their power as it drove against my shield with undeniable force.

Max stepped onto the path ahead of me and as he directed his own air magic at me too, I was left with no choice but to turn and run into the trees on my left.

I stumbled between the thick trunks as their air magic increased in pressure and the trees all around me bucked and swayed wildly in the maelstrom they were creating.

I ached to stand and fight them, unleash the full strength of the shadows on them. But my king had made it clear I wasn't to attack the Heirs or Darcy while the country was still adjusting to the new leadership. Outside of enforcing the new laws, he didn't want me to engage with them and I couldn't bear to disappoint him again. So with a growl of fury, I turned and fled.

My boots thumped over leaves and sticks in my path as I ran through the trees and for a moment, I swore I spotted a blur of movement to my right and then again ahead of me on my left. *Fucking Vampire.*

The assault of air magic didn't let up behind me though so I had no time to focus on what was ahead and with each moment that passed, my magic was being stretched to its limits as I fought with everything I had to keep my shield in place.

The trees seemed to open up ahead of me, a clear path free of debris on the ground appearing and allowing me to run faster as I took it and upped my pace.

The shadows writhed beneath my skin, but I kept my focus on my Elemental magic even as I burned through more and more of it while pushing everything I had into maintaining my shield as the wind continued to ram against the back of it.

I cast a ball of fire beside me to replenish my magic but the moment I did, the ground bucked beneath me so hard that I was thrown up in the air. I yelled out as I forgot about the flames and threw everything I had into air again to stop myself from face planting the smooth path ahead of me.

My magic was seriously depleted as I made it back to my feet by some miracle and I cursed loudly as I ran on down the path, taking a turn to the left as it curved that way, the trees and bushes either side of it far too thick for me to try and break through at this speed.

I suddenly found myself at the top of a steep hill and as my boot landed on the path again, my foot slid out from under me as I hit ice instead of mud and I fell onto my ass. But between the sharp decline of the hill before me, the slick ice and the never-ending gale at my back, there was no way for me to stop myself from sliding straight down the hill at high speed.

I threw my arms out ahead of me, trying to slow my fall with air magic, but the dull ache in my chest warned me that I was almost out and I knew there was no way I was going to be able to fight off the three assholes at my back now.

Just as my magic reserves guttered out, I crashed through an illusion that had been placed on the path making it look like there was nothing ahead of me and screamed as I was propelled straight into a heavy metal cage.

I hit the bars at the back of it hard, smacking my face and hearing bone crunch before the agony of the injury even reached me.

I rolled over, scrambling back towards the door with blood dripping down my face, but before I could even get close, Caleb shot into view, slamming the door and locking it with a metallic clang that resounded right down into my soul.

I shrieked in fury, crawling forward and throwing my hands towards him as Geraldine stepped from the trees too, a triumphant look on her face even as tears streaked down her cheeks.

Shadows burst from my palms as I directed them through the bars of the cage they'd trapped me in. But the moment the dark fog got close to the metal it ricocheted back at me, sending agony burning all the way down to my bones and making me howl in pain.

"That cage is made of night iron. The shadows can't pass through it and every time you try to force them through, the power you use is going to strike back at you instead," Darcy said grimly as she landed on the path ahead of me just as Geraldine melted the ice out of existence.

Darcy dissolved her wings, shifting back into her Fae form and making sure there was no chance of me replenishing my magic from her flames.

Seth appeared next, wearing sweatpants now with Max stalking over to stand on Darcy's other side, his face set with determination and my Atlas in his hand.

"When my king hears about this you'll all pay," I snarled at them, my gaze shifting between my sister, Geraldine and the Heirs before realising that one of them was missing.

"That's a risk we're willing to take for you, sweetheart," Caleb said, cocking his head as he looked down at me crouched in my cage.

I couldn't even stand up in this thing and when I reached out to grip the bars, they burned my shadow coated hands until I felt the skin melting on my palms and I was screaming in agony again.

"Stop, my lady!" Geraldine gasped in horror as I wrenched my hands back, panting and sweating, my body trembling with the pain.

"Let me out," I demanded but Darcy shook her head, her eyes wet with unshed tears but her expression firm and unyielding.

"You're not coming out of there until you're yourself again," she growled and before I could reply, a mournful roar sounded from somewhere overhead.

I shrieked in fear as I looked up through the bars of my cage and found Darius diving from the sky in his golden Dragon form. His gaze was set on me and the fear I always felt around him intensified as I found myself so helpless before him.

The cage juddered as his weight collided with it and I fell flat on my back as his enormous claws wound around the metal bars above me and I was suddenly lifted into the air.

I yelled and cursed and swore retaliation against all of them as he flew me up above the trees and I felt a concealment spell sliding over me and my cage as one of the others cloaked my presence from below to make sure no one spotted him kidnapping me.

The flight didn't last long and Darius landed awkwardly on the roof of King's Hollow before ripping a hole in it and depositing my cage inside the central room in front of the unlit fireplace.

I scrambled for the door of the cage as he released me from his golden talons and managed to force the shadows back enough to lessen the pain in my hands as I worked to break the lock open. But the thing was sealed up tight in some way I couldn't even begin to figure out and the longer I worked at it, the more the flesh was burned from my body wherever I touched the metal bars.

Darius dropped down into the treehouse in his Fae form and I scrambled back to the middle of the cage as I watched him warily, my gaze shifting over his powerful, naked body as fear swept through me and I wondered what the hell he was going to do to me.

He grabbed a pair of black sweatpants from a chest at the side of the room then turned to face me, his face pinched in pain like he wasn't happy to find me here. But that made no damn sense.

"What are you doing?" I growled, fighting not to show him how much pain I was in even as the blood from my nose dripped over my lips and flooded my tastebuds and the scent of my burned flesh filled my nostrils.

"Will you let me heal you?" he asked, his voice tight and rough.

"No," I growled because if there was one thing that could make my situation worse right now, I knew that it would be allowing him to lay his hands on me. All Darius Acrux ever caused me was pain and even just looking at him now made my chest ache with the memory of lightning slamming into my body and burning me alive from the inside out.

Caleb shot into the room before Darius could say anything else and he sighed irritably as he looked up at the destroyed roof before lifting his hands and using his earth magic to fix the damage Darius had done to fit my cage inside.

"I take it she won't let you heal her?" Caleb asked Darius, acting as if I wasn't even here and I narrowed my eyes on him, trying to figure out how I could get myself out of this.

"Caleb," I breathed, looking up at him through the bars as he turned to look at me in surprise. "I don't want him near me," I said, glancing at Darius whose posture stiffened at my words.

"That's just the shadows talking," Caleb growled firmly, giving Darius a look I couldn't read, but the Dragon clearly could because he clenched his jaw then stalked towards me.

I instantly shifted back, using my hands and feet to propel myself along until I knocked against the rear of the cage and I hissed at the pain of the shadows burning where the bars came into contact with me. The only part of the cage that didn't burn me was the solid base, but as I pressed my palms flat to it, it felt like it was trying to suck the energy from my freaking soul, so I had no desire to push any power into it just to have it stolen.

"Roxy," Darius growled, dropping down into a crouch and looking in at me with his brow creasing. "Please stop looking at me like that."

"Like what?" I hissed, not moving another inch but hating how vulnerable I was right now.

My whole body was coiled with tension in anticipation of what I knew he was going to do to me now that he had me at his mercy. It was all that I could do not to cower and to keep holding his gaze.

"Like you think I'm about to attack you. I fucking love you, Roxy," he growled. "Why the hell would you think I'm going to try and do something to cause you pain?"

I tried to take in what he was saying to me, but the moment I considered his words, the sharp echoes of the pain I knew he'd caused me echoed through my flesh in a keen pulse that made me wince as it bit into me.

Darius tried to reach for me and I scrambled back again, hissing between my teeth as I was pressed against the bars of the cage once more. He cursed loudly as he lurched to his feet and stormed away from me, throwing the couch over as the temper I'd known he had snapped and a roar escaped his lips.

"Darius!" Caleb barked as my skin howled in pain from the contact with the bars but I refused to move even an inch closer to him, knowing it would only be worse with him. "Calm down! What the fuck is wrong with you?"

Darius threw me a pained look and shook his head before storming towards the door. "I'm just making it worse by being here. I'll go and see what's taking the others so long."

Caleb looked torn between going after him and staying with me and I slowly eased away from the bars as I watched him come to the decision to stay. The look he gave me was pitying and the shadows rose up in me again, murmuring sweet promises into my ears, reminding me that this was my chance to escape.

A door slammed downstairs and some more tension slid from my body as I realised that Darius really had gone.

"Caleb?" I murmured, my voice low but more than enough for him to hear with his gifts. "Why are you doing this to me?"

He turned his dark blue eyes on me and moved to lift the couch back up again before rounding it to stand before me.

"I know this is confusing right now, Tory, but I swear to you this is for the best. When you reclaim your Phoenix you'll be able to fight the shadows back. Then you'll be able to think more clearly. Remember-"

"Lionel told me that the things I've forgotten cause me pain," I breathed, crawling towards him and peering between the bars. "That's true isn't it?"

"It's not that simple," he ground out, his jaw clenching.

Silence fell but I could see him wavering a little, watching me closely like he didn't know what to think so I wet my lips slowly as I tried to push him to help me. If I could just make him see how I felt now, surely he'd realise that this wasn't right. Surely he wouldn't keep me locked up in here.

"Please, Caleb, don't do this to me," I begged, letting him see how much I feared what they were planning. "I'm happy now that I'm bonded with my king. And nothing you can do will sever that bond. Besides, I want the shadows. I *need* them. Please don't let them take them from me."

Caleb groaned and dropped his head into his hands. "You're not yourself right now, sweetheart," he said. "But you will be. Soon."

Anger burned through me hot and wild and I lunged towards the bars, throwing the shadows at him with everything I had so that my whole world was consumed in a thick fog of darkness.

The impact they made with the bars had me screaming in agony within moments, but I refused to back down. I'd been reborn in suffering and pain and I could push through this torture to escape the fate they'd decided on for me.

I howled as the bars held, slamming down onto my back as my power ricocheted into me. I began to jerk and convulse with the magic I was wielding as it was driven into my body and the pain felt like magma running through my veins.

But I didn't stop. It would be so much worse than this if I stopped. If I failed my king then the torture I would endure would make this pale in comparison.

Memories of that stone room echoed around my mind. Of the jars of lightning and the metal tools that had carved into my flesh over and over. Darius had done that to me. It was all Darius. Every time I thought of him or woke calling for him in the night or screamed his name while begging for his help, that was what I'd gotten in return. He'd never come for me. He'd abandoned me to that fate.

I couldn't let him take me. I wouldn't.

I threw so much power at the cage that the whole thing shook and rattled while I jerked on my back until suddenly the darkness that surrounded me swept me up and devoured me whole.

And I was finally freed from all of it as I fell into a void of nothing.

Heat slid beneath my veins, thick and potent and full of too many memories for me to fully comprehend.

At first, I recoiled from the intensity of the flames, receding into a corner of my mind that was safe and dark and wrapped in shadow, but the stronger the fire grew, the harder it became to shield myself from it.

When I was certain I was going to burn up in the heat, my eyes snapped open and a cry of fear escaped me.

I gasped as I lurched away from the fire, but there was no escaping it, no retreating from this thing that seemed to be living inside me. I jerked around, finding Darcy looking in through the bars at me as she held a syringe tight in her fist and I looked down at my arm, finding a small puncture wound in my bicep.

"What did you do to me?" I gasped, scrambling back and crying out as I hit the bars of the cage again.

My lips parted on a grunt of pain and I slapped a hand over the puncture wound, looking around at the sea of faces surrounding me as my heart raced.

"Back up," Max growled, his hand landing on Geraldine's arm and tugging her back a step as she sobbed. "She's freaking out and she's about to lose control of her Order form."

"Shit," Seth cursed and he caught Caleb's wrist as he pulled him back too.

"Look at me, Roxy," Darius growled from my right and a shriek of fright escaped me as I found him too fucking close to the bars that contained me.

A blaze of heat raced along my shoulder blades as Max yelled something panicked and more energy than I could possibly contain rose up within me.

My body detonated into a ball of fire, wings tearing from my back and making the cage explode around me, shooting the metal bars out in every direction in a spray of deadly projectiles.

For a moment I was paralysed in fear and panic but in the midst of it, the call of the Phoenix fire in my blood centred me and I found a girl between the flames, her body coated in fire like mine and her arms outstretched to me in a silent plea.

I collided with her with a sob escaping me as she pulled me close, squeezing me so hard I was sure I would break. But I didn't. Because I had her. And she was all I'd ever needed.

My tears turned hysterical as I clung to her, my brain unable to concentrate fully on anything other than how much I'd been missing without her, how much I needed her and how much less I'd been altogether.

I wasn't sure how long we clung to each other like that, practically forming one body, two halves of the same whole. Just the way we'd been born to be.

I slowly became aware of the fire around us dying down as the tears stopped sizzling from my skin and my Phoenix withdrew, sinking within me again though staying close to the surface as it chased the lingering shadows aside.

"You're okay, Tor," Darcy was saying over and over as she held me tight against her and stroked her fingers through my hair.

"Is she under control again?" Seth's voice drew my attention and I turned my head slightly, finding him standing within a dome of ice that Max, Geraldine and Darius were all maintaining around their side of the treehouse to shield everyone.

Behind us, the entire place had been blasted apart and flames still blazed throughout the branches of the trees in the forest beyond.

"You're okay now, aren't you, Tor?" Darcy asked and I blinked up at her, drawing back a little as my brain tried to catch up to what was happening.

I was left feeling like I had to wade through a layer of cotton wool to even understand the words everyone was throwing at me.

"My lady, you may have my clothes!" Geraldine announced loudly, parting the ice beside her and stepping forward as she began to peel off her shirt, making me realise that I'd burned all of my clothes off in the shift and was crouched naked on the floor with my arms wound tightly around myself.

Darcy had clearly had the presence of mind to protect her own outfit when she shifted so I was just the naked ass chick that everyone was staring at.

Embarrassment clawed at me and the shadows slithered beneath my skin, offering me some reprieve from this feeling, but I resisted their call, looking at my sister and finding all I needed to centre myself in her gaze.

Max caught Geraldine's wrist and tugged her back before she could take anything off. "Don't crowd her," he warned. "She might blow again."

My skin prickled with the touch of his Siren gifts and I glanced at Darcy nervously as she gave me an encouraging nod. "Max will help you if you'll let him?"

I was trembling with weakness from the injuries the cage had given me and my brain felt so close to cracking that it was all too tempting to accept, but as a huge figure moved in the corner of my eye, I locked up.

Darius took a step towards me and I gasped, my Phoenix rearing up beneath my skin protectively as fear skittered through me and I tried to scramble back away from him.

"Here," he offered, pulling a hoody from a chest of clothes that had been protected from the blast by the ice shield and offering it to me.

My magic had been replenished a little by the flames of our Phoenixes and I threw an air shield up before Darius could move any closer, recoiling into Darcy's arms as a whimper of fear escaped me.

"Shit," Max cursed, glancing between me and Darius as his face pinched with sadness. "Darius...I think you should leave."

"What?" the Dragon growled, his eyes flashing with a clear refusal and his muscles rippling like he was on the verge of shifting himself.

I sucked in a fearful breath as I pushed more magic into the shield and Darcy caught my chin, turning me to face her as healing magic slid beneath my skin and eased some of the aches in my flesh.

"You don't need to be afraid of Darius, Tory," she breathed. "He's not like his father. He'd never hurt you like Lionel did-"

"Lionel doesn't hurt me," I snarled, pushing out of her arms. "He heals me. He loves me. He's my king."

Silence fell among everyone heavily then Geraldine started wailing loudly as she threw her hands over her eyes.

"Oh sweet heavens have mercy! My lady has been beguiled by a lying lizard and tricked in the most hateful way!"

"No, Tory, he's not," Darcy growled, sending a blast of magic at the shield I'd created and shattering it before using air magic to take the hoody from Darius so she could deposit it over my head. I pushed myself to my feet and it hung down to my mid thigh, a cedar and smoke scent coming from the fabric that made me feel a little safer even as I hurried to back away from Darius.

"You have your Phoenix back now. You need to use it to burn the Dark Coercion out of yourself," Darcy said.

My gaze slid to her as I opened my mouth to tell her I wasn't under the influence of any Coercion but the moment I thought about it, the Phoenix within me flared to life again, rising up and shifting beneath my skin. It blazed a path of destruction through command after command that had been placed on my mind until I was crying again with the relief of the chains being lifted from my psyche.

"What the fuck has he been doing to her?" Caleb murmured as a whine escaped Seth's throat and my gaze darted between all of them as I found myself totally overwhelmed by everything.

"Roxy," Darius breathed, stepping closer again with a hand outstretched in offering. But the moment I looked at him, my heart leapt and pounded with fear again as the memories of so much agony burning through my flesh overwhelmed me. Him. It was all him.

"Stay back," I gasped, almost calling on the shadows again as I found myself without magic once more and at the mercy of this fierce creature before me.

Darius's face tightened and something in his gaze seemed to shatter as I looked at him with fear in my soul so deep that I wasn't sure I'd ever be able to escape it.

"Everyone needs to go," Max commanded suddenly. "Cal, Seth and Gerry, fix the walls before you leave then make sure the forest doesn't show any signs of damage from the flames. "Darius, you just need to...go, I'm sorry but she can't be around you. She's fucking terrified of you. It's overwhelming her-"

"I'm not abandoning her again," Darius growled ferociously and a stab of pain lanced through my flesh at the darkness in his tone.

"I'm sorry, man," Max said, turning to him and grabbing his face, forcing him to look his way. "But you being here is...it's hurting her. I don't know what Lionel has done but every time she looks at you she feels physical pain as well as terror. If I'm gonna have any chance of fixing this, you can't be here. I hate to tell you this, but the more you're around her at the moment, the worse you're making things for her."

Darius gritted his jaw, looking like he could feel that pain in himself as he turned his dark eyes on me and I tried not to flinch this time, but I couldn't help it.

"Is that true, Roxy?" he asked, looking like he wanted nothing more than to close the distance between us and making me want to scream and leap out of the giant hole I'd blasted in the wall just to escape him.

I didn't reply but I didn't deny it and that seemed to be enough to break his resolve as grief flashed through his gaze and he nodded stiffly.

He turned and strode for the exit and Seth howled as he chased after him, Caleb only hesitating a moment longer before he raced out behind them and I relaxed a little as their dominating presences left.

Geraldine was still sobbing while patching up the wall like Max had asked but my gaze moved to the Siren as he slowly closed in on me.

"I think I can help you, Tory," he said gently, a sense of calm and understanding washing through me as he approached, his gifts filling the air around him and drawing me in like a gentle embrace.

"I don't know if-" I began, but Darcy cut me off.

"You can trust him, Tory. He'll help you. Please just let him."

My gaze met my twin's eyes and I found so much hurt and pain in them that I found myself nodding, just needing to do something to alleviate what was making her look at me that way. Memories of our childhood were bubbling up in me until I felt like I was overflowing with them. The good, the bad, the downright fucking miserable. And yet no matter what we'd experienced over the years, I'd always had this one burning light right beside me, like my very own star set to guide me back home always. Darcy. My other half. My one, truest love.

"Okay," I agreed on a breath and Max took my hands in his.

"We'll figure this out, okay little Vega?" he murmured, catching my gaze with his deep brown eyes and for some reason, I really did trust him.

"Alright," I agreed.

"I need to do this with her alone," Max said, not looking away from me for a moment. "So that my sole focus is on her emotions at all times."

Darcy looked ready to refuse and Geraldine threw an arm over her eyes as she sobbed loudly. "You'd better bring my lady back to me, you prize pufferfish. Or I'll cut your fins from your fanny and throw them in a fire!"

Max rolled his eyes at her, smiling warmly at me as his fingers tightened around mine and he continued to push soothing emotions into me.

"I don't want to leave her," Darcy growled defiantly.

"Look," Max said in a rough voice, breaking my gaze as he turned towards her. "Your sister has been through something seriously fucked up. I can't even begin to explain to you the complexity of the emotions she's feeling right now, but if you want me to have even the slightest chance of reversing this shit then you need to get the fuck out of here and let me show you why Sirens are the best fucking Order there is. Because right now I'm pretty sure time is of the essence. Her mind is fractured and malleable with the shadows pushed back and all of that Dark Coercion broken. But every moment that passes, more and more of the things she's feeling are becoming fixed. So do you want me to help her remember who she was before that motherfucker got his hands on her, or do you wanna just stand there and fuck up her chances?"

Darcy glared at him for a long moment then shot me an apologetic look. "I'll be back, Tor," she promised. "Just as soon as you're ready to see me again I'll be here."

I nodded as she grasped Geraldine's arm and tugged her from the room, their footsteps disappearing down the stairs as Max and I regarded each other.

He stepped up to me and took a deep breath as he reached out to cup my face between his large hands.

"Don't fight anything, Tory," he murmured. "Just feel all of it and I promise, I'll help you figure this out."

My heart was racing with panic and fear and I was filled with the desire to bolt and this urgent need to see my king. But as I looked into the depths of his brown eyes, something in me settled and though the tears tracking down my cheeks didn't slow, I managed to release a shaky breath that seemed to hold the weight of the world on it. And then I gave myself to the hold of his powers and let him sweep me away on a tide of pain and heartache.

MAX

CHAPTER SIXTEEN

It had taken me more than five hours of just sifting through the memories of pain and fear that filled Tory's mind before I'd even been able to get down to the roots of them. Lionel had done a damn good job of forcing her to associate every moment of torture he'd inflicted upon her with a memory of Darius.

I'd gotten a clear look at so much torture in her memories that it made me feel sick to my core and bile kept rising up in my throat as my gifts allowed me to feel every single second of it.

I could have shied away, refused to absorb the worst of it and protected myself from it, but she needed this outlet. I was certain of it. She needed to work through each and every time he'd taken her down to that room beneath the Acrux Manor and played out these dark and twisted fantasies on her.

If there had been any doubt in me at all about the depths of Lionel Acrux's depravity before, then there was absolutely no illusions left in me now.

He hadn't just cut, burned and electrocuted Tory until she couldn't even scream any more. He'd revelled in it.

Hidden deep within the memories of her pain there had been more than enough visions of his eyes gleaming with excitement while he made her scream and cry out for mercy. He'd just forced her to think of Darius time and again until she believed those memories were of his eyes. That it had been him doing that to her.

It had taken me the better part of the day to realise that he'd been using a Cyclops to assist him with a lot of his cruelty. He'd taken every dark and pain filled memory she held of Darius from when she'd first arrived at the academy and twisted the knife in the pain she felt over them until she was bleeding from the inside out. And then he'd found all of her good memories too, beating her down over and over again until she couldn't protect them anymore, though I was surprised to find there were a few things hidden within her mind still.

She was still resisting my attempts to get her to unlock them, but each time I guided her thoughts and feelings towards them, she seemed a little closer to looking at them than the last time, so I wasn't giving up.

We'd moved into my bedroom within King's Hollow after the first time she'd blacked out with the memory of the torture she'd endured, and I'd barely caught her before she cracked her head against the hard floorboards.

I'd carried her in here and laid her down on the bed beside the fireplace where I was carefully rebuilding the fire every time it went out. Using my gifts on her like this drained her magic as I fed on it, and she needed to keep replenishing her stores to keep up with how much I was taking while we worked. I was heady on the richness of her power and had had to take breaks several times to empty myself out by throwing a gale of wind into the forest outside or casting a river of water just so that I could continue to draw more from her.

She was curled in my arms, her head resting on my chest as her limbs trembled with the memory of pain that had crashed through her over and over again.

I couldn't help but feel like the monster who had done this to her in the first place as I kept using my gifts to draw this pain out of her and force her to give me every single piece of it. But I knew it was the only way. She needed to release herself from it, needed to look at it clearly and without the taint of Lionel's lies shading it in falsehoods if she was ever going to be able to move on from it.

I wasn't even going to let myself think about what it was doing to me. I was using the fullest extent of my gifts with her and she was opening herself up to them, letting me fully immerse myself in her memories so that I could actually watch them play out like I was there myself. I rarely pushed so deep into anyone's mind like this, but if I wanted any chance at all of fixing what had been done to her then I had to.

I closed my eyes as I pushed my power into her again and her cold fingers fisted in my shirt as a gasp of pain escaped her and I grunted as I felt the sharp kick of electricity slam into my own chest as if I'd been there too. I could taste blood in my mouth as she bit her tongue while she jerked and spasmed from the pain of the strike. And the hard bite of the leather straps which held her arms and wrists in place on the wooden chair she'd been strapped to in her underwear set panic racing through my limbs.

"Who do you love?" Lionel asked coldly while Clara hung off of his arm, smiling as she bared her fangs.

"You," I gasped, my voice Tory's as I relived her memory.

"What about my son?" Lionel asked, moving aside as the Cyclops stepped forward and I shook my head desperately. He had thick black hair which hung long over his shoulders and a wizened face with a jagged old scar

running through his left eye which had left the white stained red with blood even though the wound was clearly old. He called it his shadow eye, claiming he had the ability to see visions of the Shadow Realm as well as our own, and it was clear that Lionel believed him. His pupils were so dark they looked black and as he turned his gaze on me, I shuddered with fear, knowing all too well what he was capable of.

"I hate him," I said. "I hate him more than anyone I've ever met. All he does is cause me pain." But I didn't feel those words. I felt Darius's arms around me as we lay in his bed and he held me like he never wanted to let go. I felt the way my heart pounded when he looked at me and I remembered the way he'd promised to fight for me.

"Liar, liar," the Cyclops purred, reaching out and running a finger down my neck and between the valley of my breasts before hooking it around the centre of my bra and tugging lightly.

"Hands off, Vard," Lionel growled and I shivered in relief as he saved me from the Cyclops's wandering hands and he released me with a flicker of irritation on his features. "Just do your job."

The Seer huffed softly as he gave in to Lionel's command, rolling his neck in that way he always did before he shifted and making my pulse spike with fear.

"I like the pretty jewel she's wearing, Daddy," Clara breathed in Lionel's ear, pushing her hand into Lionel's pants and he growled softly.

"Now that you mention it, Clara dear, that necklace looks familiar to me." My heart thumped as they looked at the ruby necklace Darius had given me and I recoiled into my chair even though I knew there was no escape. "If you like it then you can have it."

Clara grinned excitedly but Vard moved to stand before me, capturing my attention once more as I tried to figure out who I should be fearing the most in this room.

Vard smiled toothily as his dark eyes slowly slid together, forming one huge, bulbus eye in the centre of his forehead and I snapped my eyes shut, scrunching them up as I tried to protect myself from the invasion of his mind into mine.

Clara cackled with glee as she leapt up onto the back of the wooden chair I was strapped to and grabbed a fistful of my hair, pulling hard enough to make me scream before peeling my eyelid open with her dirty fingernails digging in hard enough to make me bleed. Her other hand yanked on my necklace as she scrambled for the clasp and I felt her tug it free just as I lost the battle to keep my eye closed.

Vard caught me in his gaze and within a moment, the slimy, intrusive feeling of him slithering into my mind overwhelmed me and I swear I could feel his hot breath on my neck as he spoke inside my thoughts.

"I've seen a future where I get to touch you as much as I like, little dove," he purred. "Where my king will gift you to me and send you to my bed as often as I wish in reward for all of the visions I've gifted him. Did you know *your daddy gave me my scar? I'm going to enjoy paying his daughter back for it, over and over and over again."*

Vard drove that point home with mental images which made me gag with actual bile rising in my throat and if I'd had anything to eat today, I was certain I'd have been vomiting all down myself. Just as I felt myself start screaming at the imagined scenario playing out in my head, Vard's gifts shifted beneath my skin and he spoke a single name inside my head.

"Darius Acrux."

Before I could do a single thing to stop it, my mind whirled to the moment I'd thought of earlier, of me wrapped in Darius's arms in his bed, of how warm his skin had felt against mine and how safe it had seemed there.

But as I rolled over, I found Darius glaring at me instead of the sleepy, half smile I almost remembered. His hand snapped out and he locked it around my throat as he pinned me down against the bed, ripping open the shirt I was wearing while I fought and bucked beneath him. I couldn't scream, his grip on my throat suffocating and refusing even the slightest noise to pass my lips as he smiled cruelly and slammed a fist down into my chest.

The moment the punch landed, the force of a thunderstorm crashed into my body and I shrieked with pain as it burned me from the inside out, thrashing against the vision of Darius in my mind and the straps which held me to the chair in reality. My brain tried to keep hold of what was happening, what was real and what was a lie, but everything was blurring together as Vard used his powers until all of it merged into one and the cruelty in Darius's eyes was the only thing I was truly certain of alongside the agony in my flesh.

I fell back panting on the bed as I shrugged the memory off, tugging Tory closer to me as she trembled in my arms, helping her to see the way her memories had been manipulated to turn her against Darius while trying to contain my own emotions so that I didn't accidentally push them into her.

My body ached with the echoes of the torture she'd endured and I could feel her exhaustion as she curled against my chest and I wrapped my arms around her tighter. She needed a break. And if I was being honest then I did too because this shit was seriously fucked up. I felt like it might break me if I wasn't careful and I had to keep reminding myself of all the reasons I had to love Darius as the conditioning she'd been put through wormed its way into my head too.

I stroked my fingers through her hair, using my gifts to make her feel even more tired and pushing her into a deep, dreamless sleep before feeding her as much happy, calming energy as I could muster.

When I was certain she wasn't going to wake any time soon, I gently rolled her off of me and tucked her beneath the covers, frowning at how fragile she looked in the big bed all alone. Lionel Acrux was going to pay for what he'd done to her and Darius. Not to mention all the other reasons I had to hate him.

I left the room, but before I could even call Darius and Darcy, they appeared with Gabriel between them, the Harpy giving me a knowing look which I was clearly going to have to get used to.

"How is she?" Darcy asked urgently and I summoned the shadow of a smile for her even though the weight of everything I'd just experienced through Tory's memories was hanging so heavily on me that I felt like I might break beneath the pressure of it all.

"Better," I muttered, swiping a hand down my face. "I think she's seeing Lionel more clearly now, though the Guardian bond makes it hard for her to fully hate him. I've helped her to process a lot of her trauma, but..." My gaze slid to Darius and he nodded like he already knew what I was going to say.

"You just have to prove to her that you're not the monster she was made to believe you are," Gabriel said firmly, clapping a hand on Darius's shoulder before looking to me. "You need to rest, Max. Get some sleep tonight. I'll inform the staff that there's a bout of Fae flu going around as an excuse for you and Tory missing classes tomorrow. After that, I believe she will be able to function well enough to return."

"You really think she's gonna be able to fake it good enough for that to be safe?" I growled, feeling strangely protective over the girl I'd once sworn to ruin no matter what. But fuck putting her back in the firing line of that monster.

"It's the only way forward at the moment," Gabriel said firmly. "Any attempt we make to hide her or help her escape Lionel will fail if we try now. I've spent the entire day trying to *see* a way out of this for her, but with the bond in place..." He sighed heavily. "All isn't lost. She'll be as safe as she can be if she just keeps up the pretence of maintaining her position in alignment with him for now. But if she tries to run, the bond will force her back to him eventually and the punishment for her trying to escape will be unthinkable. This is the way it has to be."

I pinched the bridge of my nose, hating that idea but knowing that Gabriel wouldn't be pushing for it if he could *see* any other way. It seemed like fate wasn't done fucking with us yet then.

"Fine," I muttered as Darius growled beneath his breath.

"Me and Gabriel will stay with her tonight," Darcy said softly, moving to wrap her arms around my neck and squeeze me tightly. "Thank you, Max."

I was so exhausted that I didn't even hug her back, not wanting to let any of the emotions I was trying to contain slip out of me. Because she didn't need to see the details of what her sister had been through at the hands of that tyrant. I didn't want it haunting her the way I knew it was going to haunt me.

Gabriel thanked me as he followed Darcy away down the hall but Darius didn't move, like he could already tell from my expression that he wasn't going to be welcome in that room.

He waited until Darcy and Gabriel were out of sight before flicking his fingers and casting a silencing bubble around us.

"Show me," he demanded and I sighed.

"You don't wanna see it, man. Hell, I don't wanna fucking see it and I'm not in love with the girl," I tried, though I could already see how determined he was to know the extent of it.

"It can't be any worse than what I'm already imagining," he growled and I swiped a hand down my face, shaking my head.

"Imagining it and living it aren't the same. I'm begging you to leave it. Trust me to help her through it, know that it's over now and just try to-"

"Show me," he commanded, grabbing my hand and lacing his voice with Coercion even though he knew I could shove off the impulse to comply if I wanted to. But I was fucking tired and I knew he wouldn't drop it, so I showed him what he wanted to see even though I knew this was going to hit him like a stab wound to the fucking heart.

I pushed my gifts at him and he dropped his mental barriers to allow me to show him the memories I'd lived out inside Tory's head. Darius's grip on my hand tightened and the rage and grief I felt from him hit me like a tidal wave as he watched what his father had done to her.

"How often did he do this?" he snarled, his grip unyielding so he was crushing the bones in my fingers, though I was fairly certain he hadn't even realised he was doing it.

"Not as often recently. It was almost all within the first six weeks," I muttered. "He stopped once she showed fear in response to every mention of you."

Darius kept hold of me for several long minutes, his magic keeping its grip on mine as he forced me to show him as much of what Tory had suffered through as he could manage before he dropped my hand and turned away from me with a stream of smoke billowing between his lips.

"Wait," I called after him, trying to push my gifts at him to help ease some of the pain he was feeling, even as the exhaustion from using them all day almost swallowed me whole.

Darius didn't reply, ripping off his shirt and leaping out of the window before I could say another word.

The haunting roar of a Dragon in distress rattled the entire treehouse a moment later as he took off towards the sky and I felt something shatter deep inside me as my own grief over all of this threatened to tear me apart.

I swallowed thickly, taking in the empty space around me before turning and heading for the door.

As much as I wanted to stay close to Tory tonight to help her, I knew that when I slept I was going to be broadcasting all of the horrors I'd just experienced for anyone nearby to feel. Not that I was convinced I'd be sleeping at all after living through all of that. It was the curse of my kind. We took emotions from others, but it was more than just an exchange of magic. We were left with the feelings of those we drained. Their pain and memories became our own if we took too much and we could be left carrying the hurts of a hundred Fae in our hearts if we weren't careful to feed on happiness more often than sorrow. But if you took too much happiness from another Fae then you left them in pain instead of yourself which wasn't any better, unless you were a complete asshole. Which I tried not to be most of the time.

I sighed as I walked down the path though The Wailing Wood, heading for the lake and Aqua House while trying to skim whatever brief flashes of happiness that I could taste on any of the Fae I passed by just to take the edge off of what was consuming me.

But it was no good. Every time I closed my eyes, I was reliving Tory's nightmares, drowning in Darius's feelings of failure and so much pain that it made me choke.

I hardly even noticed that I was back at my dorm until I was turning my key in the lock and pushing the door wide.

I didn't even flick the lights on, just knocking the door shut behind me as I kicked off my shoes and tugged my shirt over my head. It was still damp with Tory's tears, but it hadn't felt right to dry them out with magic. They were too heavy to just wish away like that.

I noticed the door hadn't clicked shut behind me and looked over my shoulder to find Geraldine pushing it open hesitantly.

"I'm sorry, Gerry," I murmured. "I don't think I can bear to go over it all again tonight. Maybe just give me tonight to-"

"I didn't come to enquire about my lady, you bumbling beluga," she said in a soft voice, pushing the door closed behind her as she stepped inside. "I came to enquire about you."

I stilled, a lump forming in my throat as I took that in.

"I thought you didn't care about me?" I asked a little bitterly, our ongoing argument over her engagement to that fucking stuck up assbag still biting at me.

Geraldine sighed, kicking her shoes off and dropping her blazer as she padded towards me with her eyes glimmering with tears.

"Don't do that tonight, Maxy boy," she breathed. "Just let me hold you close and we can pretend the rest of the world isn't out there."

I swallowed thickly, nodding as she wrapped her hands around my waist and gently pushed me back until I was sinking down onto the bed.

Her mouth found mine as she lowered down onto my lap and I groaned softly as I fell back beneath her. Our kiss was slow and deep and laced with pain that wouldn't be fixed by anything we did now, but somehow it helped all the same.

I pulled her closer as the warmth of her body against mine seemed to soothe something deep within my soul and somehow we ended up curled together against my pillows as her soft hands continued to soothe and caress me.

I kissed her again, devouring her slowly while my heart pounded to this torturous rhythm that made me ache in a wholly different way than I had all day.

"I hate fighting with you, Gerry," I breathed as I moved my hands into her hair, letting some of my heartache slip away and worshipping her with every movement of my mouth against hers.

Everything just felt better when I was with her. She could fight away the worst demons in my mind and keep them at bay if only she'd stay here.

"Then stop talking," she breathed. "We only argue when you open your flapper trap."

I had to admit she had a point there, so I closed my mouth and gave in to what she wanted, as she pulled me into her arms. I laid my head against her chest where the solid thump of her heart beat beneath my ear and her presence eased the pain in my soul unlike anything else could have.

Her fingers stroked through my hair and there was this beautiful feeling of contentment that came from her which helped to ease the ache in my soul and stop the cycle of horrifying memories from dominating my mind.

It wasn't enough to chase out all of the dark in me. But it was the sliver of light I'd been aching for, calling me home.

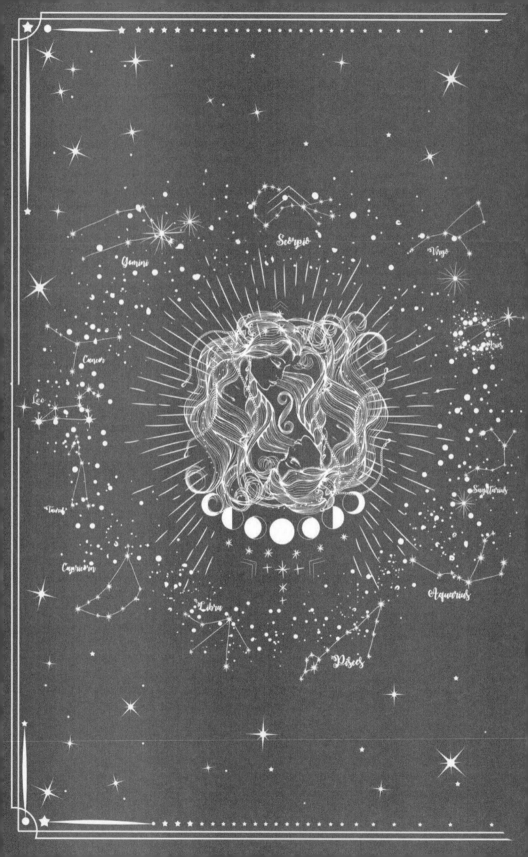

DARCY

CHAPTER SEVENTEEN

When Max returned the next morning at dawn, he made me and Gabriel leave so that he could wake Tory. I hadn't spoken to her, just curled up in bed between her and Gabriel while she slept. Me and my brother had stayed up talking half the night in a silencing bubble about Tory, the Imperial Star, Lionel's awful Orderist shit and just…everything.

I was out in the woods close to King's Hollow, pacing and practising my earth magic, making a whole tree regrow its leaves like it was in the height of summer before they all turned crisp and brown and came fluttering down around me in the air again. Gabriel had gone flying to ease his own anxiety and every now and then a shadow would cross overhead and I knew he was close.

When Max finally texted an hour later to say we could come back, I ran through the trees as fast as I could, desperate to see my sister. It had been agony waiting. And I'd longed for her to come back to me for so long. I didn't want to waste one more single second away from her.

I made it to the treehouse and Gabriel landed in front of me. I crashed into him and he wrapped me in his arms, holding me tight. Max stepped out of the door and we parted as he gave us a tight smile, his eyes ringed with darkness.

"How is she?" I begged.

"She's okay," he said, but his voice was laced with an undertone of worry. "At least, I think she will be in time."

Tears burned my eyes and I wrapped my arms around his neck, feeling his Siren power reaching out to soothe me. I let my defences down so he could and brushed my fingers over the back of his neck as I released some healing energy into his body to fight the exhaustion he must have been feeling.

"Thank you," I breathed as he held onto me for a moment before stepping back. I could never repay him for this. One look in his eyes told me what this had cost him, and there were no words which could ever encompass my gratitude for that.

He gestured for us to go inside and I ran into the tree trunk with Gabriel hot on my heels. We raced up the spiralling stairway and I pushed through the door into the lounge. I sprinted to Max's room and forced myself to stop before I just burst through it. I couldn't possibly understand what she was going through right now, and as much as I wanted to believe she would need me close, maybe I was wrong. Maybe she wanted space. And though the idea of that broke me, I knew I had to offer anything and everything she needed.

I knocked gently and Gabriel remained quiet, though he could probably *see* exactly how this was going to play out.

"Tor?" I called, my voice quavering. *Please be okay.*

"Darcy?" she called back, hope filling her voice and tears rushed down my cheeks.

"I'm here with Gabriel." I pressed my forehead to the door, letting the tears run, not bothering to even try and hold them back. "Can we come in?"

"Yes," she croaked and I twisted the door handle, pushing the door open to reveal the darkened room with a lamp switched on by the bed. She was curled up in a ball at the heart of the covers and she pushed herself up to look at us, her face blotchy from crying. I rarely ever saw my sister like that; it made me want to find Lionel Acrux this very second and make him bleed for what he'd dared do to her.

Gabriel's shoulder brushed mine as we waited for her to speak, but she didn't, she just opened her arms to us with a choked sob and I ran to her, jumping onto the bed and falling on top of her as I crushed her in my arms.

"I'm so sorry," she sobbed and I held her tighter as I fell into the space beside her, kissing her forehead and keeping her close.

"Don't be sorry for anything," I growled. "It wasn't you. It was Lionel."

She shuddered at his name and I clutched her tighter as Gabriel joined us in the bed, his strong arms wrapping around us until all of our souls seemed to connect. We just held each other and I felt the love of my family binding us all so tightly together that nothing could ever break us. Not Lionel, not the stars. They might have tried to shatter our wills and crush us beneath them, but they'd never succeed. We'd always end up back together. Where we were meant to be.

"Are you okay?" I breathed and she nodded.

"Yeah, not perfect, but I'm okay," she said. "And that's better than I've been in a long time."

After a while, a quiet kind of peace fell over us all and the wound in my heart started to heal. This would always leave a scar. But now I had Tory back, I was going to make sure nothing ever happened to her again. And that she got what she deserved. A fucking happily ever after.

"Do you want to talk about it?" I whispered to Tory as our heads lay on one pillow, facing each other while Gabriel wrapped his arms around her from behind.

She shook her head, her eyes wet, but no more tears were falling. And knowing Tor, she wouldn't let any more fall for Lionel Acrux after this.

"Not yet," she breathed and I nodded.

"If there's anything you need, tell me," I said and a smile hooked up the corner of her mouth.

Gabriel propped his head up on a pillow behind her and grinned mischievously like he knew exactly what Tory was going to ask for.

"I want to go flying," she said. "I want to fly with you and Gabriel somewhere far away from here."

"Tonight," Gabriel promised. "We can sneak off campus after classes and go together."

I clutched Tory's hand as my heart ached. "Anything else?"

"Coffee," she half sniffed, half laughed and I grinned. "And some of Geraldine's buttery bagels."

"I'll get her to bring some," I said, returning her smile but Tory caught my hand before I got out of bed.

"And I want things to go back to normal. Don't act like I'm made of glass. Promise?" she asked, the fire in her eyes saying she needed that more than anything else.

I nodded firmly, my heart squeezing with love for her. "I promise."

I took out my Atlas, shooting Geraldine a message and she replied in half a second flat.

Geraldine:

My lady will have the butteriest of bagels brought to her door this very

instant!

Gabriel sat up and Tory moved to sit beside him, resting her head on his shoulder.

"Darius is bringing coffee," Gabriel said and Tory sucked in a breath, but he went on before she could say anything. "Max has told him to stay outside. He won't see you until you're ready."

She nodded, her eyes swimming with some dark emotion, but there was love there too. The black rings in her eyes were always evidence of that these days. The way they were bound was imperfect and cruel, but it was still a mark of how absolutely meant for each other they were. And I swore on all I was, I'd help them find a way to fix it.

"Tell me the future is good, Gabriel," Tory whispered and I looked to him, needing to know that too.

Gabriel frowned thoughtfully, taking her hand and squeezing it. "The future can be good."

It wasn't a promise, but it was hope. And for now that was enough.

It wasn't long before Geraldine arrived and I hurried downstairs to fetch the bagels from her. She'd brought an entire basket, fit to bursting with bagels, butter and a whole range of jellies, toast, pastries and juice.

She burst into tears as she saw me, placing the basket at my feet and dropping to her knees in the mud. "Tell me she's well! Oh Darcy, I must hear that her spritely heart is beating and that her tongue is sharp and her wit is keen. Oh my lady, please tell me Tory is whole and sound and that the stars have gifted her with a thousand hopes and joys. Has she awoken with a sparkle in her eye and a spring in her step?" She clutched onto my legs, tipping her head back and baying like a hound.

I dropped down before her, hugging her tight as I felt her pain begin to split me apart again. "She's going to be okay. It'll take time, but she's back, Geraldine. And she's not going anywhere ever again. I'll make sure of that."

She sobbed against my shoulder for a few long minutes before finally pulling herself together and getting to her feet. "Well, we must have a stiff upper lip, hmm? Mustn't let her see us blabbering like bandicoots with our faces as wet as fishes."

I nodded, smiling at her as I picked up the basket of food. "Thanks for this."

"You are most welcome, and if you need anything more, summon me. As your most faithful friend, I shall always, always come." She turned and headed off into the trees and my gaze caught on Darius standing there with his shoulder pressed to a trunk, his eyes fixed on the window of Max's room above us.

He had a thermos in his grip and as he looked to me, he frowned. "This is for her." He held it out then pulled a packet of Tory's favourite chocolate wafers from his pocket.

I moved forward to take them and he caught the back of my neck, pulling me into a tight hug. I swear I'd never been hugged so much in my life as I had this morning, but I knew we all needed it. My gaze caught on Caleb and Seth standing further off in the trees, watching us with anxious expressions.

"Don't ever let her go again, Darius Acrux," I growled in his ear. "Don't you hurt her or let her down or make her cry. I don't know how we'll fix everything, but we will. And when we do and you two can love each other like you're meant to, I won't take any shit from you."

He chuckled in a low tone as he released me and tapped me on the nose. "It's a deal, Gwen," he said and I punched his arm playfully before turning away with a smirk.

I headed back inside and found Tory and Gabriel waiting in the lounge. I passed Tory her coffee and she eyed it for a long time when I told her who had brought it, but she didn't say anything about him.

I set about laying the basket of food on the coffee table and we all sat around it on the floor, eating the incredible freshly baked food until we were stuffed.

Once Tory had been caught up on everything that had been going on without her around, we just talked and talked about some of the good in the world. Gabriel told us about how his baby boy was growing out of his clothes nearly every month and how his wife could feed him, clean the house and do a workout in some stupid amount of time because of the gifts of her Order.

For a while, the rest of the world just faded away and for the first time in a long time, I felt truly happy.

I stood up to my waist in the warm water of the lagoon in Water Elemental class in my last lesson of the day. Tory was feigning being ill with Fae flu so she could recover a bit more today and prepare to return to lessons tomorrow and Gabriel had insisted I go to classes for the day so we didn't draw any attention to Tory.

The joy of getting her back was tainted by the fact she would now have to continue going to Lionel whenever he summoned her, pretending that she was still a slave to the shadows. I'd tried to fight it, coming up with any other option that I could think of, but in the end Gabriel had insisted it was the only option. And I really couldn't argue with him considering he had The Sight.

"That's it, Miss Vega," Washer called, wading toward me. He parted the water around him with his magic so he was walking on dry land, giving me a full view of the bulge in his tight speedo before letting the water lap in all around him again. Was that really necessary??

"Let's see it one more time," he encouraged and I turned my attention to the water, placing my hand into it and causing a whirlpool to form around it, swirling faster and faster until it started to drag students in closer and they had to fight to get out of the current.

"Wonderful!" Washer cheered, slapping me on the back one inch away from my ass. "Now pair up with Miss Grus and let's see you create a whirly wet hole together."

"Er, sir?" Damian Evergile called over to him with pursed lips. He'd pinned his K.U.N.T. badge to his swimming trunks like a douche. "You shouldn't be pairing people out of their Orders."

Washer shot him a glare. "Well Miss Vega here has no other students of her Order in the class at this moment, so what do you expect me to do?" he snapped, and I swear I'd never seen him get so angry.

Max suddenly came surfing across the water on a wave, kicking Damian in the head and Geraldine started cheering, jumping up and down as her breasts bounced in her tight swimming costume.

"Hey Gerry, watch this!" Max called, circling around the guy until he came to a halt standing right on top of his head, casually leaning on a pillar of water he cast beside him.

"Wonderful work, Mr Rigel. Take twenty points for House Aqua," Washer said as Damian started flailing, his arms flying out of the water as he struggled to get Max off of him.

Darius walked across the water on the surface, just as Max hopped off of Damian's head and dived under. He resurfaced with the boy locked in a choke hold and Darius smirked darkly.

"We'll give him some private tuition over here, sir," Darius called to Washer who smirked back.

"Ah yes, Mr Acrux, that sounds like a great idea. Make sure you keep yourselves nice and lubricated while you're working, it makes wrangling the water Element so much easier." He bent down, scooping up a handful of water and rubbing it over his tanned, waxed chest, spending extra time massaging it into his nipples. *Ergh.*

I walked over to work with Geraldine with a shudder and we started working to make a whirlpool together as the sound of Damian screaming came from behind the waterfall. I laughed darkly and Geraldine laughed like a sea witch too. Max and Darius hadn't even bothered to cast a silencing bubble, but I guessed being the son of Lionel Acrux meant no one was going to question you on shit now. The other K.U.N.T.s in the class were silent and I doubted they wanted to meet the same fate.

"That's it my dears," Washer called to us encouragingly. "Put your hips into it like this." He grabbed the hips of some unsuspecting freshman, pressing his crotch to his ass and swirling his hips in a circular motion, guiding them with his own. *Ohmagod.*

"Yep, we got it," I said. "Demonstration not needed."

Washer continued to swirl the freshman's hips a few more times before stepping back and scruffing the boy's hair, sending him on his way. The kid headed off, looking pale faced and violated, which was basically how most people looked after an incident with Washer. He was so gross.

Angelica came over to work near us, glancing our way with a tight smile. "I heard he broke up with Nova," she whispered as she cast a whirlpool of her own.

"How come?" I asked in surprise.

"He's totally anti-Acrux," she breathed. "And Nova's like an Acrux uber fan, so I guess it didn't work out."

I glanced over at Washer in surprise who was now standing up on a rock in the centre of the pool with his hands on his hips as he did lunges. I guessed that made me like him one percent more, shame he was such a creep though.

"Angelica here has started making a spectacular spreadsheet," Geraldine said proudly. "She's working out which teachers are pro Acrux and who are against him."

"Well, I wouldn't say it's spectacular," Angelica laughed, waving her off. "But it might be handy for the you know what." She gave Geraldine a wink and I frowned.

"What?" I whispered and Geraldine cast a silencing bubble over us quickly, her eyes darting left and right.

"We are starting an uprising, Darcy. In the name of the rightful queens. The A.S.S. will unite and cast an unstoppable wind through this academy that will drive out the turds."

I snorted a laugh, but realised she was deadly serious and that analogy hadn't been intentional. "Well obviously I'm up for any kind of Asscrux rebellion."

"We are stockpiling weapons, my lady. I have many an A.S.S. collecting Griffin droppings in the early morn, and I have taken a chaos crystal or two from the potions lab." She grinned widely. "Leave it all with me, I shall build an underground army ready to follow you and Tory into the depths of hell and back again. I have also sent as many of our dear Tiberian Rat friends as I could to my father before they could be taken for inquisition."

"Is he helping them?" I whispered hopefully and she nodded.

"He is leading them to secret burrows in the north," she whispered though the silencing bubble would stop anyone from hearing anyway. "As well as creating a network of friends and allies to our great and noble cause who will be at your back the moment you are ready to make your play for the crown."

My heart lifted and my spirits soared. I loved hearing that people were fighting back, that the whole kingdom wasn't just lying down and letting Lionel screw them.

"Alright, that'll do for today!" Washer called. "Class dismissed."

We headed back to the changing rooms and my heart pounded harder as I hurried to wash and change, excitement rushing through me at the thought of going flying with Tory and Gabriel.

"I have to go." I waved goodbye to Geraldine and Angelica, running out of the lagoon in my sweatpants and crop top, parting the waterfall with a wave of my hand and letting my wings spread out from my back. I took off into the sky, fire rushing along my limbs as I swept through the cold air and took a winding route toward the outer fence where I could get past the wards. I was always careful to land far enough away from it and jog the last few hundred yards on foot though, just in case I was being watched.

I found Tory and Gabriel waiting for me on the other side of the fence and I crushed Tory in another hug as she laughed. She was thinner than she had been and sadder too, but I knew the girl I loved was still here and we'd soon figure out how to make Lionel pay for everything he'd done to her. I just hoped I could help to banish that haunted look in her eyes as soon as she was ready to open up to me. Gabriel tossed stardust over us and we were transported through the stars in a tunnel of twisting light.

We arrived out at the canyon where Gabriel had first taught us to fly in the incredible jungle of Baruvia. Tory took my hand and Gabriel's on her other side, dragging us toward the edge of the canyon with a look of determination. My stomach lifted and adrenaline rushed through my veins as we all ran flat out and dove over the edge.

We free fell fast, our screams echoing around the canyon and making a flock of birds take off from the trees far below. My wings burst free the same time Tory's did and Gabriel fell a few more seconds before shifting himself.

I laughed as Tory flew around me in circles, the smile on her face filling me up with purest sunlight. I had missed her so damn much, and I was never going to get tired of seeing her smiling.

Gabriel rushed up between us and sped towards the azure sky far above. Tory and I shared a grin before shooting after him, taking chase. We climbed higher and higher, the feel of the sun on my skin like a balm on my soul.

Through all the darkness, I'd finally found something good to hold onto. My brother, my sister, my friends. I would never take any of them for granted. And Lionel had better enjoy his time on the throne while it lasted, because the true queens would soon be coming to take it back.

TORY

CHAPTER EIGHTEEN

Stepping out of King's Hollow for my first day back at school since I'd been brought back to myself felt like slipping from one reality to the next. I couldn't be myself anymore. But I wasn't Lionel's pet version of myself either. Even my memories of the time I'd spent serving Lionel's goals were thick with a fog of shadows over them and it was hard for me to fully recall the way I'd been behaving. Not to mention the idea of taking part in K.U.N.T. enforcement made my stomach turn. *Fuck my life.*

I adjusted my blazer as I walked, the material feeling claustrophobic as I drew in a long breath then released it again.

"Are you sure you're okay to do this?" Darcy murmured, taking my hand and giving my fingers a squeeze.

"I'm the asshole who went running right into Lionel's trap, remember?" I teased, though my gut knotted with anxiety. Not only that but Diego had died too and if I'd just done more to confirm that Darcy really had been missing then neither of us would have walked into that trap. I may never have ended up in Lionel's clutches and Diego might still be alive. "I brought this on myself."

"Don't say that, Tor," Darcy breathed and I shrugged.

"At least I'm in the perfect position to spy on him now," I said, trying to remind myself of all the reasons I had to give myself to this role completely. "Besides, shadow Tory was a total dick - it's not that much of a leap for me to embrace her nature."

"Stop that," Darcy laughed, slapping my arm as I smirked at her. It felt good to joke about it even if I was internally shitting myself.

"It's true. And maybe I can channel that dickish behaviour onto some people who deserve it while I'm working undercover."

"Just don't take any risks. And remember, we can meet back here tonight, so you're not really alone, even if it might feel like you are while you're playing this part."

"Don't worry about me," I said, giving her a smile that I knew was too bright before pulling her into a hug. "I'd better go on alone now though. Can't have anyone seeing us socialising."

"Imagine the scandal," she deadpanned as I released her and I gave her one last smile before turning and walking away into the trees.

I passed through the various wards and spells which were in place around King's Hollow to keep the weaker students away and tried not to let my nerves get the better of me as I headed for The Orb.

My stiletto heels clicked along the path and I lifted my chin as I walked, narrowing my eyes a little and letting my resting bitch face do the work of keeping the other students away from me.

I didn't give anyone my attention for any length of time, and I tugged on my connection to the shadows to help keep me calm as the golden building appeared through the trees ahead of me.

As I stepped out of the wood, I set my gaze on the doors to The Orb and almost didn't notice as Darius appeared, jogging up the path which led back towards Ignis House wearing a pair of black shorts and sneakers and nothing else.

My heart thumped in recognition of him and I stole a moment to run over all the reasons why I knew I shouldn't fear him. Max had helped me reclaim my happy memories of him for the most part, but he'd said the knee jerk fear I felt at Darius's presence wasn't going to be so easy to fix. I'd been conditioned to associate the sight or even mention of him with pain and violence. The only real way for me to get over that was by exposing myself to him repeatedly until I just learned not to feel it anymore. Easier said than done. Especially when the mere sight of him had me wanting to call on every drop of magic in my body to protect myself and had all of my muscles locking up instantly.

I closed my eyes, trying to focus on the real memories I had of running with Darius and wanting to see him in the mornings like this and using them to centre me. When I opened them again, I felt a little more in control and I blew out a breath as I made myself continue towards The Orb.

We reached the door at almost the same moment and I stilled as he placed a hand on it to keep it closed before casting a look over his shoulder to make sure no one was nearby.

"Morning, Roxy," he said in that low, rough voice of his and I chewed on my bottom lip as I found myself caught between the urge to run from him and move closer. The strangest thing was, I was fairly certain that had always been the way I felt about him. It had nothing to do with anything Lionel had subjected me to.

Darius's expression was guarded as he looked down at me, seeming to be trying to assess how I was taking this unexpected meeting and I wasn't even certain myself, so I couldn't exactly help him out either.

I wet my lips as I tried to quiet my thundering pulse and hunted down my voice which was hiding out somewhere in the back of my mind alongside my sanity which seemed to have departed several weeks ago.

"Hi," I replied, not having anything better to say to him than that because I wasn't even sure where to begin or if I'd even be able to find the words if I tried.

There was an endless chasm of time and unspoken pain between us and I wasn't sure how to even start trying to bridge it, let alone if we could achieve that at all.

He paused, looking like he had a thousand words waiting to tumble from his lips but then he just pulled the door wide and held it open for me instead of speaking any of them. I managed not to flinch at the movement, but it was a hard won battle and I was pretty sure he noticed.

I stepped closer to him hesitantly, my pulse picking up the pace as I was enveloped in the masculine cedar and smoke scent of him. My gaze dipped to his inked torso for a moment and I paused as I spotted a new tattoo which curved over his left hip bone and disappeared beneath his shorts.

But before I could get a good look at it, he hitched his shorts an inch higher and hid it from view.

"You're gonna have to get my pants off if you wanna see that one, Roxy," he teased and I found myself replying before I could think it through.

"Nice try, asshole."

We both paused for a moment, looking at each other like we'd somehow stepped back in time and I offered him the briefest hint of a smile before moving inside, feeling his eyes on my back as I walked away.

I tugged the shadows closer as I spotted the H.O.R.E.S. and K.U.N.T.s waiting for me, wondering what the fuck my life had come to to find myself heading into their company for the day.

I grabbed a tray and headed over to pick out my breakfast, my stomach growling loudly as I looked at the sweet pastries on offer and I remembered the bland meals I'd been eating over the last few months. The shadows were so consuming that they'd pushed out my desire for food and I'd forgotten to even eat at all half the time. But now that I was pushing them back, my appetite was returning with a vengeance.

I stacked cinnamon buns on my plate four high then moved along to the coffee machine where Darius was pouring out two mugs. He placed one on my tray as I hesitantly approached him and I stilled, looking down at it as my stomach knotted. All the memories of all the times he'd brought me coffee in the mornings came flooding back in on me at once and I was overwhelmed with the desire to reach out to him even while I fought off the desire to recoil from him.

Darius didn't say anything else to me with so many people around and I had to ignore the urge to turn and watch him walking away with my heart pounding as I headed over to join the least desirable people in the room.

"Did you hear?" Mildred asked, crumbs flying from her mouth as she failed to finish chewing her food before speaking.

I didn't respond, assuming she wasn't talking to me seeing as there were like eight other people sitting around her but as her little beady eyes swivelled over to look at me, I realised she was.

"What?" I asked, lifting my first cinnamon bun to my lips and forcing myself not to groan as I bit into it. Shadow bitch Tory didn't take pleasure from anything except shadow torturing people, so I had to pretend my food wasn't the best thing I'd eaten in months. But fuck me with a buttery bagel, this was *good*.

"Daddy was involved in a Nymph raid on a Tiberian Rat nest last night. He caught six of the little squealers trying to run and lit them up like a bonfire!" she gushed excitedly and suddenly the food in my mouth didn't taste so great anymore.

"He killed them?" I asked, my tone harsher than it should have been and I hastily reached for the shadows to help deaden the rage that ignited in me as I had to fight not to leap to my feet and scream at her.

"Of course! My family are nothing if not loyal to the crown and as the future queen, I am always encouraging him to go above and beyond in the name of our king. When me and snookums are married, I'll personally help him eradicate any and all threats to the throne and our royal line to make sure our children have a clear route to a peaceful rule," Mildred said proudly.

My gut twisted at the thought of her impending nuptials with Darius and I was gifted a vivid memory of the time I'd punched her stupid troll face until she blacked out on the floor not far from here. I had a deep and urgent desire to do it again and the shadows rose up within me, hungering for that too.

"Good," I ground out, knowing I had to seem pleased by her little announcement even as the word burned my tongue like acid on the way out.

With a force of will, I stood up and walked away from her, my face a mask of nothingness as the shadows pushed deeper into my veins and I found myself forgetting little by little. But I couldn't afford to do that. I couldn't lean into them too hard because if I let myself forget to feel anything again, I'd practically be back where I started.

The K.U.N.T.s all started laughing behind me as Mildred began to reveal more details of her story and I pushed my way into the bathroom, not stopping until I was inside one of the stalls.

Shadows flickered behind my eyelids as I danced along the line of falling into them and I called on my Phoenix to help me push them back.

I needed to get a hold of myself and make it through the rest of the week amongst these people. Gabriel had told me that I'd be able to help us work against Lionel if I could keep my poker face in place, so I just had to focus on that. I wanted to get revenge on the man who had done this to me, and I was in the perfect position to help orchestrate that. I just had to keep my head in the game.

Besides, I had plenty of practice being an asshole. I could do that. I just needed to keep my emotions in check and my face blank. If Gabriel believed this was the best thing I could do to help us in our fight against Lionel right now then I'd do it. I trusted him. I just had to be careful with the shadows, make sure they didn't drive themselves into me too deeply again and try not to give into them when I didn't have to.

But as Mildred's words echoed in my ears and my blood sang with the desire to march back out there and punish her for them, I found myself sinking into the dark again. The shadows were familiar now, comforting and calling me back to them with the promise of oblivion.

Maybe a few minutes wouldn't hurt. I could just let them have me for a little while, wipe away this pain, take away my fear…

My Atlas buzzed in my pocket and I flinched at the interruption to my emotional meltdown, pulling it out with shaking fingers and frowning at the name on the ID.

Darius:
What are you wearing?

For a moment I couldn't understand why he was asking me that - he'd literally seen me ten minutes ago and knew I was in my academy uniform. But then the twisted fog of my thoughts lifted a little, reminding me that we used to message each other a lot before Lionel took me. And his strange question was actually our own little greeting to each other which didn't require a direct answer. It was just an opener.

I chewed on my lip as my gaze moved back and forth over the words and the frantic racing of my heart began to slow a bit.

I wanted to reply, but a shiver of fear moved along my spine at the idea too and I frowned as I found myself unable to form the words I needed to say to him.

But that little message was exactly what I'd needed to drag me out of the shadows and help me see things clearly. I couldn't dive into them now. I had to keep my head clear enough to remain myself. Mildred Canopus and the rest of the K.U.N.T.s would get their comeuppance one day soon, but in the meantime, I had to focus on playing the part I'd been forced into. We could use my position close to Lionel and Clara to our advantage and I needed to keep my attention fixed on that goal.

The door banged open outside my toilet stall and I drew in a shuddering breath as I fought my emotions back into line and unlocked the door.

I stepped out and came face to face with Xavier whose mouth dropped open as he spotted me, colour rising to his cheeks as he looked around the restroom in horror.

"Ah shit, am I in the ladies?" he groaned and I couldn't help the laugh that slipped from my lips even as I fought back the urge to cry.

Fuck, I really needed to lock my shit down or I was going to ruin this plan before it even started.

"Are you...okay now, Tory?" he asked hesitantly, seeming to notice I was on the edge of some kind of brain malfunction and I guessed Darius had filled him in on the whole busting me out of the shadows situation.

I glanced at the door and flicked my fingers to cast air magic against it to keep it closed then threw a silencing bubble around us before I spoke.

"I don't know about okay, but can we go with functioning and work from there?" I asked with a hesitant smile.

"That sounds a bit like me with my Elemental magic," he joked. "Everyone expects me to be able to do magic the way Darius can even though he got four years of early training before he even came here – it's a total nightmare."

"I'm sure you're not that bad," I said and he shook his head, causing glitter to tumble from his dark hair.

"It's fine. I'll get there. And in the meantime I don't have to be in that fucking house – or palace now I guess. Point is, I'm here, I have a herd, I'm free. Or at least as free as I ever dreamed of being."

I smiled at him, realising I had to look up at him now. He wasn't just tall either, he was muscular too and his face had lost most of its boyish qualities. Genuine happiness washed through me and I found myself relaxing in his company. "I'm so pleased for you," I said honestly.

"I never really got the chance to thank you for that," he added.

"All I did was push you out of a window," I teased but he shook his head, stepping forward and yanking me into a tight hug.

"No, Tory. You saved my life. You gave me...everything. I was too afraid to do what you pushed me to do alone but now I'm out of that house, away from those sessions he was making me have with Gravebone, I'm free to be the Pegasus I was born to be. And one day I'll find a way to repay that debt to you."

I smiled into Xavier's blazer as he squeezed me hard enough to crush bones and something inside me seemed to settle. He was right, I had managed to do something good for him by showing the world what he was and freeing him from Lionel's clutches. And if I was right by that monster's side then I might have the chance to help someone else. I could listen to his secrets and use them all against him. For every life I managed to save and every plan of his I helped to sabotage, I'd be striking back against him. Little by little.

This feeling right here was what I needed to rely on to get me through the days of K.U.N.T. company and time spent by Lionel's side. For every vile, stomach churning thing I had to listen to or witness, I would find a way to counter it with something good. I'd find a way to help. And then one day, we'd be ready to strike back at him and tear him from our throne.

"Thank you, Xavier," I said, pushing out of his arms and giving him a fierce smile. "That was exactly what I needed today."

"No problem," he replied, not seeming to know what I meant by that, but he didn't need to understand. The point was that I could do this. I could go back out there and play this part and no one would suspect a damn thing about where my true loyalties laid until it was too damn late.

I headed for the door, but Xavier called out to stop me before I could pull the door wide.

"Darius never gave up on you, you know that right?"

"What?" I breathed, the mixture of confusing emotions I felt towards his brother rising up in me again at the mere mention of his name.

"I just thought you should know. All the time Father had you, he spent every single minute searching for you, fighting back against the Nymphs, letting Darcy burn him half to death with Phoenix fire just to try and remove the shadows from his body so that he could challenge Father without Clara being able to stop him. It broke him losing you... So I guess what I'm saying is that I think you should give him the chance to make things right between you two. He's been to hell and back losing you, Tory. Please don't let Father win by keeping you away from him now."

My lips parted on an answer, but I wasn't sure what to say to him so I just nodded before dispersing the magic I'd used to hide us away in here and heading back out into The Orb.

I was going to have to spend some time figuring out what Darius was to me now. And what he'd been before. But everything about him had me feeling so confused as fear and pain mixed with hope and longing and it was too much for me to cope with all at once.

Right now I needed to just get through the week and perfect the shadow mask I had to wear. Because come Friday night I was heading back to the palace and I was going to need to fool the worst monster of them all. Lionel Acrux was my priority at the moment.

Darius was going to have to wait.

XAVIER

CHAPTER NINETEEN ·

My first few weeks at Zodiac had been freaking intense. I'd made it through Hell Week and soon had The Reckoning coming up which I was studying my ass off for. I barely had time to chill out and the fact that I'd brought my Xbox with me to the academy was kind of laughable now. Any free time I had I spent flying with my new herd. And shit, it was the best fucking thing I'd ever known. Being around my kind, soaring through the clouds and feeling as free as a damn eagle was unbelievable. If it wasn't for my father being the absolute asshole of the year forcing all of the Orders to stay apart, I would have said this time had been perfect.

I didn't care that I worked my ass off from dawn 'til nightfall. I didn't care that I was exhausted and waking up early was brutal in comparison to the lazy mornings I'd been used to. I had a purpose now. And freedom that made me grab life by the balls because part of me feared how long it would last. I only got four years at Zodiac, then who knew what kind of life Father would design for me beyond that? I just hoped it didn't get that far. That Darius, the Heirs and the twins would find a way to bring him down, because we were all screwed if not.

It was difficult to see the other spares, but we made it work. All of us but Ellis anyway who seemed more concerned about breaking the law than the others. Athena, Grayson, Hadley and I had found some unused caves out in Earth Territory which we met up in as much as possible. Athena and Grayson had brought a bunch of blankets and lumen crystals for light to make it comfier, and me and Hadley had carved a few roughly hewn seats out of the rock with our earth magic.

I sat on one now, the four of us having preferred to eat our lunch here instead of at The Orb where the K.U.N.T.s watched our every move. The place wasn't very busy these days and I reckoned a lot of the other students had the same idea. I hoped most of the Fae here weren't abiding to my father's new law, but it was hard to say. The problem was, I couldn't work out anyone's allegiance. So I made sure I only spent time with the few people I trusted. And it turned out, once I'd let slip that I didn't approve of my father's shit, these guys had agreed.

Athena was floating on a cloud of air near the cave roof while Hadley gazed up at her in frustration. He'd tried to bite her again and I was pretty sure she loved evading him.

"What if you just did it as a favour to me?" Hadley called up to her. "I won't hunt you. Just help a friend out."

"Bite Gray if you want a taste of Wolf," Athena called, hanging herself upside down and spiralling through the air toward us.

Hadley growled and leapt up to try and catch her hair, using his strength to throw himself higher. She spun up and away from him again with a taunting laugh.

"If you wanna bite me, you'll have to fight me for it," Grayson said where he was lying on a blanket, tapping out something on his Atlas.

"I don't want you," Hadley muttered, pacing beneath Athena. "All of her taunting sparks the hunger in me."

"Tut tut, Had, you're not supposed to get yourself caught up in the hunt," Athena teased.

"Get down here and say that to my face," Hadley dared and Athena lowered herself to the ground like she was about to do just that. Hadley immediately shot toward her, crashing into an air shield that made him fly backwards and hit the ground on his ass. I broke a laugh, whinnying at his attempts.

"For fuck's sake," Hadley snarled, smoothing his dark hair back and pushing himself up. "Just give me a taste, Athena." He was practically salivating and I didn't like that thirsty glint in his eye.

"Nah," she said lightly, moving over and sitting down beside me.

"Hold onto her, Xavier," Hadley growled and I scoffed, casting a ring of wooden spikes to grow up around us.

"I can't be bought, dude," I said with a smirk and Hadley huffed, dropping down to sit beside Grayson and eyeing his throat like he was considering changing his mind and fighting him for a drink instead.

"Wouldn't do it, bro," Grayson said casually, his eyes still on his Atlas. "My Wolf's almost as big as Seth's now."

"I'm stronger though," Hadley said with a smirk, then dropped down beside him with a sigh. "But you're just not the snack I want."

Grayson nuzzled his head, leaving a wet lick on his temple. "Don't be too butt hurt, she'll never let you bite her. It freaks her out."

"It doesn't freak me out," Athena tsked. "I just hate being used by parasites."

"Parasite?" Hadley spat, sitting up straight and glaring at her.

She shrugged innocently, twirling a lock of dark purple hair around her finger. "That's what you are. It's like that venomous twat Highspell said in Cardinal Magic, you're one of the parasitic Orders."

"You're asking for it," Hadley warned, jumping up and raising a hand, casting a wooden club in it and smashing my wooden spikes to shit.

Athena sat there, watching him batter a path toward her before he bumped up against her air shield again.

She smirked tauntingly. "Now what, Altair? Or should I call you Al*spare*?" she purred.

He whacked his club against her shield and she scowled at him as he started using his Order strength to beat the hell out of it.

"Open up," he snapped and she started laughing.

"Never!" she cried, jumping to her feet and starting to strip off. Hadley gazed up at her, the club hanging loose in his hand as he watched her with his jaw ticking. When she was down to her underwear, revealing the tattoo of a half moon over her hip, she leapt over his head. She shifted into her huge black and grey Wolf form which kinda looked like a giant husky and sprinted out of the cave. Hadley took chase with the speed of his Order, spitting curses as he went. I laughed and Grayson howled his encouragement to Athena as he pushed himself upright.

Grayson looked to me with a smile. "So, did you understand anything Professor Zenith said about star bonds 'cause my mind is fucking blown. I don't ever wanna be cursed with that shit. Why would I give up having ten girls fight to suck my dick every night for one chick only?"

He'd built a pack solely of fangirls within a couple of weeks of being here and they all followed him around like needy puppies. It hadn't exactly slipped my attention that all of the other spares were getting laid regularly and I was pretty much avoiding any attention cast my way. At this rate, I was probably going to be a thirty-year-old virgin with a couple of house cats for company. Oh no wait, I was more likely going to be married off to some crusty crouton faced witch I had to produce Dragon heirs with. *Oh fuck, that can't be my first time. I've got to sort this out.*

The problem was, the only girl I wanted was taken. And now I'd joined her herd, her boyfriend was officially my Dom. And he made a point of keeping me under his hooves at all times. He was also a good guy, which just made it more frustrating. But I still couldn't help looking at Sofia. She'd been my one good thing before I'd come here, and now I was at Zodiac Academy which was the most incredible place ever and she was *still* the best thing in my life.

"I think we have the opposite problems," I told Grayson and his eyebrows arched.

He folded his muscular arms around his legs, scooting closer to me with intrigue in his eyes. "Who is she?"

"A girl I can't have," I said, flicking my hair out of my eyes. It was growing kinda long, but I hadn't cut it since Sofia had pushed her fingers into it the other week and told me it made me look like a real stallion.

"Spill it, Acrux, I want all the details because I'm pretty sure my heart is just another cock and I need to figure out if it'll ever want anything but multiple pussy."

I snorted, scrubbing a hand over the back of my neck. "She's in my herd. And she's older than me. And taken by the herd Dom."

"That's like the same as a Wolf Alpha, right?" he asked.

"Yeah, sort of. They mate with the most fertile female though once they take over," I explained.

"So she's the hot AFFF?" he smirked. "Hot as fuck fertile female?"

"Yeah," I snorted, ignoring the heat rising up my face.

He jumped up and smacked me on the cheek playfully. "Isn't it obvious, dude?"

"No?" I frowned.

"You have to hoof kick the Dom in the face and take his place," Grayson said with his lopsided smile. "Oh hey, that rhymed."

I grinned at that image. I couldn't deny I'd been butting up against Tyler a lot since I'd joined his herd. The instinct was there, but I knew I was holding back because of Sofia. I didn't wanna force her Dom beneath me and steal her away. Okay I did. I wanted that a lot. I was dreaming about it and becoming far more aggressive than I'd realised I was whenever I was around her and Tyler came strutting over to her like Black Beauty on Faeroids. But I wanted her to pick me for me too, not just because I was the Dom.

The bell rang somewhere off in the distance and I knew it was time to get to class. I pushed to my feet and Grayson knocked his shoulder against mine as we walked out of the caves.

"So do you get butterflies and shit around her?" he asked.

"No, it feels more like an earthquake in my chest and a thunderstorm in my head."

"Sweeeet," Grayson said. "That sounds more up my street. I should try letting a guy or two suck my cock, maybe I'm just not into girls."

"Your whole pack is literally made up of girls that you screw every day," I pointed out.

"True, but maybe I need some variety." He looked me up and down like he was trying to work out if I could be attractive to him and I elbowed him in the gut.

We stepped outside and as we headed along the path into the trees a swarm of baying girls ran out of them. They rushed around Grayson and tugged him away from me as they fought to hug and kiss him. He grinned stupidly, letting them pull him along and he tossed me a salute goodbye. "Later, dude."

I snorted at him then glanced up at the sky, biting the inside of my cheeks as the clouds called to me far above. My magic reserves rarely got depleted because I flew through them at every chance I could. I was obsessed with it. After being shut up in my father's manor for so long, I wasn't going to miss a single opportunity I got to do it. I'd even bought a Tempa Pegobag online which stretched to stay on my back whenever I shifted.

When the Wolves were out of sight, I kicked off my shoes and started stripping down, a grin pulling at my lips as I stuffed everything into my pack which was shaped like a cloud with white glitter glimmering on it – and was cool as shit thank you very much.

I put it on my back again when I was naked then leapt forward and let my Pegasus form spill free from my flesh. I whinnied loudly as my hooves hit the ground and I shook my head as glitter tumbled from my mane and my lilac wings flexed out either side of me. I started galloping down the path, my gaze on the sky as I flapped my wings and leapt off of the ground, climbing up towards the waiting clouds. As soon as I rushed through them, my magic reserves started to swell. I did cartwheels and backflips as I made my way across campus towards the Fire Arena for my next class. It was literally the best feeling in the world.

When I was above the huge amphitheatre, I circled down toward it like a bird of prey, spotting the class filing into the sandy pit below dressed in their fitted fire resistant uniforms. *Oh shit I'm late.*

I dove out of the sky and landed at the heart of the amphitheatre much to Professor Pyro's disapproval.

"Goodness!" she shouted. "Shift back this instant, boy." She threw her hand at me, her fingers twisting and the spell hit me in the chest, making me rear up angrily as a buzzing energy trickled through my veins.

My tail whipped out and I bucked as the spell rippled through me and forced me to shift.

My bare feet hit the ground and I cursed as everyone in class stared at my naked ass. I met Sofia's gaze and grabbed my junk with a groan of embarrassment and Pyro's eyebrows nearly rocketed into her hairline.

"Oh goodness, I didn't realise it was you, Prince A-Acrux," she stammered. "Please don't mention this to your father."

My brother stalked up to her with smoke pluming from his nostrils and she backed up in alarm, sputtering apologies as he laid into her for it. Which just made the whole thing worse as anyone who hadn't already been staring turned to see what he was yelling about and more heat rushed up my neck. I knew it was normal for everyone to get naked around campus before shifting, but I still hadn't gotten used to it. Especially the stares. A bunch of girls started giggling behind me and I glanced over my shoulder to find them snapping photos of my ass. *Oh man.*

Sofia jerked her head in the direction of the changing rooms and I nodded awkwardly before running off in that direction. I hurried inside and released a breath of relief as I headed to a bench, dropped my bag onto it and changed into my skin tight fire suit. It didn't do much to hide my dick anyway, but I guessed it was better than just standing out there butt naked.

I seriously had to start getting used to that. I just hadn't had the chance to adjust to herd life before coming to Zodiac. Most Orders had spent time with their kind long before they headed off for magical training. And at least I didn't have a small dick like Hubert Pluto in my herd, not that he seemed to

241

give a shit. He'd had a twenty minute conversation with me yesterday with his hands on his hips and his little dipper blowing in the breeze. Most of the herd had their bits decorated with glitter and gemstones too and I swear the big diamond at the top of his dick was always winking at me.

I'd always averted my eyes whenever Sofia stripped down, but I'd heard her talking to one of her friends about her new vajazzle the other day and the little pink gemstones she had above her clit. All this shit was so new to me and I'd never really thought about decorating my dick before. Was that what I was expected to do? Did my cock need to be sporting a bigger diamond than Hubert's to prove how worthy I was of my place in the herd? *Mindfuck.*

I dumped my bag in a locker and jogged back out to the arena where everyone had started practising their magic. Tory was working with Darcy as Pyro only paired Orders together, but since Tory was pretending to still be under my father's influence they weren't talking much. Darcy looked about ten times happier than she had in weeks though. It was a weight off of my heart as well. I didn't know how Tory was going to escape him entirely, but there had to be a way now she wasn't controlled by him completely.

"Mr Acrux, would you like to pair with Miss Cygnus, your fire magic is coming on quite well so let's see how you do with a more advanced shape cast," Pyro encouraged and I looked over to Sofia with a grin, nodding as I joined her. "Help Mr Acrux," she told Sofia and I realised this was first year stuff she shouldn't have been making her do. It pissed me off that I was getting preferential treatment. Especially if it was affecting Sofia's work.

"You don't have to," I told her and she cast a silencing bubble around us, tucking a lock of short, gold hair behind her ear.

"I don't mind," she said brightly. "I've been able to turn sand into glass for a while anyway," she said, nodding over to the other sophomores who were practising just that. "Perks of being friends with the Vegas. Their study sessions are kinda intense and I swear I learn more with them sometimes than I do with Pyro."

"If you're sure?" I asked. "I can't form anything other than simple shapes and Hadley can make a fucking rhombus." I looked over at him as he casually cast a pyramid then made splashes of fire spew out the top of it like it was a volcano. *Fucking Hadley.* The girl he was working with was so busy staring at him, she kept burning herself on her own flames.

"If you want to make something three dimensional, you have to stop focusing so hard," Sofia explained, raising her hands and creating a square of flames between them. Her fingers worked in practised movements as she cast another square beside it then let lines of flames merge them to form a cube. "The harder you try to force it, the less obedient the flames are. Think of it as like blowing on a candle. If you blow too hard, the flame will go out, but just a little and it will bend the way you want it to."

I stood beside her, stealing a glance at her pretty face and cute little nose while I cast a square with my fire magic. That was easy enough, but building anything else onto it was always the hard part. I watched her magic, then watched her, then her mouth. Fuck, her mouth. Her lips were candyfloss pink and she lightly tugged her lower one between her teeth as she concentrated.

The smell of burning reached me and she wheeled toward me with a gasp. "Xavier!"

I looked down, finding I was legitimately on fire. "Fuck!" I lurched away from her as the fire resistant uniform started somehow burning under the intensity of my flames and climbing up my arm. I waved my arm wildly which only made it fucking worse then remembered I had water magic and cast it at myself with absolutely no control. I knocked myself over with the amount I used, landing on my ass utterly drenched.

"Oh my stars, he's so fucking cute," Nina Starstruck whispered to her friend and the two of them giggled. "He's like a clumsy little Darius who doesn't even realise he's hot."

Great.

Sofia offered me a hand to help me up, but I was too mortified to take it. I knocked her hand away and got up myself, dusting the sand off my ass which wouldn't go anywhere because I was fucking soaked. I released a horsey snort of frustration and turned away from Nina who was batting her long lashes at me. I knew I wasn't like my brother, but that had always just been fine until everyone and their cat started pointing it out.

Sofia reached up and pushed my damp hair out of my eyes, tiptoeing to do so. She was so small it was just another thing I fucking adored about her.

She's taken, bro. Get the hint.

"You put the fire out at least." She laughed lightly and I couldn't help but grin at the sound.

"Yeah, I guess," I murmured and she jabbed me playfully in the arm.

"You'll get it. It'll just click one of these days."

"I just hope it clicks before The Reckoning or I'm fucked," I said.

I couldn't lose my place at Zodiac. I had to work harder and make sure I didn't do anything stupid like this when I was being assessed. I didn't work too well under pressure and Sofia always got me so worked up that I often ended up embarrassing myself in front of her. I'd done a perfect water cast just yesterday, creating a river that flowed in whichever direction I urged it to. But was she there to see that? No. She was here to see me acting like I was still on day one of my training.

I focused on creating a cube for the rest of the lesson, determined to do it and prove I wasn't actually a useless dick pigeon, and by the time Pyro called an end to the lesson, I'd not only perfected it, I'd created a pyramid just like Hadley's too. Sure, he'd moved on to casting a whole flaming flock of birds flying around the amphitheatre, but I was getting there.

I cleaned up in the changing room with Hadley, pulling my uniform back on after a shower.

"Did you catch Athena?" I asked him and he blew out a breath of frustration.

"No," he growled. "I lost her in the woods and couldn't find her." His fangs snapped out as he thought about it and I gripped his bare arm, forcing him to look at me.

"Be careful. Darius told me what happened with Caleb and Tory when he hunted her. You can't let this get to you."

"I know," he huffed. "I'm not going to hurt her. I keep myself topped up on easier prey. I just wanna catch her one time. The hunt feels so fucking good."

"Just don't do anything stupid," I pushed and he nodded.

"I won't, man." He pulled on his shirt.

"Hey Hadley, are you ready?" a guy called and I glanced over at Trent who was covered from head to toe in tattoos.

"Yeah," Hadley said, looking to me. "I'm getting a tattoo sleeve." He pointed to his right arm. "It's gonna be all the planets as skulls, Trent's a sick artist. Maybe you should get one too?"

"There's nothing I really want. Enjoy though." I put my sparkly cloud bag on my back and he eyed it with a snort.

"Nice bag," he teased.

I flipped him my middle finger with a smirk and he shot off with Trent, the guy apparently a Vampire too as they disappeared together out the door.

I headed outside and found Sofia standing there leaning against the wall. I walked over to join her, pushing a hand through my hair and her gaze dipped to my bicep, a blush lining her cheeks as I arrived. Before I could say a single word to her, a huge silver Pegasus dropped out of the sky, landing right in front of her and snorting furiously at me. Tyler trotted around her in a circle, his tail whipping out as he marked his territory and anger prickled through me.

I stamped my own foot as my Pegasus instincts urged me to challenge him.

"Chill out, Ty." Sofia patted his neck, glancing at me around him as she bit her lip again in that way that made my dick jerk to attention.

Tyler shifted into his Fae form and Sofia pulled a pair of sweatpants from her bag, tossing them at him. He tugged them on before he marched up to me and threw his arm around my shoulders.

"Hey, bud, how's it going?" he asked with a wide smile like he hadn't just gone all Dom on me and Sofia. He took his Atlas out and snapped a photo of us, tapping away as he posted it on FaeBook with the caption 'Hanging with the third in the herd.'

I hated being the third. Third best. It just didn't sit right with me.

I'd risen up through the ranks fast and now the only ones who were above me were Tyler and his mate. I kept dreaming about fighting him, burying my fists in his stomach or ramming my horn into his gut before claiming Sofia from him and forcing everyone else in the herd under my command. The idea got me seriously hard. I'd woken up with a boner over that idea so many times since I'd arrived here that I was starting to think I had issues.

I shoved Tyler away a bit harder than was really friendly and he stamped his foot as I stamped mine in return, my eyes narrowing.

He continued to smile then folded his arms. "Do you wanna hang out with us, Xavier? Me, you and my girl?" The way he said *my girl* had my anger rising and I looked over at Sofia with a hunger in me that wouldn't quit.

"Sure," I said, lifting my chin as he gave me another assessing look. *Maybe I should just challenge him? Why not, I'm strong enough. I can take him.*

My Pegasus form was as big as his and my horn could even have been a touch larger. *I should get Sofia to measure them both because mine is definitely girthier too and that has to count for something.*

"I actually need to head to the library," Sofia said. "I just wanted to give you this." She stepped toward Tyler and kissed him. My heart was obliterated like she'd just stuffed a grenade in my chest and pulled the pin. Tyler grabbed her waist, pulling her closer possessively and I stood there watching them with rage bubbling under my flesh.

My instincts rose up in me and a furious whinny escaped my throat before I shoved Tyler away from her and got up in his face, butting my forehead against his. He pushed his own forehead back against mine and I kicked out dirt beneath my feet as I refused to move.

"You wanna challenge me, buddy?" Tyler demanded with a furious snort.

"Maybe I do," I said, my chest heaving as he continued to try and force me back, but I wasn't going anywhere.

"You wouldn't," Tyler growled. "I'm your best friend."

"So you keep saying." I narrowed my eyes and he stamped his foot, slamming it down on top of mine.

I shot a sideways glance at Sofia who was biting her lip and looking between us, not stepping in. Though I was fast learning that that was the way of our kind. The guys had to fight to have the best female, and she needed to make sure she was with the right mate. So goading me into this was a standard mare move. And knowing that she wanted me to fight for her made me feel all kinds of good.

Tyler suddenly pulled away, twisting his fingers and casting a vine which tripped me up in the dirt. I raised my own hands to fight back as I hit the ground, throwing out a blast of fire. A wall of earth flew up to block it and I wasn't sure how to counter that. I just wasn't well enough trained.

Tyler stepped around it, offering me his hand and whinnying softly in an offering.

"Accept your place," he insisted and I sighed, letting him pull me up with a hard grip on my hand. I clenched my teeth as he tried to crush the bones in my fingers and I returned the favour. He lingered close to me for a moment and my gaze dropped to the hard slash of his mouth before I looked him in the eyes again with my throat thickening.

"Good." Tyler's face split into a wide grin. "I knew you'd never do me dirty, Xavier."

"I'll see you guys later," Sofia called, batting her lashes at Tyler which just made my skin run hot with anger. Hell if this was the end of me trying to win her.

She trotted off and I was left with my Dom who looked as happy as anything now he'd won a point over me. I had to give in this time, but that didn't mean I was giving up.

"There's nothing wrong with being the third in the herd," Tyler said with a grin. "You could date any of the Subs. Or all of them if you want. Why don't you ask a few of them back to your room sometime?"

"No," I grunted, my muscles bunching as we started walking down the path together.

He gave me the side eye and I could see him trying to draw his shoulders back so that he was taller than me, but even on that we were pretty dead on. We were too damn close of a match.

"Well Sofia is off limits," he warned, saying it with a casual smile, but his eyes were all murder. He glared down at me until I looked away, his status in the herd forcing me to give in. *For the star's sake.*

"Fine," I muttered and he clapped a hand to my back.

"Good. Now come and get high with me in a rainbow. There's usually a few about by the waterfall in Water Territory. And if we're lucky, some of the water Elementals will be casting rain showers so there's even more of them."

"Alright," I agreed, liking the sound of that.

He started stripping down, casually tossing me his stuff. "Put it in your Pegobag."

The direct order irritated the hell out of me, but I did as he said. I'd been beaten by him today and I had to accept that like a Fae and come back to fight another day when I was ready. My gaze dipped to his muscular chest as I started pulling off my clothes too and suddenly we seemed to be racing to do it first, the challenge in his gaze goading me on. I stuffed my clothes roughly in the bag while he tossed his shit my way. I whinnied angrily as I had to carry it like a little bitch, but he just snorted at me and tossed his head.

Furious tension rippled through the air as we pulled off the last of our clothes and I put my bag back on. He took in my body with an assessing gaze like he was trying to figure out if he was bigger than me or not and I realised for once I hadn't felt bothered about stripping off. I guessed after I'd gotten butt naked in front of all the fire Elementals in school, it had kind of gotten me over my fear.

I took in his body with an equally assessing gaze, unable to avoid looking at his dick which was ringed with silver stones at the base and a rainbow made of coloured gems sat above it on his pubic bone.

"Is this vajazzle thing something I'm supposed to do?" I asked him and he laughed wildly.

"Firstly, it's a *di*jazzle for a guy. And secondly, no you don't have to do shit." He smirked. "Nothing wrong with a plain Jane dick, buddy."

The way he said that was suspicious as hell and now I had to think that some sort of dijazzle was in order. *How do they even stick all those gems on? And was it the design that counted or just how many jewels I could stick around my junk? Do I get points for including the balls??*

Whatever it took to win Sofia's attention, I'd do it. I wasn't going to hide away from Tyler when I wanted to rise up and steal his girl. It may have been shady as shit if we'd just been friends, but we weren't just that. We were in a herd, and this was how it worked. So I wasn't going to suppress my instincts.

Tyler's eyes lingered on my chest like he was trying to figure out the breadth of it, then he turned and shifted into his huge, silver Pegasus form. I leapt after him to do the same and he started galloping away from me to prove his speed. I took chase, soon nose to nose with him as we knocked a bunch of students off the path in an effort to stay side by side.

I tried to pull ahead, but he kept pace with me no matter how hard I pushed myself. It was so fucking frustrating.

Tyler finally turned away, spreading his wings and taking off into the sky. I was hot on his heels, racing after him and squinting against the glare of the sun as I flapped my wings hard to keep up.

I may never have been an heir to anything in my life, but in this herd, I really wanted to be the king. So I was going to dethrone my Dom and take his crown. Then Sofia would be *mine*.

TORY

CHAPTER TWENTY

Somehow, I managed to keep up the ruse of my shadow identity and loyalty to Lionel all week, enduring the company of the K.U.N.T.s during the day and battling through the ache in my blood which drove me to return to Lionel as soon as physically possible too.

In the evenings I stole time with Darcy and Geraldine at King's Hollow and the Heirs appeared there more often than not too.

Caleb was always full of jokes and smiles for me which lifted my mood whenever I felt down, and Seth was overly tactile which he knew I wasn't a fan of but he wouldn't stop all the same. The Wolf also liked to bring me snacks like candy and chocolate and I got the feeling he was trying to fatten me up a bit. The only issue was that if I didn't eat them right away, he just stole them back and scoffed them himself so I'd taken to hiding a stash which he seemed to have decided was a challenge designed so he could sniff them out and steal them anyway. *Damn mutt.*

The Darius minefield was growing slightly less daunting with Max's help, but I still found it too hard to speak to him for more than a few words here and there. Darius seemed to be accepting my need to keep my distance from him, but sometimes I caught him looking at me with so much pain in his eyes that it hurt me too. I just didn't know how to do anything to fix it.

When Friday night finally rolled around, I was filled with a mixture of pure dread and unadulterated excitement at the prospect of seeing Lionel again and I hated the damn bond for messing with my mind so fucking much.

It was impossible for me to separate my real emotions and the ones that it forced me to experience entirely. I felt like I was carrying around this horrible secret all the time. Whenever one of the others spoke about hating Lionel or hurting him, a piece of me longed to scream or even attack them in defence of him. And I knew that wasn't how I'd felt before he placed this curse on me, but it was getting harder and harder to remind myself of that when the longer I spent away from him, the more I hungered for him.

Fortunately, I had a valid reason to be looking forward to returning to the palace tonight beyond my pathetic need to see the man who had tortured and abused me. Gabriel had had a vision which showed me and Darcy finding something important in the palace grounds, so we'd made a last minute plan to sneak her in through the King's tunnels so that what he *saw* could come to pass. All I had to do was make sure that Lionel was distracted while she snuck into the summerhouse where Orion was being held. Then as soon as I was certain we had a window of opportunity, I was going to meet her. Gabriel said that we'd know what to do from there. It sounded batshit to me, but I was also past the point of questioning Gabriel's visions, so I was just going to go with it.

The moment I finished my lessons for the day, I couldn't help but race back to my dorm, ditch my uniform and change into one of the dresses Lionel had given me for whenever I returned to his company. It was a blood red floor length gown with slits up the legs and though it was beautiful, it was definitely overkill. But Lionel insisted and it would be a pretty obvious giveaway if I turned up in jeans and a tank, so I wasn't going to waste energy being pissy about it.

I hurried out of my room again and quickly strode through campus as I headed for the main gates with the pouch of stardust I'd been given for these journeys in my pocket.

The moment I was beyond the border, I threw the stardust over my head and before I knew it, I was standing in front of the palace gates.

The flash of cameras started up around me instantly, but I just ignored the journalists who were always camped out here as I strode forward and got into the carriage that had been sent to collect me.

Jenkins greeted me as I stepped through the palace doors and I cast my eyes over his scrunched up face and pursed lips with barely concealed dislike. I christened that look his cat's ass face – because his mouth looked just like a cat's butthole when he did that, and the guy was an ass so it suited him well.

"The King isn't back yet," he informed me with a bit of a sneer. "He has requested that you amuse yourself while you await his return at eight o'clock."

My gut dipped with disappointment and I mentally slapped myself for feeling upset over the idea of not seeing Lionel sooner, reminding myself that this was what I'd been hoping for. *He's a big scaley dickweed who you hate more than anything in the world, so stop thinking about cuddling with him for fuck's sake.*

I nodded, not bothering to even do Jenkins the courtesy of words as I strode away from him, heading straight into the depths of the palace.

I knew where I wanted to go and I wasn't going to waste time with that old bastard making small talk.

I headed down several long corridors, through a huge glass conservatory and pulled open a door at the rear of the enormous building before stepping out onto the lawn.

No one questioned me. I was Lionel's little Vega pet after all, and he'd made it clear that I was allowed to do whatever I pleased. Mostly because up until very recently, the only thing that pleased me was serving him, so he had no reason to doubt my motivations for anything.

More fool him.

The summerhouse was set to the east of the palace, the cute little cottage partially hidden by an array of blooming flowers that were still as bright and colourful as if it were midsummer even though winter was setting in. The pool sat in front of it, forever steaming and whenever leaves floated down to lay on its surface, a magical wind guided them away.

I moved to the door, glancing over my shoulder, trying to be casual about it so no one thought I was up to anything before pulling the door wide and stepping inside.

Orion looked up in surprise from the book he'd been studying at the desk in the corner of the room and the tightness in my chest loosened as I looked at him. Shit, I'd really missed the grumpy asshole since he'd been hauled off to Darkmore and I'd been hauled out of my own damn mind and turned into a psycho mannequin.

"Tory?" he asked slowly, pushing himself to his feet as he hesitated. His hair was overgrown and his beard seriously needed a trim. No doubt Darius had already told him that I was mostly myself again now, but he was being cautious all the same.

I stepped closer, looking around to check that the place was empty and the blinds were drawn over the windows to hide us away in here.

The moment I was certain there was no one else around, I dropped my resting bitch mask, grinning at Orion in greeting and he shot towards me, a breath of laughter passing his lips as he swept me up into a fierce embrace.

I smiled like an idiot as I wrapped my arms around him and squeezed him tight as he spun me in a circle.

"I'm so glad their plan to bring you back worked," he muttered.

"Shit, dude, don't start crying on me. I thought you were meant to be an asshole?" I teased and he laughed against my hair as he gave me an extra squeeze.

"Give me a few minutes to just be glad to have you in your right mind again then I promise to go back to being a dick as soon as I can," Orion joked.

I relented, hugging him tight for a moment as we just took a second to appreciate the fact that we were both half free of our shackles, then I huffed out a frustrated breath and kneed him in the balls as hard as I could.

Orion wheezed out a cough laced with a surprised curse and I gave him a shove so he fell back onto the couch beside us as he cupped his junk.

"That's for breaking my sister's heart, asshole," I snarled, pointing a finger at him and glaring.

On the one hand, I was seriously pleased to have him back, but on the other, Darcy was my one and only priority in the world and as her big sister - by a few minutes, but whatever - it was my duty to give him a hard time. And that knee to the balls had been a long time coming.

"Fuck, Tory, why do you always go for the balls?" he groaned, cupping his crotch with his eyes half closed against the pain.

"You're lucky I left them attached to your body," I warned. "You're on my shit list, douchebag, and don't you forget it. I might be seriously happy to see your hairy face, but I'm also going to slap it every time I do until you fix this shit."

"Fix it?" he grunted. "There is no fixing it, Tory. It's too late for-"

I cuffed him around the ear hard enough to knock his head to one side and he snarled at me, baring his fangs.

"Stop," he warned.

"Bite me, asshole," I taunted and he glared at me for another moment, his gaze darting to my throat for a second like he was half considering trying that before releasing a hopeless kind of laugh.

"You know, your sister is a lot nicer than you are," he grumbled.

"No shit, Sherlock. That's why I'm kicking your ass on her behalf. She's too good to go for the balls but I swear to you now, if you hurt her again then I'm coming for yours with a fist full of Phoenix fire. Got it?"

"You're a fucking animal," he said, shielding his junk protectively and giving me a look that told me he knew I meant it.

"Yeah. And don't you forget it. Now, why don't you get me a drink and we can sit here feeling sorry for ourselves together while I wait for Lionel to get back before I have to pretend I'm a soulless vessel for the shadows again?" I dropped down on the couch beside him and he rolled his eyes at me before shooting away and grabbing a bottle of bourbon with a pair of matching glasses.

I took the one he offered me and he poured a healthy dose into it before filling his to the brim.

"I see you're back on the booze," I commented even though it had been my suggestion. But I wasn't the one who had already drunk three quarters of that bottle so my point was still valid.

"Well I have very little reason to abstain these days," he muttered.

"Cheers to that," I agreed, clinking my glass against his before sinking the lot and relishing the burn of it running down my throat. "You wanna get drunk with me and talk shit about Lionel?"

"No. That sounds fucking terrible."

"I know. But I have to sleep in a bed with him and Clara tonight, so I figure drinking myself to oblivion before then is preferable."

"Maybe you could stab him in his sleep?" Orion suggested.

"If only," I said but even those words made me feel physically ill and my heart began to race with panic at the thought of any harm coming to the man I was supposed to want dead more than anything in the world.

I rubbed at the Aries mark on my arm, trying to shake off the desire to go and check that Lionel was okay and Orion reached out to take my hand.

"One time I got so mad at Darius that I tried to punch him, but I ended up hitting myself in the face instead," Orion said, squeezing my fingers in his and I groaned as I leaned back against the couch, realising I was in the company of the one person I knew who might actually understand the way I was feeling about this shit.

I looked into Orion's dark eyes, wondering if I could admit the crazy thoughts that kept running through my head about the man who had stolen our throne. With anyone else, I felt like they couldn't possibly understand this and I'd avoided talking about it, but he knew, he'd lived with this kind of bond for years.

"At night I lay in bed trying to list all the reasons I have to hate Lionel," I murmured, embarrassment clawing at me over what I was about to admit. "But I always end up thinking about how luscious his hair is and how he smells like the best combination of iron and charcoal and... how perfect his scowl is." I was cringing as I said it, but I was also picturing that scowl and missing it so much it hurt. It was fucked up.

"His scowl?" Orion laughed and I smiled a little too even though I knew how fucking crazy it sounded.

"Well...he doesn't really smile very often," I shrugged, closing my eyes against how goddamn mortifying it was to feel like that about a man I knew deep down I freaking hated. But somehow, with Orion I didn't mind. I knew he'd understand because he had been forced into a Guardian bond too. Though at least he loved the guy he was bonded to.

"Have you ever noticed how tall Darius is? And how strong he is?" Orion asked, a smirk playing around his lips. "Or how his eyes have little flecks of gold mixed in amongst the brown?"

"Yeah," I said, biting my lip as I thought about him. There was still a trickle of fear mixed in with the butterflies I felt when he crossed my mind and it was hard for me to figure out exactly what I was feeling there, but there was no questioning the way he looked. "He's pretty fucking nice to look at."

"And spoon with," Orion added with a grin. "One time while I was in Darkmore, I drew all of his tattoos from memory alone just because I couldn't stop thinking about them. And then I stuck the pictures to the wall beside my bed so I could kinda feel like he was there while I was sleeping."

We both laughed in a hopeless kind of way and I sighed as I leaned my head back against the couch and turned to look at him.

"I'm glad someone understands my fucked up thoughts," I said honestly because it was so hard for me to be dealing with all of these conflicting emotions for Lionel while everyone else just hated him so ferociously. And it wasn't like I disagreed, but I felt like such a fucking freak for secretly looking forward to seeing him tonight and wanting to hold him in my arms while knowing that was insane.

"We'll work this out, I promise," Orion said and I nodded because I knew that we would. Either by figuring out some way to break the bond or by Lionel dying - no matter how much the idea of that made me feel sick to my core.

"I didn't just come here to socialise," I said, sighing as I leaned forward and placed my empty glass down. "I actually came to warn you to expect a visitor in a little while through the tunnels."

"Who?" he asked and I didn't miss the hopeful tone to his voice.

"Darcy," I confirmed. "Gabriel said it's important the two of us are in the palace tonight so after Lionel and Clara go to sleep, I'll sneak back out to meet her here."

"So...she's coming alone?" he asked, his throat bobbing as he glanced towards the kitchenette where Darcy had told me the tunnel emerged.

"Yeah. And if I come back here and find she's been crying, you'll be enjoying that flaming balls feeling. Got it?"

Orion shuddered, placing a protective cushion over his lap. "You're a savage."

"Damn right I am. Don't go thinking I don't mean it. Also...maybe you should get changed. I mean, it might make her feel a little better to see how much you've let yourself go, but I'm guessing you don't want to broadcast what you had for dinner to her." I pointed at the spaghetti stains on his sweatpants and he growled in frustration.

"I haven't let myself go," he complained. "I just dropped a bit of my food like five minutes before you showed up here."

"Uh huh. So what's the excuse for your shirt being inside out?"

He grabbed his collar and tugged it forward to check and I laughed at him as his eyes bugged out a bit.

"Asshole," he muttered when he realised I'd been joking.

"Seriously though, did Lionel not leave you any scissors here? Because the homeless yeti look was never in fashion, dude. And Darcy definitely won't be impressed by it," I said with a smirk.

"Alright I get it. I'm a mess," he growled. "But I don't need relationship advice from you. You've got your own shit to work out."

"Like what?" I asked, rearranging my flouncy dress as I tried to feign ignorance and he scoffed at my act, jabbing me in the arm.

"I've had Darius in my bed every night this week talking about you non fucking stop," he replied. My gut tightened as I wondered if he was exaggerating or not and I couldn't decide if I wanted him to be. "Maybe I should be kicking you in the junk too."

"Maybe," I agreed softly, not really knowing what to say about the Fae the stars had chosen for me.

"He's a good man, Tory," Orion said roughly. "Give him a chance to prove that to you again."

I sighed, not really giving him an answer to that because I wasn't sure what kind of answer I could give. I was so messed up over Darius that it was impossible for me to make any kind of decisions about him, let alone the fact that the rings in our eyes made those kinds of decisions pretty irrelevant anyway.

I glanced at the clock, seeing that it was five to eight and resisting the urge to start bouncing up and down at the thought of Lionel arriving soon.

"I need to go. Lionel is due back at eight and I'm equally dreading seeing him and so excited that I think I might puke." I released a dark laugh and stood, drawing on the shadows to help dull my nerves. If I was going to do this then I had to make sure my mask didn't slip.

"Look after yourself, Tory," Orion said, pushing to his feet and walking with me towards the door with a look on his face that said he really didn't want to let me leave, though we both knew I had to.

"You concentrate on being nice to my sister and I'll manage a dinner with the King just fine. Then I'll be back once he's asleep – Darcy will probably arrive before then."

Orion's face paled and he looked down at his spaghetti stain with a frown which made me snort a laugh as I started moving towards the door.

"Now you've just gotta decide, do you go with another sweatpants, t-shirt combo? Fancy it up to jeans? Or go all out with a suit and try to casually pretend you forgot she was coming and just happened to be wearing your fanciest shit," I joked and his face fell.

"Fuck you. I wasn't even thinking about that until you said it. Next time you're meeting up with Darius I'm gonna get in your head over outfit choices too."

"Good luck with that. Unlike you, I don't give a shit what I wear. We're not all so vain, you know?" I teased and he growled irritably.

"I'll figure out some other weakness to exploit in you then," he threatened.

"Well that's easy enough. I'm all fucked up inside, so you can just play up to my insecurities about whether or not I'm even a fully functioning Fae anymore."

"That's not funny," Orion muttered, shaking his head at me.

"I gotta laugh if I don't wanna cry, right? Now if you don't mind, I need to go cuddle up to the man who imprisoned and tortured me." I started backing up towards the door but he caught my hand in his, squeezing tight as he met my gaze.

"We're all at least a little fucked up, Tory," he said roughly. "But the people who love us don't give a shit about that. Better still – they love us even more for it."

My gaze snagged on the friendship bracelet I'd made for him all those months ago and my heart felt full as I smiled at him.

"I missed you, asshole," I said in a low voice.

"Missed you too, savage."

We exchanged a look that was a clear promise for us never to speak of this sappy as shit moment ever again and he released my hand so that I could leave.

I headed back out of the summerhouse and into the palace, walking to the informal dining room where Lionel liked to eat. It was his only real option anyway seeing as the majority of the palace was still locked up tight and he couldn't figure out how to break into any of the rooms. Which was fucking hilarious to me now that I could fully appreciate it.

My heart started pounding as I closed in on the room and when I heard the deep rumble of his voice beyond the door, I broke into a run despite my best intentions, bursting inside.

My gaze snapped straight to my king where he stood by the door and I leapt at him before I could stop myself, wrapping my arms around his neck and squeezing him tight.

"Ah, here she is," he purred in a smug voice as he wound one arm around me and tugged me against him. "My little pet."

Irritation prickled down my spine at that word, but it was tempered by the blissful relief of being reunited with him, and for several seconds all I could do was bury my face against his neck and breathe in the scent of him.

Someone cleared their throat behind us irritably and I turned to find Darius sitting at the table beside Xavier as they waited for us to join them. My gut plummeted and shame clawed at my insides, knowing he'd just seen all of that. I had to fight off a blush with a tug on the shadows that had my emotions dulling as they took hold of me.

Clara was in the seat to the left of the head of the table, dressed all in black and looking murderous as usual. I got the feeling she was holding Darius in his chair with her grip over his shadows as his jaw clenched and unclenched angrily.

"You see, Darius?" Lionel said in a voice that both made me want to throat punch him and stroke his lovely face. *For fuck's sake.* "Roxanya is thoroughly satisfied by her position beneath me. Aren't you, my dear?"

Lionel's cold gaze turned to me and I forced myself to hold his eye, reaching up to touch his face - partly to sell the bullshit better and partly because I really wanted to for some fucked up reason - as my lips tilted into a soft smile. "I'm always happy with my king," I purred, possibly laying it on a bit thick but it was that or let him see how revolted I was at this gross bond he'd put on me.

Darius didn't reply, but the way his eyes flared told me he wished he could, and I had Clara to thank for the silence.

"Come and eat, Daddy," Clara begged, patting his chair at the head of the table and he tutted beneath his breath as he drew me towards it with his arm still wrapped around my waist, his hand just barely above my ass.

I was deposited in the seat beside Darius to the right of Lionel's chair before he sat down himself and I set my gaze on my plate as a prickle of guilt washed through me. This whole thing was so fucked up and Darius had had to endure weeks of this shit, watching Lionel parade me around while I flinched every time he came near me. And now, even after I was back in most senses of the word, I still had to take part in this show. I still *wanted* to on some level too and knowing how much that hurt him just made me feel like shit.

Before any of us could say anything else, the door opened once more and Catalina walked in, her arm looped around Vard's and her face pale. I stiffened in my chair despite my best efforts not to react, but now that I had my full memories of the things Lionel and his Seer had done to me it was hard not to show fear in their presence. My bond to Lionel made it easier with him, but the Cyclops was a different matter.

Clara seemed to forget all about keeping Darius in check as Lionel sat beside her, climbing into his lap and stroking his hair in a way that half made me want to kick her in the vag so that I could take her place, and half had me relieved that he was distracted. I could already tell this night was going to be exhausting as I battled through this yoyo of emotions I felt around Daddy Acrux and I had to suppress a groan as I looked down at my lap.

Lionel didn't seem to notice as he turned his attention to the serving staff who instantly appeared with plates of food, but Darius's fingers found mine beneath the table and he ran his thumb across the back of my hand.

My heart leapt and fear shot through my veins, but as Darius made a move to withdraw his hand, I caught his thumb to stop him.

My hand was trembling, part with fear and part with something much more exciting as I touched him. I slowly slid my fingertips across his calloused palm as I extended the contact between us and he ran his thumb up the inside up wrist, sending a trail of fire racing through my flesh.

Surely that wasn't a normal reaction to someone half holding your hand, but I couldn't deny how damn good it felt to just stay there like that. Knowing he had my back.

His touch sent a shiver of longing through my skin and I had to fight the urge to look at him as I tightened my fingers around his, keeping hold of him as my pulse settled a little.

Bowls of soup were laid out alongside freshly baked bread rolls and I chanced a look at Darius as his thumb stroked over my wrist again. His eyes were fixed on me, the rage burning in them all aimed at his father and making my heart race as I looked at it. It was impossible to see anything but the dangerous creature this man was as I peered up at him and yet for once, I wasn't afraid.

My mouth suddenly felt endlessly dry and I wetted my lips as I found myself captured in his gaze while he seemed to be silently asking me what he should do. I knew that if I asked him to, he'd leap out of his chair and take his father on for me. But we also knew that between Clara's hold over the shadows inside him and the fact that I'd be compelled to place myself between Lionel and death, that wasn't an option.

Just as I felt like I might lose myself in Darius's eyes and the feeling of his hand in mine, the waiter behind me cursed as he dropped the bowl of boiling hot tomato soup he was trying to place before me. The bowl crashed into mine and Darius's hands, knocking them apart as bright orange soup flew everywhere and I sucked in a pained breath as it burned me.

Darius leapt to his feet with a curse as he got a lapful of it and Lionel snarled furiously, slamming a fist down on the table and snapping his fingers as he stole the oxygen from the waiter's lungs.

"What the hell kind of a way is this to serve food at the royal table?" he bellowed, making all of the waiters flinch in anticipation of his next move.

Clara leapt to her feet, cackling with glee as the clumsy waiter stumbled back, falling against the wall as he clutched at his throat in panic.

"Release him," Darius demanded, waving his own hand and using his water magic to gather up all of the spilled soup before depositing it back in the bowl. "It wasn't his fault, Father, I knocked his arm."

"He did," Xavier added quickly. "The waiter didn't do anything wrong."

"When I want the opinion of the talking horse, I will ask you to speak," Lionel snapped, casting a disgusted look at Xavier before lifting his soup spoon and beginning on his meal as the waiter continued to suffocate in the corner of the room.

"I said, release him!" Darius shouted, his fist thumping down on the table and making everyone's plates jump.

Catalina yelped in alarm and Xavier released a frightened whinny while Vard smiled like he'd already *seen* how this was going to play out. And if he was excited about it then I knew it could only be bad.

I looked between the dying waiter and Darius fearfully, forcing myself not to say a word despite how much I wanted to. Revealing the truth of my situation now would only make everything so much worse for all of us, but if Darius couldn't save the man's life then I didn't know what I was going to do. I couldn't let him die. He'd only dropped the damn soup because I'd been holding Darius's hand and the stars had used him to force us apart in their fucked up way.

"If you are so concerned over the life of a servant then perhaps you would like to volunteer to take a punishment in his place?" Lionel asked, pausing with his soup spoon half way to his mouth.

"Fine," Darius gritted out, his jaw ticking with fury.

Lionel smiled cruelly and released the waiter without even bothering to look his way. His face had turned blue and blood vessels had burst in the whites of his eyes, but I was fairly certain he would survive so long as someone healed him sharpish. Two more of the wait staff hurried over to drag him from the room and I held my breath as Vard tittered a laugh and Lionel returned to eating his soup.

Darius slowly lowered into his chair and it soon became clear that Lionel had no intention of punishing him yet, drawing out the suspense as he focused on his meal.

I met Darius's eye for a brief moment, hoping he could see how sorry I was for causing that problem before forcing myself to eat my own soup.

Lionel didn't break the silence again throughout the starter and only spoke once the main course was well underway and we were all thoroughly terrified of what the hell he was going to say.

"Vard foresaw something very troubling today, didn't you?" Lionel said finally and my gut tightened as I wondered what the hell his twisted Seer could have *seen*. Was he watching me closely? Was there any chance that he might know I was no longer fully under the control of him and his master?

"Yes," Vard said in that snivelling tone of his that turned my stomach. "I was blessed with a vision of a great library. One which holds more forgotten knowledge than we can even imagine."

"Where?" I asked, keeping my tone as neutral as I could.

"That's the problem," Lionel said in a tired voice. "It has been hidden away by yet another group of lowly Orders, trying to steal from their betters."

"What the hell is that supposed to mean?" Darius growled.

"You yourself know how conniving Sphinxes are, don't you, Darius?" Lionel mused. "After all, I heard you were screwing one not so long ago."

I had to fight the urge to wrinkle my nose at the reminder of him dating Marguerite and I focused on pushing my food around my plate, hoping no one was paying me much attention.

"She was trying to secure a position as your bride, did you know that?" Lionel asked with a disgusted laugh. "Her father actually had the nerve to come to me about it. He claimed you were in love and wanted to try and arrange a marriage for you. As if I'd muddy my lineage with blood like theirs."

"We should punish them for suggesting it, Daddy," Clara said excitedly and he gave her a small smile.

"I have even better reason to punish them than that," he said. "This library Vard *saw* held all manner of priceless tomes and artefacts, scriptures and knowledge long since lost to us. All stolen by Sphinxes and hidden away with the help of the Minotaurs."

"Minotaurs?" Xavier asked in confusion. "Why would they help to hide-"

"The library is underground, in the centre of a labyrinth carved by their half-shifting kind," Lionel spat. "And soon I will release this knowledge to the rest of the kingdom. Solaria will decide what we should do about these lesser creatures trying to conceal and hoard knowledge which they have no right to take from the rest of us."

"And the people will cry out encouragement to help their king retrieve it," Vard said confidently, running a hand through his long hair and licking his lips as he surveyed Catalina over his wine glass. She supressed a shudder and I watched her with a faint frown as I realised I hadn't removed Lionel's most recent Dark Coercion from her since he'd bonded me to him, the thought making my gut stir guiltily.

"So what?" Darius demanded. "Now you're going to start persecuting even more Orders? Just because this fucking...*Seer* claims to have *seen* a secret library in a vision. Even if it's true that some small selection of Sphinxes and Minotaurs were in on such a collusion, how can you possibly claim that all of them are to blame? And how come these Orders all happen to be those you despise the most - the weakest, most common Orders who you've always looked down on so fucking much? It seems more than a little convenient to me."

Lionel lowered his fork to his plate slowly and turned his eyes from Darius to me.

"I think it's time for my son to learn that lesson, don't you agree, Roxanya?" he asked in a low voice and Clara clapped excitedly as she moved to stand on her chair to get a better view.

"Punish him, Daddy! Make him bleed!" she cried.

Ice spilled through my veins as I realised he was going to make me dish out the punishment and I couldn't help but remember him making me hurt Darius before in the throne room. But it had been different then. I'd been watching through a veil of shadows, unable to feel anything, unable to care either. This was asking too much of me while I was playing this part and I didn't think I was going to be able to do it.

"Why not just do it yourself?" Darius demanded, pushing to his feet and opening his arms to make himself into an easier target. "Or don't you have the stomach for it anymore, old man?"

Lionel tutted at the goading and I looked up at Darius with wild eyes as I silently begged him to stop. I knew why he was doing it - he was trying to save me from having to be the one to hurt him, but I also knew that the more he ran his mouth, the worse Lionel would make this for him and I couldn't fucking bear that.

"It hurts you more when she does it," Lionel explained cruelly, getting to his feet and placing a hand on my shoulder. "Perhaps I should get her to use something more personal than the shadows to really drive the point home?" He lifted his steak knife between us, cocking his head thoughtfully as he looked at his son.

"Stop," Xavier begged, moving to get to his feet, but Clara flicked her fingers as she took hold of the shadows in him and shoved him back down into it.

Lionel looked like he was about to give me the knife and panic flared in me at the thought of that, but before I could figure out how to stop this from happening, Clara threw a ball of shadows at Darius with a cackle of glee.

He cursed as he was knocked back a step and a gasp escaped me before I could halt it. Luckily no one seemed to notice as Lionel nodded his approval, his eyes fixed on his son as he suffered.

"Give him more, Clara," Lionel snarled, his hand tightening on my shoulder.

His excitement turned my stomach and my magic shifted beneath my skin, urging me to do something that I knew would make everything so much worse.

Darius fell to the floor as she flooded his body with her dark power, his limbs spasming as he writhed in agony, a cry of pain escaping his lips that had ice spilling through my core.

Lionel released me suddenly and I gasped as he strode forward and slammed his steak knife straight into Darius's gut, causing him to bellow in pain.

I lurched forward a step just as the door burst open so hard that it crashed into the wall and half fell off the hinges. I only caught a blur of motion moving across the room and suddenly Orion was there, throwing a huge blast of air magic out from his palm that knocked Lionel back several paces before he managed to get his own magic up to shield himself and the rest of us.

Xavier caught my arm to stop me as I made a move to step forward, his fearful gaze meeting mine as he shook his head in a silent warning while everyone else was caught up watching this horror show play out.

"Step aside, Lance," Lionel growled with a frustrated huff.

"You know I can't do that," Orion snarled, baring his fangs as Darius cursed in pain behind him where Clara still held him in the clutches of the shadows. Orion's hair was damp and he was wearing a fresh white shirt and jeans but his feet were bare, making me think he'd been in the middle of changing when he'd felt Darius's pain and been drawn here by the Guardian bond to protect him.

"See your brother back to his accommodation, Clara," Lionel hissed, his venomous gaze still locked on his son while he bled out on the floor behind Orion.

"No!" Orion threw himself at Darius, reaching for him with green healing magic flaring in his palm a moment before Clara hit him with a shockwave of shadows so powerful that they made the air in the room ripple all around us.

The shadows in me tried to rise up to meet them automatically and I groaned involuntarily as pleasure rolled down my spine, fighting with all I had to keep them back so that I could think clearly. Catalina stared at her son in horror from her seat, seeming unable to even call out to him while she remained locked in her place.

Xavier's grip on my arm was the only thing stopping me from diving forward to help too and I choked back a sob that lodged in my throat as I fought with the desires of my heart and the desperate need we all had to keep my cover intact.

Orion still tried to crawl towards Darius, crying out in pain as Clara smiled wickedly, allowing him to get just close enough to brush his fingers against the knife protruding from Darius's gut before yanking him upright with the shadows again.

"Walky, walky, little brother," Clara purred, miming the action with two of her fingers as Orion's legs carried him towards the door despite how hard he was clearly trying to stay and help Darius.

His white shirt was stained with Darius's blood and his desperate gaze met mine with what was undoubtably a plea for me to do what I had to to save his friend's life.

Clara leapt up onto the table and ran the length of it before diving over Vard's head and scurrying out of the room behind him as Lionel advanced on his son once more.

"Don't forget your place, boy," Lionel snarled, grabbing a fistful of

Darius's shirt and yanking him half off of the ground so that they were nose to nose. "I may have use for you thanks to your brother's disgusting condition, but the moment you put an Heir in Mildred's belly, your value will greatly diminish. Perhaps you should consider making yourself more valuable to me before then."

Darius gritted his teeth against the pain of the knife lodged in his gut, grunting as Lionel threw him back down against the wooden floor and blood pooled out to further stain his blue shirt red.

Lionel slammed his foot into Darius's side as he straightened and only Xavier's grip on my arm held me in place as tears burned the backs of my eyes and I fought with everything I had against the desire to start screaming. But I couldn't do anything about it. Even now, I couldn't bring myself to truly consider hurting Lionel and the knowledge of that was cutting into me as surely as the knife piercing Darius's flesh.

"Fix my son up and see him to his quarters, Roxanya, and make sure he stays in there for the night. I'm finding the current company less than stimulating." Lionel sneered, tossing his napkin down on the table and heading from the room. "You can meet me in my chambers when you've made sure he's locked away."

Vard stood too, sighing like we were boring him before stalking out of the room after his king and allowing us to act freely.

The moment they were gone, I darted forward, dropping to my knees and pressing shaky fingers to Darius's stomach as I looked down at the blade protruding from his gut. Xavier leaned in close too, but without the training required for him to help, there wasn't anything he could do.

"I can do it," Darius grunted, reaching for the knife like he was going to rip the damn thing out himself and I smacked his hand away as I shook my head.

"I've got you," I growled, wrapping my own fingers around it and meeting his dark eyes as I psyched myself up to do this.

Darius gave me a sharp nod and I held his gaze as I pulled it free. He cursed loudly and I pressed my fingers to the stab wound as I pushed healing magic beneath his skin, seeking out the connection to his magic so that I could fix it as fast as possible.

Xavier whinnied in anguish, stomping his foot and I worked to block him out as healing magic spread from my fingertips.

It took less than a second for my magic to latch onto Darius's, that thunderous familiarity of his power calling to me like my name in the dark as I found it and I poured my power into him as fast as I could.

My eyes fell closed as I concentrated and after a few seconds, I flinched at the touch of his hand on my cheek as he sat up.

"I'm sorry," I breathed, blinking back tears as the sight of him lying there, bleeding out on the floor consumed me for an eternal moment.

"I'm fine," he promised, grasping my chin and tilting it up so that when I opened my eyes again I was forced to look at him and see the truth of those words. "I've been living with that monster for a long time. This doesn't come close to the worst he's done to me."

A distressed whinny drew my attention from Darius and I glanced around to find Xavier still hovering right behind me with Catalina standing on the far side of the table. She hadn't uttered a word though and the restrained way she held herself had me certain that she was suffering under Lionel's thumb once more too.

I pushed myself to my feet and moved around the table, taking her hand and driving Phoenix fire beneath her skin, seeking out the Dark Coercion the way I had all those months ago and finding new commands binding her mind to Lionel's will. I destroyed each and every one of them and she gasped as she was released, winding her arms around me and pulling me close as a choked sob escaped her.

"I'm so sorry, sweet girl," she breathed. "For everything he's done to you while I was forced to stand by."

I fell still in her arms, unsure what to do with a mother's embrace and feeling the weight of it right down to the base of my soul. I'd never had this. Never even come close to it. And something about it awakened a part of me I always liked to pretend wasn't even there. The part who longed for a mother who had loved her, a family me and Darcy could have called our own but would never know.

"We don't have time for this," Darius said gravely and I turned to find him on his feet, his torn and bloody shirt sticking to his freshly healed skin as he looked at me and his mother with regret in his eyes. "He told you to put me back in my suite and he'll notice if you take too long."

"Okay," I agreed, having no other choice though my mind was still reeling at what had just happened.

Darius cast a concerned look between his mother and Xavier then strode out ahead of me, leaving the others in the dining room with the half eaten meal.

We stayed silent as we moved through the busy palace towards the suites that had been allocated for Darius and Xavier on the second floor of the King's tower. There were servants everywhere, scurrying from one place to the next and ensuring we weren't really alone until the moment we reached his room.

When we stepped into the lavish suite that Darius had been given to call his own, he threw a silencing bubble up around us and slammed the door shut before pressing me back against the door and growling darkly. But I wasn't afraid. Even after all the reasons I'd been given to fear him, right then there wasn't a single piece of me that believed his fury was aimed my way.

"Say the word and I'll take my chances against him now," he growled, his voice rough and pained as his grip on my waist tightened and he pressed his forehead to mine, overwhelming me with his presence and making my breath catch in my throat.

"You can't," I breathed as the lights in the room began to flicker ominously, no doubt a warning from the stars about us being alone. "Please, Darius, don't do anything that will get you hurt."

"I'm not letting you go to him," he snarled and I shook my head as every piece of me ached with the desire to be able to stay here instead, even though the prospect of that still terrified me too.

"I have to," I replied simply, reaching for the door handle behind me as thunder boomed beyond the windows. If I lingered here, the stars would make sure everyone in the palace knew about it. Not to mention the fact that he was too close, his flesh too warm against mine, his presence too overwhelming and my scars too tender to figure out if I wanted that or not. Especially right now after I'd had to watch his father stab him. It was too much. He was too much. And I couldn't cope with it right now while Lionel was waiting for me.

"Stay," Darius demanded, his voice a growl that ripped a hole right through me even though we both knew his request was impossible.

"I can't," I whispered, twisting the handle at my back and swallowing the lump in my throat as I stepped out into the corridor, leaving him inside alone while my heart thundered in my chest.

He didn't do anything to stop me from leaving but the look in his eyes cut into me as I closed the door between us again and sealed it up with shadows like Lionel had told me to.

As the darkness writhed and twisted beneath my skin, I let the shadows delve deeper than I had all week, needing to coat myself in an armour made of them if I was going to have any hope of making it through the next part of this evening without giving myself away.

I took a moment to try and compose myself, willing my pulse to settle, my tears not to fall. I couldn't feel this right now. None of it. So I sank deeper into the shadows with a sigh of relief and let them consume every emotion burning through my blood until I couldn't feel any of it anymore.

I strode up the winding staircase of the King's tower, climbing higher and higher until I finally reached the top where the predictable sounds of Clara screaming out in ecstasy reached me from beyond the door.

I released a shaky breath and pulled the shadows even closer, letting them lick their way along my limbs and sending shivers of pleasure through my flesh. I was treading a thin line, needing to stay lucid enough to be sure I'd stick to our plan for tonight while using the shadows to deaden me to everything else. But if I was going to be certain Lionel wouldn't discover me, I had to be as emotionless as possible around him.

I just needed to make it back to Darcy. That was what I had to focus on.

"Give it to me, Daddy!" Clara screamed and I shuddered, trying not to think of the times over the summer when I'd been sitting in the room while he fucked her.

Luckily for me, Clara wouldn't hear any suggestion of me joining them during those activities which I hadn't had much feeling on one way or any other at the time, but I was endlessly grateful for now. Lionel seemed to want to keep her happy and she had made it clear that as his favourite she was the only one who would be screwing him, which he seemed to go along with to appease her temper tantrums over other issues. Considering she was the one with the real control over the Nymph army, I could only imagine he was treading a fine line keeping her in check.

I waited until I heard Lionel grunting his release, giving them a few more moments to pull their clothes on and pushed the door open before stepping inside.

Lionel was laying in the centre of the bed with a pair of black boxer briefs in place and Clara's weird shadow dress had transformed into some semblance of a nightdress too. I hadn't really given any consideration to that while I'd been under Lionel's control, but now that I thought about it, she never seemed to wear any real clothes. Even her hair seemed to be made of shadows. What was with that? Come to think of it, she never showered either. And only seemed to eat if she was joining in with our king, like tonight. *What the fuck is she?*

I headed into the bathroom, collecting a nightdress from the closet on my way and changing quickly before drawing strength from the shadows and heading back to the bedroom where Lionel had already flicked out the lights.

"Come, Roxanya," he growled irritably. "The bond won't let me settle without you close tonight."

I knew all too well how that felt and I climbed into the bed with a mixture of relief and internal disgust at my situation before shuffling up against his body and relaxing a little as the bond was finally satisfied by the contact.

Lionel leaned over me and took a syringe from the nightstand before taking hold of my arm and moving the needle towards it. I forced myself to stay calm, banishing the shadows completely as I prepared for what I'd known was coming as he drove the needle beneath my skin and dosed me with Order Suppressant once more. My Phoenix was pushed down deep inside of me and I felt so hollow without it that it stole my breath away and I had to fight not to react at all.

Mildred had already been the one to dose me midweek and now that I had full access to my memories, I'd figured out that this was the routine. Twice a week. Tuesdays and Fridays. After Mildred had first done it, I'd almost panicked, but Gabriel had shown up out of nowhere and quickly given me the antidote. He'd sworn to me that he'd be watching to *see* every time they planned on dosing me again and no matter what, someone would be ready to dose me with antidote as soon as possible afterwards. In the meantime, all I had to do was be careful to stay clear of the shadows and I should be fine.

Though as Lionel tugged me down to lay beside him and Clara shuffled close on his other side, I had to admit that my missing Phoenix was causing me more than a little concern. But I just had to wait until I saw Darcy once the two of them fell asleep and I knew I'd get it back again. So, for now, I just needed to play along.

I lay with my head on the left side of his chest while Clara positioned hers on his right and he wrapped his arms around both of us, pulling us in tightly against him. My palm was flat on his chest right above his heart and as I lay there, I couldn't help but think how I could fix all of our problems with a single blast of magic.

But the more I tried to convince myself to do it, the more bile rose in my throat and I shuddered with horror at the idea of a world without Lionel Acrux in it until I was practically choking over it.

I was broken. I knew it. This bond he'd placed on me had done something so twisted that my own thoughts and feelings weren't entirely my own anymore. But I was also a slave to this connection one way or another. And if I wanted to maintain enough of myself to stand a chance of ever escaping him, then I knew I had to accept this side of it for now. I'd lay here in a bed with my enemy and dream of the day that this nightmare would end. But until then, I was going to have to seek solace in his arms again and again and again.

As he and Clara quickly fell asleep, I just lay there, waiting until I could be certain that I could leave without them noticing and trying not to overthink how good it felt to be in his arms and how much I'd been needing this.

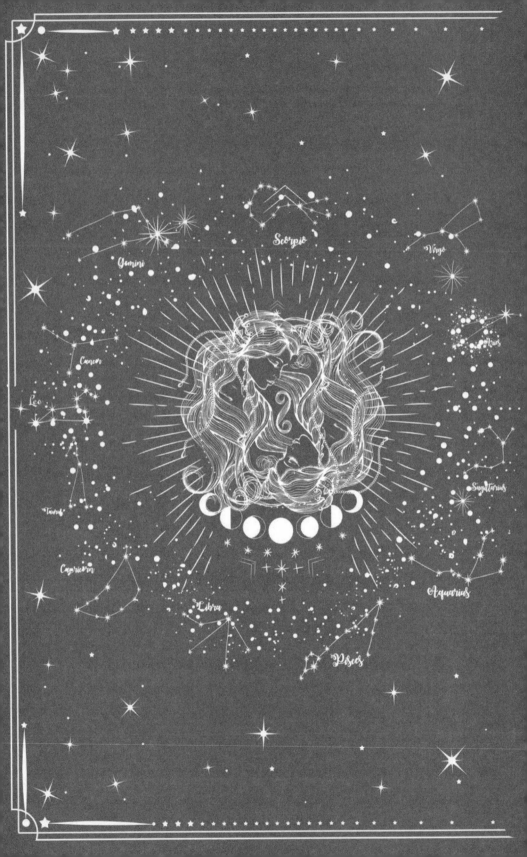

DARCY

CHAPTER TWENTY ONE

I walked along the dark tunnels beneath the palace grounds with a Faelight hovering ahead of me to illuminate the way. I was dressed in a fitted black leggings and sweater combo to help keep me hidden for when I started sneaking around later. I was still working on perfecting illusions and as Highspell was about as useful a Cardinal Magic teacher as a rotten turd, I was struggling. There was only so much I could learn from books and what I really needed was a good teacher. The Heirs were swamped with their own work and they were already giving me extra combat lessons. I couldn't take up more of their time.

Lucky you're going to see your old professor then.

The thought came out of nowhere and I immediately rejected it. I wasn't going to ask him for help. But then again…I didn't know how long I was going to have to wait with him before Tory showed up. I was going to have to say something to him. So maybe keeping our conversation on work was a good idea. It definitely beat making small talk or dipping into uncomfortable territory like all the crap that hung between us. And it would absolutely beat sitting there in deathly silence.

I headed up the passage that led to the hatch and soon arrived beneath it, hesitating as I fought away the dread in my stomach over what was waiting for me beyond it. The worst thing was, I wanted to see him. And that made me want to boob punch myself because I should have been done pining for him a long time ago.

Well I can't linger here like a bad smell for the rest of eternity.

I sighed and reached up to press my hand to the Hydra symbol on the wood. It clicked open and I pushed it up a second before someone else took hold of it and Orion appeared above, crouching down as he looked in at me.

A beat of silence passed where my eyes became stuck on his like glue and my lungs decided they no longer worked automatically. *Seriously, how do I even goddamn breathe??*

He'd shaved his beard back to a coating of stubble and his hair was cut neatly and swept back over his head. He looked how he used to before our whole world had imploded and I was captured by the need to move closer to him. But there was no chance of me acting on that urge.

"Hi," he said in a deep tone that resounded right through my bones and I gave him a tight smile in response.

"I can get out if you move aside," I said and he frowned.

"You can also get out if you give me your hand," he countered and my heart did somersaults as I gazed up at him with pursed lips.

He gave up with a sigh, standing and moving away from the hole. I cast air beneath my feet and flew up into the kitchenette, kicking the hatch closed as I landed on the floor.

The place was dark, just a couple of lamps on in the corners and my gaze hooked on a book resting open on the arm of a chair beside one of them. A bottle of bourbon was down to the dregs beside it and the scent of it hung in the air, reminding me so viscerally of him that my lungs seized up again. Whiskey and my ex were apparently a deadly combination. *Get a grip, dammit.*

I glanced at him, feeling the silence stretching already and his jaw ticked angrily as he gazed at me. Had I pissed him off? Probably. Did I give a shit? Absolutely not.

I headed away from him just so I could breathe again and I moved to examine the large blue dresser which was busy with beautiful little ornaments. I picked up a delicate seahorse carved from stone and ran my thumb along the ridges of its back, wondering how long I could stand here examining it for before I looked like a crazy person.

"Do you want a coffee?" he asked, heading to the coffee machine.

"Sure." I shrugged, stealing a glance at him and taking in the smart blue shirt that was hugging his muscles. He had smart pants on too like he was dressed for work and the way they clung to his ass was just fucking perf – *get your eyes off his ass, dipshit!* "Milk and-"

"One sugar, I know," he growled, not looking at me as he grabbed two mugs out of the cupboard, slammed them down on the counter then set about brewing the coffee like the angriest man in the world. I swear he broke the machine at one point and punched it to get it going again.

I placed the seahorse down and moved across the room, gazing at the seating options. I settled on perching awkwardly against the back of the couch, half leaning, half sort of sitting and unsure what to do with my arms. *Do they normally just hang there like that??*

"Is everything…okay?" I asked.

"Lionel attacked Darius, stabbed him with a fucking steak knife," he muttered and my breath snagged.

"Is he alright?" I gasped.

"He is now," he sighed and my breathing eased a little.

God, we needed to deal with Lionel. I hated that so many of the people I cared about were at risk all the time. Whenever Tory or Darius had to go to him, I wanted to scream. And now Darius had been hurt and it wasn't like it was the first time either. He probably didn't even tell me about half the times his father laid into him. And though Tory still hadn't spoken to me about exactly what Lionel had done to her, I'd gleaned enough from the haunted look in her eyes to know it was something terrible. It awoke a monster in me that needed cold, hard vengeance. And I wouldn't rest until I got it.

I kept my gaze on the swimming pool beyond the tall windows, the moonlight rippling across its surface as I wrestled with my demons.

Silence hung between us for so long that I swear I could hear every drop of water filtering through the coffee grains.

Orion finally walked over to me, handing me a mug with a raincloud on it and standing far too close for me to be able to think straight.

"Are you going to sit down or continue to perch there like a constipated owl?" he asked dryly and my lips dared to twitch.

"T'wit-twoo," I made an owl sound as my answer and he pressed his tongue into his cheek before walking away to stare out the window.

I cupped the coffee mug between my hands, casting a little ice on my palms to cool it down before taking a sip.

A breeze howled against the summerhouse and rattled the windows while I gazed at Orion's back before my eyes slipped down to his ass again. *For fuck's sake.*

"Can I ask you something?" Orion asked and I ripped my eyes away from his butt.

"You just did," I pointed out.

He glanced over his shoulder at me with one of his professor looks and I suddenly felt far hotter than the coffee in my mug. Not that he was going to have any idea of how much he was affecting me. I knew how to keep my emotions on lockdown these days. And it wasn't just that, I could handle them better too. He might have destroyed me when he ruined us, but he'd made me stronger as well. I guessed sometimes you had to watch your walls crack and crumble so you could figure out how to build a better kingdom.

I rolled my eyes and shrugged. "Go on then."

He turned back to face the window, taking a long sip of his coffee before he spoke. "Are you always going to hate me?"

My chest cleaved apart and I let the silence stretch as I bit my tongue on all the things I wanted to say in response to that. *I wish I could hate you, but I feel something far worse than that. A love that won't die for the man who broke me.*

He turned to me again just as the clouds drew over the moon outside and a rumble of thunder sounded in this distance, the storm drawing in. My heart missed a full beat and I tried to push down my emotions before he caught a glimpse of them.

"I don't hate you, Lance," I admitted.

He was cast in shadow so I couldn't see his expression in response to that, but he started moving closer again, his steps slow and deliberate in that way of his that suggested he was always one moment away from becoming a bloodthirsty predator.

"And why not?" he asked, his tone deadly like I was angering him. Did he *want* me to hate him?

I considered giving some bullshit answer that meant nothing, but I found I didn't want to. I'd had a thousand conversations in my head with Orion since he'd gone to prison. Conversations I'd been owed. Explanations I'd been denied. If he wanted my truth then fine, because maybe that meant I'd get his in return. And maybe I might finally get some damn closure. Because no matter how hard I'd tried to move on from him, it felt like I hadn't moved a single inch away from wanting him. I guessed the promise I'd made to him really had meant something to me, unlike it had for him.

"I don't hate you because I know what you did wasn't spiteful. Unless I've got you all wrong, I assume you didn't throw yourself into Darkmore as an easy way out of our relationship." The joke came out kind of bitter, and I couldn't say I felt bad about that.

Orion nodded, taking that in and draining his coffee before planting the mug down on an ornate silver table. "So why do you think I did it?"

I scoffed, shaking my head at him. "I don't know, Lance, you never gave me the courtesy of an explanation."

He rushed toward me at speed and I cast a solid air shield around me before he could get close. He stopped just before it, his hand brushing the barrier and he released a furious breath through his nose.

"An explanation?" He laughed a cold, mirthless laugh. "You have no fucking idea, do you?"

"About what? How you broke our promise? Or how you ripped out my heart and tore it into fifty pieces? Or was it the part where you gave me no choice in any of it?" I demanded, my temper rising as I shoved my coffee cup between the two couch cushions behind me to keep it there.

He tsked. "You think I wanted it to be this way? I had no fucking choice."

"Bullshit," I snarled, dropping my shield in favour of shoving him in the chest with a gust of air as my anger spilled over. I hadn't wanted this. I'd planned to come here and keep things simple, but maybe I should have realised that things with him would never be that. And now we were going there, I couldn't stop my rage from pouring out.

He growled as he stumbled back a step, but did nothing to counter the air I kept blasting at him.

"There's always a choice, and you chose to ruin us." I'd suppressed all of this for so long, and why shouldn't I say my piece?

He bared his fangs, his muscles bunching. "You think I wanted to give you up? You think any of this has been easy for me?"

"You were the one who made it hard!" I yelled, my Phoenix flames tingling against the inside of my skin. "You didn't have the right to make that choice for me."

"It was the only way," he pushed and I gave up on blasting him with magic, throwing my palms into his solid chest instead.

"You don't get to decide my life for me, Lance," I snapped. "You could have died in that fucking prison. And what the hell for?"

He captured my wrists as I tried to shove him once more, his eyes blazing. His skin on mine was the most tempting kind of torture, heat melting into my blood and calling me to him.

He remained silent and I yanked my hands free of his grip, turning my back on him and putting some distance between us again as I moved across the room. Rain started to patter against the windows, and I gazed out at the dark droplets smattering the glass.

Nothing. He gave me nothing. Even after all this time, he still wouldn't give me an answer to why he'd done it. It didn't matter if Darius had tried to convince me of one reason or another, the only person I needed to hear it from was Orion. And his silence spoke volumes.

My Atlas buzzed in my pocket and I took it out, finding a message from Tory saying she was on her way, but she was waiting for Jenkins to stop hovering around on the stairs.

"Is that him?" Orion grunted and I turned around again as I shot her a reply.

"Who?" I muttered, dropping into an armchair and watching the rain. Anything but look at the guy who was the reason it felt like a knife was sliding into my heart and twisting.

"Seth," he said icily, his shadow looming in my periphery as he drew closer again.

"What does it matter?" I said, following the path of a droplet as it weaved its way down the glass.

"It matters because he's a fucking asshole," he growled.

"Things change," I said firmly.

He tutted. "How? The guy cut off your hair and fucked with us for *months*."

"He also saved your life and was there for me when you weren't," I said scathingly, a part of me regretting the callous blow, but another more bitter part of me wanted to hurt him for hurting me.

He remained silent for so long that I couldn't resist looking over at him and the hurt in his eyes made my stomach knot.

"He's changed," I went on, my tone softening a little.

"Are you...happy?" he asked in a gruff tone.

"Happy?" I scoffed, glaring at him. "No, Lance, I'm not happy. I won't be happy until Lionel is dead and I know that everyone I care about is going to be okay. That everyone in the kingdom will be okay. What he's doing to people, to the Tiberian Rats..." I shook my head as emotion welled in me, threatening to rip me open.

He moved to sit in the chair opposite me, running his palm over his face as he sat back in it.

"I know," he said heavily. "It's fucking awful."

"I just feel so helpless to it," I breathed, balling my hands into fists. "And dwelling on it only makes it worse."

"Well…maybe we should talk about something else," Orion suggested and I nodded, needing that. "How's school?"

I frowned. "It's okay."

"Liar," he murmured and I sighed.

"Fine, it sucks. Everyone's miserable, the Orders are forced to be apart, I can't grasp the next level of illusion spells because Highspell won't demonstrate anything and just throws me in detention if I try to question her. She basically won't pay attention to any of the 'lesser' Orders at the back of the class and, not surprisingly, all of us back there are starting to fail."

"Why the fuck are you at the back of the class?" he snarled.

"Because I refused to go along with Lionel's Orderist bullshit," I said heatedly and a smirk tugged at his lips.

"Well fuck Honey Highspell, beautiful, I'll help you with whatever it is," he said and my throat thickened at what he'd called me. He hurried on like he was trying to ignore that little slip while I held my breath. "I mean, if you want me to." He shrugged and I tugged my lower lip between my teeth as I nodded.

Anything was better than sitting here and dying of awkwardness. His dark eyes stilled on my mouth for a second and the world seemed to fade into a blurry grey haze around me.

I cleared my throat. "I can picture just how I want the illusion to look, but whenever I do the cast it comes out wrong," I explained.

"Show me," he encouraged and I swiped his book from the arm of my chair, realising it was an old tome about dark concealment spells. I laid it in my lap and focused on the leather cover, flexing my fingers over it as I pictured a different cover until King Arthur and The Knights of the Round Table appeared over it. Only it wasn't quite right, the faces were off and the colours didn't fit. It was clear to see it wasn't a decent illusion if anyone looked close enough.

"Why did you pick that book?" he asked in surprise and I shrugged.

"It was the first one that came into my head," I said and he frowned, pushing out of his seat as he moved across the room to a bookshelf and plucked another book off of it.

He shot back over to me and knelt down at my feet, placing the book on my knee beside the one I'd disguised.

"There's a step you're missing in illusion. Honey was never any good at it in her training." He sniggered and my mouth pulled up at the corner.

"But surely she's hiding behind fifty beauty illusions, the woman shines like the damn moon," I said.

He grinned darkly, shaking his head. "It's paid for. She holds the spells of others in that ugly necklace she wears."

I released a laugh. "Please tell me she looks like the ass end of a rhino normally."

"I don't know, I've never seen her without that necklace, but I reckon she's at least got warts and a hunchback," he said.

"Maybe she has rotten teeth and a beak for a nose too."

His hand slipped to the edge of the book, his fingers grazing my thigh as he chuckled. The sound made my toes scrunch up in my shoes and I quickly flattened my smile and looked back at the books. *Nope.*

"So what am I missing?" I asked.

"You need to practise memory imprinting," he said. "The more recently you saw something, the better your memory of it is to create an illusion. But that's very limiting. Unless the memory is particularly clear, you'll never be able to create a perfect image without memory imprinting."

"How does it work?" I asked, my heart thumping a little harder as he met my gaze and I felt myself leaning closer to him without really deciding to. I mentally yanked myself back by the hair because hell no.

"You tried to conjure the image in your mind of this book from some old memory, but to become really proficient at this, you need to start building new, imprinted memories that you can access for illusions whenever you need them."

"Okay," I said slowly. "Show me what to do."

He reached out and took my hand and my stomach flipped over as he guided it onto the copy of King Arthur, encouraging me to brush my fingers over it. That was definitely not a sexual thing to do and yet heat spread between my thighs and I tried to convince myself it was to do with the buck toothed dude on the cover who was covered in chainmail. *Yup, that's definitely what's doing it for me. Not the guy who used to fuck me until I couldn't walk straight and made me come ten times before he even considered being done with me.*

"Focus on the image, let your mind relax," he instructed, releasing my hand. I did as he asked, trying my best to ignore how close he was to me or how my breathing was getting unsteady. "When you think you have it memorised, close your eyes and draw some magic up to the image. Don't let it take any form, just pull it closer to the picture in your mind until it merges."

I nodded, drawing on the well of power in me and encouraging some of that magic towards my mind. A light seemed to grow around the image I could see in my head and I sucked in a little breath in surprise.

"Got it?" he asked in a deep tone and I nodded. "Now let it go. Try not to think of it at all."

I let my mind go dark and the image seemed to snap against my brain like a rubber band. I inhaled as I reached for it again and it came into my mind's eye as clearly as if I was looking right at it once more. *Woah.*

"Open your eyes," Orion growled and I did, immediately falling into the dark well of his irises and realising my fingers were an inch from grazing his on top of King Arthur.

I curled my hand up and tried to wet my desert dry mouth as I looked down at the book of dark magic beside it.

"Try the illusion now," he encouraged, taking the copy of King Arthur out of sight.

I gazed at the other book and drew on that memory just like I'd been taught in class before rubbing my forefinger and thumb together as I cast the illusion. The cover immediately altered, and the size of the book too, everything shifting to look exactly the way the real copy of King Arthur had.

I released a squeal of excitement, picking it up and examining it for errors. But there weren't any. It was the most perfect illusion I'd ever cast. *Holy shit.*

I looked to Orion and found him watching me with an intensity that made my cheeks burn.

"Thank you," I said earnestly.

"Any time," he said gruffly, pushing to his feet. "Seriously, just text me or call if you ever need help with anything."

I didn't answer that, unsure if I should really open up a line of communication between us. But then again, I was falling behind in Cardinal Magic because of Highspell and I really couldn't afford to do that with Lionel in power. I had to make sure I passed my exams and more than that, I wanted every advantage I could gain against the Dragon Lord. But it was Orion. If I started talking to him on a regular basis, my head could get messed up. No. I couldn't do it.

A tap came on the window and I spotted Tory there, beckoning me to come out.

I gave Orion a tight smile and if I wasn't being totally crazy, I swear he looked kind of dejected. Maybe any company was better than none while he was locked up here twenty four seven.

"Guess I'll...see you in a bit," I said with an awkward smile.

"I'll wait up," he said, his throat bobbing.

I walked away, ignoring the way my heart throbbed and ached as I slipped quickly out the door. I didn't look back as Tory took my hand and pulled me along at speed, guiding me onto a path between two tall hedges before she slowed again. Her magic met mine and merged easily as we cast an air shield around us to keep off the rain.

"Did Lionel give you another dose of Order Suppressant?" I asked as I tried to reach her Phoenix with mine and came up against nothing.

"Yeah," she sighed. "And then we...snuggled. You know, usual fucked up shit."

I squeezed her fingers tight in mine, trying to get my head around the insanity of that fucking bond he'd placed on her and silently vowing for the millionth time that I'd find a way to free her from it.

I pulled the syringe of antidote from my pocket and Tory smiled at me as she accepted it and quickly injected herself.

She sighed in relief as her Phoenix returned to her and I relaxed as we kept walking.

"Everything okay?" she asked and I shrugged.

"It's just awkward with him," I murmured. "Anyway, is Darius okay? Orion said Lionel stabbed him."

"He's alright now. Lionel just went full psycho as usual. And I couldn't help. I had to just stand there and watch," she said in a choked voice and I gripped her arm.

"I'm sorry," I breathed. "That must have been awful."

She sighed, dropping her gaze. "It just makes me think how precious shit is, you know? How quickly we could lose people we care about. And look, I know this isn't the time to talk about it, but you and Orion..."

"Don't, Tor," I begged.

"But you're meant for each other, Darcy. And the two of you are so sad, I can't bear it. I swear I saw you guys for two seconds and it felt like watching a funeral procession."

A sharp lump formed in my throat and I shook my head. "He made his choice. Now I've made mine. There's no going back."

She sighed, squeezing my fingers then releasing me. "Come on then, let's go."

"Where do you think we should start looking?" I asked as we headed along the path and passed through a rose garden that was being battered by the rain. The flames beneath my skin kept the cold out but my breath still fogged before me in the air.

"Gabriel said we'd know." Tory frowned and a glimmer caught my eye ahead of us.

My breath hitched and I tugged Tory's sleeve, pointing out the large footprint shining on the path. It looked like the print of a man's boot and my heartbeat quickened as I shared a look with Tory. The rainstorm suddenly fell away as if it never was and the clouds parted above to reveal a glittering expanse of stars. The air thickened and a chill swept through me. I knew in my soul they were watching us, and they were hoping to show us something just like they had before.

Tory's hand slid into mine and we silently released the air shield around us and walked toward the footprint. It faded away as we reached it and another one appeared further ahead, leading us down a path through the gardens I wasn't sure I'd ever taken before. We moved between the bushes as we were guided across the grounds, passing through an orchard where the grass glistened wetly. Beyond it, a huge stone amphitheatre loomed out of the dark, the path leading right up to two enormous silver doors. The boot prints guided us towards it and my fingers tightened on Tory's as we made it to the entrance. The immense curved wall towered above us and my skin prickled, something about this place setting me on edge.

Tory pressed her hand to the door and it unlocked at her touch, parting in the middle to allow us access. Shadows waited for us beyond it, the only light cast by another glistening footprint waiting for us in the dark.

"Do you think it's safe?" I whispered.

"I think so," she breathed and I shared a look with her that said there was no way either of us were turning back anyway. This was important. Everything in the atmosphere told me that.

I cast a Faelight, sending it out ahead of us as we crept inside. The moment we entered, the doors shut behind us with a loud thud that echoed around the stone corridor we were in and set my heart galloping.

The boot prints headed to our right and we followed them ever on until they led us down several dark stone steps. A door waited open for us at the bottom and the cool night air wafting in told me we were going outside again. We stepped through it together and my feet met sand as we arrived in an enormous circular pit at the centre of the amphitheatre. It looked like something from the Roman empire, but the place was no ruin. Stone benches ringed the whole arena, circling high above us and far ahead of us was a huge throne set back into the stands with several smaller chairs either side of it. An archway covered them all, carved with each of the four Elemental symbols and the Vega crest at the very top of it. Around the edges of the pit were Nymph cages just like the ones we'd trapped Tory in, and the thought of what they might have been here for made my stomach knot.

The footprints marked a path across the sand to the very centre of the pit where something lay on the ground, waiting for us. We moved cautiously towards it, the air stilling as we walked, the silence pressing in.

We came to a halt in front of a shield made of polished metal, our reflections cast on its surface and we knew what to do. We knelt either side of it, sharing a hopeful look before turning our gaze to the metal. The stars had shown us our mother before, what more did they want us to see?

Our reflections changed, giving way to a scene set in the bright light of day, looking down on this very amphitheatre. A stern and handsome man sat on the throne, his eyes sharp and narrowed on the pit below him. I recognised my father, Hail Vega, looking younger than he had before he met my mother in the previous visions I'd seen of him. To his right was Lionel Acrux and beyond him were the other Councillors, all looking tense as their gazes were set on the pit.

A man was hauled to the centre of the sand in rags, his wrists cuffed so his magic was blocked. Around the edges of the arena, the black metal cages were filled with Nymphs that shrieked and roared at the crowd, the sight making my pulse spike.

"My king!" the man in the pit cried. "I'm innocent."

The crowd jeered and the guard holding him shoved him to his knees before backing up and bowing to our father.

"Who is he?" the Savage King murmured to Lionel.

"A thief, Your Highness," he whispered. "The Rat stole a hundred gold coins from my cousin Benjamin."

Hail scoffed. "Benjamin Acrux is a gambler who has brought plenty of shame on your name, Lionel."

"Be that as it may, the word of a Dragon is worth more than a Rat's," Lionel hissed and my blood burned hotter.

"Nonsense," Hail said, waving him off before calling out to the man below. "Speak your case!"

The Tiberian Rat ran a shaky hand through his hair. "I won the gold from Mr Acrux fair and square in a game of Minojack," he said urgently. "Have a Cyclops check my memories."

"This is an outrage!" cried a man who I assumed was Benjamin Acrux from the way the Rat was glaring at him.

He stood up in the crowd and looked like a squatter, uglier version of Lionel. His eyes were bloodshot and the way he swayed a little suggested he might be drunk.

Lionel leaned closer to Hail and murmured, "*You will show no mercy, sire. A Dragon's word is law. But the decision has come from you, now forget my words.*" The power of his Dark Coercion filled his voice in an undertone that made my stomach lurch.

Hail blinked, leaning back in his seat and horror filled me as he called out to the crowd. "You have been found guilty of your crime. You will be given the Fae right to fight for your life. If you live, you will face twelve years in Darkmore Penitentiary." The King waved his hand in some signal and a sword was thrown into the pit as the guard cast himself out on a gust of air beneath his feet. A wave of the guard's hand opened one of the cages and a Nymph rushed out with a bellow of rage, the hunger in its eyes clear as it raced towards the Rat shifter. He lunged for the sword, but before he even got close, the Nymph swatted him aside and the cracking of bones filled the air followed by the cheers of the crowd.

Bile rose in my throat as the Nymph stepped down on the Rat's chest and a lasting scream filled the air as it drove its probes into his heart. The vision shifted abruptly and I couldn't tear my gaze away as I absorbed the truth laid out before me.

Hail stood on a huge balcony under the light of the stars, holding something in his hand and speaking a strange word to it as a glint of light peeked between his fingers. "End the plague in Maresh," he asked. "My people are dying."

Whispers filled my head as if from the stars themselves and I suddenly realised what was in his palm. The Imperial Star. *"It is done, father of the flames."*

Hail spoke another word to it which I didn't understand before speaking to it once more.

"Protect my people from foreign invaders," he asked and the star's reply filled my head.

"They shall be protected," it whispered.

The vision faded away and my breaths came quicker as I found myself on a battlefield with Hail in bloodied armour and hundreds of dead bodies stretching out before him and his army.

Lionel stood at his side as Hail flicked his gaze to a town beyond the dead and turned to walk away. Lionel caught his arm, speaking in his ear and his voice sailed to me on the wind.

"Leave none alive, everyone in the town must die. And they must die at your hand. This is your decision, you shall forget it was ever mine," he growled, his voice thick with Dark Coercion and I wanted to cry out and stop the power from taking root in my father, but his eyes blackened and he turned to look at the town once more. He ran forward and his huge Order split apart from his skin.

His Hydra form was enormous, as large as a building as he took off into the sky on leathery wings, all the eyes of its many snake-like heads directed at the town. Screams carried from the villagers and magic twisted up into the sky as they tried to defend themselves. Lionel watched with an envious expression as the King blasted the town to ruin with purple fire pouring from his lungs.

Tears wet my cheeks as women and children were destroyed beneath his impossible power and the real monster stood observing it all with a twisted smile on his lips.

The vision shifted and Hail knelt on the huge balcony beyond his bedroom again, clutching the Imperial Star in his hand as he whispered to it in desperation. "Help me, I don't know my mind anymore. I don't know who I am. Why do I do the things I do? I need to know what's wrong with me. Let me see things clearly," he begged of the star in his palm and my heart twisted painfully as I watched our father break. He spoke words to it that I could barely comprehend, the magic in them clear as they buzzed through the air and the star shone brighter in his palm.

Whispers filled my head from it in answer. *"I lie in the palace of the flames. Where the ground is deep and the dead are old. Where the last of them lie. Only there shall you find peace."*

"What does that mean?" Father demanded. "Please, let the madness stop."

"Keep the broken promise," the star answered.

"What?" he growled, but the light went out in his palm and as he spoke a strange word to it again, it pulsed with light, but only answered him in riddles.

"Give me back my mind," he gasped at last, clutching it to his chest in desperation as he stared up at the sky. "No more shall die at my hand."

"It is not your hands," the star whispered and Hail groaned because he didn't understand. And it hurt me, because I did. I knew the truth, and it looked like he'd died without ever knowing it.

The vision fell away and we were suddenly looking at our own reflections once more. I dragged my eyes up to meet Tory's and found tears tracking down her cheeks too.

"He wasn't a savage," she rasped and I moved toward her, the two of us embracing hard.

"It was Lionel, all fucking Lionel," I growled and she cursed him with every swear word she knew.

"He has to die," she snarled, even though she looked a little ill at the idea thanks to the bond he'd put on her. "He has to pay for our mother and our father."

"And he has to pay for what he did to *you*," I said in a deadly voice and she winced as she drew back, grappling with the Guardian bond.

"But I also can't bear the thought of him dying," she croaked, clutching her heart and it pained me to see her that way.

"When he's gone, you'll be free," I promised and she nodded, though I could see the desire in her to bite back at me over that. And it killed me. "The stars wanted us to see this," I went on and her features hardened.

"How can we even trust them after everything?" she hissed as we got to our feet and I gazed around the pit which had once served as an execution ring, a shudder rippling down my spine.

"I don't know," I admitted. "But there must be a reason they showed us this. Maybe they're on our side in some ways."

"Gabriel says they don't pick sides," she muttered and I nodded. But why would the stars give us this information if they didn't want us to fight Lionel? Or maybe it was all just part of some bigger, crueller plot I couldn't see yet. I knew the stars couldn't lie, but I still never understood why they showed us what they did.

I guessed all we could do was take what we'd been gifted and use it against Lionel as best we could. Because there was one thing we now knew for sure, the Imperial Star held unimaginable power. And if Lionel ever got his hands on it and it granted his wishes, the whole of Solaria was doomed.

DARIUS

CHAPTER TWENTY TWO

I sat in my chair beside the fire in King's Hollow, my elbows on my knees as my hands trailed down towards the wooden floor. I leaned forward, letting my head hang as I just looked at the space between my feet and tried to focus on the positives. But shit, sometimes it was really hard to see any positives in the world right now with Father on the throne and nothing ever seeming to go our way in the fight against him.

It wasn't long since classes had finished, and Roxy had been taking part in them for a few weeks now without anyone seeming to realise she was no longer fully under Father's thumb. We had to keep giving her the antidote to the Order Suppressant whenever Father or Mildred dosed her, but I was just relieved that the shadows didn't suck her back in the moment she lost contact with her Phoenix. She was herself again, though she was clearly still a prisoner too. I knew it was endlessly better than it had been before, but I still despised her having to pretend.

It meant she was alone all day, keeping to herself while she sat with the K.U.N.T.s and maintained her cover. I hated that she had to do that. That after months of being cut off from everyone she was still segregated so much. But with the bond between her and my father still linking her to him, we didn't have many other options right now. I just wished I could do more about it. He had me backed into a corner and I was desperate to break free and prove to the world that you couldn't tame a Dragon.

I'd been back to visit Lance almost every night since he'd returned from Darkmore and we'd been spending time in the palace library where there were countless books on every subject imaginable. We'd begun to search through the tomes for anything that we might be able to use to break the Guardian bond. I didn't want to be negative about it, but I was having trouble maintaining any hope that we would find anything. Especially as Gabriel hadn't been able to *see* us making a discovery and we'd spent years looking into this subject in the past when trying to disconnect ourselves.

But Lance had thrown himself into it wholeheartedly, seeming glad of the opportunity to do something productive for our cause while he was stuck waiting on the full moon to reveal more of his father's secrets to him. And I was glad to have given him a task if nothing else because he seriously needed a distraction from everything that was going on in his life. The two of us were a pair of sorry sons of bitches right about now and I knew all too well the pain of being hung up on a Vega who wasn't yours.

I'd stayed with him for most of the night yesterday, researching all we could and then I'd flown back to campus instead of using stardust, preferring to stretch my wings for several hours than get back to my empty bed too soon. I didn't sleep much these days anyway. All I ever did was fall into dreams of the girl I should have been able to call mine and get caught up on the failures I'd made on her behalf.

The door opened and closed but I didn't look up. The other Heirs would all appear here at some point tonight. Darcy and Geraldine too. And maybe...

I lifted my head and found her there, hesitating by the door like she hadn't expected to discover me here alone and now didn't know what to do about it.

I didn't say anything. I couldn't. There were too many fucking words caught in my throat and too many images of the things Max had shown me of what she'd suffered through. My father hadn't wanted me to have her. So he'd done all of that just to make certain I never could. It was my fault. All of it.

The fear he'd given her for me was reflected in her eyes as she looked at me and the knowledge of that made me want to scream. I half expected her to just bolt, but Roxanya Vega wasn't built like that and she raised her chin instead, ready to face her demon. I just wished that wasn't how she viewed me.

"I...should apologise to you," she said in a quiet voice that was nothing like the girl I'd fallen for and spoke of all the hurt and trauma she'd endured because of me and my family.

"Why?" I asked, frowning at her as thunder rumbled overhead. The damn stars wouldn't even let us have this. She was ten meters away from me and my fucking heart was shredded to pieces over her, but we weren't even going to be offered the chance of a fucking conversation.

"For believing that you..." she trailed off, glancing at the window as lightning flashed outside.

While she watched the rain pouring down from the heavens, I watched her. I drank in the way her ripped black jeans hugged her figure and the bare skin of her waist which I ached to curl my hands around. Her skin was paler than it had been, her frame thinner, but Roxanya Vega had been cast by the stars to make me hunger for her no matter what shape her body was in. The cropped black sweater she wore had the words *wild at heart* written across it in swirling pink script and I was pretty certain that summed her up perfectly. Her chocolate brown hair tumbled down her spine and I was filled with the desire to push my fingers into the silken strands as I stole a kiss from those captivating lips of hers. The lips that had cursed me, caressed me, kissed me and taunted me. The ones that had always spoken her mind no matter whether she knew they'd get her into trouble or not.

She *was* wild at heart, but right now, her fire had been dampened until I barely recognised her anymore and I was left shattered in the face of what I'd done to her. Because this might have been on my father, but I knew it was on me too.

When she'd first come back here, I'd agreed to do everything I could to get rid of her. To protect our throne and our kingdom from this pair of stupid, un-Fae, practically mortal girls who I'd foolishly believed could never be strong enough to rule. But one look at her standing there after all she'd fucking survived since returning to Solaria proved how full of shit I was.

"I was a fucking idiot," I said to her, pushing myself to my feet and watching her cautiously as she turned to look at me again. She didn't flinch this time and I could have kissed Max for helping her to see what had been done to her memories of me, but I could still see some fear in her gaze as she looked at me and that cut into my heart in the worst way. Because I knew in part that she had good reason to fear me. I'd given it to her with every fucked up thing I'd done to her when she came to this academy. "The second you walked into The Orb on your first day after you were Awakened, I knew you weren't what I'd been expecting. My heart fucking leapt when I looked at you. My palms grew slick, my mouth got dry."

"Me and Darcy you mean?" she asked curiously, clearly thinking back on it too.

"No. Just you. I didn't even see her at first. I swear, I didn't even think you were who you are. For a few, endless seconds I just saw you and I wanted you. And when I did see Darcy and I realised who you were I was just so fucking angry. Because I knew I couldn't have you."

She scoffed lightly, glancing back at the rain as the storm howled outside and I knew we were seriously pushing our luck with the stars now, but I couldn't bear to walk away from her. Because that sound, that dismissive scoff and the way her posture had tightened the smallest amount was her. Not the fucked up version my father had tried to twist her into. That was my girl, calling me on my bullshit the moment I tried to give her it and I couldn't help but smile just a little as I saw that glimpse of herself.

"What?" I asked.

"That's just so typical of you," she said, looking at me again as thunder boomed overhead. "You assumed the only reason you couldn't have me was because I had Vega blood. You do realise you couldn't have just taken me if I was some normal Fae though, right? You're supposed to *ask* people if they want to be yours, not just expect them to fall at your feet."

"Is that so?" I asked, my voice teasing as I pretended to consider it like that was brand new information to me.

Roxy almost smiled then shrugged and turned to open the door. "I should go before the stars send a lightning bolt to destroy this entire place," she said, but she glanced back at me like she was holding back on saying something else and I stepped closer.

Just as I was trying to come up with some excuse to stop her leaving, an excited howl came from the stairs and Roxy stepped back as Seth bounded in in his Wolf form, a blur of movement following him a second later as Caleb leapt after him.

The two of them crashed into the coffee table so hard that it broke beneath their weight and I moved in front of Roxy defensively as Seth shifted back into his Fae form and the two of them started wrestling.

Seth was kicking and punching while snarling aggressively as Cal managed to get on top of him, taking a punch to the face before catching Seth's fist in his grip and sinking his fangs into his wrist before he could pull back.

Seth growled but it turned into a groan as Caleb reared over him, holding his wrist to his mouth with one hand, drinking his blood while pressing his other hand down on Seth's chest to keep him in place.

"Are you seriously still doing that hunting shit after how wrong it went with Roxy the last time?" I demanded, taking a step towards them, but Roxy caught my arm and I fell still as I glanced around at her in surprise.

Caleb looked up at me while he drank, his eyes filled with bloodlust as he snarled over his meal and Seth groaned again, shaking his head.

"This is on me," he muttered. "I keep making him do it. Don't be an asshole to him."

I arched a brow, not buying that shit for a moment, but Roxy's fingers were moving over the Libra mark on my arm and my attention was seriously wavering.

Caleb finally finished his fucking meal and took his fangs from Seth's wrist before standing up and offering me a guilty look as he licked the blood from his lips.

"It's not like before," he muttered, casting a guilty look at Roxy which made me bristle. "Seth is strong enough to take me on. And I don't wanna hunt weaker Fae than me anymore. It's more dangerous doing that than going up against someone on my level."

"You could just drink from willing victims like you always used to," I suggested.

Seth replied before Caleb could, pulling on some sweats and rearranging his junk inside them as he turned to narrow his eyes at me. "Yeah, and I could tie a chain around your neck and you could just fly in small circles around campus instead of flying off for miles and miles. Stop being a kill joy, Darius. You're trying to supress his Order instincts and it's bullshit."

"Fine," I grunted, my attention more on the girl who was touching my arm now anyway, though the intensity of the storm was picking up and I knew

I'd have to pull away soon. "Just make sure you're not being dumb about it."

"Maybe you could let me hunt you some time and find out what all the fuss is about for yourself?" Caleb teased which drew a growl from Seth.

"As if his lizard blood could taste as good as mine," Seth scoffed, shooting me a glare which quite clearly told me to back the fuck off as if I'd been the one suggesting it.

"There's no fucking chance of you getting me to run about like prey for you, Cal, so feel free to stick to the dog food diet," I taunted, raising a brow at Seth as he smirked like he'd just won something.

Caleb flopped down on the couch, grabbing a beer and lifting it to his lips and Seth lunged into the spot beside him and nuzzled into him. He hadn't healed the bite on his wrist for some reason, but I had too much going on in my own life to be wondering about whatever the fuck they were up to.

Roxy traced the Libra brand on my arm one more time and I gave her my full attention again as she drew my attention to the Guardian bond.

"Do you ache for Orion all the time?" Roxy murmured, taking her hand from my arm and touching her own where the Aries mark was branded to her skin.

I sighed heavily, shaking my head as I forced myself to step back and put a bit more space between us before the storm outside blew the damn treehouse to the ground.

"It's worse for the Guardian than the Ward in that regard," I said. "I do ache to be close to Lance, but it doesn't seem to eat at me the way it does to him most of the time. It was pretty bad while he was in Darkmore, but mainly because it went on for so long and he was so far away. Day to day it doesn't niggle at me as much as it seems to for him. I can distract myself from the urge more easily and I don't feel his pain like he does mine. It also gets worse for the Guardian the further you are from your Ward, so with Father away in Kerendia this week hunting down those Sphinxes, it's probably getting to you more than usual. The whole point of the bond is to ensure the Guardian stays close to the Fae they're supposed to be protecting in case they're needed. In years past, when this magic was created, the idea was for you to stay together always so that the Guardian would be prepared to defend their Ward at all times. But the Ward is supposed to be the more powerful Fae, the more important one." I cringed at the word, but it was how the magic had been created, not how I felt about Lance. "That means the Ward – my father - has more freedom so that he can make his own decisions on the things he does while the Guardian is supposed to just follow after them, dedicating their life to protecting them and nothing else."

Roxy frowned, chewing on her thumb as she thought about that and I waited while she turned the information over. "I know that I hate him," she said quietly, keeping her words for me as Seth and Caleb started discussing the Pitball match they wanted to watch this evening. "And I know that he did this to me without my consent. I know he tortured me and hurt you and has done countless horrible things, but..."

"You still want to see him all the time?" I guessed, sighing heavily. I knew this curse too well to even be surprised by the knowledge that she still pined for him even though it set my blood alight with the need to destroy him for it.

"I just wish that I could have five minutes to hate him in peace," she muttered.

"I'm not sure there is a way for you to cut off the way you feel drawn to him," I said heavily, knowing it wasn't what she wanted to hear. "The only time Lance has ever been able to resist the pull of it was when he went to hunt you and your sister down in the mortal realm."

"Really?" she asked in surprise and I straightened as that thought swept through my mind.

When Lance had agreed to be the one to go and retrieve the Vegas from the mortal realm, the two of us had been concerned about how he was supposed to stay away from me for that long. But the space between realms just seemed to mute the connection for me. And he'd been relieved of the burden of aching to return to me in the way he normally would have been with so much distance between us. When he returned, he'd said that the need to come back to me had been so much less potent while he was there that he'd actually been able to forget about it half the time.

"Roxy," I said, taking a step towards her but pausing before I could get too close and frighten her. "When we first met, I did everything wrong. I shouldn't have been the pawn my father wanted me to be. I was a coward and a fucking idiot and what I really should have done was follow my damn heart and just asked you to spend time with me. So I want us to try that. Like we should have done at the start."

"Try what?" she asked with a small frown.

"Let me take you out. I know somewhere we can go where the bond won't bother you and there are so many people that the stars won't be able to even suggest that we're alone." I offered her my hand and I didn't miss the flicker of fear that crossed her features as she eyed it.

"Where are we going?" she asked and my heart thumped hopefully because that sure as fuck wasn't a no.

"You're gonna have to trust me," I said, offering her the hint of a smirk as I dared the girl I knew to come out and play with me.

"Fat chance of that, asshole," she muttered and my smile widened tenfold. It really shouldn't have gotten me so turned on to have a girl insulting me, but I'd take Roxy Vega calling me every name under the sun over having a million compliments from anyone else.

"Come on - you said I'd have to ask if I wanted you to be mine. So I'm asking. Let me take you out."

"The stars won't let us," she said hesitantly, glancing out at the storm which had barely quieted even with Seth and Caleb here. "And even if they would, we can't be seen together."

"Just trust me, Princess," I teased, hoping it wasn't painfully obvious how much I needed her to say yes. But it had been a long, hard, miserable fucking summer without her and I needed this. I had to prove to myself that she was still her and I needed to put a fucking smile on her face to try and make up for all of the shit she'd been through when I should have been there to protect her from it.

She bit her lip as she considered it then hesitantly placed her hand in mine.

I fought the urge to yank her closer, that small point of contact between us making heat charge through my veins even though I knew it couldn't last.

"We're going out," I called to Seth and Cal as I drew her towards the floor length window by the back wall. "Don't wait up."

"But how are you going to-" Seth began but Caleb slapped a hand over his mouth.

"Don't do anything I wouldn't do," he teased and I rolled my eyes at him because I was pretty certain he had no goddamn lines so that left very little out of bounds.

I pushed the window open and the storm howled as it drove rain inside, but I used my water magic to push it back as I released Roxy's hand and tugged my shirt off.

"I'll race you to the boundary," I challenged, watching her eyes light up at that suggestion and she tugged her sweater off to reveal a racerback bra beneath and I fought off the urge to groan at the sight of her body.

She half shifted so that her wings were revealed, not igniting the flames and instead leaving the golden feathers on show. Without another word, she stepped over the edge of the balcony and let herself drop before her wings snapped out and she took off through the trees.

I grabbed a bag from the chest where we kept the clothes and quickly finished stripping as I stuffed my clothes into it before gripping the strap between my teeth and leaping out into the rain after her.

I shifted with a surge of power, my wings snapping out as my body multiplied in size and I took off and headed for the clouds, unable to dart between the trees the way she was but determined to beat her to the boundary all the same.

I raced across the treetops, circling as I moved to land in the clearing I always used when I came out this way and quickly pulling my clothes back on the moment I was back on solid ground.

The rain was fast dissipating now that we weren't together anymore, and I didn't even bother to use my water magic to keep it off of me as I started jogging up the hill.

Roxy was leaning against a tree just outside the academy fence, but she didn't even seem to notice me as I approached, leaving my empty bag in the shadow beneath an oak tree and slipping through the small gap to join her.

She was moving her fingers in a slow pattern and as I got closer, I saw the shadows spilling between them a moment before she noticed me, jerking a little as she banished them again.

"Roxy..." I began cautiously as she lifted her gaze to meet mine guiltily.

"I'm not lost to them anymore," she said, chewing on her bottom lip. "But they call to me all the time. I don't even mean to summon them but then I'll find my hands full of them. And I..." she trailed off, shrugging and I sighed as I stepped closer to her.

"You like the way they feel?"

She didn't say anything, but as her green eyes met mine, I lifted my hand between us and let the shadows slip along my skin for a moment, feeling that slice of pleasure as it raised goosebumps on my flesh before banishing them once more.

"I know," I said simply because the infection of dark magic into my limbs was anything but awful whenever I welded it. There was something addictive about it which I knew was what made it so dangerous. But with them living inside me, it was damn hard to resist them at all times.

Relief spilled into Roxy's expression as thunder boomed overhead again and I realised that she'd erected an air shield which was the only thing keeping us out of the storm now that we were alone together again. *Fucking stars.*

I took the pouch of stardust from my pocket without another word and tossed it over our heads as I concentrated hard on our destination.

The stars spun and lurched around us and I gritted my teeth as I pushed us through the divide between realms. The stars finally spat us back out in a darkened alley where the scent of fried food and cigarettes rose up around us accompanied by the sound of a large crowd and busy streets.

Roxy caught my bicep to steady herself then gasped as she yanked the sleeve of her sweater back and stared down at the Aries mark on her arm. She rubbed at it like she expected it to come off then frowned up at me in confusion when it didn't.

"I can hardly even feel him," she said, her lips parting in astonishment. "How?"

"Lance told me the mark didn't bother him anywhere near as much in the mortal realm. We guessed maybe because it's impossible to actually measure the distance, the magic is confused by it or something," I explained, drinking in the relief that filled her features as she continued to brush her fingers over the mark binding her to my father. "Have you ever been to New York City before, Roxy?"

Her eyes widened as she turned to look towards the street where bright lights lit up the far end of the alleyway and I just watched her as a smile tugged her lips up.

"No freaking way," she murmured before taking off so suddenly that I was hard pushed to keep up with her.

She jogged down the alley and straight out onto the busy sidewalk, sucking in a breath as she tipped her head back to look up at the bright lights and signs of Times Square.

A man almost walked straight into her, banging against an air shield she'd placed close to her body a moment before impact and he swore as he stumbled back.

"Get out of the way, you stupid bitch," he snapped and a growl escaped me as he stalked away while Roxy sighed in pleasure.

"Did you hear that, Darius?" she asked, turning to look at me, her eyes bright with excitement which soothed something deep inside my soul. "Angry locals swearing at people just trying to have a good time - isn't it beautiful?"

I snorted a laugh and she smiled at me a little shyly before turning and darting away into the crowd.

I was taller than pretty much everyone here so it wasn't too hard to keep track of her, but I still muttered a curse to myself as I took off down the street after her. She navigated the crowd like she knew exactly where she was going even though I was almost certain she didn't.

"Roxy!" I called as she managed to pull ahead of me, darting between the crowd and slipping around the flood of people as if they were hardly any bother to her even though I found it almost impossible to get around them.

I lost sight of her as a yammering crowd of tourists following a guide cut across my path and bit my tongue as I looked over the heads of the people all around me with my heart thumping faster as I hunted for her.

Just as I was about to roar at the people closest to me to get out of my fucking way, a warm hand slipped into mine and I looked down to find her smirking up at me with laughter in her eyes.

"Come on, country boy, stay with me and I'll get you through the carnage," she teased tugging me into motion and pulling me between the throng of bodies.

"I'm not a country boy," I growled, but the smirk on my face wasn't leaving and as she snorted a laugh at my expense, I found I didn't even care what she called me.

"Says the dude who grew up on an estate even bigger than mine which housed four people instead of forty thousand. Come on, Darius, don't try to pretend you know how to survive out on the streets. If I abandoned you now you'd end up lost within thirty minutes and you'd probably be discovered wandering around down by the Hudson in three days' time with no shoes and a wild look in your eye that said you've seen things you can never unsee."

She laughed and I jerked on her hand as I stopped walking, tugging her back towards me suddenly and making her crash into my chest as her eyes widened in surprise.

"I hope you're not trying to challenge me here, Roxy," I said in a low voice, not giving a shit about the flood of people who were muttering curses as they were forced to part around my broad frame to continue their walk down the street.

"You can't seriously think you could survive out here without any magic or money, do you, rich man?" she teased.

"I'm a big boy, people tend not to want to fuck with me," I assured her.

"Hmm." She ran her gaze over my frame slowly and I suddenly realised that I was still holding her hand and as of yet, the stars didn't seem to be doing anything to force us apart. The crowd was hiding us even better than I'd hoped and to make it even better, in the mortal realm, nobody knew who we were. "So maybe no one would dare to beat you down," she conceded slowly. "But you'd still starve to death."

"And you wouldn't?" I arched a brow at her and she shrugged innocently before pulling a handful of scrunched up dollar bills from the back pocket of her jeans. I counted over a hundred dollars as she waved it before me tauntingly.

"Well, these tourists just offered to pay for my dinner tonight. Though I might have to work a little harder if I need to pay for a hotel room - especially here in the city."

I probably should have called her out on stealing from all of these strangers where anyone might have spotted her, but we were in the mortal realm, so I guessed she wasn't really risking her reputation with anything she did here. Not that she'd ever seemed to give a damn about her reputation anyway. And I was not so secretly enjoying getting this look at the girl she'd been before she'd found out she was Fae and a princess and everything else that came with the Vega name.

"I'm not sure you've got enough there to buy yourself a dinner in one of the fancy ass restaurants around here," I teased, laughing as her nose wrinkled in distaste.

"I'm really not meant for mixing with high society," she said and I could see that she meant that in the purest possible way. She wasn't bitter about it, like a girl standing outside a grand party looking through a window and wishing she could join in - no matter how much wealth and prestige had come attached to her family name, she really had no desire to become a carbon copy of every other vapid heiress I'd ever met. Roxanya Vega was the kind of girl who pick pocketed from strangers to survive and rode fast motorcycles while calling mean bastards out on their shit and making no apologies for who she was. And I was thoroughly addicted to finding out everything about who that might be.

"Good. Because that ass of yours isn't destined to sit on the throne, so I wouldn't want you getting any crazy ideas about being above me," I taunted and her brows went up as she shook her head at me.

"So cocky, Dragon boy," she said, backing up and tugging her hand back like she was going to pull it from my grasp, but I tightened my hold, ignoring the gasp of fear that escaped her lips as I dragged her after me along the street.

"Come on," I urged as she hesitated. "If I don't feed you fast you're gonna keep running your mouth at me and I'll have to put you on your ass to remind you which one of us is more powerful."

She scoffed indignantly but let me tug her through the crowd and away from the tourist trap as we headed down side streets and I tried to remember where I was going. It had been a few years since me and the Heirs had come here for a night out, but we used to do it fairly frequently just to get a night off of everyone knowing who we were. Of course, Cal and Max had always made sure that we went to the best, most exclusive places in the city whenever we came, but I'd found a few more interesting places here too.

We finally spilled out onto another street and I tugged her along to the Mexican restaurant which was so packed that people were spilling out onto the street with food in their hands.

Roxy groaned longingly as I led her up to the door and I released her hand as the first spots of rain fell from the clouds and people around us cursed in frustration. The crowd may have been helping us to hide, but the stars were clearly taking note now and I'd been holding her hand for too damn long.

"It's over an hour wait," a server called as she passed us by, carrying a tray with two pitchers of beer and a plate of nachos on it.

I glanced at Roxy as she pouted, giving a woman's half eaten burrito a longing look. My girl wasn't going to wait for a minute, let alone a fucking hour.

"Not good enough," I said, striding inside to follow the waitress through the brightly lit restaurant.

The walls were painted a deep red colour and there were paintings of brightly coloured skulls hanging all around the place. There were tables packed end to end and little booths lining the far wall while loud music blared out over an even louder crowd.

As the waitress reached a couple in the back corner of the room and placed the beers and nachos down, I caught her arm.

"This is our food," I said, lacing my voice with Coercion as she widened her eyes on me. *"These people were just leaving,"* I added, looking to the couple and including them in my command.

Mortals had such open, malleable brains that it was no effort at all to get them to bend to my will. Maybe that made me a dick, but that was hardly news to me.

I couldn't even bring myself to give a shit about screwing them over as they scrambled away either. My girl was hungry and she wasn't gonna wait in line like some regular fucker.

I looked back around towards the door and beckoned her in as she rolled her eyes at me like I was a total douchebag. Any other girl would be falling at my feet if I'd done that for her, but Roxanya Vega somehow managed to call me an entitled prick with a roll of her eyes and I found myself loving every second of her disdain.

"Two bean and cheese burritos," I said to the waitress as I gave her my attention again for a moment, ordering the meal Roxy had been salivating over. "Plus every side you've got on offer and some tequila. *Don't make us wait."*

The girl nodded, her brow furrowing in confusion for a moment before she hurried away to get my order and I looked back across the room to my girl.

My blood heated as I spotted her in the centre of the restaurant, standing by a table full of drunk looking assholes as one of them held onto her wrist and made her stop to talk to him.

He was leering at her, loudly urging her to come sit in his lap while the guys around him all laughed their encouragement and rage lit my blood on fire as I strode back across the restaurant at a fast pace. Roxy was saying something in reply which had his friends laughing at him, but I didn't give a shit if she was already handling it. If he didn't take his hand off of her right now then I was going to break it off.

A waiter stepped out in front of me but I just shoved him back, making him drop his tray of food and not even looking at him as I stepped over his legs and finally made it to the dead man with his hand on my girl.

A few of his friends saw me coming and straightened in their chairs, pointing me out so that the asshole swung around to look at me a moment before my hands landed flat on the table in front of him. I leaned down to glare at him, certain the Dragon in me was clear for him to see.

"Take your fucking hand off of her," I growled in a low tone that had him dropping his hold on her wrist instantly and stammering apologies to me as if I was the one he needed to be offering them to. "Apologise to my girl for laying your hand on her," I snarled as several people around us started sidling away like they could tell I was about to beat his smarmy face in.

"I'm sorry - I didn't know she was yours," he gasped. "Sorry, man. Sorry-"

I reached out and grabbed hold of him by the collar, half lifting him out of his seat and twisting him to look at Roxy. "Say it to *her.*"

Roxy had fallen still and beneath the bloodlust that had taken hold of me at seeing that asshole manhandle her, I realised that she was afraid of me again. *Fuck.*

"I'm sorry," the guy gasped and I used my grip on him to toss him to the floor as I tried to fight back my temper, my gaze fixed on the girl I loved as she regarded me like she thought I might turn on her next.

But then she lifted the asshole's beer from the table and dumped it in his lap, swallowing thickly as she stepped over him and moved to my side.

"I don't need you to fight my battles," she said firmly, fighting off her fear as she folded her arms and met my eye with defiance in her gaze.

"I know," I replied and she nodded as she headed over to the booth I'd gotten us and sat down.

I followed slowly, working to try and push back the Dragon in me as the asshole and his friends scrambled out of the restaurant. The owner came bursting out of a door beside the kitchen, calling out something about me needing to leave, but it only took a couple of words laced with Coercion to send him scurrying away again.

I sat down opposite Roxy, finding the table piled up with all the food I'd ordered and eyeing her hesitantly and she narrowed her eyes on me.

"You told him I was yours," she said, reaching out to take a nacho and loading it with guacamole.

"You are," I replied simply and she held my gaze as she thought on that.

"I never said that."

"No, you didn't. But you were mine from the first moment I laid eyes on you. You're just too damn stubborn to say it out loud."

Silence lingered between us as she scowled at me and I was pleased to see she'd pushed her fear aside again.

"Maybe," she said finally before giving her attention to eating her food and I tried not to grin like a smug motherfucker as I joined her.

We didn't say much while we ate, I just drank in her company while she moaned appreciation over her food so loudly I was beginning to think her goal was to get me as hard as stone for her.

When we'd finally eaten so much that there was no chance of us managing another bite, she slammed back her shot of tequila without even flinching and eyed me with mischief dancing in her eyes.

"So what now?" she asked. "Did you have some grand plan for our evening of escaping our problems or are you just winging it?"

I shrugged because I definitely hadn't expected to take her out like this and though I was aching to get her alone somewhere, I was just happy to be in her company without shadows flickering in her eyes. And being in a crowd of strangers was close enough to alone all the time I had her undivided attention.

"Maybe we should just stay here," I teased. "Hide from all of our problems and never go back."

"It'd be that simple, huh?" she asked, glancing around the room heaving with people as if she was considering it for a moment.

"No," I replied honestly. "They'd hunt us down. There are ways to trace magical signatures which are especially effective here where there are hardly any Fae. Besides, even if we could hide from them, Fae can't live in the mortal world for long periods of time once their magic is Awakened. The balance of power isn't right here. This place slowly eats into your magic if you hang around too long. Even the Fae who work here importing goods back to our realm rarely stay more than a month at a time and even then, they pay a cost for it. We just don't belong here."

"No," she agreed, looking around at the humans who seemed so like us in some ways and yet so different in others. "What would happen to a mortal who came to Solaria then?" she asked curiously.

"They'd lose their minds," I replied. "The magic in our realm is too much for them to handle."

"Okay...so what about a couple who fell in love Romeo and Juliet style?" she asked. "A Fae and a mortal-"

"Destined for failure," I said with a mocking smile. "They can't even have children together. The magic in our blood and the lack in theirs makes it impossible."

"Good thing I'm not a romantic or the idea of that might just break my heart," she teased and the two of us fell silent as we looked at the black rings in each other's eyes. Being here with her like this felt so damn good, but I knew I was just kidding myself into thinking we were alone. There were people all around us and the stars were clearly still watching even here. But it was still pretty nice to pretend.

"So come on then, what's next?" she asked and I shrugged.

"If this was a proper date and I'd actually organised it, I guess we would have gone for a race on our bikes," I said. "I still want a re-match after the last one."

She smiled at that suggestion and my heart leapt as I looked at her. She was so beautiful. Why hadn't I just let myself see that before? I'd been so caught up on the idea of it just being lust and wanting to hate fuck her that I'd refused to see that her beauty went so much deeper than her appearance. She was everything I wasn't and everything I wanted. A princess, born to live her life in a specific way just like I had been and yet she refused to blindly follow any path. At least until my father had forced her onto one.

"Well, I guess it's on me to solve that little problem then, isn't it?" she asked, getting to her feet and pulling out the cash she'd pick pocketed before tossing it all on the table.

"What the hell are you doing?" I asked as I stood too. "You're not paying."

"Well I don't see you hiding any mortal money in those jeans," she said lightly. "So just suck up your pride and let me pay. You can be all bitch hurt over being emasculated tomorrow when I'm not around to witness the tears."

She offered me a taunting smirk and I wasn't sure whether to laugh or growl, but she didn't give me the time to decide before turning and striding out of the restaurant.

I was forced to jog after her as she led the way back up the dark street with her long hair swaying down her spine. When I called out to her to slow down she just laughed before ducking into an underground parking lot and out of sight.

I cursed beneath my breath as I ran after her, vaulting the barrier blocking the way in and heading into the dimly lit parking lot where there was no sign of her.

"Roxy?" I called and she laughed somewhere off ahead of me to my right.

I hurried past the rows of expensive cars, looking for her between all of them until I finally found her in a dark corner, crouched down beside a bright red Ducati Panigale V2.

"What are you doing?" I asked as she failed to look up at me from her position on the floor by the motorcycle.

"You promised me a ride, dude," she said, cursing beneath her breath as she kept fiddling with the engine. I couldn't really see what she was up to, but it looked like she'd made some tools using earth magic to assist her.

"What are you doing?" a voice yelled and I turned to find a guy dressed in a grey and black guard uniform pointing a gun at us. There was a radio at his hip but it was impossible to say if he'd been in contact with anyone else.

"Nothing. Leave us alone," I Coerced him and he turned away instantly,

lowering his weapon and walking off.

I looked back to Roxy with a smug grin but she pointed up at a camera by the roof which was angled right at us.

"Ah, shit," she cursed a second before a blaring alarm sounded all around the parking lot and I raised an eyebrow at her just as she got the bike started up.

"Is this what you like to do for fun then?" I teased as she hopped up and swung her leg over the bike, revving the engine at me enticingly.

"Jump on and I'll show you what I like to do for fun," she offered, patting the seat behind her.

"How about you shift your ass back and I'll drive?" I countered because there was no fucking way I was going to be her passenger.

"Oh, you can steal a bike for yourself then?" she taunted, her eyes twinkling with amusement.

"Just start one up for me," I growled, refusing to dignify that with a response.

"No," she replied with that stubborn set to her jaw which always riled me up so damn much. "Now or never, Darius, jump on the bitch seat or stay here to get caught by the cops."

"Why do I get the feeling you seriously would just ride off and leave my ass here?" I asked irritably.

"Because I would," she replied simply, shrugging one shoulder like there wasn't an alarm blaring overhead and she was in no rush at all. "Now hop on and let me show you how a real Fae rides."

I cursed as I swung my leg over the back of the bike and Roxy barely gave me time to wrap my arms around her waist before she dropped the clutch and tugged the throttle back.

My grip tightened on her before I could fall off the back and she laughed wildly as we shot away.

Roxy rode like a pro, weaving around parked cars and squeezing through a pedestrian entrance to the underground parking lot before racing out onto the street.

Her hair whipped back in the wind, catching against the stubble on my jaw as I placed my head beside hers to watch the road. The sweet scent of her skin rose up around me reminding me of the few times I'd held her close like this and my irritation over her making me be the passenger melted away as I just enjoyed it.

The heat of her body against mine had my mind filling up with ideas of all the things I'd fantasised about doing with her more times than I could even count. I'd imagined having her in each and every way conceivable and had dreamed about her every night for so long that I couldn't even remember when it had begun. And yet all of that paled into nothing when compared to the reality of actually holding her.

Rain poured from the sky in a sudden torrent and I tipped my head back, catching sight of the Leo and Gemini star signs illuminated in the sky above us before the clouds swept over to conceal them again.

We weren't free of our curse. Not even here. But Roxy didn't seem inclined to stop and move away from me either.

The flash of red and blue lights caught my eye before I even heard the sirens and Roxy laughed wildly as she put on another burst of speed.

She ducked and weaved around traffic and pedestrians, narrowly avoiding a collision with a yellow taxi as it ran a red light right ahead of us.

"The stars are trying to part us," I called over the roar of the engine and she nodded, pushing back into the cage of my arms as she kept going.

Her ass was practically riding my dick as we pressed closer to each other and I couldn't help but turn my head and press my mouth to that soft spot of skin beneath her ear. A shiver ran right through her body and she leaned back into me a little more as she sped through the streets of New York City so fast that the cops had no chance of catching up to us.

But the further we went, the heavier the downpour got until it was hard to see much ahead of us and the hazards appearing in the road were getting more and more dangerous.

A truck stopped suddenly right in our path and my heart leapt with fear for the girl in my arms as she narrowly avoided it, the tyres skidding on the wet road and only her level of skill saving us from spinning out and crashing.

"We have to stop," I called to her, hating to cut this short but fearing what would happen if we crashed. It was all well and good having healing magic, but if we died on impact that wasn't going to make a bit of difference.

Roxy growled something at me which I couldn't make out over the engine noise, but she turned off the main road and started speeding down a slightly quieter street.

I held on tighter, knowing I was going to have to let go really soon and wishing I didn't ever have to.

She pulled up sharply by the waterfront close to the Brooklyn Bridge and I climbed off as thunder boomed overhead and lightning lit the sky for a moment.

"Admit it, I ride better than you," she said as she backed up, putting some space between us.

I groaned aloud as I took in the way the rain was making her clothes stick to her frame while the adrenaline of the ride pumped through my limbs, demanding an outlet which I knew I couldn't claim.

"I already knew how well you could ride from the time you climbed into my lap on the throne," I said and her eyes widened at that reminder as I fought with everything I had to hold my ground. I knew it wasn't enough though, there was no one around us and the stars weren't going to stop until they'd driven us apart.

Roxy bit her lip, her gaze moving over my chest where my white t-shirt was clinging to every curve of my muscles. "Show me your new tattoo," she demanded and I smirked at her, loving the fact that she'd been thinking about that.

"No. You'll have to come see it for yourself," I teased and she glanced up at the sky with concern as the storm picked up even more.

She seemed tempted to come closer but the way the storm was building made it clear it was probably a bad idea.

"I guess that's our cue to head back," she said and the disappointment on her face was enough to make me want to shift and start flying huge circles through the sky.

"Come here then," I beckoned to her and she gave the bike one last, wistful look before abandoning it to come and join me as I pulled the stardust from my pocket.

I tossed it over us and we were wrenched out of the storm and into the grasp of the stars who seemed to be buzzing with even more energy than usual as they hoisted us across the divide between realms and deposited us back outside the Zodiac Academy boundary.

The sudden quiet as we landed made the energy between us crackle expectantly as I glanced up at the cloudless Solarian sky and got my bearings again.

Soft fingertips landed on my waistband and I sucked in a breath as I looked down at Roxy as she unbuckled my belt with a taunting smirk on her face that said I should have known better than to challenge her. Not that I had any complaints about her taking my pants off. I watched as she tugged my jeans down just low enough to show her the tattoo which curved over my left hip and sank down close enough to my cock to make it harden for her instantly. Not that it took much for it to do that for her, but having her hand beneath my waistband was a sure fire way to achieve it.

I watched her as she looked at the tattoo, tracing the words with her fingertips and breathing them into the silence. "There is only her." She continued to paint the marks that made up the Gemini and Leo constellations followed by the lines of the geometric design that charted the pattern of the moon and stars the night she'd said no to me. It was pretty complex, an interlinking design of triangles and interlocking lines that mapped out the alignment of the heavens on the night that had changed everything. Gabriel was the one who'd told me to get it, showing up at my room and telling me he'd *seen* it. The moment I laid eyes on the design he'd sketched out I'd known in my soul that he was right about it being destined to mark my flesh.

Distant thunder was closing in on us and I knew we'd find ourselves in yet another storm if we continued to linger here, but it was just too hard for me to pull away from her. I needed to know if she felt this too. I needed to hear the words she'd never spoken to me even though I knew I'd never deserve them.

"Are you still afraid of me, Roxy?" I asked in a low voice as her fingertips traced the tattoo and she followed the lines of the ink right along the length of it.

"Yes," she breathed, raising her eyes up to meet mine and making my gut twist with a hurt so sharp it stole my breath away. "But it's a good kind of fear."

I stared down at her with my heart pounding at those words, wanting nothing more than to pull her into my arms and taste the sweetness of her lips against mine, but she was already backing up.

And as the thunder boomed overhead once more and the earth trembled beneath our feet, I knew she had to go.

But it didn't make it hurt any less as I watched her walk away.

SETH

CHAPTER TWENTY THREE

Having Orion's new number was a treat in itself. I sent him daily photographs of me and Darcy together with captions like #sheaintblueoveryounomore and #teamDeth. He'd blocked my number after threatening to rip my intestines out and strangle me with them – amongst other murderous threats - but then I got a magical app which sent my texts from anonymous numbers so he couldn't keep me away. It was hilarious. And very intentional. Because I was officially kickstarting Mission: Get Darion Back Together.

It wasn't a complex or layered plan; it was based on one simple little emotion that made Fae fucking crazy. Jealousy. Orion had shown his cards as clear as day when I'd visited him with Darcy and Gabriel. I knew what jealousy tasted like, looked like and felt like. Just yesterday, I'd made a girl cry when I overheard her planning to sneak into Caleb's room dressed in nothing with glitter covering her naked body to ask him if he was horny for the horn. Firstly, Cal was not into that shit as far as I was aware (but I'd be the first to paint my body in glitter and strap a dildo horn to my head if he was). And secondly, no bitch. Just no. I made her do a lap of the school while some of my pack chased her with pokey sticks.

So when Orion had thrown me face first into a window, I'd had an inkling he wasn't over Darcy.

I ran with my pack in the early hours of the morning, the lasting light of the moon giving way to dawn as we made it to the pond out in The Wailing Wood. My pack slipped into the water to bathe and I padded off into the trees to be alone. I knew as soon as they shifted that washing each other would give way to fucking and I'd been avoiding that for a while now. Which made them all kinds of crazy for me, but they knew I liked fucking other Orders.

Now the law was in place to stop that I wondered how long it would be before they questioned me on it. They'd never snitch on me either way, but I actually hadn't fucked anyone else for ages. Since I'd shared Rosalie with Cal, I was more hung up on him than ever. Even though the one I really should have been hung up on was the powerful Alpha Wolf who was hot as hell and could have fulfilled everything that was expected of me.

One day, I was destined to marry someone of my own kind who matched me in power as closely as possible. Rosalie was a pretty perfect pick for that role, but the idea of tying myself to her or anyone other than Cal just made me feel all kinds of anxious. But I was probably just kidding myself and Caleb would end up with some Vampire bitch I'd resent forever. It was a shitty destiny, which was why I was actively pretending it would never happen. Denial was my best friend who liked to braid my hair and call me pretty. So yep, Cal could definitely be mine inside my head in an alternate reality I liked to call Calaria.

I'd had obsessions before. I loved a challenge. Shit, Darcy Vega had been my desire for a long time. But with her, things hadn't been clear cut. I'd been torn between my Heir bound duty and a bond between us I couldn't ignore. Then I'd inadvertently initiated her into my pack and that had let the headfuck get out of control. I was naturally protective of her. I wanted to be around her all the time. And I'd finally realised that the way I felt about her was the exact way I felt about the Heirs. Only it had been hiding under so many layers of bullshit that I'd been confused as fuck about it. She was a Vega. And I'd been told my whole life that Vegas were the spawn of evil. I'd fucked with her so bad that I was going to be beating myself up about it for a long time to come. But now I finally had a way to make up for all the shit I'd done. I was going to get her back together with the love of her life and make Lance Orion my bestie in the process. Like, not at first. Man, he was going to fucking hate me. But long term, he was a bestie to be. Either that or I really was going to end up strangled by my own intestines.

I raced through the trees with a howl toward the morning sun as it split through the foliage overhead. Adrenaline rushed through my limbs and my ears turned left and right as I felt out my surroundings. I couldn't hear anything unusual, but the hairs were rising on the back of my neck and I slowed as I reached a path, standing in the middle of it and sniffing the air.

A Wolf's grin pulled at my mouth as a masculine and tempting scent reached me in the air. *Caleb.*

I padded on down the path, pretending I hadn't noticed anything as he no doubt stalked me somewhere close by. But if he wanted a drink from me, he was going to have to fight for it.

I yawned broadly, turning off the path into the trees again and slipping between the boughs. I moved behind the trunk of a huge oak and lowered myself ready to pounce, tucking my huge body in close to the tree.

A rush of air sent fallen leaves swirling up around my paws as Caleb shot into the trees ahead of me. He stopped abruptly, turning his head left and right as he listened for me and I kept perfectly still, my ears flat to my head as I readied to launch myself at him.

I shoved my weight into my paws, throwing myself toward him and he twisted around, spotting me at the last moment. He shot away a split second before I could knock him to the ground and my paws hit the mud.

I kept running as adrenaline tore through my veins, taking off fast into the trees with a bark of laughter. He collided with my side, throwing me to the ground and the air was knocked from my lungs. I locked my jaws around his arm as he tried to pin me down and he growled in pain, but didn't let go, trying to keep me in place as I thrashed. I rolled hard, throwing him away so he smashed into a tree. I grinned wolfishly in victory but he shot upright again and casually smoothed down his hair as his arm pissed blood.

"Damn animal," he taunted.

He healed the bite and I took the chance to lunge at him again, my large paws hitting the tree above his head as I caged him in. He punched my ribs and I yelped as I fell back, uprooting him with one of my paws so he was knocked down with me.

I leapt onto him and shifted back into my Fae form, keeping him down with my weight and smirking at him. "Yield."

His fist slammed into my jaw and he rolled us over with his Vampire strength, though I didn't even bother to fight. I cupped my hands behind my head as my back hit the ground and he locked his fingers around my throat. His fangs snapped out and he grinned as he leaned down to steal his prize, pulling his hand away and driving his teeth into my neck.

I groaned audibly then bit my tongue as his muscles pressed to mine and I got rock hard for him. *Oh shit.*

He pressed me into the ground and my magic was immobilised by his venom as he crushed me beneath him. I was definitely not the submissive type, but if Caleb wanted to force me down in the mud and have his way with me, I was game. Of course, the way he wanted me was to take my blood, nothing else. I thought about what Darcy had said, wondering if I should talk to him, but surely my dick was having a whole conversation with his right now because it wasn't being subtle.

He lifted his weight half off of me, sucking in a breath and drawing away from me so he was kneeling over my thighs.

He looked down at my solid cock and no matter how many people had seen it before, nothing beat him looking at it right now, exposing me for how much I wanted him. My eyes slipped to his crotch the same time his did and the bulge waiting for me there made my heart pound out of rhythm. Caleb glanced at me in confusion, an awkward silence washing between us.

"Erm," I began and his brow furrowed just a little as he leaned back.

"Race you back to the Hollow." He got up and shot away with his Vampire speed before I could stop him and my heart lurched painfully as he just left me lying there in the dirt.

I shifted back into a Wolf, howling after him in a plea to come back. But he didn't and I had the horrible feeling I'd just fucked up everything.

I flexed my fingers, admiring the Phoenix metal gauntlets covering them. I obviously had the coolest weapon of all the Heirs. Darcy had tried to convince me to have something simple like the others, but I'd come up with this design myself after I'd dreamed of having flaming claws of death. The gauntlets were enchanted to expand when I shifted into my Wolf form, so they could pack a spectacular fire punch in Fae form and became flaming claws in my Order form.

We'd been tracking a few Nymphs out this way the last couple of nights. There'd been a bunch of reported sightings of them and we'd only managed to catch and kill three in the past two days. From the tracks we'd found tonight leading onto some old farmland, I was guessing we were about to run into a damn nest.

I moved through the cornfield behind Caleb, the others walking ahead of us following Tory and Darcy. Tory had some serious rage to vent and though it was risky bringing her on this run, it was also damn good for her. She needed to let her Order flourish and be reminded of how fierce she was, so when she went back to Lionel, she'd at least have that to hold onto.

I cast a silencing bubble around me and Cal, jogging forward to walk at his side. He glanced at me, then quickly away again, raising his twin knives. I knew talking about this now wasn't really good timing, but he'd also been avoiding me since boner gate and the last thing I wanted was to lose my friend over this.

I cleared my throat, knocking my shoulder against his. Despite how much time I'd had to decide on what I was going to say to him, I now couldn't remember any of that. *What had Darcy advised? Don't talk about my boner, or* do *talk about it?*

Her plan to feel him out so far hadn't gone too well. Apparently every time she tried to move the conversation in that direction, Caleb changed the subject. So maybe I was kidding myself thinking he really could be harbouring feelings for me. Maybe he'd gotten hard while drinking from me because blood turned him on. He was a Vampire, it made sense. So I probably just needed to Fae up, hit my feelings over the head with a sledgehammer then bury them six feet under forever.

My heart pounded harder as I stole a glance at his face, his perfectly straight nose, his eyes overshadowed and intense. I'd known him my whole life and I'd realised he was attractive some time around my twelfth birthday. It wasn't news to me that he was hot. But somehow I'd always managed to compartmentalise that from my friendship with him before. Now it was all just melding into one so all I could see was how fucking amazing he was and how much I wanted him and how it had been staring me in the face all these years. No matter how much I hungered for him though, it clearly wasn't meant to be. I just wasn't sure how to make my heart get the message on that.

"Remember when we stole your mom's fire crystals when we were kids and accidentally burned down her rose garden?" I said, wanting to remind myself as much as him that we had a whole lifetime of friendship regardless of one awkward boner moment. Nothing could break us apart. Not even our dicks.

Caleb chuckled. "Yeah, and I tried to ride on your back as a Wolf so we could get away faster."

"Dumbest idea ever," I laughed, remembering when Melinda had shot after us with her Vampire speed and dragged us both inside by the ears. She'd made us clean out the acid slug infestation she had in her gutters without any kind of magical protection as punishment.

Caleb turned to me, gripping my arm to stop me from walking on. He opened his mouth then closed it again and my heart thudded harder as I wondered what the hell he was thinking. My hand found his in the dark and I laced my fingers through his instinctively.

"Seth," he said in a low growl that could have been to warn me off or draw me closer. I guessed I wanted to believe it was the latter so I stepped into his personal space, breathing him in and trying to fool myself into thinking there really could be something between us. That I wasn't imagining it.

"Look, what happened in the woods the other day-" I started, but Tory shouted out a battle cry and the shriek of a Nymph filled the air, cutting that sentence off at the balls.

I gasped, turning to the path we'd been forging through the corn and finding the rest of our group gone.

"Shit," Cal cursed and we started running after them, pushing between the stalks and hunting for them in the dark.

"Use your speed," I demanded, but he glanced back at me with a look that said he didn't want to leave me.

Another Nymph's cry pierced the air and a blaze of Phoenix fire spiralled up into the sky a hundred yards away. We started running toward it and I shoved Caleb's back to encourage him to move faster.

A towering shadow fell over us and Caleb yanked me aside with a shot of Vampire speed just as a huge Nymph came charging through the field toward us. I leapt away from Caleb, shifting in the air, shredding through my clothes and the gauntlets around my hands expanded. They encased my front paws so that ten sharp metal claws slammed into the ground as I landed, flames bursting to life around me.

I turned and started charging back toward the Nymph, my teeth bared and my bloodthirst rising.

Caleb was running around it in speeding circles, slashing at it with the dual knives in his hands, Phoenix fire blazing along the monster's flesh. It swiped a hand through the air, knocking him away and he was thrown back into the dense corn out of sight.

A snarl of rage ripped from my throat as I leapt onto the Nymph's back, tearing at its barky flesh with my flaming claws of death and sinking my teeth into its shoulder. It reached back to try and rip me off but I held on tight, clawing my way further up until I could see over its shoulder to where the rest of our friends were fighting five more of them out in the field.

The Nymph caught hold of my tail and I yelped as it whipped me forward and threw me to the ground on my back, making pain ricochet through me. It pinned me in place by the throat with impossible strength, its long probes extended and ready to steal my magic. Fear hit me as the rattle emanating from its chest immobilised the well of power inside me. It was going to take all my magic and my life with it if I didn't get free.

I fought wildly, about to shift back into my Fae form even though I knew it would leave me vulnerable, but it might just give me room to wriggle free.

Caleb leapt out of the corn stalks with a yell of anger and sliced through the Nymph's arm, making hope spark through my blood. The severed limb fell to the ground and I rolled over, scrambling upright to get away, but the beast snatched hold of my leg and twisted until it snapped. Agony spread through me as I yelped, slashing back at the Nymph with my Phoenix claws and ripping a gouge across its face. It released me with a shriek and I ran away, keeping my weight off of my bad leg as Caleb fought to bring the Nymph to its knees.

A Dragon's roar filled the air and Darius's huge golden form swept overhead, a blaze of fire pouring from his lungs. The heat of it warmed me through as he aimed it down at an enemy of his own and the others cheered, telling me this battle was almost over.

We could never leave a Nymph alive during these fights. If they reported back to Lionel about what we were doing, he'd hunt us to the ends of the earth for defying him. But we'd all decided it was worth the risk. We needed to be doing something to fight back against him in a real way while we continued our hunt for the Imperial Star and planned a rebellion for the future.

I lunged at the Nymph's leg, slashing with my claws to help bring it down and it finally fell, crashing backwards and hitting the earth with a bone rattling thump.

Caleb dove onto it, showing no mercy as he drove one of his blades between its eyes and the Nymph burst into a cloud of shadows as it died.

He shot over to me in a blur, concern etched into his face as he ran his hand over my hind leg and healed the break.

I licked his face and he smirked at me, the sight making me howl excitedly. We sure made the perfect fucking team. And maybe I needed to accept that we were always just going to be friends, because I'd never survive losing him. But to keep things as they were, my heart was going to have to pay the price. And I was pretty sure I could already feel it breaking.

TORY

CHAPTER TWENTY FOUR

The grand ballroom at the palace where we'd celebrated last Christmas remained well and truly locked up tight against any and every attempt that Lionel made to get into it. He cursed and ranted about the palace, using every kind of spell he could think of and even getting in earth Elementals with expertise in building and architecture to try and break through the magic that was keeping him out, but it was no good. He hadn't even been able to blast his way through the door with Dragon fire.

So, much to his disgust, instead of holding his ball in there, he'd had to make use of a huge pavilion out in the east gardens for the occasion. Tonight was the annual Dragon Guild's Oath celebration which Clara had informed me was the night when every Dragon in Solaria was expected to come and reaffirm their loyalty to the Guild by remaking their oath beneath the watchful gaze of the stars. Lionel had taken advantage of that last part when telling everyone that it would be held outside, playing up to the idea of the heavens watching over the occasion, but I knew the truth. And the tantrum he'd thrown over the palace rejecting him had a smile toying around the corners of my lips.

Beyond the pompous oath nonsense, Darius had told me that this night would mostly be used by Lionel to make certain that his most loyal supporters were all still firmly on team Asscrux. The Dragons would all be making arrangements for political gains such as marriage contracts, trade deals and the like. All that standard *let's keep the rich dudes rich* bullshit that went on in fancy ass boardrooms everywhere just dressed up prettily for a party instead.

The dress I was wearing tonight was actually something I might have picked out for myself and I was going to put that down to the people who bought the clothes rather than give Lionel any credit for it. It was a deep, forest green velvet that brought out the colour in my eyes and was backless, the long sleeves covered my arms.

I walked down to the ball with Clara at my side as we followed Lionel. He had Catalina on his arm, looking stunning as always, perfectly made up in a silver dress that drew attention to her curves. Clara was pouting because he hadn't wanted her to take his other arm. Tonight was about showing his strength as a Dragon and he wouldn't be seen with anyone other than his pure blooded bride in front of all the others. But of course, Clara was petulant and childish and wasn't just going to accept that.

"Might I remind you that Guardians are only invited to this function as a courtesy," Lionel growled when she huffed dramatically for the eighth time as we passed a window with a view out to the huge wooden pavilion which was teaming with Dragon Shifters.

I looked over the hexagonal shaped building with its white roof and mid-level railings surrounding it and couldn't help but appreciate how pretty it was. Apparently it had been built for my mother so that she could have musicians come and play for her whenever she wanted.

"If you are unable to behave, then I will send you back to my quarters and you had better believe I won't be kind when I return there later on tonight," Lionel snarled.

"But *Daddy*," Clara whined. "I don't see why I can't-"

Lionel released his hold on Catalina's arm and whirled on Clara in the blink of an eye, a silencing bubble crashing over our small group as he reached out and grabbed her around the throat.

"Do you wish for Roxanya to become my favourite?" he threatened, and I fought a shudder at the implications of that.

Before I'd been brought back to myself, I'd wanted to be the favourite more than anything. But now that I was looking at it without the crazy tinted glasses, I realised the only real difference between me and Clara was that he called her his favourite and he fucked her. I might have had a need in me to please him and be close to him, but thankfully there had never been a stirring of sexual desire towards him in me. That said, I knew I would have done it if he'd told me to before. I would have gotten on my knees and done anything he wanted just to please him. *Thank fuck for possessive shadow bitch nutcases.*

"No, Daddy," Clara balked, throwing me a glare full of enough acid to melt the skin from my bones.

"Then go back to my room and wait for me there. I'll be along when I'm done with the party and you can show me how sorry you are then. Perhaps I will be merciful if you manage to do enough to appease me."

Clara looked half way between thrilled at that prospect and horrified about being banished but as Lionel's glare hardened, she murmured her agreement then shot away, wailing with tears, her sobs echoing off of the palace walls.

Lionel's gaze slid to me with a hungry kind of desire that sent a shiver of fear down my spine.

"You're going to be a good girl, aren't you, Roxanya?" he asked in a low and deadly tone as he reached out to slide his fingers around my throat the way he had to Clara.

"Yes, my King," I breathed as his nostrils flared and smoke trailed from them.

Lionel's grip on me tightened painfully and I had to fight against the urge to try and rip his hands from my throat with everything I had as Catalina released a whimper of distress.

"Sometimes I can see so much of your father in you," he murmured thoughtfully and rage built in me at the reminder of what the stars had shown us he'd done to our father.

This kingdom had never had a Savage King, it had been this hateful puppet master and his dark magic all along. All for this. He'd been plotting to take the throne even then, doing everything he could to gain the advantage he needed over the other Councillors. It made me sick to know he'd achieved all of that. And that my father may never have known he wasn't a monster.

His grip tightened until I couldn't draw breath and light flared in his eyes before he released me just as suddenly as he'd grabbed me and turned to take Catalina's arm once more.

I had to bite my tongue so hard against all the things I wanted to say to this lying, scheming sack of shit that I made it bleed and that was still only just enough to keep me quiet.

We headed out into the gardens where the path had been lit up with such a beautiful use of fire magic that I was offered the distraction I needed to pull myself together just by looking at it. The flames burned in a thousand different complicated shapes and patterns, and when we reached the enormous pavilion where the ball was being held, I couldn't help but stare at the life sized Dragon crafted from flames which perched upon the roof.

My magic flared hungrily as it was recharged by so much fire all around me and I followed Lionel and Catalina up into the pavilion, feeling slightly calmer thanks to the distraction, glad that I didn't have to call on the shadows.

A herald announced Lionel's arrival like the pretentious douche he was and to my disgust every fucker standing in the beautiful wooden structure bowed low for their king.

Lionel preened like an overstuffed peacock as the first of the simpering sycophants rushed over to join us and my gaze fell on a giant of a man as he lumbered forward. In fact, every fucker here was huge, I guessed on account of the fact that they were Dragons.

"Ah, Christopher," Lionel greeted warmly as the big motherfucker tilted his head in acknowledgement of his king. "I was hoping to have a discussion with you later about the Minotaurs living in your part of the kingdom."

"Of course," the Dragon replied, licking his lips and running his beady eyes all over Catalina without an inch of shame. "I'd be more than happy to help you rid Solaria of the vermin who have been holding us back for so long."

"Good," Lionel said. "Because there are a few favours I need of you and it would be most helpful if you could see to it that they were done sooner rather than later. Of course, I would reward you greatly for your help in this matter."

Christopher agreed to speak with him more later and another Dragon stepped forward, this one eyeing me warily as he bowed to Lionel.

"Your Highness," he said crisply, his black beard moving just enough to show he'd spoken. His eyes darted my way again and Lionel sighed.

"I'll come and speak with you alone soon, Tomas," he said. "Once my Guardian is otherwise occupied."

The bearded Dragon seemed pleased by that suggestion, bowing low before heading away and Lionel cut me an irritated look as if it was my fault his followers didn't like me being here. Technically, this was supposed to be Dragons only, but he'd said it was customary for Guardians to be allowed to attend too. It just didn't seem like the other Dragons were all too pleased about it.

I looked towards the next Dragon who was ushered up to approach us and had to hide a smile as I recognised Dante Oscura, pleased to find that there was at least one marginally more likeable person here than I'd expected. He was huge like all the other Fae here, but he wasn't like them at all somehow with his gold jewellery and causally swept back black hair, the few buttons left open at his throat and a general aura of not wanting to be here. He stood out in all the best ways and I was fairly certain he was someone I could call a friend. Or at least I could have before Lionel got his claws into me.

"Good evening, bella," Dante purred, his Faetalian accent dripping over his words as he smiled at me then turned his attention to Catalina. "And of course the Dragon Queen is looking beautiful as always." Catalina smiled graciously and thanked him as Lionel bristled at being left until last. "And finally, my lord and over-ruler, King of all of Solaria and the most powerful Fae I know," Dante said finally, his words oozing disdain and I noticed he didn't bow either.

"I hear congratulations are in order, Storm Dragon," Lionel growled. "Though I hope you don't think that your arrangement with Juniper means your other children are exempt from my rule. If they Emerge as our kind then I'll be expecting them to join to the Guild."

Dante didn't even bother to suppress a growl as static electricity washed off of his skin and lifted my hair around my shoulders.

"Well, we're actually hoping for my Wolf blood to shine through. Let's not forget I'm only a Dragon because of a gift from the stars. I doubt I'll be passing on the Dragon gene," Dante said roughly.

"Who knows what ways the heavens work," Lionel disagreed. "My blood is as pure as it gets and yet my youngest was cursed to become a Pegasus. Perhaps the stars are righting that oversight by gifting you the genetics to produce an entire army of Storm Dragons to make up for his shortcomings."

"Yes, no doubt my life and Order were all planned out by the stars to suit *your* purposes, my king," Dante replied scathingly. "We all live to serve you after all, lucertola viscida."

Lionel tsked at his tone but made no further efforts to reprimand him.

"I expect another baby in Juniper's belly by the end of the year," he said. "She's here somewhere. *I suggest you find her and put one in her before the night is over.*"

I stifled a gasp as he bound Dante with the Dark Coercion that would force him to cheat on his wife and Dante's eyes flared with the power of a storm as he glared at Lionel in outrage. A crash of thunder sounded overhead and as I looked out of the open wall of the pavilion, I could have sworn I spotted a huge, feathered wing crossing over the moon where it hung low in the sky.

I half expected Dante to lunge at Lionel and rip his throat out with the fury that was burning in his gaze as his posture locked tight and his muscles flexed within his expensive black suit, threatening to burst the seams of it.

He ground his jaw for several seconds and Lionel smirked at him like he was hoping he really would attack. I flexed my fingers, magic pooling to them while I readied myself to leap before my king if he needed defending, equally hating myself for doing it and unable to stop.

Dante growled and more static poured from him but instead of attacking, he turned to look at me and forced a smile. "Would you like to dance with me, bella?" he asked, offering me his hand and I raised an eyebrow in surprise at the sudden turn of events.

"I'm glad to see you're accepting of your task," Lionel said triumphantly looking like the cockiest, smuggest bastard I'd ever seen. "And yes, I think it might be for the best if my Guardian were to spend some time away from me so that I can speak with my subjects in private. Run along, Roxanya, dance, eat and just keep out of the way."

I agreed instantly, giving Dante my hand and letting him walk me over to the dance floor on the far side of the pavilion. Where his skin touched mine, electricity skittered against my palm and I shivered at the reminder of the torture I'd endured even though the voltage he was exuding now was nothing like the agony I'd received at Lionel's hand.

Luckily Vard wasn't here tonight either as no Cyclopses were invited so I was about as close to free as I ever got while back at the palace.

Dancers were taking their places on the floor, all of them dressed elegantly and looking supremely comfortable as someone called out to let us know this was going to be a foxtrot.

"Can I tell you a secret, bella?" Dante asked, lowering his voice conspiratorially and smirking at me like we were firm friends even though I didn't know him all that well.

"What?" I asked, keeping my tone flat.

"I don't know the steps to this dance," he whispered loudly and I had to fight a smile.

"Well then we may be in trouble, because I don't either," I admitted. "Perhaps it's better if we don't-"

"Nonsense." Dante tugged me into his strong arms and I had to fight a surprised laugh as my hand fell against his shoulder and his hand moved to hold my waist.

The music started playing and he swept me into the dance, whirling me around in circles, not seeming to give one shit that we weren't following the steps at all. I had to bite my lip to stop myself from laughing as he knocked into the other dancers, carving out a path for us and causing carnage with his total lack of shits to give. He wasn't a bad dancer, he just wasn't following the status quo and I got the feeling he enjoyed shaking it up. There was no law to say we had to do the dance that everyone else was doing anyway and I just wished I could drop my mask and laugh my way through this with him.

"Do you trust me, little principessa?" Dante asked, whirling me around and I shifted my hand in his as my mind lingered on the Dark Coercion Lionel had placed on him.

"Why are you asking if-"

"Gabby told me I could trust you," he said, flashing me a smile. "And he said that you could help me too."

My lips parted in confusion as I tried to figure out who Gabby was and Dante spun me beneath his arm suddenly, forcing another couple to stumble away from us as he almost knocked me into them. He tugged me back into his arms and my eyes widened as I found a silencing bubble pressing close around the two of us to keep our conversation private.

"What are you doing?" I breathed.

"No need to keep up the shadow twat act with me, principessa," he teased. "I see the real girl peering back at me clear as day from those big green eyes of yours."

"I don't know what you-"

"Give it up, bella. Gabby told me your secret. So do you trust me with it?"

My lips fell open as I tried to figure out what he was saying, not to mention who the hell Gabby was. I didn't know a Gabby.

"Don't tell me, he makes you call him *Gabriel*," Dante groaned dramatically. "He's such a stronzo sometimes."

The penny finally dropped and I snorted a laugh. "You call him Gabby?"

"Yeah. He loves it. Don't let him tell you different. So can you help me with my little Dragon bitch issue, principessa? Because if this Coercion makes me fuck her, my wife will cut my balls off and I happen to be pretty damn fond of them."

I had to fight my smile back so that no one else would see it as I nodded, relief spilling into me at the knowledge that I could do this for him. If Gabriel had sent him to me then there was no doubt in my mind about that.

I squeezed his fingers, my Phoenix fire crackling against the electricity in his veins as I pushed it beneath his skin and sought out the Dark Coercion binding him to Lionel's will. I burned through it easily and Dante laughed loudly, spinning me again as he bumped into a guy hard enough to knock him on his ass.

"What are you going to do about Juniper?" I asked. "If she doesn't end up pregnant then Lionel will know you didn't-"

"Don't worry about that. Gabby has a plan and I've got back up to execute it from mia famiglia." Dante smirked at me as the song ended and he turned me around, bringing me face to face with Darius who was glaring over my shoulder at the Storm Dragon like he had half a mind to shift and lay into him. "Ah here's our new prince," Dante mocked.

"You two seem cosy," Darius said in a flat tone, his gaze taking in Dante's hand in mine as the hint of a snarl escaped him.

"Calm down, mio amico, I have my own girl to keep me more than occupied. I was only dancing with your beautiful mate. But now I need to run and she finds herself in need of a new dance partner." Dante gave me a little push and I stumbled forward a step so that Darius caught me.

The feeling of his hands on my waist lit a fire beneath my skin and I drew in a breath as he looked down at me.

"Your fiancé will be a little late to the party, so you have time for a dance before she gets here," Dante added with a grin that said Gabriel had told him that too before he strode away.

Darius looked beyond me towards the throne where Lionel had set himself up to receive his subjects before his grip tightened on my waist and he drew me closer.

I looked up at him in surprise as he slid his hand around my back, his rough palm landing on my bare skin as he pulled me into his arms, his other hand taking mine as the music started up.

"Are you sure this is a good idea?" I asked though I wasn't making any attempt to pull away as he moved me out into the crowd of dancers as a waltz was announced.

Unlike Dante, Darius clearly knew all of the steps and he led me around the floor with such confidence that it was easy for me to follow him and replicate them too.

"My father enjoys watching me suffer over you," he said, pulling me even closer so that our chests were touching. "So he won't have any objections. Especially once Mildred arrives and I'm forced to endure her company for the rest of the night. Besides, being in a crowd this big might buy us a few minutes from the stars."

I probably should have said more, but I didn't want to be anywhere else so I just gave in, letting him spin me around the ballroom like a fairy tale princess even though we both knew I wasn't anything of the sort.

We danced around and around, my skirt whirling around my ankles and our bodies pressing so close that I could feel the hard ridges of his muscles through his shirt and I grew breathless as the smoke and cedar scent of him drew me even closer.

My heart was thumping to a treacherous rhythm and I was glad he held me so tightly or I was almost certain everyone in the room would be able to see that I was anything but a shell of a girl when I was in his arms.

The music dipped and suddenly his hands were on my waist as he lifted me, spinning me in time with all the other dancers and placing me back on my feet with my body pressed to his.

"When did you learn to dance like this?" I asked him and he smirked at me as we swept over the wooden floor again, the steps so fast that I wasn't even certain how I was keeping up with him.

"Around about the same time as you learned to hotwire a bike," he teased. "Some of us were raised for this life."

"And some of us learned how to really live," I taunted back.

Darius's lips lifted in amusement and I was caught in his dark eyes as he directed us across the dance floor once more.

"Are you enjoying this?" he murmured.

"Yes," I breathed, unable to deny the way my heart was hammering against my ribcage and my skin was burning up everywhere that we were pressed together.

"So it feels good to let me take charge?" he pushed and I narrowed my eyes at him.

"Don't go thinking you'll make a habit of it."

Darius leaned down so that his lips brushed my ear as he spoke his next words and a tremor ran right through me which I was sure he must have been able to feel too. "You'd love being dominated by me, Roxy," he promised. "I'd pin you down and make you scream so good you'd forget all about trying to stop me as I marked you as mine so thoroughly that you'd never doubt that it was true ever again."

A throb of need built in my core at his words and I wondered if he knew how much I wanted him to try that. I was aching for his touch on my flesh, my cheeks flushed and my panties wet as he held me almost tight enough to bruise.

But before I could give him an answer to that suggestion, a roar which sounded kind of like a pig going into battle with an angry sheep announced Mildred's arrival to the party. I flinched back out of Darius's arms as an explosion of vomit-yellow taffeta charged our way.

"Here I am snookums!" she cried as she launched herself into his arms, knocking me back and making me curse as I fought to steady myself in my heels. "No need to waste your time dancing with anyone else," she added, tossing a pointed look my way as she wrapped her arms around Darius possessively.

Everything in my being screamed at me to punch her stupid pug face and my muscles locked up as I fought to try and control my anger, cutting a glance towards Lionel on his throne.

He was watching us, his gaze on Darius and an amused smirk on his lips as I forced myself to turn and walk away. I didn't head back to Lionel though. He'd told me to dance, eat and stay out of the way so I knew he didn't want me around his Dragon asshole buddies.

I took a shaky breath as I tried to calm my pounding heart and headed over to the feast which had been laid out to the side of the pavilion. There was every kind of food you could imagine on it, beautifully presented with golden plates ready to be filled by the servants who perked up as they saw me approaching.

I told the guy who offered to get me food that I didn't care what he picked out then took it to the far side of the pavilion with the intention of hiding out in the shadows until I had to return to Lionel's bed later tonight.

Wow, my life was so fucking painful. I felt trapped in this endless cycle of lying about who I was, faking a lack of emotions about everything that mattered to me then stealing moments to be myself while still having to lie about the part of me that just ached to be with Lionel every minute of every fucking day.

Time ticked by as I stood there alone, my plate of untouched food balanced on the railing beside me as I tried not to watch Mildred pawing at Darius and failed miserably. She was all over him and it didn't even matter that I knew full well he had no interest in her. He was still destined to be hers. And unless we managed to stop Lionel by the time they graduated then he'd have to go through with the marriage too.

"You look as miserable as I feel." Orion's voice snapped me out of my thoughts and I looked around to find him leaning against the railing a few feet from me.

"Shit, you made me jump," I scolded as I glanced at his blue suit and tie while he folded his arms over his chest.

"Yeah, well, everyone is Power Shaming me so I might as well be invisible here. But *Uncle Lionel* says his Heir's Guardian had to be present so here I am."

I nodded in understanding because that was why I'd been gifted an invite too.

"Please alleviate my boredom - I need something to get me through the reality of spooning with that motherfucker tonight," I begged and Orion's lips twitched the tiniest amount as he handed me a glass of champagne before taking a long swig of his own.

"You and I both know you'll be diving in for that spooning head first," he scoffed, leaning back against the railing.

"At least allow me to pretend I've still got some dignity," I muttered.

"It's fine - I'll be in bed with Darius, no doubt listening to him talking about you incessantly while he makes me his little spoon."

"I would have pegged you for a big spoon kind of guy," I teased, not sure what to think of Darius talking about me like that.

"Yeah, well I would be if I had my girl in my bed, but the bond makes me want to please my Ward and seeing as Darius suffers from the superiority complex of a lifetime, let's just say the domineering asshole always wants to be the big one."

I smiled a little at that visual, taking a sip of my drink to cover it in case anyone was looking our way, but they all seemed too invested in their bullshit to pay attention to the unwanted additions to the party anyway.

"You said *your* girl," I pointed out, giving him a sidelong look as his brow furrowed and he sighed, casting a hopeless kind of look my way.

"Shit, you really look like her sometimes, you know?" Orion breathed, swiping a hand over his face and looking so freaking tired and broken that I kinda wanted to hug him despite all the witnesses.

"I look like my identical twin? Really? No fucking way," I teased and he shook his head.

"Yeah, well, when you smiled you just reminded me of her more than usual. Or at least of the way she used to look before I..." He trailed off, looking out over the party and my heart twisted for him, but he really had been the architect of this fucking mess between them, so I wasn't going to offer him platitudes. He needed to buck the fuck up and fix it.

I twisted my fingers where he couldn't see beside me, crafting air magic into the shape of a fist before slamming it into his junk at least as hard as I would have punched him if we didn't have an audience.

Orion cursed, doubling over and dropping his drink so that the glass shattered and several of the Dragons looked to him in shock. They hurriedly looked away again like he didn't exist and one pinched face woman loudly said, "For *shame*."

I bit my lip as I slowly took another drink, hiding my amusement as Orion tried to subtly cast healing magic on his balls while pushing himself upright again.

"Why?" he hissed and I cut him a look that said 'you know why' to which he muttered beneath his breath something along the lines of me being a fucking psychopath and feeling sorry for Darius if that was how I treated his junk.

"If you recall correctly, I offered you one chance not to fuck things up with her and promised castration if you hurt her," I said casually. "So really you're getting off lightly."

"By the stars, you're a monster," he growled.

"Damn straight I am," I agreed. "So fix it and I won't have to elevate your punishments."

"Elevate?" he asked, his voice raising an octave and making me smirk into my drink again. "If you elevate it, I won't be left functioning."

I cut him a look and mimed snipping a pair of scissors with my fingers while he grimaced, shifting a protective hand over his balls as he shook his head in horror at me.

Darius and Mildred swept around the centre of the dance floor and my amusement fell away as I watched them. She might have had a frame almost as big as his and feet which in all honesty looked even bigger than his, but she had clearly been taught how to do all of these fancy formal dances. The two of them moved around the dance floor in perfect synchronisation and as I watched them, I couldn't help but wonder what would happen if we failed to get hold of the Imperial Star. What if all of our plans and goals and aims to thwart Lionel and dethrone him just didn't work out?

Was this the life I was destined to lead forever? Watching Darius with that nasty troll of a girl as he danced with her at parties, was forced to marry her, had little pure-blooded Dragon babies with her. All while I was cursed to spend my nights warming Lionel's bed and following his every command in the vain hope that we might one day find some way to break this bond he'd put on me.

My chest tightened as I watched Mildred's vomit-yellow dress sweeping out behind her, Darius's hand resting on the small of her hairy back. His eyes met mine through the crowd and I could see that same ache there, that longing for a different life which I could see no path to. Because even if we did manage to take the throne back from his father, it wouldn't change this curse I'd put on us. We'd still be Star Crossed, destined to be alone, pining for each other forever.

Was this all my future held? Looking at him across crowded rooms and wishing I'd made the other choice?

"He really does love you," Orion said in a low voice which jolted me out of my staring and I cleared my throat as I dropped my gaze down to my feet.

"I'm not an easy person to love," I muttered.

"Neither is he. That's probably what makes you so perfect for each other."

I hmmed lightly but not really because I didn't agree, more because it seemed so pointless to even consider it. Nothing could change our fates now anyway.

"I actually came over here to hang out alone in the corner so that I could feel *less* shitty," I teased. "You're kind of a downer, you know that?"

"I'm a heartbroken criminal who has now had two careers destroyed before I've even turned thirty," he growled. "So you really shouldn't be surprised by that. Besides, what do you want me to do about it?"

"Be more fun," I joked and he rolled his eyes.

"Fine. You wanna play a game?"

"What kind of game?" I asked.

"That was a joke."

"Your delivery requires some work. Come on, you've promised me a game now. Why don't I guess what the pompous douche hats are saying to each other and you can use your bat ears to tell me if I'm right?" I suggested.

"Sure. But don't blame me when it's nothing but posturing bullshit," Orion agreed, sounding less than enthused by my idea but he was less than enthused by most things since he'd fucked up his relationship with my sister, so I was willing to ignore that.

"Okay, sooo... that big guy over there is saying; 'I just got that new butt plug you recommended, Brenda, and you're right, it does help keep the stick even further up my ass'."

Orion snorted a laugh then nodded. "First off, every guy here is a 'big guy' so I'm gonna need more to go on than that. But also, I definitely heard more than a few of them talking about those new Dragon scale butt plugs that are all the rage right now, so I'm sure you're right."

"And I heard the sticks have extra splinters which explains why they're all grumpy fuckers. Aside from Dante - he clearly had his removed."

"What about Darius?"

"Darius may have forgone the butt plug, but the stick is most likely still pretty firmly up there. But the stars won't let me get him naked to check."

"I'll be sure to tell him you want to get him naked when he crawls into my bed tonight," Orion said.

"If you must. Getting naked has never been my issue. Sex is a whole lot simpler than...all that other relationship shit. Now focus on the game and tell me what that Christopher dude is saying to Lionel. Is it something like; 'I only wish to lick your ass, oh King of the Dragons!'?"

Orion inclined his head as he trained his senses on the big bald Dragon in question while he spoke to Lionel on his throne. I watched the conversation too, noting the way Christopher nodded excitedly at something Lionel said as he placed a possessive hand on Catalina's thigh.

Darius's mom nodded robotically and Christopher grinned as she got to her feet.

"What the fuck..." Orion murmured, drawing my attention back to him as he pushed himself upright, frowning over at Catalina as she walked out of the pavilion with Christopher beside her.

"What?" I asked. "Where are they going?"

Orion looked more than a little sickened as he glanced between them and Darius who was still caught in Mildred's grasp on the dance floor.

"We have to go after them," he hissed.

"We can't," I replied and my pulse picked up as I checked around to see if anyone was paying us any attention.

"Lionel just told that big motherfucker that he could have Catalina for the night," he growled urgently. "And then he Dark Coerced her to go with him and do whatever he wanted."

My lips fell open and I shook my head, though I didn't know why I was trying to deny it. I knew exactly how much of a monster Lionel Acrux was. I knew that he'd been controlling and abusing everyone around him for years and years, so this shouldn't have surprised me but it did. She was his wife. The mother of his sons. And he was just handing her out as a favour to some gross old sleezebag to use however he wanted for the night like she was nothing?

Catalina had been on my mind a lot over the last few weeks since I'd been brought back to myself, and I'd been worried about her stuck here in this house. But I'd never once imagined she was being subjected to something like this.

"Wait," I growled as Orion made a move to leave. "Can you hear them? Catalina and that fucking pig she's gone off with?"

He paused a moment, looking around and focusing. "Yes. They're still walking back towards the palace. He's...telling her rather graphically what he plans to spend the night doing with her."

"But he's not touching her yet?" I confirmed, trying to keep my vacant mask in place as I looked out over the sea of Dragons.

"Lionel told him to be subtle about it. He said to wait to enjoy his prize behind closed doors."

"Then we have a few minutes. I'm going to make an excuse to leave. Can you slip out and meet me at the end of the path?"

"What about Darius?" Orion asked, his gaze moving to his friend who was still stuck with Mildred.

"We have to do this without him," I said. "No one cares if we're here or not, but the son of the King will be missed."

Orion cursed then agreed, shooting away from me as I took off across the pavilion, heading for the throne where Lionel still sat.

"There you are, Roxanya," he said with a smile that turned my insides.

"My King," I greeted, dipping my head even though it went against every instinct in my soul. "I miss you."

He sighed, seeming both pleased and irritated by the show of needy behaviour like I knew he would be, and he beckoned me closer as he got to his feet. "I don't plan on this party going on much longer. Why don't you head back to our bed and make sure Clara isn't up to any mischief?"

I nodded eagerly, feeling like a whipped little puppy dog as he cupped my face in his palm and placed a wet kiss on my cheek before waving me away. I turned and headed out of the party as fast as I could without drawing attention.

The path seemed abandoned as I strode down it purposefully, but as I drew closer to the palace, a blur of movement caught my gaze and I was swept off of my feet as Orion grabbed me and sped us inside.

I could hardly keep my bearings as he shot past the household staff, down long corridors and headed into the guest wing of the palace before skidding to a halt outside a closed wooden door.

He dropped me to the floor and kicked the door open before shooting inside and throwing a blast of air magic at Christopher's back before I even made it over the threshold.

The Dragon Shifter had already taken his shirt off and Catalina was in her underwear on the bed, her eyes wild as she spotted us.

Christopher stumbled back beneath Orion's attack but recovered quickly, lifting his hands and throwing a torrent of Dragon Fire straight at Orion who barely managed to shield in time to protect himself from it.

The flames ricocheted off of the shield and Catalina screamed as they were directed at the bed where she lay instead.

I cursed as I threw magic towards her, mixing ice and air into a powerful shield around her and grunting with the effort of maintaining it as the Dragon fire blasted the bed apart with a tremendous crash.

The second the flames died down, Orion hit Christopher with a shot of air so hard that he was thrown back against the wall where his head made a horrible cracking sound against the bricks before he dropped to the floor unconscious.

"Shit," I gasped as I dispersed my shield, panting in relief as I found Catalina cowering beneath it.

I hurried past Orion as he moved to make sure Christopher wasn't about to wake up and grabbed her hand, pushing Phoenix fire beneath her skin and seeking out all of the Dark Coercion that Lionel had forced on her yet again.

"Are you okay?" I breathed, looking around for her clothes and finding her dress burned to a crisp on the remnants of the burning bed.

I took her hand and hauled her up and she glanced between me and Orion with relief and fear filling her gaze in equal measures.

"You shouldn't have done that," she breathed, wrapping her arms around herself and Orion shrugged out of his jacket before handing it to her so that she could cover herself up.

"We weren't going to just let him abuse you like that," Orion snarled in disgust.

"It wouldn't have been the first time," she said, shaking her head hopelessly. "Lionel has been using me to help him secure deals for years. At first it was just flirting which I did willingly enough, but then..."

"You were Coerced to come here tonight," I said angrily. "That doesn't sound like you were willing to me."

Catalina blanched. "A few years ago, one of his political contacts wanted more than flirting from me and when I refused, he tried to pull out of a major deal Lionel had wanted to make. So, to save the deal he told me to go through with it and when I refused again, he just..."

My blood burned with fury and outrage on her behalf and I pulled her into a tight embrace as she trembled in my arms.

"I know you were trying to help me, but if Lionel figures out what happened here, he'll kill all of us," she breathed fearfully and I looked around at Orion with concern, wondering how we were going to get out of this.

A knock at the door almost made me jump out of my skin and fire blazed to life in my palm as I whirled around, finding Gabriel standing there with a grin on his face.

"Oh good, I wasn't certain if I'd get here now or after the roof caves in and I would have been a lot more pushed for time if it was after," he said like him just casually appearing right now was no big deal and there wasn't a half dead Dragon on the floor while fires burned all around the room.

"Gabriel, what the-" I began but he waved me off, tossing Catalina a hoody and a pair of sweatpants.

"Have you *seen* what to do, Noxy?" Orion asked hopefully.

"Yes, we need to add some of Catalina's blood to the fire on the bed then get the fuck out of here," Gabriel said. "Lionel will think Christopher accidentally killed her in the throes of passion and he'll be sent to Darkmore for her murder. I'm gonna fly her out of here and he'll be none the wiser."

"Where are you taking me?" Catalina asked anxiously as she pulled the clothes on automatically before handing Orion his jacket back. "I can't leave my boys. They need me, I-"

"Hamish Grus will take you in," Gabriel promised, moving towards her with a small knife in his hand. "Darius and Xavier will be able to come see you in time. But we have five minutes to get out of here or this path changes again and you need to add some blood to the bed for evidence before we can go."

Catalina looked completely overwhelmed but she took the knife and cut into her arm, her blood spilling onto the charred remains of the bed. Gabriel caught her arm when he was satisfied it was enough and healed her.

She still didn't seem entirely convinced about leaving though, so I gave her a light push towards the door, urging her to just go.

The fires were growing all around us, licking up the walls and setting the curtains alight as they spread and smoke filled the air.

"Christopher will know the truth when he wakes," I pointed out, but Gabriel just smirked like an all-knowing bastard and tossed Orion a little bottle of potion.

"Memory wipe," he explained. "And I had to give up a night alone with my wife to get my hands on that so fast, so you'd better know how much you fucking owe me for it, Orio."

"And no one's gonna question why he just conveniently lost his memory over what happened here?" I asked suspiciously as Orion shot over to pour the potion down Christopher's throat.

"Nope. Now step outside," Gabriel commanded, catching Catalina's arm and tugging her into the hall.

I followed right behind her and a splintering crack sounded from the roof of the room behind me just as Orion shot out too. A huge beam fell from the roof with an enormous crash, lumps of masonry tumbling down over Christopher where he lay on the floor and my eyes widened in surprise.

"See - no reason to question why Christopher can't remember," Gabriel said casually, tossing the door closed on the destruction and tugging Catalina into a jog as he crossed the corridor before lifting an old tapestry that hung there and pointing out a Hydra symbol on the bricks behind it.

I quickly placed my palm against it and the bricks rearranged themselves to reveal a doorway as Gabriel directed us into the hidden passage.

The rest of us followed quickly and Gabriel pulled a hidden lever which activated the earth magic embedded in the wall and closed the entrance behind us. We all fell still as the footsteps of someone coming to investigate the sounds of destruction reached us and Orion tossed a silencing bubble over us to make sure we weren't detected.

Gabriel lit a Faelight ahead of us and beckoned us into the cold passageway hidden within the walls, leading us down a long slope and on and on until we finally came to a fork in the path.

Another Faelight lit the passageway to our right and I gasped in alarm as I spotted the large figure there before Dante's features came into focus.

"Come on, Gabby, I want to get home in time to actually get some sleep tonight," he called, making me grin as Gabriel frowned at that nickname.

"What did you just call me?" he asked.

"I thought you might like your sister to have a cute little nickname for you," Dante said grinning broadly and Gabriel shook his head.

"No. No fucking way."

"I think it might catch on," Dante teased and Gabriel shook his head as he dismissed him.

"It won't. You two need to take this passage," Gabriel said, pointing to the one on our left. "Follow it to the stairs then head up one flight and exit there. No one will ever even suspect your hand in what happened to Catalina. And me and Dante will make sure she gets to Hamish safely once Darcy lets us back out of the tunnel at the far end."

"You're certain my boys will be okay?" Catalina asked, pinning me in her gaze, clearly not sure what to make of Gabriel.

"You can trust him," I swore to her. "He has The Sight. If he says this will work, then it will."

"Okay," she agreed hesitantly.

"I'm sorry, Catalina," Orion rumbled, stepping closer to her with his eyes full of pain. "If I'd known what Lionel was doing to you, I would have-"

"Shhh," she breathed, reaching out to cup his jaw in her hand and soothing him like he was her child. "I want you to know I'm sorry too. For flirting with you and making you so uncomfortable. I've never seen you that way, Lance. You're like one of my boys." A tear slid from her eye as she pulled him close and wrapped her arms around him. "I was just trying to warn you about Lionel but the spells he put on me made it almost impossible, and now it's too late-"

"It's not your fault," Orion growled, holding her tightly. "I'm sorry I didn't see it, but I swear we'll make him pay one day. You're free now. That's all that matters."

"We have to go," Gabriel said so firmly that none of us questioned it and Orion released her so that we could all go our separate ways.

Orion lit a Faelight as we hurried up the passageway and I kept close beside him, hoisting my skirt up so that I could move faster in my dress and heels.

When we reached the end of the passage where Gabriel had told us to exit, Orion caught my arm suddenly, his eyes full of anguish as he looked at me.

"She was trying to tell me," he said roughly, his fingers digging in.

"Tell you what?" I asked in confusion.

"Whenever she came pawing at me or flirting with me, she always used to say the same things over and over. Always the same words in the same order and I was so caught up in being horrified that my friend's mother was trying it on with me that I never really thought about what she was really saying."

"What words?" I asked.

"Handsome, enamouring, lovely, powerful. And sometimes she'd add unbelievable and sexy too."

"So..."

"The first letter of each of those words spells out the message she was trying to give me. 'Help us.'"

My throat tightened and tears pricked the backs of my eyes as I realised he was right. How long had she been suffering under her husband's control? How long had she been forced to do anything and everything he wanted while watching him abuse the children he wouldn't even let her show affection to?

"He's a fucking monster," I hissed, throwing my arms around Orion as I saw the devastation on his features so clearly that it made me hurt even more.

"If I'd understood sooner-" he began in a horrified whisper, but I shook my head violently.

"There was nothing you could have done. But there is now," I said fiercely. "Find the Imperial Star. We're so close, Orion. The full moon is only a few days away and then you'll be able to read your father's diary and we can get our hands on it. A few days and we will have what we need to destroy him. For all of our sakes."

"You're right," he agreed with a determined snarl. "Just a few more days."

ORION

CHAPTER TWENTY FIVE

With Catalina gone, something in me settled. But to see the woman who'd been suppressed within her all these years had left me feeling guilty and ashamed. She'd tried to ask for my help and I hadn't seen the wood for the trees. It was another black mark against my name. I wondered if the queen had told my father what I'd become. Just a nothing, nobody who made too many poor choices.

I'd spent years trying to ensure Darius could be strong enough to fight his father, my own hunger for vengeance thriving on his. But the Vegas returning had changed everything. And with hours alone with just myself for company, I started to run over all the decisions I'd made and started questioning everything. Every one of them but her. I couldn't regret her.

I should have done more to help Clara.

I should have pushed Darius harder, got him ready to fight Lionel before any of this ever happened.

I should have helped the Vegas from day one.

But I guessed if what Jasper had said was right, I'd always been on the right path. I was meant to end up in prison to meet him. I just wished it hadn't cost me Darcy.

I rubbed my eyes, draining the last of the bourbon in my glass and sighing as I knew it was the end of my supply. Darius would bring me more, even though he cursed me for it every time. I was fast slipping back into old habits, but whereas alcohol had once given me some relief from my demons, nothing could rid me of the loss of my girl. I'd considered calling her a hundred times during this evening alone, but I always ended up talking myself out of it. Just because I wasn't in Darkmore, didn't mean I was free. I was still a Power Shamed loser who would never hold any kind of position in society again.

once Lionel was done with me, I'd be back behind bars for the remainder of my sentence.

I'd considered running, talking it out with Darius over and over. But even if I made it beyond the barrier and Darius stardusted me away before I was caught, what use would I be then? Lionel would hunt me to the ends of the earth. Darius would be put under surveillance, his memories tapped into if he ever came to visit me. And there was no way he would be able to keep away with the bond tying us. Besides, tomorrow was the full moon. And Lionel had no idea that I hadn't been reading the diary all this time. So he also wouldn't realise how important tomorrow was or what I might find.

Tory had been listening in on Vard's conversations with Lionel, and she was sure he didn't seem to have any clear idea of what was in the diary or how I was deciphering it. He only knew that I needed space to work and it would take some time. Luckily for us, that meant there was a chance that I could get the location to Darius and the twins before Lionel ever figured out I even knew where it was.

Just one more day and maybe we can finally get an advantage in this war.

My Atlas buzzed and I tugged it out of my pocket, my mind going to Darcy. I'd hoped she might ask for my help with her magic, but since I'd last seen her, I hadn't heard anything from her.

I was seriously pissed that Honey Highspell was fucking up my Cardinal Magic classes. I'd never thought I'd miss teaching, but apparently it had grown on me, because the thought of that witch standing behind my desk and treating my students like shit was infuriating. Only *I* had the right to do that.

My mood took a bigger dive as I found a message waiting for me from Seth fucking Capella. It was a photo of Darcy standing on the edge of Aqua Lake in a fitted white swimming costume that emphasised her breasts. Her hair was dripping wet and shining in the sunlight so I guessed it had been taken earlier today. There were other students around her in the water and from the looks of it, this was Physical Enhancement. Underneath the photo was a caption from Seth. *Boner status: 10/10.*

My fangs snapped out and it took every ounce of self control I had not to break the Atlas in my palms as my fingers crushed it. It was my only line of communication outside of this place, but fuck. Fucking *fuck.*

Another message arrived and I snarled like a tiger as I took in the next image. Seth was standing behind Darcy, her body wrapped in a towel as he hugged her and snapped the shot of them, his head resting on top of hers. She was pressing a finger to her lips, a wild mischief in her expression that made me want to rip my own eyes out.

The caption below it said: *No law can keep me from my girl.*

I lost it, pushing out of my seat and tossing my Atlas away from me before I did anything stupid with it. I started pacing, clawing at my hair and panting heavily. I was going to kill him. Tear his fucking head off slow enough that he felt every bone snap under my hands. I squeezed my eyes shut as I tried to rid myself of images of them together. Hugging, kissing, fucking.

"*No,*" I spat, snatching up a wooden chair and launching it at the wall.

It shattered into fifty pieces, but it wasn't enough. I needed to see Seth torn into fifty pieces, not a fucking chair. I needed to make him hurt, make him fucking scream.

The sliding door opened and I wheeled around with a growl, my gaze falling on the girl stepping in.

The air rushed out of my body and my heart free fell in my chest. I'd longed for her to come and see me since I'd arrived here, but she'd never appeared. Even when Lionel had come to visit, he'd only ever brought Tory. Not her. But now my sister was stepping into this house, looking curious yet nothing like herself. Her hair was a dark sea of shadow and her body was wrapped in the same substance, the dress coiling around her flesh. I finally had her alone. And I didn't know how the fuck to act.

"Clara," I rasped, rushing toward her, but before I could get close, she locked down the shadows in me, making me slam to a halt a few feet from her.

"Hello, baby brother," she purred, cocking her head to one side as she moved further into the summerhouse. "I'm not supposed to be here." She giggled, looking around mischievously. "Daddy doesn't want me visiting you."

"And why not?" I demanded, my blood heating as she drifted through the room like a wraith.

My stomach twisted as I examined her. She wasn't herself. The shadows had consumed her. But I'd seen pieces of my sister in her eyes, so surely she could come back to me? Tory had. So why not her?

"Because you're a bad, bad boy," she said with a psychotic smile. She climbed up onto the back of the couch, tiptoeing along it as she gazed down at me with intrigue.

"Listen to me," I gritted out. "Lionel's your enemy, you're trapped in the shadows."

She flicked her hand and I yelled out as the shadows wrapped around my insides, squeezing until it felt like my organs were going to burst. I only managed to stay on my feet because she was keeping me upright with her power. "Don't you dare say a nasty word against Daddy. He looks after me, he *loves* me."

"He doesn't love anything but himself," I snarled and Clara shrieked like I'd struck her.

She leapt off of the couch, landing in front of me and grabbing my face between her hands, taking in the familiar freckles dotting her nose. Her touch was ice cold and her eyes were clouded with shadow. Beneath them was a glimmer of my sister though, just waiting there to come out. *I know you're in there.*

"Clara," I croaked. "Don't you remember me?"

Her gaze moved over my face, the anger in her features slipping away until a longing filled them instead. Tears started rolling down her cheeks and she drew in a small and hopeful breath.

"Lance," she breathed, falling forward and holding onto me. The shadows stopped controlling my body and I gasped, wrapping my arms around her, her slight frame pressing to mine. Her shoulders shuddered and her nails dug into my back in desperation. "Help me," she sobbed. "Don't let me go. Let it end here. No more, no more, no more."

Pain spilled through me at her words and I wished I knew what to do. I pressed her back, my heart thrashing as I caught her chin and tilted her head up to look at me. Her lower lip quivered and the fog cleared in her eyes, so her beautiful ebony irises shone back at me.

"Is it really you?" I asked in desperation and she nodded.

"I'm here. I'm always here," she said with a choked noise. "But *she's* here too."

"What do you mean?" I demanded, holding onto her as I tried to figure out what to do. How the fuck could I help her??

She snarled suddenly, jerking away from me and whipping a hand out. The shadows forced me to the ground on my front and her bare foot dug into my spine. "Worthless little beast, don't you touch me. Only my king can touch me!"

The shadows dug deeper, burrowing into my chest as agony splintered through my limbs. My jaw locked as I was held in their power and felt them winding around my heart, squeezing, squeezing, squeezing.

"It's going to go pop, and then you'll never upset me or Daddy again," she hissed and I fought harder, trying to get away, but her power was all consuming.

"Stop!" Tory's voice filled the air. "Our king wants him alive. He'll hate you if you kill him."

Clara paused, both of her heels driving into my back as she stood fully on top of me. "Hate me?" she gasped.

"Yes, he told me so himself," Tory said firmly and the shadows suddenly loosened, letting me go so a breath of relief escaped me. "He's looking for you."

"Oh Daddy, what have I done?!" Clara ran out the door with a burst of Vampire speed, disappearing into the dark.

I pushed myself to my feet, healing myself. "Thank you," I sighed and Tory smiled sadly, knocking the door closed behind her.

It haunted me every day knowing my sister was fucking Lionel Acrux. That she was imprisoned by the shadows. She wasn't herself. I just didn't know what to do. Tory had her Phoenix to help keep the shadows away now, but unless Darcy worked out how to drive the shadows from the rest of us, I didn't know how I could save Clara.

"I have to help her," I said heavily and Tory frowned, making me fear that she might voice what she had before. That Clara couldn't come back. That she wasn't in there. But I'd just seen it for myself. "Don't say she can't be saved," I said gruffly, turning away from her dark expression.

"I wasn't going to," she said seriously. "Actually…now I've been a slave to the shadows myself, I think that maybe you're right. But that still doesn't explain how she could be alive after all this time."

"I know," I sighed, scraping a hand over my face before looking to the empty bottle of bourbon with a need in me that wouldn't quit.

"Looking for more of this?" Tory taunted.

I turned and found an illusion shifting at her side, revealing a bottle of bourbon in her grip. I'd spent some time teaching her what I'd taught Darcy and fuck if the two of them weren't quick learners.

"You and your sister are going to surpass me one of these days." I smirked and she mirrored my expression as she offered me the bottle.

I took it, grabbing another glass for her from the kitchenette and pouring us each one, all in under two seconds. "Why are you feeding my bad habit, Tory Vega?" I asked suspiciously.

"Well I figure you can heal yourself of liver rot whenever you like so it's hardly *that* bad of a habit," she said, sipping from her glass with a smirk.

"Cheers to that." I knocked my glass against hers before draining half of mine, the burn on the way down to my stomach easing some of the suffocating pain of seeing my sister like that.

"So, I actually have another little gift for you," she said, falling onto the couch and I moved to sit in the chair opposite.

"I can't believe you remembered it's my birthday," I said in surprise and her lips popped open.

"Yeah…of course I did dude," she said, trying to play it off. "Hence all the gifts, duh."

"It's tomorrow." I grinned tauntingly and she scowled.

"Alright, whatever, I didn't remember. But I clearly get brownie points because my subconscious was like 'bring Lance a bunch of cool shit.' And I'll even let you off the dick kick today as I'm feeling extra generous. So do you want my gift or not?"

"Go on then. But unless it's a key to my freedom, the reinstating of my position of power in society, and your sister wrapped in a bow in a mood to forgive me, it's probably not gonna be what I want."

She sniggered. "Keep dreaming about the second two. But the first one…" She wiggled her eyebrows and reached into her pocket, taking out a gold ring with a red stone embedded in the top. "I found this in the King's quarters today," she whispered. "I think it was my father's."

"Oh Tory…I couldn't wear that."

The twins had told me all about the vision they'd had of their father being Dark Coerced by Lionel, and it had fucked with my head ever since. I'd hated the Savage King on principle for years. I'd wanted more than anything for Darius and the other Heirs to claim the throne together so the Vegas couldn't take it back from them, fearing the blood of their father running in their veins. But I'd been so fucking wrong. Not just about them, but about him. The whole kingdom had blamed Hail Vega for the atrocities he'd caused, and all along it had been his devious friend whispering in his ear instead. It changed everything. And nothing. Because it was done, history. But it gave me a thousand more reasons to despise the Dragon King. *As if I need any more of those.*

I'd been a total hypocrite anyway, worrying about what the Vega twins might become back then based off of their father. I'd always stood by Darius despite how awful Lionel was. Maybe bad people were born not bred.

"You can and you will." Tory jumped up. "So, the other day me and Gabriel made one of these rings for him and I decided to make you one too. I used a little binding spell to put my blood in this stone here and spelled it with some of my magic too. Which basically means this is a key to the King's passages." Her eyes sparkled excitedly and the bottom dropped out of my gut.

"I can't go beyond the shadow boundary either way," I said, my eyes fixed on that ring.

"Except, I think I can maybe let you," she said, moving toward me and reaching for my wrists. Her fingers wound around the dark rings of shadow twisting beneath my flesh and I looked up at her in concern.

"What if Clara can feel it?" I asked.

"She won't," Tory said confidently. "Because I'm not going to break the bonds. I'm going to shield them." Shadows coiled out from her palms and I felt the call of them in my bones, begging me to sink into their hungry embrace. A sigh left me as she pressed them beneath my skin and their cool touch wrapped around my wrists. The bonds were slightly larger now, but it wasn't noticeable as she shut her eyes and whispered something under her breath I didn't understand. It barely sounded like her voice at all and my blood chilled at the thought of the shadows speaking through her.

"There," she said, stepping back with darkness swirling around her irises. "That should work."

"I can't run," I told her, shaking my head. "Even if this does work, I can't leave this place. Lionel will have the FIB hunt me to the ends of the earth. I wouldn't be able to help you or Darcy or-"

"I know," she said, her brows pulling together. "But this means you can come and go without Lionel ever knowing. And when it's time to run, you can. It'll be better than him throwing you back into Darkmore, right?"

The weight of what she was offering pressed down on my heart and though I didn't like the idea of living the rest of my life on the run if Lionel remained in power, at least it was an option. And possibly a better one than twenty five years in prison. When I'd found a way to save Clara, when the twins had the Imperial Star…if it all came together, maybe then I could go.

I opened my mouth to thank her, but she spoke over me before I could.

"Let's see if it actually works first," she said with a nervous laugh, drawing me up from my seat and gesturing toward the secret hatch in the kitchenette.

I reached for the ring and she handed it over, the brush of her magic humming from the metal as I slid it onto my thumb and making me feel weirdly close to her as I looked up and gave her a smile.

"Ah, shit, you're gonna cry, aren't you?" she teased. "Suck it up, dude, I can't deal with you getting all emotional on me."

"As if," I scoffed, twisting the ring back and forth as I got used to the feeling of it sitting there. "But Darius might when he realises I'm clearly your favourite."

"Uh huh. You can tell him I got down on one knee when I gave it to you too, give him something to really get worked up over."

"I think I prefer my head attached to my shoulders thanks all the same," I joked and she nodded towards the kitchenette again to remind me of what I was supposed to be doing.

I walked over to it, crouching down and pressing my hand to the faint Hydra mark hidden in the pattern of the floor tiles. It lit up under my touch and I looked up at Tory with my heart pounding. "Well fuck me."

"No thanks, dude." She grinned as I opened the hatch.

"It wasn't an offer." I smirked.

"It's still a no." She nodded to the hatch. "Go on, see if you can get out of here. What's the worst that can happen?"

"Lionel will eat me whole in Dragon form then shit me back out just so I can continue to work on finding the Imperial Star?" I suggested and she laughed.

"If it sets off the alarm, you can shoot back here and I'll tell Lionel I got carried away torturing you and threw you across the boundary. He won't bother to question me because he thinks I'm his little lap dog."

"Alright. Fuck it." I dropped down into the tunnel and shot away with a burst of speed. I took a left as the path split, mentally mapping out the grounds above me in my mind and tearing along in the dark with a whoop of exhilaration. I hadn't run this fast in too long, it felt fucking incredible. I reached the far end of the tunnel and cast a Faelight above me, hunting around the dead end with a frown.

Another Hydra symbol caught my gaze and I shot toward it, pressing my hand to the mark so it lit up like a star. My pulse drummed in my ears as the roots above me in the earth twisted and grew down, forming a stairway that led above ground. I hurried up it, finding myself out in a dark wood that must have been beyond the palace walls.

A laugh escaped me then I raced back down the stairs, zooming along the tunnels as fast as I could before making it back to the hatch. I pulled myself out and looked to Tory who was smiling.

"Well?" I asked. "No alarm?"

"Nothing," she said then reached into her pocket and waved a pouch of stardust at me. "So if you ever need to run, you run like the fucking wind, got it?" She tossed me the pouch and I caught it.

"Got it," I said, grinning and tucking it into my pocket as I shut the hatch. "Where did you get that stardust from anyway?"

"Totally stole it from Darius. He's way too easy to pickpocket for someone who believes he's all powerful."

I barked a laugh, making a mental note to taunt him over that when I saw him later and Tory glanced at the clock with a frown.

"I've gotta go back to the palace," she sighed and my heart sank for her. "You'd better save some of that bourbon for your birthday tomorrow."

"Nah, no drinking tomorrow, Tory. It's the full moon."

"So you'll get to read that diary all night long like a total geek? Seems like your ideal day," she said with a hopeful expression and I gave her a tight smile.

My idea of an ideal day was something I could never have again. But I wasn't going to bother voicing that and dragging her into my ongoing pity party.

She headed to the door, waving goodbye before fixing on her resting bitch face and stepping outside. My chest tightened as I watched her go, knowing she was returning to the arms of Lionel and there was nothing I could do to help her or my sister. Not yet anyway. Darcy would figure out how to burn the shadows out of Darius then she would do it for everyone. I knew she could do it. And every time I suffered under the onslaught of fire she poured into Darius's veins, I knew it was worth it. Because she was going to work it out and free us all.

I headed back to my faithful friend bourbon and watched the clock tick around to midnight as I drowned my sorrows.

Happy birthday to me.

I thought over my last birthday with a longing in my soul, missing those times. I still had one of Darcy's IOUs tucked into my wallet, and I guessed it would stay there until it rotted now. She didn't owe me shit. Never had, never would.

My head grew fuzzy and I was definitely deep into the land of wasted when my phone buzzed.

I picked it up and found another photo sent from Seth that immediately raised my hackles. It was a picture of the rose quartz I'd given Darcy, sitting in his palm, a symbol of my love for her, my fucking commitment.

Seth:
Don't mind if I engrave this tonight and repurpose it, do you Lancey?
I couldn't get hold of any on short notice, but she just gave me the best blowjob of my life, so I really need to make sure she doesn't put those pretty lips on anyone else.

Another photo came in of him lying in Darcy's bed, one hand cupped behind the back of his head and the rose quartz held between his teeth as he grinned.

"*Motherfucker*," I spat, shoving to my feet and stumbling as my head spun. A roar of emotion blinded me, the hot, potent anger in me fogging my thoughts in a black cloud.

Fuck no. I wasn't going to let this stand. That mutt was not going to steal her from me.

I ignored the little voice in the back of my mind that said he couldn't steal what was already gone, but I wasn't listening. I'd had enough of his messages. He had to be fucking with me. There was no way Darcy would date that piece of shit. No fucking way.

I can just slip out of the palace, stardust to Zodiac Academy and check on her. No harm in that. I'm just looking out for her anyway. I could totally be there and back within half an hour. Just a quick check.

I glanced over at the hatch which seemed to be whispering my name, then down at the ring on my thumb which seemed to scream *go and kill Seth.* The inanimate objects all made good points.

I shot to the hatch, opening it and dropping down into the dark, pulling it shut behind me and speeding off into the tunnel. Only I actually smashed head first into a wall instead and knocked myself onto my ass. *Fucking drunk dick of a wall.*

I shoved myself to my feet, casting a Faelight which wobbled off ahead of me. Or maybe it was me who was wobbling. I tore off into the dark, speeding out to the far end of the tunnel and slapping my hand against the wall where the next Hydra mark lay, extinguishing my Faelight as it bumped into my head.

The stairway appeared, the roots winding together until I could climb out. As soon as I made it to the surface, I took the stardust from my pocket and struggled to focus. *I just need to go to Zodiac Academy. But I can't just stardust to my office like I used to. Gotta go to that other place. The place with the bushes and shit.*

I threw the stardust into the air and was yanked into the ether as I tried to focus on my destination. *Fucking Werewolf. I'm gonna break his legs and shove his head up the ass of a Griffin.*

The stars spat me out and suddenly I was falling. I was hundreds of feet up in the air and tumbling through the clouds. Aer Tower appeared far below me and I swore as I tried to wrangle my air magic to stop myself falling. I slammed into the wards around the academy and what felt like a thousand bolts of electricity exploded through my body as I was thrown away from it. I cried out, the world a mass of black and grey as I tried to figure out what way was up, my brain rattling in my head.

I managed to get hold of my air magic and pulled myself upright, standing in a cloud as the moon gazed down at me.

"Don't judge me," I slurred at it. "It's easy being you, all the way up there with your big, glowy head and your smug little crater face." I threw another pinch of stardust over myself and was transported away again, getting the last word with the moon and this time landing in a bush beyond the fence. *Ha.*

I got up off my ass and headed to the fake bar in the fence that would let me into the academy, walking fast toward it. My forehead collided with the metal and a loud dong rang out that echoed through my skull. *Nope. Not that one.*

I sidestepped, moving through the next one and onto the academy grounds. *This is definitely a good idea.*

I should probably illusion up my body though.

I lifted a hand, running a palm over my chest and face, casting some sort of illusion that would make me look like a Wolf in my Order form roaming campus. Or was it a Pegasus? Anyway, I was definitely hidden if someone spotted me. Which they wouldn't, because I could move as fast as a Harpy with its wings on fire.

I made it to the path that led up to Aer Tower, coming to a halt outside and craning my neck as I gazed up towards Darcy's room. *What if she's fucking him right now? I'm definitely going to break stuff. The window. Seth's neck. Any semblance of respect Darcy still has for me.*

Oh fuck. I gazed at the stars, shaking my head at them. *You wouldn't do that to me. Come on, I've suffered enough, haven't I? Don't let her be fucking him. I'll make a deal with you right now. You can have a limb. Any limb. Just pick a limb.*

The glittery shitbags remained deathly quietly, but I had the feeling they were laughing at me. Yeah, it must have looked so fucking funny all the way up there. With their shiny pals all placing bets on which Fae would crack first under their bullshit. *Well the joke's on you guys, I cracked a long time ago.*

Wait...

"Ahh!" a girl screamed bloody murder and I dropped my head, finding Kylie Major stepping out of the tower, her snake hair bursting from the crown of her head and standing on end in fright.

My heart lurched and I whipped my hand out on a knee jerk reaction, sending her flying away on an enormous breeze. She was thrown in the direction of The Wailing Wood and her screams faded into the distance as she cartwheeled through the sky.

She'd dropped a mirror in her wake and I hurried forward, picking it up and checking my reflection. *Oh shit.* I looked like a deranged yeti with a glittering horn poking out the centre of my face and huge fangs peeking out of my mouth.

I stared in the direction I'd launched Kylie, sure I could still hear her screams carrying to me.

I have no regrets.

I dropped the mirror and darted around the tower before using air magic to shoot myself up it at fifty miles an hour. I landed on Darcy's windowsill with surprising grace, then gazed inside, cloaking myself in an illusion of shadow as my eyes fell on the bed. The covers were pulled over a couple fucking like rabbits and my breathing grew out of control as I became nothing but a carnivorous beast looking for its next kill. I was about to force the window open and kill Seth with my bare hands, when the covers were thrown back and I realised it wasn't them at all. Just a couple of dudes having the time of their lives. *Oh, wrong room.*

I carried myself up another level, figuring out where I was then landing on the next windowsill along.

A spill of blue hair made my gut clench and I gazed in at her curled up in bed between the paws of a white Wolf. My heart fractured and my body deflated as I watched them together. My eyes tracked over her face, her expression taut like she was trapped in a painful nightmare, but then Seth nuzzled into her in his sleep and the tension in her features eased.

"Blue…" I rasped, inching forward, pressing my hand to the glass as I prepared to smash my way in there and make the Wolf bleed and hurt and beg for a mercy I was never going to give.

But then a moment of clarity gripped me.

I couldn't go in there. I'd lost the right to do that when I'd given her up. When I'd given up everything. And no matter how much I wanted to destroy Seth for this – and I really, really fucking did - I couldn't. I'd forced her away. Told her to move on. I'd just never been prepared for the fact that she'd actually listen.

I hadn't thought my heart could break any more than it already had, but apparently there was a little left of it still to shatter.

I turned and jumped off of the ledge, lowering myself down with my air magic and hitting the ground running. There was only one place I wanted to be now. I ran to Ignis House, casting myself up to Darius's room on a gust of air and feeling myself slip through his wards as they allowed me access. I pushed his window open, dropping into his room and he shot upright in bed with flames roaring in his palms.

"Who are you?!" he bellowed, his face twisting in horror at the sight of me. He launched the flames at me and I threw out a blast of water to douse them before they could burn me to dust.

"Darius," I snapped. "It's me."

"Lance?" he gasped in confusion and I nodded. "By the fucking sun, what kind of illusion is that?"

"Oh right," I muttered, waving a hand to dissolve it.

"How did you get here? Are you running? Do we need to go?" He jumped out of bed, starting to grab his stuff and a smile pulled at my mouth.

"No, brother." I shot toward him, knocking him back onto the bed and winding my arms around him. He pulled me closer with a sigh of relief as our foreheads pressed together.

"Tory found a way for me to get out." I showed him the King's ring, explaining the situation.

"You're drunk," he accused when I was done and I shrugged one shoulder.

"I'm not *not* drunk," I admitted and he pressed his fingers to my temple, starting to heal away the effects of the bourbon. With every inch my mind that cleared, the more regrets I started to have. *Ah fuck, I shouldn't have come here.*

I groaned, rubbing my eyes and rolling onto my back, my heart feeling pulverised by a blender by what I'd just seen. Darius propped himself up on his elbow, frowning down at me.

"What's going on?" he asked and I sighed.

"Seth is with Darcy. The two of them-" I pressed my lips tightly together, unable to finish that sentence as rage and possessiveness clogged up my throat. Jealousy didn't come close to describing how I was feeling. I was being eaten alive by the need to lay my claim on her and snap the neck of the motherfucker who *dared* lay his filthy hands on her.

"What? They're not together," he said and I frowned at him.

"I just saw them in the same bed," I growled.

"Yeah well, Seth does that with any of his friends when they're sad," he said with a shrug like it meant nothing. But it meant everything.

"It's more than that," I muttered, taking my Atlas out and showing him the photos Seth had sent me.

"What..." Darius breathed as he scrolled through them. "This isn't right."

"Well maybe they're keeping it a secret," I said, my breathing getting laboured as I thought of that. *I* was her deepest secret, not him. Not fucking *him*. At least...I had been.

"I'll find out, okay?" he promised and I nodded, though I knew it wasn't enough just knowing. I was never going to feel right again whether she was with fucking Seth, or some other guy. I didn't care how irrational it was, I wanted to maim and torture and destroy anyone who dared to try and claim her heart. A heart she'd given to *me*.

"I told her to move on, but I can't let go, Darius," I gritted out, my eyes fixed on the wooden canopy over his four poster bed. "I made this happen. I pushed her away. I thought I could handle it, but I can't. I didn't think anything could be more painful than losing her, but now seeing her with *him*..." My heart was slashed open, oozing blood. *I'm not going to survive losing her. It's a long and agonising death, but the end is fucking nigh.*

"Look, I really don't think they're together, but Lance...one day she is going to move on," Darius reasoned.

"I know," I hissed, venom lacing my words, my veins. "I fucking know. And I'm gonna end up with a life sentence in Darkmore for it instead of twenty five years because whoever it is is going to fucking die."

Darius grabbed my face, yanking my head around so I was looking at him. "Then don't let her go."

I shoved him off with a growl. "She's already gone. And even if in some hypothetical reality she could forgive me and take me back, what life could I offer her now anyway? I'm fucked whichever way you look at it. I'm Lionel's prisoner for as long as he wants me, then I'll be shipped back off to Darkmore for the remainder of my sentence. Even if I can run away before that happens, I'll have to live in hiding unless we can defeat Lionel. I can't re-join society as it is, I'm a Power Shamed loser. I have no future. No way to offer her anything."

"I will kill my father," Darius vowed. "And the Heirs and I will take his place as rulers of this kingdom and-"

"Wait, what? As a Councillor to the Vega queens, you mean?" I looked up at him in confusion and his expression twisted in disgust.

"No," he scoffed. "Of course not. I don't intend to let them take the throne just because we're friends now. Where the hell did you get that idea?"

I pushed myself up to sit with a growl. "Are you fucking with me right now? You're in love with a Vega. You and the other Heirs have been working with Darcy for months and-"

"And what? You thought I was just going to stand aside and give them a clean shot at my father? Let them take the throne like I'm some sort of weak Fae who couldn't claim it myself? They might be powerful, but they aren't stronger than the Heirs so why the hell would we just give it to them? That's not how it works," he said in disbelief.

"It's not about weakness," I snarled, getting up in his face. "It's about what's best for the kingdom."

"And you think *they're* what's best?" he asked in astonishment. "You're the one who's been training me up all these years to take my father's place. Now you're just switching allegiance?" he demanded.

"I'm not switching allegiance," I said seriously, gripping the back of his head to make him look me in the eye. "I want you in power, Darius. But they're the rightful queens. My father was a part of the Zodiac Guild, he protected the royals, the queen came to him with a vision that showed him the way."

"You've told me all of this," he snarled. "But you're just going on the word of some dead old man who was locked up in Darkmore for years."

"I had a letter from my father. And you know it's more than that. The twins have been gifted visions from the stars. They've *seen* the truth. The Savage King wasn't who we thought. What Hail Vega did was because of Lionel's Dark Coercion. He's been biding his time all these years, he constructed it all."

"I've been training my entire life to rule this kingdom," Darius growled, his eyes turning to the golden slits of a Dragon as smoke plumed between his teeth. "I will take down my father and I will rule alongside the other Heirs. The Vegas will not sit on the throne."

I fell quiet, seeing the blazing determination in his eyes, the stubbornness that was never going to fade.

"Rule with them," I begged, but he shook his head.

"No," he hissed. "And the other Heirs will never stand for that either. We might be friends with the Vegas, Lance, but when it comes to the throne, we *will* fight them to claim it."

I released a heavy breath, knowing I wasn't going to change his mind. I pushed out of bed, heading to the window and running my fingers through my hair.

"I'll always have your back, brother," I swore and silence pooled between us.

"I'll come home for when the moon rises tomorrow," he said at last.

341

"See you then," I said gravely, opening the window.

I cast an illusion over myself before leaping from the window ledge and racing away into the night.

I spent the next day alone, anxiously waiting for the sun to set while Darius and Xavier attended the lavish funeral Lionel had put on for Catalina. As Gabriel had predicted, there had been a brief, but very public trial for Christopher and he'd been sentenced to life in Darkmore for abducting, raping and murdering the Queen. I was actually surprised that Lionel hadn't pushed for an execution, but I was guessing he just wanted it over with and this way he could move on.

I'd watched a little bit of the ridiculously over the top funeral on TV, but the fake grief Lionel displayed had been more than enough to turn my stomach and I'd turned it off after watching the horse drawn hearse leading an enormous procession down the street.

The papers were full of stories about how beloved Catalina had been and how terribly she'd be missed, and I had to wonder what people would think if they knew the truth of the life Lionel had forced her to live.

Geraldine had told everyone that Catalina was well hidden with her father and was settling in just fine, promising to arrange a visit for Darius and Xavier as soon as possible. I was just glad that she'd escaped the hell of Lionel's company.

Gabriel called to wish me a happy birthday and told me the cards had mostly fallen in our favour today. The night would be clear, the moon bright, but he couldn't tell me about the details of what was to come in case it changed things. Everything was looking relatively good though. Luckily, Lionel was going to be away tonight, milking Catalina's funeral for all it was worth and giving Darius and I a clear opportunity to read my father's diary.

As the last rays of sunlight dripped through the summerhouse windows, my pulse began to pound. Night slid into existence and a blanket of stars spread across the sky as I waited anxiously for the moon to rise.

After a while, one of Lionel's henchmen showed up to cast a ward around the perimeter of the summerhouse and lock me in for the night. I casually flipped him the finger while he worked and he scowled at me before heading away.

The moon soon peeked out above the trees beyond the pool and I moved to fetch the diary from my nightstand with my heart rate elevating. The leather binding was etched with stars and I ran my thumb across it, feeling closer to my father for a second. I thought about him a lot lately. About all the secrets he'd hidden, about the sacrifice he'd made for the entire kingdom.

If I'd had any doubts at all about him being a good man in the past, they were thoroughly squashed now. I just wished I'd gotten the chance to know him beyond my childhood. That he could have been there when I needed him most. When Lionel had bound me to Darius, when I'd not known what paths to take.

I guessed this diary was proof that he'd had faith in me, and there was some comfort in that. But it wasn't the same as having had a parent to rely on, someone who could have offered me guidance when I was lost.

I hope I'm not a fuck up in your eyes, Dad. Even if the rest of the world thinks so.

The sliding door sounded and I turned, finding Darius walking in wearing a black t-shirt and jeans, something gripped in his hand.

"Happy birthday, Lance," he said with a slanted smile as he offered up the gift which looked like it had been wrapped by a kid. I smirked as I shot over to him and took it, ripping off the paper and finding a small box inside. I opened it, gazing down at the little glass ball inside which swirled with the colours of a sunset.

My brows arched in surprise. "Is this a memento?"

"Yeah." Darius combed a hand through his hair. "Look, I don't wanna fall out with you over the Vegas. My father forced you to be on my side no matter what by making you my Guardian and I'm not gonna make you feel shitty about making your own mind up about the throne. We'll just have to agree to disagree." His brow furrowed. "And even though my mom isn't really dead, being at her funeral today made me think about how easily you can lose the people you love. I won't lose you because I don't like your opinions on something that hasn't even come to pass yet."

I twisted the orb between my fingers, gazing at him and noticing how much of a man he'd become recently. "I'm always in your corner, Darius," I said seriously. "But I know what I'm asking of you is a lot."

"You're still asking it then?" he jibed and I grinned.

"No point denying it." I shrugged and he folded his arms, jerking his chin at the memento.

"Aren't you gonna put my ball in your mouth then?" he asked.

I laughed. "Alright, but only because you asked so nicely, sugar." I reached for his zipper and he snorted, batting my hand away.

"Get on with it, asshole," he pushed and I lifted the orb to my lips and pushed it into my mouth.

The world around me changed. I was suddenly on top of a mountain sitting on the back of a huge golden Dragon. My heart lifted at the sight of the incredible sunset beaming out toward us above a sea of cloud below. Pastel colours bled into the sky, all of it painfully temporary as the sun sank away beneath the horizon. Darius released a booming roar then took off, sending snow crumbling out beneath his talons as he carried me toward the sunset. I felt the wind on my face, the lasting heat of the sun's ray against my flesh. The memory was perfectly captured, the magic of it astounding.

Darius circled away from the sun and I gazed at the seam in the sky where night divided from day, a pool of stars chasing away the light. Darius raced toward them until it felt like the heavens were going to swallow us up and peace caressed my heart.

I took the memento from my mouth and the memory evaporated around me so I was stood gazing at my closest friend once more.

"We'll go there again one day," he promised. "Somehow, we'll figure out all this bullshit. I just wanted you to have a piece of something good. A time when things were better."

I gave him a sad sort of smile and he moved forward to embrace me. I clapped him on the back knowing with absolute certainty that, Guardian bond or not, Darius Acrux was a friend made for me by the stars themselves. And nothing would ever change that.

"Shall we find out what my father knew?" I asked and he nodded as he pulled away, tension lining his brow.

I placed the memento in the drawer by my nightstand then headed to the sliding door, following Darius outside where we moved to sit at a table next to the pool. I laid the diary down as Darius started casting illusions to hide us and a silencing bubble too.

The full moon was hidden behind a small gathering of clouds above, but as I flipped open the first page of the diary, the clouds shifted and silvery light filtered over us like a fog. Letters lit up on it in silver, shimmering like stardust as they twisted around the paper then settled into place in dark ink, the light falling away. I held my breath as I tracked my eyes over the words and the hand drawn image of a fallen star at the bottom of the page. *This is it. This is what we've been waiting for.*

Your first and most urgent task.

-

Dearest Lancelot,

It's time for you to learn the ways of the Zodiac Guild. The last of us lie dead, but I am the only one who found a grave. My death was planned meticulously for this purpose. And in my death, I can only hope you are the man Queen Vega foresaw you to be.

It is time for you to resurrect the Guild. You will take Ling Astrum's position as Guild Master and initiate your most trusted, loyal friends to its cause.

The Imperial Star awaits you in my tomb at The Everhill Graveyard. Know this, it can only be wielded by a reigning sovereign, so it must stay out of Lionel Acrux's hands if he has ascended to the throne.

If things have gone as hoped, you will have access to the rings of the Vega Princesses. Both are needed to open the tomb, but be warned, this ancient graveyard is heavily protected. Only those proficient in dark magic can enter.

Go now while the stars are in alignment.
You can do this, my boy.

Holy shit. My dad had a grave. I recalled my mom telling me he'd been cremated. She even had an urn on her mantlepiece. Had it all been a farce?

"Well this has been a waste of time," Darius sighed and I looked up at him.

"What?" I balked.

"The moon isn't doing shit," Darius said, gesturing to the diary with a frown. "Maybe it needs to lay in the moonlight for a while?"

"You can't see it?" I asked in surprise.

"Wait, you can?" he gasped, shifting closer.

I nodded, a laugh escaping me. "I guess it's for my eyes only. Actually, my dad mentioned something about that in his letter to me-"

"What does it say, asshole?" he demanded.

"It says where the Imperial Star is," I whispered, my heart pounding excitedly. "And we need to go get it right fucking now."

I stood from my seat, pushing the diary into my pocket and Darius jumped up with a dark, unbridled wildness in his eyes. I'd continue reading tonight just as soon as we had the Imperial Star.

"Fuck yes."

"The only thing is, it looks like we won't be able to use it. It says only a reigning sovereign can wield it," I sighed.

"Well let's at least keep it the fuck away from my father," Darius said firmly and I nodded.

"You'd better remember everything I taught you, because my dad says we'll need dark magic to reach it. Have you kept all of my artefacts?" I asked.

"All of them," he confirmed. "They're at the academy."

"We need the twins' rings too, the ones their mother left for them," I said and Darius nodded, his brows pulling together. "Alright. Do you know where we're going?"

"Yes, my dad has a tomb at The Everhill Graveyard in western Lacrovia. The Imperial Star's with him," I said with a grin, remembering visiting the place as a boy. My dad had taken me there to steal bones, using his gifts to gain access to some of the crypts and graves that were less protected, though he'd always warned me not to attempt it at night. And never alone. We didn't have much choice but to go this second though; there was no time to waste with Lionel out of town and the stars in alignment for us.

"Fuck yes. Then we'll go to Zodiac. You can get into King's Hollow and you'll find all of the artefacts in the chest in my room while I get the ring from Roxy," Darius said.

"Okay," I agreed, my heart pumping with excitement for the first time in a long time. "Let's go and get one up on the King."

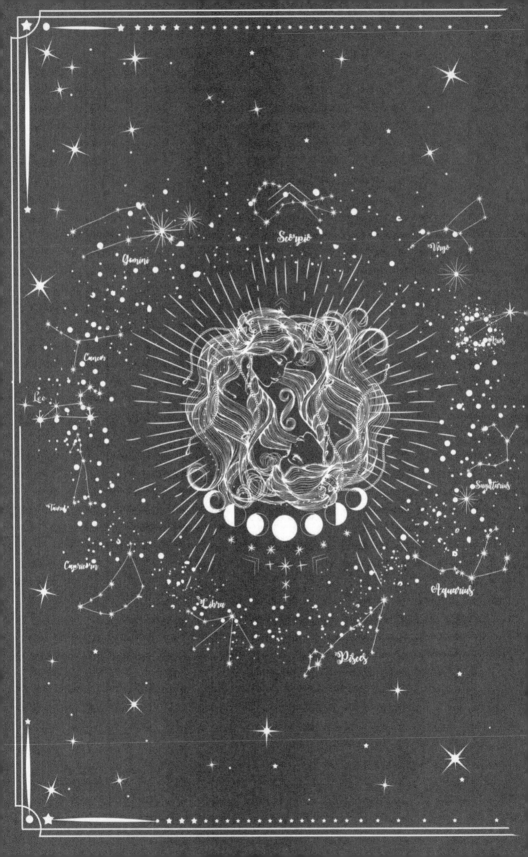

DARCY

CHAPTER TWENTY SIX

"I can feel your amusement from a mile away," Max drawled from his seat as me and Geraldine tried to sneak up on him with an orb of water cast between us, hanging over his head.

"You can feel no such thing, Maxy boy," Geraldine said airily. "I am feeling nothing but contempt for you, you salacious sealion."

"Bullshit." Max twisted around in his armchair and Geraldine and I dropped the water on his head.

He threw out a palm, casting it away from himself at the last second as he wrangled the Element and we dove to the floor as the water went crashing over our heads while we squealed. Caleb shot out of its path just as Seth burst through the door behind him into the Hollow, taking the full brunt of it and tumbling back down the stairs.

We all burst out laughing and Seth came running back into the room with a vine in his hand which he struck like a whip, breaking a hole in the floorboards. "Alright, which one of you water Elementals did it?" He narrowed his eyes at me and Geraldine on the floor, then looked to Max who had slipped casually back down into his chair like nothing had happened.

"Right, c'mere." Seth whipped the vine and grabbed Geraldine by the ankle with it, dragging her toward him.

I caught her hand with a laugh as she wailed like a banshee and I was hauled across the floor with her.

"Let me go, my lady!" Geraldine cried. "I shall go into the eternal night for you. You must live on to produce many a babe with the most handsome of kings!"

"Well that would be me then." Caleb shot forward, diving onto my back and clinging on as Seth heaved us all across the floor.

"*Caleb*," I laughed as he tickled me to try and make me let go of Geraldine.

"Let the Wolf have her!" Caleb cried dramatically and I lost my grip on her, leaving Seth to yank Geraldine across the floor at his feet and he started binding her with more vines.

"Fungal festoons!" she wailed. "I die in the name of my queens! I will be remembered as Grus the Great. The most loyal of friends, fiercest of allies-"

"Not today, Gerry!" Max leapt over me and Caleb, running at Seth, his footsteps pounding across the floor.

He blasted Seth with a gust of air that sent him stumbling back and Seth howled as he cast vines at Max's legs to trip him up.

"I'm your real enemy!" Max cried.

"*You* did it?" Seth feigned shock with a snort of amusement then Max Pitball tackled him as he leapt over Geraldine and they started wrestling on the floor.

Caleb shot to his feet, whipping me up and throwing me over his shoulder before racing over to toss me into the dog pile, diving into it himself. Seth's teeth sank into my arm and I yelped, smacking him with a laugh.

Geraldine broke her binds, launching herself at us with a yell and grabbing a fistful of Seth's hair, wrapping her legs around his waist from behind as she fell backwards to wrench him away from me. My leg got caught under hers and Max's face smooshed into my stomach as Caleb kicked him in the head. We were a tangle of limbs and we all started belly laughing as none of us could get up.

The door flew open and my laugh stuttered out like a car running out of gas as I stared up at Orion in the doorway, gazing down at us all in shock. *Ohmagod.*

"What the fuck?" Max balked, managing to get up and pulling me after him.

I knew that Tory had given him a way out of the palace, but it still didn't make me any less surprised to see him here. What the hell was going on?

Geraldine leapt up, lifting her chin and pointing at Orion. "Treacherous lech! Why are you here?" she demanded.

"Watch it, Grus," Orion said in a low voice, his eyes moving over the rest of us and pausing on me.

"What's going on?" I asked, stepping forward as worry hit me. Was it Tory? Darius?

"I need to talk to you. Alone," he said, glancing at the others like he was hoping they'd all fuck off.

"No," I said immediately. "Whatever it is, you can say it to all of us. We don't keep secrets anymore."

His jaw ticked and Max folded his arms beside me, saying he was going absolutely nowhere.

"She's right, dude," Caleb said. "Spit it out."

"Or are you just here to try and convince Darcy to take you back? Because this dramatic declaration is pretty lame so far," Seth threw in, making heat rise in my damn cheeks.

"Shut your mouth," Orion snapped at him. "I'm here about the Imperial Star."

"Did you find something in the diary?" I asked, my heart jackhammering in my chest.

He nodded, his jaw grinding as he gazed at the others, then seemed to decide he had no choice but to trust them. "I know where it is. I need you and your sister's rings. The ones your mother left for you. Darius is getting Tory's."

"What's it for?" I asked in confusion.

"I think they'll let us gain access to my father's tomb," Orion explained. "That's where the Imperial Star is. But it'll be dangerous-"

My heart jolted. "I'm coming with you," I said firmly, no room for negotiation.

"No. Me and Darius can go," he said. "No one else needs to put themselves at risk."

"I'm coming whether you like it or not," I growled and a crease formed between his eyes.

"Isn't that what you said to me last night, babe?" Seth joked and I ignored him as Orion bared his fangs, but didn't take his eyes off of me.

"It's not safe," he said firmly.

I stepped forward, lifting my chin as I gazed up at him. "I'm a Phoenix who can destroy Nymphs, who has four Elements, who's fought the shadows and won. And I will not be told no by anyone, Lance Orion."

His throat bobbed and a beat of silence passed before he snatched my hand, tugging me forward. "Fine, you can come." He pulled me down the corridor into Darius's room and kicked the door shut, which opened one second later as Geraldine threw it wide with the Heirs at her back.

Her chest was puffed out like a peacock and she had a look of war in her eyes. "You will not dismiss us, you vainglorious Vampire! Where my lady goes, I go. And though these men may seem tricksome and can be downright scallywags, they are also loyal and steadfast. If there is danger afoot, there is no better band of knights than these to follow one of the true queens into the night."

"I'm not following anyone anywhere," Max growled. "We're going for the Imperial Star, that's it."

"To stop Lionel," Caleb agreed.

"Yup," Seth added and Orion growled, his hand still tight around my wrist.

I prised his fingers off, giving him a firm look as my flesh tingled from his touch. "It's not up for debate."

"Fuck, *fine*," Orion hissed. "But you'll all do exactly as I say because this place is protected by dark magic and the spells we're gonna need aren't in the damn curriculum."

"You can't boss us around anymore, *sir*," Seth mocked. "You're just a Power Shamed nobody. You're lucky we're even acknowledging your existence and you know it."

Orion opened his mouth to snap at him again, but I got there first.

"Shut up, Seth. Do as he says. We're not fucking this up. We need to get the Imperial Star," I demanded and Seth growled at my tone, but didn't bite back.

When I turned to Orion again, I swear he was smirking, but it was gone a split second later so I couldn't be sure.

Orion gave me an intense look. "We won't be able to wield it against Lionel."

"What, why?" I asked, my heart sinking.

"It can only be used by a reigning sovereign," he said and the others cursed.

"Well so long as Lionel doesn't get it, it doesn't matter," I said firmly, though it was infuriating to know we were this close to so much power and it wouldn't be able to help us.

Orion nodded then strode over to the solid gold chest at the back of Darius's room, opening it up and taking out a wooden box of Pitball cards I recognised. He retrieved a draining dagger from it and I stiffened. I'd seen Orion stabbed with a blade like that. Tory had succumbed to the shadows so many times because of one too. I didn't want that shit near anyone I loved ever again.

He packed it up with a bunch of bones and tools in a backpack before shouldering it. Then he met my gaze and I stepped toward him, fighting away any fears I had about using this stuff, because we had to get the Imperial Star. And I'd do anything to make sure we got it before Lionel did.

"What do we need to do?" I asked.

"What happened to you and me going alone, brother?" Darius's voice boomed as he stepped into the room with Tory a few steps behind him.

I smiled at her and she grinned, pushing through the Heirs to reach my side.

"Seriously?" Orion groaned.

"Well you didn't really expect me and Darcy to just bow out, did you? I thought you'd have learned your lesson about that a long time ago," she said airily.

Geraldine let out a squeal of excitement, clapping her hands. "The Vega princesses shall never bow to anyone!"

"Uhuh," Darius said then muttered something else under his breath which sounded suspiciously like 'we'll see about that' before continuing in a louder voice. "Let's go. Get your weapons." He turned around and headed out the door, revealing the axe strapped to his back that glinted with the flames that lived within it.

"That reminds me." I looked to Geraldine in excitement. "Me and Tory made you a weapon."

"Gracious!" she gasped. "What unworldly thing could I have possibly done to deserve such a gift?"

"You're you, Geraldine," I said with an earnest look. "That's enough."

"Never change," Tory added with a smile, grabbing her hand and towing her out of the room after the Heirs.

I went to follow but Orion caught my arm, turning me back to face him with a look of uncertainty.

"Can I…" He had a long box in his arms and he placed it down on the bed with an expression of longing. The wood was carved with the Orion constellation which I'd engraved in it myself. My breath snagged in my lungs and I stepped past him, opening the box and taking out the beautiful sword forged in Phoenix fire. The one I'd made for him as a gift the night before he'd been arrested. I'd tried not to think about that night, but it was written into my soul as clearly as the zodiac was written into the stars. There was no escaping it. No way of hiding how much it had meant to me. But it only made his betrayal sting deeper.

I held it out to him with a taut frown. "It's yours. Always. Just because we're not…well, just take it, okay?" I handed it to him and his fingers brushed mine as he accepted it, an arrow of electricity firing through me from his touch.

"Tentacles on a tuna fish," Geraldine exclaimed from the other room. "Look at me go!"

I gave Orion an awkward smile and jogged out of the room, finding Geraldine with the flail we'd made for her, the spiked ball of metal swinging on a chain at the end of the huge stick. She swung it around her head, under her leg, over her shoulder, all with impossible skill.

"I've flung a flail or two in my time," she announced. "It is absolutely divine, my ladies. I couldn't be more grateful. In fact, perhaps a song is in order?"

"We don't have time for songs," Caleb growled, glancing at Darius. "Right?" His eyes were pleading and Seth slung an arm over his shoulders, his hands wrapped in his metal gauntlets.

"Don't be a killjoy, bro. Let's sing that Vega song about them sucking our cocks," Seth said with a smirk and Geraldine bristled, pointing her flail at him.

"Do not besmirch my beautiful lyrics ever again, you foul mouthed mutt!"

Max laughed and Geraldine rounded on him with a growl.

"And what are you chuckling at, you overgrown sea cucumber?" she demanded.

"Calm down, Gerry," he said.

She looked like she was about to explode, but Orion shot to the centre of the group with the sword in its scabbard at his hip. "We're leaving. Stop bickering or some of you will get left behind when we stardust out of here."

"Pfft, as if Darius would leave any of us here," Seth said but Darius folded his arms with a look that said he would and everyone fell into line.

Orion strode to the door just as my Atlas buzzed and I took it out, finding a message from my brother.

Gabriel:

The K.U.N.T.s were out in force when I stardusted home an hour ago. Let the Vampires take you and your sister to the boundary. The others won't be stopped.

Good luck tonight.

He started sending a bunch of pictures of his baby and family and my heart squeezed. Dammit that baby was cute. I just wanted to squeeze his chubby cheeks and tickle his round belly and – *oh right, I've got a life or death mission to go on that needs my attention.*

"Lance," I called to him, jogging over and showing him the message before letting the others see.

"Caleb, take Tory," Orion commanded then scooped me up before I could disagree and shot off down the stairs.

I clung to him, stifling a scream as he clutched me to his chest and moved at the speed of light, sprinting faster than he ever had with me in his arms before. I couldn't draw a single breath until we stopped and the world spun. We were standing beyond the fence of the academy and the cool night air whipped around us.

I stared up at Orion as his eyes roamed my face and my toes curled.

"You can put me down now," I said breathily, my heart hitting a wild beat and I tried to convince myself it was from the speed we'd been moving at. But who was I kidding?

He placed me on my feet and silence rippled between us as I remained snared in his eyes.

"Happy birthday," I forced out.

I'd been considering messaging him all day, but hadn't been able to bring myself to do it. Now he was right in front of me, I didn't want him to think I'd forgotten. Maybe I should have been a dick about it, but he was already spending this day as a prisoner with nothing to do and nowhere to go. Well, until now I guessed.

"It's not as happy as my last," he murmured then Caleb arrived with Tory, setting her down beside me, leaving me trapped in a happy memory of the past and wishing I could go back to it.

"Did you really need to do a lap of the whole academy?" Tory tutted, flattening her messed up hair.

"I needed to limber up before we go into battle," Caleb said with a smirk.

"We're not going into battle, we're going to a graveyard where all kinds of bullshit spells are waiting for us," Orion said.

"Well I limbered up for creepy spells then." Caleb shrugged.

Seth appeared in Wolf form with Darius and Max on his back and they all slipped through the gap in the fence. Seth shifted back, putting on some sweatpants and sneakers as Max threw them to him and pulling his hair up into a topknot. Geraldine appeared in her Cerberus form, one of her three large brown dog heads jamming between the bars as she tried to squeeze through. She was damn huge. Bigger than Seth in his Wolf form and he could barely fit.

She shifted back into her Fae form with a laugh, her breasts squashing against the bars as she moved through the gap.

"By the sun, Gerry," Max snapped, stepping forward to try and shield her from view.

"Oh do stop being a possessive porpoise, Maxy boy. It really is unbecoming." She took her clothes from him, pulling them on before snatching her flail from Darius who'd been carrying it for her.

"Let's go to war," Seth said excitedly, knocking his shoulder into Caleb's as he howled.

"We're not going to fucking…argh, never mind," Orion said, stepping closer to me and Tory. "Have you got the rings?"

"Yup. Here you go, dude." Tory held hers out, but I grabbed it before Orion could, pushing it onto my finger beside the other ring.

"Wherever these go, I go," I said with a challenge in my voice. If he thought he was going to ditch me at any point tonight for my own safety or some bullshit, it wasn't gonna happen. I was going to personally make sure that star was brought back here no matter what.

"Dammit," he muttered and I grinned triumphantly. *I knew it.*

Tory laughed. "You can't get one over on her anymore, asshole."

"I wasn't trying to-" Orion stopped himself mid-sentence, shaking his head. "Let's just fucking go." He took out some stardust, throwing it over us before anyone could say another word and we were dragged away into the stars.

My feet hit the ground, but I didn't stumble, blinking around at my friends then to the huge black metal fence rising up ahead of us. Silence fell and I could feel the power of this place humming in the air, sending a trickle of anticipation running down my spine.

Behind us was a dense forest, the shadows between the boughs as black as night. A low, doggish howl sounded somewhere within the trees and everyone stilled.

"Darius," Orion growled, a warning in his tone I didn't understand.

"What is it?" Tory hissed as I stepped closer to her.

"Reaper Hounds," Darius revealed darkly.

"They're bound here to protect the perimeter," Orion explained, casting a silencing bubble around us. "No one look them in the eyes, they'll rip the soul right out of your body if you do."

"They'll do fucking what?" Max balked.

"Rip the soul from your very being, Maxy boy, do keep up," Geraldine said, raising her flail. "All of you should go ahead, I shall face these villainous fiends for my queens. I'll dive into the dark forest and return these beasts to the hell from whence they came."

"No Geraldine," I gasped. "You're not going anywhere."

"No, you're not. Everyone needs to shut their eyes right now," Orion commanded as more howls sounded out in the trees and my heart thrashed at the noise. "Don't engage them, no matter what they do. Don't open your eyes, don't run, and do *not* fight back."

"Even if one rips my arm off?" Seth questioned. "Because I can't make any promises in that scenario."

"They won't attack unless provoked," Orion growled. "So feel free to jab one in the eye, Capella, but do it somewhere away from the rest of us."

A growl came from the trees and I caught sight of a huge black figure moving between the boughs before I slammed my eyes shut. *Oh shit.*

"Everyone hold hands and follow me, we need to get to the gate, the wards wouldn't let us stardust any closer than this," Orion said and his rough palm grasped mine.

My other hand slid into Tory's and we all started walking as more howls rang out in the forest.

My heart galloped in my chest as we walked, leaves crunching underfoot as we went, sounding like gunshots in the quiet. A snarl sounded right beside me and my breathing quickened as sniffing filled the air and the padding of heavy paws passed close by.

Hot, rancid breath made my hair flutter and my face warm. The beast must have been huge standing at least as tall as me, and the scent of rot clung to it, making my stomach turn.

"We're almost there," Orion muttered.

"You'd better not be opening your eyes," I hissed and his fingers squeezed mine.

"Someone's got to look, might as well be the Power Shamed nobody," he said under his breath and my nails dug into his flesh.

"You're not nobody," I growled seriously. *You're one of the most important somebodies I know.*

"Are you ready, Darius?" he called, not responding to me.

"Ready," Darius confirmed and a snapping noise sounded somewhere behind me.

"What's he doing?" I whispered, then another growl sounded by my ear and I flinched.

"He's casting a dark spell on a Fae bone," Orion murmured. "Reaper Hounds can't resist the scent of death."

A whoosh reached me as Darius threw the bone and the dogs howled and bayed. It sounded like a large pack of them were racing away from us, the ground shuddering beneath me as they went.

"Hurry!" Orion barked. "Everyone keep close. You can open your eyes but if there's any sign of them returning then shut them immediately."

I cracked my eyes open as Orion pulled his hand from mine and Darius raced past me. We stood in front of a huge gate which had deadly looking spikes at the top of it. Written in the iron across the middle were the words

The Everhill graveyard.

Orion passed Darius a draining dagger, holding another of his own. They both sliced into their palms before starting to move the blades in perfect synchronicity with one another, seeming to cut into the air itself. The movements were complex and each slash lessened the magical tension in the air.

A furious howl split through the night and sent a tremor of fear through me.

"I think they've figured it out," Seth hissed.

"They're coming back," Caleb said urgently, but Darius and Orion were lost to a trance as they worked to break the wards.

"Get your weapons ready," Tory gasped and everyone did so as the thumping of paws drew closer once more.

Tory and I raised our free hands, keeping our other ones locked together. My Phoenix fire burned hot against the inside of my flesh and our power instinctively merged, an inferno spinning between us, ready to be unleashed.

I shared a look with Tory then clamped my eyes shut, the howls drawing nearer and nearer.

The paws were thundering toward us at a furious pace and from the snapping of teeth and terrifying snarls, I had a feeling Seth was right. They knew what we were doing. And they were coming for blood.

"Devils of death, I will flail you into the afterlife!" Geraldine cried.

A growl sounded then a yelp followed as a blow was struck against one of the beasts and my heart lurched.

I kept my palms raised, flames curling between my fingers as I waited to attack, pushing my earth magic into the ground as I used it to sense their approach.

A snarl sounded right ahead of us and I felt Tory press closer as we raised our hands together and stepped away from our friends to make sure we didn't hurt them. I could feel the hound's breath, taste its sickly scent on the air and feel the shudder of its paws in the ground through my magic. We released the power of our Phoenix in an explosion of fire, a rush of adrenaline scoring through my veins. The flames blazed through my eyelids as it wheeled away from us and one of the beasts yelped and screeched.

"Fuck yes!" Tory whooped and a grin spread across my face.

Our victory was short lived though as howls sounded out in the woods, revealing more beasts waiting in the dark.

"Get back!" I called to the others and Tory and I cast a wall of fire ahead of us to keep the hounds at bay.

My back hit Darius's and suddenly I was falling, stumbling backwards and passing through the wards surrounding the graveyard.

"Get inside!" Orion roared, grabbing my arm and keeping me upright as he steered me around and I dragged Tory after me. The sound of clanging metal filled the air then my feet hit softer ground. "Open your eyes," he commanded and I did, finding myself looking up at him, his brow etched with concern.

I wheeled around, checking everyone was okay and, miraculously, they were. I shared a look of relief with Tory before gazing around the dark graveyard we were standing in.

Tombstones stretched out ahead of us, all of them ancient and crumbling, marked with zodiac symbols and the names of the dead. There were larger tombs deeper into the graveyard, spreading away up a huge hill and a large stone mausoleum stood at the peak surrounded by trees.

I realised my hand was still locked with Orion's and quickly pulled it free, my pulse thumping at the base of my throat as my palm continued to tingle from his touch.

"No one look back. We need to salt the earth to keep them out. It won't last forever, but it should give us long enough," Orion said and he and Darius moved back to the gate while we all kept our eyes forward. When it was done, they reappeared with dark expressions, talking in low mutters together.

"So?" Tory asked. "What's the plan?"

"We're in the outer ring," Orion said, pointing out the gap that parted the outer graves from those further in. "The protection will be weaker here. The further in we go, the darker the spells will become."

"And let me guess, your daddy's tomb is somewhere in the middle?" Seth said with an arched brow.

"The graves are placed by levels of power," Orion replied coldly. "So yeah. He'll be somewhere towards the middle. If you're too pussy to head that way, then feel free to stay here."

"Have you got something you wanna say to me, asshole?" Seth growled, stepping toward him with his shoulders squared. "Because your attitude is bullshit."

"I have nothing to say to you," Orion hissed.

"Oh yeah?" Seth growled. "Well apparently the only pussy around here is you then."

"What the fuck is that supposed to mean?" Orion's fangs snapped out and I stepped between them with a growl of my own.

"Stop it," I snapped. "We have to move."

Seth's eyes slid to mine and he backed down with an innocent shrug. Orion looked between us with a grimace I didn't understand, but said nothing more.

"Come on," Darius growled and Orion fell into step with him as they led the way through the first line of graves.

I walked beside Tory behind them and felt the prickling of dark magic in the air, charging the particles around me. The second we reached the inner circle, the hairs rose along my flesh and my breathing stalled at the power in this place.

"Do you feel that?" Caleb growled behind me and we all nodded.

The ground started to tremble beneath our feet and I gazed around at the graves surrounding us uneasily. Geraldine screamed as a skeletal hand burst through the earth to her right and fire exploded from me on instinct, blasting it to pieces. But more and more of them were fighting their way from their graves, hundreds of dead bodies scrambling out of the dirt. Fear and horror wound through me as the undead rose and I planted my feet as I prepared to fight.

Darius swung his axe as a bony figure lunged at him and he smashed it to bits with one heavy blow. The moment the bones hit the ground, they started drawing back together and the corpse pushed to its feet once more.

"What the fuck?" Tory's nose wrinkled and the two of us moved closer together, readying to blast them all back to hell.

"Find the tomb!" Darius barked at Orion.

Everyone started wielding their weapons against the skeletons as more and more of them crawled out of the ground. Some of them looked fresher than others, their bodies sinewy and rotting. And as one of them raised their arms, fire magic burst from them and sent a flaming ball towards Seth.

He shifted fast, landing on all four paws as a Wolf, ducking the fireball and slashing the skeleton to pieces with his Phoenix fire claws.

"Go!" Darius commanded and Orion looked to me, a decision in his eyes.

"Wai-" I started but he shot forward, throwing me over his shoulder and tearing away deeper into the graveyard, leaving the others behind.

CALEB

CHAPTER TWENTY SEVEN

A corpse clawed its way out of the ground before me and I raced at it, swiping my twin blades as I moved with the speed of my Order and cutting it apart so it fell into a heap of bones at my feet.

I blasted the remains with my fire magic to finish it off, but as the flames burned out, I found the bones still intact, the magic in them pulling them back together already as it reformed itself.

I cursed as I bent down, ripping an arm free from it and throwing it away from me with the full strength of my Order before tossing a leg in another direction. I tore the skull from the neck and its teeth sank into my finger, causing me to yell out before I hurled it like a Pitball destined for the Pit.

But it didn't land in the Pit. It hit a white Werewolf in the ass and bit down, causing him to yelp in pain as it clung on tight.

Seth twisted around, snapping his jaws as he tried to rip the thing off of him, but it was impossible with the position of it.

I made a move to race over and help him, but another corpse lurched into my path, this one with more skin on its bones and some intelligence lingering in its soulless eyes. I swung at it with my dagger and severed an arm, but it had lifted its other arm already and a blast of water magic hit me in the chest.

I was hurled off of my feet and thrown across the graveyard, crashing to the ground on my back and skidding through the mud until I smashed into a huge gravestone which knocked the air from my lungs.

I coughed out a breath as I rolled over, but before I could get to my feet, hands burst from the soil beneath me and I yelled as I was dragged down into the dirt.

I kicked and flailed as sharp teeth bit into my arm, ripping a chunk of flesh free as I slammed into a coffin and soil cascaded down all around me, pressing in on every side, drowning me in the dark.

I lost my grip on one of my daggers while I was unable to swing my arm to use the other and I yelled in pain as more teeth sank into my leg.

I thrust my hand into the soil, conjuring earth magic to bind to my will as I filled the space around me with razor sharp stones and blasted them away from my body with a surge of power.

The corpses were ripped away from me and I grunted out a curse as I began to shove the soil aside so that I could climb out of the grave and get back to the fight. But as I started to make my way up to the surface, I found two white paws tearing at the soil as Seth dug for me from above.

The dirt parted and I came face to face with Seth's Wolfy snout, his tongue swiping straight up the centre of my face a moment before he shifted back into his Fae form and heaved me to my feet.

"Shit man, for a second there I thought you were a goner." He gave me a shake like he was making sure I was definitely okay before turning and ripping the skull from his ass cheek where it was still clinging on by the teeth.

I grabbed the skull and hurled it as hard as I could towards the fence where those Reaper Hounds were waiting, hoping it cleared it and they could finish the thing off for me.

"Sorry about that," I laughed. "And you didn't need to worry. It's harder than that to kill me," I promised him before slapping my hand over the bleeding wound on his ass and healing it for him.

"It had better be," Seth snarled, shifting back into a Wolf again and racing back up the hill towards the fight.

I paused, reaching out with my earth magic to hunt down the dagger I'd lost beneath the ground before flinging it back out of the dirt and catching it deftly. I shot up the hill to catch up with Seth then kept pace with him as he tore into more of the corpses with tooth and claw beside me.

Geraldine was standing on top of a stone sarcophagus whirling her flaming flail like a freaking baton of death as she crushed skulls and hollered to the moon.

"Come for me you ghastly cads!" she roared. "For I am true of heart and forged in steel! I wield a weapon created by the true queens of Solaria and none who stand against them shall ever succeed! They are the light of the rising sun and I am the shadow at their backs - you will never pass me!"

A flaming arrow shot past my ear and I whipped around to spot Max suspended on a tower of air magic as he took shot after shot with his bow, hitting the corpses dead in the centre of their chests where their hearts should have been. When they fell they didn't rise again and I guessed that made sense. Magic resided in the heart after all so that must have been where they were drawing their power from.

I grinned as I leapt onto Seth's furry back before launching myself at the closest corpse and slamming my dagger down into its chest. Brittle bones snapped, sinew parted and the light went out of its undead eyes before it crumpled to the ground at my feet.

Seth howled in excitement as he charged into the thick of the fight, bowling into the crowd of corpses trying to climb up to Geraldine and knocking a group of them flying before he pounced on them one after another, crushing their chests with his huge, flaming paws.

Darius and Tory were fighting further up the hill, him swinging the huge double headed axe with all the power of his Order and carving the undead apart while she sent spears of Phoenix fire flying at targets further away from them.

I spotted a group of the undead charging up the path Orion and Darcy had taken and I sped around the gravestones to intercept them.

I charged straight towards them with a snarl of bloodlust and my daggers raised but one of them sent a blast of air magic crashing into me before I could cut them down and I was thrown away again.

This graveyard was the most prestigious in all of Solaria and the corpses here had all been powerful Fae once upon a time. Hell, I was probably fighting against my great, great grandpa in amongst the masses and all of them had clearly held onto that strength in death.

There was a reason why most Fae were cremated upon death. Our magic stayed in our bones and it was all too tempting for grave robbers to come and steal bones to be used in dark magic. Hence the insane security around this place. Of course, it would have just made sense to cremate all Fae, but powerful assholes like my family always liked to do things the hard way just to prove they could.

I shot back into the fight with a snarl of determination as the group of undead continued to charge up the path, seeming to know exactly where they were going as they raced after Darcy and Orion, leaving the rest of our group behind to fight the others.

But I wasn't going to let them catch up to them. They needed to get the star and my job here was clear cut. Those creatures had to be stopped.

I holstered one of my blades and tugged the earth beneath their feet into my control, bucking it wildly and sending them all flying as I sprinted into their midst.

My blade found a home in the hearts of three of them before they even realised I was there then another wild blast of air magic crashed into me, hurling me away again.

I hit the ground hard, tumbling downhill then leaping to my feet again as I shot back towards the dead.

A wall of fire bloomed into existence before me and I dove behind a tall gravestone to take cover before lifting a hand and fighting to gain control over the Element.

The fire was wild and cast without purpose beyond getting in my way and I managed to steal control of it quickly, turning it to my will and stoking the flames as they whirled all around me in a burning vortex.

I built the flames higher and higher then launched them down the path, ripping through the corpses and sending them all crashing to the ground before shooting over to them once more and driving my blades through their hearts one after another.

The moment they were all incapacitated, I whirled around and shot back towards the others, the sound of a pained howl cutting through the air and urging me to move even faster.

I found Seth backed up against an imposing stone mausoleum, fighting like mad against at least twenty of the undead creations as they teamed up to try and take him down. They were too close to him for me to cast fire at them so I used earth instead, ripping the dirt out from beneath their feet and causing a group of them to fall to their knees.

Seth took the opening to slash his claws through the chests of several of them, incapacitating them for good, but it gave three of them the opportunity to leap onto his back.

I cursed as Seth howled in pain, kicking and thrashing as he tried to dislodge them and they sank their teeth into his flesh.

I raced forward, driving my blade into three corpses in quick succession before an enormous blast of fire magic tore through all of us from one of them and knocked me off of my feet.

I threw my hands up, controlling the Element with my own power and keeping it away from me but I'd lost track of Seth and as he howled in agony, my heart damn near ripped right out of my chest.

I released a roar of rage as I threw all of my power into forcing the flames into my grasp, seeking out the shape of Seth's body amongst the corpses and drawing the fire away from him as fast as I could. Then I made the fire burn hotter and hotter as I used it to rip through every single skeletal body around us, the heat of the flames almost unbearable as it pressed in on me. But I didn't stop, raising them higher and higher as fury tore through my flesh that was so potent, it stole all thoughts and focus from me. And the sole desire left to me was to protect Seth from any more harm that could be aimed his way.

The flames burned white hot and furious as they devoured the corpses and I was left panting and almost tapped out by the time I guttered the flames.

Seth was back in his Fae form, lying in a ring of green grass surrounded by charred and blackened soot in every direction for as far as I could see and I shot to his side in the blink of an eye.

I dropped down beside him, cringing at the burned and blistered flesh coating his body as a pained howl escaped him and I snatched his hand into mine.

My magic connected to his as easily as breathing, the power of a tornado crashing through my veins and the heavy weight of his earth magic merging with mine like they were one and the same and had always been destined to join this way.

Healing magic sped from my body into his and he groaned as I pushed it in faster and faster, urging every burn and blister to heal as fast as possible while he crushed my fingers with a death grip.

The moment he was healed, I released his hand, gripping his face between my palms and kissing his forehead before pulling him against me.

"Fucking hell, Seth, don't ever do that to me again," I growled as my heart beat out of rhythm and I had to blink repeatedly to force the image of his burned body from my mind.

"So long as you don't do it to me, we have a deal," he laughed and I could have fucking kissed him to hear his teasing tone again.

His arms wound tight around my waist as he held me close for a moment before I shot to my feet and hauled him up with me.

My hands were trembling with the lack of magic in my veins and my fangs snapped out as my gaze caught on the thumping pulse at the base of his throat.

"Stop eye fucking my neck and just bite me already, Cal," Seth said, his earthy brown eyes tempting me closer as he lifted his chin. "We have a fight to win and I've been running beneath the full moon all night. My magic will be replenished in five seconds flat once I shift again so stop holding out on me and do it."

He reached out to grip the front of my shirt and tugged me towards him forcefully and I smirked as I lunged for his neck.

The groan that escaped his lips as I bit him had my hands locking around his waist. I pushed him back against the smoke stained wall of the mausoleum and the taste of his power on my lips sent a shiver of pleasure tracking down my spine.

His fist tightened in my shirt as he tugged me as close as possible and I drank deeply as my fingers dug into his flesh and I clung onto the fact that he was here, solid and present with me just like he should be.

I drew back when I'd had enough, the stubble on my jaw grazing against his and my chest rose and fell heavily as I looked into his eyes again, the moon reflected in his dark pupils as if it was watching me too.

"Cal," Seth rasped, his mouth so close to mine that I felt the movement of my name on his lips.

"Yeah?"

"I..."

He still held my shirt tightly like he thought I might run if he let go and I hadn't released my grip on his waist, my thumbs shifting over the hard curves of his abs as I adjusted my hold on him.

My heart was pounding to this deep and rhythmic beat that seemed to want me to stay right where I was and for a moment, I had the insane idea to just lean forward and-

A scream of pain ripped through the air from the others back at the fight and Max roared so loudly that I felt his fear and rage as his gifts sent a flood of his emotions tearing out over the entire graveyard.

"Geraldine," I gasped, turning from Seth and shooting away to help her.

But as I raced back into the battle, my gut plummeted with disappointment and I couldn't help but wonder, what would have happened if I'd spent a few more moments alone in my best friend's company?

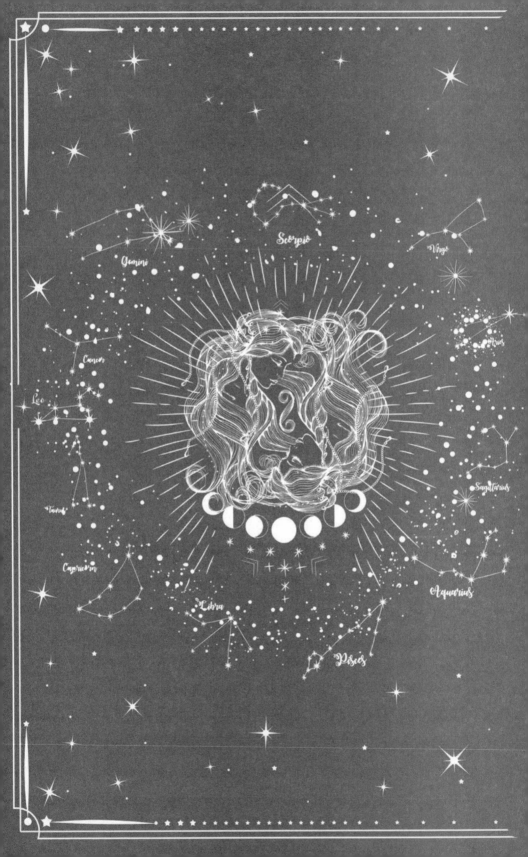

DARCY

CHAPTER TWENTY EIGHT

I jogged after Orion through the graves surrounding the huge stone mausoleum at the heart of the cemetery. Statues of the star signs stood around it and we moved past a creepy looking Capricorn ram as we examined the large stone sarcophaguses circling it. A rattling came from within them that said the dead were trying to get out, but I guessed they couldn't lift the stone lids. The shouts and cries carrying from our friends said they were still facing them. So we needed to hurry our asses up.

"Are we close?" I whispered.

"I don't know," Orion murmured.

"Didn't you ever visit his grave?" I asked in confusion.

"No, I thought he was cremated," he said, his brow pulling down.

"Oh…well, they're all Capricorns here," I said and he frowned at the nearest stone coffins.

"They must be laid out by star signs," he said, grabbing me and I cursed as he whipped me into his arms again, racing around the mausoleum at high speed. He planted me down beside a large statue of a set of weighing scales and I shoved out of his arms.

"Quit doing that with no warning," I hissed, but my point was lost a little as my foot skidded down a muddy bank.

I was about to cast air to push at my back when he threw out a hand at lightning speed to catch me. He yanked me back against his chest and I tilted my chin up with a scowl.

"Stop it," I snapped.

"I'm never not going to catch you," he growled and I pulled away from him, rounding into the group of graves beyond the statue and hunting for Orion's name.

"I would have caught myself," I said firmly.

"Sure you would."

His eyes slid over my head and I opened my mouth to rebuke him but he blurted, "That's it," and rushed past me.

I twisted around, spotting him running toward a huge stone tomb standing under an arching willow tree. The name Lancelot was etched beside a Libra symbol above a round stone door.

"How do you know?" I asked as we stopped in front of it.

"Because my dad used to call me that," he said then brushed his fingers over two small holes in the centre of the door, overlapping like an infinity symbol.

I took the rings from my hand with a buzz of excitement in my veins and stepped forward, pushing the first into the deeper hole then the other into the one that overlapped it.

There was no sound of the door unlocking and I glanced at Orion in concern as he pushed against it, but it didn't budge. He ran his fingers over the stone, his eyes shutting in concentration and I glanced over my shoulder anxiously, hoping the others were okay.

"What's wrong? How do we get in?" I asked and he sighed, opening his eyes.

"It's bound with blood magic. But it doesn't just want my blood..." His fingers moved across the stone, brushing the rings. "It wants a Vega's too."

"Do you think my mother *saw* this? Us standing here together?" I asked in shock.

He swallowed, glancing at me. "Looks like it." He held the draining dagger up to his palm, slicing it open and pressing his hand against the stone.

I took the dagger from him, feeling the call of the shadows within it. But I knew what I was doing, and my Phoenix wouldn't allow any of that darkness into me again anyway. I cut my palm open and Orion's fangs snapped out as he watched, a low groan leaving him.

I arched a brow at him then placed my hand on the door beside his, my breaths coming quicker in anticipation. It threw me for a loop knowing my mother had *seen* us together and had told Orion's father. Did they think we were allies, or did they know we'd been more than that?

A heavy grinding of stone sounded from within the tomb and the circular door swung inward. Magic washed over me from inside and I felt something calling to me, begging me to come closer. I gasped, rushing into the tomb, needing to reach whatever it was and Orion was right at my side as he hunted for it too. It pulsed like a second heart beating close by, one that ached to be in my hands.

The door twisted shut with a loud thunk that made my bones rattle and my magic inside me fell still, blanketed by some power and not allowing me to access it.

"Oh shit," I breathed, casting a red and blue flame with my Phoenix fire in the corner of the tomb and my gaze fell on a huge sarcophagus ahead of us.

The effigy of a man was carved into the stone lid, holding a sword against his chest which had all the constellations etched into its surface. His eyes were closed like he was in an eternal sleep and I was struck with recognition at how much he resembled his son.

Orion shot forward and lifted the lid, carrying it with the strength of his Order and placing it against the wall. A corpse lay inside which was nothing but bones and Orion moved to look down at his father with an ache in his eyes that hurt me.

"Hey, Dad," he murmured.

"I'm sorry," I said gently, moving closer to look down into the coffin.

"Don't be," he sighed. "He died a long time ago."

"That doesn't mean it's not sad anymore," I said with a frown, moving to his side and brushing my fingers against his arm. He glanced at me and our eyes met, the air thickening between us.

He reached down into the coffin, carefully checking around the body. I moved along the edge of it, hunting the dark space, urging Phoenix flames in my hands to see by.

"It's not here," Orion growled.

"It must be," I insisted, starting to move around the tomb, searching everywhere.

Orion shot around too, checking anywhere that could hide a compartment, but there was nothing, just four cold stone walls.

"Why would the diary lead you here if it's gone?" I asked in frustration, carefully searching around the body again. "Could someone have gotten here before us?"

"There's no way," he growled fiercely. "How could they have gotten through that door?"

I shook my head, confused and furious as I continued hunting, but there was no compartment or hatch or anything. It was just an empty tomb and the sarcophagus.

"There has to be something we're missing," I said stubbornly, looking to Orion but he didn't have an answer. "Maybe you needed to come here with Tory…"

"No," Orion growled. "It was meant to be you, I'm sure of it."

"Why?" I balked, moving to the door and pressing my hands against it, shoving with all my strength, but without my air magic I had no chance of opening it. *Shit, how the hell do we get out?* "It could be her. Or both of us, or-"

"It's *you*," he snapped. "It's me and you, that was how this was meant to be."

"Says the guy who abandoned me," I scoffed. "We clearly weren't *meant* to be anything."

"I didn't abandon you," he said in disbelief, shooting to my side as he shoved the door too, adding the power of his Order, but it wouldn't give. *Shit.*

"Right," I said bitterly. "You just thought heading off to Darkmore and leaving me to pick up the pieces of our ruined relationship was a great way to show your support for me?"

"I had no choice," he snarled and I wheeled around to face him.

"If you say that one more time, I'm going to blast your head off with Phoenix fire."

His eyes darkened, narrowing to slits. "You don't understand," he hissed.

"I understand perfectly actually. I understand that you betrayed me, that you broke my trust. The one thing you knew was nearly impossible for me to give you. But I did, because I thought I could rely on you, that you would always be there. But you stopped fighting for me and I was the idiot who was actually surprised."

"I never stopped fighting for you, Blue," he growled, boxing me in against the wall and my heart clenched at the use of that name. "I just stopped fighting for *us*."

"Same difference," I said icily as fire blazed in my palms in warning, but he didn't back down.

"Wrong," he snapped in his damn professor tone and I held my breath, wondering if he was actually going to give me an explanation at last. "Everything I did was for you. And I would do it again and again, because despite how much this fucking kills me, you're still on the right path to become a queen of Solaria. And if I'd done anything different, you would have lost your place at Zodiac Academy, your name would be ruined by your relationship to me. I was going to prison either way, and I saw one way that wouldn't drag you down with me. So I took it. And if that makes me an asshole then I don't give a fuck. If you hate me for the rest of my life, I will swallow it because I will *not* be the reason you lost your chance to claim the throne."

Tears blurred my vision but I blinked them back as anger welled up in me. "You had no right to make that choice for me."

"I know," he said in a grim tone. "I didn't take pleasure in it. But I'd still make it every time."

I shook my head at him, my heart thundering furiously against my ribs. "And didn't you even consider what you going to prison would do to me? How much it hurt knowing you were in that fucking place, that you could have died in there, and that everyone in the kingdom thinks of you as some goddamn predator who manipulated me?" I shoved him to try and get by, to get some air, but he didn't step back, refusing to let me go. And I was one second from forcing him to.

He gripped my chin, his chest crushing me back against the wall and suddenly the air was thick and hot and another pulse was pounding in time with mine again somewhere in the tomb. But I couldn't focus on it through the fog of my mind, my hands sliding up to grip his biceps and squeeze as anger gripped me in an iron fist.

"I don't care," he said, his breath warm and enticing against my mouth. "I knew I could never keep you, Blue. I knew it from the first time we kissed,

I just fooled myself into believing it for a while. So when it came to us or you, I chose you. Because I woke up to reality. And real life isn't nice or easy, it's fucking quicksand that tries to drag you down the more you fight it. Love doesn't conquer all this time, because we're on two different paths. You're heading to the stars, beautiful, and I'm staying down here in the dirt. That's just the way it is."

"It didn't have to be," I hissed, hating him, loving him.

"Well it's too late for regrets," he said darkly. "And I'm sure you'll enjoy the view of the sky up there with Seth Capella beside you."

"What?" I balked, my thoughts totally derailed by that comment. "What's Seth got to do with it?"

"Oh, come on," he scoffed, his fangs on show as he leaned down into my face and my hands grew scoldingly hot against his arms in a threat. "Are you going to deny it right to my face?"

"Deny what, asshole?" I snapped, my hands blazing hot now, but he still didn't move, taking the burns rather than letting me go.

"That you're together. He likes to send me the updates to rub my face in it," he spat and the heat slid away from my hands as I saw the hurt in his eyes. "To be honest, you being with anyone else would have broken me, but did you really have to choose the one guy who tried to rip us apart?"

I reached up to brush my fingers across his cheek, hating the raw pain I saw in his eyes. It cut into me like a knife. "I'm not with Seth, Lance. Never have been, never will be. He's a friend. That's all."

He tsked like he didn't believe me and I scowled, my anger rising again. So my word just meant *nothing* now?

"You think I'd screw him after what he did to me? We might have resolved our differences, but I wouldn't just forget that he cut off my hair or that he tried to ruin me at every chance he got. That he messed with us and made it so much harder for us to be together. Do you really think that little of me, Lance Orion?"

His brow creased, his eyes scouring my face, pausing on my mouth. "No...I think the world of you, Darcy Vega."

He grabbed a fistful of my shirt, yanking me forward and suddenly pressed a demanding kiss to my lips. He surrounded me, consumed me. My heart was fit to burst as I tasted the man I'd pined for for so long and I was frozen in shock, torn between wanting him and needing to pull away. But I gave in, falling into temptation as I took a bite of the juiciest apple ever presented to me. I clawed at him as he pinned me back against the wall, a low groan of desperation in his throat making an earthquake roll through to the centre of my being. He tasted like broken promises, but of purest sunlight too. The shattered pieces of my heart sat like broken glass against my tongue, and the longer I kissed him, the more those pieces seemed to draw back together. But it was too late for that. We'd had our shot. He'd hurt me. And he hadn't once even apologised for it.

I broke the kiss, furious at myself for giving in and his face was cast in shadow as I looked up at him, my lips bruised and tingling.

"We can't," I breathed.

"Fuck," he rasped, stumbling back a step. "No."

I didn't know what to say, but I knew this was the last thing on earth we should even be doing right now. The drumming pulse of magic sounded in my head again and Orion took another step back, his hand going to his throat.

"Darcy," he begged and I shook my head.

"We have to figure out how to get out of here," I said, my cheeks still burning and my lips stinging.

"No, *Blue*," he said, a fierce warning in his tone and I frowned as I realised his fangs were glinting at me in the dark. The power of this place closed in on me on all sides and I twisted around as I realised he was looking at something over my head. Words lit up across the door in glowing blue letters and my heart juddered in fear as I felt the spell they cast, spilling through the air.

Royal Vega blood tastes the sweetest.

Does the monster or the man in you run deepest?

"Get out of here!" Orion roared, his pupils dilating and fear ran through me as I raised my hands. His upper lip peeled back, the bloodlust in his eyes making his face seem wholly animal. "Darcy - run!"

GERALDINE

CHAPTER TWENTY NINE

"Come and get me you rambunctious heathens!" I cried, glaring around at the hoard of undead scallywags set to drag me to the netherworld where I'd fallen.

The Flail of Unending Celestial Karma, as I'd christened it, had fallen from my grasp when the stone sarcophagus I'd been standing upon had crumbled like an underbaked scone and I'd tumbled down here like a fish on a Ferris wheel only to find myself alone in this dark chamber.

The corpses raced at me while I held firm, my chin high and my water magic keeping them at bay as they tried to swarm me. But I was no floundering Florence, and I wouldn't fall prey to these scoundrels.

With a battle cry loud enough to set the heavens ablaze, I raced for my glorious flail, diving into a roly-poly and snatching it into my grasp before swinging it at the noggin of the closest devil who'd come to try and taste my flesh.

"Not today, good sir!" I bellowed. "For I fight with the fire of justice beneath my wings and the shining light of my ladies leading me to success. I will never be vanquished by the likes of you!"

I swung the heavy spiked ball of my flail overhead and smashed the skull clean off of one of the braggards before another leapt upon my back.

"Geraldine?!" Max bellowed, his voice echoing down to me from above.

"Fight on, you slippery eel!" I called to him. "Take your place defending my lady Tory in this hour of need and turn your mind from my endeavours."

"I'm coming down to you - just hold on!" he shouted as if he was

But I had no time to chastise him as more of the soulless hooligans came for a taste of Grus.

"No you don't, you skeletal scoundrels!" I cried, swinging my flail over my head, the flames of glory pouring from it as it blazed with the power of my ladies and I knew that the luck attuned to such a treasure would never fail me.

I fought with the fluidity of my water Element and the strength of my earth just as my dear papa had always taught me, channelling the pure will of the stars through my every movement while knowing I fought the good fight.

If I died today in defence of my ladies, then I would go on to join the stars knowing that my sacrifice had been worthy. And yet I had no plans to leave them now. I would be there, watching their ascent to the throne and bathing in the glow of their eternal reign over our kingdom.

Bone splintered, magic flared and rotting bodies fell apart around me as I fought with the fury of the warriors of old and a fierce determination to get back to my lady and stand firm at her side.

Just as the final upstart met his doom at the end of my heavy ball of wrath, a salacious salamander dropped down into my cave with a look of relief filling his deep brown eyes.

"Holy fuck, Gerry, I thought-"

"There is no time for lollygagging!" I cried, placing a flat palm to his puckered lips as he leaned towards me like he thought a moment such as this was the time for smooching. "We must get back to my lady."

I raised a hand, wielding the earth to my command and creating a platform which rose us back up towards the graveyard where the battle raged on.

"I was really worried about you, you know," Maxy boy growled as he moved closer, cupping my jaw in his grasp and causing an earthquake that raced right down to my nether regions.

"I follow the true and just path of the Almighty Sovereign Society," I said lightly as we rose ever higher. "There is no need to worry for my wellbeing."

He shook his head like he couldn't understand me and crushed his mouth to mine before I could protest again.

I gave him a moment of surrender as we rose up to ground level and tore away from him as the moonlight touched our skin again.

"In the name of the true queens!" I bellowed as I raced back into the melee with my flail swinging in wide arcs around my head. "May the stars shine ever upon them!"

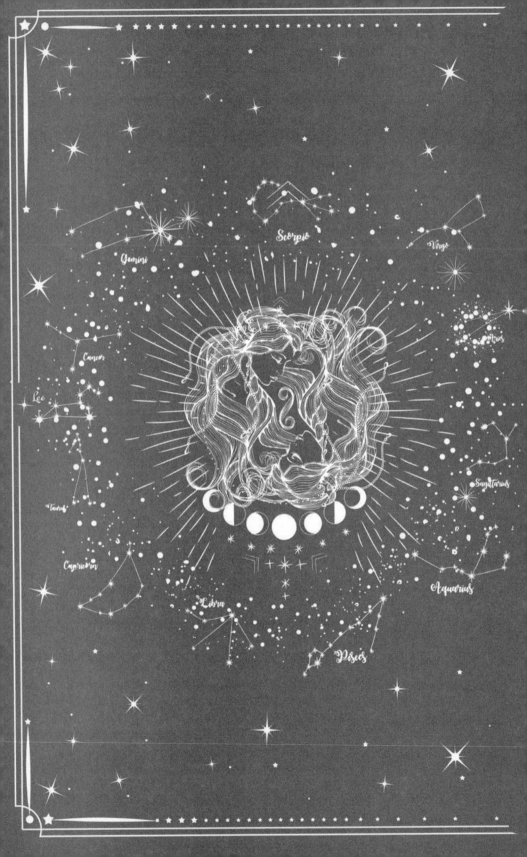

DARCY

CHAPTER THIRTY

Orion rushed at me again and again while I used my Phoenix fire to try and keep him back. But I didn't want to hurt him, so I cast flash fires at his feet, trying to slow him down enough to just keep him away. I could feel the power of the spell he was under, and there was nothing I could do to stop it.

There was no way out. Nowhere to run.

I backed up against the far wall, casting an arc of fire in front of me to try and hold him off.

"Lance, stop!" I screamed as he lunged through it and I extinguished the flames fast so I didn't kill him. The only thing worse than ending up dead myself, was him dying instead.

His hand wrapped around my throat and he pinned me to the wall, his fangs bared and his eyes swirling with nothing but hunger. He wasn't there. He was a vessel starving for blood and I was terrified that there was only one way this would end.

He lurched forward, shifting his hand to try and get his teeth into me, but suddenly I was falling, the wall behind me spinning backwards. I stumbled into a hidden passage and managed to kick him hard enough to knock him off of me.

I twisted around and sprinted away down a steep set of stairs that spiralled off into the pitch darkness.

Orion shot after me and I released a flash of fire behind me with a cry of fright, making him growl like a beast and fall back. My feet hit the bottom of the stairway and I ran, finding myself in a winding maze, the corners tight and pressing in closely either side of me. The flames in my hands were the only light as I took turns at random, hearing a rush of air as he raced after me with the speed of his Order and I threw fire in different directions to throw him off the hunt. He growled in fury as he took wrong turns, but he was so close, his heavy breaths reaching me from just beyond the wall to my right. The only thing keeping me alive was pure luck, but it was going to run out. It had to.

I ran faster, left, right, left, right, my mind spinning as I got lost in the endless passages. I moved as quietly as possible, but every footfall I made sounded like a thunderclap in my ears. Terror bled through me and clouded my thoughts. *Just keep going. Don't stop.*

I raced around a final corner as the rush of air behind me drew nearer. I had a second to act as I sprinted out into the centre of the maze, finding rows and rows of statues ringing a large sarcophagus. The statues were made of stone, standing tall and imposing in the shape of warriors.

The sound of the pulsing, pounding magic filled my head again, louder than my own heartbeat and I knew in my soul the Imperial Star was close.

I dove behind one of the statues and held my breath, making myself as small as possible as I tried to hide. I extinguished my flames and was plunged into darkness just before Orion shot into the space.

I heard him moving through the statues, hunting me down and fear rippled through me. The only thing keeping me safe was the thundering magic from the Imperial Star which must have been veiling the sound of my heartbeat. But if I couldn't find a way to stop this spell he was under; he was going to find me. And I was surely going to fall prey to his fangs, because I'd rather die than kill the man I loved.

TORY

CHAPTER THIRTY ONE

I hadn't felt this alive in months. The pure, unadulterated power of my Phoenix was burning through my limbs with such intensity that my freaking veins were humming with it.

Molten fire burst from my hands in a mixture of red and blue and I revelled in the heat of the flames as they stoked my magic and filled me to the point of bursting.

Darius fought like a warrior beside me, swinging his axe with a two handed grip and carving through the bodies of the dead like he was felling trees. His muscular frame flexed with the power of the blows and my gaze kept travelling to him over and over again.

A ferocious howl caught my ear from the direction of the gates and I froze as I whirled around to look down the hill in that direction. *That wasn't Seth.*

My blood chilled as I spotted the figures racing up the path towards us, the sound of the pack of hounds baying for our blood making fear wash through me in droves.

"The Reaper Hounds just broke down the gate!" I yelled, loud enough for everyone to hear me as I pointed in their direction.

They were too far from us for me to have to worry about looking them in the eyes yet. But their mountainous black bodies stood out as darker shadows within the graveyard, their monstrously large size impossible to miss as they looked more like horses than dogs.

"We need to run for the tomb!" Darius commanded in a tone that brokered no arguments. "We can make a stand there if we have to and I'll fly us out of here the moment Orion and Darcy return with the Imperial Star."

The others were still fighting the undead who continued to crawl up out of the ground and I urged my wings to burst free of my flesh as I took to the sky.

"What are you doing?" Darius demanded, reaching for me as I swept over him and I pointed towards the pack of dogs charging this way.

"I'm going to make it as hard for them to follow us as I can," I said, ignoring the way he was shaking his head in refusal as I swept away from him over the heads of our friends and further down the path with fire burning in my limbs.

The moment I was past Max and Geraldine, I swept my hands out either side of me and cast a blazing wall of Phoenix fire across the path to slow the hounds.

As soon as it was in place, I dove back to the ground, casting a sword made of nothing but Phoenix fire into my hands as I banished my wings before swinging it at the head of the closest corpse and barking at the others to start running.

Seth raced up the path ahead of us in his white Wolf form and Caleb shot between the headstones, stabbing corpses with his twin daggers and sending them tumbling to the ground before they even knew he was upon them.

Geraldine and Max came to run with me and we charged through the crowd of undead, with our weapons swinging and power blazing through the air which made it crackle around us.

I'd lost sight of Darius and I hunted for him through the throng of corpses as we fought our way up the hill, my heart racing as I looked left and right with fear taking me captive.

The sound of the Reaper Hounds reaching the wall of fire behind me made my pulse skip as they howled their fury at the sky and I looked back over my shoulder, my gut lurching as one of them leapt right through the flames and landed on the path at the foot of the hill.

"Oh fuck," I gasped, putting on a burst of speed and dropping my hold on the sword I'd created as I wielded air instead.

I created a shield around myself, Max and Geraldine then threw it out from my body with the full strength of my power so that the corpses surrounding us were blasted back and we were gifted a free run up the path.

"Have heart, my lady!" Geraldine cried. "We are true of honour and have the stars at our backs. We cannot fail."

"The stars are never at my back, Geraldine," I grunted as I ran on. "Those sparkly motherfuckers only ever send me bad luck."

Geraldine didn't get a chance to answer as we crested the hill and found ourselves surrounded by the undead once more.

"Brace yourselves!" Darius bellowed and relief filled me as I spotted him standing on top of a stone Dragon that was guarding the entrance to a tomb.

He had his hands raised before him and I threw more power into the air shield protecting the three of us just before he sent a tidal wave of water crashing through the crowd of the undead.

The corpses screamed for our blood as they were swept away and I whooped in triumph as the wave crashed over my shield, leaving the three of us in place on the path.

I chanced a look back down the hill as the Reaper Hounds leapt on the corpses, tearing into them savagely, ripping bones free and devouring them with snarls and howls as they fought over their meal.

Darius leapt down onto the path ahead of us and my gaze fell to his bare arms, the ink slick with a sheen of sweat that made my heart race as I got caught up in the idea of being crushed in his firm hold. There was still some fear lingering in me every time I was around him from what Lionel had done to me, but I was starting to crave the rush of it, always hungry for the little shivers of adrenaline I got by being close to such a dangerous creature.

He took his axe from the sheath at his back and waited for us to catch up to him, giving me an assessing gaze that sent my heart racing before we ran on in search of Darcy and Orion.

"Over here!" Caleb shouted from somewhere up ahead and I spotted him and Seth who had shifted back into Fae form and pulled some sweatpants on. Max always carried spare shit for his friends; he probably had a whole outfit change in his bag for me too if I needed it.

They were all stood in front of an enormous tomb beneath an arching willow tree and we ran to join them.

"You only have to say the word and I shall charge down yonder to delay those beasts, my lady," Geraldine said, swinging her flail as she moved into position by Seth's side.

"No one's going anywhere, Geraldine," I commanded. "Just stay beside me and let's try and not have our souls sucked out, yeah?"

I looked around us to get my bearings and spotted mine and Darcy's rings lodged in the round stone door of the tomb, marking Orion and Darcy's passage inside. The door seemed to be shut tight and I couldn't hear any sound coming from inside, but they must have been in there.

"Close your eyes, Roxy," Darius commanded as the baying howls of the Reaper Hounds signalled them taking up the scent again.

"You close your eyes," I bit back as he moved to stand in front of me with his axe raised. "I can use air and earth magic to sense where they are and flames clearly don't bother them that much, so maybe you should just stand behind me."

"Not a fucking chance, gorgeous," he said, smirking at me tauntingly before turning his back on me and hefting the axe in his hands.

"If I die, don't let my mom clear out my room," Seth muttered. "There's like soooo much porn beneath my bed."

Caleb snorted a laugh as he closed his eyes, the earth Elementals all tapping into their connection with the ground to let them feel the Reaper Hounds coming.

"By the guiding light of the moon, I know we will prevail," Geraldine said, her eyes closed as she swung her flail at her side and my heart raced as the sound of the pack drew closer.

As the first of the huge, black beasts crested the hill, I snapped my eyes shut and used my connection to the earth to buck the ground beneath their feet.

Caleb, Geraldine and Seth all joined me as we felt every place their paws met dirt and we thrust spears of rock and wood up into the paths of the oncoming beasts.

The scent of rot and death washed over us as they ran closer and my friends yelled out as they fell into battle with the beasts come to drag us to hell.

I kept my eyes clamped shut as I felt for every movement against the ground, every stirring of the air and I cast deadly magic at them time and again.

Darius was swinging his axe with savage blows as the beasts reached us and I could feel the ripples of his movement rebounding through the air every time he moved.

The need to open my eyes was overwhelming and I had to fight it with every scrap of self control I had. But as Darius grunted in pain, I couldn't help but crack an eye open to see what had happened to him.

My breath stilled in my chest as he fell to his knees before a monstrous beast, his eyes wide and locked in the blood red gaze of the creature. His axe fell slack at his side and my heart fractured.

The Reaper Hound prowled forward, teeth bared and drool sliding from its jaws as its rotting flesh was stretched into a hellish snarl.

"No!" I roared, racing towards him as the beast's red eyes flared with power and I ripped the axe from Darius's grip before swinging it with every scrap of strength I held in my body.

The axe fell on the hound's neck, bone snapping and a huge thump sounding as I severed its head with a furious scream as I refused to let that monster steal him from me.

Darius gasped as he rocked back onto his heels, suddenly freed from its monstrous power.

Max roared a challenge to the sky and a huge air shield was blasted into existence surrounding all of us as he fought to keep the creatures back.

Seth raised his hands too, strengthening the magic as the hounds dashed themselves against the shield, barking and snarling in wild fury as they tried to break through it.

I lunged at Darius, dropping the axe by my feet and slamming into him hard enough to knock him back onto his ass as I landed in his lap.

"Is it you?" I demanded, looking into his dark eyes and grabbing his face between my hands as I held him still, searching for the man the stars had chosen for my mate. "Are you still you?"

"It's me, Roxy," he said roughly, his hands moving to grasp my waist as he looked at me like I was the answer to every question he'd ever asked of the world.

Relief spilled through me in an overwhelming torrent that made me sag forward as I pressed my forehead to his for the briefest of moments before rearing back again.

"You fucking idiot," I snapped, punching him in the chest as I realised he was okay. "Why the fuck were your eyes open?"

"Because I wasn't going to risk them getting past me to you," he snarled like that was the most obvious thing in the world and I punched him again.

"And what would I do without you?" I demanded, making his eyes widen with surprise before I even realised what I'd said, but fuck it.

I didn't even want to think about the answer to that question or the implications of me asking it, so I just tipped my chin up and climbed off of him, closing my eyes tight as I raised my hands and added my air magic to the shield.

I cursed as the hounds crashed against it, trying to force their way in and the entire thing rattled with the strength of their power.

"How long can you hold it?" Caleb demanded from my left.

"Longer if we power share," Max grunted and Darius grasped my left arm instantly.

The moment I felt his magic pushing up against the barrier of mine, I opened myself to it, the feeling of his power merging with mine the most natural, exhilarating sensation in the world.

But if I'd thought that was a rush then it was nothing compared to what happened when he connected his magic to Caleb's then Seth's and the barrage of their magic flooding into my body almost knocked me from my feet.

I gasped aloud as I fought to contain so much power at once and when Geraldine grabbed my other arm and her and Max's power joined with ours too, my knees almost buckled from the weight of all of it.

"Ho-ly fuck," Caleb groaned.

"This might just be better than sex," Seth gasped and I made a sound of acknowledgement which came out as a breathy moan.

"Good golly lobsters," Geraldine sighed and for once I knew exactly what she fucking meant.

The Reaper Hounds continued to throw themselves against the shield and I grunted with the effort of holding them back as we all flooded our magic into keeping it in place.

"Come on, Darcy," I growled, hoping for some miraculous twin instincts to give her the message to hurry the fuck up, because even with all of our combined power holding this shield up, I knew it wasn't going to remain in place forever. And I wasn't sure I liked our chances against the Reaper Hounds once it broke.

ORION

CHAPTER THIRTY TWO

My mind was clouded by bloodlust as I hunted the blue haired girl through a sea of stone statues, the call of her blood like nothing I'd ever known. I needed it. I had to have it, rip into her veins and drink every last drop. There was a thundering noise in my head drowning out all sounds of her, but she had to be close. I could sense her here, hiding in the dark.

I shot around the room as fast as I could and finally my gaze fell on her huddled behind a statue.

I grabbed her off of the floor and she screamed as I threw her against the statue to try and pin her in place. It toppled backwards from the force I used, smashing into pieces and I snarled as I lost my grip on her. She hit the floor among the rubble and scrambled away, casting a ring of blue and red fire around herself to keep me back. But nothing could. I'd burn for her, I knew that in the remnants of my sanity. I'd stand in the flames of hell and die for this girl's blood, but first I'd sate this thirst in me that devoured me from the inside out.

"No! Lance – stop!" she cried as I dove through the flames, pinning her beneath my weight on the ground.

The scent of my own burned flesh slid under my nose as her hands pressed against my arms to try and keep me away, her skin blazing with the heat of the sun but I refused to flinch away from the pain of it.

Her blue hair fanned out around her and I gazed at the thrumming pulse at the base of her neck, knowing with absolute certainty that I was going to drink. My fangs pricked my tongue and her hands clawed at me as she tried to stop me, but I was one of the strongest creatures in this world. She couldn't escape. She'd have to kill me first.

"Lance!" she screamed and I growled against the pain of the burns she left on my arms.

I captured her chin, forcing her head sideways to expose her throat and dropped my mouth to her flesh. The vein in her neck was pulsing with the rapid beat of her heart, desperate for me to sink my teeth into it, but the scent of her made me pause.

She was the sweetest thing. Honey and sugar and all things good. She reminded me of a fairground, a school, a secret.

Another growl raked against my throat as the beast in me begged me to bite, but a different part of my soul was holding me back.

I saw memories scrolling through my mind of this girl. Her standing before me for the first time, her hair dipped in blue, her eyes wide and curious. Then her sitting in my class, me stealing looks at her I had no right to steal. The taste of her lips against mine for the first time, hidden at the bottom of a pool, then the way she'd looked dripping wet outside my front door with a single word on her lips. A word that meant everything to me. Because it meant her. My girl. My queen.

"*Blue*," I groaned, releasing her chin so she turned her head to look at me with fear in her deep green eyes.

I couldn't bear her looking at me like that and in the haze of my mind, I leaned down without really making the decision as a thread of fate seemed to drag me toward her. I pressed my mouth to hers, transfixed.

Her hand slammed into my cheek and I grunted as my head wheeled sideways.

"What the hell?" she demanded, panting as she tried to shove me back.

The spell finally let go of me fully, the power in the air dissolving, freeing me, returning my mind to me. And clarity was a bitch.

"Shit." I kneeled back, pulling her up to sit and anxiously checking her over for injuries, snarling at the bruises I found.

"Did I hurt you?" I asked in a panic, a weight crushing my chest at what I'd just done.

She gaped at me then shook her head. "Are you...you again?"

"Yeah," I growled. "I'm so fucking sorry."

"It's alright. But what the hell happened?" she breathed and I swallowed the dry lump in my throat. A thumping rang in my ears, the noise like a Siren's song that called to me. But nothing in this world could make me turn away from Darcy right then.

"I don't know."

"You're hurt," she said in a choked voice, brushing her hands close to the burns on my arms.

"I'll heal," I promised. "We just need to get out of here and get our magic back."

"*You've passed the test. A new Master of the Zodiac Guild is born,*" an ethereal voice filled my head and Darcy stiffened as she heard it too. "*Protector of the royal line, safe keeper of the heart.*"

Light shimmered from under the lid of the sarcophagus at the centre of the room. It shined brighter and brighter as I pushed to my feet and helped Darcy up beside me. We walked together and when I took her hand, she didn't pull it free. I glanced at her as we approached it and I pushed the lid open to see inside. An object sat in the empty grave, illuminated with a brilliant whiteness. I reached out toward the blinding light, my fingers brushing a rough stone.

I wrapped my hand around it when nothing bad happened, taking it into my palm and a jolt of white hot energy ran through me. I looked down at my forearm in shock, finding the shimmering mark of a sword igniting beneath my flesh. It was the exact same as the one Jasper had had and my mind spun with all that meant. *The new Master of the Guild? Holy fuck.*

"Vega princess, half of one whole. Seek the palace in the deep. Where the last of them lie," the voice spoke once more.

"Please tell me you're also hearing the star talking to you?" Darcy whispered and a low laugh escaped me.

"Yeah, I hear it. Fuck, it's pretty." I turned it over in my palm, the rock rough and glittering like diamonds.

"Son of my last keeper," it whispered to me. *"Do what the King could not."*

"What couldn't he do?" I asked in confusion.

"Do what the King could not," it repeated then the light faded and the star sat peacefully in my palm like it wasn't a magical talking rock that had come from the heavens.

I held it out to Darcy and her eyes widened.

"It seems like it wants *you* as the keeper," she said.

"I can't take it home to Lionel, beautiful," I said with a smirk, my mood going through the roof at the fact that we'd actually pulled this off. We'd gotten one over on that fucking asshole at last.

She reached out and took the star, brushing her thumb over it before pushing it into her pocket.

"We need to get back to the others," she said firmly but paused, suddenly reaching into the sarcophagus and picking up a single Tarot card. The Chariot.

Shock rattled through me as I recognised the swirling silver writing on the back. It was another message from Astrum. Darcy moved closer so I could read it too.

You've found the final card.

The stars have aligned, my duty is done.

When all hope fails, Vega Princesses, find courage in the light.

"That's it," she gasped. "This is the last one."

"The Chariot means taking control," I said hopefully. "Taking the reins and-"

389

"Getting on the path to victory," she finished with a wide grin then tucked it into her pocket. "Let's go."

I scooped her up and shot out of the room, racing back through the maze of tunnels and up the stairs into the tomb.

The sound of grinding stone said the door was opening and Darcy urged me on as I rushed forward to get out.

A cacophony of noise reached me as I found our friends holding off a pack of Reaper Hounds right outside the tomb. My heart lurched and I slammed my hand over Darcy's eyes as I shut my own.

"We're here!" I shouted and an earth shattering boom sounded before a Dragon's roar filled my ears in a clear command.

"The rings," Darcy said urgently, trying to fight her way out of my arms, but I wasn't letting her go, not for fucking anything.

I turned, cracking my eyes open and grabbing the silver rings from the tomb door and the whole thing sealed itself once more.

"Get on!" Tory screamed and I shut my eyes again as I turned back towards the sound of her voice. Her hand curled around my arm as she dragged me and Darcy toward Darius.

"Shut your damn eyes," I snapped as Darcy begged her to as well.

"They are shut, I opened them for like one millisecond," Tory growled.

I pushed Darcy up ahead of me as I placed one hand on the hot scales of my friend and boosted Tory up after her. I climbed on and a hand found mine which I knew was Blue's by touch alone. I sat behind her and felt Geraldine slide into place behind me, knowing it was her by the way she breathed, "Holy guacamole, I'm upon the loins of a lizard."

Warm magic swept out from Darcy's hand and the burns on my body healed over. I immediately pushed my own magic back into her veins, healing any bruise or mark I'd left on her in the tomb. It made me sick that I'd done that. I knew I'd been under a spell, but fuck, that didn't make me feel any better about it.

Geraldine's arms slid around my waist as Darius shifted beneath us. "Holy abs, whose man muscle am I holding onto?" she cried in my ear and I snorted.

"It's your old teacher," I called to her.

"You're only as young as you think you are," she said then Darius took off and she wailed like a banshee, her hands sliding up to grip my pecs and squeezing hard.

"By the stars," I swore, pulling Darcy against me as Geraldine nearly clawed my nipples off.

I opened my eyes just as Darius sailed over the gate far below and flew across the forest as more furious howls rang out while the pack chased us. Darcy's midnight blue hair fluttered against my face and I held her tighter, relief filling me at getting the fuck away from that graveyard.

"By the light of the moon upon my Great Aunt Delia's bosoms, this is the most magnanimous ride of my life!" Geraldine yelled.

Seth started howling and Max and Caleb joined in as we soared up toward the full moon.

"Wanna loosen your grip there a bit, Grus?" I growled as her fingers clamped tighter over my pecs.

"A strapping man like you can handle a little light lady-handed squeezing," she insisted and Darcy craned her neck to try and see what the fuss was about, bursting out laughing as she realised what was going on.

"Are we stardusting out of here or what?" Max called.

I adjusted my grip on Darcy, pushing a hand into my pocket and pulling out a pouch. "Ready Darius?" I yelled to him and he nodded his large head.

I threw it ahead of us and Darius flew us straight into it. We were wrenched away into the ether, travelling a hundred miles across Solaria where we were spat out beyond the fence of the academy.

Darius shifted back before we landed and we all fell in a heap on the grass. I extracted myself from the pile up, tugging Darcy up by the hand and hooking her sister out of the mess too.

"Did you find it?" Tory asked anxiously and Darcy reached into her pocket, taking out the Imperial Star to show her with a triumphant smile. Everyone crowded closer to see and pride swelled in my chest. We'd fucking done it.

"Have mercy!" Geraldine wailed, honest to shit tears rolling down her cheeks as she gazed at it. "It's more beautiful than the sunset diamond of Tullissia."

"Make it do something," Seth urged, bouncing up and down excitedly.

I made a mild attempt not to despise him, but failed. If Darcy had been telling the truth about them then he had a fuck ton of explaining to do. And I was not a forgiving kind of guy.

"Let's not," Darcy shot back, pocketing the star. "We don't know how it works and fucking with stars has caused us far too much trouble before now."

"Seconded. Let's just get to King's Hollow. I'd rather not piss off any more celestial beings in my lifetime," Tory said, shooting a look at Darius as he finished pulling his clothes back on.

"It's a shame we can't use it to make my father's head blow up though," Darius said with a frown.

"That's too quick of a death for him," Max reasoned. "He should be cursed to eat a field of thorn bushes then be smothered inside a Griffin's asshole."

"Oh what fun," Geraldine guffawed, slapping her thigh. "I'd like to make that odious beast stand in a pool of ravenous fishes who feast on his scrotum and tallywacker until there is nothing left of him downstairs but his questionable morals."

I barked a laugh and she grinned at me. "What would you have him do, Professor?"

"Lance," I corrected firmly. "And I'd be happy if I could just beat him to death with a Pegasus horn."

"So come on, tell us what happened in the tomb while we were all fighting the undead?" Caleb asked me and Darcy.

We shared a look before explaining the crazy shit that had gone down in there – barring my really poorly timed kiss and the headfuck I was left with since. I mean, really? *That* was what I'd decided to do? What the fuck was I thinking? That I could just kiss away all our problems? Darcy deserved better. Hell, she deserved everything. And I was the exact opposite of everything.

I had to cut myself to show them the Zodiac Guild mark on my arm just like Jasper had shown me, and Geraldine all but fainted when I did. Not because she was squeamish, but because the Zodiac Guild was apparently 'the most sensational society of all the societies in the land and she'd give up three limbs to be a part of it.'

"I have to go back to the palace," I said miserably, looking to the paling sky.

A guard would come and check on me just after dawn and remove the wards meant to keep me in the summerhouse overnight. The thought of leaving made my heart sink, but we had the Imperial Star now. And Lionel wasn't going to get anywhere near it. That was something to be happy about.

Darius drew me in for a hug and murmured in my ear, "Not much longer, brother. We'll beat him now. Fate is swinging in our favour."

He let me go, stepping back and Tory hugged me next, taking me by surprise. "We're gonna hit him right where it hurts."

"I'm not sure one of your kicks to the balls will help, but maybe if you attach the Imperial Star to your shoe while you do it, you'll break them right off," I said dryly and she laughed, releasing me.

Geraldine threw herself at me next, taking me even more by surprise. "Oh, you loyal Master of the Guild, you're a true royalist, you have always done what is right for my queens. I see that now," she sobbed, earning me harsh glares from the Heirs. *Ah shit.*

I patted her shoulder awkwardly, but she clung on tight as I tried to press her back, releasing a mournful sob.

"Can't you fix things with my lady Darcy?" she whisper-shouted completely unsubtly. *By the fucking stars.*

I met Blue's gaze over her head and my throat tightened. I had so many damn things I needed to say to her, but I didn't know when I'd get that chance or if she'd even want to hear them. I'd kissed her like a fucking idiot – *twice*. At least she'd kissed me back the first time. But not for long. And I doubted she ever would again.

I stepped away from Geraldine, giving her a taut smile, knowing this was the last thing I needed to be focusing on right now.

"I'll come home tomorrow," Darius said as he stepped through the fence and Max tossed me a salute while Caleb just turned away. Our Order meant we were never going to be anything but rivals, but I wasn't going to cry myself a river over lost friends. It was a miracle I could count myself more than three anyway.

"Stay safe," Darcy said with a tight smile and I caught her hand before she could escape.

She turned back to face me, looking up at me with a question in her beautiful eyes. I took the rings from my pocket, placing them in her palm, wishing I didn't have to let her go. But I did. I always fucking did from now on. My heart hurt though because I knew the second I released her, I wouldn't know when I'd see her again.

I let go, having no choice and she turned away with a word of thanks, heading through the fence without looking back.

Seth went to follow last, but I caught him by the collar, wheeling him around to face me with a snarl.

"You and me need to talk," I growled as he yanked himself free of my grip and folded his arms.

"What about? Me following Darcy back to Aer Tower and fucking her blind?" he asked casually and my fist snapped out, clocking him in the jaw and making him stumble backwards with a doggish yelp. I relished the bite of pain against my knuckles. Fighting Fae in Darkmore had taught me to enjoy a physical brawl more than I'd imagined. And if I was going to inflict pain on this fucker, I wanted to inflict it first hand.

He swore then came at me like an animal, grabbing my shirt in his fist and yanking me forward so I was nose to nose with him. I bared my fangs, unphased. I'd relish a fight. I'd take pleasure in feeling his bones break under my fists.

"Jealous, asshole?" he taunted and I shoved him back a step with the force of my Order, making him nearly fall over before he caught himself at the last second with a gust of air.

He laughed viciously, tipping his head forward as he growled.

"You're not with her, she told me herself," I said and he laughed again.

"Well she would say that, wouldn't she?" he taunted. "I know I have a lot of making up to do before I earn her trust, but I will do it *Professor*."

"I'm not your professor, Seth, so I have no problem murdering your hateful ass and burying your body. It would make my fucking day. And what's a few more years on my sentence now anyway, huh?"

His face split into a grin and he jumped at me with a joyful bark. I threw a solid punch into his gut as he wrapped his arms around me and licked the side of my face as he wheezed out a breath.

"What the fuck are you doing?" I snapped, shoving him off, but he just kept coming, trying to lick and nuzzle me until I punched him in the face again and shot away several paces with my Vampire speed.

His man bun had come loose and he casually retied it as he smirked at me, healing his bruises. "Right, I'm off to fuck your girl. Oh sorry, I meant *my* girl."

I lunged at him again, but hit an air shield this time. "She's not fucking you. She has more class than that."

"Thing is, Lancey, as much as you wanna believe that, a tiny part of you is doubting her, isn't it? After all, she hid her relationship with you for long enough. And obviously we're keeping it low key considering the current laws. She couldn't risk Lionel finding out the truth from you if he ever decided to have a rummage in your head with one of his Cyclops pals. In fact, do you think she'd ever trust you with a secret again?"

I didn't want his words to get under my skin, but they did. They worked their way into me like rats burrowing into my heart. But who was I going to believe? Darcy Vega or this piece of shit?

But dammit the piece of shit has a point.

He smiled widely. "Right, well enjoy stressing about me screwing her. I think tonight's the night I'll fuck you out of her for good actually." He headed away through the fence and I threw a blast of ice at him that made his air shield tremble, but it didn't break.

I took two heavy breaths, my chest heaving as I considered going after him. But it was almost dawn and what the fuck was I going to do? *Killing him* would *solve my issue...*

I pictured making him scream for a long moment before snatching the stardust from my pocket. *Probably not worth making Darcy and Darius hate me. Besides, fuck if they'd just give me more time in Darkmore for that. They'd execute me on the spot.*

The stars carried me back to the woodland near to the palace and I ran to the huge tree, pressing my hand to the Hydra mark there and slipping down the stairway into the underground passage. I shot back to the summerhouse at high speed and opened the hatch, pushing it open and slipping into the kitchenette. All was quiet and I took a steadying breath just before the sliding door sounded. My heart lurched and I shot into the bathroom faster than I'd ever moved in my life, tearing my clothes off and diving into the shower. I set it running, washing away any trace of the night.

"Lance!" Lionel's voice boomed.

Holy fuck. What if he knows?

Fear rocked through me as I pushed out of the shower, wrapping a towel around my waist and fixing a flat expression onto my face. I had to act for my life, because there was no way I was going to let him find out we had the Imperial Star.

Lionel was wearing an emerald green coat and looked like he was heading off to the city.

He gave me a dark look, walking toward me with his shoulders pressed back and rage in his posture.

"I am growing impatient," he hissed. "Vard has told me to give you time, but you have had plenty. Where is the Imperial Star? You must have something tangible by now."

Relief rushed through me that he didn't know I'd left the property. It felt fucking amazing to get one up on him. And I had the best poker face of anyone I knew. Except maybe Tory - that girl was a pro at bullshitting people.

"I found something today," I lied, shooting over to a drawer in the kitchenette and taking out the replica of my father's diary I'd made.

It was filled with nonsense symbols and diagrams which looked totally fucking convincing and meant absolutely nothing. I pointed out one of the maps I'd hand drawn. I'd copied it from an old kid's book I found in the library, changing a few of the details so it wasn't completely recognisable. Not that I expected Lionel to pick up a copy of The Fae Who Flew to Flamoo any time soon. But you never knew what psychos lulled themselves to sleep with at night.

"I think the Imperial Star may be hidden in this mountain, but it's not clear where it is." I pointed to the nonsense symbols above it which were all smudged - thanks to me. "The name isn't readable, but I've been working through ancient maps of Solaria to try and match it."

Lionel took the diary from me, frowning at the picture as he tried to place it. "It does look familiar...perhaps Vard can *see* more."

Oh fuck, he might see Flamoo.

"I doubt it. It says it's a long forgotten place protected by dark spells to conceal its location," I sighed and Lionel narrowed his eyes at me. I kept my features taut, frowning like I was trying to figure it out. But the only thing I was really figuring out was how best I'd like to see him fall from grace. Burned to a crisp in Phoenix fire, or torn to pieces in the jaws of his son? Thrown into a vat of hot tar, or churned up in a blender? "I found this too." I turned the page and showed him an image of a sceptre which I'd traced from a book on ancient artefacts – plus added a few embellishments including a stone set into the top of it. I'd based it on one of the many ancient stories about where the Imperial Star had been kept in the past, so it was pretty convincing. "I think the star could be hidden in this sceptre."

He eyed it, a hungry glint entering his gaze like he was picturing wielding the sceptre and destroying people with it. *I wonder what age Lionel turned into a fully fledged psychopath, or if he was born deranged.* "A sceptre...yes it makes sense for it to be set in something like that. Keep searching. I want it in my possession soon," he growled, a warning in his tone.

He turned like he was going to leave, but I caught his arm, an idea coming to me.

Lionel looked back at me with a snarl, eyeing my hand on his arm and I withdrew it quickly, figuring I didn't want to lose a limb tonight.

"Uncle Lionel..." I laid it on thick. "I know we don't see eye to eye sometimes, but you've always watched out for my family." I dropped his gaze and felt him scrutinising me closely. I was going to get a Golden Leo award for this if I pulled it off. "It kills me not being around my sister. Can she come and visit sometimes?"

If I could spend more time with her, maybe I could find a way to bring her back, make her remember herself.

Lionel sneered, stepping away from me. "No."

"Why not?" I demanded as my blood heated. "I've done everything you've asked me to, let me have this one thing. Let her have some damn happiness."

"Happiness?" he laughed. "The girl is more content with me than she is with any other Fae in Solaria. She couldn't care to spend time with you, Lance.

Even if I cared to allow it. Which I do not."

A growl built in my throat as an acidic rage burned through me. I knew it was a bad idea to poke the Dragon, but I was also valuable to him, so what could he even do to me? Imprison me? Yeah, been there done that, got the 'I survived Darkmore' cap.

"She isn't herself," I snapped. "How can you lay your hands on her? It's the shadows that want you, not her. She would never touch you."

I expected him to strike me, but he didn't. He just laughed, a cold, empty laugh. "Your sister was sucking my cock long before she ever went into the shadows, boy. Even before I Guardian bonded her to me."

"Liar!" I snapped, lunging at him with nothing but hate driving my actions as I cast a blade of ice in my palm. It shattered against his air shield before I even got close, and his eyes darkened to deadliest nightshade.

He whipped out a hand, a blast of air throwing me across the room so I hit the wall hard and pain exploded through my head. He wrapped a tendril of shadows around my throat and held me pinned there, slowly walking toward me like a murderous beast and carefully pushing his blonde hair back into place.

"She is attracted to power and I let her have a taste of it because she was useful to me. Don't go trying to convince yourself that I forced her or abused her. You want to know how it first started? I found her waiting naked in my bed one night when Catalina and your mother were staying in the city for some charitable function. I will admit that I was surprised, but she is a beautiful girl and I wasn't going to embarrass her by turning her away. And it wasn't long after that that I realised how useful she could be to me. Now she is useful once more, so I will fuck her and use her and devour her if the notion takes me, boy, because she is mine – quite willingly so. She no longer cares about her waste of perfectly good oxygen brother who has done nothing but brought shame on her family. You are an embarrassment to your parents," he hissed.

"Only to one of them," I managed to croak out and his eyes narrowed.

"Your father was a loyal servant of mine, despite how his wife pined for me," he laughed again, taking joy in my pain, but he didn't know anything.

My father had deceived him. Let him think he was his ally, when he'd actually been the ally of the royals. His loyalty had lain with them, and no one else. And when it came to it, he'd sacrificed himself to ensure this asshole of a Dragon had a weakness. The Imperial Star, the twins, me. Maybe they'd even known about Darius too.

"You should really show more respect for the man who arranged the marriage of your mother and father," he snarled, releasing me from the shadows so I hit the floor. "You wouldn't even exist if it wasn't for my interference."

"Lucky me," I ground out, pushing to my feet and he raised his chin.

"It's time you learned your place, Lance Orion. You're nothing anymore. You gave up your Faehood when you fucked a Vega and landed yourself in prison. Pathetic really. When you've found the star, I will be more than happy to put you out of your misery if you want. I'm sure you'll be begging for death soon enough."

"Fuck you," I snapped and he turned his back on me, heading to the exit.

He said nothing more as he stepped out of the door and it whipped shut behind him with a swipe of his hands, locking tight.

My heart bunched up in my chest and I roared my anger at the world over Clara. But I had to hold on to the fact we had the Imperial Star now. And somehow, some day soon, Lionel was going to meet his end and I would make damn sure I was there to watch.

TORY

CHAPTER THIRTY THREE

With all of us in King's Hollow, we were seriously lacking in space with the two armchairs and a three seater sofa between the seven of us so I escaped to the kitchenette. My plan was to make coffee for everyone while Darcy and Seth started bickering about who had claimed the armchair first, but I stalled as I realised I wasn't actually sure how to do that.

Although I'd been staying here pretty often since I'd been drawn back from the shadows, I'd been treated like an honest to shit princess by the others because they were all keen to look after me after my time spent trapped in Lionel's fun company. And I kinda didn't hate that because drinks had been fetched on my behalf a whole hell of a lot as well as tasty food and snuggly blankets.

Caleb had bought me a pair of fluffy slippers and Seth was still on the feeding kick, bringing me candy all the time. Of course, Geraldine had me swimming in bagels every morning and Max was basically my emotional crutch, ending up sleeping in my bed with me half the time to help with my nightmares.

Darcy was my other half so just her being with me was all I needed, but of course she'd been pampering me nonstop too and we stole as much time together here as we could get away with.

And Darius…well, Darius was just there whenever I needed him. I couldn't be alone with him obviously and we couldn't get close physically for any real length of time, but he found other ways to be close to me.

Like the way he always set a fire blazing in my room before I even thought about heading to bed. Or the way there was a perfectly brewed coffee with my name on it waiting for me every damn morning without fail, even if he slept at the palace with Orion. He'd even bought me my own mug – not that he had given it to me to unwrap or anything like a normal person. My coffee had just started appearing in it every morning without him saying a word. It was baby pink with a golden R printed on it, a crown casually hanging from the top corner of the letter and a pair of wings spread wide around it. Not me at all - totally girly, princessy, OTT on the cuteness and with the complete wrong initial printed on it like he'd been trying to make sure I freaking hated it…and yet if anyone else dared to drink from it I kinda felt like burning their face off in case they broke it, so maybe I loved it. Not that I'd be telling him that.

In fact, he was so in tune with my caffeine needs that I hadn't actually made myself a coffee once in all the time I'd spent here. So now I was standing looking at the over engineered piece of garbage they called a coffee machine, wondering what the fuck I was supposed to do to it to get my caffeine fix. Where were the instant granules? Hell, where were the mugs kept? And the sugar? I hadn't slept all night and I was going to start getting the twitches if I didn't feed my habit soon.

My skin prickled with awareness and I stiffened as I felt a large body moving up close behind me.

"I can help you out if you're not sure how to use it," Darius said, leaning around me and fiddling with some of the buttons and shit on the machine as his chest pressed to my back.

"Erm, thanks," I said, trying to concentrate on what he was doing so that I'd remember next time while being utterly overwhelmed by his mere presence instead.

He was saying something about beans and moving a funny looking handle thing from one part of the machine to another, but all I could think about was the heat of his body pressing to mine and the way his stubble was grazing my temple as he leaned over me while he spoke.

"Got it?" Darius asked as he finished putting the frothy milk into the coffee. So much for the instant shit I used to buy back in the mortal realm. I had been wondering why it tasted so much better here and I guessed I had my answer, but I still had no idea what he'd just done so I shook my head. *Nope, I was distracted by how damn good your body feels against mine and wanting to lick your tattoos.* Damn, it had been a long time since I'd gotten laid.

"Maybe you make it and I'll hand them out?" I suggested, drawing a laugh from him.

"You want me to show you again?" he offered, pressing closer so that my ass drove against his crotch and I bit my lip to hold back a gasp.

"Make mine a triple shot, I'm dog tired over here," Seth called and I looked over at him just in time to see Max punch him in the bicep. "What? Don't you get it? Dog tired - because I'm a-"

"You're ruining the moment, jackass," Max growled and I quickly ducked out of my space crushed between Darius and the counter as I grabbed the coffee he'd already made and took it over to Geraldine.

"Oh my gracious," she gasped. "My lady you should not be reduced to a serving maid for a wretch such as I - leave the running around to one of these lowly Heirs. They are much more suited to the task of servitude-"

"Like fuck we are," Max growled and I just waved her off with a laugh as I moved back to grab the next cup from Darius.

Every time he passed me a mug, his fingers brushed mine and I couldn't help but bite my lip against the stupid ass smirk I was fighting. It was like we were playing a game against the stars, trying to figure out exactly where we crossed the line between them not noticing our interactions and them doing something to intervene. And I wanted to play it all the damn time.

When everyone finally had coffee and Max had pushed an energetic feeling over everyone to help us perk up after being out all night, Darius and I moved over to sit down with the others and found there was only one spot left on the end of the sofa.

Seth and Caleb were sitting on the other two couch seats, Seth leaning low in his chair so that his head was pressed to Caleb's side while his feet were propped up on the coffee table.

Darcy had taken the armchair to the left of the fire and Max was on the right with Geraldine perched on the arm of it with her feet in his lap.

I took a step towards Darcy, but Darius caught my arm and tugged me down on the couch instead, placing me carefully in between his legs as he hung one over the arm and spread them as wide as possible in that my-dick-is-too-big-to-function way of his. It meant we weren't actually touching but I was practically in his lap at the same time.

He slung an arm over the back of the couch and took a sip of his coffee, maintaining eye contact with me as I looked over my shoulder at him and he raised an eyebrow as if daring me to make a fuss.

I decided against that and turned to look at the others instead, pretending not to notice the way they were all watching us as I drank a bit of my own coffee.

"Let's see it then," I said as Darcy raised her eyebrows at me, twinunicating the fact that she wanted to discuss the Darius situation with me asap while I arched an eyebrow, letting her know I expected all the details about her and Orion in that tomb.

She cut a glance at the others, gave me the hint of a nod then pulled the Imperial Star from her pocket before holding it out for all of us to look at.

Seth released a low whistle, leaning forward to pluck it from her hand and holding it up so it caught the light of the rising sun as it came through the window.

"This would look damn good in a sceptre," he said, tossing it up and down a couple of times so that a rainbow of light spilled across the room. "Why doesn't anyone carry a sceptre anymore? Maybe I could bring it back."

"Nah," Caleb said, leaning forward to pluck it from his grasp. "This belongs in a big ass crown."

"You mean to suit your big ass head?" Darius teased, leaning around me to place his mug down on the table beside mine before reaching for the Imperial Star and Caleb tossed it over to him.

Seth flopped back, dropping his head into Caleb's lap and whimpering as he gave him the puppy dog eyes and Caleb began stroking his fingers through his long hair while shaking his head like he didn't really want to. But he could have just said no, so I was gonna call bullshit on that.

Darius sat forward, his arm winding around my waist as he handed over the star and I sucked in a deep breath as the power of the thing hit me like a solid weight landing on my chest.

"Holy shit," I breathed as it tingled against my fingers and my magic rose up to caress it like it was aching for the chance to use it. "That feels incredible."

"I know, right?" Darcy grinned while Seth cocked his head in confusion.

"It just felt like a rock to me," he said, glancing up at Caleb who nodded.

I exchanged another look with my sister as I passed it to Geraldine who dropped to one knee in front of me before accepting it.

"Of course none of you unworthy buffoons can feel the power within the weapon of the royals," she exclaimed as she held the Imperial Star up over her head like she was afraid of it getting too close to the ground. "You do not have royal blood running in your veins and therefore are not able to tap into the power that resides within. Only the true Queens can feel it!"

"I felt something," Darius put in. "It wasn't a lot, but it was more than nothing. Like there was power laying in the heart of it behind a veil I couldn't see through."

Geraldine gasped, almost dropping the star as she clutched her pearls - which she was honest to shit actually wearing - and glared daggers at Darius behind me.

"Your unworthy usurper of a father has placed his scaly behind on the throne and crowned himself King. His blood runs in your veins which must make you a...a...a prince of darkness."

All of the other Heirs shifted uncomfortably at that announcement and I frowned as I realised there was some truth to it. They might have all been evenly matched before Lionel had gifted Darius the shadows, but now that he had them, he was technically stronger. And with his father on the throne, he was next in line...

"Calm down, Geraldine, I'm not a prince of anything," Darius growled. "I would never claim to be the heir to the throne. My intentions have always been clear and have never faltered. I stand with my brothers united."

The other Heirs relaxed at that while Seth snorted a laugh. "I know you'd never turn on us, Darius. You're too hard pressed for friends as it is - without us you'd have no one and nothing."

"Except a comfy throne and shiny crown," Caleb joked and Darius laughed dismissively while Max leaned forward to pluck the star from Geraldine's hand.

"Well, I can't feel anything," he said with a shrug. "But if you girls can then maybe you can wield it after all?"

He tossed it across the coffee table and Darcy caught it as Geraldine screamed in horror, throwing the back of her hand over her eyes.

I couldn't help but laugh and Max scooped her up off of the floor, dropping her in his lap as he murmured at her to calm down.

"The diary said only a reigning sovereign could use it," Darius said.

"Well, it's worth a shot. Give it a go," I urged and Darcy frowned as she looked at the shimmering stone in her palm.

We all fell silent as we watched her and I flinched in surprise as Darius's hand landed on my shoulder blade before he scored a line down the exact spot where my wings emerged when I shifted.

A breathy moan slid from my lips which I hurriedly covered with a cough as the others looked our way and Darius chuckled before doing it again.

Ho-ly fuck, why did that feel so incredible? He needed to stop. And never stop. And oh shit, he was doing it again…

I tried to ignore what he was doing as Darcy stared at the star for a bit longer before giving up with a sigh.

"Nothing," she said. "I can feel the power of it, but it's kinda like Darius said, there's something standing between it and me and I can't seem to merge my magic with it or get it to respond at all. It sounds crazy, but back in the cave it spoke to me and Lance. It said we need to seek the palace in the deep where the last of them lie. And…that we need to do what the King could not."

"Sounds like gibberish to me," Seth said and Geraldine scoffed.

"The voice of a star is sacred, it must mean something of upmost importance," she exclaimed.

"We heard it talking in the vision of our father," I said, trying to recall everything we'd heard it say. "Didn't it mention a palace then too?"

"Yeah," Darcy said. "The Palace of Flames." She looked to the Heirs to see if they might be able to shine some light on that, but no one had an answer. My sister reached into her pocket, taking out a Tarot card and my heart beat harder.

"Is that-?" I asked and she nodded, sending it over to me on a flutter of air. I gazed at the picture of a man riding in a chariot accompanied by two Sphinxes and turned it over to read the message.

"It's the last one," Darcy said and I smiled, tracing my fingers over the lettering.

We'd done what he'd wanted, and I guessed if these Guild people had wanted us to be able to find the Imperial Star then maybe it made sense for them to use this frustratingly annoying way to show us where it was. But still. We had it at last. So maybe the old guy had been onto something when he'd left a trail of magical Tarot cards after his demise. Totally batshit, but pretty helpful in the long run.

Darcy gazed at the star again in her palm. "I guess we really would have to claim the throne to use it."

"No chance of that then," Darius muttered and we all stilled, casting looks at each other as we were all reminded of the huge divide that still sat heavily between us.

It may have seemed like we were getting along like one big happy family these days but in reality, we were just united in our goal to dethrone Lionel. After that, all bets were off.

"You rotten, dirty scoundrels cannot seriously still believe-" Geraldine began but she was interrupted by a knock at the window and we looked up to find Gabriel standing on the balcony with his black wings fluttering in the breeze.

Seth used a bit of air magic to open the window for him and he hopped inside, his wings fading out of existence as he shifted back into his Fae form.

"Oh my, I'll never know why I didn't suspect your royal blood before the truth was revealed, dear Gabriel," Geraldine said, fanning her face with her hand. "The cut of your physique is clearly that of a true, blue blooded specimen. The broadness of your chest alone-"

"Put a shirt on dude, you look cold," Max snapped, using air magic to whip a shirt out of the chest at the side of the room and tossing it into Gabriel's face.

Darius ran his thumb down my shoulder blade again but I shrugged him off, frowning over the throne comment and reminding myself of all the reasons I had not to be getting so damn comfortable with him. Gah, he was so frustrating. Why did he have to be so freaking tempting even though I knew that when it came down to it, we would never truly be on the same side? We would always be waiting for the other to bow and that could only end in a fight and a loser.

"I *saw* myself coming here but I don't know why," Gabriel said, tossing the shirt aside and moving to lean against the fireplace.

"We retrieved the Imperial Star tonight," I said, grinning at him as his eyebrows rose and Darcy lifted the glittering stone to show him.

"You what? How...I *saw* you heading off campus and knew it was something that mattered, but I didn't..." Gabriel's brow furrowed. "Something this important happening to the two of you should have had my head spinning with visions all day. How is it possible that I didn't even realise that you were heading out to get it last night?"

"Sorry dude, I should have told you," I said. "But I just kinda assume you know everything, so it didn't really occur-"

"I don't know *everything*," Gabriel said with a shit eating grin lifting the corner of his lips which said he pretty much did. "But I do have a damn good handle on the stuff that counts. And something this big happening to my sisters-"

"What does that mean?" Seth interrupted him and Gabriel cocked his head as he looked at the stone.

"I'm not sure. Can I have a look at it?"

Darcy passed it to him and we all watched as he turned it over in his hands, brushing his thumb back and forth over the rough stone then closing his eyes as he concentrated.

"I can feel great power in it, but I can't access it," he said.

"How the hell can you feel it?" Caleb demanded. "I thought it was only people with royal blood and you're not the Savage King's son so you shouldn't be able to feel it any more than I can."

"Our mother was a princess where she came from. Maybe as her oldest son, Gabriel technically has a claim to that throne?" Darcy suggested.

"Oh, what sense this makes!" Geraldine gasped. "I have long since admired what a dashing and magnanimous figure you cast and now knowing that you are indeed a prince-"

"Let's not get carried away," Gabriel interrupted as Max muttered something about him not being that dashing. "I'm part of a royal line, not a prince and I don't *see* any future where I even travel to our mother's home country let alone have any interest in claiming some foreign throne. My heart and my family are in Solaria and I intend to stay here and stand by my sisters' sides as they rise up and claim the throne. Then I'll serve them as their Royal Seer. That's it. Anyway, back to the point at hand, I can't *see* anything about this star. Nothing. I can't even *see* which one of you will take it from my hand. So I'm almost certain that it's shielded from my visions in the same way as all of the stars' decisions are. They gift me The Sight when it comes to things that affect people I know or love, but they don't allow me to *see* their movements with things such as Elysian Mate bonds and this feels the same."

"So Vard shouldn't be able to *see* it either?" I asked hopefully.

Gabriel's upper lip peeled back at the mention of Lionel's choice for a Royal Seer. "No. That two bit con artist doesn't have a tenth of the control over The Sight that I do. I'm willing to bet the only reason he even manages to *see* anything at all is because he's sitting his unworthy ass in the chair in the Royal Seer's Chamber and using the power of it to amplify his meagre abilities tenfold."

"So how come you didn't just sit in it and *see* everything you could ever want to *see* during the summer while Darcy still lived in the palace if it's so amazing?" Seth asked, giving Gabriel an accusing look and Gabriel sighed.

"I did. I sat in it multiple times and tried everything I could to get it to work for me, but it's enchanted to only work for the Royal Seer and seeing as I am not that and Darcy couldn't give me the title unless she claimed the throne, it wouldn't work. Believe me, I tried everything I could think of to make it work for me, hoping it would show me some way for us to get to Tory."

Gabriel's pained gaze moved to me and my heart twisted at the thought of what they'd all been through while I was held by Lionel in his manor. I knew they'd done everything they could and I couldn't imagine how much it had hurt my siblings to know there was nothing they could do to save me while terrified of what was happening to me. It would have sent me insane.

"So if we can hide the Imperial Star then there should be no way for Lionel to ever even find out we have it?" I asked and Gabriel nodded.

"Let's just test my theory about me not being able to *see* it first. I'll close my eyes and one of you throw it at me. My Sight always warns me of something aimed my way like that so if I don't *see* it then we know it truly is shrouded by the stars."

Gabriel closed his eyes and Seth snatched the star from Darcy with a gust of air magic before launching it at Gabriel's chest way harder than necessary.

I sucked in a breath as it smacked against his pec and he grunted a curse as the rough edge of it cut his skin open while Seth saved the Imperial Star from falling to the ground with his magic and guided it back down to the table.

"*Ow*," Gabriel snarled, opening his eyes and narrowing them at Seth.

"How can we be sure that proves anything?" Caleb asked. "I know you *think* you would have seen that coming, but maybe you wouldn't really *see* anything we threw at you and the Imperial Star is no different."

Gabriel tutted as he healed the cut on his chest before levelling a look at Caleb. "If you want me to prove it then throw whatever else you like at me," he taunted, closing his eyes again and waiting.

Caleb smirked as he leaned forward, lifting his hand and casting round stones into his palm before throwing them at Gabriel one after another. My brother caught each of them with ease, never once opening his eyes and somehow having his hand in the perfect place to make the catch no matter what way Caleb shot them at him.

"Satisfied?" Gabriel asked, smirking cockily and I grinned at him. That shit was stupid cool. I seriously had the best siblings.

"Okay, so we just need to hide it then," Darcy said thoughtfully. "Should we leave it here somewhere or-"

"Oh my lady, I don't believe it should ever be out of sight of one of the Vega Princesses. This is of tantamount importance in the fight against our evil overlord," Geraldine said hastily.

"One of you should wear it then," Max suggested.

"I have a chain that you could hang it from," Darius said, lifting me into his arms for a moment so that he could get off of the couch before placing me back down and heading across the room to the chest where he kept his treasure.

"You should wear it, Darcy," I said. "It's too risky for me to be bringing it near to Lionel whenever I go back there."

"Okay," she agreed, accepting the silver chain from Darius as he held it out to her.

He didn't actually let go of it though, a soft growl escaping him as he tried to fight his Dragon nature to hoard all of his treasure for himself.

"I could find a different chain if you don't want me to have this?" Darcy asked, looking amused as his muscles bunched with the effort of trying to make himself part with it.

I got to my feet and moved over to him, taking his hand in mine and meeting his dark gaze as I slowly peeled his fingers out of his fist one by one.

"Bad Dragon," I chastised and he almost smirked at me until the moment when I actually tugged the chain out of his hand.

He snatched my wrist suddenly but I'd already tossed the chain to Darcy. I could feel all of our friends watching us as he fought against his

Dragon nature while staring down at me with all the intensity of the fire that burned in his soul.

"You shouldn't have done that, Roxy," he growled and a shiver of fear tracked through my core at his words which both made me want to run for the hills and move even closer to the danger in his eyes.

I forced myself to push through the fear, tiptoeing up and placing a kiss against the rough stubble lining his jaw, my lips just brushing the corner of his mouth as my heart galloped in my chest.

"You'll forgive me," I teased and his eyes flared with liquid heat as he slowly relaxed his grip on my arm and let me go.

I stepped back with my pulse pounding and turned to Darcy as she crafted an amulet out of earth magic to hold the star on the chain before hanging it around her neck. It was beautiful, but nothing about it gave away what it truly was, and I grinned at the knowledge that we'd finally gotten one up on the lizard asshole who had stolen our throne.

"So what now?" Seth asked eagerly and I looked around at everyone, wondering if any of them might have an answer to that.

"Well, Orion won't be able to read any more from the diary until the next full moon," Darius said. "And it's not like we can actually use the Imperial Star. So I guess we just keep looking into ways to break the Guardian bond, fighting Nymphs and hunting for any more advantages that we can get over my father between now and then."

"Well I suppose in that case, it is time for me to hit the hay," Geraldine announced, getting to her feet. "We should all try to rest our noggins awhile to refresh ourselves before class."

"I'll walk you back," Max announced, getting to his feet and heading out of the room with her.

"You wanna come for a sleepover with me?" I asked Darcy, giving her a look that let her know I was going to be getting answers about her and Orion the moment we were alone.

"Sure," she agreed and we said goodnight to the others as we headed out of the room towards the bedroom I'd claimed for my own here in the Hollow. We couldn't stay here together nearly as often as I liked in case one of the K.U.N.T.s noticed her absence, so she often had to return to Aer Tower and I relished the chance to remain here with everyone now.

I ducked into Darius's room as Darcy moved into mine and I looked around for a moment before snagging one of his hoodies from the end of his bed and taking it with me. I wasn't going to let myself overthink the fact that I slept better when I was wrapped up in his clothes than I did without them. They were just warmer than mine. And comfier. And smelled all kinds of nice.

Darcy was already showering when I made it inside and I pulled my clothes off, using my water magic to wash instead of waiting for a turn then using air to dry myself off again before pushing fire though my veins to warm up. Then I pulled on Darius's hoodie and made myself and Darcy little crowns made of white rose vines just to use every Element before crawling into the bed and waiting for her. It was pretty damn cool having all the Elements and I was in the mood to celebrate our win.

There was a fire burning in the grate and I bit my lip as I looked at it, trying to figure out when Darius had managed to sneak in here and get it going for me since we'd returned. It wasn't like I needed any help in lighting a fire, but the room was always so nice and warm when it had been burning for a while and the constant flames meant that I always woke up with my magic fully replenished every morning too.

When Darcy reappeared wearing a pair of my pyjamas, I grinned as I tossed the crown onto her head and she laughed as she settled herself back against the pillows.

"Look at us, practically queens already," I joked, grabbing a huge bar of chocolate from my nightstand and tossing it to her before cursing as I realised my second bar was gone. Fucking Seth. I knew it was him. Always sniffing about my snacks. I was gonna have to set up some kind of snack trap to keep him out of my shit if this kept happening.

"Can you actually imagine it?" Darcy asked, breathing a laugh. "Us ruling a damn kingdom?"

"I've been thinking about it and I have some ideas," I said seriously. "Like first of all, I'm thinking there could be some pretty epic race nights at the palace if we build a circuit through the grounds. And every month I can beat Darius's ass at the race."

"Sounds good. No need to worry about all that political crap."

"Nah," I agreed. "We'll make the Heirs our Councillors and let them deal with that shit. Make me queen of partying and I'll be a happy duck and you and Orion can fill the palace with little baby Vampires to satisfy the kingdom's need for more Heirs."

"As if," Darcy balked. "There is no me and Orion. Not anymore."

"Right. So why are you blushing? Do you wanna tell me what happened in that tomb or are you gonna make me guess?" I teased.

Darcy groaned loudly, slumping back on the pillows as she took a big bite of chocolate. "I dunno, Tor. We were looking for the Imperial Star and then somehow we were arguing about everything that had happened and I was just so mad at him all over again then suddenly he was just there and he...I..."

"So you're telling me that while we were all out there fighting for our lives you two were making out in the dark?" I teased and she groaned, yanking a pillow out from under me and covering her face.

"No, it wasn't like that," she protested, her voice muffled by the pillow and I snatched it away from her again.

"So what was it like? Are you getting back together?" I asked hopefully and her face scrunched up angrily at that suggestion.

"Fuck no. He doesn't just get to rip my heart out, stamp on it, leave it to rot for six months then dust it off and start it beating again. We're just...he's just...I'm just...nothing."

She looked so broken by that statement that it cut into me and my heart twisted with sympathy for my twin as I burrowed down into the covers beside her.

"Maybe you should think about forgiving him?" I suggested in a small voice.

"What?" she gasped like she never would have expected to hear that opinion from me and I grimaced at the words too, but I stood by them.

"Look, I know I'm always the first to tell people to get fucked if they cross me. And I'm the first to kick a dude in the dick if he even thinks about crossing you - which I have been doing repeatedly to Orion by the way - but my situation has made me realise that maybe, sometimes, it's worth letting your pride slip and thinking about forgiveness.

If I hadn't been so stubborn when it came to Darius then maybe things could have turned out differently for us. But now that I know what it's like to ache for a love I can never really have, I just don't want that for you. And I know Orion fucked up and deserves every punishment you want to dish out and he should have to grovel so hard that he becomes the king of grovelling but..."

"But?" she asked, looking at me like she was hoping I might have the answers she needed even though we both knew I sucked at this stuff more than anyone we knew. But I guessed I was an expert in what *not* to do, so I could give her my advice on that much.

"But if you think there's a chance that the love between you could be repaired or that you might be able to forgive him one day then maybe you should open yourself up to the possibility of that? Because I once thought I could never forgive Darius for the things he's done to me and maybe I still haven't, but I wish I had the choice to try. And I don't want to see you left pining for the man you love when there's a chance for you to find happiness with him, even if it's only the slightest glimmer of hope. At least there *is* hope."

Darcy's eyes filled with tears for both of us and I smiled sadly as I pulled her into my arms and we lifted the covers over our heads like we used to when we were little kids.

"I'm not sure there is any hope," Darcy whispered in the darkness.

"I know," I said. "But not sure is better than being certain there's not. So just think about it, yeah?"

"Okay," she agreed. "I'll think about it."

XAVIER

CHAPTER THIRTY FOUR

I jogged out to Earth Territory for my Order Enhancement lesson, excited to fly with my herd. I was in a fucking awesome mood today. Since I'd passed The Reckoning, shit just seemed to be getting better and better. Darius and the others had found the Imperial Star, my mom had escaped my father, and my horn had grown two centimetres in the last week. Life was sweet. And to top it all off, I'd spent yesterday evening dijazzling my junk with shiny topaz rhinestones and a big ass diamond which now adorned the base of my dick.

I wasn't sure I'd done it right exactly, but I'd figured it out from an article in Zodiass Weekly. And I couldn't wait to show it off. Getting naked was kinda second nature now and all the other stallions were showing off their glittering bits all the time to get the females' attention. So it was time I Faed up and did it too. It didn't feel completely right on me, but I was sure I'd get used to it in time.

I hurried up the hill where all the other Pegasuses were gathering for class. Professor Clip-Clop – whose name was actually Clippard but he seemed to like his students' little nickname for him - was there with his violet hair, square chin and narrow shoulders, already stripping down as he prepared to shift.

"Morning Xavier!" he called brightly. "Ready to get into the sky?"

"Yes, sir." I grinned, heading over to join my herd but my mood took a dive as my gaze fell on a shirtless Tyler whispering in Sofia's ear and kissing her neck. She was in rainbow coloured underwear that made my dick twitch happily, but the way he was touching her made my lips tighten. He was such a possessive asshole, with his muscles and his hair that always looked casually windswept like he'd just flown through the freshest, fluffiest cloud. I just wanted to punch him in his damn face.

Sofia waved me over and I pulled my shirt off, revealing my broad chest which I'd been working on daily in the Lunar Leisure gym.

Before I made it to Sofia, Liselle jumped into my way, her silvery hair running down her spine and her large eyes framed with blue glitter that matched her shifted form.

"Hey Xavier, wanna fly beside me today?" She batted her lashes and I looked over her head to Sofia.

"Yeah, sure," I muttered as she ran her finger up between my abs.

Sofia snorted indignantly and my heart lifted as she glared at Liselle. Was she...jealous?

Liselle tiptoed up to draw my attention back to her. She really was pretty, with full lips, dark skin and a scent that reminded me of candy canes. But there was only one girl I craved and I planned on claiming her and this herd just as soon as I could.

Liselle pushed her fingers into my hair, tipping her head to one side. "You'd look good with a long mane, have you ever thought about growing it out fully?"

She was suddenly ripped away from me by the hair and I found Sofia there, knocking her to the ground and turning around to kick dirt over her. *Holy shit.*

"Brutal, baby," Tyler laughed, taking out his Atlas to record it.

"You classless hinny!" Liselle shrieked, diving at Sofia, but my girl was ready, kicking her hard in the gut and sending her flying back onto the ground. Sofia did a victory trot around her and my gaze followed her ass as more of the males drew closer.

Hubert's arm brushed mine as he stepped in beside me. He was a head shorter than me with a waxed chest and a colourful tattoo of a fairy over his right pec. He was naked, his small, sparkly dick proudly on display. Which was fucking stiff as he stared at Sofia.

I snorted angrily and shoved him to the ground, making him whinny at me in fury. He didn't get up as I postured over him though, turning his head down submissively.

"Let's get into the sky, gang!" Professor Clip-Clop called and I knew it was now or never to show off my new dijazzle. Man, I never thought I'd enjoy decorating my dick over playing Fortnite, but things had changed.

Nerves warred inside me as I kicked off my shoes and dropped my pants and boxers, stepping out of them and pressing my shoulders back as I looked to Sofia. She'd moved back to Tyler's side, but her eyes were firmly fixed on me, widening as they fell to my flashy dick.

A few of the lesser females cooed but I didn't have eyes for them. I just wanted Sofia's approval, and as she bit her lip and stepped toward me, my heart raced.

"Looking good, Xavier," she purred and I tried not to get hard, but shit I was a sucker for this girl.

412

Tyler stamped his foot as the rest of the females started crowding around me and Liselle even reached out to try and touch it before I smacked her hand away.

My head was about to explode with pride when I felt one of the gemstones come loose and drop into the grass. *Oh no.*

Another fell after it, then another, until a cascade of rhinestones were tumbling down to land between my feet and everyone around me stared on in shock. *No, no, no! Abort, abort!*

I whinnied in alarm as the last of them fell and finally the diamond plopped off and that was that. Silence fell, and I swear an obnoxious tumbleweed rolled by.

Tyler burst out laughing first, the sound making rage flood through every inch of my being. "What kind of useless sticking spell did you use, buddy?"

Heat burst through my cheeks as I tried to maintain my dignity, but others were laughing now and I was tempted to open up a hole in the ground with my earth magic and let it swallow me away.

"I just used Begluezzle glue," I murmured then wished I hadn't because Tyler just laughed harder.

"That stuff is like sugar water," he chuckled and I stamped my foot in anger as more people joined in laughing.

Tyler lifted his Atlas, about to document this and make me the laughing stock of the whole school. But fuck that. I released a furious neigh then charged at him full pelt. He wasn't quick enough to get out of my way and I tackled him to the ground, headbutting him hard.

I threw my fists at him and he fought back with an angry whinny, struggling to try and roll us over. His knuckles crashed into my jaw and I twisted my head, biting his arm and he neighed loudly, forcing us to roll at last. I let the shift run through me, refusing to let him get the upper hand as my body twisted into my lilac Pegasus form. I kicked him away with my hooves and he shifted too, tearing through his pants and landing on four powerful silver legs.

He came at me with his head low and his horn glinting sharply. I swung my head toward him and our horns collided with a sharp ringing noise. I wanted to snap this asshole's horn right off and beat him down until he submitted to me. Nothing was going to stop me this time.

I reared up, trying to kick him but he reared up too, his hooves cracking against mine.

Sofia whinnied excitedly nearby, clapping as she bounced on the balls of her feet. Tyler's hoof smashed into my shoulder and I neighed in fury, returning a hard kick to his chest.

"Alright now, off into the sky!" Clip-Clop called, running forward and smacking my flank.

I reared up again in anger but he stared me down with a look that said he was gonna throw us into detention if we didn't obey. He went to slap Tyler's ass too, but he galloped away, neighing a command for the rest of the herd to follow. I galloped behind him and Sofia soon caught up with me in her sparkly pink form, her nose in line with mine as we chased Tyler.

I had to let him go, hating that this fight was over. But the war had only just begun.

Sofia whinnied and nuzzled her face against mine for a moment before charging ahead to run at Tyler's side. Mixed messages was definitely her middle name. But apparently the sparkling shower of gemstones which had fallen from my junk didn't mean it was game over for us just yet. *So I had to take it as a win.*

I sat in Tarot with Hadley on my right and Grayson on my left. It was one of the few classes where we weren't divided up into our Orders, and Professor Nox conveniently foresaw anyone's death in the stars if a single K.U.N.T. made any kind of fuss about it.

I'd finally mastered a silencing bubble thanks to Darius mentoring me on it, so me and the guys could talk undisturbed within it as we read the cards for each other. Athena sat with Ellis across the room, looking bored as hell by whatever Max's sister was saying, occasionally throwing us wistful glances. The four of us had become really tight recently, meeting at the caves every lunchtime and evening, our hideout now filled with all kinds of shit we'd stolen from around campus. Grayson and Athena had even managed to get a few beds down there, sneaking them out of Aer Tower in the night with their air magic and stowing them in the caves.

Despite my attempts with her, Ellis didn't ever seem inclined to hang out with us, and we'd pretty much accepted that she wasn't interested in being our friend. Or maybe she was just too afraid of Lionel's Orderist law to thwart it. Occasionally she tried to draw me into a conversation about how great my father was and I fed her a few bullshit lies that implied I agreed before making a hasty exit. She'd probably be joining up to the K.U.N.T. one of these days.

Grayson elbowed me in the ribs as he took his Atlas out. "That witch has banned Halloween, I fucking knew it," he growled, showing me the announcement on the screen and I realised most people in class were checking their Atlases. Even Gabriel Nox was looking at his with a scowl that could have broken glass.

> *All students are reminded that social events are restricted to Orders and parties are forbidden to no more than three students at a time. Halloween is a sacred occasion intended for remembering the passing of the dead. Ensure you spend your evening respecting those lost. Costumes are strictly banned. Any*

student seen dressing up or pretending to be anything other than
their blood born Order will face severe consequences.
    Have a wonderful day.
    Glory to the star-chosen King.
    Principal Elaine Nova.

A bunch of students looked my way, some of their expressions hateful, others fearful, some adoring. I despised being Lionel's little prince. I wished I could make a stand and tell the world I wanted nothing to do with him and publicly reject everything he stood for. But that would be the same as placing a noose around my neck and jumping off a bridge. I didn't wanna die. And at least I had Sofia and the other spares to confide in. But I could never be too careful about who I aired my opinions to.

The class broke out into chatter and I disbanded the silencing bubble around my friends.

Professor Nox tucked his Atlas into his back pocket and folded his arms. "Quiet," he said in a commanding tone and everyone obeyed. "You heard the rules. All joy is cancelled tonight. Class dismissed."

Everyone stood from their chairs and I shared a frown with Hadley who looked ready to go on a killing spree.

"It's our freshman fucking year and we've literally had no fun," Grayson grumbled.

"Capella twins, Mr Altair and Mr Acrux, stay behind please," Professor Nox said sternly and I looked down at my half filled out Tarot worksheet on the desk. *Shit.*

Everyone headed through the exit, moaning about the giant dump that had just been taken all over Halloween.

"This year sucks." Grayson kicked a chair. Nox arched an eyebrow at him and he whined like a dog.

"Take your anger out on someone else's furniture, Grayson," Nox warned and he folded his arms with a huff.

"You're such a pup sometimes, Gray," Athena teased.

"Shall I call your mommy up and tell her you wanna go home and suckle on her teats?" Hadley jibed and Grayson lunged at him with his teeth bared. Hadley shot calmly out of his way with his Vampire gifts, appearing behind Athena where she was sitting on her desk. He lunged forward with his fangs bared, excitement in his eyes, but slammed into a close-knit air shield she'd erected and stumbled away from her again with a curse.

"Not happening, Hadley," she said lightly and he growled.

Professor Nox moved to shut the door and cast a silencing bubble around us, making me frown.

"What's going on?" I asked in confusion.

"The stars have gifted me a vision about you four," he said with a smirk.

Darius had told me this dude was trustworthy and I knew he was a friend of Lance's, so I felt pretty certain that he was on our side. But it was still weird for a teacher to be all friendly and shit.

"What did you *see*?" Athena gasped, swinging her legs excitedly.

"That you will all be attending a party tonight after all." Nox grinned conspiratorially.

"Fuck yes, where?" Grayson asked, bounding towards him, having no trust issues whatsoever.

"Do you know Geraldine Grus?" Nox asked.

"The crazy Ass lady?" Hadley balked and I stamped my foot at him.

"Don't call her that," I demanded and he raised his eyebrows at me in surprise.

I hadn't been able to tell them my mom wasn't actually dead and had taken refuge with Geraldine's father. It was too risky letting anyone know about it, but I sure as shit wasn't gonna stand for anyone badmouthing any of the Gruses. They'd taken my mom in and not once questioned her loyalty. I owed them everything for that. Besides, I knew crazy and it wasn't them. It was my Uncle Benjamin who'd lost the plot when my father had banished him from the Dragon Guild after apparently losing over two hundred gold bars and three hundred bags of stardust in a game of Minojack. The guy had shown up at our door a bunch of times over the years, begging for forgiveness while jacked up on some sort of drugs, promising he could win my father the world if he just leant him a few auras.

"Woah, chill man," Grayson said with a smirk.

"Geraldine is looking for recruits to a good cause," Nox explained.

"I'm not becoming a part of her loony royalist society," Hadley said coolly.

"You don't have to. Her cause runs far deeper than that," Nox explained then lowered his tone to a whisper. "A rebellion."

My heart rate ticked up in excitement as I shared a look with my friends. "Like, against my father?"

"Exactly," Nox said, his eyes glittering mischievously. "And as faculty I am absolutely not allowed to be involved. So of course, I have involved myself up to the neck and am working hard to *see* who may make suitable recruits."

"Are our brothers in it?" Athena asked.

"Yes," Nox said and I pursed my lips at not being included sooner. "They're having a party tonight. Head to the northern door of the Pitball stadium at seven and tell Geraldine that Agent Foxy sent you." He sighed as we laughed. "I didn't pick it, Geraldine did. I tried to change fate before she decided but she's a very stubborn girl."

"Fuck yes," Grayson whooped and Athena howled excitedly.

Hadley watched her with a hungry look as he shot to my side and I gave him a taunting smile. We headed out of class and had to split up as we walked back to our Houses. The K.U.N.T.s were out in force tonight, but that just made me more excited about sneaking past them later on. I really wanted to feel like I was defying my father, and this seemed like the best opportunity yet.

At half six I showered and packed my Pegobag with some clothes for the party and lay on my bed with a towel wrapped around my waist, anxious to go. I'd styled my hair back and pushed some shimmer wax through it that made it glitter.

I was wasting time Faegling dijazzles on my Atlas, still mortified as shit over what had happened yesterday. But I wasn't gonna call it quits. I was going to have the best looking dick in the herd, I just had to figure out how to make that happen...

I tapped on a link for the ten hottest dijazzles of the year and my brows shot up as I scrolled onto number eight. Instead of gemstones, the guy had pierced his dick with crystals and it looked pretty damn sweet.

A message popped up at the top of the screen and my heart thudded harder.

Sofia:
I'm a little drunk.
Halloween is my favourite holiday.
I'm naked right now.

I sat upright with a stupid grin, tapping out my answer. Two truths and a lie was our game and as much as I wanted option number three to be true, I didn't think I was that lucky of a guy.

Xavier:
The third one is the lie...

Sofia:
You're right. Are you disappointed?

My dick tingled at her words and I sucked my lower lip, about to respond when a bang sounded against my window followed by a groan.

"What the fuck?" I jumped up, finding Hadley clinging to the frame outside.

"I came at it too hard. Let me in," he called, rubbing his nose and I snorted a laugh as I opened it for him.

He dropped into my room dressed in a crisp white shirt and slacks, his dark hair pushed back. He had a look of his brother Caleb tonight, everything about him dripping cockiness.

"Why are you naked, man? Get dressed."

"I'm gonna fly there." I pointed to my Pegobag and Hadley scowled at it, swiping it up.

"No. You need to look hot tonight." He shook my clothes from inside it which consisted of a pair of jeans and a t-shirt, then clucked his tongue and walked past me to my closet.

"Er, why?" I asked in confusion as he rifled through my things, taking out a black shirt and smart pants before throwing them at me.

"Because you need to get your cherry popped," he said with a grin and I scowled.

"Who says I haven't-"

"Everyone," he deadpanned. "Literally everyone says you haven't so maybe you should fix that. Like stat."

I didn't answer as heat climbed my neck, pulling on the clothes he'd picked out for me.

"Yeah, that'll do it." He clapped me on the shoulder. "Now get on my back, I'm your ride for the night, sugar."

I whinnied a laugh. "You're an asshole."

"Yeah, but assholes get laid," he pointed out, turning around and patting his shoulder. "Come on, hop on."

"There's only one girl I want, man," I muttered and he sighed.

"I know, I know, but Sofia is taken. And if you wanna steal her then you also wanna impress her in bed, right?"

"Well yeah, but-"

"No buts, you need to fuck as many girls as you can as practise," he said casually and I frowned. "Then you can lay on the charm, show her your magical dick and bam, she'll be yours for as long as you want her."

"I don't just wanna fuck her. I want her to be *mine*," I growled and he glanced back at me with a derisive look.

"Seriously? You want to settle down with this girl when you haven't even screwed any other Fae?" he asked.

"You're starting to sound like Grayson," I said.

"Grayson's pack of fangirling mutts don't appeal to me," he scoffed. "I like a girl who's a challenge. But once I've had her, then it's time to find new prey. Maybe you're like that too? Once you've had Sofia and she's fucked you until you shit glitter, you'll get over her."

"It's not like that with her," I said, a growl to my tone that was almost Dragon worthy.

"How would you know?" He arched a brow and dammit I didn't have a fucking answer to that. "See? You're an Alpha, it's in your blood like it's in mine. But you're gonna be an Omega in the bedroom if you don't get laid multiple times. And preferably before you try it on with a girl you actually like."

Maybe he had a point. But I also couldn't see myself wanting any other girl. There was just something about Sofia. And whenever I saw her in Tyler's arms I wanted to force him beneath me and take her away from him. Make her want *me* instead. But what if Hadley was right? What if I managed to take her then had no fucking clue what to do with her body? *Oh shit, I could mess up everything. What if I accidentally put it in her butt?*

"Let's just go," I muttered, moving to get on his back.

"I'm gonna run at my top speed," Hadley warned as he climbed out of the window and stood on the small ledge beyond it. The three floor drop below made my gut swoop, but I was more than used to heights by now. "Ready?"

"Ready," I said with a smirk then he leapt forward, plummeting through the air before softening the earth to break his fall and charging off across campus.

The world became a blur around me and I laughed at the rush rocketing through my blood. This was *insane.*

A thrill buzzed in every piece of my flesh before he jerked to a halt on the north side of the Pitball stadium, stumbled down a hill and we went crashing into the mud. I neighed a laugh as he rolled, pushing himself to his feet and looking down at himself in horror.

"*Fuck,*" he hissed.

"It's okay, I got you." I leapt up, moving toward him. "I learned a cleaning spell this week." I reached out, starting to syphon the mud off of his clothes and his eyes widened hopefully. "Who are you trying to impress anyway?" I taunted as he fixed his hair and his muscles bunched.

"No one. But we're not gonna get laid looking like shit," he growled pissily. His hot head went off more times a day then I could count, but I'd lived my whole life under the roof of the angriest Dragon in Solaria, so it was nothing I couldn't handle.

"Right, that's why you look ready to break someone's neck," I commented with a sideways grin and he shrugged, his scowl in place to stay.

I finished getting the mud off of us and we headed up to the metal door in the tall wall of the stadium. I rapped my knuckles against it, my heart cantering in my chest as we waited for an answer.

A slot whipped open in the centre of it and two bright eyes peered out. "Speak your names!" Geraldine cried.

"Xavier Acrux," I said.

"Hadley Altair."

"You're not on the list, away with you heathens," she hissed.

"Agent Foxy sent us," I said quickly and her eyes narrowed.

She finally stepped back and flicked her fingers through the slot. A spell hit me in the chest the same time it hit Hadley and we were forced back a step by the strength of it. A chill ran along my skin and I shivered.

"What was that?" I demanded.

"It unveils any illusion you may have been disguising yourselves under," Geraldine explained. "You have passed the test. Come hither!" The door flew open and Geraldine stood there in lacy mask that covered the top half of her face and a flowing bubblegum pink gown which clung tightly to her figure. "Oh my dear Xavier." She pulled me into a tight hug, squeezing me tight. "I am overjoyed that you have joined us at last."

"Thanks," I said as she released me and I gave her a bright smile. When I got a chance later, I was going to get her alone to ask about my mom, but I couldn't risk saying anything right now.

Hadley pulled the door closed behind us and I gazed down the long corridor, nothing but silence meeting my ears. Where the hell was everybody?

"You're the last ones in," Geraldine said, stepping forward and casting a spell on the door which I guessed was to lock it. "You'll need these." She plucked a couple of masks from between her breasts and passed us one each. "I am utterly aggrieved that we can't all dress up in our most outrageous costumes, but the A.S.S. committee agreed it wasn't worth the risk of getting caught out and about across campus in our frillies tonight." She sighed heavily. "Our identities must all remain hidden to protect each other though. So we shall don our masks and stick it to the big man while we're here all the same."

"Yeah, fuck my father," I said with a grin as I put my mask on.

"All this defiance gets my wet Wanda working," Geraldine exclaimed as she led us along dark corridors before pushing through a door into a stairwell and guiding us down a couple of flights.

"How did you get on the Pitball team, Geraldine?" Hadley asked. "I wanna try out next term."

"You must have the heart of a lion and the balls of a bull, young Altair," she said seriously, lifting her chin as pride gleamed in her eyes.

"Check and check," he said with a smirk and I rolled my eyes at him.

We headed through a door and my heart leapt as Geraldine let us into a silencing bubble and the sound of a crowd exploded in my ears. We were in a huge underground space the size of the Pitball pitch. It must have been right underneath it. The whole place was decorated with earth magic so it looked like a jungle, moss and vines covering the roof and floor, trees dotted around the place with ornate wooden stools ringing them. A band was playing in front of a dancefloor and to one side of it was a long bar stacked high with alcohol.

"Woah," I breathed.

"I shall see you soon, boys, I'm off for a romp on the dancefloor." Geraldine headed away, soon joining Max Rigel and swishing her hips to knock aside a girl who was dancing close to him. The other Heirs and who I guessed was Darcy were beyond them, all drinking shots and jumping wildly to the beat. I only recognised the Heirs because I knew them so well, but they'd all changed their hair and had cast illusions over their appearances to blend in.

"This is fucking awesome," Hadley growled.

My gaze suddenly locked on Sofia in a pastel blue dress, her blonde pixie cut shimmering with glitter. I knew it was her from the deep connection I felt in my chest the moment I laid eyes on her. She was at the bar with a group of girls and there was no sign of fucking Tyler for once. *She's here. And she looks like a damn dream.*

"I'm gonna go say hi to Sofia," I said, turning to Hadley, finding his gaze locked on someone and his brow drawn low.

I recognised Athena sitting on one of the stools around the nearest tree, wearing a black dress that split up one thigh. Hadley's friend Trent sat beside her without a mask on, his hand on her knee and Grayson was beyond them, talking animatedly as his pack of females all sighed or laughed at every word he said.

"You good?" I nudged Hadley and he grunted.

"See you in a bit," he muttered then shot off ahead of me, dropping into the seat beside Athena, his shoulders squared at Trent. If I wasn't being totally crazy, it kinda looked like he was jealous. Or maybe it was just a blood thing. He was desperate to sink his teeth into Athena and Trent probably was too. I'd never understand the Vampires. The idea of drinking blood made me wanna vom. Give me a sparkly rainbow cloud any day of the week.

I started walking through the jungle toward Sofia, my pulse thumping against my eardrums as I went. Hadley's advice kept haunting me as I walked. That I should hook up with some random girls just so I wasn't a complete inexperienced virgin when it came to claiming Sofia. But as I drew closer to her, I didn't even see anyone else. How was I supposed to screw another girl when it felt like this one already owned every piece of me? I knew it was fucking crazy. But I just couldn't get her out of my head. She was my lucky star. And maybe she'd get over the fact that I wasn't like the other guys she'd been with when I stole the title of Dom and crushed the rest of the herd beneath my hooves.

I walked straight up to her before I could second guess myself, planting my hand on the bar and gazing down at her as the other girls backed up around me.

"Hey," I said, my eyes falling down to her lips as they parted in surprise.

"Xavier," she gasped. "You're here."

"Guess I'm part of the club now," I said with a smirk worthy of Hadley. I could totally do this cool dude act. Though a drink or two might have helped.

"I guess you are." She grinned.

The other girls started giggling, and I recognised Liselle as she stamped her foot in irritation, trying to catch my eye.

"Do you want a shot?" I asked Sofia, ignoring the others, my whole world consumed by this beauty before me.

She battered her lashes beneath her mask which were laced with pink glitter and nodded.

I grabbed a bottle of tequila and two wooden shot glasses from a stack at the back of the bar. It seemed like a help-yourself-deal so I was gonna help myself to as much alcohol as it took to stop my nerves giving me away.

I poured us one each and our eyes remained locked as we knocked them back. I had two more before I felt myself starting to relax and I soaked in the rock music from the band as I took a step closer to Sofia.

"Tyler's not a part of the club?" I asked, resting my hand on her hip and she moved into the arc of my body immediately. *Fuck yes.*

"Yeah he is, but he went off with Hubert and Brutus earlier," she said with a challenging smile.

I nodded slowly, fighting the urge to look around for him. If Tyler got pissed I was making a move on his girl again, he was going to have to fight me. Because my instincts were burning and I wasn't going to ignore the way they drove me toward her. As a prospective Dom, she had to take my interest seriously; it was the way of the mares. But I technically hadn't officially challenged Tyler yet. I'd wanted to settle into the herd first and make sure I wasn't kidding myself. But I didn't think there was any point waiting on it now. I'd do anything to claim her. And more than that, I wanted to lead the herd. It was in my blood.

"Dance with me," I all but ordered, capturing her hand as she nodded and pulling her toward the dancefloor.

We moved through the crowd and she wound her arms around my neck as I tugged her close, our bodies pressing flush together. My dick liked that a lot and I smiled darkly as we started moving to the beat. I guessed grace had always been in my nature, plus years of attending boring ass balls with my family meant I knew how to dance. And Sofia seriously did too.

Her fingernails raked against the back of my neck in the most enticing way, my forehead falling to hers as her curves melted against my muscles. It felt so damn right, I wanted to shout it to everyone in this room and proclaim her as mine. But I knew I couldn't do that without beating Tyler down first.

"You didn't answer my question earlier, Phillip," she teased, using the name Darius had given me when she'd texted me through all those months.

She'd been a total lifeline to me in my solitude. The one glimmer of hope in a sea of dark. I'd known nothing of my Order, been unable to shift unless I was alone somewhere long enough, but never able to fly. She told me everything about Pegasuses, she'd made me love being one, made me ache to cast my shackles off and come join her in the sky. My wish had finally come true. And it was better than I ever could have dreamed it would be.

"What question?" I asked, my mind blanking as I traced her features, from the curve of her lips to her big blue eyes. She was pixie sized and fucking perfect.

Her lashes lowered half way, framing her gaze in glitter as her mouth quirked up at the corner. She tiptoed to whisper in my ear and her breath against my skin sent a quiver right through me. "Were you disappointed I wasn't naked when I texted you?"

My throat bobbed as I turned my head, brushing my lips against her candyfloss scented skin. "No," I admitted. "Because I thought you might be with *him*."

Her fingers pushed into the back of my hair, her body arching against me so her breasts pressed to my chest, getting me rock hard for her just like that. *Oh shit.*

"And what if I wanted to be naked with you?" she whispered.

I was a goner. My dick was making itself known and she leaned back with a little gasp of excitement, her eyes boring into mine.

"Do you wanna go somewhere quieter?" she asked and I nodded because hell yes I did. *But oh fuck the stars I don't know what I'm doing.*

She snagged my hand and towed me off the dancefloor, my gaze falling to her ass in that tight dress, making me want to bite down on my knuckles. She looked so edible, maybe I could understand Hadley's needs after all because right now all I wanted to do was sink my teeth into this girl and taste her.

We slipped through a side door into a stairwell and Sofia pressed her back to the wall, reeling me in by the hand. I observed her with a fierce desire as I took my time to memorise every inch of the way she looked tonight, and she bit her lip in anticipation.

I pressed one hand to the wall above her head, running my fingers along her jaw with my other hand as I angled her lips up toward mine. I may not have screwed a girl before, but I knew how to kiss one. I'd made out with girls at my old school before Father had kept me home after my Order had Emerged.

Her breath caught and the air seemed to spark like a livewire hung between us. "You are the most beautiful creature I've ever seen," I growled and she reached out to fist her hand in my shirt. "And you gave me something to look forward to when I thought I had nothing in my future. I dreamed about meeting you every night, Sofia. And it didn't come close to the reality. You're my sunshine in the dark."

She yanked me closer, but she didn't have to, I was already moving, crushing her to the wall and pressing my lips to hers. Her mouth parted for me and I slid my tongue in to taste her, her tongue meeting mine with hungry strokes as we devoured each other.

My hard on ground into her thigh and she reached between us, running her palm up and down it and making me groan needily. I wanted to touch her too, but I also didn't want to fuck it up and make her realise how much of a virgin I was. But if I didn't touch her, what was she gonna think?

I focused on kissing her until she was panting and I swear I was gonna come in my pants with the way her fingers grasped and caressed my cock. My head was spinning and I couldn't get enough.

I reached down to hook her thigh over my hip and she sighed my name, the sound the best thing I'd ever heard.

"Do you like that, baby?" Tyler's voice cut through the fog in my brain and I jolted in surprise, my lips parting from Sofia's as I whipped around, shielding her from him and stamping my foot in anger.

"By the stars, Tyler, how long have you been standing there?" Sofia demanded, not seeming remotely bothered that he'd just caught her with her tongue in another guy's mouth.

She moved to my side, straightening the skirt of her dress and folding her arms, totally unphased.

"Long enough to work out that Xavier here is a virgin," Tyler said with a wicked smirk and I neighed furiously. "I've had my suspicions for a while, but now I'm positive."

"Fuck off," I snapped.

"It's not a big deal," Tyler said placatingly. "You don't mind, do you baby?" He looked to Sofia and heat swept up the back of my neck. I couldn't face her, or deny it or do anything but just stand there like a lump of awkward.

"Why would I mind that?" she replied and my heart thumped powerfully at the conviction in her words.

Tyler strutted forward like the big I am and hooked Sofia toward him by the waist. "Guess this means I've got to win you again, huh?"

She nodded, a smile playing around her lips. "Sorry, babe, Xavier's just so…" She looked at me in a way that made my insides squeeze and it felt so fucking good. "And we have a connection."

"I know," he purred, brushing her hair behind her ear and glaring over her head at me. "Oh well, I kinda enjoyed beating down the lesser stallions before." He dropped his mouth to hers, kissing her fiercely and a furious whinny built in my throat which I didn't allow out.

She moaned as she arched into him just like she had with me and my dick got even harder. I didn't know why, but watching them together made me as horny as it did furious. I pushed Tyler away from her when I couldn't stand it a second longer, whirling Sofia around to face me and drawing her in for another passionate kiss. I could taste Tyler on her mouth and I grunted angrily, kissing her harder, bruising her lips. Tyler pressed up close behind her, pulling her hair sharply to break our lips apart then angling her head around to kiss him again, his eyes remaining on me with a dare in them. One I was more than willing to rise to.

His hand slid down her dress, squeezing her breast and my throat thickened as she moaned. Sofia reached for me, taking my hand and placing it on her other breast and my heart hammered like crazy. I was way out of my depth, but I wasn't going to walk away. No force in the world could make me do that. *Just don't fuck this up.*

I had to do it better than Tyler, it was the only thing I could think of. So I tugged her dress down, freeing her breast from her sparkly bra and lowered my head, capturing her nipple between my lips and sucking. She cried out, her fingers pushing into my hair and knotting tightly as she kept me there and excitement pounded through me. I wasn't fucking it up. She liked it. She actually liked it!

Tyler suddenly shoved my head away and I stood upright with a neigh of rage. Sofia rested back against his chest as he locked his arm around her possessively.

"Is this an official challenge, Xavier?" He narrowed his eyes and I lifted my chin.

"Yeah," I said, with no doubt in my voice. "It is."

His gaze darkened and he nodded, acceptance filling his expression. "Okay…" He nuzzled into Sofia's neck, dragging his teeth across her flesh and making her shudder in his arms. "I wonder if the virgin can do this to you, baby." He slid his hand down her body once more, pulling up her skirt to reveal her sparkly pink panties before sliding his fingers inside them. I swallowed the razor sharp lump in my throat as I watched, unsure what the fuck to do as he started moving his hand and Sofia gasped in pleasure, dropping her head back against his shoulder.

Tyler gazed at me tauntingly and I fought the urge to squeeze my dick through my pants to relieve some of the pressure that was building in me. This was so hot and so infuriating all at once. And I might have been a virgin, but I was also a quick learner so fuck if I was just going to stand here.

Sofia's eyes widened hopefully as I closed the distance between us and butted my forehead against Tyler's over her shoulder. I slid my hand into her panties, following the line of his fingers and meeting her wet centre. *Holy fucking stars.*

My fingers slid between his and I pushed two inside her to join Tyler's, making her whinny for me. I grinned, learning from the movements of Tyler's hand and matching his rhythm as she panted and gasped between us. He pushed his forehead hard against mine, but I didn't give an inch, forcing him back just as hard so our eyes were locked.

My breaths came heavier with my own need for release and the sound of Sofia moaning had me aching to claim her.

"Come for me, baby," Tyler demanded, shoving my head with his own and I shoved his back, making us all stumble a few steps in his direction.

"Come for *me*, Sofia," I growled and she pawed at my chest with one hand while cupping the back of Tyler's neck with the other.

"Oh my stars," she gasped.

Her pussy tightened around our fingers and she moaned loudly as she came, my gaze falling to her face. I drank in her hooded expression and realised her skin was actually shining. Fuck she was beautiful.

I kissed her, tasting her heat, her flesh and removing my hand from her panties just before Tyler did. She panted between us, holding us both close and I kept my attention on her instead of the douche behind her.

"It's on, Xavier," Tyler warned, drawing her away from me and she tugged down her skirt with a breathy laugh.

"Wait." She tugged her hand free of his, running back to me and pressing her mouth to mine. I grinned against her lips, kissing her slow and trying to draw it out.

Tyler pulled her away again and she pouted sadly, her hand holding onto mine before he turned her around and marched her toward the exit.

"See you soon," she called to me, biting her lip and Tyler dragged her out the door before I could follow.

I looked down at my rock hard dick with a sigh and moved to sit on the stairs, figuring I needed to think some unhappy thoughts to make it go away before I went back to the party.

Mildred's hairy back, Mildred's hairy back, Mildred's hairy back.

I sat in the shadows with exhilaration rushing through me and realised I wasn't even as pissed at Tyler as I should have been. Something about this challenge just felt right, natural. And I relished the idea of beating his ass and making her mine officially in front of the whole herd.

My boner was being stubborn as hell, mostly because it was impossible for me not to replay what we'd just done over and over again. I felt like one percent less of a virgin which was totally sad and yet seriously ace at the same time.

The door suddenly flung open and Athena marched through it before Hadley shot after her and caught her wrist, wheeling her around.

"What's your problem?" she demanded, yanking her wrist free and glaring at him.

"He had his hands all over you," Hadley snapped.

"So? What's it got to do with you?" she asked in disbelief.

"He's a Vampire. He's trying to claim you as his Source," he growled. "And I'm not having it. If you're gonna be anyone's Source, you're *mine*."

She narrowed her eyes at him, falling deathly quiet in that way she did when she was about to get scary and I decided remaining here in the shadows was a good plan.

"I'm no one's Source," she said in an even tone. "I'm not a blood bag for you to drool over. I'm supposed to be your friend."

Hadley shifted his weight from one foot to the other, seeming agitated. "You don't understand," he snarled.

"Well explain it to me, Had, because you're one second away from me cutting you off for good. I'm sick of this," she said calmly, a deadly glint in her gaze.

"I need a taste. Just one taste, Athena. Then I can get you out of my head. Please. I'll do whatever you want in return," he said, sounding completely unlike himself as he begged her.

She surveyed him with her eyes narrowed. "You'll do anything I want?" she asked with intrigue.

"Anything," he swore, stepping closer to her like he'd already won, but she pressed a hand to his chest to hold him back, mulling over her next words.

"You'll be my bitch for the week," she decided with a playful smile. "You'll do whatever I ask, carry my shit and fetch anything I fancy for me."

Hadley fell quiet with a low growl in his throat then he lunged at her, bouncing off a tight air shield around her body. Silence thickened the air and she looked like she was about to walk away and be done with him forever. I didn't like the thought of that. I loved the group we'd formed.

"Fine," Hadley spat at last. "I'll do it. But you have to let me bite you where I want, as much as I want. Right here, right now. You're mine Athena."

"For five minutes," she sighed.

"Ten," he snapped.

"Four," she countered with a smirk.

"Five then," he growled, pacing left to right with his hands balled at his sides. "Drop your shield."

She looked nervous for a moment, taking a breath then flicked her fingers as she released the magic. He leapt at her, grabbing a fistful of her dark, purple-streaked hair and dragging her head to one side, driving his fangs into her throat. She gasped and he groaned like he was riding the best high of his life, holding her in his arms at his mercy.

He growled like a beast as he fed from her and her eyes fluttered closed. For a moment I thought she might be about to pass out and I almost pushed to my feet, but then she released a breathy moan that was a total game changer.

Hadley chuckled mirthlessly, clutching her closer as he pulled his fangs free of her throat then dropped his mouth to her breasts and started feeding once more. She fisted his hair as he drove her against the wall and when he was done, he dropped to his knees, throwing her leg over his shoulder and driving his fangs into her inner thigh. I didn't know what the fuck to do at this point so I just sat there, hoping Hadley didn't decide to pay attention and pick up my heartbeat, but I reckoned the fact that he was on cloud nine right now meant he was too distracted to notice.

"Fucking hell, Hadley," Athena growled, tipping her head back against the wall. For a girl who hated being fed on by so-called parasites, she sure as hell seemed to be enjoying herself.

Hadley finally stood up, wiping a line of blood from the corner of his mouth and sucking his fingers. He got up in her face and she raised her chin defiantly, masking the bliss on her face I'd seen a few seconds ago.

"Are you done?" she asked icily and he shook his head, checking his watch.

"I've got you for another full minute."

Man, I really needed to leave.

"You taste like a summer's day," he said breathlessly.

"Well I imagine you taste like the dead of winter," she said with a shrug.

"Do you wanna find out?" he murmured then lowered his head to look her in the eyes, pressing his hands either side of her on the wall as he caged her in. "You can taste me if you want, Athena. I won't tell anyone."

"I'm good," she said lightly. "And you've got about ten seconds left before you become my little bitch, so are you finished being a leech?"

He snarled then lunged forward and took her lower lip between his teeth, drawing blood and making her wince. She swallowed visibly as he released her lip, their mouths grazing and his body pressing flush to hers. Their eyes were locked and for a moment I saw a hint of something more in Athena's eyes as she gazed at him.

"Time's up," she said with a victorious smile.

"Worth it," he said heavily.

"Carry me back to the party, little bitch," she commanded with a smirk and he rolled his eyes before whipping her off of her feet and shooting away through the door.

My boner was officially dead so I got to my feet, waiting a few seconds before following, planning to keep what I'd seen to myself. I was no snitch, and I didn't like drama.

My gaze fell on Sofia again, dancing with Tyler beside Darcy, Geraldine and the Heirs in their masks. My brother caught my eye, jerking his head to beckon me and I smiled as I jogged over.

"Nice hair," I taunted, eyeing the long golden locks hanging around his shoulders.

"Nice lipstick," he tossed back and I quickly wiped my mouth with a furious whinny.

"Join us Xavier!" Darcy called and I realised Geraldine was teaching her, Seth, Caleb and Max some sort of crazy dance involving a lot of weird hand movements.

"It's the Crockenberry Jive," Geraldine announced like that might entice me into it. It kinda did to be fair.

Sofia pulled away from Tyler to learn it too and I dove into the fray with a grin, copying the wiggling hand movements Geraldine was doing as she circled her hips.

Darius drank his beer, shaking his head at us but the ghost of a grin hid at the corner of his mouth.

Sofia's hip bumped mine and I smirked down at her.

"You sure you can keep up, Xavier?" she asked, her eyes glittering with mirth.

"Yes, little mare," I teased. "I can keep up." And not just with this dance, but with Tyler too. I'd be running our herd soon enough, and he'd be bowing to me with my girl by my side. And once I won her, I was never going to let her go.

MAX

CHAPTER THIRTY FIVE

"That's it!" Washer cried as he waded through the water in the Aqua lagoon to come and see what we were doing. "But if you really bend into the motion and thrust your hips you would get better drive on the cast."

Darius arched a brow at me as Washer came to stand beside us, bending in half at the waist so that his head was almost submerged in the water before flicking upright and thrusting his hips forward. The bulge in his budgie smugglers was front and centre as he threw his hands out and cast the magic. A shudder of disgust ran down my spine which I absolutely let him feel with his Siren gifts. A surge of motion rippled beneath the waves before four perfectly casted horses leapt above the surface entirely crafted from water and galloped away from us.

He had something of a point; water magic was fluid and worked best in motion, so adding movements to your body could increase the power of the cast - but that was something weaker Fae needed. With the kind of power we were packing, we really didn't need to do anything like that, and if he thought I was gonna bend over with my ass in the air then thrust my junk towards the sky as I lunged upright, he had another thing coming.

"Come on, I'll show you," Washer insisted, moving behind me with his hands held out like he actually believed I'd let him hold onto my hips while he showed me how to thrust in that tiny fucking speedo of his.

"I think I've got it, thanks. That visual you gave me really helped," I said firmly and he bumped against the air shield I'd put up between us with a pout on his face.

"Everyone needs a little help sometimes, Max," he insisted, pressing himself up against my air shield so that his chest was pressed hard against it like it was a pane of glass and his nipples were smooshed until they looked like a pair of pink fried eggs. "Even Heirs need a teeny weeny bit from time to time."

"I think I'm good," I insisted and he sighed dramatically before plodding away, looking like a dolphin who'd been slapped by a seal.

"Are you sure you don't want the extra tuition, Max?" Darius joked. "I heard you can get some real power into your moves with a mega thrust like that."

"Yeah and I heard that Washer keeps a photo of you in his wallet and calls it his cheeky boy piccy," I tossed back.

"Sure he does. I signed it. We all know that the Fire Heir has the most fans."

"Psh, I don't think so, I got like fourteen pairs of panties sent to me this week," I replied casually. I mean it was kinda gross but still true.

"I'm not really interested in your choice of underwear, dude. But some crazy chick was arrested for breaking into my car and laying herself out naked on the back seat last Sunday," Darius said.

"What car?" I asked with a snort of amusement.

"That Faerarri I never drive. One of Father's servants takes it out once a week to make sure the engine doesn't go to shit from lack of use and I guess she recognised it somehow when he parked it up in town. I don't think she was banking on a middle aged Manticore with a moustache to find her – apparently she threw a fit and refused to get out of the car unless I came to get her."

"That's fucked up," I sniggered. "Was it that crazy stalker one again?"

"Yeah, Cindy Lou something," he said with a dismissive shrug. "The FIB said they'll inject her with a tracker if she tries to come near me again but I'm not all that worried about some deluded psycho. Anyway, point is – I've got a stalker and you don't. If that's not proof that I'm more popular then I don't know what is."

I barked a laugh and threw a fistful of water at his face which he dispersed with a wave of his hand before diving through it and tackling me.

His big ass Dragon body slammed into me and I was knocked beneath the surface of the water where I instantly locked my arms and legs around him and used my control over the Element to shoot us back towards the shore like a torpedo.

As we made it to the sandy beach that ringed the lagoon, I propelled us out of the water and managed to flip us over so that I landed straddling him in the sand. Darius laughed as I threw a punch into his ribs with a snarl as my heart raced with adrenaline.

Darius took the hit with a grunt but the second time my fist came down, pain splintered through my hand as my knuckles met with a layer of ice that he'd used to coat his flesh.

I reared back with a curse of pain and he lunged upwards, flipping me beneath him and wrestling me down at the edge of the water where the waves crashed over us as we fought.

Darius shoved my head beneath the surface and I laughed as I cast a bubble of water around his head. I could have shifted or used air magic to help me breathe, but this was a water Elemental lesson after all so I just entered into the drown-off with the hopes that I could hold my breath for longer.

Darius held me down and the two of us glared at each other through the blurry water dividing us, daring the other to flinch first.

My lungs began to burn and bubbles slid from my lips as the seconds ticked past and neither of us let up on our positions for a single second.

Just as I was sure one of us was going to have to crack, a whip of water slapped down across my thighs so hard that the pain broke my concentration and my hold on the water surrounding Darius fell apart. He released me in the same moment and I lurched upright, sucking in a breath as I found Geraldine standing over us with a water whip held in her hand poised to crack again.

"You pair of wet Wallys will get yourselves killed with this machismo lollygagging one of these days, mark my words," she announced, raising the whip threateningly.

"I should put you on your ass for that," Darius growled as he stood, offering me a hand and as he pulled me up I noticed a pink whip mark crossing his back where she'd hit him too.

"I'd like to see you try," she scoffed, lifting her chin. "Some of us actually pay attention in class, so I'm sure that I'll be above you in the pecking order soon if I'm not already."

"You wanna put your money where your mouth is, Gerry?" I teased, casting some water over myself to remove the sand from my skin.

"Why are you always trying to tangle your tentacles around me, Maxy boy?" she demanded.

"I'd have thought that was pretty obvious by now," I said in a low voice.

"Oh hell no," Darius growled drawing my attention to what he was glaring at on the far side of the lagoon.

Tory and Darcy were working on lifting whirling water up above the surface into mini cyclones, and Tory was lost in the movements of the work, trailing her fingertips so that the water swirled all around her legs while she moved in circles to draw it up around her. As she worked, Washer was closing in on her, whirling his hips around and around in circles like he was using a hula hoop and shouting, "Rotate! Rotate! Gyrate!"

Darius took an angry step towards them but Tory beat him to it, sinking her fingers into the water and pushing more magic into it before the cyclone took off, leaving her behind and crashing into Washer. It scooped him up and spun him around while he wailed something about the powerful thrust she'd created then he was launched away from her towards the centre of the lagoon.

She did a pretty good job of keeping her bitchy shadow girl mask in place, but as she turned and looked at Darcy, a smirk escaped her hold and the tension ran out of Darius's limbs.

While I'd been distracted, Geraldine had taken the opportunity to stride away from me and I sighed as I watched her go, my gaze finding her ass in the tight swimsuit she was wearing as I sagged in defeat.

"Dammit, why is she always walking away from me?" I grumbled but Darius had ditched me too, heading over to Tory with water magic swirling around his arms before he cast a field of liquid flowers to bloom all around her.

Tory's lips twitched as she stole control of the water and created a miniature city instead, the Empire State Building rising up in the centre of it. Enough lust was pouring from the two of them to make my skin tingle and I decided to leave them to it.

I made the decision to hound after Geraldine, but before I could, my little sister stepped in front of me, arms folded and chin raised in a challenge, causing me to sigh as I felt the lecture coming even without using my gifts. She really was her mother's daughter.

"What do you want, Ellis?" I asked her in a tired tone.

"Mom said you had to help me master my water magic, Max," she said haughtily. "And you haven't even helped me once. Am I going to have to call her and tell her all you do is hang out with the other Heirs and laze about all the time?"

"Do what you want, Ellis. I don't have to teach you shit, especially when you're being a little snot bag. Go cry to Mom about being a single Elemental who needs extra tuition, because it's not my job to help you make something of yourself."

Sometimes I felt kinda bad about the relationship I had with my sister. Her mom had forced her into rivalry with me from the moment she was born, always showering her with more love and praise than me, comparing us and finding me wanting, making comments about the way Ellis was a more natural leader just to rile me up. But I knew the real reason for all of that didn't have anything to do with my so-called mother's low opinion of her son. It was all about the fact that she wasn't my birth mother, and it ate her up that her own kid wasn't going to be the one in power after my father retired from his spot on the Council.

There had been a time when that had worried me a lot, that I'd been genuinely concerned about Ellis being stronger than me even though we both would have inherited our power from our father as he was the strongest of our parents. But not anymore - especially since she only had water magic. The idea of her taking my place now was practically laughable.

"Don't walk away from me, Max," Ellis snarled as I turned to do exactly that.

I chuckled just to piss her off and kept walking. But as the water around my ankles was drawn away and I felt her anger crashing against my senses, I threw up an air shield at my back.

A tidal wave crashed over my shield as she screeched in anger and threw all of her power at me in an unrestrained, wild act of fury which made my blood boil.

Who the fuck did she think she was to be attacking me in public like that?

"Do you really wanna play this game with me, Ellis?" I asked, turning back to face her with a taunting grin plastered in place as pretty much everyone in the lagoon turned to look our way.

In reply, the cocky little brat swept her hands through the water and flung another huge wave at me like she seriously thought she could take me on.

I widened my smile, flicking my fingers and parting her wave as I walked right through the centre of it with my feet stepping on the surface of the water.

Ellis shrieked at me as she threw more unshaped water at me with nothing but brute force and I laughed as I slapped it aside with a casual gesture then dunked a torrent of ice cold water over her head.

I would have left it at that, but she ran at me, screaming furiously and making the water all around me rise up like she intended to drown me with it.

With a twist of my wrist, I lassoed the back of her swimsuit in a rope made of water and lifted her up by it so that the material was pulled right up her ass, giving her a mega wedgie as I carried her over to the sandy beach.

Ellis kicked and flailed wildly, looking like an octopus on killblaze as she tried to fight her way free. But I just dropped her face first onto the beach, using my magic to force her head beneath the sand so that she was left there with her ass in the air for everyone to see like a turtle set to lay its eggs.

The sound of laughter tore out all around me and I caught sight of a couple of girls filming from just outside the changing rooms, where I guessed they'd run back to grab their Atlases when our fight started. Maybe that had been a dick move, but it had also been a necessary one. The only people in Solaria powerful enough to face me were the Vegas, the Heirs and their siblings.

The spares weren't likely to pose much threat with their lack of training, but they had just as much magic in their veins as us and if they wanted to claim our spots then they only had to challenge us and win to take them. It didn't happen often, but it had been done more than once in the history of the Council and I wasn't going to allow so much as a whisper of a rumour to get out suggesting that Ellis might be able to match me one day.

The bell rang to signal the end of class and I turned and strode out of the lagoon, leaving my little sister to scramble back out of the sand, coughing and spluttering as she wrenched her swimsuit out of her butt crack. My power swelled with the rush of amusement and cruelty that I drew in from the surrounding crowd and my smile widened as I headed back inside to get changed.

I pulled my uniform on to a chorus of sycophantic praise from the dudes who had just seen me put her in her place and wanted to make sure they made their loyalty clear. It was political bullshit but I still lapped it up.

When I opened my Atlas and found myself tagged in a post which

435

included a video of me handing Ellis her ass, I couldn't help but laugh aloud.

Tyler Corbin:
It looks like the Water Heirs decided to have a throw down during class today and I just received this video from an anonymous classmate of theirs. It's just a shame that @EllisRigel made such an ASS of herself looking like an ostrich with a plucked butt after @MaxRigel was done with her. Are we sure she's a Siren, because she might have lost control of her Order form and I'm pretty sure I saw a camel toe.
#fullmoontonight #watershame #whoissheanyway #feelingbutthurt #mindthecrack #spareforareason #camelshifterindisguise

Lucy Burfoot:
Do you want some cheese on that butt cracker? – maybe a slice of camelbert?? #shesgotthehump

Sophie Ruddock:
They might have room for you at the court of Camelot, Ellis! #knightoftheroundtoeble

Annemarie Mclaren:
Watch your mouth, Corbin! The only one who's going to end up with a plucked butt is you just before the true king roasts you and eats you for dinner. #Pegatwat #lesserFae

Tyler Corbin:
Could you tell the King thanks for the offer, but if he wants to spit roast me he should really eat my ass beforehand, not after. Besides, I don't fancy getting split in half by his monster dick #longdongsilver #kingdong #Lionellongschlongenstein #dicktator

Erica Collins:
@TylerCorbin no way! He's so big headed, he's definitely overcompensating for his tiny todger #lillionel #minimeat #hunglikeadragonfly #dinkypinky

Telisha Mortensen:
@EricaCollins his junk so small that when a Lionel dick pic got leaked everyone thought it was a photoshoot for a Lagulian Worm Shifter #hiswormmakesmesquirm #canhiswormevengetfirm

I woke up in the middle of the night in King's Hollow to the feeling of Tory's panic and fear slamming into me and I shoved myself upright with a curse as I stumbled towards the door.

She was sleeping in the room beside mine which had become a habit since we'd pulled her back from the shadows and her nightmares were the reason for that. At night it was harder for her to keep the memories of her torture at bay and they often crept up on her, disturbing her sleep and slowing her recovery.

I pushed her door open just as Caleb stepped out of his room down the hall in a pair of white sweats and yawned as I waved a hand at him, letting him know I was on it. But as I headed into her room, using my gifts to calm her down, he slipped in behind me.

"Does this happen every night?" Caleb breathed, his brow furrowing as Tory tossed and turned in the sheets, her skin lined with a sheen of sweat and little whimpers of fear escaping her.

"Not when she sleeps with Lionel," I muttered, telling him what she'd told me. "He trained her mind so that she feels safe in his presence, but the longer she's away from him the worse this gets."

"Does Darius know?" Caleb asked as I reached out to take her hand and push more calming energy into her. Her fingers gripped tight around mine and my breath caught as her power slammed into me, forcing a full memory into my head even though I hadn't been trying to look at one.

"Whose fault is this?" Vard asked as I found myself peering out of Tory's eyes in that same cold, stone room with the beige walls and single lightbulb hanging overhead.

I blinked up at him through the pain in my body as I tasted my own blood on my lips. I couldn't look down at my flesh to see what they'd done to me, the sight was enough to turn my stomach and if I threw up then the punishment would only be worse. But the pain consuming my flesh told me well enough how bad it was.

My lips parted on a word that stuck in my throat and Lionel tutted irritably.

"You're strong of spirit, I'll give you that, Roxanya," he commented, moving to stand before me as Vard stepped aside with a bow of deference. "But that's only making this take longer. Tell me who you love."

"You," I gasped out as he reached forward to caress the side of my face, smiling like he was proud of me as healing magic slid into my skin and a whimper of relief crept past my lips.

"Good girl. You know how much I hate seeing you like this, Roxanya. I only wish to look after you, but I can't help you until you give Vard what he needs. Don't you want to please me?"

I nodded mutely and his soft touch on my cheek grew firm as he moved to grasp my chin tightly in his big hand and turned my face so that I was forced to look straight into Vard's single Cyclops eye with no warning.

"Darius Acrux," he spoke inside my mind and I fell into a memory of kissing him before I could even try to fight it.

The second my mind latched onto the memory, pain burrowed into my body so deep and fast that a scream tore from my lips, ripping my throat raw.

I blacked out, falling into the soft embrace of oblivion willingly as I begged it to take me away, but I woke again with a gasp as ice cold water crashed down over me.

"Whose fault is this?" Vard asked as I recoiled in fear, the chains

binding me to the chair not letting me escape.

"Darius," I breathed and he nodded, stepping back as Lionel moved forward.

"It's alright, Roxanya," Lionel purred, placing his hands against the bloody wounds on my stomach and healing me as I choked against the pain. "I'm here now. I'll take care of you."

The chains holding me down came loose and I sagged forward into his arms as he picked me up easily and held me against his chest.

"Who do you love?" he murmured as my tears slowed and I curled against him.

"You, my King," I whispered, leaning into him while my limbs still trembled with the memory of pain. "Only you."

I grunted a curse as I took control of her memories with my gifts, gently reminding her of the truth and separating my psyche from hers as I soothed away her fear and pain until her breathing settled.

As I drew back into myself, I realised Caleb's hand was on my shoulder and I turned to look at him with a frown, finding his face pale as he slowly stepped back.

"Did you see that?" I asked, a little pissed that he'd done that without asking.

"Yeah," he muttered, his gaze straying to the girl sleeping in the bed as her brow furrowed again. "I'm sorry. But you were broadcasting bits of it without me touching you. I was getting flashes of screams and pain and I just... sorry."

"It's alright," I said, releasing a heavy sigh. "But you might want to apologise to her in the morning - it wasn't my memories you snooped on."

Caleb nodded, his throat bobbing as he looked down at her again and I swiped a hand over my face.

"You're taking that fear and shit away from her like this a lot?" he guessed, eyeing me as I cringed a little.

"Yeah...well if I don't she just gets worse and I-"

"That's gotta be fucking with your emotions though," he said, knowing too well how my Order gifts worked and the way I was affected by the kinds of emotions I fed my power with.

"A bit," I admitted. "It's not too bad doing this once or twice a night, but she won't really settle unless I sleep in here with her and then I end up automatically feeding on it all night. It makes for a kinda sucky night's sleep." I shrugged as I moved to get into the bed with her and Caleb caught my arm.

"You want me to stay too? I'm not exactly laughing my ass off, but I've probably got some lighter emotions than that going on in my head to balance you out."

My shoulders dropped as some of the tension spilled from me and I gave him a smile as I nodded. "Yeah, you're nowhere near as deep as Tory. So if you've got the magic to spare-"

"I had a snack earlier," he said with a smirk, pushing a hand into his

438

blonde curls and I caught a taste of laughter, joy and lust on him as he thought about that which made me grin.

"Come on then," I urged as I pulled the blankets back and moved to get into the bed with Tory, lifting her a little and moving her across the sheets to make room for us. She was more than used to me doing this in the night now, so she didn't wake, but the tension in her body relaxed as I laid my head on the pillow beside her and drew her back against my chest.

Caleb climbed in behind me and slung an arm over me too as a tendril of amusement slipped from him.

"You're my little spoon, Maxy pad," he laughed and the taste of his joy to counter Tory's fear was enough to make me let that name slide as I used my gifts to make us all sleepy and we drifted off.

An incessant buzzing against my thigh woke me and I groaned groggily as I frowned at the dream I was currently taking part in. Caleb and Tory's subconsciousnesses had clearly connected to mine to create a weird ass jumble of thoughts. I snorted a laugh at the sight of Mildred Canopus getting her ass kicked by Tory while a shirtless Seth whooped and cheered in between doing a strip tease to Milkshake by Kelis. Caleb and I danced on the back of a golden Dragon while Gerry's voice intermittently called out types of fish in a seductive voice.

I groaned as I managed to pull my Atlas from my pocket, frowning at the messages I'd received and the notification that I'd been tagged in multiple news stories.

Tory mumbled something sleepily and I wriggled out of the bed so as not to disturb her, managing to catch Caleb's knee in the gut before I made it out.

I paused and pushed more sleepiness over the two of them as they rolled towards each other before slipping back out into the living area and opening up the messages I found there.

I had eight missed calls from my dad and a bunch of texts from him telling me to phone him and I quickly tapped on the newspaper links to see what the hell was going on.

A headline stared up at me, slapping me in the face as I took it in.

Water Heir Max Rigel not really an Heir at all.

What the fuck? I clicked the next link and my gut plummeted as I realised exactly what this was.

Max Rigel - bastard! The truth about the Water Heir's hidden parentage and everything you need to know about his secret Minotaur grandfather.

Shit. This wasn't good. Especially right now while Lionel had half the country believing that the Minotaurs were in on some secret plot with the Sphinxes to steal and hide knowledge from the rest of the Fae population.

My Atlas rang again and I answered my dad as I sank down onto the couch with my heart racing.

"Max? I take it you've seen?" he demanded.

"Yeah, Dad," I said in a hopeless kind of tone. "Who the fuck leaked it?"

There was a long pause before he replied. "You...already knew?"

"Yeah. I found out years ago so I'm not freaking out over that. And believe me, I'm not upset that that bitch you married isn't my mother, but... this is really fucked up timing, isn't it? I mean, it would have been a scandal before but with Lionel going after the Minotaurs-"

"I've already got all of my people on this," he growled. "Don't you worry. Besides, you still have my blood in your veins which is what really counts. Everyone screws around before they get married, so the idea of a bastard being a scandal is absurd in this day and age. You're still my Heir as far as I'm concerned and you're more than powerful enough to fight off anyone who tried to challenge you for your place which is all that really counts anyway. Fae fight for their position and no one is strong enough to unseat you. Don't worry son, we'll weather this storm."

I smiled weakly, endlessly grateful to my father for standing by my side like this. "Thanks, Dad."

"Nothing to thank me for. Now we just need to focus on damage control. We'll play down the Minotaur thing as much as we can. What about the other Heirs, how will they take it?"

"They already know, Dad," I admitted. "They don't give a shit. We're loyal to each other." I'd gotten over the fear of losing my place amongst my brothers the moment they'd found out the truth about me being a bastard. They didn't care about my bloodline - they cared about *me*. We were family, unbreakable, united always. And knowing that took away some of the fear I held getting through this shit.

"Well that will make this a lot easier then," Dad said firmly. "Assuming they're willing to say that publicly?"

I opened my mouth to say they would but then I paused. "I'm pretty sure they will, but I guess it depends on what their parents' take on it is... I wanna think that Cal and Seth won't be any issue, but I guess if Lionel tells Darius he doesn't want him speaking out in favour of someone with Minotaur blood-"

"I'll be making house calls to Melinda and Antonia today. If we're united then hopefully our *king* will see sense and back you up too.» I couldn›t help but doubt that and I didn›t miss the way Dad spat the word king.

"Do you know who leaked it?" I asked, knowing there was no point pursuing that topic right now.

There was a pause then Dad sighed. "Not for certain, but... Your mother was-"

"Not my mother," I growled, glad at least that I wouldn't have to pretend about that shit anymore even if everything else was fucked.

"No, I suppose not. Well, she was most upset about those videos that were circulating yesterday of you and Ellis," he said heavily. "Of course I told her that was just usual Fae on Fae posturing and that Ellis needed to figure out how to handle it without coming crying to us but Linda wasn't satisfied with that. She wanted me to force you to make a formal apology and said that I should make you give Ellis private tuition daily to improve her magic at an accelerated rate. When I told her you needed to concentrate on your own studies and pointed out that Ellis wasn't the Heir anyway, not to mention the fact that she was only gifted one Element so she really isn't ever going to be-"

"The bitch decided to go public," I summarised. "You think she's going to try and push Ellis to challenge me for my place one day?"

Dad grunted an agreeing noise. "Well she does have very high ambitions for her and of course I love Ellis dearly, but the girl just isn't cut from the same cloth as you, son. You're my oldest and my strongest. There's no doubt in my mind over who the Heir is. We just need to make sure the rest of the kingdom stays in agreement with us over that."

"Okay," I agreed, trying not to feel too hopeless. "I'll see if I can get the Heirs to release statements in support of me and let you get on with damage control."

I made a move to cut the call, but Dad called out to stop me.

"I love you, Max," he growled. "We'll fix this."

The line went dead and I smiled a little even as panic consumed me at the knowledge that this secret was out. One thing was for certain though - I wouldn't be helping Ellis learn shit. If she seriously thought her single Elemental ass could take me on then she could come at me like Fae.

For now, I was going to have to work on damage control and just hope that this didn't all go to hell.

DARIUS

CHAPTER THIRTY SIX

I flew a short circle around the academy grounds with the drizzle in the air sticking to my scales and my breath rising in a fog even though I wasn't breathing fire. It was one of those depressingly damp and cold winter days that were better off spent inside, but I'd had trouble sleeping and so I was out in it all the same.

I looked over the sea to the horizon where the sun was rising, wanting to leave the protective wards that surrounded the academy and fly for hours, really stretching my wings. But that would require me to land and exit via the gate before heading off and then Father would be informed that I'd left the grounds. And I couldn't really sneak out either because it was pretty hard to hide the passage of an enormous golden Dragon through the sky. I was fairly certain I was the only golden beast of our kind currently alive and people talked when they thought they'd spotted an Heir.

I'd asked Father why the wards were even still in place now that he had control over the Nymphs and we were no longer at war. He'd told me he was concerned about the threat in the north where there were rumours of small villages being entirely wiped out over night, houses found empty and bloody with no sign of the Fae who had once lived there.

I suspected him of course. He'd marched squadrons of his so-called tame Nymphs up there to counter the threat and I didn't trust that one bit. But the attacks seemed to come at random. Little towns all over the place were struck out of nowhere. I thought it was strange that none of the Fae living in any of the destroyed towns had ever even managed to get a phone call out, but without any survivors to ask, it was impossible to understand what the reason for that could be. And Father certainly had very little interest in discussing it with me. There had been next to no newspaper coverage on any of it either which stank of conspiracy to me, but there wasn't much I could do unless we managed to get a lead on a town when it was being attacked so that we could go there and figure out what was doing it. Gabriel was looking out for information with The Sight, but he hadn't *seen* anything useful yet. And as it wasn't affecting anyone he knew closely there was little chance of him *seeing* what was going on, especially while he was watching so many other things closer to home.

I wanted to head up to one of the destroyed towns and investigate it, but so far between classes, the obligations Father put on me, my research with Orion and the Nymph hunts we were still sneaking out on whenever we got the chance, I hadn't been able to find the time.

I spotted a white Wolf racing through the trees close to King's Hollow and tucked my wings as I dove from the sky to intercept him.

I was silent as I shot towards the ground and the moment Seth bounded out into a grassy clearing, I reached out and plucked him from the field in my talons.

Seth yelped in surprise as he was hoisted off of the ground and I snorted a Dragon laugh as he began to buck and kick before sinking his teeth into my foot.

I almost dropped him, lurching towards the ground as I scrambled to keep my grip and he shifted in my hold so that he slid between my talons in Fae form and used his air magic to land safely on the hillside below.

I circled around before landing too and I shifted back at the edge of the clearing, shooting him a taunting grin.

"You wanna go?" he called out in a challenge, thumping his chest like a dudebro who had sunk too many beers and wanted to fight everyone in the vicinity.

"You wanna wrestle me naked?" I teased as I stalked towards him through the long grass which brushed around my waist and he smirked as his gaze moved down my body for a moment.

"I mean...I've had worse offers in my life."

"Let's just eat first," I suggested. "I prefer to do my ass kicking on a full stomach."

"Race you back to the Hollow then?" Seth didn't give me the chance to reply before he took off into the trees and I cursed him as I took chase.

The moment I stepped out of the clearing, I knocked against an air shield and barked a laugh as I almost fell back on my ass before blasting it down with fire magic and tearing after him.

The asshole sent vines to trip me, rocks bursting out of the ground in my path then a huge hole tore open in the ground beneath me, my gut lurching as I fell.

I managed to cast water beneath me before I could hit the bottom of the pit and I cast a bridge of it above the ground, running on the liquid as I spotted Seth's bare ass just about to reach the entrance to the Hollow.

A flick of my wrist set an explosion of fire to life right in front of him and as he flinched back, using air to steal the oxygen from it, I knocked him from his feet with a blast of water from his right. He howled as he was washed away through the trees and I laughed as I charged over my water bridge and made it to the door.

I reached out to wrench it open and my fist slammed against solid air again, my knuckles crunching at the impact. I growled as I attacked the shield with fire while my instincts prickled to let me know he was right behind me already.

Seth's shoulder slammed into mine as he tried to knock me aside to get to the door, but I didn't move, planting my feet and using my Dragon strength to hold my ground as he yanked the door open.

The two of us lunged through it at once, our shoulders jamming in the frame as we both burst out laughing before tumbling through together.

"I guess we're still evenly matched then," Seth joked as he nuzzled against my arm affectionately and I shoved him off with a snicker.

"Put your dick away before you start pawing at me, mutt," I joked, opening the cupboard beside the door and tossing him some clothes as I pulled a pair of cream sweatpants and a grey tank on.

"I hope Geraldine brought some bagels already," Seth groaned, sniffing the air hopefully, but seeing as it probably wasn't even six am yet, I doubted it.

"I keep meaning to talk to you actually," I said to him, realising that this was coming pretty damn late after I'd promised Orion I'd have this chat with him, but I'd had a lot on my mind. Besides, I really didn't think there was anything to this anyway and I'd kinda forgotten about it. Which possibly made me a terrible friend, but at least I was getting around to it now.

"Oh yeah?" Seth asked casually.

"Yeah. What's going on with you and Gwen? Lance seems to think you're a thing, but from where I'm standing, I don't see it. So is he just being a jealous, heartbroken asshole, imagining things or what?"

"Let me grab my Atlas and I'll show you," he said mysteriously and I held my tongue as I wondered what the hell he was up to.

Seth sniggered as we jogged up the stairs into the front room of the treehouse and I moved to shove some bread in the toaster for us while he put himself on coffee duty. The room was dark, the fire in the hearth burning low, though I coaxed it back to life with a flick of my fingers as I waited on Seth's explanation.

He pulled open a drawer and grabbed his Atlas out before opening it up onto his messages with Orion and passing it over to me to look at.

Seth Capella:
I still haven't made her bow to me, but I got her on her knees last night.
Open mouth emoji *aubergine emoji*

Seth Capella:
What do you call a washed-up professor with no job and no girlfriend?

Seth Capella:
Nothing. Because she can't remember your name.

Beneath that was a selfie of Seth lying next to Darcy in her bed while she was sleeping with *#allfuckeredout* beneath it.

"Get it?" Seth asked with a grin. "Like all tuckered out but with fuck because I want him to think I stuck my dick in her."

"But you didn't?" I clarified, not sure what the hell all of this was about.

"Nah, man. It's not like that with me and her. I mean sure, there was a time when I thought about it a bit, but now my fantasies are a lot less Phoenixy and a bit more – Well anyway, if she wanted to give me a pity blowy, I wouldn't be totally against it because my balls are feeling about as blue as her hair recently and it doesn't look like there's much chance of me getting what I really want, so-"

"Rewind to the bit where you said it's not like that and yet you're still sending Lance this shit," I said, unsure if I should be growling or laughing and feeling altogether lost over the whole thing.

"Right. Yeah, so, I'm fucking with him to send him into a jealous rage that will force him to tell her how he feels and therefore make her listen and forgive him and then they can be endgame, happily ever after and all that shit. I expect to be best man - sorry dude but Lancey is gonna love me the most when I'm through here and you'll be relegated to groomsman, or maybe page boy. You could get a cute little bowtie and shit though."

I couldn't help but laugh as I scrolled over a few more of the messages he'd sent then tossed his Atlas back at him. "You're fucking insane and he'll probably try to strangle your ass for this," I said.

"*But?*" he prompted.

"But, I'm onboard with it. The two of them need to sort it the fuck out and get back together. So if he asks me again, I'll play along."

Seth grinned widely and we grabbed our plates of toast before heading to eat on the couch.

I took my usual armchair beside the fire and Seth moved to the couch but as he went to sit down, he jerked back up again and I barked a laugh as I spotted Max emerging from a heap of blankets.

"Ah shit, did I fall asleep?" he slurred, reaching for Seth's coffee and draining it before Seth could even realise what he'd done.

"Hey! Did you just force me to be generous?" Seth accused and Max gave him a weak smile which pretty much admitted it before swiping a palm down his face.

I upped the light in the room with a few Faelights to see him better by, noticing the generally feelings of concern and worry slipping from him as his gifts spread through the room.

"Why the hell were you sleeping out here?" I asked him and he groaned.

"I wasn't meant to be. I got some bad news and I was using my gifts to make myself calm down so that I could think through my best course of action. I must have upped the voltage a bit too much and made myself sleepy instead."

Seth snorted as he grabbed himself some fresh coffee and a second mug for Max who seemed like he needed it.

"What was the bad news?" I asked, biting into my toast as Max grimaced.

"My sweet sister and evil stepmother decided to out me to the world last night, most likely in payment for me making Ellis look like a fucking fool. A story was leaked about my bastard blood and my Minotaur grandfather on my real mother's side and I'm basically expecting a whole world of shit today. Especially as Lionel has half the kingdom hating Minotaurs right now."

"Fuck," Seth said heavily. "But on the bright side, now it's out we can just deal with it and move on. I mean, you might be the cause of a bit of a political scandal for a while but at the end of the day you're still your father's son, there's no law against bastards claiming their place and you're still a million times stronger than Ellis. So she's no threat to you or your position as Water Heir."

"What tactics are you planning on using to counter the gossip?" I asked and Max looked between us uncomfortably.

"Well, when I spoke to Dad he said that it would help to have clear backing from you guys. A statement or whatever. But I know that with Lionel's stance on Minotaurs he probably won't want you doing that, Darius. And I understand that you and Cal have to check with your parents too, Seth," he said with a helpless kind of shrug.

"Fuck my father," I growled. "What loyalty has he ever shown me? Give me your Atlas and I'll record a statement in support of you. We'll make it clear we've known about this for a long time and tell them the only reason it was kept secret was to protect your stepmom from the scandal of the world knowing your dad cheated on her. Simple."

"Seriously?" Max asked, raising his brows at me. "But Lionel will punish you for that if it's not what he wants."

"So what? Fuck him. Fuck his Orderist bullshit and fuck the idea of me ever letting anyone think I believe in his screwed up hate speech either. He won't kill me without another Heir to replace me and I've lived through enough of his punishments to know that trying to follow his rules won't save me from them. So I might as well earn them doing something I believe in." I reached for Max's Atlas and he slowly handed it over.

"I don't want you getting hurt on my behalf," he said, clearly conflicted over what I was offering.

"Look, I either make the recording for you to give to your people to use in the best way they wanna release it, or I'll go live on FaeBook now and tell the world myself," I said.

"Alright. Shit, man, I owe you for this," Max said.

"No you don't. We're brothers and this is what we do for family. No question. No debts. We're just here for each other when we need to be."

I lifted his Atlas and made a recording, speaking clearly and honestly about my love and support for him and saying in no uncertain terms that the addition of Minotaur blood to his heritage made no difference to me at all. Max was the only real candidate for the role of Water Councillor when we all ascended to our positions, and I wouldn't be hearing any suggestion of anyone else taking on the job.

I finished up my breakfast while Seth made his recording too and Max was looking a lot more confident about his situation by the time he finished up.

"Where's Cal?" I asked. "We'll get his statement and you can send them to your team with one of your own."

"Still in bed," Max said, pointing vaguely towards the corridor as he started playing back the videos to check them over and Seth leapt up as I headed away to wake Caleb.

"Let's wake him up by dog piling him," Seth suggested with a grin and I smirked at that idea, casting a silencing bubble over us as we headed to Caleb's room.

But when Seth pushed the door open, we found it empty.

"Where is he?" Seth asked and I frowned in confusion as I looked around at the corridor, noticing one of the doors ajar. Roxy's door.

A prickle of apprehension ran down my spine and a low growl built in the base of my throat as an idea formed in my mind which I just couldn't get rid of. She hadn't been at Ignis House last night and I knew she'd been sleeping here a lot. And if Caleb was missing from his room then what if...

I swear it felt like the stars were nudging me towards that door, stoking the flames of jealousy and anger in me even though I had no right to feel anything like that yet. Or at all, really. She wasn't mine. But she was. And if he'd fucking touched her again, I'd rip his cock off and set it alight.

I clenched my jaw and strode over to her room, pushing the door open without bothering to knock or release the silencing bubble that concealed me and Seth who followed right on my heels.

The world stopped spinning as my gaze fell on the bed where the two of them lay, her head on his chest and his arm around her. There was a dull, echoing thump taking place somewhere in the depths of my mind and a ringing in my ears that wouldn't quit.

I couldn't even move for the longest moment, my body tensing with a rage so potent and powerful that I was afraid I'd burn up in it the moment I unleashed it from my body.

Seth was whimpering, pacing back and forth beside me as he clawed his hand into his long hair, his gaze fixed on the two of them like he was just as destroyed by this as I was, but I couldn't concentrate on that. Because I was about to murder my best friend.

The shadows rose up within me and I dropped the silencing bubble as a roar of fury escaped me and I lunged towards the bed, intending to drag Caleb out of it and beat his pretty face in until he stopped moving.

A shriek of fear escaped Roxy as she lurched awake and I crashed

448

into an air shield before I could get my hands on the motherfucker who had touched what was mine.

The Dragon in me was out for blood and my flesh burned and itched with the desire to shift. But I fought it back with a furious determination, knowing I wanted to feel his body break beneath my fists, not my claws.

"What the fuck?" Caleb yelled as he scrambled upright beside my girl, the blankets shifting to pool at his waist and reveal his sweatpants. But my brain was more focused on the urge to rip his head from his neck than his clothes. "I didn't touch her!" he added, clearly catching on to the reason for me looking at him with murder in my eyes.

"Is that what you think?" Roxy balked, shoving the covers aside and getting to her feet as she glared at me in a black tank that was clearly meant for a man and hung down around her thighs. "Fuck you, asshole," she snapped, pointing at me and I yelled something incoherent again as I tried to force my way past her magic by coating my fists in flames and punching the living shit out of the shield dividing us.

"Stop hiding in there, you fucking coward!" I roared, my gaze fixed on Caleb as Seth snarled beside me, seeming to have my back.

"Nothing happened, man!" Caleb yelled. "Max was in here with us. He was helping with her nightmares and I was helping him because he was struggling with taking on so much negative energy all the damn time!"

"I didn't even know he was here," Roxy added angrily, her glare fixed on me. "But thanks for trusting me, you piece of shit."

"You're in her fucking bed!" I roared, aiming all of my rage at Caleb because I couldn't bear to point it at her. "The two of you are half naked!"

"It looks pretty fucking suspicious, dude," Seth added bitterly, folding his arms over his chest while his jaw worked furiously like he was holding back on saying more.

"Well it's not," Caleb snapped, giving Seth a pained look which pissed me off because his focus should have been on me.

I struggled against the bloodlust and rage pounding through my veins as I looked between the two of them, my gaze snagging on her as a hopeless, desperate kind of longing filled me.

The Dragon beneath my skin was ready to rip this place apart, Caleb most of all and a fierce, relentless agony started up in my chest because I realised that even if it wasn't him, it was going to be someone some day. She wasn't just going to remain celibate because we couldn't be together. How could I expect her to do that? I might know that she couldn't find love elsewhere, but we already knew that it was perfectly possible for her to fuck someone else despite this bond. Someone in particular in fact.

My gaze snapped back to Caleb and I bared my teeth as potent rage flooded my body and my eyes shifted to Dragon slits. I was going to fucking kill him if he'd touched her again. If he seriously thought that he could lay his fucking hands on my girl and keep them attached to his body then-

Roxy moved across the bed until she was standing right in front of me, her position meaning she was eye to eye with me, her own anger lining her beautiful face as she dropped her air shield and shoved me in the chest as hard as she could. It wasn't enough to move me, but I could feel the force of that shove and knew that had been her intention.

"Get it through your dumb head, asshole - nothing happened. It's not like that with me and him. Not anymore," she shouted.

"Then why the fuck are you all snuggled up in bed together?" I demanded, smoke spilling between my lips as the urge to shift overwhelmed me and I turned my furious gaze on Caleb once more.

"It's *you*, dumbass," Roxy snapped, shoving me again and making me growl even louder. Why the fuck did she think it was a good idea to bait the beast in me when I was ready to- "It's only you. Even though it can't be, it fucking is."

"What?" I asked, my brow pinching but her mouth was on mine before I could further form that thought.

All the heat of the sun flared between us as she wrapped her arms around my neck and leapt up onto me, her legs tightening around my waist as a groan of pure fucking need escaped me and she pushed her tongue between my lips.

I growled hungrily, kissing her harder and gripping her ass as I held her up against me. I tasted every slice of jealousy that I'd ever felt over her in that kiss, every inch of pain I'd suffered in wanting her and knowing I could never have her.

She wound her fingers into my hair as she tugged hard enough to hurt. I bit down on her full bottom lip with a growl that told her I was still a wild beast and I wasn't about to be caged any time soon. Though if anyone had a chance of caging me then it was her.

I turned her around and drove her up against the wall, my hard cock driving against the wet material of her panties as I groaned for her and I was vaguely aware of Seth and Caleb leaving the room. But I didn't give a shit about them. I'd forgotten all about them and whatever fucking insane jealousy the stars had so clearly wanted me to feel when they drove me into this room because it was her. And there was only her, just like she'd told me there was only me. So fuck the stars for always wanting to part us. Fuck them for thinking they could stop this, stop *us*. There was no stopping us. She was it for me and even if I could never truly have her, I wasn't ever going to stop wanting her. I wasn't ever going to stop belonging to her.

Roxy kissed me harder, demanding more as my skin burned with the fire of my Dragon and my rage turned into something so much more primal.

She was mine. Destined to be mine by the stars. The girl who should have been my Elysian Mate and was so much more besides. I needed this. I needed her. I'd been like the moon without the light of the sun without her all this time. Cold and pale and void of life. But she lit me up and made me burn. And I never wanted to stop burning with her.

I dropped her onto a chest of drawers, knocking shit flying from it as she clawed at my chest and a boom of thunder crashed overhead.

But I couldn't let go. I wouldn't. *Fuck*, I didn't even care if they struck me down where I stood so long as I was in her arms when I went.

She shoved my sweatpants down, her fingers dragging across the tattoo I'd gotten for her and making me growl even louder before she wrapped them around my cock and I pushed her wet panties aside.

"I can't be without you anymore, Roxy. It's killing me. It's going to kill me," I groaned against her mouth and she whimpered with need, pulling me closer so that the head of my dick was pressed to her slick centre.

But before we could make good on that intention, a bolt of lightning slammed into the roof above us and she screamed as the entire treehouse lurched to one side, flames bursting to life across the wood and yells coming from our friends in the other room.

"Fuck!" I roared, tearing myself away from her and yanking my sweatpants up again before my need for her got her killed.

"Darius," Roxy growled in a clear demand for me not to lose my shit, but I was so fucking angry, I could hardly hear her.

I slammed my fist into the wooden wall hard enough to bust a hole in it and a roar spilled from my lips that was all Dragon as thunder crashed overhead again.

I threw one last, lingering look at the beautiful girl who owned my heart, wishing more than anything in the world that I didn't have to walk out on her then tearing my own soul in two as I did exactly that.

The other Heirs all tried to reassure me as I made it back to the front room, but I couldn't listen to it, dropping my sweatpants as I threw the window open and diving out into the storm instead.

My Dragon form burst from my flesh and I flew hard and fast towards the gap in the fence with flames tearing from my lips, consumed by the loss of everything I should have had with my girl.

When I made it to the hole in the fence, I shifted, crossed through it and shifted again before taking off in the direction of the mountains, using the storm clouds to hide me. I needed to be as far away from anything and everyone as I possibly could or I was going to lash out at someone who didn't deserve it.

I beat my wings and flew as fast as I could, leaving the academy behind and my heart right along with it. My mind was filled with images of a beautiful girl with eyes full of fire and lips that tasted like sin and the twist of fate which was always going to keep her from me.

The storm didn't let up as I flew, never looking back, just racing on and on through the sky and welcoming the misery of the freezing rain as it crashed down on my burning hot scales.

My mind was swimming with every awful thing I'd ever done to her, reminding me of all the reasons why I deserved to suffer like this until regrets and self hatred threatened to drown me more thoroughly than all the water pouring down on me.

I finally landed in a huge clearing between two mountains, the flat plain being pounded by the rain and my claws digging into the damp soil.

I roared at the stars even though I couldn't see them amongst the clouds, but I did it all the same, cursing them just like they'd cursed me and breathing out a giant plume of Dragon fire in an enormous fireball which blossomed right up to the sky.

I hung my head, watching the flames as they slowly died out before me and my heart stuttered as I spotted a figure stepping through the smoke as it cleared, her long hair falling all around her and a dark look on her face that told me she was pissed as all hell.

"Don't you run away from me, Darius Acrux," Roxy snarled, striding right up to me in that tank top which I just now realised was actually mine.

Her feet were bare and her golden wings were flexing at her back, glinting with the fire of her kind despite the pounding rain.

An air shield closed over me as thunder boomed through the heavens again and lightning struck it, splintering over the dome she'd created and lighting her up as if she was the one wielding it.

I shifted back into my Fae form, my muscles bunching with tension as I fought between the desire in me to go to her and the need to protect her from the wrath of the stars.

I stood totally still as she strode towards me, her eyes flaring with danger and determination.

"You know, when I was dragged out of my life and brought to your world, people kept telling me over and over again about the way the stars choose our destinies. They told me that our fates are set in stone and sealed by those twinkling little dots of light way off up in the sky. And I told them I didn't believe in fate. No matter how many times predictions and horoscopes and all of it was proved right, I kept scoffing and telling them I didn't believe it."

"That's not a surprise, Roxy. You're the most stubborn Fae I've ever met."

"Said the pot to the kettle," she growled and a ripple of anger burned in me at the tone she used with me. Even after all this time she was still just as disrespectful, just as rude and cutting and fierce as she'd been on the first day I'd laid eyes on her. Maybe even more so now.

"Well if you find me so obnoxious then why did you chase me out here?" I challenged.

"Because, from the moment I arrived here I swore I wouldn't let anyone decide my fate for me. So despite the fact that you're literally the rudest, most pig-headed, infuriating asshole I have *ever* met, I still want you. So fuck the stars. Fuck the moon and the meteors and the fucking clouds. Let the sky watch me as I tell it to get fucked. Nothing up there or down here gets to tell me what to do. You told me I was yours and I think that you›re mine too.»

"You *think?*" I asked. "I told you I love you. I tattooed it on my flesh, Roxy, I feel like I've made my feelings pretty clear. You're all I want for myself. The only choice I wish I could make and the only one I can't. So you don't *think* anything. You *know* I›m yours, every damn piece of me. But you›ve never told me what you want out of owning me or if I own you too.»

Thunder roared in the sky but Roxy ignored it entirely as she held her air shield in place, not even flinching when lightning crashed against it repeatedly.

"I'm the girl no one ever loved, Darius," she said. "No one but Darcy, my whole life. And though I never let it show, I used to dream of finding someone who would love me like a prince in a fairy tale so I could be their princess. But I don't love you like a princess. There isn't anything soft or sweet or easy about us. It's wild and unpredictable. It hurts more than any pain I've ever felt and consumes me more completely than anything I ever could have predicted. You make my heart race with all the best kinds of fear and my gut clench with the angriest butterflies I've ever known. I have hated you more than I even knew I could hate a man and I think if I love you with as much fury then I'll burn up in it."

"So you don't want to let yourself love me?" I asked, looking down at her as she stopped barely a meter from me and the heavens raged in fury at the way we were defying them.

"Maybe not," she agreed and my gut fell, but she lifted the hem of my tank and my gaze was drawn to the movement of her hand as she dragged her thumb up the front of her thigh and removed the concealment she must have had in place over her skin there.

A lump formed in my throat as my gaze tracked the lines of ink on her flesh. I knew the design because it mirrored the one Gabriel had told me to place on my own skin. The lines which dictated the position of the heavens on the night she'd told me no. The night when everything could have been so different if I'd only followed what my heart wanted sooner. The words which ran down her thigh to the left of the design in delicate script were a mirror of those on my own skin. *There is only him.*

"I think I'm already burning, Darius," she breathed. "And it's time I stopped pretending I'm not."

I stepped forward and caught her face between my hands, kissing her in a hard and demanding plea for that to be the truth. Because if I had her then I knew I had it all. And I didn't care if we really would have to tear the stars out of the sky to force them to give us our tomorrow. I'd do it. I'd pay any price they asked of me just to make this feeling last. Just to truly have her.

Give me this, I begged them as I lost myself in the feeling of her mouth against mine, her hands on my skin and her pulse thundering to the same heady rhythm as my own. *Give me her and I will pay any price you ask.*

The thunder seemed to crash even louder like the heavens were denying my pleas, but I soon forgot all about the stars and everything they were doing as I lifted Roxy into my arms and kissed her like this might be the only chance we got. And maybe it fucking would be. Because it was clear she was planning to hold off the storm with her magic for as long as physically possible and who knew if the heavens would ever let us get this close again.

We were standing in the middle of a muddy field which meant there were only so many options available to us, so I sank down onto my knees before sitting back on the ground with her in my lap.

Her tongue chased mine as she kissed me harder and my magic danced against the edges of my skin as it ached to be joined with hers. My barriers fell away and hers followed, a moan escaping her as the weight of our magic colliding flooded through us.

She was so powerful that it stole my breath away, this endless, unstoppable ocean of power which roared to a rhythm I hungered to drown in.

My hands moved up her spine, shoving at the material of my tank which she still wore, but it caught on her bronze wings, refusing to move for me and making me growl with frustration until my fingers met with the silky soft texture of her feathers.

A shiver ran through her entire body and she drew back with a gasp as I stroked my fingers over her wings, her pupils dilating as she looked at me.

"Do it again," she commanded, her eyes flashing and bringing a smile to my lips as I did as she wanted, caressing the ridges of her wings before circling my fingers over the spot on her back where they connected to her flesh.

She moaned as I repeated the move and I leaned in to kiss her neck, tasting her sweet skin as the ground beneath us began to rumble with the next wave of the stars' defences against us.

Roxy drove her knees down into the soil either side of my hips and through the connection of our magic, I felt the way she harnessed power over the earth beneath us, forcing it to still once more with a flare of magic.

I released my hold on her wings, sweeping my hands out around us and casting flames into existence in a ring surrounding us so that she could replenish her power while we stayed here like this, giving her all she needed to shield us from our fate.

I moved my hands down her body as I continued to kiss her neck, feeling her hard nipples through my tank and groaning as I closed my mouth over them one after the other.

Roxy moaned my name and I swear that was the best sound in the entire world.

She pushed me back and I let her, lying on the wet, muddy ground as I grasped her waist and moved her to kneel over my face so that I could kiss the ink on her thigh. I traced each and every line of that tattoo with my tongue, my heart racing at the knowledge that she'd placed it on her skin permanently for me.

My hands slid up the backs of her thighs and over the round curve of her ass as I ran my mouth over the tattoo before hooking my fingers into her panties and bringing fire to my hands to get rid of them.

Roxy gasped as the flames kissed her skin, but the Phoenix in her wouldn't let her burn.

I turned my head from her thigh to the centre of her, gripping her ass tightly and bringing her down over my mouth as the sweet taste of her desire met my tongue.

Thunder boomed so loud that the air within the shield rattled, but her magic held, protecting us here so that we could defy the stars.

I ran my tongue over her clit, loving the way she shivered in pleasure at my touch and her bronze wings flared wide either side of us, the flashes of lightning reflecting off of them and making her look like a fallen angel. And I was the demon who'd cast her to ruin. I just couldn't bring myself to regret that for a single second.

I used my grip on her ass to rock her hips and she obeyed my instructions, riding my face as I devoured her, the hard bite of my stubble grazing her soft skin and my tongue dragging through the centre of her over and over again.

She was so wet for me that it made my cock throb with the need to fill her and I growled against her pussy, making her gasp as she rocked her hips more urgently and my tongue worshiped her clit.

When she came for me, she cried out in bliss, her wings spreading wide and the fires all around us flared brighter, warming my skin.

I could feel the earth trembling again beneath us, the entire plane we were lying on seeming to shudder with the might of the earthquake the stars had sent to force us apart. Roxy's magic tugged on mine even harder as she forced her control over the Elements to keep us safe and I couldn't help but marvel at the strength in her.

The rain was crashing into her air shield so hard that I couldn't see beyond it aside from the constant deluge of water running over its surface. It felt like she'd created this one tiny paradise for us here where nothing beyond the two of us existed and I intended to make full use of it for every moment that we could steal.

I grasped Roxy's waist and flipped her off of me, tossing her down on her back in the mud and she banished her wings with a filthy laugh as I moved on top of her.

My mouth found hers and she kissed me hard, the taste of her orgasm dancing between our lips as I drove her down into the mud beneath me.

I found the hem of the tank she was wearing and ripped it up and over her head. But as the material caught around her arms, I twisted it to keep them trapped within it, pinning them above her head and smirking down at her as her green eyes flashed with anger.

She arched her back like she meant to fight back against me, but my cock found her entrance with the movement and as I drove into her, she forgot all about that idea.

"Shit, Darius," she panted as the perfect tightness of her pussy closed around my shaft and I pushed in harder, loving the sound she made as I filled her and the way her entire body arched against mine.

I captured her lips again, kissing her hungrily as the ground continued to judder violently beneath us and the thunder crashing overhead made the whole word vibrate.

The moment she melted into my kiss, I drew my hips back and thrust in again hard, keeping her hands pinned above her head and dominating her body as I fucked her with the desperate need to make her mine irrefutably.

Dragons were hardwired to find the most priceless treasure they could and make it theirs and she was the most prized possession I could ever hope to own. She was beauty and strength and bravery and hope and if I spent every day for the rest of forever making her mine then I'd gladly do it.

I was going to fuck my name into every inch of her skin, brand her with my kisses and mark her with my love until not a Fae in the world could deny it and even the stars would be forced to allow it.

My free hand moved over the curves of her body as I slammed my cock deep inside her over and over again and her flesh was painted in muddy handprints which I never wanted her to wash off.

Every scream that escaped her lips urged me on as I thrust harder, deeper, wanting her to come for me again and again until she couldn't see straight or think straight and all that was left in the world was me and her and nothing else.

She gave in to me for several ecstasy filled minutes as I dominated her, making me growl with pleasure as her body bowed to mine the way I'd always wished I could get her to submit.

But of course, she wasn't just going to let it be that easy.

With a sharp tug, she yanked her arms free of the shirt and my grip and moved her hands to my chest as she tried to push me to make me roll beneath her.

I growled a refusal at her, liking the feeling of owning her like this way too much to give it up and hooking her knee into my grasp so that I could fuck her even deeper. I watched her moaning and writhing for me as I pounded into her harder and harder, her hands pawing at her breasts and squeezing her nipples, painting every inch of skin with mud.

But just as I was certain I had her at my mercy, she reached up again, pressing a hand to my shoulder and knocking me back with the shadows that lived inside her.

I groaned as the darkness in me responded keenly, filling my entire body with pleasure as the shadows within us merged and pulsed with a keen need to be joined and I somehow found myself on my back beneath her.

Darkness pooled all around us and I dug my fingers into Roxy's hips as I drove my cock up into her, making her take me so deep that each thrust stole her breath.

The shadows were whispering something in my ear, making me ache to spill my own blood to intensify the pleasure they were feeding me as they beckoned me deeper into their hold.

But as my hooded gaze stayed fixed on the girl on top of me, I focused on fighting them back instead, knowing I could never need anything the way I needed her.

Roxy's eyes flared with Phoenix fire and the shadows raced from her body, the flame that lived within me rising up too and helping me banish them as she tipped her head back in pleasure.

My grip on her hips tightened and I leaned up, meaning to flip her beneath me again. But her hands landed on my chest as she denied me so I sat up instead, kissing her hard and fucking her deep.

I found her clit between us and her fingers pushed into my hair as I rubbed it in time with my thrusts deep inside her until she was panting and screaming and coming on my cock so hard that I couldn't help but come with her.

I thrust in firmly one last time, making her cry out as her tight pussy clamped down on me and I spilled my hot cum into her with the growl of her name on my lips.

The thunder that crashed overhead was full of rage and ominous predictions as bolt after bolt of lightning hit her air shield and she flinched as she fought to maintain it, dragging so much power from me that it made my breath hitch.

We stayed there, joined and panting, kissing softly and sweetly instead of hungrily and desperately and I ran my muddy hands up and down her spine, knowing this was the end of it. But I didn't want her to go. I didn't want her anywhere but in my arms, always.

"I'm yours, Darius," she breathed, her voice barely audible over the storm. "And you're mine. No matter what."

I kissed her once more, not wanting this to end, not wanting her to go. It felt like it would break me all over again if I had to watch her walk away from me again and yet I knew that this was the most we were ever going to be able to have. It was so much more than I thought we could take, but it was nowhere near enough at the same time.

I kissed her swollen lips one last time and she ran her fingers over my jaw like she wanted to memorise the lines of it before finally pulling back and getting to her feet.

The moment our bodies were no longer connected, the flow of our shared magic was cut off. I groaned at the loss of her power within me while she gritted her teeth as she fought to maintain the air shield with her power alone.

I stood too, stumbling a little as the force of the earthquake rattled through the ground beneath us.

"Can you hold the shield while we fly above the storm?" I asked her, the lightning which was slamming into her magic making my skin prickle with discomfort.

"I think so," she agreed, pulling my filthy tank back on before shifting into her full Phoenix form, her body covered in red and blue flames.

I shifted too, the Dragon in me bursting free of my fresh and I leapt into the air after Roxy as she took off towards the sky.

We flew hard and fast, lightning striking Roxy's shield over and over again, making my heart pound with the idea of what might happen if one of those bolts managed to break through. But she just flew harder, driving a path into existence between the clouds until we emerged above them and we were suddenly bathed in sunlight.

The air shield surrounding us fell away and we exchanged one last look before she took off in the direction of the academy once more and I was left to watch her go with my heart breaking a little all over again.

But this time the fissure wasn't so deep. Because despite the fact that the stars were determined to keep us apart, we'd managed to fight back and claim a slice of our own happiness right out from under their noses.

I just hoped they weren't the types to hold a grudge. Because if they were, then I had the feeling that destiny would be turning against us now and fate would make sure it got the last laugh.

I strode out of Jupiter Hall at the end of the day, my mind full of my girl instead of the lessons and I almost didn't notice the gold coin sat on the path in front of me until my foot was about to land on it.

Smoke coated my tongue as I looked down at it. That wasn't just some random coin. It was a four hundred and thirty-eight year old solid gold aura from King Agrien's reign.

I smirked as I bent down to retrieve the treasure, my inner Dragon chortling happily as I mentally added it to my treasure pile. Technically I probably should have made some effort to find the original owner and return it, but fuck that. This coin was mine. *Mine.*

The other Heirs had already headed to The Orb and I started making my way there, keeping my pace casual as I tugged my Atlas from my pocket and sent Roxy a message. We hadn't really gotten back to messaging each other like we used to yet, but after we'd denied the stars to be together, I was hoping we were back on track at last.

Darius:
What are you wearing?

Our unusual conversation starter made my heart race as I thought about how little she'd been wearing out in that field in a thunderstorm sent to tear us apart by the stars, and I almost didn't notice the glint of gold at the edge of the path to my right. But the Dragon in me wasn't going to miss treasure when it was up for the taking and my head snapped around almost of its own volition as I spotted another coin, this one even rarer - a ten aura piece from Queen Alanara's reign.

I smirked as I picked it up, rubbing the gold between my thumb and forefinger and enjoying the little thrill of magic I gained from it.

Just as I was about to turn away from the path, a deep blue gemstone caught my eye further into the trees and I grinned as I headed over to claim it.

My Atlas pinged as I grabbed the sapphire from the ground and the Dragon in me tasted the hint of water magic lodged in the stone. This wasn't any old sapphire - it was an aqua sapphire, pretty damn rare. *And pretty damn mine.*

I added the gemstone to the collection in my pocket and lifted my Atlas to find Roxy's message for me.

Roxy:
Just my uniform ;)

There was a photo attached and I swallowed thickly as I opened the image of her with her skirt removed and her school shirt unbuttoned, revealing her black underwear alongside her knee length school socks and the stilettos she'd taken to wearing to class recently. Her thigh was bare and she'd removed the concealment from her skin so that I could see her tattoo.

I wanted to go to her so badly that an actual groan escaped me and I just stared at the photo for way too long, wondering if I could convince her to fly out to some remote field somewhere again even though I knew that was a bad idea. If we kept riling up the stars and fighting against the fate they'd dished out for us, I was certain they'd strike back at us somehow. But I also knew I wasn't going to be able to stop. And I was quietly hoping that the stars would eventually see that they owed us a second shot at our destiny if we kept defying them, even if that was dumb as shit.

Roxy:
You never did finish telling me that story about you and Max doing that photoshoot at the beach last year...

I sighed as I realised I had to rein my dick in and forget about the fact that she was dressed up like a wet dream right now. Besides, even if my cock wasn't going to be getting any action from her, I had her attention and I planned on keeping it. If that meant catching her up on stories about me and Max getting mobbed by a group of horny women and having to use our magic to ski away into the ocean, then I was more than happy to do that.

But as I went to type out that message, a glint of silver caught my eye and I turned to look further into the trees, noticing a delicate necklace hanging there, swaying gently in the breeze.

It wasn't normal to find treasure scattered through the woods. With a frustrated grunt, I stowed my Atlas in my pocket and narrowed my eyes on the necklace before stalking forward to claim it.

If ever a trap had been laid for a Dragon, then this was definitely it. But as I lifted the one of a kind, platinum piece of jewellery from the branch, I couldn't help but grin again. *All mine.*

Further into the trees, I noticed a golden broach cut with the shield of the Omega family who had died out around a hundred and ninety-six years ago. *Nice. Mine.*

I continued on, keeping my guard up as I stalked into the shadows and collected treasure after treasure, unable to stop myself from smirking as I thought about adding them to the chest at the foot of my bed when I got back to my dorm later.

I finally stepped into a clearing where a golden tiara sat on a rock. A cursory glance told me it was over three hundred years old, encrusted with air crystals and crafted with deft precision. Probably from King Hector's reign. *Stunning. Mine.*

"And with one fell swoop, the Acrux Heirs did perish!" Geraldine cried as she dropped a concealment spell that had been hiding her to the side of the clearing and did some kind of weird flourish thing with her arms.

"What are you playing at?" I asked, noticing Xavier looking a little sheepish behind her as I resisted the urge to place the tiara on my head and added it to the collection in my pocket with the rest of my new treasure. She sure as fuck wasn't getting any of that back.

"You both fell prey to my lurings," she said smugly. "If I had been of wicked intent then likely you both would have perished."

"*Not* likely," I disagreed. "I was well aware I was walking into a trap and I was more than prepared to fight off whoever the fuck thought they could take me on. You forget I'm one of the most powerful Fae in the kingdom, Grus."

"Second," she said haughtily.

"What?" I questioned.

"One of the *second* most powerful Fae in the kingdom. Although now I'm thinking on that, I wonder if you're third really as my ladies jointly claim two places at the top." She tipped her head up towards the sky and placed a finger on her lips as she pondered on that and I arched an eyebrow at her.

"We disagree on that little nugget of shit, and you well know it. When the Vegas manage to put me on my ass and stand over me in victory, I might consider your point valid. But seeing as that day is unlikely to ever come, I'll sleep happy at night knowing the Heirs and I outrank them."

Geraldine burst into a fit of laughter, doubling over and clutching her stomach as Xavier raised his eyebrow at her like he was wondering if she was even sane and I folded my arms as I waited her out. It took a long time.

When she finally straightened again, all signs of mirth had fallen from her face and she looked fierce enough to shift into her Cerberus form and try to rip my head off.

"The day fast approaches, Master Lizard. Beware the bell that tolls," she said seriously, glaring at me.

"What?" Xavier asked. "Is that a prediction or something?"

"No, fine steed, I am not blessed with The Sight, but I do have a river of faith and a mountain of belief in my ladies. Now, quit lollygaging and let us set off." Geraldine took off into the trees and I arched a brow at her retreating back.

"Where the fuck do you think you're taking us?" I asked.

"I assumed you wished to visit your mother," she called back without bothering to look at us again and I exchanged a more excited look with Xavier before taking off into the trees after her.

"Really?" Xavier asked, hurrying to catch up to Geraldine and making me quicken my pace too.

"Of course. My dearest Papa is expecting us, and he has been making sure she is quite well looked after during her stay at our abode. I am certain you will be most pleased to see how well she is doing," Geraldine explained and I really hoped that was true, because our mom deserved the chance to be happy after so many years chained to that monster she'd been married to.

We kept pace with Geraldine as she headed through the trees towards the gap in the fence and I nudged my brother to get his attention.

"What did she lure you into the trees with?" I asked him, knowing his instincts wouldn't have made him follow treasure the way I had.

"Oh, erm." Xavier blushed a little and I was enough of a dick not to let him off the hook, waiting for the silence to stretch out before he admitted the truth. "Carrots."

I snorted a laugh and he did too, pulling a juicy orange carrot from his pocket and grinning as he took a large bite from it.

When we made it beyond the fence, Geraldine took some stardust from her pocket and swept us through the heavens to land outside her family's property. It was a huge white manor house set amongst a garden filled with every kind of tree and shrub imaginable, the clear use of expert earth magic making flowers bloom even though it was winter so the whole place was bursting with colour and life.

Geraldine led us through the gate, using her magical signature to open it and explaining that they'd given the staff the evening off to hide our visit as we walked up the gravel drive.

I found myself filled with anticipation as we drew closer to the place our mom had been hiding, wishing I could have come sooner and trying not to focus on all the horrendous shit she'd been through.

We entered the house and I was surprised to find that despite its huge size, the place was homely and cosy, full of warm features and the scent of freshly baked bread in the air. I knew Hamish Grus had been alone since Geraldine's mother had died years ago so I was guessing that he had kitchen staff whipping up the delicious smelling food and I was hoping we would be fed while we were here.

Geraldine kicked her shoes off and gave us a pointed look which made us follow her lead before delving into the depths of the house down a narrow corridor.

The smell of cooking food grew stronger the further we went and the sound of laughter drew a smile to my lips. This place wasn't just a house like the one we'd grown up in - it was an honest to fuck *home*. And I found I really liked the idea of my mom being here.

"Don't tease me, Kitty," Hamish Grus's rumbling voice carried to us from beyond the door at the end of the hall. "You have me drooling over here and I'm going to need a taste."

I wrinkled my nose, wondering if Geraldine's dad was fucking one of his staff then wondering why the fuck Geraldine was still walking right towards the door where the sound was coming from.

"You'll spoil the anticipation," Mom's voice came next and my frown deepened.

"You know I can't wait, I am such an impatient porcupine," Hamish groaned.

"Open your mouth then," Mom said with a soft laugh and I growled, shouldering past Geraldine with every intention to rip her father's head off. My mom had come here to escape lecherous old men, not fall prey to another one.

I threw the door open ahead of me, snarling loudly just as my gaze fell on my mom where she stood beside the oven and Hamish Grus who was sitting in a chair next to a wooden dining table laid out for five. He was a big man, thick with muscle with a shining bald head, a black handlebar moustache and bushy mutton chops which were certainly a choice. Though somehow he managed to pull the look off with an air of 'I don't give a fuck'.

He was leaning back in his chair and had his mouth open and Mom tossed him a bite of bread which he caught between his teeth like a dog, grinning widely as he chewed.

While I tried to figure out what the fuck I was witnessing, Mom turned to look at me with a squeal of excitement and darted across the room to pull me into a hug.

I remembered a beat too late to hug her back, smiling as she squeezed me tight and trying to adjust to the difference in her since she'd been freed from Father's control. My chest tightened at the thought of all of the years we'd missed out on. All of the love I'd been lacking while he kept her from me and my heart ached at the thought of it.

Xavier appeared beside me and she released me to hug him next before falling into a tirade of 'look how big you both are', 'oh and so muscular too', 'my tiny babies are bigger than me now', 'oh look how perfectly you shimmer in the light, Xavier', and so on. We just drank it in, grinning at her and letting her fuss and fucking loving it even while we pretended to groan and downplay her compliments.

She looked good. Damn good. Her complexion was richer, her eyes bright and full of life and her long, dark hair spilled down her back in waves. I'd never seen her looking like anything aside from the plastic perfection Father expected and it only made me realise how little we'd gotten the chance to know the woman she truly was. She was at home here, wearing a green apron over a sweater dress with a pair of fluffy socks on her feet and a smile bigger than I'd ever seen on her.

While we stole her attention, Hamish and Geraldine set to work dishing out a huge pot of stew with bread rolls, butter and bottles of wine with a homemade label which said they were made from the Gobblesome Grus Grapes which I was guessing indicated home brewed.

Mom ushered us to sit down at the round wooden table and we all filled our own plates, not a servant in sight. And from the easy way Hamish handled himself in the kitchen, I got the impression that that was the way it was here. It clearly wasn't like he lacked the funds for staff, but he seemed content to keep his home for his family and I found I really liked that.

"Thank you for this glorious and most splendiferous meal, Kitty Cat," Hamish said, smiling warmly at my mom as she took a seat beside him and beamed proudly.

"You know I was only able to cook it because you taught me, Hammy," she teased, smacking his arm playfully and batting her eyelashes before turning to watch me and Xavier take a bite of our food.

It was nothing like the pretentious shit that we always ate with Father. This meal was warm and wholesome and full of love and I grinned in appreciation across the table at my mom. "This is amazing," I told her honestly.

"Freaking perfect," Xavier agreed and she beamed before tucking into her own food.

We stayed there throughout the evening, demolishing our meals and listening to all the fun things Mom and 'Hammy' had been getting up to since she'd come to stay with him.

They'd been working to build up a list of Fae who were unhappy with Father's rule which Hamish kept referring to as 'la rebellion' without explaining his need to add the 'la'.

Mom was actually really helpful as far as figuring out who my father's enemies were because she'd spent years by his side, attending events with him and seeing the relationships he had with many powerful Fae. Father liked to listen to the sound of his own voice, so he'd also vented to her about Fae he didn't like and given her plenty of ammunition to use against him when Hamish approached them now.

They were being careful to keep my mom's involvement out of everything, not letting anyone know she was alive aside from him and I found myself really warming to this man who owed us absolutely nothing and yet had taken her in when she needed help without so much as a question over her loyalty.

The rebels had been creating networks across the kingdom to help hide the persecuted Orders and get them to safety and they even had the beginnings of some plans to break the Tiberian Rats my father had imprisoned in his Nebular Inquisition Centres free.

Geraldine gushed about the A.S.S. and how they'd been secretly meeting up still and between the two of them it sounded like there was a strong rebellion growing out of sight, ready to come and stand against my father as soon as we were ready to strike. I mean, yeah, they intended to back the Vegas for the throne, but they were also happy with the idea of me and the other Heirs continuing on as Councillors. They'd just have to accept the fact that the Vegas wouldn't actually be wearing any crowns when the time came for the kingdom's new rulers to ascend. Because to claim the throne they'd have to prove they were stronger than us and I had trouble believing that day would ever come to pass.

Aside from their work against my father, Mom had thrown herself into being domesticated. She was learning to cook and bake and spending time with Hamish while they worked on honing their earth magic - hence all the beautiful plants everywhere. In short, she was happy. And the knowledge of that soothed the pain and heartache in my soul in a way I hadn't even realised I'd been needing.

She gushed about getting to choose what time she woke up in the mornings and picking her own clothes and the evening she'd spent reading a book just because she felt like it, and my heart ached for the life she'd been trapped in. But here she was finally free, and it felt so damn good to just have something to be happy about for once that I bathed in it for the entire evening, never wanting to leave this little place of contentment.

The Gruses might have been pretty damn weird at times, but they were seriously good people and I owed them a debt that I would never be able to pay back. So I'd have to settle for killing my father and making sure this bubble of peace was able to extend beyond these walls one day.

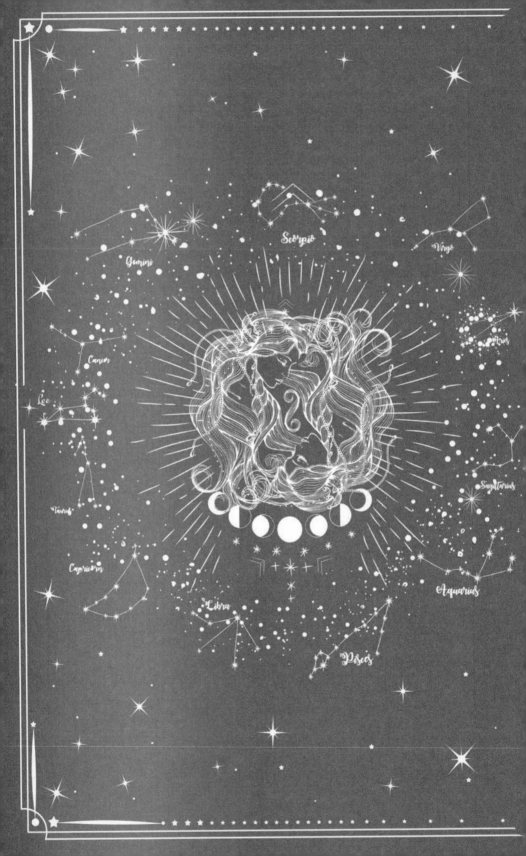

DARCY

CHAPTER THIRTY SEVEN

"Tuck your hineys!" Washer called as we did squats in the mud, the rain beating down on us on the Pitball pitch.

We never shielded from the weather while we were training so we got used to all conditions during a match. No magic could be wasted for that when we had to reserve it all for fighting the opposition. Washer had had some mercy on the cheerleading squad at least after making them rehearse in the pouring rain until their costumes were drenched, and he'd finally let them head off to the changing rooms to shower.

"Do we really need to do any more of this shit?" Darius barked at Washer who was casting the rain away from himself as he sat on a fold out chair in some lycra shorts and a yellow turtleneck sweater.

He'd taken over Pitball training since Professor Prestos had been overwhelmed by all the extra classes she was teaching. He didn't even freaking like Pitball and his grasp on the rules was next to none.

Nova apparently didn't give a damn if our team went to the dogs. She probably hadn't even noticed, what with her head being so far up the King's ass. I got the feeling she'd assigned Washer to this role to punish him for breaking up with her too. But the only ones really getting punished were us.

"No, you're quite right, Mr Acrux," Washer called: "Pair up. Boys with girls. That's it, you can pair with Mr Capella, Miss Vega." Washer directed Seth over to me while wetting his lips thirstily, giving me the chills. He paired up the rest of the team, taking his time over deciding who went with who like it mattered. "Mmm that's it, now all the girls get on your backs and stretch one leg as far over your heads as you can. Boys, press your weight down on their thighs to really widen the stretch."

"Are you fucking kidding me?" Caleb barked.

"Pipe down, Mr Altair. Flexibility is an important part of any sport," Washer said. "Now hurry along and get those legs in the air girls."

I dropped down into the mud with a huff, stretching my leg up as far as I could over my head and Seth bent over me to push it further, keeping his weight off of me so this didn't get super weird. Although, I was pretty sure this was already in that territory.

Geraldine lay in the mud beside me with both of her legs stretched over her head with no freaking bother. "Come on then you wet willy, help me stretch out my quads," she demanded, lifting her head up to shout at Max between her thighs. He smirked and dropped his weight onto her, gripping her ankles and driving them into the mud above her head as his crotch ground against hers. *Jesus.*

I looked up at Seth with a snort and he sniggered at his friend.

"Push the girls harder, boys!" Washer called. "Use your weight to get a nice *deep* stretch. You're not using your weight, Mr Capella." A torrent of water hit Seth in the back and he was knocked over me, his heavy body falling onto mine. I hissed as he forced my leg to go far further than it wanted to and I was drenched in the icy flow of water too.

"Ow ow ow," I pushed him back and his hand slipped in the mud as he tried to get up.

"I'm gonna kill him," Seth growled, turning his head to bare his teeth at Washer as he managed to raise himself off of me.

"Less of the attitude, Capella, or you'll lose your extra credit for this term," Washer warned.

"Fucking asshole," he snarled, turning back to face me. "Sorry, babe, you're gonna have to take one for the team."

I growled, shoving his chest. "Just let me swap legs, this one's officially broken."

He laughed, kneeling back and letting me swap out before pressing his weight down on me again, but not much. He cast a subtle silencing bubble around us, his eyes darting over to Caleb who was further down the line.

"So…have you spoken to Cal again?" he whispered as my ankle went over my head and I winced.

"Yeah, but whenever I try to steer the conversation toward you, he changes the subject. I dunno how to break him," I said with a frown.

"I swear he feels something," he murmured.

We'd been over every detail since the graveyard incident, of how Caleb had saved his life then leaned in, gazed at Seth's mouth and almost seemed like he was gonna kiss him.

Seth had acted it out moment by moment so I had a pretty good visual, though the Wolf had a tendency to dramatize things which meant I couldn't be entirely sure how accurate his account was. But there must have been some truth to it.

"Maybe you just need to ask him," I suggested, knowing I was sounding like a broken record by now, but really, what other option did he have?

"*Or* maybe we need to make him jealous. Watch his reaction," he demanded, dropping the silencing bubble before I could agree then grabbing my wrists and pinning them above my head with one hand.

"*Hey,*" I hissed.

"Max, take a picture of us." Seth wrangled his Atlas out of his pocket, tossing it to his friend who was now rocking his hips back and forth while Geraldine held onto his head and shouted wild encouragements to him. He looked like he was having the time of his life.

Seth's Atlas fell into the mud and Max looked over at us in a daze. "What?"

"Get a photo," Seth snapped.

"I don't want a photo," I yanked at my wrists, opening my palms and readying to blast him off of me with air if he didn't obey.

Max laughed, snatching up the Atlas and snapped a photo just as Seth leaned down and pressed his lips to mine.

"*Ah!*" I released a storm of air, forcing him off of me and sending him flying away into the mud with a hard thwack.

I wiped my mouth with the back of my hand, sitting up with a snarl before pushing to my feet. "What the hell, Seth?"

He got up, clutching his stomach as he laughed and I charged him down, using my earth magic to pelt huge balls of mud at him. The first one slapped him right in the face, killing his laugh dead, but he threw up an air shield before I could land the second one.

The earth quaked beneath my feet as I prepared to bury him, but Caleb suddenly shot between us and Washer started blowing his whistle.

"What's going on?" Caleb demanded of me, like it was my damn fault Seth didn't have any boundaries. But I had to admit, maybe Caleb did look kind of jealous.

"He kissed me," I growled, pointing an accusing finger over Caleb's shoulder at the mutt.

Caleb whipped around to look at him and I couldn't see his expression as Seth shrugged innocently.

"She was begging for it," Seth said with a smirk. "She kept saying 'oh you're getting me so wet, drag me back to your Wolf den and put it in my ass'."

An earthquake split away from me as I snarled and the ground tore in two. *I'm gonna kill him.*

Seth rose himself up on a cloud of air as Caleb jumped out of the way of the hole opening up in the ground.

"That's enough!" Washer called. "I know this new Order law is causing a lot of sexual frustration, Miss Vega, but we must all try to restrain ourselves. I can always help syphon off some of that rampant energy if you need an outlet."

I shuddered, rounding on Washer as Seth and Caleb did too.

"Why are you such a damn pervert?" I snapped at him before I could stop myself and Washer's mouth dropped open.

"I do beg your pardon, Miss Vega?" Washer held a hand to his heart, looking utterly offended.

"No, she's right," Seth snarled. "If you talk to her like that again, I'll deal with your ass myself."

"I don't need your help," I tossed at Seth, but I guessed his solidarity was sort of sweet.

"Oh-ho!" Washer gasped. "You'll deal with my ass will you, Mr Capella?" he asked, making it sound like a completely different kind of threat and I grimaced.

"I'm gonna get you fired if you don't back down, you old creep," Darius barked, walking over with Max at his back, water streaming from their hair and making their uniforms cling to their muscular bodies. I'd noticed he'd point blank refused to take part in the stretching shit and I knew that was because of Tory. He didn't let any of the fangirls even get close to him these days and there was something stupid cute about that.

Caleb laughed obnoxiously and Washer looked between us all in shock then took a step back, chuckling nervously.

"I meant no harm. You've got the wrong end of the stick," he simpered, cowering under the gaze of all of us.

"Good," Darius growled. "Then in the words of Lance Orion, the best damn Pitball coach this team has ever had by the way, class is fucking dismissed."

We all turned away from Washer, heading to the locker rooms and Geraldine guffawed as she came prancing along beside me.

"That'll show that brackish ballbag where to stuff his stationary," she said with another loud laugh and I grinned.

"I don't think he'll ever stop being creepy though," I said as we headed inside and I urged my Phoenix fire into my veins to warm me through.

We split away from the boys, walking into the girls' changing room and we were soon showered and dressed in warm clothes and I adjusted the necklace holding the Imperial Star over my shirt carefully. I put on the Gemini bracelet my brother had gifted me too, liking the way it made me feel closer to him.

I'd wanted to go flying with him and Tory tonight, but the weather was only getting worse. When I checked my Atlas, I found a text from my brother saying there were storms all across the kingdom, but the sun would be out tomorrow so we should go then instead.

I pulled a navy hoody on over my sports bra, leaving the zip open as I dried out my hair. The last of the other girls filed out of the room and I looked over to Geraldine who was putting on makeup in the mirror.

"Going somewhere tonight?" I asked curiously.

"Justin and I are meeting up for a late supper," she said, powdering her nose.

"Oh, like a date?" I asked curiously and she shook her head.

"Oh no my sweet Darcy, I do not date. I spread my lady seed as far and wide as I can until my days of unshackled courtship come to a close. My marriage to Justin, the little worm, will be the end of it, but sometimes…"

"What?" I asked as she sighed heavily, her shoulders heaving and dropping.

She glanced at me with emotion glazing her eyes and I rested a hand on her shoulder as my heart tugged.

"Well, lately," she lowered her voice. "My Lady Petunia craves to have her garden watered by one single devilish dandelion."

"Max?" I whispered, excitement running through me. I knew Geraldine's political stance was holding her back from giving herself to Max, but I wished it didn't have to. They were polar opposites but somehow they found a balance between them that just worked.

She nodded, sucking her lower lip then suddenly fell to her knees and wailed. "Oh, my Queen, I have wronged you by that admission! He is an Heir – a ghastly *Heir*! And I would never align myself with such a lout! Never!"

"It's okay, Geraldine." I drew her to her feet as she released a croaking sob. "Max is a good guy. Screw politics. If you like him, then go for it. Tory and Darius are meant for each other, so why not you and Max?"

"Oh my lady, if only it were so simple. And my lady Tory and her Darry man are an exception chosen by the stars themselves. He will eventually inevitably bend the knee when she puts a pin in his astoundingly large head." She sniffed and I really hated that politics had to mean so much to her and that she wholeheartedly believed some pre-arranged engagement had to be stuck to. I didn't care who she dated. Alright, I wouldn't be thrilled if she joined the Clara party and started dating Lionel and calling him Daddy, but pretty much anyone else in Solaria was fair game. *Except Orion. Nope, go away unwanted thought.*

The door pushed open and Seth came walking in like he owned the world in just a pair of sweatpants with a bag slung over his shoulder. "Wanna walk back to Aer Tower with me, Darcy?" he asked. "The guys have gone."

I looked to Geraldine and she nodded, waving me away as she turned to the mirror to reapply her makeup. "I'll see you in the morrow. I shall have a feast of buttery bagels ready in the Hollow at dawn."

"You don't have to," I said like always, but she waved me off again, because she always would. She was too damn good of a friend.

I headed out of the door with Seth, walking through the quiet halls together, relishing breaking Lionel's little Orderist law. Ever since Orion had helped me with my illusion spells, I was getting seriously good at them. I could make myself look like a fluffy grey Werewolf padding along at Seth's side whenever I liked, so hanging out with him and the other Heirs around campus had become a little easier.

"I wanna go for a run before we head back, I thought you might like the ride?" Seth asked and I scowled.

"I'm still pissed at you," I reminded him.

"Oh right," he said, cocking his head to one side and giving me a puppyish look. "Forgive me, babe. I just wanted to make Cal jealous. And did you see him run over? I think it might have worked."

"I don't think you should play games like that," I said, clapping him in the ear. "It's not cool."

He whined low in his throat. "But jealousy is so fucking efficient at making people show their real feelings," he reasoned.

"True, but it's also game playing. Caleb doesn't deserve that," I pushed and he considered my words before nodding.

"Dammit, you're right. Why are you always right?"

I laughed, tossing my hair jokingly. "It's because I'm one of the true queens."

He growled and I grinned, but he didn't bite the bait. We all avoided the fact that we'd have to fight for the throne one day. It was simpler that way. Besides, with Lionel in power, that future seemed so far off and impossible it was easy to forget we might all clash again eventually.

We reached the exit and Seth pulled off his sweatpants, putting them in his gym bag which I took from him, hooking it over my shoulder. He opened the door, leaping out of it and shifted into his huge Wolf form.

I jogged forward to climb on his back, quickly casting an illusion over myself so no one would see anything but swathes of white fur in my place. Then I cast an air shield around us to keep us dry and he took off across the wet grass, his nose in the air as he breathed in the scents of the evening.

I clung to his fur, keeping low on his body as he ran faster and faster, tearing past the Earth Observatory and circling around to The Wailing Wood. The darkness was thicker between the trees and there were other Orders out too, creeping amongst the shadows.

Seth raced on through the wood, weaving between the large boughs and making my heart leap with exhilaration. We soon arrived at Aer Tower and he slowed his pace, padding up to the door while I raised a hand to cast air at the Elemental symbol above it. Seth nosed the door open and started running up the stairs, knocking people aside as he took several steps at a time.

There were posters on the wall warning of some sort of wild monster man that Kylie keep harping on about it, saying it had attacked her one night a few weeks ago. I guessed it was just a way to try and get attention, but it hadn't worked. The only Fae who gave her any notice these days were the others K.U.N.T.s. And even *they* didn't spend actual quality time with her. But whenever I felt remotely sorry for her sitting on her own pining for a friend, I vividly remembered her up on that stand in court, telling the whole kingdom that she had been the one to catch Orion and I. I would never forgive her for that. And if she spent the rest of her time at Zodiac alone because of it, then she was getting off lightly.

Seth slowed as he reached the corridor that led to my room, waiting for the students around us to file away before charging down it. I slipped off of his back, unlocking the door and turning to say goodnight but he pushed into my room.

"Damn Wolf," I muttered as I followed him inside, shutting the door and locking it tight before casting a silencing bubble around us.

Seth shifted back into his Fae form and I tossed him his bag. He took out some boxers, pulling them on before throwing himself onto my bed and making himself comfy. He didn't always stay here, but I had to admit I slept better when he did. With Tory having to pretend she was still controlled by the shadows, I couldn't stay with her unless we slept at King's Hollow. And without company, I barely got a couple hours sleep. So as weird as this was, I also wasn't going to make him leave.

I kicked my shoes off, grabbing an elastic from my nightstand and pulling my hair up into a ponytail then dropping down beside him on the bed.

"Don't you miss your pack when you stay here?" I asked as I hooked an Astrology textbook out from under my pillow and propped it up on my knees.

Professor Zenith wanted us all to study the Seventh House for a pop quiz she was throwing tomorrow. We'd been studying it all week, and as it was ruled by Libra and Venus (Orion's star sign and the damn love planet) I was constantly reminded of him. The Seventh House's other name was the House of Partnership too so that was just a bundle of coincidences I didn't need right now.

"Not really," he said, looking guilty as he rolled toward me and rested his head on my arm. "Do you wanna know something I've only told the Heirs?"

"Always." I placed my book down, looking to him curiously.

He glanced up at me with a slanted grin. "They're my real pack. The ones I count on over anyone else. The ones I'm there for before anyone among my Wolves. I know it's fucked up, and I do love my pack. But they're not family. The Heirs are. And so are you now. Your sister is too…though I don't think she likes me that much."

"Well you keep bringing her snacks and then stealing them back."

"That's a game we're both taking part in," he said defensively. "When I was on the moon the other Fae used to hide all the best snacks for me to sniff out and steal. They loved it."

"That kinda sounds like you just stole their food."

"Trust me. They loved it. Tory does too," he insisted.

"Err, no. Tory is like a bear when it comes to food. She doesn't share often and she definitely doesn't like it being stolen from her," I said and he just scoffed.

"She loves it," he insisted even though I knew for a fact he was wrong. "But aside from that, she still doesn't seem to wanna snuggle with me much, so there must be something else holding her back."

"Well, you peed on her that time," I pointed out. "People don't just get over being peed on."

"Yeah…" he said, a soft Wolfy whimper escaping him and I took pity on him as I went on.

"She doesn't hate you anymore. She just needs to get to know you better," I said and he chuckled in a low tone.

"Maybe I need to work on that," he replied, shoving my Astrology book aside so he could curl up against me better, yawning like a tired pup.

I'd never had a pet dog, but I imagined it was kinda like this. Which was totally weird, but there was something about him lying on me or the way he did with the Heirs that just seemed natural. It was the way of his kind and he had such a soothing aura when he wasn't being an asshole. Which these days tended to be pretty often. At least to those in his inner circle. I'd never really imagined there could be this much good in the guy I'd once hated with all my heart.

"So, are we ever gonna talk about what happened between you and Orion in that tomb?" he asked out of the blue and my heart jolted.

"What?" I blurted, heat rushing up to my cheeks. "Nothing happened." Great, that sounded really convincing.

"Pfft, you came outta there looking guilty and confused as fuck. I know something happened," he insisted. "I just assumed you might bring it up eventually, but apparently you still don't trust me."

I groaned, rubbing my eyes. "It doesn't matter, it didn't mean anything."

He gasped, sitting upright and knocking my hand away from my face. "Holy fuck, I didn't think anything actually happened, I was just testing you! Tell me everything."

"You asshole." I punched his arm and he laughed, grabbing my wrist and grinning like a maniac. I sighed dramatically, giving in as I tugged my arm out of his grip. "*Fine.* It was just one stupid kiss that's all." Tory was the only one I'd confided in about it and the only one I normally would. So this was a stretch for me.

His eyes lit up like I'd just told him Christmas was coming early and I frowned in confusion.

"Why do you look so damn happy about it?" I asked.

"It's just exciting," he said with a shrug, but I wasn't buying it.

"Seth," I warned and he sighed, dropping down to sit beside me and rest his head against mine.

"Fine, I want you two to get back together. Is that a crime?"

I wheeled on him, surprised that he was echoing what my sister had said. "You what?"

He shrugged innocently. "You're fucking made for each other, and come on, it's been months since he was gone and you're not over him. Not even one percent over him," he implored and I hated him calling me out like that. It put me on the defensive and I spluttered a non response while he just gave me a patient look that said he was waiting for me to admit it. Goddammit he was annoying sometimes.

"Even if I wasn't over him, which I am, I could never be with him after what he did," I said, but even as I said it, I knew it wasn't entirely true anymore. Since Orion had explained himself, I kept running over his words in my mind. They were too sincere, too fucking sweet.

"You mean when he sacrificed himself for you so you might have a chance to take down Lionel? So that you wouldn't lose everything including your place at the one academy capable of training up a Fae of your power level and giving you a real chance for the throne? By the stars, what an asshole," he growled mockingly and I pursed my lips. "No, you're right, Darcy. I won't stand for it. How dare he throw himself into the most dangerous place in Solaria and face months of hell in Darkmore because of how much he loves you? How fucking dare he."

"Stop it," I snipped, but he just kept going.

"How *dare* he ruin himself as far as any Fae can possibly ruin themselves for you."

"I didn't ask him to," I said heatedly. "I never wanted him to."

"I know," he said, his smile falling away as he took my hand and squeezed. "And you have a right to be mad at him for that. But not forever, babe."

A lump burned my throat as emotion welled up in me. I dropped his gaze, unable to face the blazing truth in his eyes. "It's all so messed up."

"But it's not unfixable," he urged. "Look, I love hanging out with you, Darcy. Staying here with you feeds my inner Wolfiness, but I'm only here because I can feel your pain. Not in the way Max can, but..." He reached out, brushing his knuckles across my collar bone with a dark frown. "It's instinct, I guess. I just know you're hurting. And that hasn't changed since he left. Even since Tory came back, I know you're happier but it's not enough. And if I'm honest, I don't think it's going to change unless you two fix this."

"I don't know if it can be repaired, Seth," I said, the pain in me splitting open like a sealed box cracking in my chest.

He cupped my cheek, giving me an intent look. "If you both want it enough, it can be."

I ripped my gaze from his, not wanting to face what he was asking of me. But I knew I needed to. I just wasn't sure I could ever let go of this hurt Orion had left in me. I couldn't see a reality in which I could trust him again, and if I couldn't trust him, then there was no hope for us.

I sat in my last class of the day, scowling at Highspell as she handed out fat chocolate brownies to the 'higher' Orders at the front of the room, spending particular time chatting with the boys and casually running her fingers through their hair. Her skirt was almost short enough to see her snake hole and she made a point of bending over in front of any guy she took a liking too.

I felt sorry for Tory having to sit up there and pretend she was a slave to the shadows. She was probably working to restraining herself from tit punching Highspell right about now. As amazing as it was to know she was mostly free of Lionel's control, it sucked that I couldn't spend more time with her. We had to always be careful in case anyone suspected anything. And as much as I missed her, I wasn't going to risk Lionel finding out she was no longer a walking zombie.

There was one thing keeping my spirits high today though, it was another full moon at last. And Orion would be able to read more of his father's diary. Maybe my mother had *seen* more of what we needed to do to face Lionel.

I tried to cast a levitation spell on the three kilo weight sitting on my desk and it raised up a few inches before I let it tumble back onto my desk again. Highspell didn't let us have anything above five kilos for this, while the front of the class were already lifting up to fifty. She'd vaguely given an explanation to the whole class of how to cast the spell then spent the rest of the time moving between the 'higher' Orders and showing them how to do it in more detail. And everyone back here was unsurprisingly failing this subject hard.

My Atlas buzzed and I took it out. Highspell rarely paid any attention to any of us in the back rows, so I didn't bother to hide it as I found a message from Darius. Of course, if she *did* decide to look this way, she'd punish the hell out of me for it. But I didn't give a damn.

Darius:
Can you go to Lance's tonight? He might need help and I'm busy.

My heart missed a full beat.

Darcy:
Busy doing what?

Darius:
Stuff and things. Be there by seven, shrew.

I shot him a gif of an angry Minotaur shouting 'NO!' and he replied with one of a shrew running away from a torrent of Dragon fire.

I pursed my lips, wondering where the hell he'd found such a gif before tossing him one back of a Calonian Octopus Shifter with Fae hands on the end of every tentacle putting its middle fingers up.

Darius:
Have fun!

"Asshole," I muttered.

Right, well if I was going, I definitely needed a buffer. I wasn't gonna spend an evening alone with a guy I craved like a drug and who was just as bad for me. So I shot a message to the group chat asking for help.

Max:

No can do, little Vega, Gerry's sneaking over to my place tonight.

Darcy:

How did you pull that off??

Max:

I stole all the bagels from the school supply and stashed them in my room. If she wants breakfast tomorrow, she has to come. Literally.

I snorted a laugh but it fell dead as Seth's reply came in next.

Seth:

Can't come tonight. Cal's hunting me.

Caleb:

I am?

Seth:

Yup. *crossing swords emoji*

Seth:

Shit that was meant to be a battle axe emoji.

Caleb:

Seth:

Anyways, sorry babe, we're out. Good luck, let us know all the juicy deets... about the diary.

I gritted my jaw in annoyance, looking over to Tory, but I knew she couldn't join me. She only went home to Lionel at the weekends and there was no way I was going to make her head back to the palace any more than she had to.

My Atlas buzzed and I found a message from the only other person I could have called on.

Gabriel:

No can do, I'm heading home for the night for Faetalian Tuesdays. I'm cooking. I'll freeze you some!

Great. It looked like it was on me.

It wasn't like I didn't want to see Orion. Hell, that was *all* I wanted to

477

do. But being in a house alone with him seemed like a terrible idea. Especially since we'd kissed. I'd worked really hard convincing myself it meant nothing, and I didn't want to be proven wrong.

I moved my thumb onto the new number in my contacts for Orion, his name saved as Starboy just like it used to be to hide the fact that we were talking. I guessed some things never changed. I hadn't messaged him once since I'd gotten his number, but I figured it was only right to tell him I'd be showing up later.

Darcy:

Hey, I'll be over at 7. Darius thought it would be best if someone is there

with you.

P.S. Full moon woo!

Full. Moon. Woo??
God why would I say that?
Three little dots appeared to let me know he was typing a reply and I couldn't believe how much that made my heart backflip.

Starboy:

And Darius thought the best someone would be you?

P.S. I think you're spending too much time with Werewolves for the moon to

get you that excited...

I rolled my eyes, but I was also struggling to flatten my grin as I replied.

Darcy:

He's busy doing 'stuff and things' apparently which I'm gonna assume means

counting out his gold and checking all the locks on his doors to make sure no

one ever steals it.

So I guess you're stuck with me.

P.S. No more time than I do with Sirens, Vampires, Cerberuses and Dragons.

Starboy:

I can think of worse fates.

P.S. They don't sleep in your bed though, do they?

My heart lurched into my throat as I stared at those words. How the hell did he know Seth slept in my bed? Had Darius told him?

"Miss Vega!" Highspell shrieked and I looked up in surprise, finding her storming toward me like a bat out of hell. Her eyes turned to green slits and the necklace around her throat glowed brighter as she closed in on me. "How dare you disrespect me in my own classroom?" she hissed and I tucked my Atlas into my pocket.

"I don't need to disrespect you, miss, you manage that all on your own," I said lightly, poking the beast.

Tory met my eye across the room, a grin tugging up the corner of her mouth ever so slightly. I noticed her fingers flicking under her seat and Highspell suddenly tripped over like a whip of air had caught her legs, sending her tumbling to the floor ass over tit. Everyone roared with laughter including me. *Yes, Tor.*

The bell rang for the end of the lesson and I sprang out of my seat, leaping over Highspell as she struggled to get up and running for the door.

"Darcy Vega stop this instant!" she roared and I knew I'd pay for it tomorrow but I didn't care.

Tonight was the full moon and I was not getting landed in detention. I laughed as I ran full pelt down the corridor and ice suddenly blasted over my head. *Oh shit!*

"Stop this second or you'll regret it!" Highspell screamed and I spotted Caleb walking up the stairs ahead of me.

"Cal! Zoom me out of here!" I called and he didn't even question it, shooting towards me and throwing me over his shoulder, laughing as Highspell came racing toward us on her high heels.

Caleb flipped her the bird then shot away at high speed, shooting across campus and making my head spin. We both cracked up as he placed me down and I realised I was beyond the outer fence.

"You'd better keep running, sweetheart. She's gonna have every K.U.N.T. in school hunting for you." He smirked, taking out a pouch of stardust and tossing it to me.

"Thanks." I grinned. "What about you?"

"She's got a thing for me." He winked then stepped back through the fence. "I'll just flirt my way out of trouble. Oh, and I'll slip her a memory potion to get you off the hook too. See you later." He shot away and I was left smiling as I took a pinch of stardust between my fingers. It really paid off being the Heirs' friend these days.

My mouth grew dry and I looked down at my school uniform with a frown. Not exactly the outfit of dreams for tonight. But I didn't really have much choice now.

I threw the stardust over my head and pictured the woodland outside the palace as I was tugged away through the stars.

I landed in the mud – without a single stumble thank you very much - and started jogging down to the tree where I could access the passage into the palace. I never stardusted too close to it just in case someone happened to be out here when I showed up. I didn't think it was likely, but I was always cautious just in case.

I headed up to the gnarled tree, my breath fogging before me in the cool air as I pressed my hand to the Hydra mark and it shone beneath my palm.

I thought of my father with an ache in my soul, wishing I could have had a chance to know him. But more than that, I wished he could have been saved from what Lionel had done to him. It haunted me knowing his fate. I just hoped he'd known happiness alongside my mother at least.

I walked down the stairs the roots formed, descending into the tunnel below before they retracted and the lasting light of the day vanished. I took out my Atlas, figuring I should give Orion a head's up that I was early, but found I had no signal. I swore under my breath as I tucked my Atlas away and cast a Faelight to see by as I jogged along, willing heat into my veins to fight away the cold.

When I reached the hatch, I cracked it open and peeked out with my heart pounding. The sound of the shower running reached me and I climbed up, gently dropping the hatch back into place and moving into the living room. The door to the bathroom was half open and my pulse went haywire at the sight of Orion in the shower. His back was to me and water rushed down his broad shoulders and the muscles tapering at the base of his spine before washing over his ass.

I remained stock still, not daring to breathe as he carved his fingers through his hair.

I should move.

I should do anything but stand here and just stare.

Heat burned a path through my body until I felt like I was melting. I forced myself to take a step away, but the floorboard creaked beneath my foot. His head whipped around and I nearly swallowed my own tongue as he met my gaze. *Shit shit no shit.*

I panicked, all rational thought going out of my head as I fled. It was stupid and childish but I didn't give a damn because I just needed to get back into the tunnel and leave, come back later if I had to, but right now I just had to embrace my inner coward and run like a maniac to escape.

I almost made it to the hatch when Orion shot in front of me with a towel wrapped loosely around his waist, his naked body dripping water as he smirked at me. Fucking *smirked*. My heart collided with my throat and I folded my arms as I tried to regain some composure, but I was pretty sure I'd lost that the moment I'd freaked out and acted like the house was burning down.

"Where are you running off to, Blue?" he asked, his eyes glittering darkly and everything tightened between my thighs. Why had he started calling me that again? Why did I like it so much?

"I'm early," I stated the obvious, because that was an awesome idea obviously.

"I see that," he said, his fangs glinting at me and I wondered if that little chase had woken his Vampire up. Despite all the recent evidence to the contrary, I wasn't, in fact, prey. And I needed to remind him of that fast.

"Were you spying on me?" he asked, amusement written into his features and I pressed my shoulders back.

"No. But maybe you shouldn't shower with the door open, idiot. I wasn't planning on seeing the crack of dawn twice today," I tossed at him.

He barked a laugh and it was so damn infectious that a smile hooked up the corner of my mouth. His dimple dented his right cheek and I had the urge to reach out and run my thumb over it. An urge I quickly squashed.

He took a step toward me and I fought to keep my eyes on his face as his gleaming abs begged for my attention. "Don't leave," he said in a low growl which made my toes scrunch up in my shoes. "I'll get dressed."

He shot away across the room and I glanced over my shoulder as he dropped his towel by a set of drawers beside the large bed. I snapped my head around again fast enough to give myself whiplash. "Are you quite done being naked?"

"So long as *you're* quite done with it," he said teasingly and pockets of heat burst in my cheeks.

"I was done a long time ago, Lance," I said lightly, though I was probably way past looking innocent at this point. I really should have texted before I went into the tunnel. My Horoscope had warned me about making rash decisions today. *'Think before you act, Gemini'.* Well that advice had gone to the dogs.

He shot past me into the kitchenette in some grey sweatpants and a white wifebeater, starting to make coffee.

"The moon won't rise for another couple of hours," he said, glancing at me. "Why are you early?"

He sounded kind of pleased that I was and the idea of that warmed me through. "Let's just say I'm on the run."

"From who?" he asked with a low laugh.

"Highspell," I said, wrinkling my nose.

"Well you can hide out here away from that witch anytime you like," he muttered, brewing the coffee and handing me a mug. It had a little ray of sunshine peeping through a cloud on it and I wondered if the set had been my mother's.

"Thanks." I blew on my coffee for something to occupy myself with, but despite me walking in on him butt naked, this somehow didn't feel as awkward as the last couple of times I'd been here.

And this time I at least had some idea of what to say to keep the conversation moving. Which was kinda sad seeing as we'd never had trouble talking before. But opening up to him was difficult now and I wasn't sure I wanted it to become easy again. Tory and Seth had planted a seed in my head about Orion though and it just kept growing a little bigger each day. With all I knew about his reasons for what he'd done, how could I stay angry at him forever? Especially after everything he'd been through since. He'd been punished plenty for it. But the idea of forgiving him opened up more questions I wasn't ready to face. Even if I admitted that I still loved him, what then? He wanted me to move on. He didn't see a future for us. He'd made that clear enough. *Ergh, what a mess.*

"Any chance you want to help me with another spell?" I asked, hoping we could focus on that for a while and stay away from uncomfortable territory like *us*.

"Sure," he said, sipping his coffee and watching me over it. "What has Honey Highbitch failed to teach you this time?"

"Levitation," I sighed. "I can do small objects, but she won't let me practise on anything bigger than five kilos in class because the students at the back of class aren't 'capable'. But even when I've tried on my own, I can't seem to grasp it. Tory said she'd talk me through what the bitch showed her when we get a chance, but it's hard to find the time together when she's pretending to be shadow controlled all the time."

He frowned angrily at that, placing his coffee down on a table and beckoning me over. "Come here."

I placed my mug down too, walking over and the scent of cinnamon carried from his flesh, making my mouth water. I missed that scent more with every passing day. One time, Max had found me sobbing in my room at the palace in a heap of Orion's clothes which I'd made Darius give me. His scent had finally left them and I knew that was it. The last time I'd ever smell him. But now it turned out I'd been wrong. And I wasn't sure which fate was worse. Having him this close knowing I could never have him, or never being near to him again.

"Turn around," he instructed and I did so as he moved up close behind me. He lifted my right hand, angling it toward the couch and his breath against my shoulder was definitely not distracting. "Levitation is a mind game. You can only lift five kilos because you believe you can only lift five kilos. Highspell is holding you back on purpose by teaching this spell that way," he said in a furious tone.

A growl of anger left me as I absorbed that.

"Do you really believe a Vega princess can only lift five kilos?" he asked in my ear, making goosebumps rush down my arms.

"No," I said in realisation, raising my chin.

"You could lift a mountain, Blue," he murmured and I felt his belief in those words trickle into me too.

He angled my hand towards the couch then released it, letting me do the work. I brought my thumb in against my palm as I urged magic to the edges of my flesh and focused on the furniture in front of me. I let Orion's belief in me and my belief in myself fill me up to the brim, leaving no room for doubt.

I can do this.

The magic left me in a wave and I yanked back on it as it met the couch, keeping the power attached to me the way I'd learned so I could control it.

The whole thing lifted a foot off the floor and I gasped in excitement, magic tumbling out of me and all the furniture in the room started lifting up to join the couch. The bed, the coffee table, even the pictures on the walls. Everything in the room was floating and it was easy, easier than forcing myself to lift a tiny weight one at a time and fear that was all I would ever be able to manage. This was how my magic was meant to be cast. Freely with complete, utter belief behind it.

I twisted around with a laugh, throwing my arms around Orion's neck and he pulled me tight against him. My heart tried to beat its way out of my chest as I was reminded of what it was like to be held by him again and it was nearly impossible to pull away. But I did. I backed up, turning around and lowering everything back to its place.

"You didn't answer my question earlier," Orion said darkly and I moved to sit down on the couch, picking up my coffee and frowning over at him.

"What question?"

He rubbed his hand across the thick stubble on his jaw, dropping into a chair opposite me. "About the Wolf sleeping in your bed."

My gut clenched and I stole a few extra seconds drinking my coffee before I answered. "Who told you that?"

"Does it matter?" he shot back.

"Fucking Darius," I muttered.

"You said you weren't together," he said and I sighed, not wanting to get into an argument again.

"We're not. He just sleeps in with me sometimes," I said like it was so simple, but it probably didn't sound that way.

"And kisses you on the Pitball field?" he snarled and my jaw literally dropped.

"How the hell do you know about that?" I gasped, but his teeth snapped together. *Goddammit Darius.* "He kissed me because he was trying to-" I stopped myself there, not wanting to give away Seth's secret about Caleb. "He just wanted to make someone jealous, that's all."

His jaw ticked as he rested his elbows on his knees. "Do you really have to lie to me?"

"I'm not lying," I said in disbelief, my tone getting harsher as I failed to keep myself calm.

"You lied about us, so why not him?" he threw at me and outrage hit me like a punch to the chest.

"I *had* to lie about us," I snarled and he blew out a breath.

"For fuck's sake, that came out wrong. I mean, you have reasons to lie about him too. There's a law banning Fae of different Orders from dating, your sister might disapprove and-"

I pushed out of my seat in fury. "I'm going to say this one last time, Lance. And if you don't believe me then that's your problem. But I am not with Seth Capella. And I wouldn't make the mistake of lying to my sister ever again."

My Atlas started ringing before he could respond and I took it out, finding Gabriel calling. I answered, holding it to my ear as I rose from my seat as my stomach dipped.

"Hey, everything okay?" I asked, concerned he might have *seen* something bad.

"All good, Darcy, can you put me on speaker? Lance needs to hear this too."

Damn psychic. I wondered how much he *saw* of me sometimes. Could he just figure out wherever I was by turning his mind to me? *Probably.*

I hit the speaker button, lowering the Atlas from my ear and Orion frowned curiously.

"I've had a vision," Gabriel said, sounding excited. "It's an opportunity. One we really mustn't miss."

"What is it, Noxy?" Orion rose from his chair, moving to stand in front of me so the Atlas was held between us.

"Lionel's hosting a party at the palace on Christmas Eve," he said. "And there's going to be a chance for me to get inside and use the chair in the Royal Seer's Chamber that night. The stars are going to grant me this one opportunity to use it even though I don't officially hold that title."

I sucked in a breath. "That's great."

"Yeah," Gabriel said. "And I think we might have another opportunity at the same time too..."

"Like what?" Orion asked.

"Stella's going to be at the party, which means you two could try and get onto her property. I can't *see* how that might go unfortunately, she still has Nymphs stationed there and they're keeping it concealed from me with the shadows."

"Why us?" I asked, glancing at Orion then back to my Atlas.

"Because you're the only two who won't be invited to the party. Besides, you can break the wards, Orio, and Darcy, you know where to look for Diego's hat."

My heart beat harder and adrenaline coursed through my veins as I accepted he was right. "Okay. Shit, let's do it." I looked up at Orion with a grin and he smirked back at me.

"I'll talk to you tomorrow," Gabriel said. "The moon's up."

He hung up and I turned to look out the window, my smile widening as moonlight spilled across the patio.

"Fuck yes." Orion shot away, grabbing the diary from his nightstand drawer and I jogged to the door, sliding it open just before Orion ran past me, catching my hand and towing me after him at speed.

He planted me in a seat at a patio table and dropped down beside me, placing the diary in front of us. I started casting a concealment spell around us and Orion helped until we were totally hidden then he threw me an addictive kind of smile.

He opened the diary and the moon bathed the pages. Light shimmered across it and words appeared in dark, swirling handwriting.

"Is that the Imperial Star?" I breathed, pointing to the image at the base of the first page as I raised a hand to brush my fingers over the necklace and Orion whipped around to look at me.

"You can see the words?" he asked in surprise.

"Yeah, can't you?" I frowned.

"I can," he said. "But Darius couldn't."

"Oh," I breathed. "Well...the tomb let us both in. So maybe it's a Vega and Orion thing."

"Yeah...actually, my father's note said the diary would be unreadable to the disloyal. He must have meant loyalty to the royals," he murmured with a small smirk as he surveyed me for a second before looking back to the diary and turning the page. I guessed that was proof he was loyal to me and Tory. Did that mean he no longer backed Darius and the other Heirs? He'd encouraged me before, but seeing this truth laid out for me made my heart squeeze with emotion.

I leaned close to him to read the next entry, our shoulders pressing together.

Congratulations, my son.

If all has gone to plan, you passed the test we laid for you in the tomb. Merissa Vega assured me you would protect her daughter no matter what spell you were under. Pride doesn't come close to what I feel toward you right now. If you have gained the Imperial Star, then I know you are the man I hoped you would become.

Now, the star must remain hidden. Only your most loyal of friends can know its location. A star cannot be seen by Seers or divined by the arcane arts. So long as you protect the knowledge of its location, it can never be discovered by Lionel Acrux.

This brings me onto your next task. You must reform the Zodiac Guild. Choose those strong of heart, mind and soul to swear an oath to protect the Vega royals. They will need a strong following to help them ascend, Fae who they can trust with their lives. Choose wisely.

To bind new members to the Guild, you will need the Chalice of Flames, an item that has long been in my possession.

Spill your blood beneath the light of the full moon to summon the chalice.

Orion flipped the page over and the image of a beautiful chalice was drawn there with a postscript beneath it.

The Chalice of Flames holds an ancient Phoenix flame within its core. It is indestructible, cannot be tarnished and must be protected by the Master of the Zodiac Guild. All who drink the royal elixir from this cup and speak the words inscribed upon its surface will be bound to the Guild, sworn in to protect the Vega line.

Orion placed his thumb in his mouth, cutting it open on his fang and holding it up to the moonlight bathing us. Light glittered across his palm and a shimmering silver chalice appeared in his grip, making my lips part in awe. The words inscribed on it were written in what looked like Latin and I had no idea what they meant, but I could feel the power of this object practically calling to me.

"Can I hold it?" I breathed and Orion passed it to me without hesitation. The metal was warm, kissing my palm and I gasped at the feel of the flame curling within it, sensing some long lost connection to the Phoenix who'd placed it there.

"It's beautiful," I sighed, passing it back to Orion and he placed it down in front of us as he started reading the next page. I leaned forward to do the same.

The elixir of the royals is laid out on the following page. It will take six weeks to brew, and during this time, you have the sole responsibility of ensuring the Imperial Star is protected. Merissa informs me that with the help of a dear friend, you will see *the way to keep it safe until the Guild can be reformed and your allies can help protect its location.*

I smiled, thinking of Gabriel and feeling closer to my mother than I ever had before. Knowing that she'd *seen* us gave me some comfort, like we held a connection to each other. That Tory and I hadn't just been strangers to her in our adult lives. She'd known us to some extent through her visions. And I wished I'd known her too.

Your final task is the greatest of all. You must ensure the Vega twins are crowned. They must become true Queens so that they are able to wield the Imperial Star. Meanwhile, you must safeguard the knowledge in this diary. Each spell the star can cast is accessed by a powerful word. Words which are contained within these pages. You must memorise each one, ensure the Vegas know them by heart and never, ever forget them. You must not try to use them on the Imperial Star yourself or allow the Vegas to attempt it before they are crowned, for only a reigning sovereign can wield the Imperial Star. All others will <u>perish</u> if they attempt it.

Orion turned the page and a word ran across the centre of it in curling script.

Immunisia
Immunity.
This spell grants lifelong immunity to all illnesses.

"Holy shit," Orion breathed and I turned to him with laughter bubbling in my chest.

"This is crazy."

His eyes met mine and his fingers brushed my hand on the table, sending a line of fire through my body. "You're gonna need to polish your crown, Blue," he teased.

I breathed a laugh, leaning a little closer and whispering, "I need to take it back from a Dragon king first."

TORY

CHAPTER THIRTY EIGHT

Christmas Eve had crept up on us before we knew it and I'd spent the day in the Palace of Souls with Lionel, trying to hide my nerves about what we were planning to do tonight.

Gabriel was confident that everything was coming together despite all the reasons we had to fear this going wrong and he was certain that we would have a decent shot at sneaking him into the palace during the party.

Then we just had to get him to the Royal Seer's Chamber and sit his ass on the chair so that the stars could gift him with the vision they'd promised. Why they had to be dicks about it and insist on him coming to the palace was beyond me, but he seemed to think it was perfectly acceptable for the twinkly bastards to set a challenge if we wanted to be rewarded with knowledge from the heavens.

I personally thought they were just being vindictive little assholes, but maybe I was just a salty bitch over the way they'd repeatedly fucked up my life.

I also had no idea why the stars had decided to allow him to make use of it tonight after months of him trying while I was trapped in Lionel's grasp – maybe they just didn't like me very much - but I did trust that he knew what he was talking about. And hopefully this would be the key to us moving forward with our plans against the so-called king so I was more than willing to run with it.

Over the past month we'd all been helping gather the ingredients Orion needed for the royal elixir to initiate members to the Zodiac Guild. It was complicated as shit and the bubbling potion in his closet which gave off a weird almond smell apparently needed a full week in darkness now before we could add the next ingredient. Which was something called rothium grass and it only grew on one special mountain which had apparently been blessed by some old Vega prince hundreds of years ago. Frankly, the whole Guild thing kinda made me uncomfortable. But maybe that was because I was assuming all royalists were like those in the A.S.S. who liked to stare at me and my sister, taking photos on their Atlases when they thought we weren't looking. I didn't want people swearing shit to me and making promises on the damn stars which they couldn't take back. Maybe it wasn't like that though. Because I couldn't picture Orion suddenly waiting on me hand and foot and bursting into song when I entered a room. *He might for Darcy though...*

Damn, I forgot to dick kick him today.

The dress I'd been given to wear to the ball tonight was golden and shimmered as the light touched it, looking like a spill of liquid metal over my curves as it fell to my feet. My arms were bare and the neckline plunging which would have left me cold in the current weather aside from the fact that I could use my fire magic to keep me warm.

Lionel had managed to force entry into the grand hall - which my father had apparently used for trials during his reign - and had chosen to hold this party there. No one dared ask why we weren't using the extravagant ballroom and it was a matter of quiet joy that I knew the palace still wouldn't open all of its doors to him.

I'd already silently suffered through the reception line where Lionel made every guest at the party file past him and bow while he sat on the throne. He kept a host of Nymphs at our backs the entire time just so that he could boast about his control over them, but everyone who came had eyed them warily.

The Nymphs had stayed in their shifted forms the entire time, standing stoic and statuesque at our backs, but the whole thing had left me fighting to stave off a shudder. I didn't trust them. Even though I knew Clara had full control over them, that didn't stop me from expecting them to attack at any moment. Knowing Diego had been good only eased my fears like one percent. Because of all the Nymphs I'd come into contact with, he was the single one who hadn't looked hungry to eat my magic, and who had tried to help us. So I was assuming he was an anomaly. *Oh Diego.*

Clara was in her element tonight, prancing around on Lionel's arm, cooing and clucking about how sad she supposedly was over Catalina's death while making less than subtle hints about her desire to be Lionel's new queen.

I stayed silent, only responding to anyone who addressed me directly and ignoring all the suspicious looks I was drawing. People didn't know what to make of me anyway so they never really had anything to say.

The Heirs and their parents were here tonight too and I'd caught their gazes more than once, taking some comfort in knowing that I had friends here even if I couldn't speak with them.

Lionel was oozing smugness in a cloud so thick that I was choking on it as I hung from his arm and I was just glad that I'd been in the habit of keeping my face blank as a shadow bitch so that I didn't have to fake smile along with his bullshit.

I was listening though. Every word that spilled from his lips, all the lies about Tiberian Rats and Minotaurs and Sphinxes and all the plans he had to bring them to heel was absorbed and noted. Then anything that might be able to be used to counter his vile plots was passed on to Hamish Grus and his rebels who might be able to do something about them.

More often than not, Lionel had already carried out his atrocities before I reported them, rounding Fae up and holding them in the Nebular Inquisition Centres before anything I passed on could be of any help. But occasionally, Hamish and the Fae he'd gathered around him who wished to stand against Lionel's tyranny would help get people to safety before the King could get to them. And every time I heard that something I'd passed on had saved a life, it made this role I had to play a little easier.

"Ah, if it isn't my first born son," Lionel called, breaking me out of my thoughts as Darius strode out of the crowd dressed all in black.

Black suit, black shirt, black cufflinks, the whole lot. The darkness of the outfit just made him seem even bigger and more intimidating than usual, highlighting the black rings in his eyes and drawing attention to his ebony hair and the stubble on his jaw. I mean shit, he was freaking edible. It had been too damn long since we'd stolen that time alone together from the stars and I was seriously tempted to ask him if he wanted to try for round two somewhere soon. Maybe somewhere less muddy, though it had to be somewhere open… like a desert. Sun, sand, sex…but then there would be sand everywhere and that was never fun. No one wanted a sandy vag. *Dammit stars, why do you have to be such fucking V blockers?*

"Father," Darius said curtly, his gaze sliding to me for a lingering moment that made heat rise in my cheeks as I decided I'd totally risk a sandy butt crack for him before he dragged his eyes away again.

"Where is your beautiful bride?" Lionel asked him, looking around curiously.

"She got a sudden bout of the shits," Darius replied with the hint of a smirk that told me exactly who was responsible for that. "And let's not bullshit by calling her beautiful, Father, we all know she looks like the rear end of a warthog that's been hit by a bus."

I snorted a laugh before I could stop myself, trying to cover it with a cough and drawing Lionel's attention to me as I worked to school my features.

"Does that amuse you, Roxanya?" he asked, narrowing his eyes on me which wasn't all that surprising as I generally only laughed if I was shadow torturing people in my fucked up shadow dick state.

"It has a ring of truth to it, sire," I replied, giving him the adoring eyes and running my hand up his arm and over the curve of his bicep. It had the strange effect of making me buzz with joy at being so close to him and feel a little like puking up the alcohol I'd consumed. Which admittedly might have been too much on an empty stomach.

Lionel's gaze roamed over my features as I gave him my most simpering look and he nodded lightly before looking back to his son.

"Well, seeing as you're not occupied with your bride, why don't you take Roxanya to get some food? She has a habit of forgetting to eat if not reminded and I'm too busy tonight to fuss over her."

Darius's jaw locked and he shrugged. "Do you enjoy torturing me with her company, Father?"

"I would have thought that you'd appreciate the chance to spend time with her. You were most thorough in your hunt for her throughout the summer after all. Or has your idealistic fantasy of love finally run its course? Perhaps you've given up on trying to tempt her back from the dark?"

"Never," Darius growled, offering me his arm and I glanced to Lionel for his approval before I took it.

"Then see her fed and stop complaining about your lot in life. I'm handing you a throne here after all - I won't tolerate your ungrateful attitude much longer."

Darius sketched a mocking bow and I stepped forward, wrapping my hand around his forearm and letting him draw me away.

My skin heated where we touched but I didn't dare look up at him, simply walking at his side until we reached the buffet laid out on the far side of the room. I swear I could feel Lionel's eyes on us the entire way and when I turned to look back over my shoulder, the look he was giving me sent a shiver of fear down my spine.

"Eat, Roxy," Darius commanded, accepting a plate of cakes and hand crafted cookies from one of the serving staff and holding it out to me.

"So bossy," I muttered, accepting the food and biting into a cookie, suppressing a groan at the deliciously sweet taste. "Do you think Lionel suspected anything?"

"Hard to tell with him. He's always suspicious. But I think if he had then he would have called you up on it there and then." His brow furrowed with concern for me and I gave him a small smile.

"I'm sure it's fine. Max has been teaching me to shield my thoughts from Cyclops interrogation anyway so even if he gets Vard to-"

"If he or that psychopath ever lay a hand on you again then I'll rip them apart with my fucking teeth," Darius growled, catching my wrist and squeezing hard enough to bruise.

"I can handle it," I said firmly.

It wasn't like I enjoyed the idea of being brought back to that room they'd used to torture me and turn me into Lionel's plaything, but I was well aware I might have to face another visit to it at some point. I just tried not to think about it and made sure to prepare myself as much as I could with Max's help.

Lionel moved out of sight, heading into an antechamber across the room with a man who I was fairly certain was another Acrux and I nudged Darius to draw his attention to them.

"Gabriel said the opportune moment would present itself," I pointed out, quickly eating another cookie because they were to-fucking-die-for and backing away from the food table.

"I'll meet you out in the west corridor," Darius murmured and I nodded, watching him as he strode away through the crowd.

I lingered for another few minutes then turned away too, spotting Seth and Caleb by a side door and walking towards them with purposeful steps.

Seth was tossing olives into the air and catching them in his mouth and Caleb threw me a wink as I skirted past them.

"We'll keep an eye out, sweetheart," Caleb promised in a low voice I was sure no one else heard and I nodded once before heading out of the room.

My heart was thundering as I walked to meet Darius so that we could open up the secret passage to get Gabriel into the building.

He'd been confident that this part of our plan would go well. But from here on out, we'd be flying by the seat of our pants, too many possibilities for him to be certain what course we'd land on.

So for now I'd trust in his vision. And as far as everything else went, I was just wishing for the best.

ORION

CHAPTER THIRTY NINE

Darcy and I stardusted to the outskirts of my mother's property, the icy air whipping around us as we stood in the dark woodland. I listened for sounds of anyone close by, but all was quiet. Darius had messaged to say the Nymphs were at the palace as his father wanted to show off his control of them to his pious followers. For once, we were lucky he was such a vain, prideful bastard. Because his peacocking had opened up a window of opportunity for us. So Blue and I were climbing through it, about to piss all over him. Metaphorically speaking, obviously. But I wouldn't have minded taking a piss on the Dragon King if I ever got the chance.

We were both dressed in black, but it was just an extra precaution. I'd make sure we were shrouded in concealment spells as we moved. It was going to be an in and out job. No time wasting. And as a Vampire, that was kind of my fucking forte.

"Do you remember where you last saw Diego?" I asked Darcy and she frowned thoughtfully. The moonlight highlighted her face in profile and my gaze slid over her small nose and full lips. Lips I wanted to score my thumb across before claiming, marking, biting – *concentrate, asshole.*

"I'll recognise it when we get closer to the house. It's somewhere over that way I think." She pointed off into the trees to our right and I nodded.

I stepped toward the wards, feeling their energy humming close to my flesh as I reached out and angled my palms towards them. My mother's magic was powerful, but her blood ran in me – much to my misfortune – so I could get onto the property if she hadn't restricted my access. And as I'd been a prisoner for months, I was betting that she wouldn't have bothered. As my hand slid through the invisible barrier, I grinned triumphantly, pressing my magic into it and creating a doorway for Darcy to pass through.

"Your carriage awaits, ma'am." I beckoned her forward and she stepped through the gap.

"Are *you* my carriage?" she asked.

"Yeah, I forgot my saddle, but you can ride me bareback, right?" the joke slipped out as easily as if we were still a couple and I immediately regretted it.

She punched my arm, but a smile played around her lips and my regrets instantly went away.

"So that's a yes?" I taunted and she rolled her eyes.

"Stop wasting time," she muttered, walking ahead of me but she was definitely trying to hide her smile from me. And that made me feel all kinds of good.

I glanced between the dark trees. I needed to mark this area out so we could find it again. I didn't want to leave anything too conspicuous, but I also wasn't going to take any risks. If we had to run, or if we got split up, Darcy needed to find her way back to this place.

I used my water magic to cast glinting icicles on the nearest tree, the moonlight just highlighting them if she came looking.

"That's your way out if things go to shit," I told her and she gazed up at the icicles in concern. But her expression quickly hardened into resilience. "It won't go to shit. We'll find the hat and be gone before you know it."

I started casting concealment spells and she helped, adding to my magic until the darkness clung to us.

"Okay, let's go," she breathed and I turned around.

"Hop on, beautiful," I instructed and she jumped up onto my back, wrapping her legs around my waist. The warmth of her body against me felt so fucking good and I was seriously not complaining about being her steed for the night.

Her knee nudged the diary which I'd concealed in my pocket, shrinking it down and using an illusion to make it look like a silver coin. It was too important to ever let it out of my sight and I double checked that it was still in place before getting ready to run. I held onto Blue's thighs as she wound her arms around my neck and leaned in close, her breath on my neck sending a line of heat straight to my dick. *This is not the fucking time.*

She cast a tight silencing bubble around us and I shot off through the trees, focusing on the task at hand.

It wasn't long before we made it to the edge of the treeline and I slowed, letting Darcy get down as we hid in the shadows and gazed out across the yard toward my old home. The house was dark, not a single light on inside and that gave me some comfort. No one was here.

The house had obviously been rebuilt since Lionel had levelled half of it, and I noticed a few embellishments and rooms that hadn't been a part of it before. I hated that my home had been ruined for me. It was where most of my memories of my dad existed, and my mom had managed to tarnish them all. It had once been a place of happiness, but now it was just a place that homed a wicked witch and nothing but misery.

"It was somewhere over this way," Darcy said and I followed as she led me through the trees, my skin prickling as I listened, keeping my ears trained on the wood. The hoot of a far off owl was like a klaxon in my head and the sounds of nocturnal creatures scurrying and scratching reached me from all directions. That was good though. Nothing was off. It was when the animals went quiet that we had to worry.

Darcy paused as we made it to a more open patch of woodland, gazing around with a taut frown.

"It was here," she breathed sadly. "This is where Clara fought us. If Diego shifted into a Nymph then he must have left his clothes somewhere."

"I'm sorry I wasn't there for you that night. All of you," I admitted, my chest tightening.

It had haunted me ever since I'd found out about it. I'd known something was horribly wrong that night after I'd experienced the agonising pain of Darius fighting Lionel. The need to go to him had driven me insane. I'd tried to fight my way through five guards and ended up locked in isolation for the night, going crazy with worry. I'd broken both hands trying to batter my way through the steel door and had eventually had to be sedated so a medic could heal me.

Being unable to protect my Ward was an agony I never wanted to know the taste of again. But finding out Blue had been there too after Darius had come to explain what had happened had left me in pieces. That day had spiralled into one of the worst weeks of my life. I'd grappled with regrets while facing the bad luck from the stars, ending up in more fights than I could count. Some of Gustard's unFae assholes had shanked me in the showers and I'd nearly bled out. There was nothing like almost dying on a cold, dirty, wet floor in prison to put your life into perspective.

Darcy gazed at me with an echo of hurt and I knew there was nothing I could do to heal it. I'd fucked up. I hadn't been there when she'd needed me most. Some part of her probably hated me for that. Even if she'd never admit it.

"You couldn't have known," she said with a sad look as she gazed into the trees. "Let's get looking."

She set off to search and I started hunting the ground, kicking over leaves as I tried to block out the voice in my head reminding me of how much I'd failed her. But there was one thing I could do at least. And that was find this damn hat. We couldn't use a summoning spell on it as it was bound to the damn shadows, but it had to be around here somewhere.

We moved methodically across the ground, skimming the debris on the surface as we hunted. I felt the time ticking by and every faraway crack of a twig had my fangs lengthening and my hackles rising.

I hadn't known Diego all that well, but I'd been starting to like him. At least he'd died valiantly, and in the arms of a girl who adored him. I couldn't imagine a better way to go myself. And I'd come pretty close to doing it once too. Maybe barring the valiant part.

When we'd turned over every rock and leaf in the area, Darcy gave me a frustrated look that creased her brow.

"It could be anywhere in these woods. What if he shifted a mile away?" she aired her thoughts in frustration, looking out into the shadows between the trees.

"What did he say to you exactly?" I asked.

"Nothing…he just said to take the hat," she said with a pained frown as she looked to a place on the ground like she was reliving the memory of his death.

I hated seeing that grief in her eyes, it awoke a monster in me that wanted to fight her demons and lay them dead at her feet. This girl didn't deserve to have so many wounds on her heart. She deserved peace and happiness and a life without pain. If I could have one wish from the stars, I'd wish for that. Alright, and for Lionel to have his power blocked and be kicked off of a two hundred foot cliff. Small dreams and all that.

"Well, it was important to him, so maybe he left it somewhere he would find it easily," I said thoughtfully and she nodded, biting her lip as she considered that.

"Maybe he hung it somewhere." She looked around to the trees in the space and I nodded, striding forward with purpose.

"Get on my back again, we'll do a circuit. There's no one here, if we use a Faelight we might spot it easier."

"Alright," she agreed, climbing onto my back and casting a Faelight in her palm. I locked her legs tight around my waist then started running while she angled the light at the trees and the ground as we searched for any sign of it.

Come on Diego, where did you stash your abuela's damn soul hat?

DARIUS

CHAPTER FORTY

I sat at the foot of the stairs in the central entranceway to the Palace of Souls, waiting for my girl with my heart thumping to a steady rhythm and my senses tuned on the surrounding area.

I'd cast detection and repulsion spells all around us while Roxy headed into the secret passages her father had once used to meet Gabriel. He'd *seen* this much going smoothly and was certain we'd make it to the Royal Seer's Chamber without being discovered, but after that, the stars wouldn't give him a clear answer as to whether or not we'd get away with this.

I swiped a hand down my face, rubbing at the stubble lining my jaw as I leaned against the bannister and watched the empty patch of wall where Roxy had disappeared. I hated having to let her head down there alone. But even during the walk here, the ground had begun to tremble, making pictures shudder on the walls and a waiter had opened a kitchen door so fast that he'd crashed into us, sending his whole tray of champagne flying everywhere. I'd managed to catch the liquid with my water magic before it had drenched us and Roxy had given me a pissy look which had cut short the way I'd been laying into the dude too.

Apparently it wasn't cool for me to yell at the pawns the stars used to force us apart, but it was also pretty much the only outlet I got for my frustrations so it was hard not to.

I had to fight off the urge to start pacing and I straightened as I felt a Fae's magic brushing against my repulsion spells beyond the door that led to the east wing of the palace.

The sound of someone muttering reached me and I stiffened as I recognised Jenkins, my father's asshole butler.

"I was sure I needed to go this way..." He mumbled something else, seeming to wonder if the King was responsible for his change of heart and I cursed as I realised he'd detected my magic. I smirked to myself as I pushed more power into the spell, making him feel a desperate urge to take a shit and he cried out as he began to run in search of a bathroom. I fought down a laugh as I hoped he ended up shitting himself before he got there.

The sound of grating stone announced Roxy's return and I straightened as a hole opened up in the wall and she stepped through with Gabriel at her side.

The two of them were laughing and my skin prickled as I watched them, hungering for the chance to make her smile like that more often. The only other person I'd ever seen her truly let her barriers down like that for was Darcy and though I knew Gabriel was her brother, it still rankled at me to know there were walls she wasn't letting down for me yet.

Not that I could claim to have let her see all of me either, but I was trying. And I guessed she was too. So if the stars would just stop getting in our fucking way then I was certain we'd have a real shot at something here.

"Hey," I said to Gabriel, jerking my chin in greeting while my eyes stuck to my girl.

She looked intoxicating in that gold dress and I'd been caught up in fantasies about dragging her off to the throne room ever since I'd first laid eyes on her.

There had been something seriously exciting about being with her in there of all places. Like we were mocking the stars for pitting us against each other over who got to sit their ass on it. Of course, they got the last laugh by cursing us though.

"We need to get going," Gabriel said, barely greeting me and I noticed he looked away from me pretty fast too, like he had little to no interest in my presence.

"This way," Roxy said, taking his arm and tugging him down a corridor to our left.

I eyed the casual contact with a hint of jealousy. I was jealous of anyone who could be close to my girl without repercussions. Which meant I was basically a hot mess of envy at all times which was threatening to burn into rage at the slightest provocation.

I followed them down the corridor and Roxy glanced back over her shoulder at me with a small smile that made my gut lurch and I found myself smiling back like some happy little elf at Christmas. If I wasn't careful that girl was going to make me fucking soft. Problem was, I didn't have any inclination to stop her.

We reached the door to the Royal Seer's Chamber and Roxy opened it carefully.

Cool air washed out of the dark room and her high heels clicked on the marble floor as she stepped inside.

With a wave of her hand, Roxy lit a series of sconces set into the walls with her fire magic and a long chamber was revealed to us.

I moved in behind them as Gabriel headed to the left wall, tilting his head back to look up at the portrait of an elderly man holding a crystal ball, his eyes glazed as he foresaw something.

The walls were all hung with huge portraits of past Royal Seers, men and women, sometimes royals in their own rights, others just powerful Fae gifted with visions of the future.

Roxy strode to the far end of the hall and stopped beneath a portrait of a stunning woman staring up at a midnight sky with a silver tiara placed on her head.

"She was almost as beautiful as you," I murmured as I came to stand behind her, gazing up at Queen Merissa, Roxy's mother and the last great Seer known to roam the world.

"Sometimes I wonder what it would have been like to know her," Roxy said softly, her voice laced with regrets. "To have grown up loved by parents who wanted us and cared for us."

"We would have been raised together," I murmured, because I knew it was true. "You and Darcy would have been with the four of us from the start, night and day, Awakened early, trained to lead."

She looked up at me then, arching a brow. "And in that scenario you would have been happy with that?" she asked me. "For us to be your queens and for destiny driving you to be our Councillor?"

I looked at her for a tension filled moment as I considered it then nodded. "If your mother and father had been alive then there never would have been an alternative. You would have been raised for the role. You would have been perfect for it."

"But because your father killed my parents and tried to kill us, abandoning us to the foster system in the mortal realm, we're just a pair of dumb girls who will never be fit to rule in your eyes?" she challenged, that argumentative glint in her eyes which I equally loved and hated.

"I didn't say that," I growled.

"So you're ready to bow to me then?" she taunted and my spine straightened in a clear refusal of that.

"I don't want to fight with you," I said in a low tone and she scoffed.

"And yet all the time this hangs between us, aren't we always going to be fighting deep down? When it comes down to it, your family betrayed mine. Your father took everything from us. A chance to grow up loved in the world where we belong, the chance to come into our powers early and learn all the things you were gifted so easily. And even after everything that's happened, you still want to keep stealing from us, don't you? You still believe that you and the other Heirs are more suited to sit on the throne than we are. Even though it's *our* birth right. Even though we are more powerful than you. Even though we had to lose everything to get to where we are." Her eyes flashed with emotion which she rarely allowed anyone to see and I was caught between wanting to hold her and shake her.

"Roxy," I said in a rough voice, stepping forward and making a move to catch her arm as anger prickled through my flesh at her accusations. But she shifted so that I couldn't touch her, my hand grasping nothing as she drew back and the beast in me growled angrily. "If I could go back and change it, I would. But that doesn't alter the reality we now live in. The Heirs and I have the political knowledge, strength of character and magical training to assure that we are the only realistic candidates to rule this kingdom once my father is dethroned. If you'd just stop being so damn stubborn and look at it logically then you'd see-"

"Enough," Gabriel snapped, stepping between us and fixing me with a furious glare which begged for me to smack it off of his face. "If this descends any further we will be discovered here and your bickering won't resolve anything. You're too stubborn and pig headed for that." His words could have been aimed at us both but the way he was glaring at me made it clear who they were intended for.

"Do we have a problem?" I snarled at him, but instead of rising to the bait I was laying for him, he just sighed.

"I deal with much more irritating men than you on a frequent basis, Darius, you won't rile me into a fight just because your pride is wounded. We came here for a reason and we need to see it through." He cast a pained look up at the portrait of his mother then strode away from me towards the chair which occupied the centre of the room.

It was a throne in its own right really, cut from glass which caught the light and seemed to sparkle with endless magic. It was inlaid with silver gemstones which I was certain were fragments of meteorites which mapped out all of the constellations over its surface.

Roxy moved after him, not wasting any more time on me and I muttered curses at her and myself in my mind as I followed on behind them. The sooner she accepted she was going to have to bow to us the better.

Gabriel fell still before the glass throne, reaching out to brush a finger over the armrest and stiffening as his gaze glazed with a vision for several seconds before he pulled his hand back and shook his head to dismiss it.

"We don't have long," Gabriel murmured and Roxy took hold of his hand, squeezing his fingers tightly before he looked over his shoulder at me. "You should record this," he said. "Because I don't know what I'm about to *see*, but I do know that it's quite possibly the most important vision I am going to have in my entire life."

I arched a brow and silently took my Atlas from my pocket before setting it to record.

Gabriel pressed a kiss to Roxy's head then guided her a few steps back from the glass chair before turning his back on it and slowly lowering himself to sit upon it.

He sucked in a sharp breath and the fire in every sconce in the room guttered out under a supernatural wind which kissed my skin and made me shiver. As we were plunged into shadows, Roxy's hand found mine in the dark and I held her tightly, blinking as I tried to see through the pitch-black. I flinched as deep blue flames burst to life in the sconces, lighting the place in an eery colour.

All of the gemstones set into the chair began to glow with some inner light and the constellations they made up were projected all around us, covering the walls, ceiling and floor as if we were floating amongst them ourselves.

Gabriel's hands clasped the arms of the throne, his knuckles turning white as his pupils seemed to glow with golden light until all that I could see in his eyes was that rich, golden colour like I was looking upon the face of a star.

"Hear me now, for his prophesy could change the course of fate itself," he said in an ethereal voice that wasn't his at all and Roxy's fingers tightened around mine as she sucked in an alarmed breath.

"Look east to the heart of the rising star when the wind calls to you and find the origins of your legacy," he said firmly before his voice seemed to multiply and resound off of the walls of the room and I was certain this next part was the prophesy he'd been waiting on.

"Two phoenixes, born of fire, rising from the ashes of the past.

The wheel of fate is turning and the Dragon is poised to strike.

But blood of the deceiver may change the course of destiny.

Beware the man with the painted smile who lingers close to your side.

Turn the scorned. Free the enslaved.

Fear the bonded men. Many will fall for one to ascend.

Suffer the curse. The hunter will pay the price.

Do not repeat the mistakes of the past. Keep the broken promise.

Mend the rift. All that hides in the shadows is not dark.

Blood will out. Seal your fate. Choose your destiny."

The blue fire went out in a wave and the light from the crystals in the throne extinguished too as Gabriel's panting breaths came from the throne.

"Gabriel?" Roxy gasped, releasing me and darting forward as she lit a fire in her palm, the light from it blazing bright enough to illuminate her brother half collapsed on the throne.

I shut off my Atlas and moved forward to help her heave him to his feet.

"We have to go *now*. Vard is on his way here," Gabriel grunted, barely seeming able to stand as he stumbled towards the door.

"What's wrong, do you need me to heal you?" Roxy asked worriedly but Gabriel shook his head.

"It's not that. There are just so many visions pouring in on me right now that I can hardly bear the weight of them. I need to contain them for now and get somewhere I'll be able to pull them apart and *see* them all one by one," he explained.

"Let's get out of here then," I said.

I wrapped my arm around his waist and threw his arm over my shoulder before heaving him upright and propelling him towards the door, almost entirely supporting his weight on my own.

Roxy hurried ahead of us and pulled the door open before extinguishing her fire magic and stepping back out into the corridor.

"Not that way," Gabriel muttered as I went to turn right and I wheeled us around, half carrying him as we started jogging in the other direction.

Vard's voice caught my ear from behind us just as we turned a corner. Gabriel pointed at a tapestry depicting a Hydra standing on a mountainside before Roxy tugged it aside to reveal a staircase behind it.

I hauled Gabriel inside the servants' passages, hoping none of them were currently using them and Roxy threw a silencing bubble over us as we started down the steps at a fast pace.

We took a turn and Gabriel reached out to open one of the King's passages with the ring Roxy had given him so that we could slip into the safer tunnels where no one else would find us.

"You need to head back through there, Tory," Gabriel said, pointing at a bare patch of wall to our right. "Then you can circle around to the party though the gardens. Darius will head back another way."

"Are you sure?" she asked, her eyes flaring with concern as she looked from her brother to me.

"Yes," he insisted. "*Now,* Tory. This way should work. I'm almost certain."

She didn't look like she thought that was good enough, but she agreed before looking at me and meeting my gaze.

"Get back safe," she commanded me. "I'm trusting you with my brother, too."

"I'm on it, Roxy. You can count on me," I promised her and she nodded firmly. She clearly believed that much of me, even if I could tell that she was still a bit pissed about the divide we still felt over the throne. But she'd forgive me. She couldn't help herself.

She moved forward and pressed a kiss to Gabriel's cheek before turning and placing the briefest of ones on my lips.

My heart leapt in surprise and I barely even leaned into it before she'd broken away and was heading towards the hidden door again, leaving my lips tingling and my heart thrashing.

"We can finish that argument later, asshole," she said, her eyes lighting like the idea of that excited her. "In the meantime, just get Gabriel out of here."

I smirked in agreement to that challenge and she was gone a breath later.

"That way," Gabriel commanded, pointing down the sloping tunnel and I started moving, helping him along though he seemed to be leaning on me less already.

We took several turns and he finally stopped beside another blank patch of wall, taking his arm from my shoulders and breathing in deeply as he straightened.

"You good?" I asked him and he nodded before levelling me with a dark look.

"Yeah. But I wanted a word with you alone about Tory," Gabriel said, rolling his shoulders back as he straightened up.

"Oh?"

"Just don't fuck this up," he warned, fixing me with a death glare. "Because I *see* a series of scenarios playing out for the two of you and in at least half of them you act like a fucking ass. If you break her heart a second time, she'll never give you the chance to claim it again. Do you hear me?"

"You seriously think I don't already know that?" I growled. "I don't wanna hurt her. Not now or ever. But you can hardly expect me to just roll over and offer her the throne after all the-"

"I'm not talking about that shit," he said, waving a hand dismissively. "I'm talking about you and her. Just do it right. And the next time you wanna defy the stars to be with her maybe give me some warning so I can take a sleeping potion or something," he added with a look of disgust.

"What's that supposed to mean?" I asked.

"That I caught way too many flashes of the two of you rolling about in the mud and I don't wanna see that shit. I can block those kinds of things out most of the time, but that was damn hard with the heavens so fucking angry at the two of you and all of their attention fixed on ripping you apart."

I smirked at the reminder, shrugging a shoulder at him. "Well it wasn't exactly planned."

"I know. But if the two of you are determined to go up against the will of the heavens over this then I think you should know that you'll be making plenty of enemies amongst them along the way."

"She's more than worth it," I assured him and his pissy mask broke into a smile.

"Good. That's all I needed to hear. Now fuck off back to the party before your father misses you." Gabriel used his ring to open the hidden door and I clapped a hand on his shoulder, feeling like we actually saw eye to eye on something for once.

"Are you gonna be alright getting out of here?" I asked him and he nodded, frowning slightly.

"My head is so full of visions at the moment that I can hardly make sense of them, but my family helped me build a room at our winter cabin which helps me to focus. I'm fighting the visions off for now but once I get there, I'll sort through them and hopefully we will have more to go on."

"I can stay with you and make sure you get out of the palace safely," I offered as his gaze seemed to slide in and out of focus with the visions that were pressing in on him, but he shook his head.

"I'll be alright. I have another Dragon waiting for me at the far end of the tunnel out in the trees. You need to get back to the party."

I nodded my agreement, watching him as he started to walk away until I was confident that he could manage alone before slipping through the hidden door and heading back out into the corridor within the palace.

At the first opportunity we could get, we were all going to have to try and figure out the meaning of that prophesy. I just hoped that it was good news. Because it sure as fuck hadn't sounded all that promising.

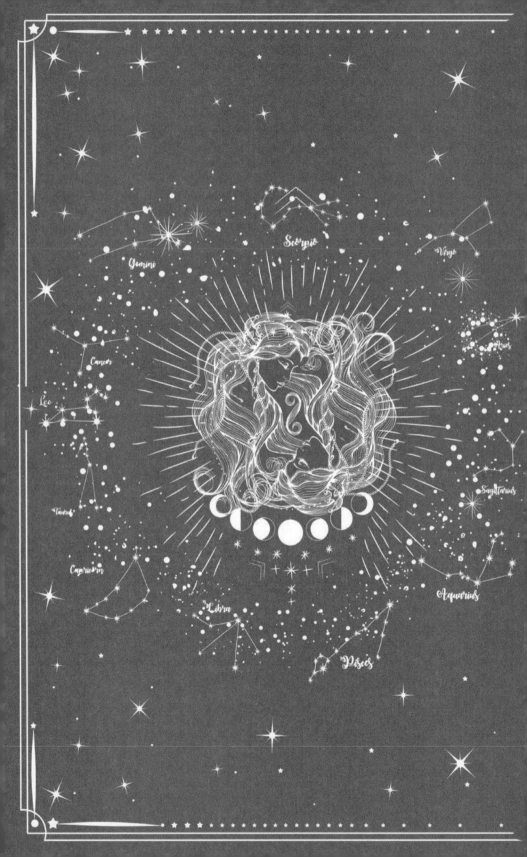

DARCY

CHAPTER FORTY ONE

We'd hunted nearly every inch of the forest when my Faelight lit up something ahead of us.

"There!" I called, pointing it out and Orion shot over to it, letting me down off of his back.

He plucked the hat from a jutting out branch which was low on the tree trunk and my heart lifted as he passed it to me, a sigh of relief falling from my chest.

My foot caught on something on the ground and I bent down, pushing the leaves aside and finding Diego's clothes there. My heart split apart as I pulled them from the mud and grief held me in a cold, unyielding grip. He'd tried to help us. And he'd died keeping Clara away from us. I would never be able to repay him for that and I missed him every day.

"Extinguish your Faelight," Orion growled and his tone sent a tremor of fear through me as I quickly complied.

I got to my feet, meeting his anxious gaze as he listened to something out in the forest which I couldn't hear.

"Get on my back," he hissed and I hurried to jump up, holding on tight to his shoulders as I pushed Diego's hat into my pocket.

"What is it?" I breathed, though our silencing bubble was hiding our voices anyway.

"I'm not sure," he answered. "But we need to go." He sprinted away through the trees, racing for the boundary so fast that the world became nothing but a blur of darkest greens and blues around me.

The glint of the icicles appeared up ahead and I pulled the stardust from my pocket, readying to throw it over us the second we cleared the wards. We were twenty feet from it, ten, five-

The world was ripped out from under me as Orion fell and I was thrown from his back with a scream, tumbling over the hard ground and casting a wall of moss to stop myself from rolling any further. I had no time to dwell on my panic though, I had to move. Fast.

Orion groaned in agony and I leapt to my feet, running back toward him in fear. He was on his back, writhing under the onslaught of some power I couldn't see, but a sliver of moonlight gave me a glimpse of his eyes and they were swirling with shadow.

"No!" I gasped in horror, grabbing his arms and hauling him backwards toward the boundary.

We were so close. I could get him out. I could make it.

"*Run,*" he gritted out, but there was no way I was leaving him behind.

I flicked my fingers, focusing hard and casting a levitation spell to get him off the ground, my pulse thrashing against the inside of my skull. I started running, guiding him behind me, tugging on my magic to keep him close as I raced for the gap in the wards.

Something slammed into me with the force of a battering ram and I was thrown to the dirt on my back, a body pinning me down as adrenaline tumbled through my body. My magic was severed with Orion so he hit the ground somewhere beyond me and I knew I had no time to waste.

I twisted my hands up to fight as my heart thundered madly and Phoenix fire flared under my flesh like an inferno.

"One spark of magic and my brother dies," Clara warned, leaning back so I could see her pale face in the moonlight and the shadows crawling beneath her skin. She smelled like ash and death, the power of the shadows radiating from every inch of her. "Don't test me, little princess," she hissed and a demon peered from behind her eyes that sent terror daggering into my heart.

Orion cried out in agony and it took everything I had not to try and destroy the girl sitting on top of me. My breaths came heavily and I balled my hands into fists as I held back the fire in my blood.

I looked over at Orion in desperation as he jerked on the ground under Clara's power. *What do I do? How do I get us out of this?*

"Maybe you shouldn't have been so cocky by coming here," Clara spat at me then her face split into a grin. "But never mind, let's have some fun before Mommy arrives. She'll be quite surprised when she realises who triggered the shadow alarm I cast up by our house."

I growled at that. No wonder we hadn't been able to detect it with our magic. Shit, we had to get out of here. I had to find a way to save us.

Clara got up, pulling me to my feet and brushing a leaf off of my shoulder, smiling at me like we were best friends. "Don't look so sad, it's playtime. We're going to have fun! Come on little brother, up you get."

Orion stopped jerking, rising to his feet with his face twisted in raw anger. But he didn't say a word and maybe he couldn't because he just stared at me with anguish in his eyes. I wanted to tell him it would be okay, but fear was winding through me and I couldn't think of a way out of this. If I attacked

Clara, she'd kill him. And I couldn't risk that. Not for anything.

Clara lunged toward me, picking me up and throwing me over her shoulder. I gasped as she shot off into the forest and I heard Orion tearing after us.

When I was placed down again, we were inside Stella's kitchen, the space large with beams running across the ceiling and wooden worktops beneath large cream cabinets. Clara jumped up to sit on the edge of the huge table at the centre of the room, flicking her fingers so Orion came up behind me, wrapping a hand around my throat. I stilled in his hold, my breaths coming heavier. I couldn't panic. I had to think straight. Find a way to escape.

Do not fucking panic.

Clara swung her legs as she observed us and I glared back at her with venom in my eyes.

"If you fight him off, he dies. If you fight me, he dies. If you make me angry, he dies," she sang. "Do you understand the game?"

"Yes," I hissed poisonously. "What do you want?"

"Hmmm, no one has asked me that in a long, long, long, long time," she said in delight, her hair floating around her like it was caught in some ethereal wind. "I suppose I want what every princess wants. What *you* want too, Vega girl."

"What's that?" I demanded, figuring it was best to keep her talking until I could work out how to get us out of this. But unless I could kill her before she could kill Orion, I didn't know what to do. And one failed attempt would equal his death. She was so powerful, I had no idea what it would take to destroy her.

"To be a queen," she sighed longingly. "Daddy's going to marry me."

I wrinkled my nose and she shrieked at my expression. Orion yanked me back against his body, his grip on my throat tightening painfully. I clutched his arm, fighting my instincts not to use magic and force my way free.

"Don't look at me like that!" she yelled, her voice taking on a deep, demonic quality that made the hairs on my arms stand on end. "I'm destined for greatness. Daddy says it himself. He loves me. Just like my brother loves *you.*"

Orion twisted me around in his arms, closing two hands over my throat and the fear in his eyes nearly broke me.

Clara shot over to us, watching my face with a bright smile. My lungs burned for air and my nails dug into his hand as magic tingled my fingertips, begging me to use it against him. But I wouldn't. There was no force in this world which could make me risk his life.

Orion suddenly released me and she grabbed his hand, making him dance her around the room like a puppet on strings. I held my sore throat, gasping down a lungful of air as I buckled over. My Phoenix roared beneath my flesh, desperate to try and destroy her and it took everything I had to hold it in check. *One spark and she'll kill him.*

"How did you get out of your prison, I wonder?" Clara mused, cupping Orion's face between her hands. "How very curious. Daddy won't be pleased.

But he's having a party and I mustn't disturb him during his parties. Mommy will know what to do though. It'll be a family reunion!"

She wheeled away from Orion suddenly, directing him toward me and he shot forward in a blur, grabbing me from behind.

"I wonder how she tastes," Clara breathed and Orion grabbed my arm, forcing it out towards his sister. My muscles tensed as hatred snaked through my flesh. But I couldn't fight.

"Get away from me," I snarled as Clara moved toward me like a wraith, licking her lips. "Don't move, little princess. Or he'll be deader than dead."

I bit down on my tongue as she grabbed my arm, bringing my wrist to her mouth, my stomach twisting from her touch. Her fangs snapped out and I shuddered as her cold mouth pressed to my flesh. Her teeth sliced into me with force and I gasped in pain as she bit down, tearing into my veins like a savage and drinking greedily.

I felt my magic being sucked away into this void before me as she drank and drank, gulping more and more of my lifeforce into her. My Phoenix was warring inside me, my skin growing hotter and hotter as I could barely contain it. How fast could I kill her? What if I failed?

I can't risk it.

She ripped her fangs free only to tear them into my flesh further up my arm, making me cry out as she broke the skin again and again, blood pouring out from the deep wounds. The ruby necklace she'd stolen from Tory dragged against my skin, the warmth of it calling to me like it was begging for me to rip it from her neck and I wished I could.

Clara's nails scraped down my throat and over my collar bone. She was so close to the Imperial Star, but she had no idea. I just prayed she didn't look closer at the amulet around my neck, that she didn't sense anything from it.

Another cry escaped me as she split my skin open once more and she leaned up to lap away the blood from my chest with hungry moans. I clenched my jaw through the torture. I could bear the pain so long as she didn't hurt Orion, but I needed to get us out of here before she decided to kill us both regardless.

My head was starting to spin as Clara drove her fangs into my throat and continued to drink and drink. It was too much, she was taking far too fucking much and my magic reserves were ebbing away along with my own strength.

I have to hold on.

I pressed back into Orion's arms, his body surrounding mine as my breaths became shallower. I couldn't die like this. I had to protect us. *I have to do something. Anything!*

The door whipped open and Stella came striding in with Diego parents, Drusilla and Miguel, at her heels. They weren't in their Nymph forms but their eyes glinted red as they saw me bleeding out, their hunger for my magic clear.

"Clara what on earth is going on?" Stella gasped, looking from me to Orion in shock.

She was dressed in a fitted purple dress, her short dark hair styled and the scent of rose perfume carrying from her. The Nymphs were dressed up in fine clothes too, Drusilla in a black gown and Miguel in a formal suit and I guessed they'd been at Lionel's party too.

"Is that a Vega?" Stella balked, throwing out a hand that made the front door slam.

Clara yanked her teeth free from my throat, wiping away the blood dribbling from her mouth, her face looking monstrous and contorted. "Hello Mommy."

Stella's throat bobbed, approaching her with caution and glancing at her son with a flicker of concern in her eyes. "This is quite the surprise, Clara."

"They were trespassing on your property, I felt them break my alarm, aren't I good girl for coming here to catch them?" Clara cried, rushing over to hug Stella and smearing blood across her cheek. She grimaced, patting her daughter's back as she played along, but it was clear even she was uncomfortable with Clara's behaviour.

While they were distracted, I subtly pressed my fingers to my palms, casting healing magic through my veins and fighting back the wooziness in my head. My magic was down to the final dregs so I would have to rely on my Phoenix to protect us. I just needed an opportunity to use it without risking Orion's life.

"I've seen you in my son's memories," Drusilla spoke, her eyes narrowing on me as she approached. "You're the one who turned him against us."

"No, Diego decided that all on his own," I growled, my heart pinching at the memory of him. Of everything he'd shown me of his beastly mother and his Uncle Alejandro.

Miguel's expression was vacant as he looked around, not seeming particularly interested in anything that was going on.

"What do we do with her?" Clara asked Stella excitedly. "Bake her in a pie and feed her to our army of Nymphs?"

"Don't be ridiculous," Stella scolded. "We'll take them to Lionel, he'll know what to do."

"Daddy is busy!" Clara shrieked. "We can't disturb him or he'll be angry."

"He will want to know about this," Stella threw back, stepping past her and taking me in with an arctic expression. "Why are you here in my home with my son? How did he get out?" she demanded.

I came up with a lie on the spot, needing to cover for what we'd really been doing here. They couldn't find Diego's hat no matter what.

"Lance said there could be something of his father's here that could free him from the shadows. Something that could help him run away for good," I said, feigning being beaten down so they thought I was telling the truth. I even faked a lip tremor pretty convincingly.

Stella's eyebrows arched with intrigue. "What exactly?"

"I don't know," I said, shaking my head. "I just wanted to help free him."

"Clara, let my son speak," Stella demanded and her daughter huffed dramatically.

"She's lying, can't you tell Mommy?" Clara spat. "Nothing can free him from my shadows." Clara moved closer again, glaring at me with my blood still wetting her lips. "You fought them off with your dirty little Phoenix powers, but you can't do it for him, can you? Or you already would have," she taunted, flicking a finger and using a tendril of shadow to grab a sharp kitchen knife from a block across the room. She placed it in Orion's hand and he immediately pressed the tip against my heart, making my body go rigid. "The shadows can't be beaten," she whispered excitedly. "I could have him cut out your heart and lay it in my palm if I wanted. And maybe I do..."

I winced as Orion applied pressure and the tip of it pierced my flesh.

"All that pretty blood," Clara purred, licking her lips. "Your heart would taste sweeter than all the others that have filled my belly. And I'm owed vengeance against the Vegas, so maybe this would be fitting."

Eat my fucking heart??

Stella gripped my chin and pulled my head around to face her as panic flashed through me. "You will tell me what you came here for or I will let my daughter do whatever she wants to you. Be honest, and I will have mercy."

"*Mercy*," Drusilla scoffed. "She's a Vega. Let me drain her power just like my brother Alejandro drained her father's. I want the power of the royals in my veins."

"Quiet," Stella snapped, her nails digging into my chin. "Tell me the truth." Her voice was laced with Dark Coercion, but the Phoenix fire in my veins flared in my mind and quickly burned it away.

"Okay," I panted, pretending her power had affected me and preparing to act for our lives. "It's...the Imperial Star. Orion and I believe it's being kept among his father's things. We thought maybe it was here, in the basement..."

Stella's eyes widened in glee. "Where?" she demanded, getting close to my face as a rampant hunger filled her expression.

"It's disguised as a sceptre," I lied, keeping to the bullshit story Orion had been feeding Lionel. "I don't know more than that."

Stella grinned like a kid on Christmas day, twisting around and running out of the room. I'd hoped Clara might be tempted away with her, but she remained there, twirling a lock of shadowy hair around her finger.

"This is foolish, we have the rogue Vega standing before us. Let me have her, Princess. Please," Drusilla asked, stepping toward me hopefully.

"You could have a little I suppose, but I don't think there's much magic left," Clara mused and I shuddered as Drusilla's right hand shifted into long, Nymph probes as she approached, a rattle sounding from her that made my blood chill.

"Get away from me," I snarled as Orion slid the blade up to my throat. A deep rattle in Drusilla's body washed over me and my magic started to shut down as she drew nearer.

Clara started singing up on the kitchen table, her song tuneless and twisted. Orion's muscles bunched and I could feel his hand shaking as he fought against the power holding him in place. But I'd been under its influence myself before and I knew the absolute control Clara could take of your body. Once she had you, there was no way out.

Only, there had been for me. My Phoenix had forced the shadows from my body. I'd found a way to escape, and maybe I could offer him that. I'd failed countless times with Darius, but I had to try.

I reached up, clutching Orion's arm and willing my Phoenix to the edges of my skin, trying to hide what I was doing as I pushed the fire into his flesh. Drusilla pressed her sharp probes to my chest and they drove into me, making me scream in blinding agony. I forced my fire deeper into Orion's veins, trying to spread it everywhere and chase away the shadows. But just like with Darius, they kept pushing back.

"Wait," Clara growled suddenly, spinning on her heel and staring at me.

Drusilla didn't stop, licking her lips greedily as she drove her probes in deeper and an ice cold pain shuddered through my chest. My magic was fully asleep, waiting to be taken. And I couldn't let that happen. This wasn't going to be it. Regardless of the pain, the fear, I wasn't giving up. I refused this fate.

I fought against the shadows in Orion once more, feeling them recede and the blade suddenly pulled away from my throat. His hand came down hard and I stiffened in fear, expecting the slice of its sharp point, but the knife slashed across Drusilla's probes instead, severing them off with a clean slice.

She wailed in agony, stumbling back, clutching the bloody mess of her hand to her chest in horror. The monstrous probes were still sticking out my chest, the pain of them agonising, but her power was cut off. I hurriedly twisted around in Orion's arms, pressing my hands to his chest and forcing my fire deeper into his body, making the shadows recoil from his heart, knowing this was the only chance we had now.

"He's dead!" Clara yelled. "Dead, dead, dead!"

Orion was still mostly under her control and I felt the shadows fighting back against my fire in a rush of power as they tried to kill him. But I wouldn't let them hurt him. I placed my fire between them and his heart, keeping it safe from their touch as she tried to destroy him.

"Kill her!" Clara demanded. "Stab her, cut and slash and spill her blood, little brother!"

His hand slammed into my side and it took two full seconds to feel the pain, the shock of the freezing blade hilt-deep in my flesh. I clutched his shirt with a gasp of agony, refusing to let go, needing to keep fighting back the shadows in him. But my knees were buckling and suddenly Orion was falling down on top of me, drawing the blade out and ramming into my side once more as he released a strangled noise of anguish.

I screamed so loud, my throat was rubbed raw but I didn't let go. I held onto him with every ounce of strength I had left, refusing to let the shadows creep into his chest as they took control of his limbs and she wielded him against me. The knife slammed into my side once more and Phoenix fire twisted out from me in furious, billowing blaze, all of it rushing into his body at once. I felt my Phoenix connect to some deep source of power within him and the blade clattered from his hand as he groaned. My fire combined with that piece of him and rushed through his body, his eyes glinting with it as it spread like wildfire and drove out every shadow it found. *Please be safe. Please be free.*

He fell over me, holding me tight like he was trying to protect me from something and suddenly a twisting storm of fire exploded out from me and him, blasting through the room like a bomb going off.

Clara screamed as she shot away at full speed to escape it, but I couldn't see anything else as flames framed my vision.

When they finally died down, Orion leaned back to look at me. His eyes cleared until they were just his again, deepest midnight blue and full of terror. But not for himself. For me.

I couldn't even feel the pain anymore, a numbness seeping into my body, but the growing pool of heat around me told me there was a lot of blood. And I suddenly found I had no strength at all.

It didn't matter though. Because he was okay. The shadows no longer had hold of him and they never would again.

His mouth formed my name as he shouted, but the darkness was pulling me down, down, down and death whispered sweet promises in my ear. It would have been so easy to take its hand and let it guide me away, but somewhere in my mind, I felt a tug on my soul, binding me to a girl who was the other half of me. I couldn't leave this world without her. Or the man who was calling my name.

Light shifted across my vision, red, orange, gold-

"Blue!"

Warmth surrounded me, but my eyelids weighed a thousand tonnes. I didn't think I could open them any easier than I could hold the weight of the sky on my back. But I did. Somehow, I did.

And he was there, holding me in his arms as he stood in the burned out husk of the kitchen. Drusilla's body was cast to ash, the remnants of her clothes laying in tatters on the floor.

"She's coming back!" Miguel shouted from the doorway, one side of his face burned as he stared in at us. It was the most emotion I'd ever seen on his face, panic, desperation, and a glint of a soul that had been absent from his eyes up until now. I didn't understand it and there was no time to either.

Orion shot away with me held against his chest like a child, tearing through the front door and sprinting into the trees. I held onto him, feeling the kiss of his healing magic still tingling beneath my skin. Clara was suddenly at his side, keeping pace with us and I threw out my hands with a yell of rage and determination, my Phoenix flames tearing away from me in the shape of wings.

Clara fell back to avoid them, but I could hear her chasing us still.

"Lance!" she cried, her voice throaty and more real than it had sounded before. "Get away! Run!" she begged. "I can't hold her off much longer."

I didn't know if it was the real her or some trick, but she didn't attack us and it hurt me to think she was still in there, trapped by the shadows.

Orion clutched me tighter, releasing a groan of distress as he sped on and suddenly we were through the wards. My hand was sticky as I pushed it into my pocket hunting for the stardust, but Orion was already throwing some over us and we fell through a sea of stars.

They gleamed down on us brighter than ever and I felt some of their strength filling me up. Whispers drifted through my head and I could have sworn they were saying our names.

Orion's feet hit solid ground, still holding me tight against him and as I tried to get down, he refused to let go.

"It's okay, I can walk," I said, but his jaw was locked shut and he didn't look at me as he walked through a gate and I felt the trickle of magic slipping over me. "Lance, it's okay. Put me down."

I glanced around to try and see where we were, a vineyard stretching out either side of us, but then he sprinted onward with his Vampire speed again and the world was lost to me.

He stopped on the porch of a huge house which stood in the shadow of a large mountain. It had pale blue walls and a Christmas wreath hanging on the door. Orion pressed his hand to it and it opened at his touch. I knew where we were. It was a place of happiness, family and peace.

It was Gabriel's home.

CALEB

CHAPTER FORTY TWO·

A flash of gold caught my gaze and I nudged Seth as I spotted Tory strolling across the room with shadows coiling all around her arms and her gaze vacant. At least they'd made it back without us having to cause some kind of distraction.

"Is it me or is she scary as fuck when she goes all shadow freak?" Seth muttered and I snorted.

"A bit," I agreed. "But she can be scary as fuck without the shadows too."

"I guess she'd need to be to keep Darius in line," he joked.

"Is that so?" Darius's voice came from behind us and I turned to look at him with a less than innocent shrug.

"You're high maintenance, dude. You gotta admit it," I teased.

"Yeah, everyone knows brooding bad boys are the hardest work when it comes to boyfriends," Seth agreed. "But all the angry fucking usually makes it worth it."

"Usually?" Darius asked, looking amused.

"Well, I don't have first hand experience of your cock to judge by, so I can't be sure unless you wanna go somewhere more private?" Seth teased and irritation prickled down my spine.

"If anyone is going to be pinning you beneath them tonight, mutt, it'll be me," I warned him, flashing my fangs and watching as Seth's smile widened.

"Wanna bet?" Seth challenged, always so cocky about his ability to fight me off and yet whenever we played this game, my fangs always ended up in his skin.

"Are you challenging me to chase you around the palace like we're a bunch of badly behaved kids whose parents can't reel us in?" I asked.

"No. I'm challenging you to chase me around the palace like a bloodthirsty

Vampire who spends his nights dreaming about the taste of me," Seth goaded, tipping his drink back into his mouth and grinning as he looked towards the door.

"You wanna come play with us?" I asked Darius. "You can help me hunt if you like, but the prey is all mine."

"Nah," he replied, using his chin to point across the room to where Max's step mom was standing, looking like she had a bad smell beneath her nose while Max remained stuck in her company. "I think I'm gonna go over there and let her feel my contempt for her with my gifts and then steal Max away to get drunk with me while I keep an eye on Roxy."

"Catch, you later then, dude." I raised my drink to my lips as I headed away from him with Seth at my side, the two of us cutting each other looks as we snuck off to get up to no good. My pulse hitched with excitement at the idea of doing this here.

We escaped the stuffy party and strode away down echoing corridors, casually taking turns left and right until we were lost in the depths of the palace and I had no idea where the hell we even were.

"Are you ready?" Seth teased, nudging me hard enough to knock me a step to my right and I flashed my fangs at him as I released a primal growl.

"I'm really thirsty tonight," I warned but instead of balking in fear, his eyes flashed with excitement.

"Let the hunt begin," Seth said with a taunting smile that had my fangs tingling and my tongue running over my lips. "This is fast becoming my favourite pastime."

"Are you sure?" I asked, cocking my head at him as he started unbuttoning his grey dress shirt. "It seems like the rules of the game are changing."

"You know me, Cal," Seth purred, finishing with his buttons before pushing his shirt wide and letting it roll off of his broad shoulders as he revealed his muscular body. I caught it as he tossed it to me and tucked it into the back of my pants. "I never played by any rule in the first place. So if you wanna change the limits you're putting on yourself then I'm ready."

I swallowed thickly at the implication in his tone and my heart pounded as I watched him unbuckling his pants.

"Why bother shifting?" I challenged. "You know I'll catch you anyway."

"Oh really?" Seth taunted, a smirk lifting his lips and drawing my gaze. "Come and get me then, if you think I'm such easy prey." He began to back up, fastening his belt again and offering a taunting grin which made my pulse skip with the desire to hound after him.

I shrugged like I wasn't a predator on the verge of attacking then lurched towards him, jolting back hard as I yanked against the vines he'd managed to snake around my jacket. I cursed, pulling my arms free of the material before shooting forward again only to crash into a solid air shield. I hadn't even seen the asshole cast and I snarled as I bared my fangs at him in clear warning of what I was going to do when I got my hands on him.

Seth barked a laugh then turned and ran off down the corridor in his Fae form, lifting a hand to flip me off over his shoulder as he went and howling the moment he was out of sight around the next corner.

I brought fire to my hands and started punching the air shield with the speed and ferocity of my Order, striking it again and again until it finally shattered and I was able to shoot down the corridor.

I focused my gifts on my sense of hearing, cursing as I failed to detect anything. Damn asshole must have had a silencing bubble in place. But if he thought that was enough to stop me then he had another thing coming.

I shot back and forth as fast as I could, throwing open doors and speeding around the rooms I found as I hunted. He might have been sneaky, but his speed had nothing on mine and there were only so many places he could hide around here.

I threw open the door to an enormous music room and paused. It had a vaulted ceiling hand painted with effigies of the constellations and instruments were laid out around the space, making plenty of hiding places for a sneaky Wolf.

I almost turned away again, but as I looked back towards the door, movement in the corner of my eye gave him away and I whirled around as he leapt out of the shadows from the top of a grand piano. I shot aside as he landed, skidding in his fancy shoes with a laugh spilling from his lips as he stood his ground and magic crackled through the air.

I shot towards him, throwing fire at the shield he'd created then darting out of the way as he tried to catch me in a net of air magic.

"I think you've gotten too comfortable thinking you can get a drink from me every time we play this game," Seth taunted, his eyes tracking my movements as I sped around him, looking for an opening.

"I think you like it when I bite you," I tossed back. "You like the rush."

"Oh yeah?" he asked, smirking as the air magic he was wielding tossed his long hair around his shoulders.

I kept shooting from place to place, aiming fire magic his way over and over again as I looked for a weakness in his defences and I quickly cast an illusion of myself into existence before hiding behind a giant horn.

Seth fell for it as the fake me shot towards him and as he directed his magic that way, I sped out of my hiding place and threw a javelin of fire at the back of his shield.

He wasn't dumb enough to have weakened it while focusing on the fake me, but with his attention taken from the area I was attacking, and the full weight of my power thrown into the strike, I managed to break through.

I slammed into him, knocking him from his feet and sending the two of us rolling across the floor as we laughed and fought, punching and kicking as we both struggled to get the upper hand.

We were so caught up in our scrap that we didn't even notice we'd rolled right over to the carefully lined up instruments. We crashed into a cello which went flying into a tuba and the next thing we knew, the whole orchestral line up came crashing down like a row of dominos.

The two of us froze, lips parted and staring at the carnage we'd caused as Seth pinned me to the wooden floor and the sound of a guard shouting in the distance caught my ear.

"Come on," I hissed, shooting to my feet and wrenching Seth onto my back before zooming out of the room and away through the palace corridors as fast as I could run.

I picked a door at random once we were far enough away and I burst into a dark kitchen as we fell about laughing.

"You should have seen your face," Seth mocked. "You looked about ready to shit a brick, Cal."

"You think?" I grabbed him and flipped him around, shoving him back against the worktop and fisting a hand in his hair as I tilted his head aside to bear his throat to me. "Kinda like the way you look when I have you at my mercy like this then?"

Seth snarled, grabbing my waist and shoving me around until he was driving me back against the counter instead, moving his hand to grasp a fistful of my blonde curls too. "Maybe you need a reminder of who you're playing with," he warned.

I snorted a laugh and lunged at his neck, but I crashed against an air shield he'd constructed tight against his skin and he smirked at me.

"Cheat," I grumbled, the ache in my fangs growing to a desperate throb as I eyed the thump of his pulse beneath his skin.

"No rules, remember?" Seth taunted.

My gaze moved up from the constant thrum of his pulse, sliding over the roughness of his jaw and lingering on his mouth for several long seconds before I lifted my gaze to meet his.

Seth's eyes were the richest brown I'd ever seen, like the deepest, warmest tone of chocolate with little flecks of gold buried amongst them and a soul so rich and caring lying within them.

"You know…" I said slowly. "The whole world thinks you're an asshole. In fact, like ninety nine percent of the people you meet would agree with them because you can be a total Alpha mega dick when you want to be."

"Keep talking like that Cal and you're gonna get me weeping," he teased but I only lifted the corner of my lips in a smile at him.

"I'm just saying that beneath it all, you're actually the best of us. Once you let someone in, you feel their pain like it's your own. I've heard you howling for Darius and Tory, seen you sleeping in with Darcy night after night just because you know she's sad and all alone without Orion. And you let me hunt you because you know I'm weak and I can't resist it, and you know what it would do to me if I hurt someone the way I have before-"

"Or maybe you were right the first time," he teased, seeming a little uncomfortable at the compliment I was giving him. "Maybe I just like the way it feels when you bite me and I'm really just a selfish motherfucker, using the excuse to get your mouth on my skin."

He delivered it like a joke, but it fell flat somehow and my gaze shifted down his bare chest slowly before I met his eyes again.

"Maybe you don't need an excuse," I said carefully. "Maybe if that's what you want you should just say it."

Seth swallowed thickly, his eyes flicking back and forth between mine like he was hunting for some answer from me even though I knew full well I didn't have one. But I liked the way his hands felt on my skin and I liked the way he tasted. Shit, I just liked every fucking thing about him and maybe I was crazy, but I was starting to wonder if-

Seth used his grip on my hair to tug me down to his neck, baring his throat to me and dropping his air shield so that I could feel the warmth of his blood reaching through his flesh against my lips.

I inhaled slowly, not biting down, just running my mouth up the curve of his neck to the corner of his jaw.

I loosened my grip on his hair, my fingers pushing into it gently instead of fisting it roughly and a shiver ran through his body as I dragged my fangs back down his throat.

"By the stars, Cal, you're gonna be the fucking death of me if you don't get to the point soon," he said in a rough voice and I chuckled against his skin, nipping lightly but not puncturing it.

"And what's the point?" I questioned, wanting to hear the answer to that way more than I should have.

Seth hesitated, a soft, canine whimper escaping his throat.

"Don't tease me, Caleb," he murmured. "Not if you don't really..."

"Don't really what?" The movement of my mouth on his neck made him growl softly and I felt that noise all the way through my body.

His grip in my hair tightened and he drove my head down harder, demanding I get on with this and I gave in to him, sinking my fangs into his skin and groaning as the delicious richness of his blood and magic spilled over my tongue.

He was still pinning me back against the counter and he ground against me forcefully, the hardness in his pants rubbing against my hip.

He tried to move back, but I dropped my hand from his hair and caught his waistband, yanking him close again and holding him there as I felt his arousal driving against me and found I liked that a whole hell of a lot.

My other hand slid down the hard ridges of his chest and he drew in a ragged breath which made my skin prickle.

"Oh, erm, sorry - I didn't mean to interrupt," Xavier's voice came followed by a horsey snort of embarrassment and I drew my fangs back out of Seth's neck as I looked over at Darius's younger brother with a flare of irritation.

He was standing by the door to the kitchen and had a half eaten sandwich on a plate which he waved at us as Seth growled beneath his breath.

"Dudes, I totally thought I just caught you doing something else," he laughed, looking at my fangs as I licked the last of Seth's blood from my lips and banished them. "I came in here looking for more mayo because they're all out in the main kitchen and here you are in the dark, half dressed and all over each other and..." He cleared his throat as neither of us spoke and gave us an awkward smile. "But err, you're obviously just feeding - is there like some protocol I'm missing here about interrupting a Vampire mid feast or-"

"Nah man," I said, slapping on a grin as I reached up to heal the bite from Seth's skin. "Like you said, I was just feeding and Seth was gonna shift before – which is why he's shirtless."

My gaze met Seth's and a soft whine slid past his lips before he turned and grinned at Xavier too, but it looked all kinds of false and I couldn't help but feel like I'd just said the wrong thing. But what was the right thing? 'Yeah I was just biting him, but it felt like a lot more than that and if you'd interrupted us ten minutes later then I'm not really sure what you would have found.' That was fucking crazy. Right?

"Yeah. If you'd caught us fucking, Cal would have been pinned beneath me screaming my name in ecstasy," Seth joked.

"Err, I think you'll find Seth would have been on his knees moaning something that could be my name, but you wouldn't be sure because his mouth would have been so full of my dick," I added with a dark grin.

"Haha, yeah," Xavier said, laughing a little too loudly as his cheeks pinked. "One of you would have been all like 'oh baby put your mega dick in my...ear while I recite the alphabet to make sure I don't come too quick and then I'll totally destroy your...knees on the hard floor...'"

"Shit, dude, don't ever say that to someone you wanna fuck," I said laughing as he flushed from strawberry to scarlet and quickly yanked the fridge open to find his mayo.

Seth looked at me with a question in his eyes and I frowned, unsure what he was asking for one of the first times ever. I tugged his shirt from the back of my pants, handing it over to him in offering and he frowned as his gaze fell to it.

He snatched it from me kinda roughly and shoved his arms into it like the thing had offended him.

"Do you guys want a sandwich?" Xavier offered, holding out a bag of carrots and I opened my mouth to reply, but a pain-filled scream met my ears before I could, making me freeze where I was standing.

"Did either if you hear that?" I asked in a sharp whisper.

"Hear what?" Xavier asked, looking back at me around the fridge door with his cheeks a little less red.

"Someone screamed," I murmured, training my gifted hearing on everything all around us as I frowned in concentration.

"When I was on the moon," Seth began. "There was sometimes this sound kinda like a scream when-"

I shushed him aggressively as I heard it again, but this time there was a man begging for someone to stop what they were doing alongside the scream.

"Come on," I commanded, running from the room and hurrying along the corridor outside before taking a sharp turn onto a servants' staircase that led to the underground portion of the palace.

"Where are we going?" Seth growled, seeming kinda pissed at me and I shot him a frown.

"Someone down there is screaming for help."

That wiped the irritable expression from his face and he hurried his pace as I led them down to the foot of the stairs before pausing to listen again.

"Are you sure there's someone here?" Xavier asked, looking a little concerned but determined to stick with us all the same. He still had half a carrot and mayo sandwich in his hand which he quickly ate as I glanced at it.

"Yeah," I said, waiting for the screams to come again and frowning when they did. "It's still coming from beneath us."

"I've explored the palace a fair bit and I haven't seen a level beneath this one," Xavier said in a low voice as he swallowed down his snack.

I frowned as I looked around us, placing my hand on the stone wall at the foot of the stairs and ignoring the impulse to shoot off and take a piss as it crept over me.

"There's a repulsion spell here," I grunted, focusing hard on trying to pull it apart as the need to pee made me feel like I was about to piss myself. "Someone strong created it."

"Father?" Xavier asked in alarm.

"No," I said as I forced my magic into the spell and broke it with a shove of power. "It would have been harder to bypass than that if it was him. I can feel a space beyond the wall now."

Seth moved to my side, his arm brushing mine as he ran a hand over the wall too, feeling it out with his earth magic and I nudged him slightly in the way he normally did when he could tell something was up. He glanced at me for a moment, a smile catching the corner of his lips as he nudged me in return. It turned into a grin as he found the catch holding the door in place and pressed the brick into the wall.

There was a sound of grinding stone as a doorway was revealed and flickering orange light from somewhere below lit up a curving staircase.

I threw a silencing bubble over the three of us then looked at the others. "Whatever is down here isn't good. Last chance to turn back."

Seth scoffed dismissively, but we both knew my offer had really been for Xavier who raised his chin defiantly.

"I'm coming," he said, stamping his foot like it was a hoof and I was gifted a vivid memory of him doing that exact thing when we'd all been playing together as kids. How no one realised he was a Pegasus before he Emerged was a mystery to me in hindsight.

"Alright then, let's see what you've got, pony boy," Seth joked and I smirked as I led the way into the dark stairwell.

We jogged down the stone steps, the cold air seeping into my skin and making me use fire magic to warm myself. I reached out for Seth's arm behind me and gifted him some fire too as he was the only one amongst us without it, and he leaned forward to lick my cheek in thanks.

I batted him off with a snort of laughter but quickly forgot our playful crap as another scream came to us from much closer this time and the two of them sucked in gasps of alarm.

We broke into a run, heading down to the foot of the stairs where the firelight burned brighter and a huge room opened up before us.

Seth threw a concealment over us as we stayed hidden in the shadows at the foot of the stairs and we looked out over the stone chamber where several medical tables were laid out with surgical equipment beside them.

A short man in long red robes stood over a guy who was strapped to the table in the centre of the room, his white hair almost shining in the firelight as I looked at the back of his head.

"I know him," Xavier hissed, horror lacing his tone. "He's the Order Conversion Therapist Father got for me after I Emerged as a Pegasus. His name is Gravebone."

"What the fuck is that when it's at home?" Seth asked.

"A sick motherfucker who tried to make me believe I was a Dragon and not a Pegasus. I never could work out what the point of it was, but his methods were scarily effective. For a while, I almost began to believe the shit he was feeding me." The rage and disgust in his voice was clear and I laid a reassuring hand on his arm as I gritted my teeth in anger at the way he'd been treated just as Gravebone started to speak.

"Rats are such dirty creatures," he purred, his voice as slick as oil and his attention fully on the man who was struggling against his bonds beneath him. I spied a pair of magic restricting cuffs around the man's wrists which were clearly being used to stop him from fighting back. "Such little, pointless, scheming *vermin*. No one would wish to be such a lowly Order. *You* certainly don't."

"There's no shame in being a Tiberian Rat!" the man on the table hissed. "You won't convince me I'm a fucking Medusa so stop trying."

"The procedure will go much more smoothly if your mind is in alignment with it," Gravebone said, sounding resigned. "But if you won't even *try* to adapt to your new reality then there is much less chance of success-"

"Fuck you!" the Rat snarled before spitting right in Gravebone's face.

The creep flinched back, growling loudly as he swiped a red sleeve over his cheek to remove the spittle. "Let's try this again." He lifted a scalpel from a small table beside him, but Seth threw a hand out before he could use it, casting a thick web of vines into existence which snapped tight around his hands and immobilised his magic.

I shot forward in the next breath, earth magic pulsing in my veins as I sped around Gravebone several times while he cried out in panic, binding him in vines of my own. He yelled out for help before falling to the ground with a hard thump but with my silencing bubble surrounding him there was no chance of that coming.

"Oh my stars, are you here to rescue us?" the guy on the table gasped, his pasty blonde hair sticking to his forehead as he looked at me like I was some kind of hero.

And I guessed maybe that was exactly what we were here for, even though I hadn't given it much thought until this exact moment.

"Us?" Xavier asked as he rushed over, heading straight towards the Rat dude like he intended to unstrap him, and I held an arm out to slow him down.

"Hang on a second," I said, my palm hitting Xavier's chest as he looked at me in alarm. "We can't make it obvious we were here."

"Fat chance of that!" Gravebone shrieked from his position on his back on the floor. "I've seen your faces - your father will hear of this Xavier!"

Xavier snorted in fury, kicking out at Gravebone's head and making him shriek in pain as his nose shattered. I caught Xavier's shoulder to stop him before he could do any more, still unsure of the best way to proceed.

I filled Gravebone's mouth with dirt to stop him from speaking again and smiled cruelly down at the terror in his eyes as he fought to breathe around the obstruction.

"Untie me!" the Rat begged. "Please - I know who you are. You're Caleb Altair-"

"Everyone knows who he is, buddy," Seth said, moving to stand beside me with a contemplative frown on his face.

"Yes, but, I went to Aurora Academy with Elise. Please, my name is Eugene. Eugene Dipper. I swear I didn't do any of the things they said I did. I didn't steal the midnight amethyst stones from anyone. I was just a collector, I never hid that, I swear!"

I exchanged a look with Seth, the guy having even more of my attention now as I wondered if I should try to call bullshit on his claims by finding out if there was any truth to them. If he'd known Elise then I guessed that gave me even more reason to help him out, but I didn't have any intentions of leaving him here anyway.

"Calm down, man," I said. "No one is leaving you here. We just need to figure out how to cover up our involvement in this little incident. I need it to look like you got yourself free somehow."

"H-he - Gravebone has the cuff key in his pocket," Eugene gasped. "Perhaps if it looked like I got a hand free then maybe it could seem like I'd gotten hold of it and freed myself and my magic without help."

"Doesn't help us with the witness issue though," Seth mused, giving Gravebone a casual kick which drew a muffled grunt of pain from him.

"That's why we need to kill him," Eugene growled and I was surprised to hear such savagery from the little dude, but he was more than clear in his thirst for blood here. And I guessed if I'd been strapped to a table and tortured while some freaky asshole tried to convince me I was a Medusa, I would be out for blood too.

"What the fuck is the point of all this anyway?" Xavier asked indignantly. "Even if you believed you were a Medusa, you wouldn't suddenly become one so-"

"Gravebone and V-Vard have been doing experiments," Eugene said, a sob catching in the back of his throat. "C-cutting Fae open and trying to steal their Order forms before re-replacing it with another. I've been down here for weeks and watched them kill countless Fae of my kind with their twisted experiments. It's never even come close to working but they just start again as soon as they fail. They're sick."

"There are more of you here?" Seth asked sharply and Eugene bobbed his chin towards a door on the far side of the open space.

"M-more than I can count. Tiberian Rats, Sphinxes, Minotaurs - all of the Orders the Dragon King has deemed lesser than whatever he requires for supremacy. You have to help us. You have to!"

"We're getting to it," Seth said, glancing at me and I gritted my teeth as I tried to think about the best way to do this.

"We need to cover our faces so they don't all see us, in case any of them are caught," I said, glancing at Eugene and wishing I'd thought of this sooner. "Then we let them out and give them a chance to run for it. They can punish Gravebone however they see fit."

Gravebone started to thrash and kick on the floor at my feet, knowing full well the victims of his torture wouldn't be merciful if we let them decide his fate. But that really wasn't my problem. If they wanted to get revenge on him for what he'd done then they had the right to.

"If we just let them make a run for it they'll be caught again," Xavier protested angrily and I ran a hand over my jaw, knowing that there was a fair chance he was right about that.

"I don't see what else we can do," Seth said. "I mean, the Rats could shift and maybe sneak out, but the Sphinxes and Minotaurs..." He shrugged. "At least this way they'll have a shot."

"That's not good enough," Xavier demanded, stamping his foot angrily again and I opened my mouth to argue just as the sound of stone grinding on stone announced another secret door opening behind us.

I whirled around, fire blossoming in my fists as I felt Seth's air shield lock into place around us and my heart nearly fell out of the pit of my stomach as a door slid open in the wall and Gabriel stepped through it.

"I *saw* that you needed my help in getting some people out of here," he said with a cocky grin which he totally deserved to be sporting.

"Fuck yes," Seth whooped and Xavier sagged with relief as I set my focus on setting these Fae free.

I bent down and hunted Gravebone's pockets while he bucked and fought beneath me, but he was so well tied that there was no chance of him getting away. I pinned him down with an irritated grunt, finding the key to the magic restricting cuffs in his pocket followed by a thick metal key which I was guessing would set the Fae beyond that door loose.

I swiped a hand over my face as I cast the concealment to hide my identity and Seth quickly did the same for him and Xavier. Gabriel followed our lead and once I was certain no one would recognise us, I grabbed hold of the leather cuff tying Eugene's wrist to the table and tugged on it with a surge of my Vampire strength. The damn thing almost didn't give but with a grunt of effort, I broke it, leaving Eugene to unbuckle the rest of his limbs as I raced towards the door on the other side of the room.

The key I'd stolen from Gravebone opened it and I found a row of cells full of Fae who all shrieked and cringed away from the bars at the sight of the door opening.

"I'm here to get you out," I called, my voice disguised by the concealment spell as I moved to the closest cell and quickly unlocked it.

I decided that them knowing I was a Vampire wouldn't really risk my identity and quickly shot around using my gifts to unlock the rest of the cells as fast as possible. The Fae inside all poured out, calling their thanks, some of them sobbing as they ran for the exit and a freedom I was guessing they hadn't expected to ever see again.

By the time I returned to the main room, Seth had unlocked most of their cuffs and Gravebone was well and truly dead. His blood was seeping over the floor and his mangled body so pulverised I was willing to bet they'd beaten him to death instead of wasting magic on him.

I dispersed the vines I'd created to hold him and Gabriel ushered the escapees towards the dark tunnel he'd emerged from.

"Go now," he barked at us. "Caleb needs to run you back to the party within the next thirty seconds or you'll be missed. I can get everyone away from here safely. Hamish will help them hide from there."

I didn't need telling twice so I gave Gabriel a firm nod before shooting forward and hooking an arm each around Xavier and Seth before speeding out of the hidden chamber.

I only paused to close the concealed door again then hoisted the two of them into my grasp and carried them back to the party, skidding to a halt at the side exit we'd used to escape it.

Xavier looked half inclined to puke from the speed we'd just travelled at and Seth shook his head like he was trying to stave off some dizziness. I dispelled the illusions over us and we pushed the door open, slipping back inside.

My heart was thundering as I led the way towards the buffet and my mom's voice drew my attention to her as she called my name.

"I've been looking for you!" she chastised half-heartedly. "Come on - I want you to speak with the leader of the Falhurst company. He's doing some really impressive things with predictive charts that I just know you'd love to hear about."

I smiled politely at the Falhurst dude who Mom was clearly trying to impress for some deal and painted on my Heir face as I moved over to join them.

Had we just gotten away with freeing a bunch of prisoners right out from under Lionel's scaly nose without anyone even realising we'd ducked out on the party?

Hell yeah we had. And it felt really fucking good.

DARCY

CHAPTER FORTY THREE

Istood in a huge shower which seemed big enough for eight people as I washed the blood from my skin, examining the places on my stomach where the knife had cut me open. There was no sign it had ever happened, yet I could still feel the icy lick of it imprinted in my memory.

I shuddered, turning the water off and stepping out into the large bathroom onto a fluffy white mat, using my air magic to dry myself off before wrapping myself in a towel. Gabriel's family were away at a cabin for Christmas in their usual tradition and Gabriel would be joining them there too after tonight. He'd given me access to his house a while ago and had given me permission to come here if I was ever in trouble. I guessed he'd done the same for Orion.

My bloody clothes were bagged up in the garbage and Diego's hat rested by the his and hers sinks with my Atlas. I picked them up, finding a text from Tory in reply to the message I'd sent her to say we had the hat and we were okay, but we'd had to run after Stella and Clara had shown up. I'd tell her the rest when I saw her next. At least for now, we were safe.

Tory:
Lay low. Lionel will send the FIB looking for Orion as soon as he realises he's escaped. xx

My throat thickened as I let that knowledge settle over me. On the one hand, I was glad he was away from Lionel but on the other, the idea of the FIB coming for him was terrifying. What would they do to a convict on the run? How many more years would they add to his sentence if he was caught? There was only one plan we could make. They could never, ever catch him.

I dressed in a pair of soft lilac sweatpants and a white crop top I'd borrowed from Gabriel's wife then opened the door, putting Diego's hat and my Atlas in my pocket. Orion immediately pushed off of the wall opposite me, his eyes full of anxiety. He'd washed and changed, wearing what I guessed were a pair of Gabriel's navy sweatpants. He didn't stop coming, dropping to his knees in front of me and pressing his mouth to my bare stomach. I gasped in surprise, fisting my hands in his hair as desire spilled through my flesh.

He hugged me against him and looked up at me with his brows drawn low.

"I'm sorry," he rasped, a haunted look in his eyes that made my heart squeeze painfully.

I knelt down too, leaning into his touch as he cupped my cheek. "It wasn't you."

His upper lip peeled back, his fangs glinting as hatred shone in his eyes. But I wasn't sure who it was aimed at, only certain it wasn't me. His fingers pushed through my hair like he was trying to reassure himself I was still here, and I let myself bathe in his touches despite knowing it would only make it harder to pull away.

"I'm okay," I promised and his Adam's apple rose and fell.

"I'm not," he replied in a deep growl.

"I'm sorry too," I breathed, pain caving in my chest.

"Don't you dare be." He looked at me with an intensity in his gaze that made my breath catch. "You freed me from the shadows. You saved us. I was the one who…" He laid his mouth on my throat where the knife had kissed my flesh and a shiver darted down my spine.

"Stop," I said but it came out husky, more like a plea for him to continue than anything else. After coming so close to losing him again, all I wanted to do was pull him nearer and never let go. But there was still an abyss parting us that couldn't be crossed. "It wasn't your fault."

He pushed to his feet, not letting go of my hand as he towed me after him with a harsh and distant expression dawning on his face. I eyed his wrists, noticing the shadow cuffs were gone and it made me feel so fucking good that I'd finally been able to free someone else from Clara's dark control. And maybe I'd be able to do it again.

We walked through the large, empty halls of Gabriel's house and I peeked into the beautiful nursery with light blue walls and an array of stuffed toys in the cot from a giant snake to a fluffy lion with a dark mane. Orion was quiet and brooding, his jaw continually flexing as if he was struggling with some demon inside him. We made it downstairs to a large kitchen built of beautiful honey wood and cream fixtures. He led me to a stool at the island with five seats, picking me up and planting me on it before heading to the fridge. I frowned in surprise, gazing at the taut muscles of his back as he started taking out food and piling it on the counter.

"I'm not hungry," I said, taking Diego's hat from my pocket and laying my Atlas on the island. "We need to-"

"You're gonna eat," he growled in his bossy professor tone and my lips pursed.

"No... I'm going to try and find out what Diego wanted us to *see* through his hat." I moved to put it on but he shot toward me, snatching it away and shoving it into the back of his waistband.

"You're gonna eat first," he reiterated, placing his hands on my thighs to keep me in my seat, making anger and lust wash together inside me. He was intoxicating when he was up this close, his breath on my skin making me heady. But I wasn't going to give in to the raging emotions in me because if I fell for his allure tonight, I'd never stop falling.

I pushed his hands away, slipping out of my seat, but he didn't move a single inch so I was caged in by his arms and trapped in the delicious cinnamon scent of his bare chest.

"Give it back," I growled, fighting to keep my voice level. I was not in the mood for an argument after all the shit we'd just been through.

"No," he said simply, grabbing my hips, lifting me up and planting my ass back on the seat, crowding in even closer to me. Dammit, I didn't want a fight but he was asking for one.

"Lance," I warned, holding out my hand. "Give it back."

He leaned near to my face, his breath brushing against my lips and tasting like a cardinal sin. "Not. Until. You. Eat."

I reached around his back to try and grab the hat and he shot away with his Vampire speed. The second he stopped running, I used a whip of air magic to pluck it from his waistband.

I caught it and cast a dome of air around myself as he sprinted forward to try and grab it again. I smirked as he crashed into my shield and he growled. He opened his mouth, no doubt to try and boss me about so I lifted the hat, defiantly tugging it on.

Everything went dark and I was half aware of falling off of my chair before my mind drifted into the pitch. Someone's hand was gripping mine as the power of the shadows drew me into them and something in my soul told me it was Diego. Emotion clutched my chest and I was caught between sadness and joy at feeling his presence again. My friend. A boy who'd given his life for me, for the whole kingdom really. He'd tried to stop Clara and shown what his soul was truly made of.

The shadows wound around me but couldn't get beneath my skin as they carried me down, down, down into an eternal darkness. Orion's presence drifted closer and I felt him pulling on my consciousness demandingly. But I wasn't going anywhere. I exerted my will, forcing him to come with me as I fell into the black and suddenly a cloud of white opened up ahead of us, flashing with the memories of the past.

I felt the weight of it in the atmosphere, a thousand lives, a string of ancestors stretching back hundreds of years. The hand slipped from mine and I glimpsed two dark eyes among the mist a moment later, my heart tugging with recognition.

"*Diego*," I said, but the name only sounded in my head. I reached for the cloud of memories, a deep need filling me as I searched for my friend.

I felt his hand wrapping around mine once more, pulling me in and I sensed his need to show me what waited in the fog.

I tumbled into a memory, seeing through the eyes of someone who was playing with shadows in their palms, sitting in front of a large fire. There were Fae sitting around it on logs and an old woman perched on her left, adjusting the girl's palms as the shadows danced along her skin.

"*That's it, Lavinia," she said, tugging a fur tighter around her shoulders. "You have such a talent for it."*

"*I still can't wield them like, Nisar," I complained, my voice Lavinia's as I relived the memory from her point of view.*

I scowled over at the boy who always held everyone's attention with his gifts and a bitter jealousy filled me.

"*You're only fourteen, in time you will wield them better than anyone in our tribe," the old woman said. "You're destined for greatness."*

"*Do you really think so?" I asked.*

"*I know so. It's written in the stars."*

"*Don't tell her stories," a large, bearded man called over with a scowl. "My daughter is destined to produce babies and take care of her future husband. Just like all the women in our tribe."*

"*I don't want that, father," I growled coldly. "I will be a warrior."*

"*You will be whatever I tell you to be," he answered, drinking his ale and an icy hatred ran through me. A hatred I'd felt for a long time for a man who had always favoured my brothers. Always thought of me as nothing.*

The vision changed and I sensed that a few years had passed as I watched through the eyes of Lavinia again.

I snuck through the tents of the tribe with a knife in my grip, slipping into one where my father was passed out drunk in a bed with two women. I crept up to the bed of furs and wielded the shadows as I'd been practising day and night. My power over them had grown immensely and as I felt them out in my father and the whores, I locked them down tight. Father jerked awake, but couldn't move as I held onto that power in him, a thrill buzzing through me at how easy it was. I smiled viciously, climbing onto the bed and toying with the blade in my hand as Father's eyes flashed with fear.

"*You never should have underestimated me, Father." I leaned down, holding the tip of the blade of his chest.*

He jerked against the power of the shadows but I was immensely gifted. More gifted than anyone in the tribe. I stabbed him hard in the chest, then again and again before striking at the women too, relishing their pain. Blood coated my flesh and I licked it from my lips as I destroyed the man who'd kept me down, who refused to acknowledge my greatness. And I whispered my deepest desire in his ear as he died, "I will be a queen."

The vision changed once more and sickness filled me as I could still taste the iron tang of blood in my mouth. I felt myself slipping into Lavinia's memory once more.

I rode a horse, charging across a battlefield with my hands raised and shadows tearing around me, ripping through the hearts of other Fae who wielded their Elemental magic against me. I turned my head and my heart swelled at the sight of the huge army of magnificent beasts running behind me, smashing through our enemies.

Shock ran through me. The tribe weren't Fae at all, they were Nymphs. And so was Lavinia.

I cast the shadows at the Fae ahead of me, cutting through their bodies. They looked poor, their clothes worn and their faces gaunt. Though they tried to fight, nothing could stop my power and they were soon bleeding and screaming for mercy. A mercy I would not give. I was the ultimate power in this land, and I would do whatever it took to claim my rightful place as Queen.

The Fae were forced to surrender and the Nymphs declared victory before the vision changed once more, showing Lavinia and her tribe moving into their new territory, claiming the town as theirs and killing any survivors. I watched through Lavinia's eyes as she callously murdered a family hiding in a barn and my stomach turned as I wished I didn't have to see it.

The bodies fell into the mud and a cold laugh left my throat as the Nymphs around me gazed on in fear and respect. I thrived on it, death and power feeding the darkest piece of my soul and making me hunger for more.

The vision changed once more and I sat on a throne made from the curving bow of a tree, placed at the top of a large hill with an ornate stone gazebo standing over it.

A man was escorted toward me, flanked by two Nymphs in their shifted forms while other guards stood watching closely. The man was tall and blonde, his eyes deepest green and I recognised him as the Dragon Master, Octavius Acrux. He was handsome. A man I respected and had quietly coveted from afar.

"Princess Lavinia." He bowed lowed. "I bring a gift from my family. An offering of peace from the Dragon Guild." He stepped aside and a large, rectangular object came floating forward on a gust of air he cast. He placed it upright in front of me and moved to tug the silk free from it.

A beautiful gilded mirror was revealed, the frame silver, twisting like vines around its edges, covered in delicate roses. I stood from my throne and gazed at my reflection.

The girl staring back at me was stunning, her hair long and raven, her eyes two purest marbles of blue. She was beautiful, her lips full and wide and her features strong. She looked like a warrior, her body clad in armour, scars marking her arms.

"We want to offer you an alliance," Octavius said, moving to stand beside the mirror as I admired it. "I know you are seeking to claim the throne from the Vegas, but you haven't got the numbers behind you to face them. Uniting with the Dragons would make us all strong enough to achieve it together."

Hope stirred in my chest as I looked to him, but suspicion too. "And how am I to trust you?"

The man dropped down to one knee with a smile, taking out a wooden box and offering me a ring. "Marry me and make a promise on the stars. Our families will be bound by the powers of the heavens. Acrux and Umbra. Our Seer has had a great prophesy. Gaze into the mirror so you can see for yourself." He gestured for me to step forward and I did so cautiously. I needed this, I wanted to be a queen more than anything else in the world. But I had never wanted to share my throne...

I stepped in front of the mirror and the image twisted, showing me sitting on a large throne in a room full of burning sconces. The throne was made of a deep, ruby red glass, glinting in the firelight. The place was beautiful, the high walls towering and seemingly built from the earth itself. Beside me in another throne of deepest sapphire was Octavius Acrux, his robes crimson and his eyes shifted into reptilian slits, gazing at me adoringly. Across my lap was a beautiful silver sword with a glittering stone in the hilt. I looked happy, in love. So maybe sharing my throne wasn't unfathomable. If ever a man were to capture my heart, it wouldn't be so bad if it were this one.

The vision in the mirror faded and I looked at Octavius in awe. "I'll have the Imperial Star?"

"It will be ours," he growled. "The Vegas will fall, we'll claim the Palace of Flames and destroy the last of the Phoenixes."

"But how will we defeat the Queen?" I asked.

"I know of a dark curse that even her power cannot overcome," he said with a twisted smile. "Once her army is defeated, you can use the power of the shadows to ensure we can destroy her at last."

Excitement swelled in my chest and I nodded keenly, accepting the ring from him and the vision changed once more.

I was on a bloody battlefield and Nymphs were falling all around me, Phoenix fire tearing through their bodies and casting them to ash. They raced through the sky on flaming wings, raining down hellfire on their enemies. I fought against Fae on the ground with everything I had. They weren't just using their Elements to counter my attacks, they were using dark magic, fighting the shadows of my Nymphs with power wielded through bones to enhance their natural magic.

Hatred spilled through me as my gaze fell on the Phoenix Queen hovering above her army, her dark hair spinning around her in the breeze, her face fixed in a snarl. She wore a silver crown on her head and in her hand was the huge sword which held the Imperial Star and had all the constellations of the sky etched into its surface. She held it up, speaking a word to it which I couldn't hear, but which made the air pulse with shockwaves of power.

A Dragon soared toward her, but a Phoenix man swept past his queen to hold it off, fighting it with huge blasts of fire from his palms.

Though it was day, the stars suddenly shone in the sky, glittering brightly down on the world as blood and chaos reigned.

I panicked as a huge wave of power blasted out from the Imperial Star, sweeping over the entire battlefield. The Nymphs fell prey to its power, crashing to their knees and I fell too, grasping at my chest as some fierce magic took root in me.

A huge fissure opened up in the sky at the command of the Phoenix Queen and the shadows started pouring into it from my army as the dark power was drawn from them, stolen away and cast into the abyss. I screamed in anguish as the shadows were taken from me too, ripped from the centre of my soul and leaving an empty hollowness in my chest which I feared would never be filled again.

When the last of them were drawn into the hole in the sky, it closed up and the Imperial Star stopped shining in the hilt of the sword.

"There will be no more war!" the Queen cried, her voice carrying across the quiet field, desperation in her tone. "And there shall be no more dark magic and no more shadows in our land ever again. From this day forward, it is outlawed. And those who call upon it will face my wrath."

"No!" I screamed, pushing to my feet. "We need the shadows to survive, we're not like your kind!"

"You will find a way," the Queen sneered, calling a retreat to her people, leaving the Nymphs powerless on the ground.

A huge red Dragon swept towards us and my heart lifted as I saw Octavius coming to aid me like he'd promised, backing me to the end and offering one final chance for us to turn this around.

But instead of charging in with tooth and claw to save me, he roared an Order to his army and they turned on my Nymphs, burning them to soot with huge billows of fire from their lungs.

"Octavius!" I cried in horror as the Dragons decimated my army, betraying me and his promise, breaking my heart in two.

How could he do this? He'd promised me the world, made love to me, spoken endlessly of all the things we would have together. How could he betray me after telling me he loved me? Was it all a lie? Some great deceit to lure me here and destroy my kind?

The Dragon Master led his beasts to land beneath the Phoenix Queen, bowing to her as they all roared. She nodded to them and my heart shattered as I watched the world fall around me. My chance at true power stolen away.

The Queen landed before me in her golden armour, her flaming wings folding behind her as she gazed down her nose at me. "This is the end of your reign of terror, Lavinia."

"You can't just kill me," I gasped. "I'm a princess of my kind. There is no other left to lead them."

"You are nothing but a princess of the shadows now, so you will die with them," the Queen growled, clutching the Imperial Star in her hand and murmuring something to it.

I pushed to my feet, raising a knife from my hip, but the Queen melted it with nothing but a flick of her hand. Another twist of her fingers sent a blast of air magic crashing into me and I flew back, thrown through a rift between worlds opened up by the Imperial Star once more, dragged away into nothing but shadow.

The dark Element wrapped around my body and consumed me whole, tearing through my flesh until I became one with it. I didn't die as I expected, as that vile queen expected.

And through the fog and haze of all that pain and power, I hungered for vengeance and the king I'd been promised in an empty, endless land of darkness, swearing that one day I'd return to claim it.

I was pulled out of the vision, torn from the cloud of memory and suddenly I was wide awake, laying on my back with Orion panting beside me.

"Oh my god," I breathed. "That's her. The Shadow Princess."

"Somehow she's bound to my sister," Orion said, clawing a hand over his face.

My heart was still racing like crazy as I pushed myself upright, taking the hat off, the power of it quiet now. I pushed it into my pocket and turned to look at Orion, his chest rising and falling frantically.

"She's trying to fulfil her prophesy, even after all this time," I said in shock and he nodded, looking to me with a crease between his eyes.

"I have so many questions," he said, his gaze alight with all the information we'd been fed.

That dark magic had once been used by all those Fae. That the Nymph Princess and the Acrux Dragons had been aligned once before.

I got to my feet and started pacing as excitement ran through me.

Orion sat up, watching me pace with a hopeful smile and my gaze snagged on the dimple in his right cheek. "This proves my sister is still in there. She's being controlled by the princess."

"We'll save her," I swore to him as I had once before. "We'll find a way. Maybe the hat will show us more."

"Blue," Orion said as I continued pacing, but I couldn't stop.

"Maybe there's some answer here, something that can help us. Did you see all those Phoenixes? They must be my ancestors-"

"Blue…"

"But what happened to them? Did the Dragons eventually destroy them? But how?" My mind ran through everything at a hundred miles an hour. I felt excited, like we were on the cusp of knowing something life changing but I didn't know what.

"Blue," Orion shot in front of me, gripping my crop top in his fist.

"What?" I demanded, looking up at him in surprise as my heart juddered.

"You're going to be a queen," he growled. "Just like your ancestor. I can feel it, I fucking *know* it."

"How do you know?" I asked, doubt flitting through me.

But I knew I wanted it. I needed Lionel to fall, and right now it felt more possible than ever. We had the Imperial Star. We had a connection to a sea of memories which could hold answers to defeating the Shadow Princess, to unravelling the power Lionel currently held in the kingdom.

"I've known since I crowned you in my car. Just don't ever forget you were *my* queen first." He yanked me forward and his mouth met mine, his kiss urgent and furious and I couldn't help but give in to it for two whole seconds. I felt urged toward him as if by the stars themselves and I remembered what it was like to have him as my will was broken down inch by inch.

But then I pulled away, shaking my head, unsure of myself, of him, of anything.

"Tell me no. Say the word," he growled and my lips parted but it didn't come out. Why wouldn't it come out??

I stepped away, backing up as I tried to get my head straight. But it was crooked as shit.

He stalked after me, slow and intentionally and I couldn't ignore how every fibre of my being burned for him. "I thought you were done with me, Blue, I really did. I hoped it too even though that knowledge would have destroyed me. But then I found out you were sleeping with the dog."

"We've been through this-" I started in exasperation but he spoke over me.

"I almost lost all hope for us, beautiful, even though I wasn't meant to have any in the first place. But I did, I just hid it really fucking deep, denying it to myself that I still dreamed about a future where you were mine, no matter how impossible that seemed. And after you told me you weren't his and kissed me back in the tomb, fuck, I've not thought of anything else since. Nothing but your mouth on mine and you pulling me closer. But I still kept away. Because I can't give you anything. Nothing's changed. I know that in my heart. I know it and I still can't accept it. Because tonight I found out what it was like to have you dying in my arms and nothing has ever terrified me more. *Nothing*, Blue."

"So what are you saying?" I demanded as I rounded the couch and put the coffee table between us, my heart jack-hammering like crazy.

He shot toward me and raked his thumb up my cheekbone. "I'm saying I fucked up everything. And it's not getting unfucked any time soon. But I also can't stay away from you any longer."

"You don't get to just decide you want me again and expect us to pick up where we left off." A snarl left my lips as I shoved him in the chest and he pushed back against me, grabbing my hips and yanking me closer.

"I know," he said on a furious breath. "I wish there was a future where I could offer you everything you deserve, but there isn't. That life doesn't exist for me. Fate closed the door on it, but some part of me is still foolishly scratching at it trying to find a way back in."

"Lance you're so fucking stupid," I snapped and his brows pulled together like he damn well knew that, but I didn't think he even understood it in the way I meant. I knotted my fingers in his hair, leaning up and staring him in the eyes. "You're the best man I know, the best, fucking stupidest, most frustrating man I know. Whether you're a professor, a convict, a fugitive, a power shamed Fae or all of the above, there isn't one thing you could be that wouldn't make me want you. But I just can't trust you."

"You still want me?" he asked like that was all he'd heard.

I wanted to fight and claw and scream to get through to him, but I just stood there trapped in the gaze of the man who'd captured my heart so completely that it barely even felt like it belonged to me anymore. It had never healed when he'd left. And now he was asking me to surrender for some finite amount of time, and the worst thing was that my heart wanted it too.

I pushed away all of the doubt and fear inside me over us and just took one sweet moment for myself, surrendering to this love and letting it consume me like fire. The second I pulled him closer, he groaned in desperation and my heart beat like powerful wings as his mouth fell against mine. I knew nothing was fixed between us, that it possibly couldn't ever be, but I'd craved him for so long and I couldn't think. I wanted it to be us again. Just one more time.

His tongue moved with mine and I felt the stars colliding somewhere above us as he put his hands on me, raking them up my back with a growl of need. His fingers dragged between my shoulder blades and I moaned, shivering all over from his firm and demanding touches. Phoenix fire sparked from my flesh and I couldn't control it as he grasped my hips and the heat of his chest moulded against my body.

I didn't dare break our kiss as he lifted me so I wrapped my legs around his waist. Little fires blazed in my periphery and his hand shot out to douse them with water before the whole place went up in flames. He sped across the room, knocking over a lamp as he crushed me to the wall and the wallpaper went up in blaze. He broke the kiss and slammed his hand to the wall, sending ice spilling up and away from us, coating the whole room and turning it into a shimmering winter wonderland.

"Oh shit," I breathed, looking at the mess we'd made of Gabriel's home.

"You can burn the house to the ground if you want, beautiful, I'll happily rebuild it brick by brick when you're done with me." He captured my chin, yanking me back to look at him and my breathing faltered as I fell into the endless depths of his eyes. The truth sat on my tongue, weighing it down as heavily as lead. That I'd never be done with him. I loved him too completely. In every minute of every hour, right down to the space between seconds.

This was a terrible idea with a million repercussions that I'd have to face tomorrow. But weren't all the best ideas that kind?

I gripped the back of his neck, drawing him toward me, my palm sliding down to his chest to feel the furious, desperate beating of his heart.

The whole world came crashing down around us, the roof shattering above and I cast an air shield with a scream as Orion clutched me to his chest and started running. Dragon fire spilled through the air, tearing across the room and ringing around us in a blaze that melted the furniture. Orion didn't slow as he ran at the flames, but the heat sweeping toward us told me he'd die if he tried to get through. I did the only thing I could think of to stop him, ripping his legs out from beneath him with a whip of air. He hit the ground and we tumbled toward the fire before I threw up a wall of air to stop us before we rolled into it.

Orion wrenched a pouch of stardust out of his pocket, tossing a pinch over us but it fell in a cascade of glitter around us without us going anywhere. "The wards aren't completely down," he cursed.

Debris tumbled down from above as a huge shadow blocked out the light of the moon and Lionel's Dragon form dropped out of the sky, landing on the shattered roof and glaring down at us, his jaws wide and fire flickering in the back of his throat. Panic bled through me as I cast air beneath us the same time Orion did, grabbing onto each other as we propelled ourselves over the flames. Lionel snapped his jaws at us and I blasted out a line of Phoenix fire at him before we hit the ground, making him rear away.

Orion lifted me up again and started running once more, blasting a window apart ahead of us and diving out of it. A huge wall of shadow stood in the sweeping vineyard ahead, ringing the entire property and trapping us in.

"No," I gasped.

Clara stood between the vines with a crazed smile on her lips and the awful Seer Vard stood just behind her.

"Now, my King!" he cried and Lionel released a huge blast of fire which crashed over our combined air shield.

I yelled in exertion as Orion and I threw more and more of our power into the dome surrounding us, the fire spilling everywhere until it was all I could see.

I acted fast, casting an illusion of the two of us standing in our place then blasted the ground apart as Orion helped to conceal the hole. He shot down into the tunnel I carved as I held onto his back just as the fire surrounding us fell away. The illusion wouldn't last long, but it might give us just long enough to get beyond the wards and stardust out of here. Lionel must have broken through them somehow, despite the strength of them. And my gut told me Clara had had a hand in it, her power unimaginable. It made me sick to think Vard had *seen* us here. That we actually thought we'd been safe.

The tunnel was completely unstable, collapsing in behind us as I blasted through the earth, casting a Faelight to see by as we moved faster and faster. One falter by either or us and we were done for.

A tremendous roar above ground told me Lionel was coming for us and an awful thundering, ripping sounded through the earth over our heads.

"Faster!" I screamed, clinging to Orion with one arm while tunnelling deeper, further.

Light spilled over us as the earth was cleaved apart above and tendrils of shadow clawed through it, digging us out.

I felt the tingle of magic against my body, the ward surely just ahead. But something wound around my waist, dragging me backwards and wrenching me above ground.

I was flung into the vineyard and I rolled at speed, the air knocked out of me as I crashed through the vines, softening the earth with my power a second too late. I got to my feet with my head spinning, not hesitating as I spotted Lionel in his Fae form, a dark robe wrapped around him as he raised his hands and the force of a hurricane blasted at me. I threw my own air against his, digging my heels in to stop him forcing me back, desperate to turn and look for Orion. But I couldn't take my eyes off of this monster.

Vard strode up behind him, glee twisting his features as he watched and whispered in Lionel's ear, giving him an advantage I couldn't counter. But I had to damn well try.

I held my shield up with one hand then cast Phoenix fire toward him with the other, a tunnel of flames racing away from me. Clara shot into his path, throwing out a swathe of shadow which swallowed up the fire before she was thrown backwards with a shriek.

"Fight me like Fae!" I roared at Lionel.

"Now, sire!" Vard barked then a whip of air slammed into my shield, cracking through it like a nut.

I cried out, blasting more Phoenix fire away from me as Clara shrouded Lionel in shadow. I couldn't see where any of my enemies were as I continued to throw my power at the Dragon King. Another whip of air caught my wrists, twisting them violently to the sides and I screamed as Lionel snapped every bone in my hands.

Orion suddenly crashed into me from the side, carrying me away from them once more as fast as he could possibly go.

"Heal me!" I gasped in a panic, unable to cast anything and he reached up to press his hand to my arm. His power washed into me and the bones started snapping back into place, but his magic was waning and fear hit me.

"Fuck," he growled.

He'd used too much magic tonight and he hadn't fed. I should never have let my guard down. I should have let him feed as soon as I'd replenished my own magic back at the house.

His power stuttered out and he put on a final burst of speed, giving everything to just getting us beyond the wards.

We reached the wall of shadow and I turned my hands to it, blasting out as much Phoenix fire as I could to carve a hole in it.

Something collided with Orion's back, knocking us down in a tangle of limbs and I groaned in pain as I was crushed beneath him. Clara dove on us with a cry of elation and something sharp slammed into my neck before I could turn my flames on her once more. The strength faded from my body as my cheek pressed into the damp earth and my heartbeat started to slow, my limbs as heavy as boulders.

A bare foot pressed against my side, kicking me over and I found myself looking up at Lionel as my body continued to shut down. Orion's hand brushed mine, but I couldn't turn my head to look and see if he was okay.

"Medusa venom," Clara announced with glee in her eyes. "Uncle Vard's idea. Isn't he a clever little Seer?"

Vard stepped into view, smiling proudly with his chest puffed out and hatred rippled through me.

"Your visions are finally paying off, Vard." Lionel smiled smugly but it turned into a sneer as his gaze dripped over me.

He reached down and panic made my blood run cold as I was sure he was going to take the Imperial Star from me. Instead, his fingers wrapped around my throat, his eyes filled with a promise of death. "Take one last look at the night sky, Gwendalina. The next time you see the stars, you'll be up there with them."

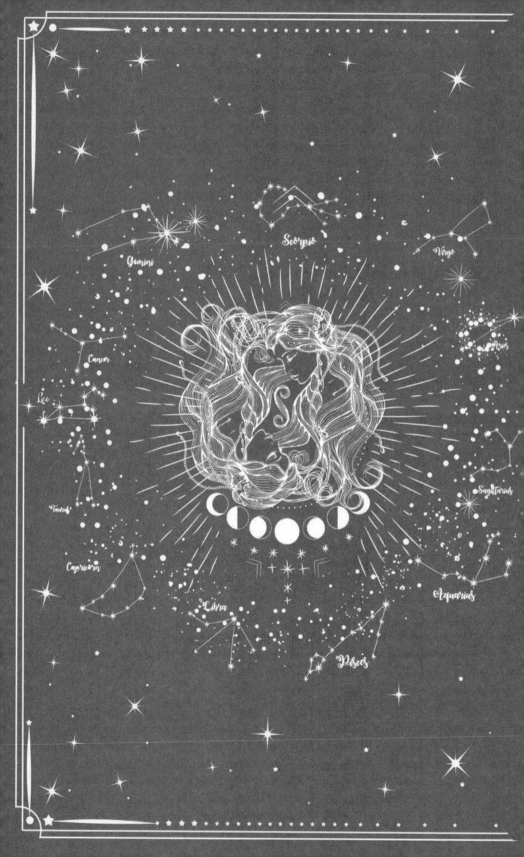

TORY

CHAPTER FORTY FOUR·

I sat on a chair to the side of the sweeping room where the party was being held, more than a little lost for what to do as the hours slipped by and I began to wonder if I'd been forgotten. Lionel had disappeared alongside Clara and Vard ages ago without any explanation, just telling me to wait here until he returned. So I was left to sit with my shadow bitch mask in place while the Heirs and Xavier made small talk and the Fae who had come to spend Christmas Eve with the King were left to their political schemes without him.

More than a few of the Fae here had approached me on and off, but I warded them away with flat looks and bored expressions. The stars only knew how I was ever supposed to win them back around to following me if we ever managed to take Lionel down. I could see what they thought of me - some vapid pawn he'd overpowered. But I'd show them. Before this was over, I'd make them see that nothing could tame me for long.

My gaze swept towards the huge clock on the wall just as it ticked onto midnight and my heart squeezed as a chime rang out and the guests all paused in their political scheming to cheer for Christmas Day.

This was the first time I was ever going to wake up on Christmas without Darcy. For as long as I could remember, we'd slept in bed together on Christmas Eve and she'd woken me up, bouncing around like an excited little puppy dog even though we didn't have presents to open or shit like that.

Santa tended to forget foster kids who no one wanted. We'd always managed to get something for each other though - Darcy usually spent weeks hand making me a gift and because I sucked at stuff like that, I just stole shit she needed like good socks or new underwear. One time when we were fifteen, I'd stolen her this beautiful navy coat right off of a mannequin in a store window. It was lined and soft and seriously warm which was exactly what for the long walk to school in the winter. But she only got to wear it once because our foster mother at the time saw it on her and flipped the fuck out, accusing us of thieving and threatening to call the police and social services on us. She didn't though. She just started wearing the coat herself and let Darcy walk to school shivering every day. Fucking bitch.

I was so lost in my thoughts that I didn't even notice Darius walking up behind me until he leaned down to speak in my ear, his stubble grazing my jaw and making me crave so much more from him than just that.

"Such a beautiful girl shouldn't be sitting on her own at Christmas," Darius murmured and I turned to look at him as he pulled up a chair beside me and placed two glasses of champagne on the table.

"Trying to get me drunk?" I teased, keeping my expression neutral in case anyone was looking our way.

"Never," he disagreed, tipping back his own glass and leaning back in his chair as he surveyed me and casually flicked a silencing bubble up to surround us. "I hate seeing you all alone at things like this."

"It's a travesty that I'm not dancing on a table while trying not to puke," I agreed, keeping my face as neutral as I could manage in case anyone was paying us any attention. "You owe me a proper night out after this is all over."

"'This' being my father's reign of terror and you having to constantly pretend to be his little pet?" he asked with a note of bitterness to his tone.

"That's the one," I agreed. "Shouldn't be long now."

Darius snorted a humourless laugh and I almost smiled.

"What are the chances of me stealing you away for an hour tomorrow?" he asked.

"You want to sneak off to some field in the middle of nowhere and see if we can battle the stars for a hook up again?" I teased.

"Well, I was going to suggest Darcy sneaks into Orion's summerhouse and the four of us have a mini Christmas celebration, but your offer does have a certain appeal."

I bit my lip as a smile tugged at the corners of my mouth and Darius gave me a look that said he'd fucking destroy me given half a chance. And if it was my choice I'd happily give him that chance. But the stars were a pain in my ass like always and I was going to be spending the night in his father's bed instead. *Gross.*

The double doors on the far side of the room banged open dramatically and Lionel strode in with Clara and Vard either side of him, a smirk playing around his lips that said wherever he'd been he'd been up to no good. Stella scuttled in a step behind them, trying not to look like a butt hurt bitch over it, but I'd spent enough time around her to see through that shit. She hated that he'd traded her in for her daughter. And I mean, she had a point – it was pretty mortifying and totally puke worthy. But she was hungering for that place on his arm and even while she tried not to let it show, I could see through her bullshit.

"I hope you've all had a wonderful evening," Lionel called, opening his arms to encompass everyone in the room with that statement. "But it's getting late and I'm sure you all want to get back to your homes for Christmas tomorrow."

The music was cut off abruptly, and I exchanged a look with Darius before I could stop myself, wondering what had prompted this sudden end to the evening. I mean, sure it was late and all, but Lionel had been missing for a good hour or more and it seemed strange to reappear just to tell everyone to fuck off.

The guests hurried to leave, the other Heirs waving at us as they followed their families out. Darius straightened in his chair as Lionel cut through the crowd, ignoring everyone else and aiming straight for us.

"Still pining after my Guardian I see, boy?" Lionel asked, cutting Darius a look of disdain as he moved to stand over us.

"I think he loooooves her," Clara cooed, hopping up onto the table and placing her bare foot right on top of a cheesecake that had been left there without seeming to mind that at all.

"*Love,*" Lionel scoffed, his upper lip peeling back. "What a weak concept."

"Isn't love supposed to conquer all?" Darius asked casually, not seemed to care at all that he was baiting the monster.

The last of the guests filed out and Vard closed the double doors before leaning back against them and watching us with a hungry expression on his face that could only spell trouble.

"Let's put that to the test then, shall we?" Lionel asked, flicking his wrist so that a spear of shadows bolted from his hand and struck Darius in the chest, knocking him backwards out of his chair and crashing to the floor.

I leapt to my feet with a gasp of alarm but managed to stop myself from moving any further than that as I felt Lionel's eyes fix on me.

"What is it, Roxanya?" he asked in a soft tone which urged me to look his way.

But I knew my fear for Darius would be written all too plainly across my face and my heart thundered as I kept my eyes on him instead, watching as he writhed on the floor beneath the torture the shadows were inflicting on him.

"I asked you a question, girl," Lionel snarled and I reached for the shadows as a jolt of fear spilled through my body. I dove into them head first and let them consume me before I turned to look at him with darkness spilling across my vision.

My lips curled up into a cruel grin as he watched me and I moved a step closer to him, trying to think of the answer he wanted while shivering from the kiss of darkness inside me.

"I was just watching his pain," I said, a touch of amusement colouring my words even while they burned my tongue with bile.

Lionel considered me for several more seconds, reaching out to clasp my chin between his thumb and forefinger and I looked straight back into his eyes as he assessed me.

"Don't ever hesitate when I ask something of you again," he growled.

"No, my King," I agreed.

His gaze narrowed on me then he broke a smile which made my heart lighten because of the damn bond, but also made me relax as his attention moved off of me.

"Get up," Lionel snapped at Darius as he withdrew the shadows from his body and his son rolled over onto all fours, panting to regain his breath.

I was desperate to run to him, hating Lionel, Clara, Stella and Vard with a fury that was unrivalled by any other feeling I'd ever succumbed to. One of these days I would go full Phoenix on their asses and burn them all to soot. But until then, I hated myself with almost as much ferocity for having to stand by and watch them hurt so many people.

Darius gripped the edge of the table as he hauled himself to his feet, his teeth bared at his father and smoke spilling between his lips.

"You're a fucking coward," Darius snarled. "You hide behind the shadows and the girl you bonded to yourself against her will and you refuse to fight me like Fae. Everyone here knows it's because I would beat you. And you're so fucking terrified of that day coming that you just keep finding more barriers to place between us. But one day, I'll break through and prove your fears correct."

Lionel snarled right back, the pungent scent of his smoke slipping from him as he stepped up close behind me and placed both hands on my shoulders, his grip bruising as he clasped me tightly.

"I think it's time you go to bed, boy," Lionel purred and I frowned as he failed to do a single thing to reprimand Darius for speaking out. "You're clearly drunk and the rest of us are tired."

Darius looked like he wanted to argue against that but I shot him a pleading look, begging him not to. I couldn't bear to stand by and watch Lionel torture him and I was guessing he understood what I was asking because he muttered some choice curses and stalked away from us.

"Escort my son back to his room, Stella," Lionel commanded. "He's clearly drunk and needs some time to sleep it off."

"Yes, my King," she cooed, smiling sweetly before trotting after Darius towards the door.

Vard stepped aside so that Darius and Stella could leave the room and Lionel turned me to look at him as the door closed once more, smiling like a doting parent as he ran a finger down the side of my cheek.

"Such a clever little thing, aren't you, Roxanya?" he asked softly, stroking me again and I hated how much I liked him praising me like that and how I enjoyed the heat of his hand on my skin.

"She's not as clever as me," Clara muttered, but Lionel ignored her, smiling at me before taking my hand and leading me towards the door.

I walked at his side as we approached Vard and he smirked at me with his blood red shadow eye seeming to flare with darkness for a moment, making my stomach knot with tension.

"I'm still the favourite aren't I, Daddy?" Clara whined as she hurried after us and I huffed irritably, letting the stupid bond guide my reactions as Lionel led me through the palace towards his chambers.

"Do you still wish to be the favourite, Roxanya?" he asked in a low voice, leaning close to murmur in my ear, his hot breath washing over my nose and making my stomach roil.

"Yes," I forced myself to say, even the draw of the bond not making it any easier to utter that word.

"Then perhaps you're in luck."

I almost tore my hand from his grasp at that suggestion, managing to stop myself from doing it but still flinching enough to make him cock his head at me as he noticed.

I drew on the shadows as I fought not to react, hoping he would dismiss the involuntary motion as nothing more than a muscle spasm.

We started up the spiralling staircase to his chambers and my heart pounded harder with every step we took towards the top of the tower. I listened to Clara's shrieks of protest over him giving me more attention than her with a desperate hope that they'd be enough to make him give in to her.

"It is time, Your Highness," Vard announced as we reached his chambers and I looked around at him in confusion as Lionel tugged me into the massive room at the top of the King's Tower.

Though I probably should have been relieved to have the creep follow us inside. Lionel wasn't into voyeurism as far as I was aware, so I doubted he was planning to fuck anyone with Vard in the room.

"Daddyyyy," Clara whined loudly as Lionel moved me to stand in the centre of the room before stepping back to look at me with a critical eye.

"Clara, if you do not stay silent and learn your place then I will be forced to punish you," Lionel growled. "And not in the way you enjoy."

Clara looked about ready to pitch a fit and my eyes tracked her movements as she turned and ran to the bed, flinging herself down on it dramatically as she sobbed.

"Remove your dress, Roxanya," Lionel growled, his gaze fixed firmly on me as he ignored Clara altogether.

"What?" I balked, my gaze slipping to Vard as he took up position by the door once again, a cruel smirk twisting his features.

"Your dress. Don't you wish to please me?" Lionel challenged and I had to fight not to let my mouth fall open as I just stared at him blankly for way too long and smoke plumed between his teeth. "Is there some reason that I should know of for why you suddenly seem reluctant to show me your love?" he pressed and I quickly shook my head.

I reached for the straps on my golden dress and hurriedly tugged them down my shoulders without answering. Underwear I could cope with, but if he tried to lay a fucking hand on me then I was going to go full Phoenix, burn his cock off then run for the freaking hills. Cover be damned - I wasn't going to fuck this motherfucking asshole no matter what happened.

I dropped my dress and it slid from my body, leaving me standing in my stilettos and black underwear as Vard chuckled like some gross old lech in the corner of the room.

"Good girl," Lionel purred. "Now come here."

I hesitated a beat before walking towards him, Phoenix fire lighting a path through my veins and promising me safety even as fear lit me up from the inside out.

The shadows slid over my skin as I fought to keep my mask in place externally and I stilled in front of Lionel as I waited to see where this was going.

He reached out casually, pushing his fingers into my hair and shoving the pins free that had been styling it as he roughly combed them through it like he was hunting for something.

I stayed still, focusing on the fact that I'd never seen him do anything like this to Clara before fucking her and trying to calm my thrashing heart.

"What is it?" I breathed as he pulled his hands back, his gaze sliding over my thin underwear critically.

"Turn around," he commanded coldly and I forced myself to swallow my complaints as I turned my back on him.

My hands curled into fists which ached to burst into flame as I stood staring through the window at the star filled sky beyond while I waited to find out what this was about.

A sharp prick stung my thigh and I gasped in alarm as the fire in my body shrank away like someone had blown it out and my Phoenix fell away from me into the dark.

"I had to be certain you didn't have the antidote on you before I gave you a fresh dose of suppressant," he supplied, tossing the needle aside as I realised too late that I was in serious trouble.

Lionel's hand caught my throat as I tried to lurch away, his grip tightening as he yanked me back against his chest and I cried out in panic.

I tried to call on my magic to fight him off, but I was overwhelmed with horror at the idea of hurting him as the Guardian bond on my arm burned in outrage at the suggestion.

"So, so clever," he sneered in my ear, his hand squeezing my throat until I couldn't draw breath at all and even then I couldn't force my body to fight back against him.

Someone grabbed my hand and I wheeled my gaze to my left, spotting Vard there and managing to blast him with fire magic before he could snap the cuff he was holding around my wrist.

Lionel snarled angrily at my back, squeezing my throat so tightly that spots began to swim over my vision and my high heels scrambled uselessly against the wooden floor. I brought my hand up to clasp his arm where he held me, but I couldn't even force myself to try and tear his hand off of me as the bond forced me to let him do this.

The stars beyond the window seemed to mock me as the darkness drew in even closer and I felt the magic restricting cuffs snap closed around my wrists just as I was certain I was going to black out.

But before I could escape into oblivion, Lionel threw me away from him with the full strength of his Dragon.

My forehead slammed into the corner of the nightstand on my way down and the pain of it almost blinded me as I crashed to the floor, gasping for breath with blood streaming down my face.

Clara cried out in victory, jumping from the bed before kicking me in the side with her bare foot and sending more pain splintering through my body.

She kicked me twice more before I managed to catch my breath enough to try and fight back.

I caught her ankle as she aimed another kick my way, yanking hard and unbalancing her so that she fell to the floor with a shriek of rage.

She dove at me and I punched her in her stupid shadow twat face with a snarl of fury for everything that her and the men in this room had done to me. Something cracked beneath the force of my blow and she screamed in pain before driving the shadows into me like a thousand knives peeling my flesh from my bones all at once, blinding me in agony.

My back slammed hard against something as I screamed and when she finally withdrew the shadows from my flesh, I found myself strapped to the chair from my nightmares, bloody and panting and filled with a fear so pure it was paralysing.

"My foolish son has been worming his way back into your heart, hasn't he?" Lionel sneered as he stood over me and I lifted my chin before spitting right in his face. It was over now anyway. He knew. So fuck him and fuck this bullshit half life I'd been living beneath him.

Lionel flinched as blood and saliva ran down his face then growled at me as he grasped my throat again in an iron clad grip. He reached down to score a line of fire across my thigh with a single finger, burning through the concealment spell I'd placed on my skin to hide my tattoo.

"How sweet," he purred as he read the words marking me as Darius's before wrapping his hand over the ink and drawing Dragon fire to his palm.

I couldn't help but scream as the ink was destroyed alongside the flesh on my thigh and the sickening scent of burning skin filled the air. When he finally withdrew his hand, I almost passed out from the pain of it.

Vard drew close behind him as Clara's laughter filled the air and my gaze caught on the ruby necklace she was wearing. The one that Darius had given me which she twisted between her fingers to taunt me with.

Tremors racked my body as I tried to remember everything Max had taught me about evading Cyclops invasion. But with so much pain in my flesh it was almost impossible to force my thoughts to align enough to prepare for it.

Vard licked his lips as his mismatched eyes slid together and Lionel grasped my chin as he forced me to turn and look at his Seer.

I gritted my teeth and forced my mind to lock all of the secrets I was keeping away in the dark. He wasn't going to find them. I'd die before I gave my sister up, my brother, my friends. I would keep everything we'd been doing to fight back against this monster secret and conceal the location of the Imperial Star no matter what. He wasn't going to break me. But he was definitely going to try.

The last thing I heard before I fell into the chasm of Vard's power was Lionel's voice thick and heavy in my ear. "I think it's time you were reminded of who you truly love, Roxanya."

DARIUS

CHAPTER FORTY FIVE

I sat eating my breakfast at the huge dining table beside Xavier, waiting for Roxy to arrive while my gut knotted with tension over how late they all were to appear.

I wasn't sure how much longer I was going to be able to go on with this ruse. I hated it. Fucking loathed it. And we still hadn't made a single bit of progress towards finding anything that would free her from the bond my father had placed upon her.

The last time I'd spoken to Orion about it he'd suggested we figure out a way to trap her and Clara somewhere, leaving my father vulnerable and them unable to run to his aid so that I could finally force him to face me like a true Fae. And I had to agree.

The only problem with doing that would be in actually tricking the two of them and managing to hold them for long enough to enact it. We wouldn't even be able to tell Roxy our plan or the bond would force her to thwart it and the idea of locking her up somewhere without her even knowing why made me feel all kinds of uncomfortable. But I knew she'd understand after it was done.

Clara was the main issue. She never left Father's side and seemed to have no desires beyond pleasing him, so trapping her was going to be damn near impossible to orchestrate without him realising what was going on. And while he could still call on the Nymphs to protect him too, we really needed to make sure he was alone somewhere and unable to call on them in time to save himself.

There wouldn't be any mistakes this time. We couldn't afford for it to go wrong again.

I'd been calling Orion repeatedly while sitting here too, wanting to hear more about how everything had gone with Diego's hat, but his Atlas was just going straight to voicemail. And thanks to the fact that I'd snagged a bottle of rum and taken it back to my room to drink myself into oblivion after the party last night, I'd woken up too late to head over to the summerhouse in person.

Father had made it clear he expected us here for Christmas breakfast at eight, but it was almost nine now and he still hadn't arrived.

The door finally opened as Jenkins pushed it wide for my father with a simpering bow and the man who had sired me strode into the room. But instead of Roxy walking in by his side like she did every morning that she stayed here in the palace, he came alone. Even Clara was absent, and the strangeness of that fact put me on edge immediately.

"Oh no, boys, don't stand on account of your father," he said disdainfully as neither I nor Xavier made the slightest attempt to move from our positions sitting over our plates of food. "I'm just the man who gifted you life, who brought you into this world, who raised you to be strong and fearless and take what is yours like a true Fae. I'm only the one who gave you the shadows and elevated you above all others. Just the man who has assured that you will be king in my place one day, Darius."

"Where's Roxy?" I asked, ignoring his bullshit rant. I hadn't asked for a single one of those things from him and he knew it.

Xavier straightened beside me and put a hand on my shoulder in warning, but I didn't care if I was punished for my insolence. I needed to see my girl.

Father clucked his tongue and sighed heavily as he moved to take a seat directly opposite me.

"Merry Christmas, Darius," he said with a cruel smile. "Wouldn't you like to know what your gift is?"

A growl built in my throat as I met his gaze, the Dragon in me shifting uncomfortably like it had already figured out what he was talking about even while I stayed rooted in my position, having no idea.

"I don't want anything from you," I replied but his smile only grew as he slowly took his Atlas from his pocket and placed it on the table before sliding it towards me.

"Last night was very interesting for me," he said casually, brushing some invisible speck of dirt from his cuff before levelling me with that hungry look again. "So many lies brought to light. It got me thinking about the things I need to do to secure my hold on the throne."

"Like what?" Xavier breathed and Father shot him a disgusted look like he'd only just realised his second son was here at all.

"Do not speak unless you are spoken to, horse," he snarled before his gaze flicked back to me.

"Don't talk to him like that," I growled, my eyes flickering to reptilian slits and back as the beast in me hungered for his blood.

"It's fine," Xavier insisted, gripping my arm like he thought I might lunge across the table at the scum sitting before me, but I hadn't entirely lost control yet.

"You would do well to remember that I am not above filicide. The unsightly specimen beside you is not and never will be an Heir of mine. He may have my blood running thick and fast in his veins, but his worth has been lost with this twisted curse sent from the stars. No Heir of mine will pass on equine DNA. You are just lucky that you are my son, Xavier, because believe me, when I had it checked, I was hoping to find out you weren't. And then I would have drowned you like the runt you clearly are."

I slammed my fist down on the table with a loud bang as I pushed out of my chair and growled at him, a clear challenge in my gaze.

"You don't speak about him like that," I snarled as Father surveyed me with a wild glint in his eyes.

"You, on the other hand, Darius are a truly fine specimen, aren't you?" he commented, looking over my huge frame and smiling to himself like he could claim all responsibility for everything I was and call it his own accomplishment.

"Apologise to Xavier," I demanded, but I may as well have been talking to myself because he just went on with his fucking monologue.

"Tall, broad, stronger than any other Fae physically and magically, ferocious and bloodthirsty, single minded and cruel," he listed as if those words could sum up the total of what I was. "And above all, *powerful*. Almost powerful enough to rival me in fact."

"You and I both know I outmatch you," I said in a dangerous tone as I leaned forward over the table. "You'd be dead by my hand if you hadn't used Clara to save your miserable life."

"Power comes in many forms, son," he replied with a shrug of his broad shoulders, not seeming the least bit concerned about me leaning over him with his death in my eyes. "The sooner you admit that, the sooner you will grow into the man I need you to be and stop with this foolish nobility. We're Fae, not field mice. We see what we want and we take it if we can. The strongest naturally rise to the top. You cannot deny that is who you are through and through. It is why you fight me so hard after all. You want things that I own - my crown, my power...even pretty little Roxanya Vega who stole your black heart and corrupted your dark soul with that crippling curse."

"What curse?" I asked with a sneer, not buying into his bullshit for a moment.

"Love," he replied simply like it was a dirty world that stained his tongue. "It's why I took her, you know? Because you wanted her so much. The Fae in me saw how precious she was to you and I took her because I could. Because I'm more powerful than you, which is true for one single, undeniable reason."

"What's that?" I asked.

"You're debilitated by your emotions. Your love for her makes you weak. If you truly wanted to kill me, you could have done it already - you only have to cut through her to get to me. But you won't, will you?"

"Never," I agreed, not bothering to try and hide how I felt about her because he already knew anyway.

"Pity," he said with a sigh. "But I'll burn that weakness out of you in time. Aren't you going to open your gift?" He pointed at the Atlas which lay forgotten between us on the table and I growled as I looked down at the black screen with a play button illuminated in the centre of it.

"What is that?" I asked, wondering again where the hell Roxy was and fear knotted in my gut.

"A reminder," Father shrugged. "Of who I am and what I am capable of. You may need to work to keep your emotions in check when you play it though - if you lay so much as a claw on me in reaction to it there will be dire consequences for your brother."

I glanced at Xavier who still sat in his chair, glaring at our father with his chin raised defiantly like he was willing to take whatever punishment he chose to dole out. But I refused to be the architect of his pain.

I snatched the Atlas from the table and hit the button to play the video. Roxy's screams filled the quiet room the moment I did and the camera moved to show her strapped to a wooden chair in the centre of my father's chambers. She was in her underwear, her flesh carved up with countless cuts and stab wounds and her brow was lined with sweat that made her dark hair cling to her face.

"Again," Father's voice came, making it clear he was the one recording this and Clara shot forward from the corner of the room with a bloody knife in hand before slamming it into Roxy's stomach.

Horror washed through me in a wave so potent that I couldn't draw in another breath as I stared at the images, my chest seizing up and my muscles locking with fury and a desperate desire to go to her, rescue her, go back in fucking time and stop this from happening.

Clara stabbed her again and again and she screamed in agony before Vard moved to stand before her, his single Cyclops eye boring into her tear filled gaze as he licked his lips hungrily.

"Who freed you from the shadows?" he purred, his voice slick and oily and turning my stomach.

"Fuck you," Roxy hissed between her teeth, panting heavily as she began to bleed out and she sagged against the restraints holding her in place on the chair. "I freed myself."

Clara backhanded her so hard she fell back against the wood with another curse of pain and the video was cut off just as my father demanded more.

"We had a rather long night," he said, stifling a yawn as I fought with everything I had not to shift and attack him even while my flesh trembled with the need to destroy him for this. I had to hear him out, because he still had her and I didn't know where Vard and Clara were or what the fuck might happen to her if I leapt across this table right now and ripped his miserable head from his shoulders.

"You're a fucking monster," Xavier breathed, but he was ignored entirely.

"I announced a new law this morning," Father went on like this was just a normal conversation to have over breakfast. "Fae no longer need to wait until graduation to get married. I'm done waiting around for you to fall into line, Darius, so I'm making this simple. Today you will marry Mildred and then you will fuck her. You will fuck her day and night until you put an Heir in her belly to secure my legacy and the purity of our bloodline."

"Mildred?" I choked out, trying to make my thoughts align as they stayed fixed on my girl and the desperate need in me to get to her and save her from this fucking animal.

"Yes. I don't care what you have to use for motivation to get your cock hard for that troll of a girl, but believe me you'll figure it out. Perhaps you'll get lucky and she will fall pregnant quickly for you and give you nine months reprieve before you'll need to put another Heir in her belly."

"I'm not marrying her," I hissed. "I won't. I love Roxy and I'm never going to be with anyone else."

Father sighed heavily like I was testing his patience. "You will. Because every night that oaf isn't pregnant is another night your sweet Roxanya gets to spend like that." He pointed at the Atlas in my hands and I tossed it away from me in disgust so that it thumped down onto the table. "And if that's not motivation enough, then Vard has been hungering for more of a taste of her, so perhaps I'll start sending her to his bed as well."

"You can't," Xavier breathed in horror and Father just huffed a breath like his mere presence was offensive.

"Of course I can. I'm the King. I can do whatever the fuck I want. But I can be kind, too. In reward for you putting an Heir inside the Canopus troll, when I find it, I'll use the Imperial Star to stop the heavens from colliding every time you are alone with Roxanya. You can have her too, in reward for good behaviour that is."

"Have her?" I asked in confusion, my brain struggling to keep up with this fucking mess that had unfolded all around us.

"Phoenixes are useful and there is deep power in her blood. I think it is worth allowing crossbreeding in this one circumstance. Any children you sire with her can be Guardian bonded to the Heirs you make with Mildred. This way you can have it all. I think I'm being more than fair."

"Fair?" I balked. "You can't seriously believe-"

"Enough!" Father roared suddenly, the air vibrating all around us as his power flared with his rage. "I won't have any more complaints or insolence from you, Darius. You have a wedding to attend and if you don't go through with it, I will personally carve Roxanya's heart from her chest and lay it at your fucking feet."

He stood abruptly and stormed from the room, throwing the door open wide and letting it crash against the wall as he left me there, drowning in fear and the most suffocating realisation that I was going to have to do this. There was no way out of it.

"Darius?" Xavier's voice seemed to come from far away and I couldn't even bring myself to look at him until he started shaking me, barking an order at me to fucking listen to him. "There has to be some way out of this," he insisted passionately. "I'll go and get Lance. We'll figure it out. We will. Promise me you won't give up."

Words failed me for several long seconds and in my mind all I could see was the girl with the long brunette hair and eyes which could peer straight into my dark soul without flinching away from it. She was the owner of all that I was and I knew I'd make any sacrifice I had to to save her.

Movement by the door drew my attention and I looked up as Vard strode in, followed by a group of servants who were carrying suit bags and styling products and my gut lurched as I realised this really was happening.

"His Majesty requests you arrive at the chapel within half an hour for the ceremony," Vard said politely, combing his fingers through his long, greasy black hair as he strode closer and I stood to face him.

Xavier muttered something about needing the bathroom and scurried from the room, tossing me a look that said he was going to find Lance and though I desperately hoped that my best friend might be able to come up with some way out of this for us, I didn't hold out much hope.

Vard smirked cruelly as he shifted, his eyes merging into one as he tried to draw me under his power. I didn't resist, knowing I had to comply with everything Father commanded until I figured out how to rescue Roxy from him.

"Your bride is beautiful," his voice spoke inside my head, pushing my mind onto an image of Mildred with her undercut jaw, moustache and seriously masculine features, not to mention her vile personality. She was ugly right down to her core and everyone knew it. But Vard managed to seek out images of Roxy within my mind and he tried to merge the two like he seriously thought he could manipulate me into feeling desire for that hag.

He kept nudging inside my brain to try and make me more compliant for a few more minutes, but the moment he withdrew, the Phoenix Kiss Roxy had gifted me flared to life beneath my skin and burned all of his manipulation out of me.

Fuck him for thinking he could just make me forget my girl and want that fucking bitch Mildred. But the worst thing was that it didn't even matter that he'd failed. I was still going to marry her. I had to. Even though it broke me and I feared it would break Roxy too, I had to do it.

Father hadn't been lying. I knew him too well to think he'd value her over his desire to force me into line. He'd kill her alright. He'd probably force me to watch too. And I couldn't allow that. Even if the cost of protecting her meant betraying her like this.

I stayed silent as I let the servants dress me for my wedding in a perfectly tailored black suit with a black dress shirt and cravat beneath it. Someone styled my hair and another even laced my fucking shoes and I just let them do it, not giving a shit about any of it and just wishing Lance would appear with some answer I couldn't see.

But when Xavier returned, his eyes were wide with desperation and as he hurried over to me, I found I already knew what he was going to say before the words left his lips.

"He's not there. It doesn't look like he's been there all night. Do you think Father would have done something to him?"

"Of course he has," I growled, rubbing my thumb over the Libra brand on my left arm and wishing that Lance could feel it via our connection even though I knew it was pointless.

Xavier looked utterly crestfallen and I just closed my eyes, trying to pretend that none of this was really happening while racking my brain for any idea that might help my girl.

"Time to go," Vard commanded and my eyes snapped open as I levelled a glare on him that would have seen weaker men piss themselves.

"One of these days, I'll rip you open and tear your intestines out," I swore to him. "And then I'll hang you up by them and let the crows finish the job."

Vard's eyes glazed over with a vision and the way his face paled let me know that he'd just *seen* a path to a future where I made good on that promise. And I really hoped it came to pass.

While he tried to fight off the fear that flickered over his features, I turned and strode from the room. I knew where the fucking chapel was and I wasn't going to be dragged there like some snivelling coward.

Xavier ran to meet my pace, a pained whinny spilling from his throat as he tried to catch my eye but I just stayed focused on my destination. I had no choice. Father had set this trap too well.

We made it through the palace quickly and I stepped out into the fresh snowfall beyond the doors to the rear of the building before heading away to the west of the grounds where the chapel lay.

For a moment I just looked at the snow, thinking of how Roxy had told me her only Christmas tradition was a snowball fight with Darcy and remembering the way she'd laughed with me when we'd wrestled in the snow exactly a year ago in the grounds of this very place.

I should have told her then how much I wanted her. I should have been a true Fae and owned up to all the shit I'd put her through and just told her how much I admired her, hungered for her, needed her.

But I'd known I wasn't good enough for her. Even then I'd known it, so rather than just tell her how I felt I'd hidden it. And look where that had gotten us.

I'm so fucking sorry, baby.

My heart was thumping to this horribly final rhythm that felt like a fucking death march as I walked towards my fate and all I could do was keep walking.

The chapel was set on the edge of the river which wound through this part of the grounds. There was a huge oak tree beside the beautiful stone building which was decked in fresh snow like everything else. It would have been stunning if I wasn't here for such a fucked up reason.

Someone pulled the doors wide for me as I arrived and Xavier snorted in distress as we stepped into the pretty little building.

There were six stained glass windows running along either side of the chapel, each with a different zodiac sign represented and my gaze snagged on the Gemini twins for a moment as my heart twisted sharply at the thought of what I was about to do.

The minister was already waiting for me before the altar and I took in his watery eyed face and white hair before dismissing him. He was just another tool my father was wielding against me.

Father rose from a seat in the front pew and my heart leapt as he tugged Roxy up beside him, yanking her to his side as he gave me a look that said he knew he'd won.

It was only us in here, and I wasn't sure if that was because he hadn't invited anyone else or if he just wanted a moment to twist the knife in my gut before letting them in.

Roxy's face was pale and I found fear and pain in her big eyes, the echoes of what he'd done to her last night still lingering even though he'd healed her now. He'd put her in a white dress just to fucking mock me and the way the lace clung to her body made me ache for this to be some other reality. For it to be me and her standing here alone while I promised her everything I had to give.

She was breath taking to the point of pain and looking at her felt like there was a knife carving right through my heart because she would always be mine and could never be mine.

"Roxy," I breathed, looking into her eyes and trying to convey everything I was feeling to her without words.

I wanted to rip her from his arms, drag her away with me and just run and run until we were so lost that no one could ever find us again.

"Darius, I'm sorry," she began and I was relieved to see he hadn't managed to crush her with the shadows this time, but that just meant she was feeling every bit of pain he doled out to her.

"Drink this, Roxanya," Father commanded, holding out a vile of red liquid and making her take it into her hand.

"What is that?" I growled, wanting to snatch it away from her and throw it as far as I could.

"Drink it or I'll kill Xavier," Father added casually and I growled loudly as I stepped between him and my brother who whinnied in fright but still stood firm with me.

"It's okay, Darius," she insisted even though we both knew it wasn't.

I reached out to snatch it, but I wasn't fast enough to stop Roxy from unstoppering the bottle and drinking the contents down.

"What was that?" I yelled, not caring if the fucking minister was watching or not.

"Just a little essence of autumn bloom. So long as she drinks the spring shine elixir I have prepared within half an hour it won't be fatal. I wanted to be sure you didn't get any theatrical ideas about making some grand gesture during the ceremony," Father said casually like he hadn't just forced her to drink a deadly potion.

I shook my head, trying to deny that this was seriously fucking happening. Spring shine elixir took four days to brew and I didn't know of anywhere that I could find some faster than that. He'd stolen the last inch of hope I'd been holding onto thinking I might find some way out of this.

"Cheer up, Darius," Father said, his gaze flicking over me, assessing me like he was absorbing all of my pain. "I'll give you two minutes with Roxanya to say what you need to before the rest of the guests arrive and then I won't hear any more of this foolishness. If you wish to have her to yourself again after that then get an Heir in your bride and learn to behave yourself."

He gave Roxy a shove towards me and I caught her face between my hands, creating a silencing bubble around us as my mind whirled with a desperate desire to find some way out of this.

"Tell me what to do, baby," I breathed, looking into her green eyes, hoping she might have thought of something I hadn't.

She swallowed thickly and shook her head. "There isn't anything," she breathed, a tear slipping down her cheek as she looked up at me. "I'm sorry, Darius. I don't want you to have to do this for me."

"I would do anything for you," I growled fiercely, swiping the tear from her cheek as it felt like my entire chest was caving in and I tried to linger in this moment forever, never wanting it to end and for the future I couldn't escape to come to pass.

"I'm yours," she breathed, her mouth touching mine with her words. "Whatever you have to do...even if Mildred really does have your-"

"I can't be with her like that," I growled. "I can't be with anyone but you. It would fucking kill me, Roxy."

She smiled weakly, reaching up to hold my cheek in her palm as her other hand fisted my shirt over my heart.

"You're mine where it counts, Darius. And I'm yours. Nothing can change that."

Her lips met mine and I tasted her tears and my grief between us for the sweetest, most painful moment I'd ever known.

Something heavy knocked into my leg and I cursed as pain shot through the limb, breaking away from Roxy as I stumbled back.

I looked down at the fallen lectern which had hit me as the minister gasped his apologies for somehow knocking it over.

But it hadn't been him. Not really. That was the fucking stars stealing her from me again and as Father tore her away and pushed her down into the pew at the front of the chapel, I knew that we were never going to truly be allowed to be together. And the fact of that coupled with the knowledge that I couldn't protect

565

her broke something inside me that hurt so much I couldn't fucking breathe.

Xavier caught my arm, squeezing tightly as he tried to reassure me and the minister directed me to stand to the side of the aisle to await my bride. My fucking bride. What the hell had I done to the stars to deserve this? Were they really that pissed about me and Roxy managing to be together despite their best efforts to keep us apart that they felt I deserved this fate? On fucking Christmas? Who the hell would do something this fucked up on Christmas?

Clara, Stella and Vard entered the chapel amongst the few guests Father had invited, alongside a handful of his favourite Dragons and my heart fell as I realised he hadn't even invited the Heirs and Councillors. They had no idea this was happening to me. And that was the very last hope for help I'd been holding out on.

When everyone was in their seats, the door swung open once more and Mildred's unmistakable frame darkened the doorway.

She was wearing a voluminous white dress and thankfully had a veil pulled down to cover her mismatched features, but it wasn't much comfort. I was still going to have to lift that thing and look upon her star-damned face as I swore to be her fucking husband.

Fuck only knew how I was supposed to get an Heir in her belly. But if I didn't figure it out then Roxy's suffering may as well have come from my own hand. And despite what she said, I knew this would break us in ways we couldn't repair. We might still own each other but if I had a child with that monstrous girl how could Roxy ever look at me the same way?

Mildred took her sweet time walking up the aisle, almost falling out of her high heels more than once before stopping at my side.

She leaned towards me like she expected me to lift her veil, but I just stood there, scowling, giving no shits if everyone could see how much I didn't want to marry this fucking woman. I felt like I was rooted in place with an iron rod through my spine, no choice but to follow through on this twisted fate while every inch of my being begged the stars for a different fate. But the heavens had forsaken me a long time ago and it was clear they weren't done punishing me yet.

Mildred giggled and lifted it herself, grinning broadly at me and revealing the brown lipstick she'd smeared across her mouth and teeth. I had no damn idea why she had decided to start taking Faeroids or when but the effect they'd had on her body was beyond grotesque. What was to say she could even get pregnant with all of that shit affecting her so much?

My dick was going to shrivel up inside my body before it would ever end up inside this fucking specimen. She batted her spiky eyelashes at me and I shuddered as I looked away from her, my gaze finding Roxy as I spilled a thousand silent apologies into the air that hung between us while the ceremony began.

The ringing in my ears grew too loud for me to focus on the words that were spoken to me as the minister read out the vows and promises and I only jolted out of my reverie when he nudged me to make me clasp Mildred's hand for the binding.

Her hairy knuckles brushed against my fingers and I swear her fucking hands were bigger than mine. She gripped me so hard I felt my bones grinding together and my cock retreated further at the thought of her getting her death grip on it.

"You must now both speak the words of the binding," the minister announced and the words seemed to push their way into my mouth unbidden as I spoke in unison with Mildred.

"I choose to bind myself to you in marriage. Let us both enter this union with clarity and honesty and forever be linked by the stars."

I felt so sick at the finality of those words that I didn't even feel the clap of magic that must have accompanied them, locking me in marriage to the woman I'd sworn I'd never wed.

My gaze found Roxy again, but before I knew what was happening, Mildred had lunged, her moustache was brushing over my upper lip and her thick, wet tongue was swiping across my mouth. She gripped my head so fucking tightly that it felt like she might bust my skull open and I could only keep my mouth stamped firmly shut and wait for her to fucking stop.

The motherfuckers watching this farce were clapping when I finally wrenched myself away from her and I swiped a hand over the back of my mouth to remove that fucking brown lipstick from my face.

"You are now bonded in a marriage everlasting in the eyes of the stars. May fate never tear you asunder and may destiny always shine on you kindly," the minister announced with a flourish and my gaze met Roxy's once more as a weight heavier than any I'd ever carried before seemed to fall around my neck.

Father smiled widely as I looked at him, pulling the vial of spring shine elixir from his pocket and handing it to Roxy so that she could heal herself before the autumn bloom took root in her heart and killed her.

Father stepped up to me as Mildred squealed in delight, hanging off of my arm and posing for photographs that I wasn't even looking at.

"Well done, boy," he purred, clapping me on the back. "Now go and fuck her before you come and join us for the rest of the celebrations. I want that Heir on the way as soon as possible - and don't think I won't know if you lie about it. Mildred is a virgin and we'll be making sure that's no longer the case once you're done with your marital duties."

"What celebrations?" I asked, refusing to comment on the horrors of what I was going to have to do next and picking up on how excited he'd looked when he mentioned that.

"You'll see," he replied elusively. "But I can assure you, it will be a day to remember for all of Solaria."

Before I could reply, Mildred yanked me away from him and I stumbled against her muscular frame as she reached out and grabbed my junk in her massive hand and squeezed.

"Come on, lover boy, I'm going to rock your world," she promised as I managed to knock her fucking hand off of me.

She still had hold of my arm though and she dragged me towards the door at a fast pace, clearly desperate to get to the next part of this while my heart was racing with the horror of it.

I couldn't go through with it. How the fuck could I? She was vile and vulgar in every single way and even if she hadn't been, she wasn't my girl. I didn't want her or anyone else. Only Roxy. Only ever her.

I twisted to look around at my girl as Xavier stood at her side, his fingers curled around hers. The pain in her green eyes as she watched me go fractured something in me that I wasn't sure would ever be mended. I'd sworn I'd never hurt her again and here I was tearing her heart out when I wasn't even worthy of owning it.

I tried to dig my heels in, Roxy's name catching in my throat as I ached to call out to her, rip my arm free of Mildred's death grip and run back to her. But as Father stepped up behind her and placed a hand on her shoulder, I knew it was no use. I had to do as he said if I wanted to save her, but how could I go through with that when I was certain it would destroy us?

Mildred clearly didn't share any of my concerns as she dragged me back towards the palace and I was forced to leave my girl with that monster yet again, I began to wonder if I was seriously going to end up doing this.

If I thought the wedding had been awful then I had no fucking idea how I was supposed to survive the consummation.

I'm so sorry, Roxy.

DARCY

CHAPTER FORTY SIX

I'd expected to die, not to wake up cold and shivering in a damp, dark cell. My eyes cracked open and I groaned as I pushed myself onto my knees, my heart clenching as I found my wrists bound in glowing blue magical blocking cuffs. My Phoenix lay dormant inside me and there was a needle puncture wound in my arm that spoke of the Order Suppressant I'd been given.

Basically, I was fucked and as I looked around the dank space, from the ancient bricks curving up around me to the iron bars in front of me, I knew there was no way out.

I reached up to my throat in a panic, but found the Imperial Star miraculously still hanging there. Lionel didn't know. *He doesn't know.*

"Blue?" Orion's anxious voice reached me from beyond the wall to my right and I wheeled around in hope, rushing toward it. "Are you awake?"

One of the bricks was missing between our cells so I could see into his. His hand shot through the hole and clasped mine, tugging it through to his side, his mouth pressing to the back of it. The heat of his lips was like a bonfire, burning through the cold clinging to my bones. I rarely felt the cold these days, always able to use my Phoenix to keep me warm and I'd almost forgotten how deeply it could bite.

Orion's magic cuff bumped against mine as our fingers locked together and panic sliced a path through my chest. I had no idea how long it had been since Lionel had captured us or where we were or what that bastard had planned. And the unknown was worse than the fear. Worse than even this dungeon we were locked in.

I pulled my hand free, looking through the gap instead and his gaze met with mine.

"I won't let them hurt you," he swore, but whatever Lionel had planned for us, we weren't going to be able to fight. Without our magic and Orders, we might as well have been mortals.

"Don't make promises you can't keep, Lance," I breathed hopelessly.

He growled, swiping his hand over his face as tension lined his features. He looked desperate, lost to a sea of fear, but the way he kept glancing at me told me that fear wasn't for himself.

"I know I broke your trust before," he said with pain coating his voice. "But only because I thought it was the right thing to do. I wouldn't break a promise to you unless the alternative was worse. So when I did it, I was sure it was."

I rested my forehead to the wall above the hole, taking in a breath. "I know," I admitted.

At some point during our time together these past few months, I'd come to see the truth in how he saw things. It didn't make it right, or better. But the bitterness over him abandoning me had become less sharp. Now we were sitting in the Dragon King's dungeon awaiting an inevitably terrible fate and there was so much left to say.

Why we weren't dead yet was a mystery, but maybe Lionel planned on torturing us first. If he had any inkling that we knew the location of the Imperial Star then maybe that was what he was after. But why weren't we strapped to some torture device right now if that was the case?

I traced my finger over my necklace and Orion shifted closer, sharing an intent look with me.

"I wish you could use it," he sighed.

"I'd have to be a queen," I said sadly.

"You are," he growled and the ferocity in his voice made me wrap my hand around the Imperial Star. There was a faraway echo of power thrumming within it, but there was no way it could answer my call.

"You always had so much faith in me," I said sadly. "I'm so grateful for that."

"I would have been horrified at myself once if I'd seen what a royalist I'd become," he laughed humourlessly. "Master of the Zodiac Guild," he scoffed at himself. "No regrets when it comes to that though, beautiful."

"Do you still have the diary?" I asked him and he nodded, patting his pocket. As it was concealed to look like a coin, I guessed Lionel hadn't bothered to take it from him. I quickly pushed my hand into my pocket, finding Diego's hat there and a sigh of relief left me.

"Darcy, I..." He shifted closer to the wall, reaching through it once more and I laced my fingers between his as my heart ached. "If this is my last promise, please know I won't break it. I swear that no matter what happens, I will fight to save you."

Tears burned my eyes as I gripped his hand tighter. "I'll fight for you too," I swore. Just like we had all those months ago. Before I'd lost everything.

"I know this means nothing now, but if I don't say it I'll hate myself," he said, his voice dark and rough. Silence stretched for a long moment as I waited for him to continue. "I love you, Blue. I loved you then, I love you now, I'll love you tomorrow even if I'm no longer on this earth. No time exists where I won't love you."

"Lance, please don't say goodbye," my words caught in my throat as pain burrowed into my core.

"I have to," he rasped. "Just in case. I'm so fucking sorry for everything I did to you. To us. I ruined everything. And I know it can't be fixed. That I made it nearly impossible for you to trust me when we first met, and when you finally did and I earned your heart, I broke that trust irreversibly."

"Maybe it was always meant to be this way," I said heavily, my chest tight. "You wouldn't have accessed the diary if you hadn't gone to prison. Your father knew that. It was where you had to end up for us to get the Imperial Star."

"But it cost me you," he said, his tone full of loss and regret.

I clutched his hand harder as tears spilled down my cheeks, accepting that I had to open my heart one last time, because I may never get a chance to do it again.

"Lance," I said, my voice breaking, shattering. His words were the sweetest poison, tailor made to kill me. I wiped my tears away and summoned the courage to tell him what needed to be said, but then the sound of a door opening reached us and heavy footsteps pounded this way.

Orion's grip on my hand tightened painfully and I peered through the hole as a Faelight illuminated his cell and fear yanked on my heart.

A clunk sounded as his cell door unlocked and two large men strode in wearing the uniforms of the King's Taskforce.

"Hey look, it's the princess fucker," one of them sneered and a growl built in my throat. "You're on trial again, you power shamed piece of shit," the other one said, smiling cruelly. "My bet's on the King showing no mercy. You'd better say goodbye forever just in case."

They lunged at Orion, dragging him to his feet and his hand was ripped from mine. He tried to fight, throwing furious punches, but without magic, they quickly tied his hands with a vine and hauled him to the door. One of them slammed their knuckles into his gut, making him snarl and my breathing stuttered.

"Wait!" I cried as panic tore at my heart with sharp claws. "Take me too! Take me with him!"

They started laughing, ignoring me as Orion turned his head to meet my gaze with an agonised expression as they dragged him away.

I started screaming his name with a raw desperation, because I had a horrible, heart-breaking feeling it was the last time I was ever going to see him.

DARIUS

CHAPTER FORTY SEVEN

Mildred practically dragged me through the palace until we made it to a suite in the guest wing that I guessed Father had given to her. She unlocked the door and I frowned as she tugged me through magical wards and a silencing bubble until we stepped into an enormous white and blue suite laid out with a massive bed in the centre of it which was covered in red rose petals.

"I've got a surprise for you," she breathed in what I was guessing was maybe meant to be a seductive voice, but it came out more like a snake hissing as spittle flew between the gaps in her teeth and I cringed.

"Maybe we should just get this over with," I grunted, not having any desire to do that at all, but I still had no fucking way to get out of this.

Unless...maybe I could just bend her over and force her ugly face down into the pillows so she couldn't see what I was doing. Then I could create a magical illusion of a cock to fuck her with and she'd never even know we hadn't really done it.

That wouldn't help me with the Heirs issue, but I didn't want her having my fucking kid anyway. And maybe if I could just buy a bit of time, we could get Roxy away from my father somehow.

It wasn't much of a plan but it sure beat sticking my dick in her.

Mildred grabbed my hand and tried to drag me across the room, but I growled at her and used my strength to whirl her around and toss her down on the bed instead.

She bounced with the force I used and her eyes widened as I stalked after her, my jaw gritted with determination.

"Wait - I haven't shown you the surprise!" she gasped, her voice sounding even more masculine than usual, but I needed to get this done, not engage in conversation with her or indulge her with fucking surprises.

"Stay quiet," I growled, grabbing her waist and flipping her face down before lifting her hips up to point her flat ass at me.

I shuddered as I used water magic to create ice so that her arms were frozen to the headboard and the angle I stretched them at forced her face into the pillows like I'd planned.

I flipped up the massive skirt she was wearing as I tried not to give too much thought to what I was about to find beneath all these layers of fabric.

At least I'm not really fucking her. I repeated those words over and over in my head as I hunted through the fabric for her panties. My hand suddenly ran over a bulge between her legs and I reared away in alarm.

"Woah, hold the fuck on - you're a *guy*?" I balked, but it actually did make a lot of sense now I thought about it. "Is this your fucking surprise?" *Holy shit, maybe this is my way out. I can't impregnant a man.*

Her big ass foot suddenly slammed into my chest and knocked me flying back against the table beyond the foot of the bed.

"What the fuck?" I roared at her, my temper fraying as she melted the ice restraints off of her arms and rolled over.

But instead of finding Mildred there, I found fucking *Gabriel*, grinning at me like some crazy asshole as he removed the illusion spells he'd put in place to make himself look like Mildred.

"Hey, husband," he teased, gripping the front of the wedding dress and ripping it right down the front so that he could climb out of it. "Were you really about to fuck me without even telling me you loved me?"

"What...how...I just married you!"

"Not quite," he disagreed. "I'm already married more than enough, though it's sweet you thought it was a possibility." He waved his wedding ring at me and I just stared in confusion as my brain tried to catch up to my eyes.

"I don't understand," I growled, trying to figure this out, was I *not* married? Holy fucking shit, was that possible?

Gabriel rolled his eyes and got to his feet, kicking off the stilettos and crossing the room in his boxers with his tattoos all on display. My gaze caught on a Dragon which curved over his shoulder blade and looked suspiciously like me.

"I *saw* what was going to happen today and this is the only chance we had to stop it. And seeing as you vowed to marry Mildred in 'clarity and honesty' but I was really just a disguised dude in a dress, those vows don't mean shit. Didn't you notice the lack of magic binding you after you made them?" he asked, pulling open a drawer and tugging a pair of jeans and a black sweater on.

"I guess I was more focused on being forced to marry that beast while the girl I really love had to watch," I growled, but even though I felt seriously pissed, his words were slowly sinking in. "Wait, so...I'm not really married?"

"Nope. And as fantastic as I'm sure you are in bed, I've got some pretty strict rules about not getting fucked by a Dragon, so I had to stop you," he joked.

"How the fuck did you pull this off?" I demanded, a grin spreading over my features as I realised he'd just saved me from a fate I couldn't escape. Though I still had no idea how the hell I was supposed to get away with it long term.

"Well, if you'd let me show you the surprise instead of groping my dick then you'd know." Gabriel strode across the room, swiping the brown lipstick from his mouth with the back of his hand and I made a mental note to kick his ass for committing to the role so damn much at some point. But right now I could forget that disgusting kiss in the face of my gratitude and curiosity.

He moved to the closet door and tugged it open, stepping aside with a huge grin on his face as he revealed Mildred hog tied in the bottom of it with magic restricting cuffs glowing blue around her wrists. She was grunting and cursing around a ball gag in her mouth and I burst out laughing as she glared at me with her little round eyes.

"I arrived here in the early hours and with the help of a friend of mine, we managed to convince her to remove the protections in place to stop anyone from impersonating her. Luckily he happened to have these ropes and the cuffs and the gag...and I promised to buy him replacements because clearly he won't want those back now. Anyway, I'm just going to give her a memory potion so she forgets all this shit and then we need to go," Gabriel said, dropping down to unclasp the ball gag before forcing a little bottle of potion into Mildred's mouth.

She fought and squealed like a pig as she thrashed against her restraints and I sniggered as Gabriel used his water magic to force the potion down her throat. Her eyes went glassy as it took effect, and he snapped the ball gag back into place before closing the door on her and turning to face me again.

"You wanna tell me why you decided to kiss me and grab my fucking dick while I believed you were her?" I asked, unable to shake the feeling of Mildred's moustache grazing across my lips from my memory even though I now knew it had been him in disguise.

Gabriel smirked, stepping forward to look me right in the eyes and I was surprised to find he matched my height because there weren't many men who did.

"You remember when my little sister came back from the mortal realm and you made her life a living hell?" he asked me in a low growl, darkness shifting in his gaze. "Remember how you burned all of her clothes off and made the whole kingdom think she was a sex addict and almost drowned her in that fucking swimming pool?"

"You were punishing me?" I asked, my brows rising at the smug look on his face.

"It was the least you deserved, don't you agree?" Gabriel slapped my cheek a couple of times and I jerked back with a growl but he just held his ground, seeming to be so certain that I would agree with him that he wasn't afraid of me lashing out. And maybe he was fucking right about that.

"Alight. I get it. I fucked up and you're not gonna let me forget it," I muttered and he nodded.

"We have more important things to discuss than that though."

"What?" I asked, sensing the shift in his tone and he frowned.

"When I finally got back to my family's winter cabin last night, I went to my amplifying chamber and managed to *see* a whole hell of a lot of things that my time in the Royal Seer's Chair opened up to me. And there was one prophesy which I can't *see* any way around but this."

"But what?" I asked in concern, frowning at him as he stepped closer to me with his brow furrowing.

"One of my sisters is going to die today. And the only possible chance we have to save them is by me bringing you to the caves of the forgotten."

"The what of where?" I demanded, my heart racing at the idea of Roxy or Darcy not making it through the day as I tried to figure out what the fuck was going to happen that could mean they might not.

"It's an ancient set of caverns in the far south of Solaria, hidden within a jungle and long since forgotten by our kind. My visions led me there once before and I found a ring which saved my life. The stars won't show me what will happen when we get there or anything at all other than to whisper that it is the only chance there is for both Vega Princesses to survive the day. So are you with me?" he asked urgently and I could see how serious he was about this as I nodded.

"You're sure the best thing I can do for Roxy is to go with you now?" I demanded. "And how is Darcy involved in this?"

"Your father captured her and Lance last night. I was so lost in the visions the stars had flooded me with that I didn't *see* him coming for them until after it had already come to pass. I'm more sorry for that than words can express. I called the other Heirs and told them what's happening. But if you and I don't head to the caves now then I know that one of my sisters will die."

"Why?" I balked, stepping forward and grabbing his shirt as I tugged him closer to me. "How? Where? Let's just go and get them now and-"

"No," Gabriel snapped, shoving me off of him and making my panic turn to anger. "I told you, we need to go to the caves if we want to save them. It's the only chance we have. If you let your hot head get the better of you and try charging off to rescue them then you'll bring their deaths about. I want you to come with me willingly, but if I have to beat the shit out of you and drag you there hog tied like Mildred then I will. Because I'm not gonna let anything happen to them. So are you with me or not?"

I glared at him for a long moment as those words sank in and I forced out a hard breath as I accepted them. I might have wanted to run to Roxy, but if I could have ripped her out of my father's arms then I would have done it already. Gabriel was by far the best Seer I'd ever met and though he kinda irritated me a lot of the time, I did trust him, especially when it came to the Vegas.

"Alright," I agreed firmly, knowing enough about his visions to trust that he really did know what he was talking about with this. "Let's go."

Gabriel nodded firmly before moving to a bookcase set against the wall and using the ring Roxy had made for him to open the King's Passages there.

I stepped into the dark behind him, putting all of my faith into him as I left Roxy behind and followed him out of the palace. But if this was what it took to save her or Darcy then I'd do it. Whatever it took.

ORION

CHAPTER FORTY EIGHT

The two assholes who'd dragged me out of my cell had taken me through dark tunnels then shoved me into a stone room with a door ahead of me and behind, the only light the blue glow from the cuffs that restricted my magic. Before they left, one of them had jabbed a needle into my neck and my Order had awakened not long after. I'd tried to break my way out of this place, but magic made it strong and without my own powers to unravel it, I was fucked.

All was silent, too fucking silent for my heightened senses and I guessed I was held within a damn silencing bubble. I expected Lionel to show up at any minute with some plan, some explanation of what was about to happen. But he didn't.

The fear of parting from Darcy was suffocating. Not knowing if I'd ever see her again made me lose my mind with misery, fear, panic. I had to get out. I had to save her from whatever was about to happen.

I threw my weight at the stone door ahead of me again and again, trying to force it to give and suddenly the whole thing swung open and I went stumbling out. My feet hit sand and as I passed through a magical barrier, a tumult of noise crashed down on me. I was blinded by the sun after so long in the dark and I raised a hand to shield my eyes as the wild cheers of a crowd surrounded me.

"Lance Orion!" Lionel's voice boomed out as my vision sharpened and I found myself standing in the pit of an enormous amphitheatre.

There were cages made of night iron ringing the circular space, each of them holding a Nymph in its shifted form, their gleaming red eyes watching me hungrily.

Dread tangled with the very root of my being as I spotted Lionel up on a large throne in the stands with Tory on one side of him and Clara on the other. Xavier stood beyond Tory and Vard was next to him with a bloodthirsty smile on his lips. With a cold clarity, I realised where I was. This was the amphitheatre used for trials and death games during the reign of the Savage King. A place which had been closed by the Councillors, outlawed, forgotten. But of course this monster would bring it back into use. Probably more than half the Fae who'd died here during Hail Vega's reign were because of him.

My pulse thundered in my head as I took in the crowd of people in fine robes and gowns and I could practically taste their desire for my suffering.

Tory jerked forward where she stood beside Lionel but one glance from my sister forced her back. From the look of Xavier's rigid posture, I guessed he was held in place by the shadows too. But where was Darius?

"You are on trial for escaping my custody, thwarting your prison sentence and colluding with an enemy of the Acruxes," Lionel announced and boos sounded out around the stadium. "Do you have anything to say for yourself in your defence?"

"Fuck you," I snarled, spitting on the sand at my feet and heckles rang out from the crowd.

Lionel regarded me with a grimace. "Very well. As punishment, you will fight for your life. Your Order has been returned to you and you may use any of the weapons available to you in the ring." He gestured to the middle of the pit where a rusty sword, a knife and a wooden bat lay on the ground.

Excited laughter sounded from the bastards watching and my skin prickled all over. Anger and hate twisted up inside my chest, possessing every inch of me.

I shot toward the weapons, picked up the rusty piece of shit sword and launched it with the full strength of my Order at Lionel Acrux's smug fucking face. It smashed into a magical shield protecting the crowd and gasps rang out before everyone started clapping and laughing.

Lionel's face shifted into a dark and furious scowl that spoke of my defiance. He hated that he could never truly get me under his heel. But he didn't know that we had the Imperial Star, or that I'd been feeding him bullshit lies for months. If he really planned on killing me now, then had he given up hope of finding it?

"You will suffer for your crimes against me," Lionel snarled and a hushed silence fell over the crowd as they listened.

"So kill me!" I roared. "Have your lump of flesh, you piece of shit."

He considered me with a knowing look that sent a shudder clawing down my spine. "It is not *your* flesh I crave."

A grinding of stone sounded behind me and I twisted around, finding Darcy stepping out of the door in her sweatpants and crop top.

The crowd gasped and clapped, pointing between us as they discussed whatever lies they believed about us. But they knew nothing.

"Gwendalina Vega made an attempt on my life last night," Lionel called to the crowd who bayed and shouted angrily.

My heart crushed in my chest as Darcy lifted her chin defiantly, glaring at the worthless man who dared to call himself king. I shot to her side and our hands clasped together automatically, making the crowd angrier as they booed and swore at us.

"Today, this traitor of the crown dies!" Lionel boomed and Tory jerked forward once more, her eyes full of terror, but Clara forced her back again. "Do you dare to speak in your defence, Gwendalina Vega?"

Her fingers tightened on mine and her upper lip peeled back, her expression that of a fearless warrior. I nearly burst with pride to be standing beside her. If she died today, so would I. I wouldn't stay a single second longer in this world without her. But even considering that fate for her was unbearable. And I would do everything in my power to stop it.

"You are unFae and unworthy to sit on my father's throne," Darcy called, her voice ringing around the amphitheatre. "I know what you did, I know how you Dark Coerced Hail Vega, how you poisoned his mind and turned him against his own people."

The crowd started muttering, exchanging curious glances and Lionel sat up straighter in his seat.

"Your father was a heartless, mindless fool, and no true Fae would ever bow to his filthy bloodline ever again," Lionel growled.

"All hail the Dragon King!" Vard cried and an answering call fell from the lips of everyone in the stands.

"All hail the Vega Queens!" I bellowed in response and dropped to my knees, bowing for my queens in an act of rebellion which would likely be my last.

"Release the Nymphs!" Lionel roared and the cages clanged as they opened all around us. Darcy yanked on my sleeve to get me up and I stood, pulling her closer as my heart thundered against my ribcage.

"Any chance they awakened your Order, beautiful?" I murmured and she shook her head. *Fuck.* "You'd better get on my back then."

She lunged toward me, tiptoeing up and kissing me fiercely for two short, sweet seconds before running around and climbing onto my back. And something told me that might be my last good moment in this world.

"I love you, Lance," she whispered in my ear and her words filled me all with the strength I needed to face down the five Nymphs coming our way.

I shot to the centre of the arena, hefting the bat into my grip and tucking the knife into my waistband. I knew the odds of this game were vastly weighed against us. But I would fight until my very last breath to keep my girl safe. Death would have to try and rip her from my arms itself if it wanted her, and even then, I would not let go.

DARIUS

CHAPTER FORTY NINE

The stars spat us out in the middle of a sweltering jungle and I sucked in a breath of the humid air as Gabriel started off through the trees at a fast pace.

"There are still ancient wards around this place," he said without looking back at me. "But they allowed me to pass them by and I've *seen* you entering them too. I just thought I should warn you, because you'll know all about it when you pass through them."

"Okay," I agreed, striding after him as he used his earth Element to force the foliage to part for us, creating a path through the dense jungle.

I stripped out of my heavy suit jacket as I walked, tossing it aside without a care before ripping the fucking cravat off too. It was sweltering here and I didn't want to wear the fucking thing anyway, it was only a reminder of the twisted fate I'd just managed to escape.

"You're sure this is where we need to be?" I asked anxiously, hating that I was so far from the people I loved most in this world when they obviously needed my help.

"This is one of the clearest visions I've ever had. The only chance we have of both of my sisters surviving the day is by being here. There are so many paths to death for the two of them today that I'm getting constant flashes of one or the other dying repeatedly. This is how we save them," Gabriel said firmly and I could see how much the fear of those visions coming to pass was weighing on him.

"Let's hurry then," I growled, focusing on the task at hand and refusing to let myself get caught up in worries. If this was what I had to do then I would.

Gabriel upped his pace and suddenly the air all around us seemed come to life with energy. I gasped as tiny pinpricks of light sparked and zapped everywhere and my skin buzzed from the contact as the ancient magic pressed in on my skin, stealing my breath.

"Acrux," a voice spoke in my head which was soft and feminine and yet fierce and full of power too. *"Descendent of the oath breaker. Harbinger of doom. The blood in your veins runs thick with lies and betrayal."*

The power surrounding me grew denser and more potent, immobilising me as I gasped for breath and the zaps of energy began to burn against my skin.

"I see two paths before you, blood of the deceiver. Choose wisely."

The power released me so suddenly that I fell to my knees, sucking in a shaky breath and my limbs trembled as I fought to regain my composure.

"Told you you'd feel it," Gabriel said as he stood over me and I forced myself to my feet with a grunt of pain.

"What the fuck was that?" I snarled.

"Something far older than us," he supplied before turning and leading me on through the trees again.

I hurried after him, tugging open the buttons at my throat as sweat lined my skin and I used my water magic to cool down.

Gabriel suddenly stepped through the trees ahead and I glanced down at my feet, noticing the bronze pathway peeking out between the foliage before I pushed through behind him and found myself standing at the entrance to an enormous cave.

"Are you ready, Darius?" he asked me seriously and I shrugged.

"I guess we're about to find out."

We strode into the darkness of the cave, but before I could cast a Faelight to see by, huge, silvery runes illuminated on the wall. Gabriel nodded at me to go ahead as I looked to him in question.

I stepped forward and brushed my fingers over them, gasping as a surge of power flooded beneath my skin, seeking out my magic and seeming to weigh its worth before retreating again.

Before I could ask what we were supposed to do now, more of the ancient runes lit up along the wall, twisting away down a passage that turned right.

"They'll show us the way," Gabriel said and I broke into a run as I chased after them.

Our footsteps echoed heavily along the wide, stone tunnels and I spied ancient relics and treasures along the way, some so precious that the Dragon in me ached to stop and claim them for my own. But there wasn't a single treasure on this earth more precious than the girl I loved and I wasn't going to be distracted from what I needed to do here.

The tunnels angled downwards and the deeper we delved into the caves, the more powerfully the magic of this place seemed to hum around me. It was beautiful and terrible and somehow hauntingly familiar to me too.

We suddenly burst into a cavern which opened up all around us and as the runes illuminated all over the walls, I found life and greenery flourishing everywhere.

A small, trickling waterfall ran down the cave wall on our left from somewhere high above us and a stunning tree had grown up beside it, its roots spreading out all over the cavern. Little white flowers blossomed everywhere on thick green vines that covered the stone walls and I gaped at the place, wondering how the hell all of this had flourished so much beneath the ground in the dark like this.

Was the magic here so potent that it had taken on a life of its own? Not needing the hand of a Fae to guide it? Or was this some creation from centuries past, the magic that had created it so strong that it still held power here?

The runes pulsed and flickered, and my gaze was drawn to the far side of the cavern where a round, stone door sat closed against the wall, the wheel of the zodiac surrounding it and every symbol illuminated in silver.

I stepped closer, afraid to break the silence as I held my breath and approached the door, knowing with a certainty that ran soul deep that my destiny lay beyond it.

"This is as far as I go," Gabriel said darkly, reaching out to grasp my shoulder and causing me to turn and look at him. "I can't *see* what you're going to find beyond that door, Darius. I only know that once you're inside, whatever happens will twist the wheel of fate in a fundamental way that could change many things. So many that I can't even begin to *see* them all."

"But if I do something right in there, the Vegas will survive?" I asked, needing to know it without any doubt.

Gabriel hesitated, reaching out to brush his fingers over the stone door, making it quiver and illuminate with his star sign for a moment before he drew back. "Yes. You can save them by going in there. But I can't *see* any more than that. This is a test for you alone."

"Then I'll be certain not to fail it," I swore, clapping him on the shoulder and stepping forward to look at the door.

I placed my hand against the rough stone and the Leo symbol lit up brighter than all of the others, magic rumbling through my limbs as the zodiac wheel began to rotate until my star sign sat above the entrance and the door swung open.

It was dark beyond the door, but I refused to balk, raising my chin and striding inside.

"Acrux," the ethereal voice spoke in my mind again. *"Your destiny awaits."*

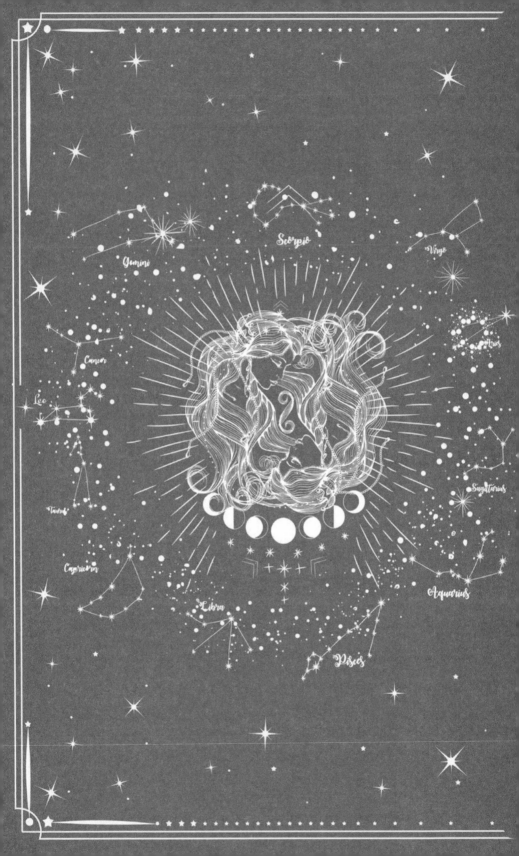

DARCY

CHAPTER FIFTY

O rion shot around the stadium, launching himself onto the back of a Nymph just as another cast fire at us in an explosion of uncontrolled power. The fire slammed into the beast we were fighting, hitting it squarely in the chest so it screeched and stumbled backwards, about to fall.

I yanked the knife free from Orion's waistband as he clung onto its neck and I reached up, stabbing it with all my strength in the back of the head. It exploded into shadows and I let go of Orion before we hit the ground, his weight knocking the wind out of me.

We'd taken out two Nymphs already, but for every one we destroyed, another was released into the pit and I knew we couldn't keep this up forever.

A tower of fire billowed from the probed hands of the closest Nymph which had large, curving horns on its head and a blackish star between its eyes. It was scarily strong, the stolen Fae power in its veins terrifying, and the only advantage we had was that it couldn't wield it with much skill.

Orion scooped me up, racing away as the fire flared across the ground where we'd just been laying. We made it to the other side of the pit and I jumped down from his arms, hurrying around to get on his back as a Nymph came at us from the right. I kept the knife in my grip as Orion lifted the bat with a snarl and the crowd called out encouragement to the beasts heading our way, hollering for our deaths.

Orion breathed heavily as he caught his breath and I wished I could offer him healing magic, but I was useless. All I could do was hold onto him and do my best to ensure we survived. But the longer this went on, the more I feared we were moving closer to our end. It was a miracle we'd survived so long.

"Hold on tight," Orion growled, lifting his bat higher as our enemies circled.

"We can't go on like this," I said, looking to the stands where Lionel watched us with amusement twisting his features.

Tory stared back at me with desperation in her eyes as Clara kept her locked in place and I silently communicated to her that I wasn't going to give up. Not ever.

The closest Nymph sent a blast of water magic at us, ice shards shooting everywhere and Orion raced away, hissing between his teeth as one of them tore along his arm. I gasped, clutching the wound, my fingers coming away wet with blood.

"Keep running," I begged in terror.

He continued to rush around the pit as magic was thrown at us from all sides and I placed my entire faith in Orion to see us through it.

He shot up behind the Nymph with water magic, whacking it hard in the backs of the legs with his bat and the creature stumbled down onto one knee with a roar.

Orion twisted around, hefting the bat over his head and smashing it down on the Nymph's skull with a furious blow. The creature hit the ground with a dying groan and burst into ash and shadow around us.

"*Yes*," I hissed, kissing Orion's cheek.

More Nymphs spilled into the arena from a set of stone doors across from us and Orion ran at them full pelt to try and get inside. But just as we were about to dive through the doors, we hit a magical barrier and were thrown backwards amongst four of the giant beasts, rolling away from each other across the sand.

My heart thundered in my chest as I pushed myself up, lifting the knife and slashing at the legs of the closest Nymph before driving it into one of their stomach's.

A huge probed hand smashed into me, sending me flying further away from Orion and I hit the sand hard enough to bruise my spine. Fear and determination collided together inside me as I shoved to my feet once more with a snarl, rearranging my grip on the knife as I ran back to where Orion was savagely wielding the bat against three of the monsters.

He fought with furious, unyielding blows, but they soon got the upper hand and one of them knocked him to the ground, slamming a foot down on his chest and reaching toward his heart with its outstretched probes.

"No!" Terror seized me and I sprinted toward him with a scream of defiance, slamming the knife into the Nymph's back over and over and over, making it twist around in alarm to face me. Another beast caught me around the waist, throwing me down beside Orion and the knife was knocked from my hand, bouncing away across the sand. My heart thrashed, my hope receded.

A sea of grotesque Nymph faces gazed down at us as they pinned us in place and Orion fought with everything he had to get up, making it half way only to be pushed down again by more and more Nymph hands as they battled to be the ones to probe him.

"Get away!" I cried, reaching for him as sharp probes scraped down the length of my body and the scent of my own blood ran under my nose.

I had to get to Orion. I wouldn't stop until I was with him.

If we have to die, at least let us die together.

"Darcy!" a piercing scream came from my sister and pain spread through me at that sound, confirming what I already knew. It was over. The Nymphs were fighting over which one would steal our magic and we couldn't get free as they surrounded us.

I'm sorry. I love you.

The crowd were shouting excitedly, chanting for our deaths and life seemed to close in all around me, narrowing down to a few final moments.

My hand found Orion's and he yanked me tightly towards him, trying to get free with all his might. But the Nymphs were crowding in and as he somehow made it to his knees, one of them took hold of his head. I reared up and tore into the beast's hands with my nails, sinking my teeth into its probes and biting the hard bark of its flesh until I tasted blood.

It lurched back with a screech, but another took its place and held him still. Orion's eyes met mine, unblinking, like he didn't dare see anything but me in his final moments and I didn't dare to close my eyes either. Grief splintered through my body as another Nymph got hold of me and Orion and I were forced closer together as they started fighting to get their probes into us first.

Tears slipped down my cheeks and I barely felt the pain of my injuries at all as I gazed at my mate in front of me. A man I had chosen for myself, regardless of stars and fate and laws. He was mine and I was his. Now and always. In the end, he'd kept his promise to me after all and I'd kept mine. We'd fought for each other until we couldn't fight any more.

I breathed him in and cursed the world for not giving us a chance. Or maybe we'd had one and this was the price of screwing it up.

"Don't let go of me," I begged against his mouth.

He held me tighter as he tried to get up once more, but too many of them were pinning us down. "See you in the stars, Blue," he swore, his lips brushing mine.

Thunder cracked overhead and a flare of lightning ignited the stands before a crash sounded as something was hit. I felt death leaning closer, surrounding us like a cloak.

"Argggggghhhh!" a woman cried from somewhere beyond us and the crowd gasped and cried out just as four enormous white paws slammed into the Nymphs holding us down. The front two were clad in Phoenix metal and fire blazed out from his claws, killing two Nymphs in quick succession.

We were knocked over and Orion pulled me to his chest, surrounding me with his body as Seth leapt over us and ripped through another Nymph with teeth alone. Geraldine was riding him, dressed in some kind of gleaming bronze warrior armour complete with pointed silver boobs.

She whipped her flail around her head, smashing through Nymph skulls as shadow and dust burst from the Nymphs as they fell. Through the pain and the weakness in my body, I could barely summon the strength to hope.

"For my most glorious majesties!" she cried. "Peril calls my name and my name is Geraldine Gundellifus Gabolia Gundestria Grus! Hear. Me. Roar!"

Caleb tore into view, dressed in black, dropping down into the sand before us and pressing his hands to my back where the Nymph's probes had cut into me. I whimpered in pain as he healed me before moving to heal Orion whose fingers were locked around mine. When it was done, Caleb jammed a needle into my arm without a word and I gasped as the Order Suppressant antidote rushed into my veins.

"I got you," he growled, unlocking my cuffs with a key before tossing it to Orion.

"Thank you," I said breathlessly.

"Up, fight, run, that's the plan – oh and don't die," Caleb said, taking a huge sword from his back that I recognised as the one I'd made for Orion. He passed it to him before tearing away in a blur.

Magic rushed to my fingertips and I pulled Orion closer while the Nymphs were distracted by our friends, drawing his mouth firmly to my neck. He hadn't fed since we'd been at Stella's house and he must have been starved for magic.

"Drink," I commanded as I cast an air shield around us and he did, his fangs slicing into my throat as he recharged his magic with my own.

I barely had time to be relieved as chaos descended around us and the shadow of a huge Storm Dragon flew overhead. The crowd were screaming and death was spilling through the amphitheatre on furious, ravenous wings as Dante's lightning powers blasted the stands and more and more of our friends appeared.

"For the true Queens!" Hamish charged through the crowd, pulling his clothes off before shifting into a huge black Cerberus and snapping his jaws at the Fae who'd come to watch us die. There were Tiberian Rats, Minotaurs, Wolves. It was beautiful, terrifying havoc. And I drank it all in with hope building in my chest and my strength returning in a furious wave. I couldn't see Lionel behind a swarm of shadow as Clara fought to hold back anyone who dared try to get near him. But my sister was up there. And I had to get to her.

When Orion was done, we hurried to our feet, healing our wounds and I raised my hands as Phoenix fire rippled through my being. A dark and vengeful smile hooked up my mouth. The shield was down above the pit and our friends were here to save us. Fate had offered us a second chance. And I was going to make the most of every second of it.

As Seth and Geraldine tore through the Nymphs ahead of us and Orion shot forward to cut more down with his sword, I held out my palms and released a huge burst of Phoenix fire, letting it carve through Nymph after Nymph until half of them started running to try and escape. But I would show no mercy. It was time for the King and his army to fall. And the Vega Queens to rise.

MAX

CHAPTER FIFTY ONE

My deep blue scales coated my body as I launched myself up above the amphitheatre on a gust of wind and held myself suspended above the crowd of screaming, fighting Fae.

Dragons roared as they shifted and took to the sky in defence of their king and I dove into the deep well of power that my gifts contained as I sought out each and every one of them with my psyche.

I latched onto mind after mind, their shifted forms making them even easier to grasp with their magic out of play and I conjured up all of the deepest, darkest feelings of fear, hopelessness and terror that I could and drove it into them with force.

Men screamed in panic as the might of my gifts crashed over all of them and the more they feared me, the more that fuelled my own power.

Lionel was still hidden beneath a veil of shadow in the stands below me and I cursed him as I spotted Caleb trying to blast a way through them to get at him.

Dante Oscura roared ferociously as he swept overhead in his navy Dragon form, the might of a storm tearing from his jaws as lightning struck with fatal precision, slamming into Lionel's supporters and obliterating them time and again.

He wheeled towards the ground beyond the huge stone structure where Lionel's sick games had been held and I used my air magic to push myself through the sky after the Storm Dragon. I closed in on him, pumping courage and confidence into the rebels clinging to his back as he landed to let them down so that they could join the fight.

As they leapt from his back, they shifted, most of them turning into a pack of enormous wolves with one gigantic Nemean Lion racing into the fight amongst them, roaring so loudly that the sky seemed to tremble with it.

A blast of magic slammed into the shield I'd constructed around myself and I snarled with anger as I tore my gaze away from the rebels and found Vard standing beneath me on the wall that ringed the stands, casting fire in his palms as he raised his hands to shoot at me once more.

I ripped the bow from my back and took aim at him, smiling savagely as I let him take his shot, the full force of his magic crashing against my shield and making it vibrate with the force he'd used.

But I was an Heir to the Celestial Council, one of the most powerful Fae in the world, and he really should have known better than to take me on.

I let my shield flicker out of existence half a breath before I let my arrow fly and a trail of fire spun through the air as my aim sent it careering straight for his heart.

Vard threw his hands up, blasting his fire magic at the arrow with all he had and knocking it off course just as the shot of air I'd been preparing slammed into his gut, the moment he thought he was safe.

He fell from the wall with a shriek of fear, but I couldn't be certain that he'd broken his fucking neck because a rusty red Dragon dove from the sky towards me with a furious roar and stole all of my attention.

I shot aside as the Dragon released a ball of fire aimed straight for me and I channelled all of my gifts into making him tremble in fear at the mere sight of me.

The Dragon roared, trying to fight against the terror I was awakening within his soul and I shot spears of ice into his side as he was paralysed by the fear for a second too long.

The beast roared in agony as his wing was shredded and blood poured from the wounds. His eyes widened with panic as he tumbled from the sky, shifting back into his Fae form before hitting the ground with a sickening crack that signalled his end.

The deep rattle of the Nymphs drew my attention to the pit in the centre of the amphitheatre again and I sped back that way, wrapping my air magic around the arrow I'd shot at Vard and returning it to my hand as I went.

Geraldine fought beneath me with a bellow of fury passing her lips as she swung her flail around her head over and over again, yelling at the Nymphs in challenge and blazing with all the confidence of the sun.

"I am the fair demon who haunts your nightmares, shadow fiends! Feel the kiss of justice when I strike you down and banish you to the depths of the nether world!" she cried, racing forward fearlessly and cracking the spiked ball at the end of her flail against the skull of one of the creatures.

The Nymph shrieked in agony as the Phoenix fire imbued in the weapon set it alight and Geraldine laughed loudly before running for her next target.

She was so fucking beautiful that it set my heart racing and I chased her through the sky, working to help her take on the Nymphs as she dove into the fray once more.

I pushed confidence and bravery into my friends as they fought, but they didn't even need it, each of them fighting with the pure fury of justice as we battled for our lives and those of the ones we loved.

But as I took aim with my bow once more, an all too familiar, pained howl called to me and set my heart racing with panic. I whipped around to hunt for Seth amongst the fighting bodies, my heart dipping as I failed to find him.

I cast an amplifying spell as I heard him again and I dropped to the ground as I started running in the direction his howls were coming from. I just hoped I wasn't going to be too late.

SETH

· CHAPTER FIFTY TWO ·

Two Nymphs cornered me against a wall, pinning me down beneath them as I fought furiously to try and get free. The one with curving horns was throwing fire at me, burning my side with a sadistic, raking laugh as I howled in agony.

I clawed at them with my paws, but the bastard didn't stop even as I sliced into its side with Phoenix fire.

I heard Darcy yelling my name and red and blue fire billowed up into the sky from somewhere across the pit, telling me she wasn't going to get here in time. A gap opened up between them and I dove forward to try and get free with a bark of determination, but another Nymph blocked my path, its large probed hand cracking against my face and knocking me back down.

They rattled deep and hungrily as the three of them fought to pin me in place, each of them desperate to be the one to steal my power as they killed me. Fear hit me as they forced me onto my back in the sand and the huge one with the horns reached down to rip my magic from my heart. *Fuck, no, I've got too much life to live. I never told Cal how I feel.*

An arrow slammed into the skull of the one holding my paws and it exploded into shadows as a second arrow narrowly missed the horned Nymph above me. The large beast roared a challenge, leaping over me and running toward Max as he descended from the sky, casting a huge blast of fire from its hands.

Max shielded with air as I scrambled onto my paws, yelping from the aching burns on my side, the scent of singed flesh and burnt hair reaching me from my injuries.

I lunged at the final Nymph with a fierce savagery, tearing into its throat and shaking it ferociously as it screamed and shrieked in my jaws.

My muscles trembled as the pain of my injuries began to overwhelm me, and my grip on the Nymph slackened for a moment as I almost passed out but with a determined growl, I managed to fight the feeling off and cling on.

With a vicious jerk of my head, the Nymph's neck snapped and it burst into shadow as I staggered, my front legs giving out. I tried to push myself up, but darkness curtained my vision and I stumbled instead, crashing into the sand with a whimper of pain.

A blur of motion ran toward me and my heart lifted as I raised my snout, readying to greet Caleb. But it was Orion who slowed in front of me, dropping down and pressing his hands to the burns covering my body. The pain ebbed away as he worked and I let out a low whine as I wheeled my head around to lick his face, making him grunt in annoyance. *Lance Orion came for me. He loves me like a pack mate.*

"This is only because Blue would hate me if I let you die," he growled and I gave him a Wolf's grin, my tail pounding against the sand. *Sure it is.*

When he finished healing me, I jumped to my feet and jerked my head toward my back in a clear offering for him to get on.

"Not in your lifetime, mutt." He shot away from me, cutting down a Nymph with a furious blow of his sword and I sighed internally. *There goes my future best friend.*

I took off across the sand as a few of the Nymphs retreated towards a wide doorway that led beneath the amphitheatre and Max worked to break down the shield stopping him from following.

Darcy fought with the horned Nymph with the savagery of her father and I howled my joy before turning and leaping out of the pit into the stands.

I snapped at the heels of the crowd as they fled, knocking them down with my huge paws and spotting Rosalie's beautiful silver form ahead of me, leading a pack of Oscura Wolves. I howled to her in greeting and she turned her head, barking in reply.

I sprinted through her pack until I reached her at the front and we ran side by side, trampling any unlucky piece of shit who got in our way.

I hunted for Caleb in the madness, but there were too many Fae running all over the place. It was impossible to find him. I just hoped he had made it to Tory already, because we had to get her away from Lionel. Then maybe one of us would be lucky enough to get a shot at killing him.

TORY

CHAPTER FIFTY THREE

I stood by Clara's side, locked in place by the shadows she wielded to stop anyone from making it close to attack us. Lionel paced before us, glaring down at the fight taking place in the pit while the sound of the rebels and Dragons clashing outside called to us where we stood in the royal box.

My muscles were rigid with tension as she forced me to remain utterly still, even my jaw locked tight against any words I might speak while Xavier received the same treatment on her other side.

"How long until my Nymph army arrives to crush these traitors?" Lionel demanded.

"They're coming, Daddy," Clara assured him, the shadows coiling around her wildly. "Some will be here soon. Some are very, very, very, very, very far away-"

"You're the one who told me they needed fresh victims. I only sent them north because you insisted they be given the chance to claim magic for themselves and now they aren't here when I need them," he snarled, pointing an accusatory finger at her. "If they fail me now, you'll be the one I blame."

Clara whimpered pathetically, turning to me and slapping me across the face as hard as she could, making my head wheel sideways and my lip split as the shadows stopped me from fighting back.

"Your sister is making Daddy sad!" she shouted, pointing in my face and I just smiled at her to let her see how I felt about that while she still refused to let me speak.

Clara shrieked as she lunged at me but Lionel caught hold of the back of her dress to stop her before she could reach me.

"This is unacceptable," Lionel snarled. "I won't stand for it anymore. If the Nymphs don't finish the job down there, then I'll do it myself. Every

Fae who has shown up here to fight in defence of that Vega girl has proven themselves to be disloyal to the crown. They're traitors and this is an act of treason, the penalty for which can only be death."

My skin prickled at his words but I refused to let them fill me with fear. The Heirs were here, the rebels too. Darcy could make it out of this, I believed in her.

Clara parted the shadows so we could see down to the battle below and Orion shot across the sandy pit below us, swinging his sword with a cry of fury. My lips twitched in triumph as the Nymph he struck split apart into shadows with a shriek of agony as it died.

"Enough!" Lionel roared, his voice echoing off of the stands as the Dragon in him showed through. "Clara, get down there and end this now. I won't stand by and watch it play out any longer."

"Yes, my King," she purred excitedly, moving straight towards the wall that lined the balcony and hopping up onto it before leaping over the edge.

Shadows rose up all around her as she used them to float down into the middle of the battle which was raging below us and I was left alone with Lionel and Xavier.

My eyes locked on my sister as she fought furiously and that shadow whore moved straight towards her with a terrifying grin on her face as her darkness built and writhed around her.

The shadows released their hold on me as Clara focused on the fight and I gasped as I took several steps away from Lionel, catching Xavier's arm and tugging him towards the door to the side of the balcony.

"You can't leave me, Roxanya," Lionel scoffed, not doing a damn thing to even attempt to stop me. "We are in the middle of a battle. My life is in danger. The bond will keep you by my side and ready to die in my defence whether you want it to or not."

"Then I hope I die," I spat at him. "And the last thing I see is my sister cutting your fucking head off."

Lionel scoffed as the taste of those words on my tongue made me feel physically sick. I cursed the bond as it thrummed with life between us, urging me closer to him even though I knew in my heart I didn't truly want that at all.

I tried to take another step, but found I couldn't, the need to protect him building up in me until there were no other thoughts left in my head.

"Tory, come on," Xavier urged, tugging on my arm but I shook my head as I threw a protective shield up over Lionel, easing some of the bond's demands as I gave in.

"You go," I choked out, the pressure in my skull lessening a little as I stumbled back to Lionel's side and he smirked at me triumphantly.

"I'm not leaving you here," Xavier growled but before I could try and insist, a blur of motion in the corner of my eye made me whirl around.

Caleb vaulted over the balcony and shot towards Lionel so fast I could barely even make out the movement. He bounced off of my air shield at the last moment and stumbled back with a furious snarl as my heart lurched with panic for my king.

"Hey, sweetheart," Caleb said, holding one of his flaming daggers in his hand as he looked between me and Lionel for a moment. "Wanna step aside for me?"

"I can't," I grunted, moving to block his view of Lionel as the bastard laughed behind me.

"Your mother will be so disappointed when I send her your head, Caleb," he sneered. "Whatever will she think to find out you're a traitor to the kingdom you were raised to rule?"

Caleb didn't waste time engaging in bullshit with him, shooting around me instead. He ripped a chunk of stone from the seats above us using his earth magic, raining the heavy lumps of masonry down over Lionel's air shield.

My hands snapped out and I threw a fireball at Caleb before I could even consider holding back, the blast of magic exploding against the wall where he'd been standing and making my heart leap with fear for him.

"Nice try, sweetheart," Caleb teased as he shot behind me and I sucked in a sharp breath as I whipped around to face him again.

"I can't let you hurt him, Caleb," I warned, holding my hands up again and coating them in air with the hope that at least I wouldn't set him alight if he wouldn't back off.

A blast of air magic shot past me as Lionel took aim over my shoulder and Caleb sped away again, throwing fire in a wild arc that crashed against Lionel's shield.

"Fight like a Fae!" Xavier roared at his father, making the stone around us shudder as he wielded earth magic. "Stop hiding behind her and face your enemies yourself!"

"As if a herd creature such as you would even understand the meaning of true power," Lionel spat as I was forced to shoot a blast of air at Caleb to stop his attack once more. "Using Roxanya *is* me being Fae. If you can't even see that then I can see that there isn't any hope for you. You're nothing but a mistake I should have dealt with a long time ago."

Xavier roared a challenge as he ran forward with his hands raised and I screamed a warning at him as he released a blast of pure fire magic which was so hot it seemed to set the air alight all around us. It crashed into my shield hard enough to make it rattle but it held and I swore, wishing I could have just forced myself to drop it.

There was nothing I could do to stop myself as I blasted him with a bolt of air and his lack of training meant Xavier hadn't even shielded against me.

I cried out as the blast hit him with the force of a meteor, lifting him from his feet and slamming him against the wall with a sickening crack. Blood spilled and he fell to the ground unmoving as a sob lodged in my chest.

I caught a blur of movement shooting towards us again and fought with everything I had against the bond, trying to stop myself from shielding Lionel as I clung onto every reason I had to hate him.

A blast of fire shot from Caleb's hands and I leapt in front of it, not even shielding myself as I threw all of my magic into protecting Lionel and my skin burned without my Phoenix to protect me.

I fell to the floor with a cry of pain and the flash of Lionel's fire magic blasting over my head was all I could see as I quickly smothered the flames burning into my white dress.

I grunted as I healed myself, pushing to my feet again before I'd even finished, creating a whirlpool of water magic all around myself and Lionel to keep Caleb away from us.

"That's it, Roxanya," Lionel encouraged as he brushed my hair back over my shoulder and stepped so close that his breath made a shiver run down my spine. "Now prove to them where you true loyalties lie and kill him for me."

The command was like an arrow piercing my heart and a fire lighting in my soul at once.

The bond wanted to please him more than anything, urging me to destroy Caleb for daring to stand against my Ward while my heart ached and shattered at the thought of hurting him.

"I won't," I breathed defiantly as the whirlpool fell away beneath my command.

But as I stood ready to face Caleb again, I held a dagger forged from ice in my hand and I was filled with the desire to plunge it into his heart.

Caleb eyed me warily as I positioned myself between him and my king, a tear slipping down my cheek as the need to kill him burned brightly within me and I silently begged my friend to just turn and run.

But of course he didn't. He was an Heir. And they'd been bred to be cocky and self-assured until the very end. I just prayed I wouldn't end up becoming that end.

"Oh, I think you will," Lionel purred and I had the horrifying feeling that he might be right.

DARIUS

CHAPTER FIFTY FOUR

The chamber I was in was dark and cold but somewhere ahead of me, golden light spilled into the shadows, guiding me closer.

My skin was tingling with the power in this place and my pulse thumped to a sultry beat that seemed to be lulling me deeper into the cave.

As I took a step forward, a golden rune illuminated beneath my foot, the symbol twisted and beautiful and seeming to whisper its meaning into my ear.

"Truth."

I took another step and another rune lit up beneath me, this one breathing, *'fortune'* on the air. As I continued on, more runes illuminated and more of their meanings were whispered to me.

"Honesty. Virtue. Life. Growth. Strength. Sacrifice. Power. Death. Destiny. Fate."

As the echoes of the last word fell from the air and I was plunged into silence once more, I found myself standing before a huge stone which glowed ever so faintly in the dark.

It hummed with a power so visceral that the hairs along the back of my neck stood on end.

I reached out for it hesitantly, my fingertips brushing against the rough stone before a jolt of power slammed into my chest and I was drawn undeniably closer.

I sucked in a deep breath as the entire thing began to glow with a deep, golden light which reminded me of my Dragon's scales when the setting sun hit them just right. It was rich and vibrant and so full of power that it stole my breath away.

The entire thing seemed to hum with a power so ancient that I felt utterly insignificant standing before it as it scrutinised every dark corner of my soul.

"Acrux," it breathed, its voice deeper now that I was touching it and my pulse galloping as I felt like it truly knew me.

In the centre of the stone was a perfectly smooth hole and I slid my hand down to touch it, finding coins, jewels and other small tokens that had been left there in offering so long ago that even the earth beneath my feet could hardly remember the Fae who had left them. But it was clear to me that this had been a place of worship once and this relic was crafted with the deep and ancient magic our kind had long since forgotten.

The space surrounding us was pregnant with expectation but as the voice failed to speak again, I was struck with the need to offer up something of my own in payment for its words, the way that others had clearly done before me.

I ran my hands over my pockets uselessly, cursing as I found nothing at all in my possession that I could offer up aside from the clothes on my back. And a suit made for a wedding I hadn't even wanted to attend didn't seem like much of a sacrifice to me.

I frowned as I tried to think of something I could offer it, going over all the tales Orion had told me about ancient magic when teaching me how to wield my draining dagger and cast blood magic. The things he knew were relics of the magic from long ago according to his father. So much knowledge had been lost to time and with dark magic being outlawed, even more of it had fallen from memory.

But some knowledge had remained. Like the power of blood.

I twisted my fingers in a subtle pattern, creating a blade with my ice magic before lifting my other hand and placing it inside the hole in the centre of the stone.

I closed my eyes for a moment, holding the dagger ready and hoping that I wasn't losing my damn mind before scoring it straight across my palm and slicing deep.

Blood welled in the wound, splashing down inside the hole and I gasped as the entire cavern was lit up by the bright golden light and my arm was dragged deeper within the stone by some unworldly magic.

"The price of knowledge is power. The price of power is great. Every bargain has a cost. What will you trade for a different fate?"

The voice rebounded off of the walls, driving into my skull until I was crying out from the force of it, desperately trying to tear my hand back out of the hole as the stone drew more and more of my blood from my body and I could feel it feeding on my power too.

I cursed as I fought to free myself, beating at the stone with my free hand and finding myself unable to cast any magic, as if it were a Vampire using venom to immobilise it.

Strength began to leave my limbs and I scrunched my eyes closed as I hit the stone until my knuckles were busted open and my mind was filled with an image of the girl I loved.

Of her in my arms, wrapped up tight in my bed with me, her eyes filled with laughter and her hands on my flesh. She stroked her fingers down my jaw and looked into my eyes, consuming me with the warmth in her expression and making me feel content in a way I never had before. Roxy tugged the white sheet up over our heads and we were lost in a cocoon of white.

"I love you, Darius," she breathed, her words so pure and real that they made my chest ache with the most desperate desire to truly hear her say them. "I love you, Roxy," I growled in reply, my words echoing in the cavern as I spoke them aloud and not just in the vision. She leaned forward, pressing the sweetest kiss to my lips as my hand moved down over the swollen curve of her stomach as an ache unlike anything I'd ever felt before consumed me.

The vision fell away and the voice spoke again. *"You wish for love with the girl who denied you. But fate has other designs in mind."*

I was thrust into a series of visions, one after another, some just flashes and others lasting longer as I saw the people I loved most in this world engaged in a battle at the amphitheatre in the palace grounds. My heartbeat thundered desperately as I saw each of the Heirs hurt or dying, Orion skewered on the probes of a Nymph, Darcy screaming as Clara tore her apart with her teeth and blood flowed hot and fast, too much for her to possibly survive losing. I saw my brother dashed against a stone wall with a blast of magic and finally Roxy fighting to save my Father's life against her will, only to have him stab her in the back the moment the fight was won.

The vision lingered on her face as she dropped to her knees, my name on her lips as the brightness dulled from her eyes and she collapsed to the floor beneath him, red blood staining her white dress as my entire world was torn away from me.

"What would you give for them, Darius Acrux? What would you sacrifice to see them survive?"

ORION

CHAPTER FIFTY FIVE

A Nymph fell beneath the might of my sword and I twisted around, seeking out Darcy to check she was alright, but my gaze caught on Clara racing toward us. Shadows burst out from my sister, swallowing me and Blue and my pulse hammered in my ears.

I couldn't see. I'd lost sight of the battle, my girl, everything. Whispers filled my head and all sound was lost to the dark magic consuming the world around me, the only light the glittering fire burning on the edges of my sword.

"Clara!" I called into the dark. "Show yourself."

The darkness swept out around me so I found myself standing in a dome of shadow arching over me. Clara was kneeling at the centre of it, clutching her chest and sobbing.

"Clara?" I breathed hopefully, stepping closer to her cautiously.

"Oh Lance," she said, her voice cracking. "Please help me."

I reached for her shoulder and her head whipped around, her eyes as dark as pitch as she lunged at me with her fangs bared. My heart lurched and I threw her away from me with the strength of my Order, but a tendril of shadow caught my legs and flipped me onto the ground on my back.

She jumped on my chest and I snarled, throwing her away from me again so she went tumbling over the sand. I leapt up to fight, raising my weapon in defence, but how could I strike her when I knew my sister was in there?

"Lance!" Darcy's voice reached me from somewhere out in the shadows, and my chest tightened.

"Blue. Stay away!" I roared, but she called my name again like she couldn't hear me.

"I could crush her, little brother," Clara said lightly as she rose up on a tower of shadow ten feet above me, glaring down with venom in her eyes. "I could squeeze her in the shadows until her head went bang."

I clenched my jaw, running forward and slicing the sword through the shadows beneath her. She shrieked, falling down and hitting the ground. I lunged for her, trying to grab her hair but my hand passed through nothing but darkness.

"You can't hurt her, she's stronger than you," I snapped and she waved a hand.

Darcy's screams rang in my head and fear sped through my body.

I ran towards Clara, but she shot away into the shadows and I took chase, running as fast as I possibly could to catch her.

"Blue!" I bellowed, but no reply came. I was lost in the dark again, running through an endless sea of it, unable to find my queen or my sister.

"Blue!" a mimicry of my voice sounded off in the mist and my heart lurched in panic.

"I'm coming!" Darcy's reply came.

"No! that's not me!" I shouted, but the sound came thundering back into my own ears, not seeming to go anywhere at all.

Clara's high pitched laugh filled my head and I ran faster through the shadows as I searched for Darcy.

"You've been very mean to me, little brother," Clara's voice followed me everywhere as I sprinted, my arms wheeling back and forth beside me as I ran harder and faster. "And now you've chosen this dirty little Vega over me and my shadows. They were a gift, how dare you let her get rid of them?"

"Shut up!" I bellowed. "You're not my sister. You're Lavinia. A Nymph princess."

"Ohhh!" she cried in glee. "Lavinia, yes, yes, yes. I'd forgotten my name. How pretty it is. La-vin-ia. I love it, I love it. Thank you, little brother."

"I'm not your brother," I snarled viciously.

"Yes, you're right I suppose. But Daddy isn't my daddy and I rather like calling him that. I think your sister liked it too once," she chuckled cruelly. "Clara is here. Do you want to say hello?"

My breathing stuttered and I slowed my pace. "Yes, let her out. Let her be free, Lavinia. Please. She has nothing to do with this."

"Lance," Clara sobbed. "Please end it. Save me."

I growled angrily, turning as my sister's voice sounded right behind me. Two familiar eyes met mine between the shadows and I lunged for my true sister, reaching for her hand, but she immediately dissolved into the mist.

Lavinia's dark laughter sounded once more, rattling through my skull.

Darcy screamed somewhere off in the fog and panic tore at me. *What do I do? How do I find her?*

"Daddy wants you alive," Lavinia cooed at me. "But you can't be alive and not be punished. So I'm going to make your life hurt, little brother. You'll suffer and suffer and suffer until you beg me to take away the pain. You'll want to return to the shadows and be by my side forever. You and me. Family.

Doesn't that sound nice?"

"Fine," I snarled. "Hurt me, punish me, do whatever you like, just let Darcy go."

"And why would I do that?" she chuckled. "Pain makes you suffer in the now, but I want you to suffer in the always."

"Blue!" I called again in desperation and my voice echoed everywhere.

No reply came and fate seemed to close in, narrowing down until there was only one path to follow. And it wasn't going to end in my favour.

"Let her go," I demanded.

"Alright," Lavinia chuckled. "Which will it be then, your sister or the Vega princess?"

"Both," I hissed, my heart beating fiercely.

"Ah you little witch!" Lavinia screamed suddenly and the shadows tightened, suffocatingly thick. I was being dragged forward, guided toward something as tendrils of shadow bound me and I slashed at them over and over with my sword to try and free myself.

"Fuck you," Darcy snarled and Clara shrieked again.

"Ow ow ow! You're hurting. All that fire is ouchy," Lavinia begged then started laughing and laughing. "Stay in there in the dark, I'm talking to your lover boy."

"Lance!" Darcy cried but the sound was muffled and as she started shouting again, her voice faded away.

I battled the shadows holding me, more and more of them wrapping around my flesh and several locking around my arm as they tried to prise the sword from my grasp. But I wouldn't let go.

Lavinia appeared before me, peering at me from behind my sister's eyes, her head cocking to one side as she regarded me and I tried to lunge at her, finding myself unable to move.

"I need a little something," she said with a smirk, drifting toward me and gripping my chin. "You're a clever thing, do you know much about shadow curses?"

"No," I said, my voice thick as the word curse sent fear dripping down my spine.

She reached out, grasping my throat and I fought harder against the shadows, trying to tear myself free of them. Her touch was ice cold as her hand slid down my skin then her fingernails drove into my flesh. "It requires some blood. And I'm fresh out." An icy blade slashed across my arm and I snarled in pain, shoving her away, but not before she coated her hand in the blood from my wound.

"Clara," I breathed, trying to get my sister's attention, seeking her out in this monster's eyes. "I'll save you. I'll find a way."

She sneered, but then her expression shifted and I was sure I was looking at my true sister. Her ebony eyes were filled with endless pain and it broke my heart to see her suffering.

"I'm here, look at me. You can fight her off, I'll help you. Darcy will help you," I promised and she released a sob that hurt me.

"I can't come back," she choked. "Please free me." Then she disappeared into the dark once more.

CALEB

CHAPTER FIFTY SIX

I shot around the balcony for what felt like the hundredth time, my magic beginning to wane as I threw it at Lionel time and again.

But Tory got between us more often than not and even when she didn't, his shield deflected my blows as he focused on maintaining it. Every time Tory was exposed to fire, her magic swelled, but Lionel's had an expiry on his just like mine did. And though the golden crown on his head would have been offering him some power, I knew that Dragons couldn't gain a lot fast from a single piece of jewellery like that.

I just needed to wear him down and outlast him. Then I'd prove to him that the Acruxes weren't any more powerful than the Altairs.

Tory's eyes were full of pain as she was forced to fight me over and over again and I silently apologised to her as I just kept coming. This was where I needed to be in this fight and even if I'd wanted to spare her from having to go up against me, I couldn't turn back now I was here.

Lionel roared as he threw a fireball at me with so much force that I chose shooting away over trying to deflect it, only realising it was heading straight for Xavier's unconscious form at the last second.

I shot in front of him, throwing a wall of dirt up to surround the two of us and heaving him over my shoulder as the flames crashed overhead.

The moment they died down, I ran away, leaping from the balcony and casting a few wooden spears over my shoulder to keep Lionel back while I ran.

I shot up the stairs of the amphitheatre and cast a concealment spell to hide us from the Dragons and Nymphs fighting on Lionel's side of this battle. I laid Xavier down on one of the stone benches and pressed my fingers to his head to heal the bleeding wound there, my power waning as I drew close to the end of it. I needed blood, like right now.

An explosion of fire and lightning clashed overhead as one of Lionel's purple Dragons went up against the Storm Dragon and I couldn't help but tip my head back to the sky as they clashed in a furious tangle of claws and teeth.

Dante roared ferociously, sinking his teeth into the other Dragon's neck just as he released a blast of lightning from his jaws which drove into his opponent, barbecuing him from the inside out.

Xavier yelled in alarm as he came to and spotted the purple Dragon tumbling from the sky right towards us and I snatched him from the ground again before shooting out of the way of the crash zone.

The dead Dragon slammed into the stands with enough force to make the whole structure rattle and I paused as I turned to look around at the body as it shifted back into Fae form in death and a naked man was left in its place.

There were rebels everywhere now and my cousin shot past me, running in the opposite direction with a whoop of triumph for the Storm Dragon as he roared his victory to the sky. Dante dove low as he heard her calling out to him and she used a shot of air magic to propel herself up into the sky so that she could land on his back, the two of them racing away into the fight again.

I ran on, still holding Xavier then skidded to a halt at the edge of the pit, glancing down into the raging fight below for a moment before giving my full attention to him.

"I need to get back to Tory," I told him.

"Come on then, let's-"

"No. You should get down there and show these motherfuckers why they shouldn't underestimate a Pegasus. But first - I'm gonna need a drink." I lunged at him and he swore as my fangs sank into his neck, the rich combination of the power in his blood sliding over my tongue as I swallowed greedily.

"Asshole," he muttered as he gave in. "I heard you were horny for the horn, but I never knew it was true until now."

I almost yanked my teeth from his neck as I snorted a laugh at that before growling to cover it. I hated that fucking rumour - but in this one instance it might have been funny.

Xavier Acrux tasted damn good. But he was no Alpha Wolf and I drew back as quickly as I could, needing to get back to the fight with Lionel.

"Come on then, shift," I commanded and Xavier nodded firmly.

"Good luck, Caleb," he said seriously, tugging his shirt over his head as his skin began to glimmer with lilac glitter.

"I don't need luck," I teased. "I'm invincible."

Xavier's brow pinched like he was going to tell me off for tempting fate like that, but I just laughed and shot away to take on his father.

He was just an evil Dragon overlord with control over dark shadow magic and two powerful Guardians working alongside him after all.

I could totally kick his ass.

Maybe.

DARCY

CHAPTER FIFTY SEVEN

"Lance!" I cried for the hundredth time, using my fire to burn away the shadows as I sought him out in the endless ring of darkness I was lost in.

"Lance, Lance, Lance!" Clara's voice mocked me and I growled, raising my palms and burning back more of her power.

I couldn't risk tearing right through the fog of shadows in case I hit Orion, but the second I saw that bitch again I was going to burn them right out of her.

"You're pretty, just like *she* was pretty," Clara cooed somewhere behind me and I wheeled around to try and spot her. "But all Vegas are nasty, nasty. You're just like she was, that foul queen who cast me into the dark."

"I saw what you were," I called. "I know what she did to you."

"Oh you know, do you? So you know the Nymphs were persecuted by that evil fire queen?"

"She was just trying to end the war," I growled.

Clara snarled furiously. "She ruined my kind, made us into monsters and turned the entire world against us."

"What do you mean?" I demanded, keeping a ring of fire tight around me to hold back the shadows closing in.

"We're sisters, see?" she said forlornly. "Sisters are so very precious. But the queen betrayed all of her sisters."

"I don't understand. You were related to her?"

"Not in that way, oh don't you see, little Vega princess? How very naive you are, and how arrogant too."

"Lance!" I called again and she laughed shrilly.

"Lovers in my spider's web," she sang. "Well I'd best get on with it before this blood dries upon my palm. It'll hurt a little now, then later it will hurt a lot."

"What are you talking about?" I snarled, pushing my fire further away from me as I tried to carve out a space to see ahead of me.

Time was dissolving in here and I feared what lay beyond this, my sister, my friends, what was happening out in the battle?

"I'm going to do to you what I wanted to do to her," she cackled. "I spent so long learning this spell, but I never got a chance to curse her like I wanted. It's rather exciting actually. How many, many, many years I've waited for revenge and I'm going to draw it out slow and long and oh so sweetly."

I pushed my fire deeper into the shadows, my pulse accelerating at her words.

"Come out here and face me," I demanded, readying to fight for my life.

"I'm going to put a little fun twist on it too," she went on like I'd said nothing. "Oh, it's going to be so much fun to watch you both break when you find out what it is. I'm going to make sure you live long enough to see me rise. Daddy will be mad, but I am to be his queen, and maybe it's time I started making my own rules."

"Fight me!" I roared, letting fire billow upwards to carve a hole in the shadows above. I cast air beneath my feet, racing toward the sliver of sky that opened up, but it closed away again as the darkness pressed down on me, forcing me back. I hit the ground and snarled as I started running, sending flash fires out ahead of me as I carved a path.

"Lance, where are you?!"

"Darcy!" he cried somewhere close by and far away.

I ran harder with frantic, desperate breaths, needing to get to him. As soon as I was near, I could blast away this net of shadows and free us.

A heavy magic licked my skin and Clara started chanting words that made the hairs on my body stand on end. I couldn't understand the dark language she was speaking, but I'd heard it spoken in the shadows before and it sent chills right down to my core.

"Ambres tenus avilias mortalium avar," she hissed. "Irexus tu neverendum."

I burned through the shadows that tried to cling to me, running faster and faster as the curse pressed down on me, enveloping my body then pushing deeper and deeper as it tried to take root in me.

I urged my Phoenix fire through my veins, trying to burn it away, but the dark magic slipped past it and I couldn't stop it as it buried itself deep inside me. This was something I couldn't fight and the thought of that terrified me.

"Novus estris envum magicae," she breathed. "Avilias avar!"

An ice cold hand pressed to my arm and I wheeled around, blasting fire toward Clara before she disappeared into the dark once more with a shrieking cackle.

I looked down at my arm in fear, finding a bloody handprint wrapping around my bicep. The mark turned black and my head spun as the power from it rushed into me like a tsunami.

I stumbled, my vision darkening as the power gripped me and I found myself unable to fight off whatever was happening. I forced my Phoenix fire against it with everything I had, but it did nothing to stop it. And in the deepest regions of my heart, I knew nothing could as I fell to my knees and an ocean of darkness stole me away.

ORION

CHAPTER FIFTY EIGHT·

Lavinia's laughter rang out everywhere as I pushed through the sea of shadows, feeling it drag at me like I was wading through the thickest of bogs. No magic could hold it back except the power of the sword, so I cut and fought my way forward with it to find Darcy even as my muscles burned and my strength was pushed to its limits.

"Blue!" I shouted, my voice getting hoarse from calling for her.

The shadows suddenly opened up, releasing me and a path ran through them all the way to where Darcy was lying on the ground, looking terrifyingly still as her dark blue hair spilled out around her in a fan. Panic split through me and I sprinted toward her with a yell of desperation, but before I made it there, the shadows closed up once more and she was lost in the dark.

"Lavinia!" I bellowed. "What have you done to her?!"

Laughter rang around me, mocking me and chills spread everywhere through my body. I heaved in breaths, cutting through the shadows as I forcibly tried to get to my girl. *She's not dead. She's not fucking dead.*

"Calm down, it's just a little curse," she said with a laugh that made my blood chill.

"What kind of curse?" I roared, whipping around as I hunted for her and finding nothing but shadow yet again. *What has she done to her?*

"My army is here," Lavinia whispered close by and I swung toward the voice with a snarl. "Your friends are dying." The pressing silence of the shadows lifted for a moment and screams and shouts of terror called out all around me, making my heart stammer with concern.

I heard Geraldine screaming in pain and fear crashed through me before the sound was stolen once more by the darkness closing in on me.

Two cruel eyes appeared in the dark and I slashed my blade toward them in a warning to keep her back. Lavinia shrieked then released a breathy sob that pulled at my heartstrings.

"*Lance*," she spoke and I knew it was my sister this time. "She's getting too strong. You have to end this. Please. Kill me. I'm already dead anyway. I can't come back, deep down you must know that."

"No," I growled in denial, reaching for her in the dark and her cold fingers found mine, though I still couldn't see her.

I tried to pull her towards me out of the fog, but she couldn't be moved.

"I'm so sorry," she cried. "For everything. But you have to see the truth. You know it in your heart."

"Please don't say that," I begged, the thought of losing her all over again too much for me to bear as panic made my heart hurt and I fought to deny her words.

The shadows closed in around me and flashes of images ran through my mind until I was dragged into memories racing through my head of the night I'd lost my sister.

Clara stood in the desolate land of the Shadow Realm naked and frozen, her arm still bloody from the sacrifice Lionel had made her offer before the dark stardust had consumed her.

"Hush," Lavinia's voice filled the air and shadows coiled around her, cloaking her body. "I am here." They wound tighter and tighter and Clara gasped in fear as they sank beneath her flesh, taking root in her. "Go quietly, Fae girl, your body is mine."

Clara screamed and thrashed as the shadows possessed her until she was forced to her knees and blood dripped from her mouth as the shadow spirit of Lavinia ate its way into her body.

Sickness ran through me and I was half aware of releasing a shout I couldn't hear.

Wounds opened up across her skin and blood poured out from her in wave after wave, washing across the ground and rushing back through a fissure which was torn into the air. A portal ripped open by Lionel Acrux as a part of the ritual he'd forced us to bear witness to all those years ago, sacrificing my sister just for this.

Clara started crawling back toward it in desperation as a horrid scream left her which made my entire being seize up with grief.

She fell still before she made it to the portal and the shadows settled inside her, claiming her body, her soul. Lavinia took control of Clara as the wounds across her body healed, her features twisting as they lost the gentleness of my sister and took on the ferociousness of a Nymph Princess.

She scrambled to her feet and rushed toward the portal, but it closed up before she made it and Lavinia released an inhuman shriek that echoed through my skull. Then she fell to the ground, lapping at the blood that lay there like a monster until my stomach turned and my chest hollowed out.

I was released from the vision and a noise of grief left me as the weight of the truth fell over me.

"I was dead the moment she found me," Clara whispered in my ear and I felt the brush of her thumb against my hand, her fingers still clutching mine. "My soul is trapped, unable to join the stars. And if you don't destroy her, I'll never be free. Please, Lance. Please do this for me."

Her hand was torn from mine and Lavinia snarled, sending the shadows crashing into me and I was thrown to the floor. I cast air beneath me to right myself and hit the ground running, cutting a path deeper into the dark as my mind whirled and a terrible decision was laid at my feet.

"I've seen what she'll do," Clara gasped like she was in pain.

"Shut up!" Lavinia screamed.

"I've seen her plans," Clara called in a tight voice. "You must destroy her before she completes the curse."

"There's still time?" I gasped in hope.

"Enough!" Lavinia roared and I felt her anger sparking through the atmosphere.

My foot caught on a soft body and I hit the ground, scrambling back toward her, my heart thundering as I sliced the sword through the air to clear away the dark. Darcy lay there with her eyes closed, her expression peaceful, and her skin warm.

"Thank the stars," I said heavily, hearing her heartbeat pounding solidly in my ears.

I was about to pull her into my arms when the shadows drew away and I found myself looking up at Lavinia, scowling down at us with her upper lip peeled back. The fire ruby necklace that belonged to Tory shone around her neck, looking starkly red against her near translucent skin.

I pushed to my feet with fury in my heart, placing myself in front of Darcy as I held the sword higher and gritted my jaw.

"Stay still," Lavinia growled, wetting her lips. "You didn't give me enough blood." She rushed at me and I held the blade steady as my pulse thundered in my ears.

I planted my feet, refusing to let her get close to Darcy, protectiveness driving my actions as she came for me. I was about to strike her with the blade, but then I thought of my sister, playing with me in the garden as a kid, laughing and joking. We'd loved each other with every piece of ourselves. We were inseparable. Lionel had ripped us apart, but even if just a part of her was left in this body, how could I hurt her?

Lavinia collided with me, knocking me back a step and her hands clawed at me.

I snarled, trying to shove her away as her fangs sliced into my arm as she bit me savagely, tearing open my flesh so hot blood ran across the skin.

"Lance – now – do it now!" Clara screamed in a pained and desperate voice and my heart broke apart, cleaving down the middle.

My hands trembled around the hilt of the sword and her eyes met mine as she managed to lurch away from me. I could see her fighting to hold onto herself as Lavinia battled to regain control. I had seconds to act. Seconds to strike her, seconds to free my sister, to save Blue.

"I'm sorry." I swung the blade up, making the decision with a suffocating pain in my chest as I drove it into her gut. I tore through flesh and bone and shadow as I impaled her on it and Lavinia and Clara screamed as one.

The shadows wrapped around me, clutching my throat, my chest, my stomach and forcing the air out of me as they tried to kill me, crushing me like a rat in the grip of a python. But I didn't let go of the sword, driving it deeper with a shout of utter fury and grief.

Phoenix fire suddenly flared around me, burning back the shadows as Darcy's power aided me from behind.

The shadows receded, rushing back into Clara's body in a huge swirling cloud as the fire burned them away. A tornado of flames surrounded us, my girl's power exploding from her in an endless wave of destruction, devouring every shadow it found.

The cries of the battle fell in on me once more, daylight illuminating us and burning my retinas.

I wrenched the sword free and my sister collapsed to the floor beneath me with shadows coating her flesh. I fell to my knees, tugging her against me and cupping her face as she peered at me with a blissful smile on her face. She reached up to run her fingers over my cheek, brushing my tears away as my heart broke and I faced a goodbye I'd never gotten the first time I'd lost her. A goodbye I'd never wanted to have to give.

"Thank you," she sighed, looking to the sky as if she could see the stars shining back at her. I hoped she could see our dad, that she was going to be reunited with him and the two of them would wait for me beyond the Veil until it was my time to join them. And I hoped Dad knew how sorry I was that I couldn't save my sister.

"I love you," I rasped, holding her tighter and her lips moved, repeating the words to me, but no sound came out.

Her eyes fell closed and I squeezed her in one final, heart breaking embrace before her body turned to dust, the shadows pluming out and away from it as she was parted from them at long last. Tory's necklace lay on the ground where she'd been and I took it, pushing it into my pocket as grief made me buckle forward.

"Lance?" Darcy's voice sounded from behind me and I twisted around to see the girl who made my existence on earth worthwhile.

But my heart lurched in terror as the shadows reared up behind her, gathering together and reforming until a girl stepped from them, the darkness within her making the air crackle with power. "Quendus novlia andrenis," she spoke in a commanding tone and Darcy groaned, unable to get up as she fell under the dark power of those words.

"No!" I shot toward her to get her out the way but tendrils of shadow burst from Lavinia, forcing me to the ground and binding my limbs.

Lavinia looked down at her own arms, admiring her true form as she scraped her long, black fingernails over her pale skin. Her long hair danced around her, alive with shadows and her eyes were wicked and red as her gaze snapped up to lock onto me and the girl I loved. I felt like I'd been hit by a truck as I stared at the Shadow Princess, somehow still here. Still fucking alive. And I got the horrible feeling that now that she was free of Clara's body, she was more powerful than ever.

Lavinia lurched forward with unnatural speed, grasping Darcy's arms and smearing them with blood. *My* blood.

"Stop!" I roared, fighting with everything I had, but the power holding me was immense.

"Nevellius combra asticious levellium mortus!" Lavinia cried as I twisted the sword in my grip and slicing it through the shadows binding me. The fire flared along its length, slicing through the shadows and suddenly I was free. I shoved to my feet, running forward frantically, my breaths falling furiously from my lungs as I powered toward them, my sword poised to kill.

Darcy screamed as she was held in the grip of Lavinia's dark curse, her Phoenix fire flickering weakly against her fingertips.

"Watch me rule as Queen, little Vega princess," Lavinia laughed as she shoved Darcy towards me. "I shall offer you death when you come begging me for it."

I launched the sword at Lavinia with a shout of effort, throwing all of my power behind it and it wheeled end over end towards the Shadow Princess. She evaporated into a cloud of shadow, tearing away from us into the battle and my sword thumped uselessly onto the sand beyond where she'd been. I dragged Darcy to her feet and she fell against me with a shuddering gasp.

I held her close, pouring healing magic into her body while maintaining an air shield around us to keep us safe as the battle raged on and hope faded everywhere I looked. The Nymph army was pouring into the amphitheatre, crushing the rebels with sheer numbers.

Darcy steadied herself and stepped back, strength starting to return to her eyes and that gave me something small to hold onto. My gaze fell to the black handprint on her arm and my heart turned to dust.

"What has she done to you?" I dragged her closer, examining the mark, but Darcy reached for the wounds on my arms, sending healing magic out into my skin. Fear pressed in on me as I stared at her, not knowing what that vicious witch had done to her.

I just had to focus on the fact that she was alive, and here. Whatever curse had been put on her, I would break it. I vowed it on every constellation, every galaxy, the entire universe.

"I don't know, but we have to get out of here." She turned to look for her sister up in the stands, her eyes full of worry as a swarm of Nymphs raced towards us.

I readied myself for one last fight, sending healing magic through my veins, keeping her close as I moved to grab my sword.

I was exhausted and aching and running on fumes. But I would not give up. Clara may have been gone, but she was with the stars now. And I would grieve her later when this was done.

For now, I had to ensure no more of my loved ones were lost to our enemies.

DARIUS

CHAPTER FIFTY NINE

My mind was ablaze with visions of all the people I loved in this world falling prey to horrible twists of fate and my heartbeat thundered in my ears as the deep magic of this place seemed to drive its way right into my soul.

"Tell me," I growled. "What will it take to save them?"

"Sacrifice," the voice breathed, making the air around me tremble as countless runes illuminated on the walls surrounding me.

The hole in the rock suddenly released its grip on my arm and I stumbled back a few steps as I withdrew my bleeding hand. My magic returned to me as I stood panting before the huge stone and I felt like I'd run a marathon from whatever it had just done to me.

"Will you save them?" I demanded and a rustle moved through the room which almost sounded like distant laughter. My skin prickled as if a hundred eyes were on me but I couldn't tear my gaze from the glowing stone before me.

"The life of a Fae means little to the stars. Fate changes, destiny isn't always set in stone. The gift on offer isn't life. It's freedom. A chance. A possibility to change the stars again."

I opened my mouth to ask what that meant as another vision filled my mind.

Roxy was fighting for my father, compelled to give everything she had in his defence by the bond he'd forced on her. But as I watched, she fell still, the Aries brand on her arm fading to nothing and her mind clearing of the bonds' control.

Her eyes flashed with power and vengeance, but the vision fell away before I could see that path play out. I was filled with one certainty though - if that happened then he wouldn't be able to stab her in the back, that possibility would be gone and her life would be saved. She would survive this day at least and right now I wasn't sure how much more I could even hope for.

"One year," the voice breathed. "To love her like you ache to. To be the best of yourself. One year and no more."

"You want me to buy her life with my death?" I asked, my voice rough as I realised that was the price. That was what it would take to re-write the stars, save her life and release her from my Father's hold.

My heart pounded desperately within my chest as if I was standing looking my death in the eyes right now and a shiver of fear ran through me at the thought. I didn't want to die. I wanted to live. With her.

But if her fate was already decided and this was the only chance she had, then what other choice was there for me to make? If she died now, I may as well die anyway because I knew there was no joy in the world for me if she didn't exist anymore.

Solaria needed strong rulers, but Xavier could take my place on the Council. And she would have her sister after I was gone.

"All bonds?" I clarified as the visions of her dying pressed in on me again, warning me that time was running out for her, that I had to make this choice fast.

"A fresh start," the voice confirmed. "Every bond placed upon the two of you by the stars wiped away."

"But all I get is a year?" My heart was thrashing desperately now, adrenaline begging me to do something to save myself, but this wasn't an enemy I could fight. It was destiny in the making.

"A year to live the life you yearn for. A year to find out if you really are the man you wish to be."

My lips parted on an answer but the air before me shimmered and I saw myself in a vision of the future. I was standing with Roxy beneath a huge Christmas tree, my lips pressing to hers in one final, desperate kiss before my time ran out one year from now.

Her arms curled around my neck, drawing me closer as I held her so tightly that I was certain not even the stars could tear us apart.

But as the clock struck midday, my muscles locked, the magic within me stilling. And even as I fought with all I had to stay there with her, my fate was already sealed and it tore me away all the same.

Roxy screamed as I fell to my knees before her, the power of the stars coming to collect the price I'd promised to pay. The sound of her grief cut into me and the idea of causing her so much pain made me ache with a desperate desire to shield her from it. But there was no alternative. She could have a life without me or no life at all. And I couldn't bear the idea of her being taken from this world before her time no matter what price I had to pay.

I fell back to the floor in the vision and Roxy refused to release me, falling on top of me as she pressed another kiss to my mouth and begged the stars to change their minds.

Her tears washed over my cheeks as my final breath slid past my lips and I was forced to leave her behind. I fought to hold on to her as I was ripped away and my heart tore apart at the thought of leaving her all alone. If I got my way I knew I'd never leave her again.

But as I fell into the dark embrace of death, my heart was light with the love I'd felt in that year. Of having that time with her as my own like I'd yearned for for so long.

It wasn't enough time. But no amount of days, months or years with her would ever be enough. And I knew that all the time in the world would be empty to me without her in it if she died now.

The price was too high. But I would pay it twice over for her.

I closed my eyes and thought of her as I placed my bleeding hand upon the surface of the glowing stone again, the magic in it calling to me as I made the only choice I could. It was a sacrifice I wished I didn't have to make with every single part of my soul. But I'd known that I would give my life for my girl for a long time now. So it really wasn't a choice at all.

"Blood of the oathbreaker," the voice came again, rich with even more power now as the energy in the cavern made my entire body tingle. *"Descendant of the deceiver. Son of the destroyer. Do you offer your life in payment for the breaking of the bonds?"*

My hand trembled where it pressed to the stone and I closed my eyes against the golden glow emanating from it as I filled my mind with images of the girl I'd gladly give it all up for, silently apologising to her for being so selfish in making this choice. Even though I knew there was no other choice that I could make.

There was no me without her. And I'd have given my life for hers even if I had to die right now. I'd make this year count. I'd make up for every awful thing I'd ever done to her and I'd destroy my father to make certain that she would be safe from his tyranny when I was gone.

In the end there was only her for me. I'd inked it onto my skin and it was branded on my heart. She owned me entirely and I was never going to make any other choice.

"I accept your terms," I growled in a deep voice that echoed with finality. "And I offer my life in payment."

TORY

CHAPTER SIXTY

Fire blazed all around me as I stood before Lionel, gritting my teeth in desperation while I tried to stop myself from attacking Caleb. But it was no use, the bond forced me into action no matter how hard I fought it.

I held an air shield tight around myself and Lionel and the thump of my pulse in my ears was enough to make my head spin.

Caleb shot to my right with a determined yell and I lifted my hands to blast him with water magic, but just as the power reached my fingertips, an enormous blast of energy almost knocked me from my feet.

I staggered back a step as I sucked in a sharp breath, my magic pulsing through my skin in an unfamiliar wave of motion, feeling like sunlight against my flesh in the brightest summer's day and an echo of something dark and forgotten brushing up against my soul.

My left arm burned in a way that sent shivers of pleasure racing through my skin and as I looked down at it, I found the Aries mark Lionel had branded me with fading as the shackles within my mind began to fall away.

I sucked in an astonished breath as my power surged within me and I swung my head around to look at the man who had stolen my crown.

The shield I was using to protect us disbanded as the compulsion to protect him left me. Lionel grabbed my wrist, shouting something I couldn't make out as I narrowed my eyes on him, finally feeling nothing at all but hatred for this monster who had imprisoned and tortured me.

From the corner of my eye, I noticed a blur of motion shooting towards me, taking advantage of me dropping my shield for the first time and I gasped as a sharp prick smacked against my arm.

Caleb was gone as fast as he'd appeared, but the effects of the antidote he'd just given me sped through my body like wildfire as my Phoenix woke up and fire danced within my soul.

"What the hell have you done?" Lionel bellowed, his grip on me tightening as he felt the bond between us falling apart too.

But he clearly hadn't figured out that that was what was happening yet, and this single moment was the only one I needed.

With a roar of fury, my Phoenix form burst from my skin and I was swathed in flames which burned hotter than the surface of the sun as I shifted.

Lionel screamed as his hand was engulfed in the flames where he held me and a blast of air magic slammed into my chest so hard that I was thrown clean out of the royal box and down to the pit far below us.

The stench of burning flesh stayed with me as I fell, his magic driving against me so powerfully that I slammed down onto the sand within the pit before I could even try and fight it off.

The sand felt as hard as rocks as I hit it and my wings were crushed beneath me as my flames flared around me, agony ricocheting through my spine.

I gasped against the pain in my body, healing myself of the worst of it as I found myself in the thick of the battle taking place down here, though none of the Nymphs had turned their attention on me yet.

I cursed as I scrambled to my feet, and a charred, blackened hand fell from my wrist where his fingers had still been curled around me, thumping down onto the sand. A wild and savage smile filled my lips as I looked up at Lionel where he stood screaming down at me from the royal box, a blistered stump where his right hand should have been and his face filled with utter panic as he spotted the charred lump of flesh before me.

He threw a blast of magic at me, but I was far faster as he struggled to wield his Element single handed through the blinding pain of that injury and his attack ricocheted off of my air shield without effect.

Magic surged in my veins as I looked up at him, seeing my chance to end this once and for all and the flames coating my body built up all around me in a blazing inferno, gathering in my palms as I prepared to destroy him.

But before I could obliterate him, a woman clad in shadow leapt between us, shrieking my name in fury as she spotted me and yanking on the shadows which were latched to my soul, fighting to force me under their control once more.

But I was done being a plaything for the shadows and that motherfucking Dragon bastard. And as the shadows reared up within my veins and she tried to force me to fall still under her command, the Phoenix within me flared brighter and brighter. My entire soul was forged in fire and as I gave myself to the heat of the flames, they chased beneath my skin, hunting down the dark power which never should have been mine in the first place. The flames burned through the shadows one after another, freeing me from each and every one of their shackles until every single scrap of darkness within me was banished.

I gasped as the last of them was burned from my soul, standing taller as the weight of them released me and I was finally returned to myself.

I was free.

My smile widened and the shadow bitch screamed furiously as she realised what I'd done, shooting towards me with her fangs bared like she was planning on ripping me apart with her fucking teeth.

I threw a blast of Phoenix fire at her, forcing her to halt her advance as she called on more and more shadows to defend herself. But she didn't stop there. Darkness billowed from her body in a cascade of endless shadows, coiling around her and crackling with dark power which seemed to suck all of the joy out of the air and sent the rebels closest to her falling to their knees in the sand as they screamed in agony.

I looked all around for any sign of Darcy or my friends, but my attention was caught on the Shadow Princess again as she managed to fight off my flames and draw even more dark magic to herself.

The cloud of black smoke began to whirl around her in a maelstrom which only built higher and higher as she smiled wickedly, preparing to destroy us all with the full force of her power.

"Get my hand!" Lionel bellowed as he threw a blast of magic at Caleb who was fighting him once more, managing to knock him back far enough to offer up a chance for him to escape.

Lionel cast a blaze of fire behind him to keep Caleb back and leapt from the royal box, casting air to propel him towards me as I threw my flames towards the shadow bitch, trying to break through the shadows before she could do whatever the fuck it was she was building up to.

But fuck that. Lionel wasn't going to be healing from that wound if I could help it. I'd promised to pay him back in blood and flesh for all of the agony he'd gifted me and this was just the beginning.

With a surge of Phoenix fire which burned its way right through my soul, I blasted the blackened hand which lay on the sand with the full force of my gifts, obliterating it with a yell of fury and bathing in the agonised roar Lionel released as he saw what I had done.

Reattaching and healing a limb was possible. But growing a new one? No fucking chance.

The shadow bitch screamed so loudly that I swear the entire sky almost tore apart as she threw shadows away from her in a deadly arc that slammed into the rebels, causing everyone they hit to shriek in agony.

An earth shattering roar broke through the clouds overhead and I couldn't help but look up as the Storm Dragon swooped towards us, lightning crashing from him in an enormous blast that threw Lionel back towards the swirling shadows that engulfed the far side of the amphitheatre.

Dante swung around to chase after him, but the horned Nymph leapt at him from the stands, its probes slashing down his leg and tearing through scales and flesh as the Dragon roared in agony and wheeled away through the sky.

I'd lost sight of Lionel in the shadows and I threw a wild blast of fire magic towards the Nymph, forcing it away from me as I turned to try and get my bearings.

I threw a shield up over myself and turned desperately, searching for my sister amongst the carnage, knowing in my soul that if we were going to have any chance of surviving this then it needed to be together.

I spotted her blue hair first as she finished a Nymph with a roar of fury and she turned to look at me as if she'd felt my gaze on her.

I shifted back into my Fae form as we started running to meet each other and my heart ached with the need to be reunited with my other half. If our power merged then I was certain that there was nothing in this world that could stop us. Not evil Dragons or psychotic, shadow wielding bitches.

This fight wasn't over. But we were going to end it together.

Darcy

CHAPTER SIXTY ONE

I ran to my sister, our hands clasping together and she looked to me, realising something was wrong as my Phoenix didn't immediately rush to meet hers, the lasting power of the curse making me feel exhausted and weak. Confusion rushed through me as I found her eyes clear, bright and green, the black Star Crossed ring around them gone.

"What-" I started but a huge navy Dragon landed beside me with a guttural roar and electricity sparked off of his skin as he wheeled his head around to look at us.

"Dante," Tory gasped, running to him and healing a jagged wound on his leg.

"Lance!" I called and he shot to my side in a flash, looking at me in dismay as he lowered the sword in his grip.

"We have to go," he said urgently. "The Nymph army is here, we're all going to die if we stay. You have to call a retreat before we're overrun."

"Me?" I scoffed.

"Yes. This is your army. They'll only listen to you or Tory," he said firmly, his eyes flaring with how much he believed that. I wasn't so sure, but I guessed it was worth a try. I didn't want anyone else dying today.

He reached out to cast a spell over my throat and I shared a look with Tory who nodded her agreement.

I tipped my head back to shout, the sound amplified tenfold by his magic. "Retreat!"

Hamish howled up in the stands, calling his friends after him as he led the way through a hole carved into the side of the amphitheatre as they turned from the fight and fled.

"My ladies, you must both leave this instant!" Geraldine came running forward with Max beside her and Seth shifting back into his Fae form at their heels.

Shadows swirled out all around the stadium as Lavinia tore through the retreating rebels, cutting them down with her ferocious power which seemed stronger than ever before, making the ground shake beneath our feet.

Lionel suddenly took off into the sky in his Dragon form, clutching one stumpy front leg to his chest as a hoard of Dragons leapt after him, shifting and protecting him as they flew over the crowd, releasing jets of fire from their lungs.

Orion threw up a shield and I pushed my magic out from me with an effort that made my legs quake, helping him protect us as Max, Seth and Tory all added their power too. Caleb shot out of the shadows towards us and we let him in just before the shield closed up entirely.

"Where the hell is Darius?" Tory demanded as Orion hunted for him in the stands.

"He's not here. He went somewhere with Gabriel," Seth said, casting some earth magic over his legs to cover his junk up with a pair of leaf pants.

"Come fair warriors, we must retreat so that we can live to fight another day!" Geraldine demanded.

Xavier whinnied at us from the sky as he swept overhead, his wings beating furiously, his horn bloodied and his eyes fierce.

Dante growled an order at us, jerking his head at his back, telling us to get on. We scrambled up onto his back and Orion clutched me against his chest as I wrapped my arms around Tory in front of me.

Dante took off into the sky while we all continued to shield him and I gazed down at the carnage below in complete despair. The amphitheatre was burning and the rebels were running for their lives. Rosalie Oscura howled as she led her Wolves away across the palace grounds with a huge golden Lion racing amongst the pack and a group of people clinging to his back.

Shadows consumed the entire stadium below in a display of power so immense it sent fear spilling into my chest.

"What has Darius done?" Orion questioned heavily, leaning forward to show me his left arm where the Leo mark no longer shone.

I gasped, clinging onto him and my sister tighter than before.

"I have no idea," Tory answered, showing us the bare patch of skin on her arm where Lionel's star sign had once been branded too. Hopeful tears filled my eyes as I prayed some good had come from this day.

A flare of power rushed through the handprint Lavinia had left on my bicep and I held in a gasp as I clutched it, biting my lip as the ominous feeling of the curse radiated through me.

Orion pressed his mouth to my temple then spoke in my ear. "Whatever she's done, I'll do everything in my power to fix it, Blue." My heart squeezed as I leaned in to his touch, hardly able to believe we'd both gotten out of that pit alive.

Lionel roared, wheeling through the sky as he spotted us and took chase with Lavinia riding on his back and an endless expanse of shadows billowed out around her.

I swore as I threw all of my magic into our combined shield, ready to fight if I had to while praying we could outrun them.

Xavier flew beside us, his wings beating furiously as he kept pace with Dante and stayed within the protection of our shield.

Dragon fire spewed toward us as the Dragons loyal to him raced into formation at his back and we found ourselves fleeing from an entire army of them with only our combined shield standing between us and death.

"Get beyond the palace wards!" Tory cried in encouragement as Dante raced through the sky and Dragon fire bled over our shield, making it quake and rattle as we fought to maintain it.

The tingle of magic ran over us as we made it beyond the wards and I turned my head, seeing Caleb ready with a pouch of stardust.

Caleb threw the stardust into the air ahead of us and Lionel roared angrily as Dante flew us into the particles and we were tugged away by the stars.

Dante dropped several feet as we arrived in a different, blissfully silent sky somewhere far away from the palace and relief crashed through me as I clung to my sister and she gripped my hand tightly in return.

We raced up into the clouds with Xavier flying alongside us and Dante released a mournful roar which I felt down to the pit of my soul.

Tears blurred my vision for everyone lost today. And as we soared into the endless blue sky, I didn't know where we were going, only that we couldn't go back to Zodiac Academy. We couldn't go anywhere that Lionel would find us. The Heirs had stood against him, we'd all shown our cards. And the Dragon King would have every loyal Fae and Nymph in Solaria hunting for us by nightfall.

We were all fugitives now.

And if any of us were ever caught, the price would be death.

AUTHOR'S NOTE

Heeeeeey, how was that? Are you feeling calm and collected? Did you just release a big breath, look up to the sky and thank the stars for keeping all your faves alive? So far. When Caleb was tempting fate did you think he was about to become Vampire sushi? I hope you kept the faith. You know we'd never do you dirty like that...right?

On a scale from stumble off of a kerb to faceplant off of a mega cliff of doom how did we do? Third floor splat onto concrete? Tripping over in front of all your peers and landing face first in a plate of Kipling cake? Somewhere in between?

There was some fun in here though too, right? We honestly had a lot of fun writing some of the stuff in this one (and yeah okay we cried a bit writing others but that's okay). Who wants to see a dijazzle in person? Did you die inside for poor Xavier when they all started falling on the floor? Do you think he should rock the banana piercing in future? That would have to win him some Dom points wouldn't it?

And we gave you a wedding too. Who doesn't like a wedding? We knew you'd be hoping for one and you can't say we didn't deliver.

See, we're nice to you. So you can totally forgive us for a smidge of heartache, a curse or two, the shadow bitch, a couple of torture scenes, a little bit of emotional trauma, Catalina's fucked up life, Lionel, the Daddy love, that Star Crossed thingy, Geraldine's fiancé, Orion getting stabbed, Tory getting stabbed, Darius getting stabbed, Darcy getting stabbed... and Washer.

Ahem.

But on a slightly more serious note, we really do want to thank you so much for continuing down the fictional rabbit hole with us once again (I'm assuming this isn't the first book you've read by us because choosing book 6 in a series would be a bit of a mind fuck but if you did then no judgement). The road to this place in our careers has been a seriously crazy ride and we couldn't have gotten here without your support and continued love for our stories and each and every one of you means so much to us.

2020 has been an interesting year for all of us and I know we are all hoping to see a lot of change for 2021 but I hope in the meantime we've helped you escape into books from time to time and that we haven't caused too much heartache.

But if we have then feel free to come shout at us about it in our reader group. Seriously, we thrive on the abuse, the more we get the more ammunition we have to throw at our characters so it's a win-win. Unless you have some objection to us killing off fictional people or something...

As always, we adore you and hope you think we're mildly likeable too. Book 7 won't be too long in the making, so go grab yourself a buttery bagel and relax while you can because it's sure to be one hell of an ending.

Love, Susanne & Caroline

ALSO BY

CAROLINE PECKHAM

&

SUSANNE VALENTI

Brutal Boys of Everlake Prep
(Complete Reverse Harem Bully Romance Contemporary Series)
Kings of Quarantine
Kings of Lockdown
Kings of Anarchy
Queen of Quarantine
**

Dead Men Walking
(Reverse Harem Dark Romance Contemporary Series)
The Death Club
Society of Psychos
**

The Harlequin Crew
(Reverse Harem Mafia Romance Contemporary Series)
Sinners Playground
Dead Man's Isle
Carnival Hill
Paradise Lagoon

Harlequinn Crew Novellas
Devil's Pass
**

Dark Empire
(Dark Mafia Contemporary Standalones)
Beautiful Carnage
Beautiful Savage
**

The Ruthless Boys of the Zodiac
(Reverse Harem Paranormal Romance Series - Set in the world of Solaria)
Dark Fae
Savage Fae
Vicious Fae
Broken Fae
Warrior Fae

Zodiac Academy
(M/F Bully Romance Series- Set in the world of Solaria, five years after Dark Fae)
The Awakening
Ruthless Fae
The Reckoning
Shadow Princess
Cursed Fates
Fated Thrones
Heartless Sky
The Awakening - As told by the Boys

Zodiac Academy Novellas
Origins of an Academy Bully
The Big A.S.S. Party

Darkmore Penitentiary
(Reverse Harem Paranormal Romance Series - Set in the world of Solaria, ten years after Dark Fae)
Caged Wolf
Alpha Wolf
Feral Wolf
**

The Age of Vampires
(Complete M/F Paranormal Romance/Dystopian Series)
Eternal Reign
Eternal Shade
Eternal Curse
Eternal Vow
Eternal Night
Eternal Love
**

Cage of Lies
(M/F Dystopian Series)
Rebel Rising
**

Tainted Earth
(M/F Dystopian Series)
Afflicted
Altered
Adapted
Advanced
**

The Vampire Games
(Complete M/F Paranormal Romance Trilogy)
V Games
V Games: Fresh From The Grave
V Games: Dead Before Dawn
*

The Vampire Games: Season Two
(Complete M/F Paranormal Romance Trilogy)
Wolf Games
Wolf Games: Island of Shade
Wolf Games: Severed Fates
*

The Vampire Games: Season Three
Hunter Trials
*

The Vampire Games Novellas
A Game of Vampires
**

The Rise of Issac
(Complete YA Fantasy Series)
Creeping Shadow
Bleeding Snow
Turning Tide
Weeping Sky
Failing Light